CALLA Cthulhu™

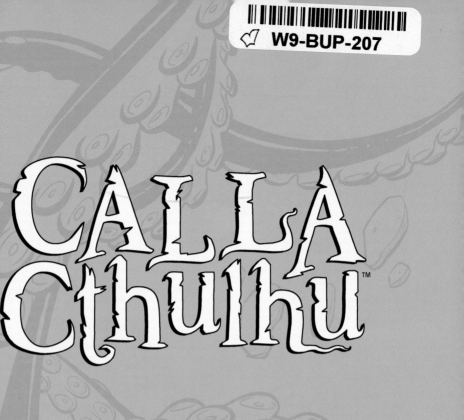

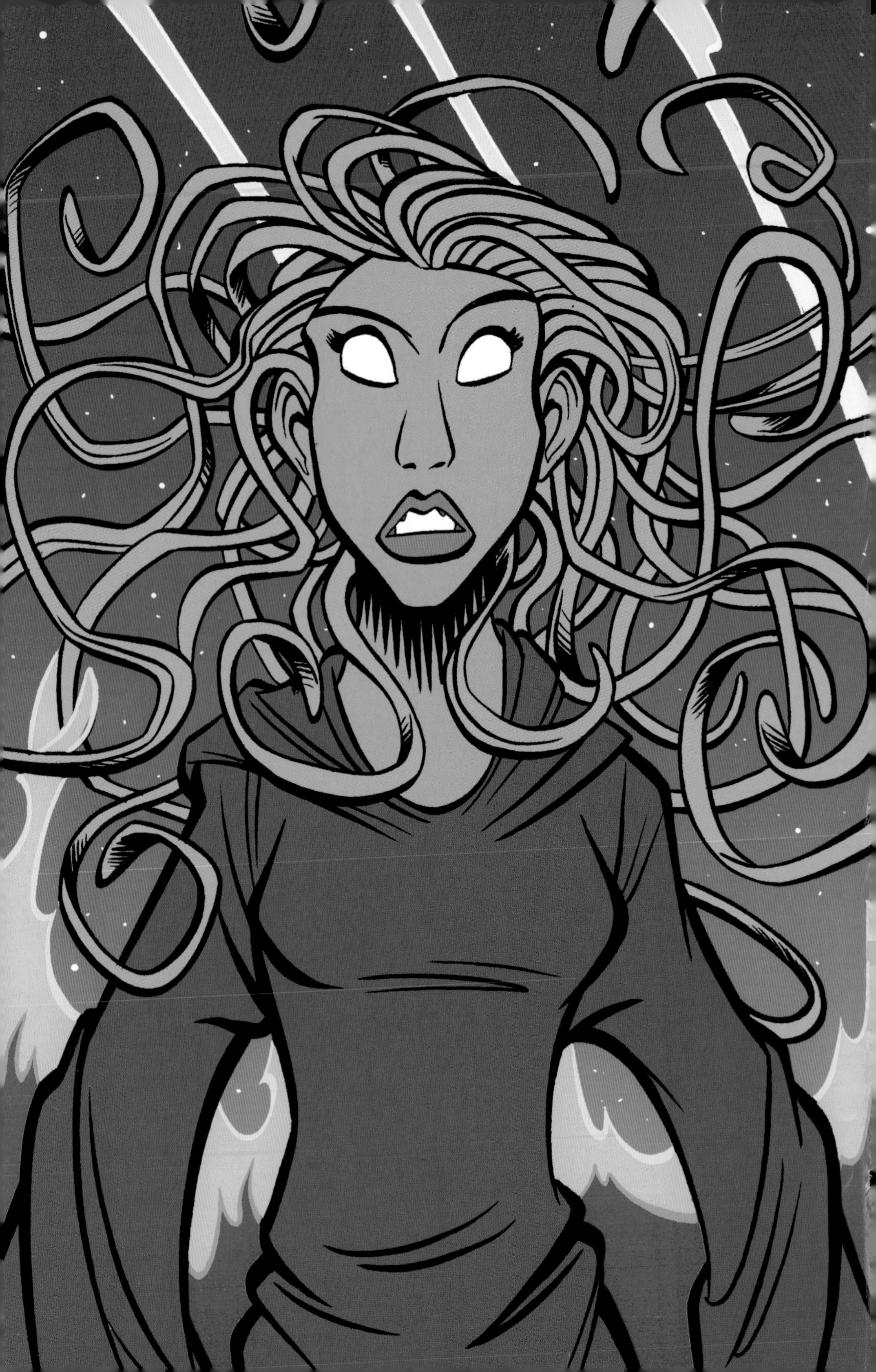

CALLA Cthulhu™

Script
Evan Dorkin and Sarah Dyer

Pencils
Erin Humiston

Inks
Erin Humiston (PAGES 7–44)
Mario A. Gonzalez (PAGES 45–225)

Colors
Bill Mudron

Lettering
Nate Piekos of Blambot®

DARK HORSE BOOKS

President and Publisher **Mike Richardson**

Editor **Daniel Chabon**

Assistant Editor **Rachel Roberts**

Designer **Brennan Thome**

Digital Art Technician **Christina McKenzie**

Originally published in digital format by Stela. Thanks to our publishers and editors: Sam Lu, Ryan Yount, Jason Juan, Jim Gibbons, Roxy Polk, and James Tao. Special thanks to Propnomicon.Blogspot.com for consultation on signs and symbols. Special thanks to Alice Dyer for color assists and creative input.

Published by Dark Horse Books
A division of Dark Horse Comics, Inc.
10956 SE Main Street
Milwaukie, OR 97222

DarkHorse.com

First edition: August 2017
ISBN 978-1-50670-293-3

10 9 8 7 6 5 4 3 2 1
Printed in China

International Licensing: (503) 905-2377 | Comic Shop Locator Service: (888) 266-4226

Library of Congress Cataloging-in-Publication Data

Names: Dorkin, Evan, author. | Dyer, Sarah, author. | Humiston, Erin, artist.
 | Gonzalez, Mario, inker. | Mudron, Bill, colourist. |
 Piekos, Nate, letterer.
Title: Calla Cthulhu / script, Evan Dorkin and Sarah Dyer ; art, Erin
 Humiston ; inks, Mario A. Gonzalez ; colors, Bill Mudron ; lettering by
 Nate Piekos of Blambot.
Description: First edition. | Milwaukie, OR : Dark Horse Books, 2017. |
 Summary: "Calla Tafali finds herself battling supernatural monsters,
 human assassins, and her uncle, The King in Yellow, while resisting his
 call to embrace her own chaotic heritage and join the family business"--
 Provided by publisher.
Identifiers: LCCN 2017008212 | ISBN 9781506702933 (paperback)
Subjects: LCSH: Graphic novels. | CYAC: Graphic novels. | Monsters--Fiction.
 | Genealogy--Fiction. | Supernatural--Fiction. | Coming of age--Fiction. |
 BISAC: JUVENILE FICTION / Comics & Graphic Novels / Horror. |
 JUVENILE FICTION / Comics & Graphic Novels / General.
Classification: LCC PZ7.7.D68 Cal 2017 | DDC 741.5/973--dc23
LC record available at https://lccn.loc.gov/2017008212

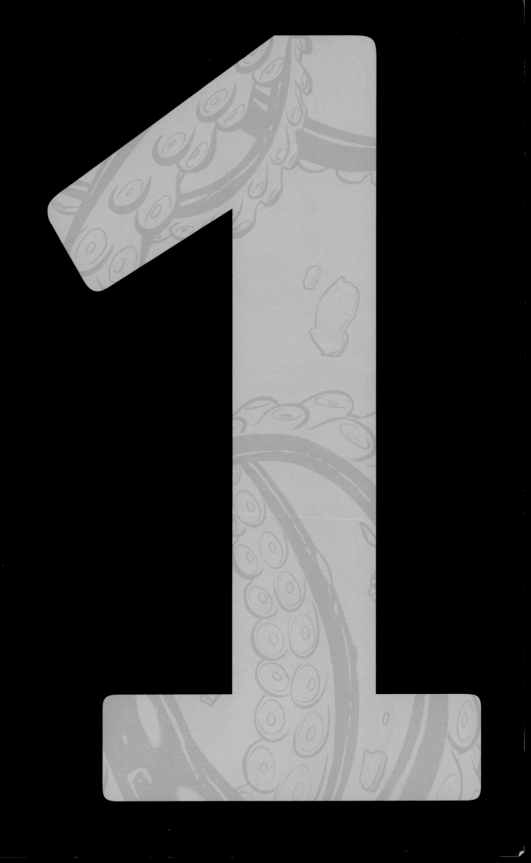

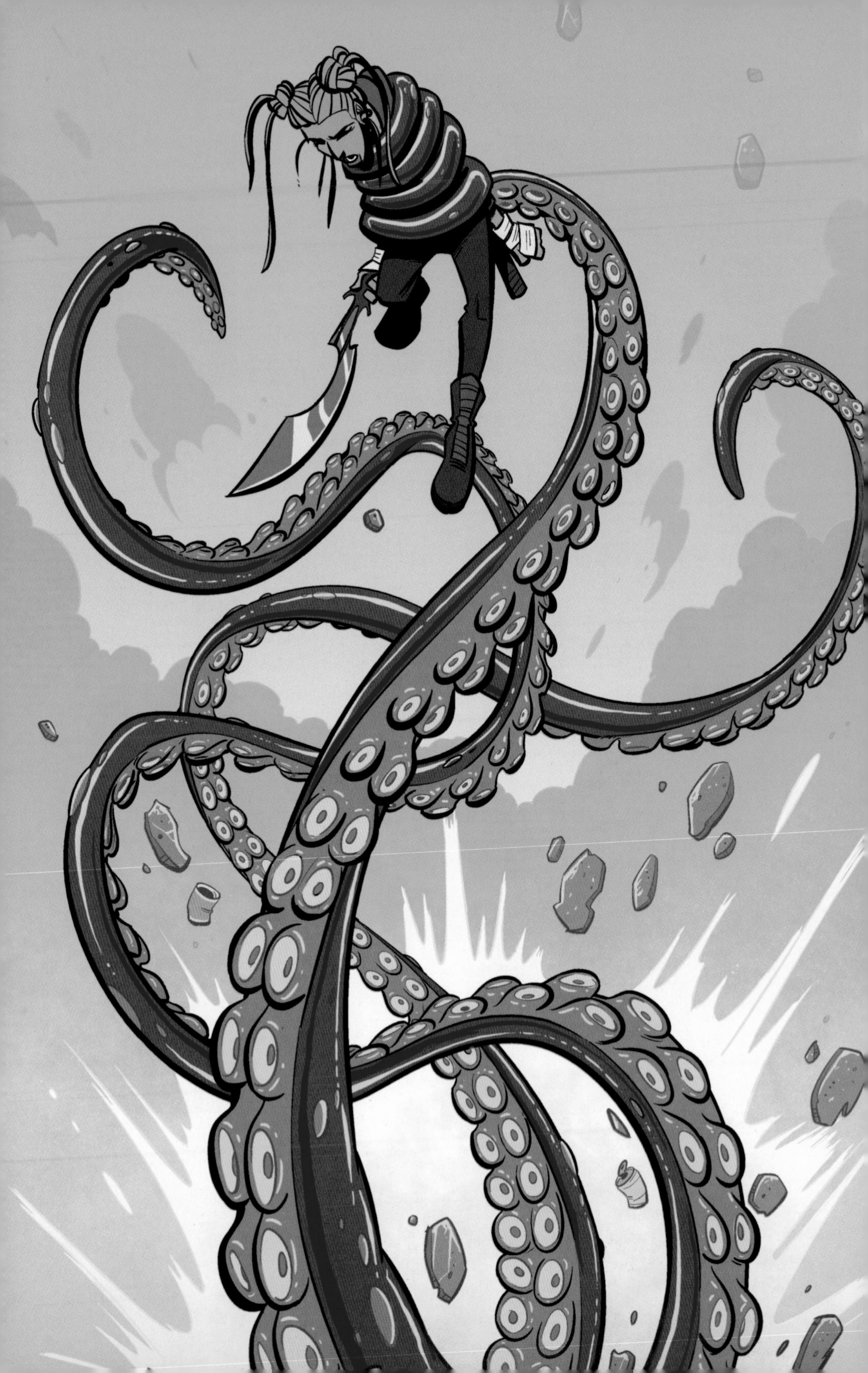

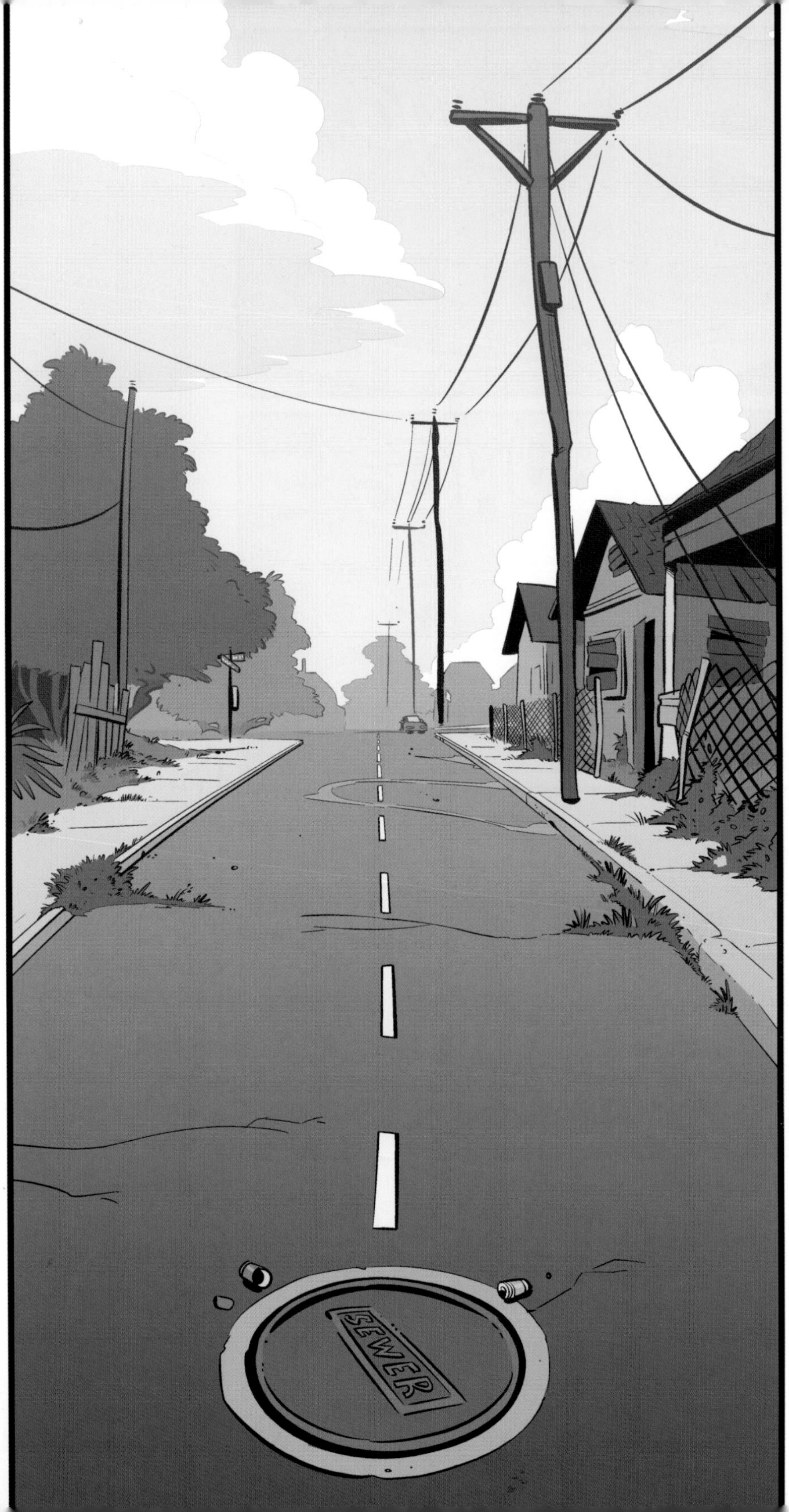
SEWER

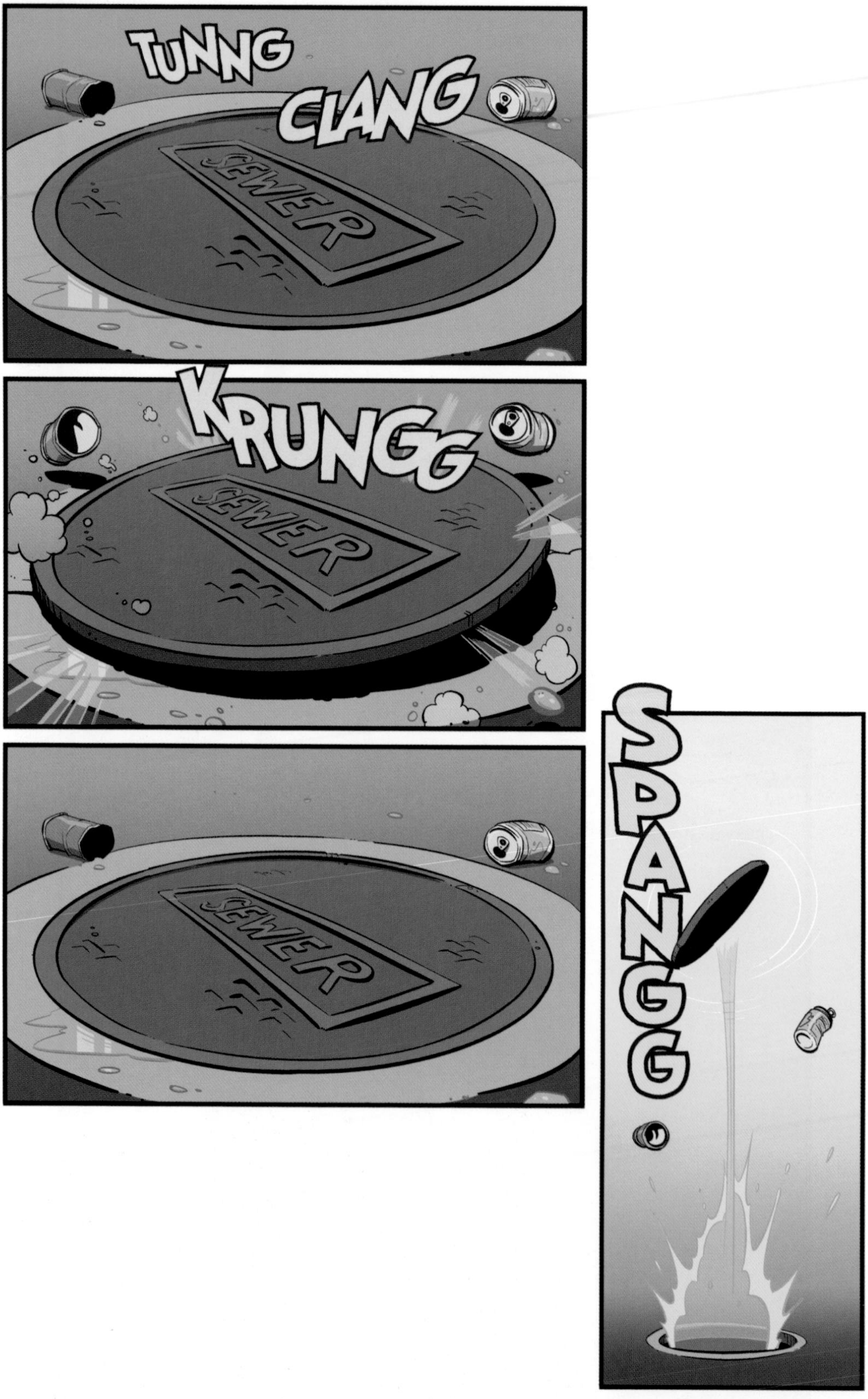
TUNNG
CLANG
SEWER
KRUNGG
SEWER
SEWER
SPANGG

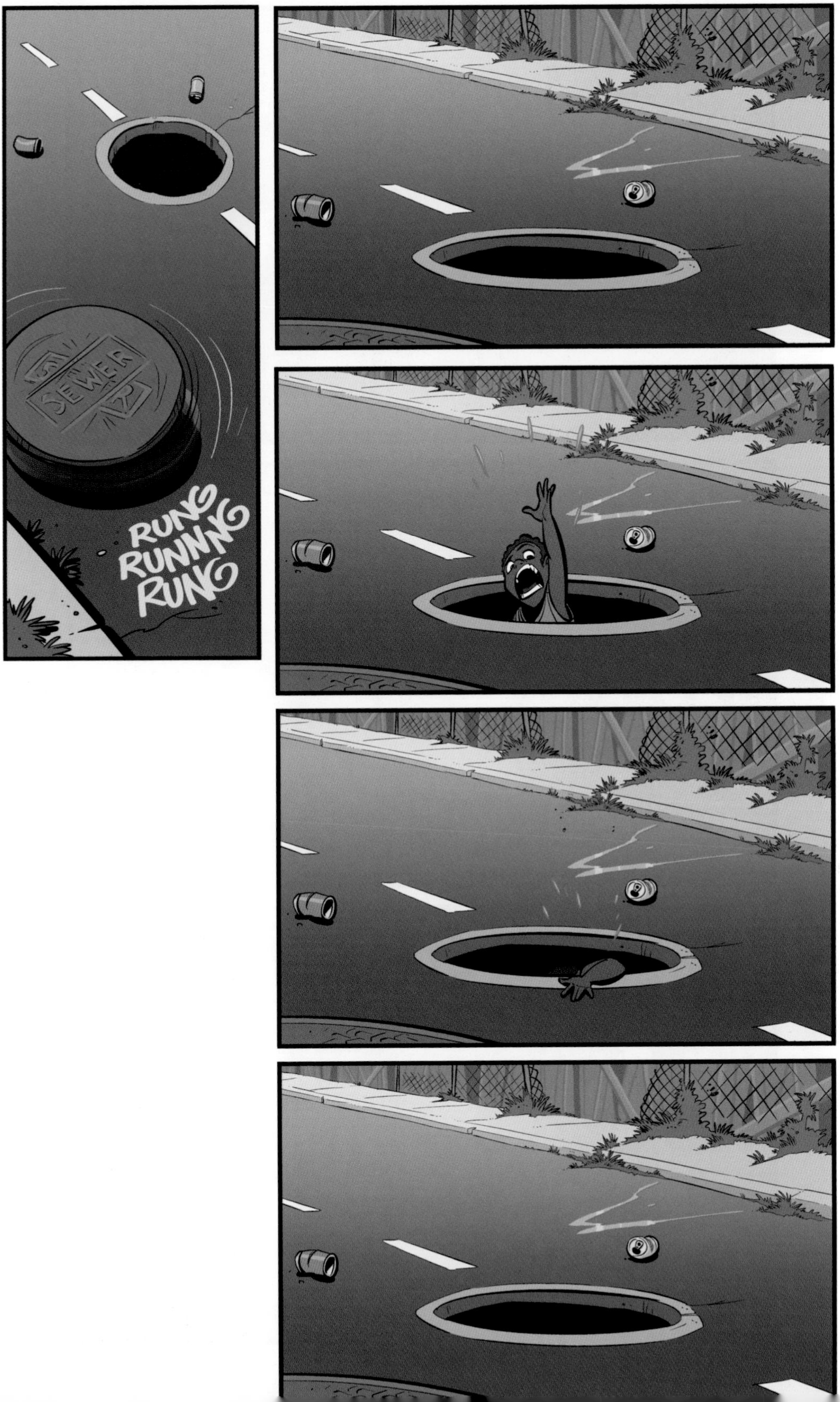
RUNG
RUNNNG
RUNG

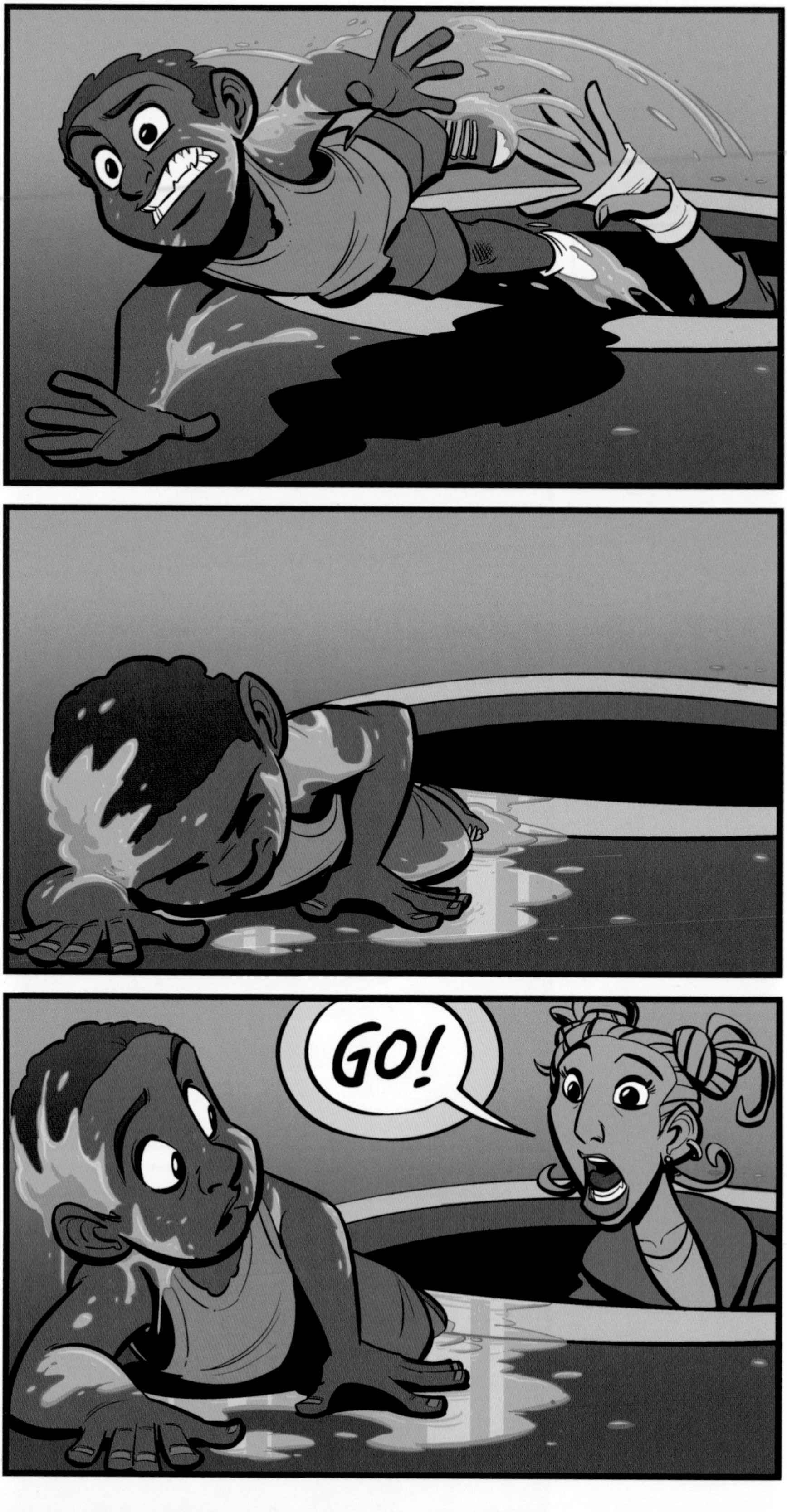
GO!

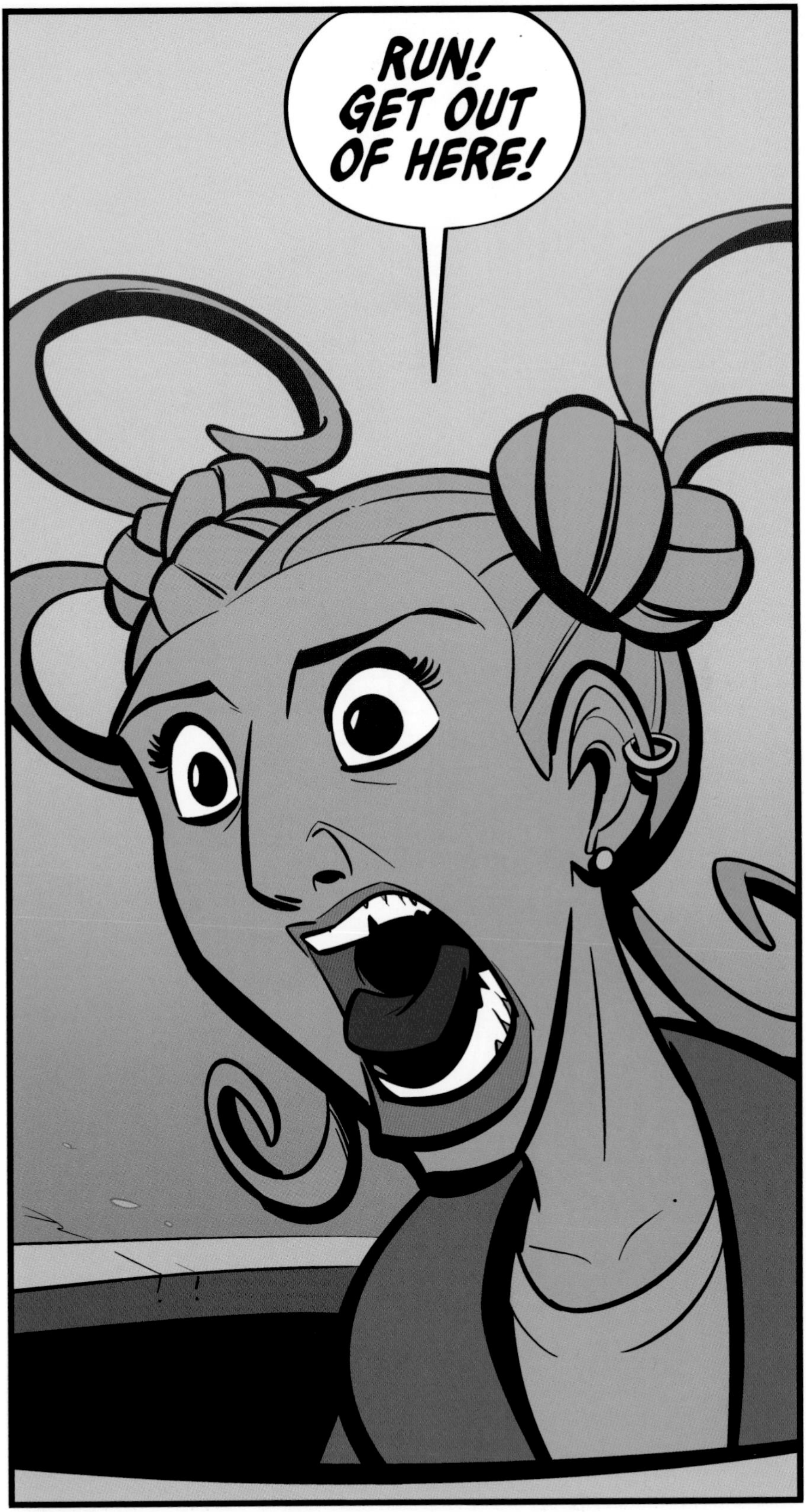
RUN! GET OUT OF HERE!

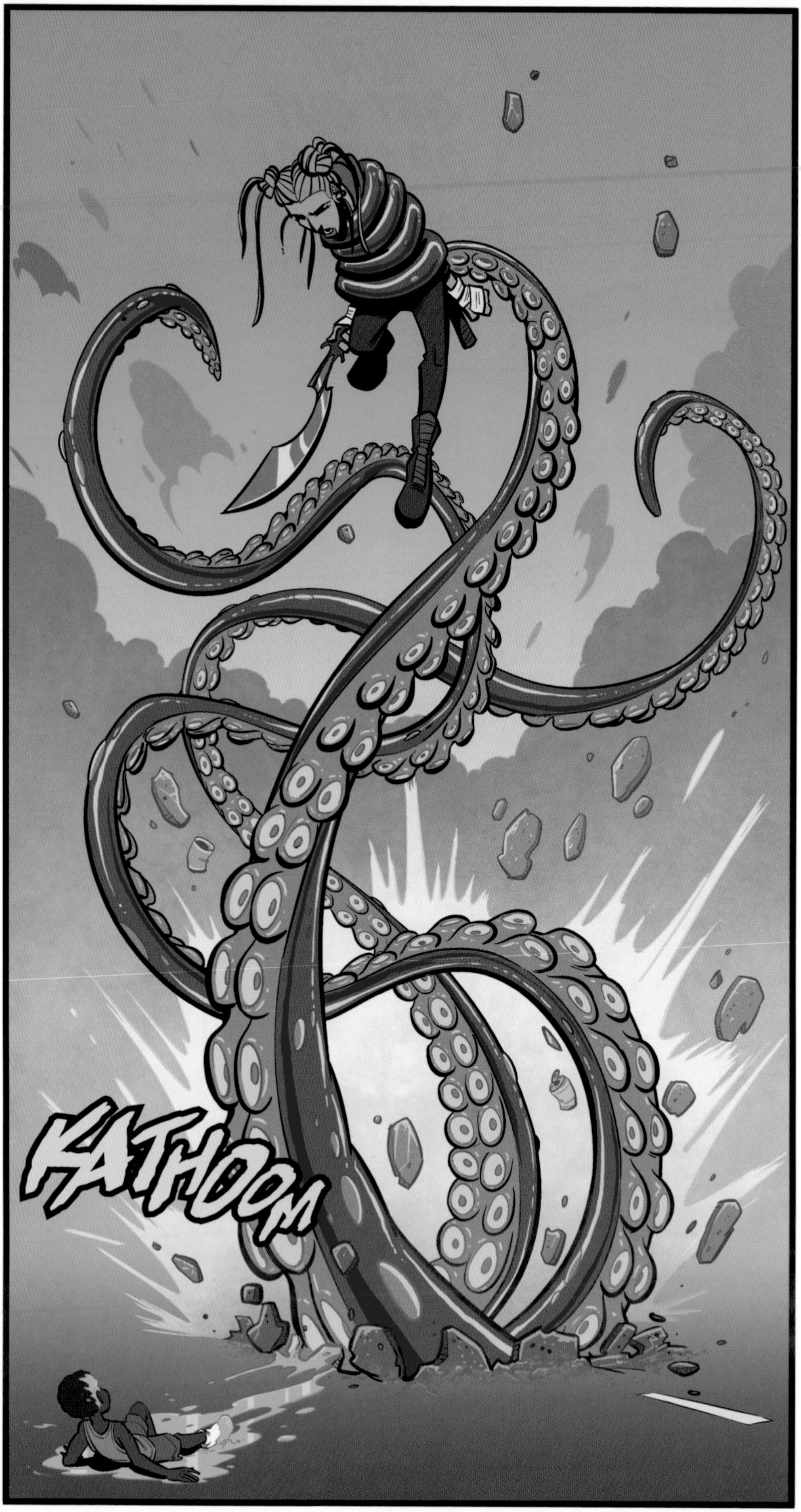
KATHOOM

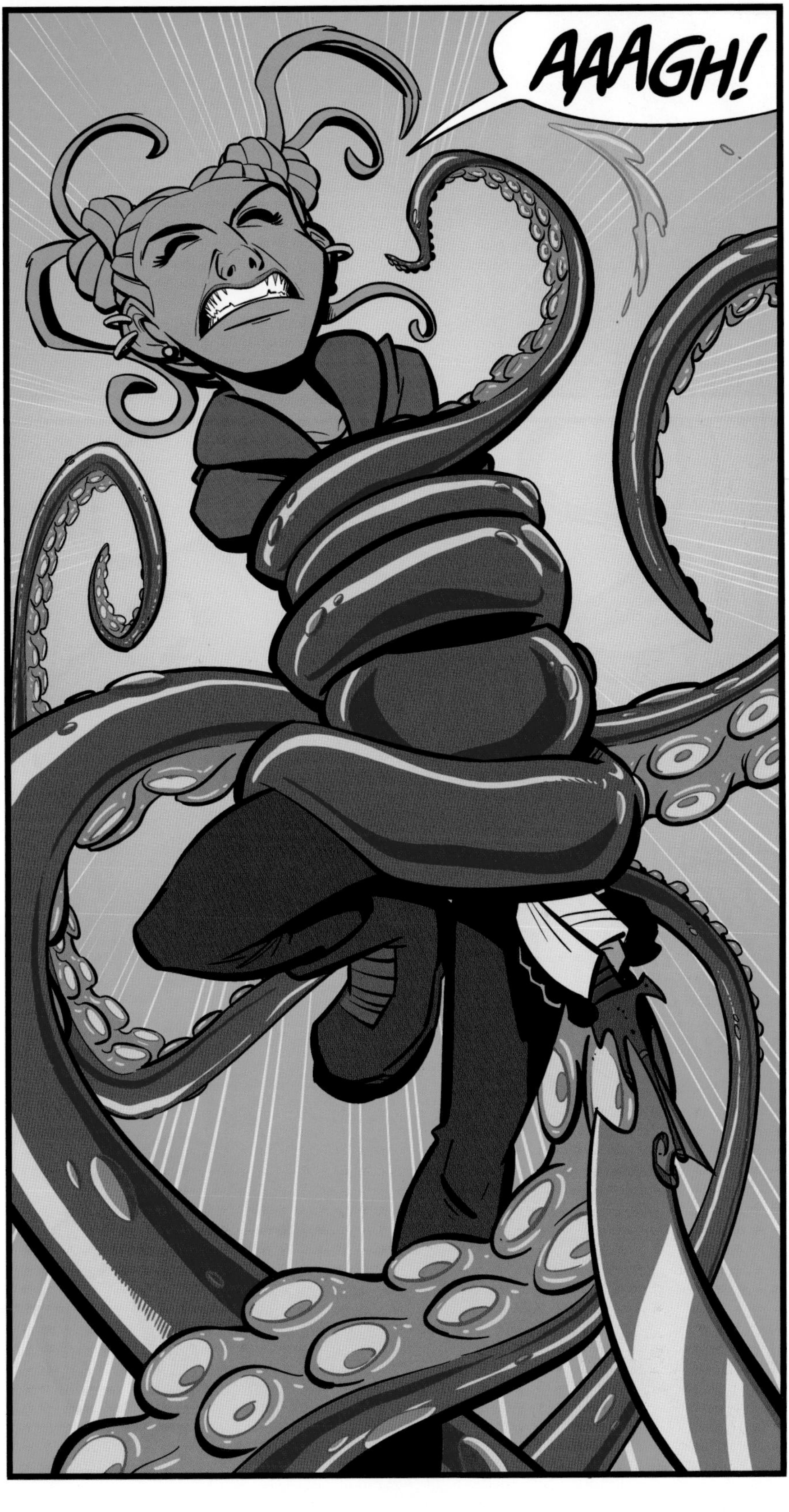
AAAGH!

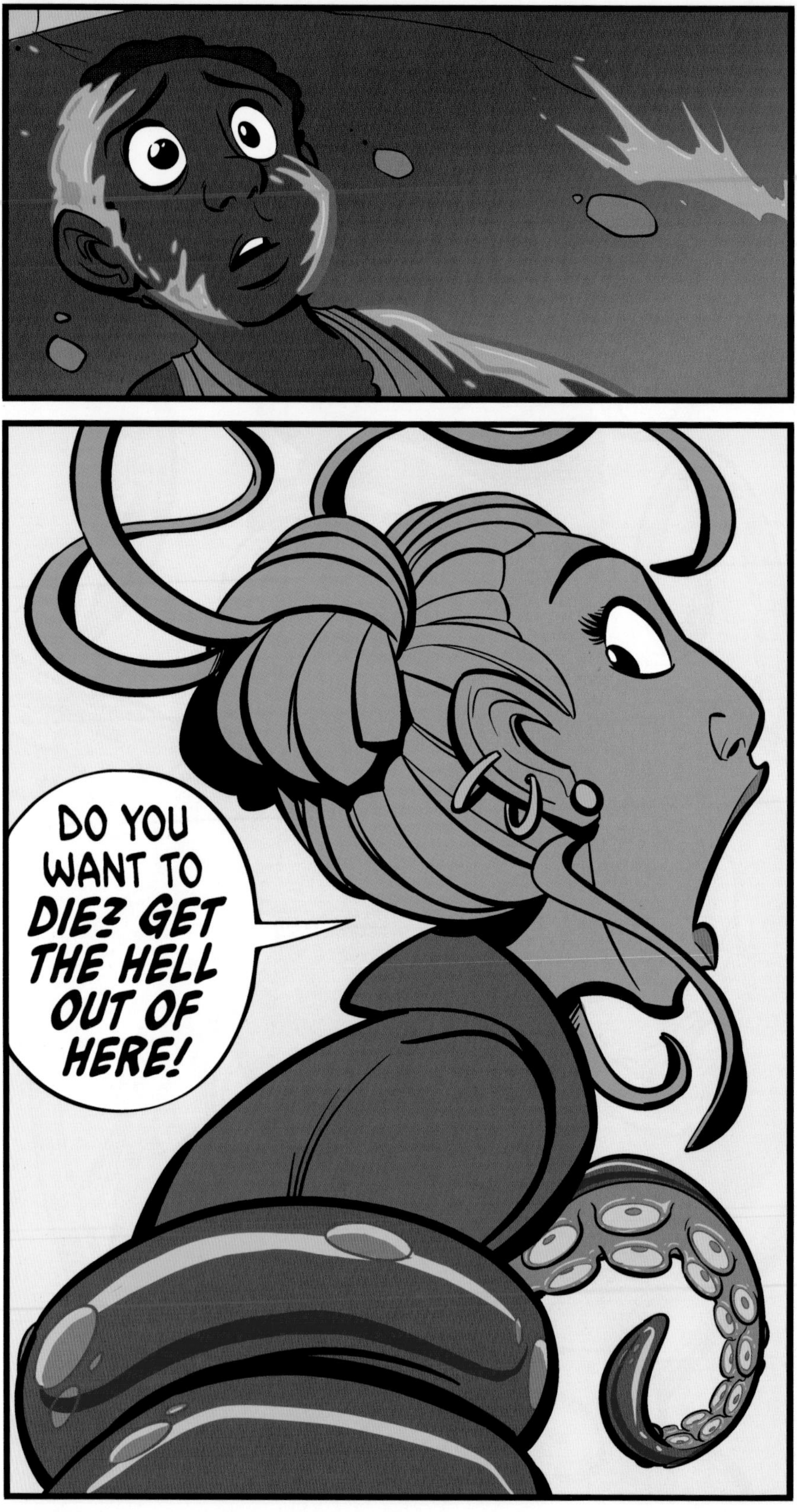
DO YOU WANT TO DIE? GET THE HELL OUT OF HERE!

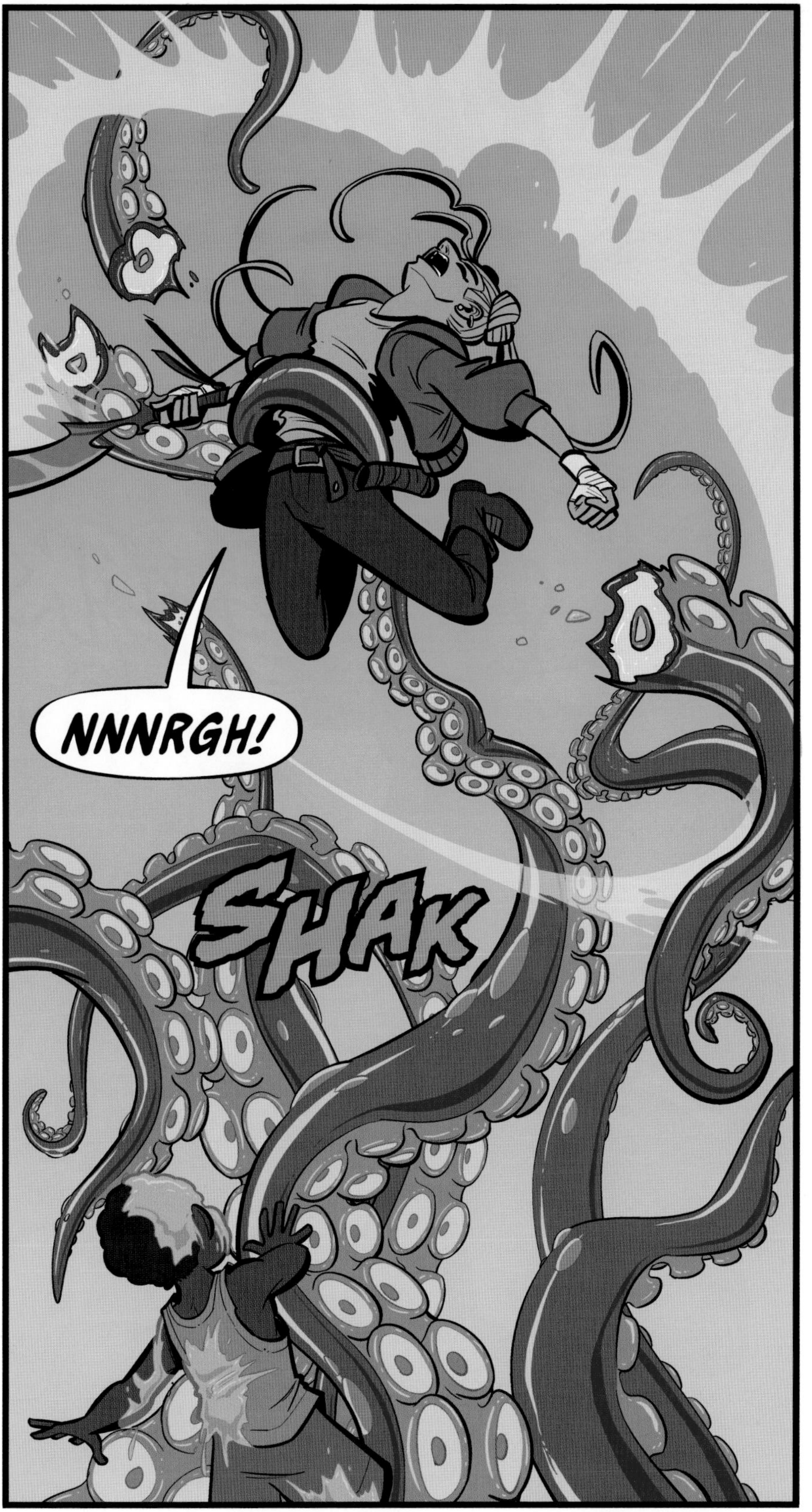
NNNRGH!
SHAK

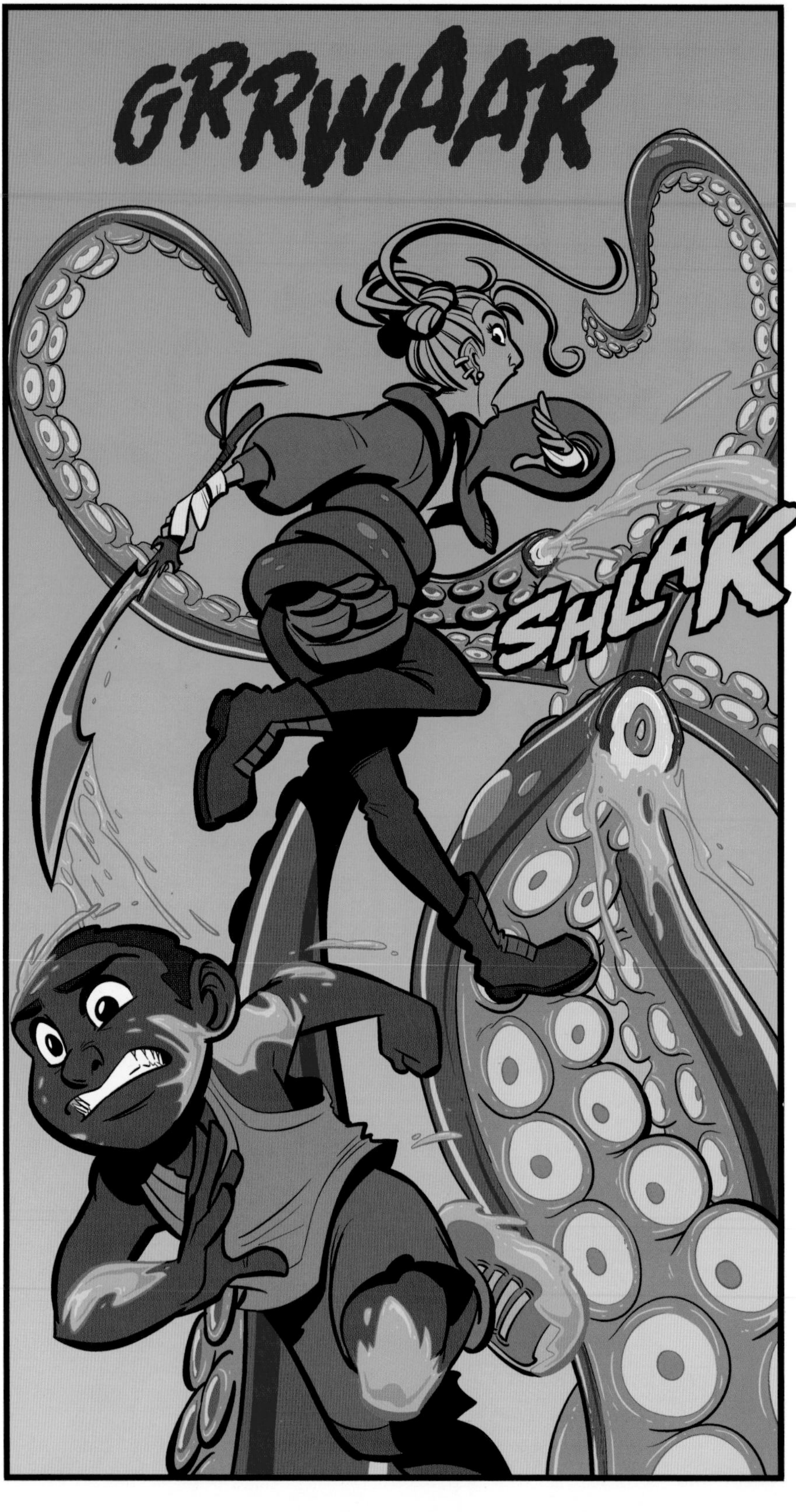
GRRWAAR
SHLAK

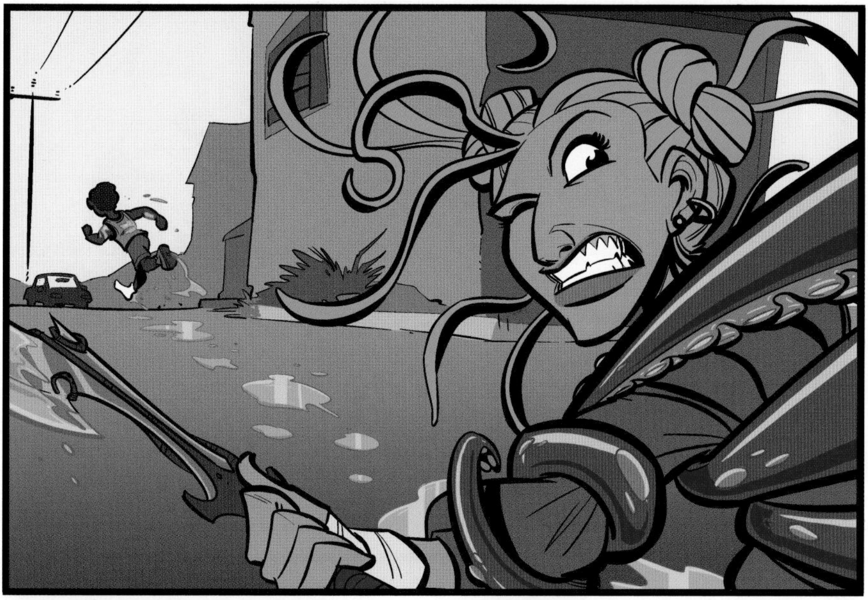

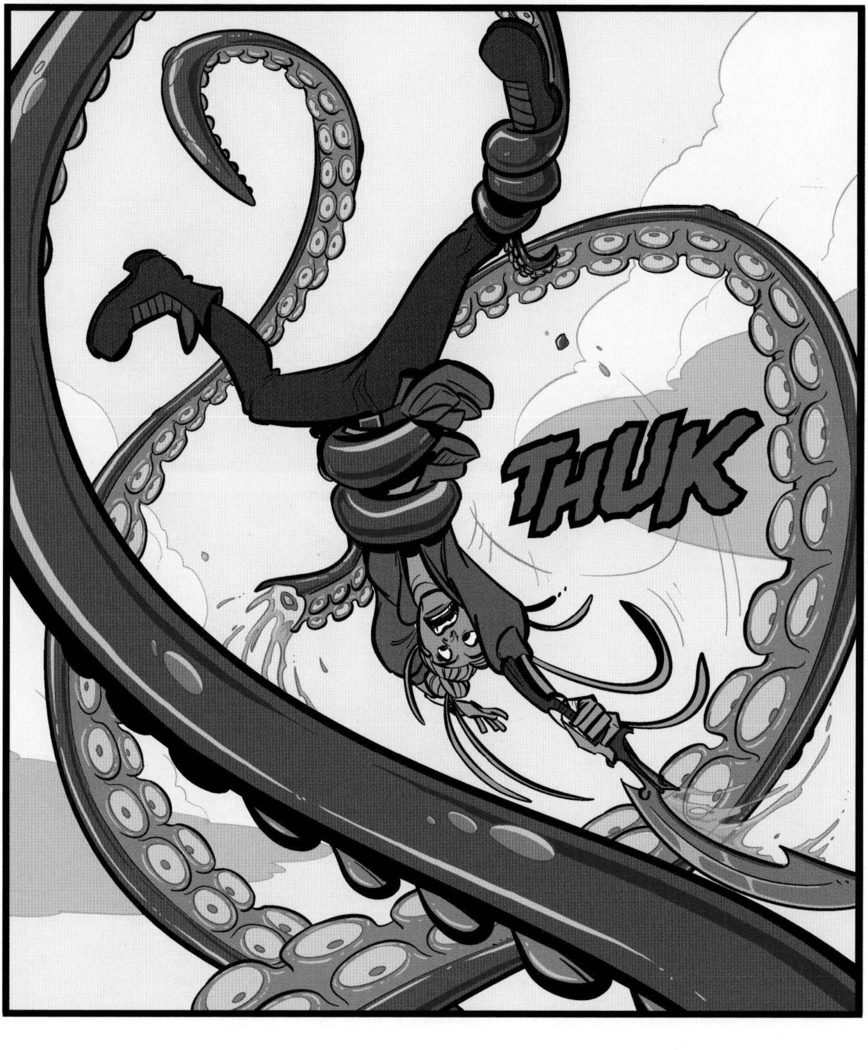
THUK

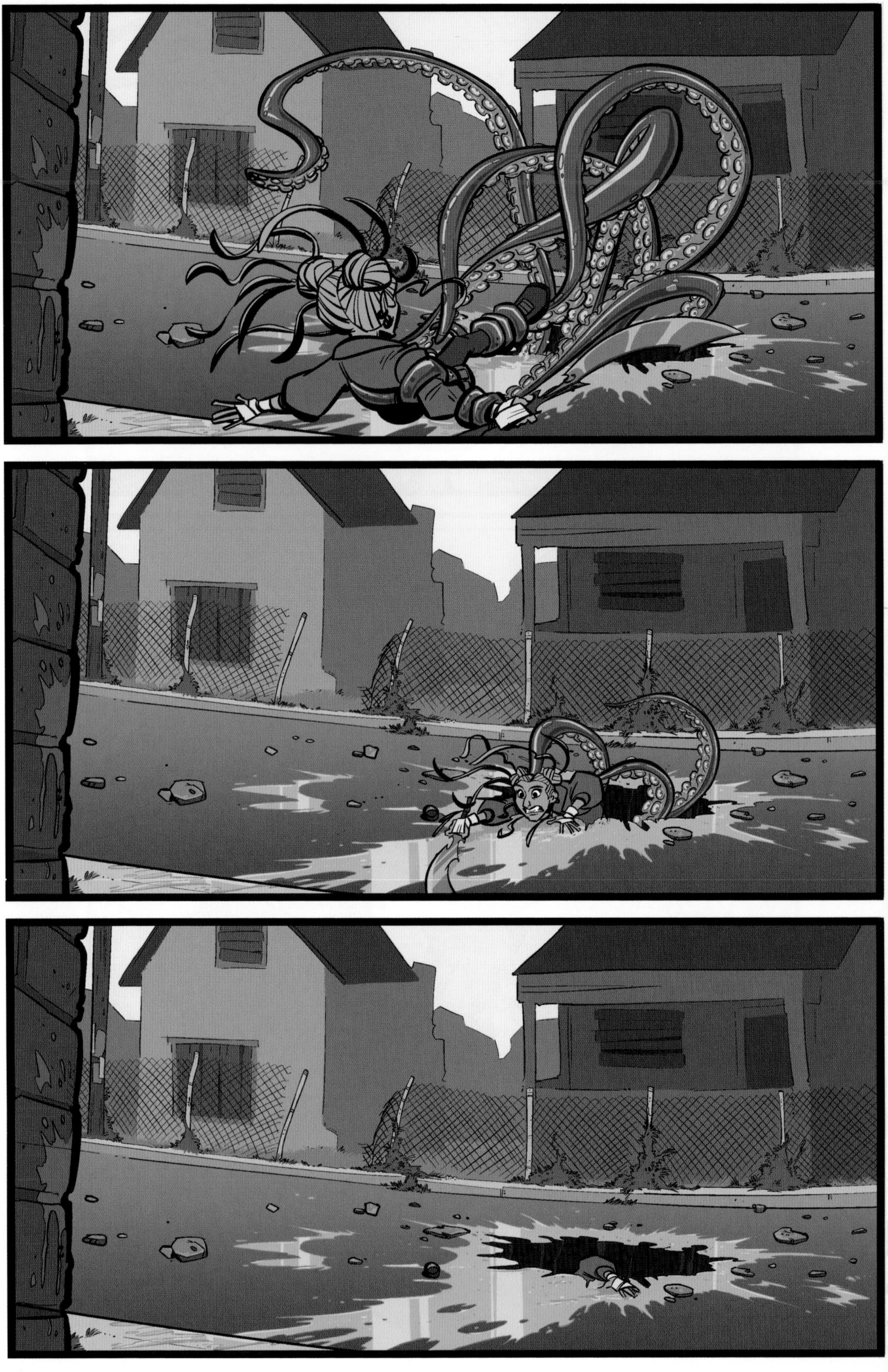

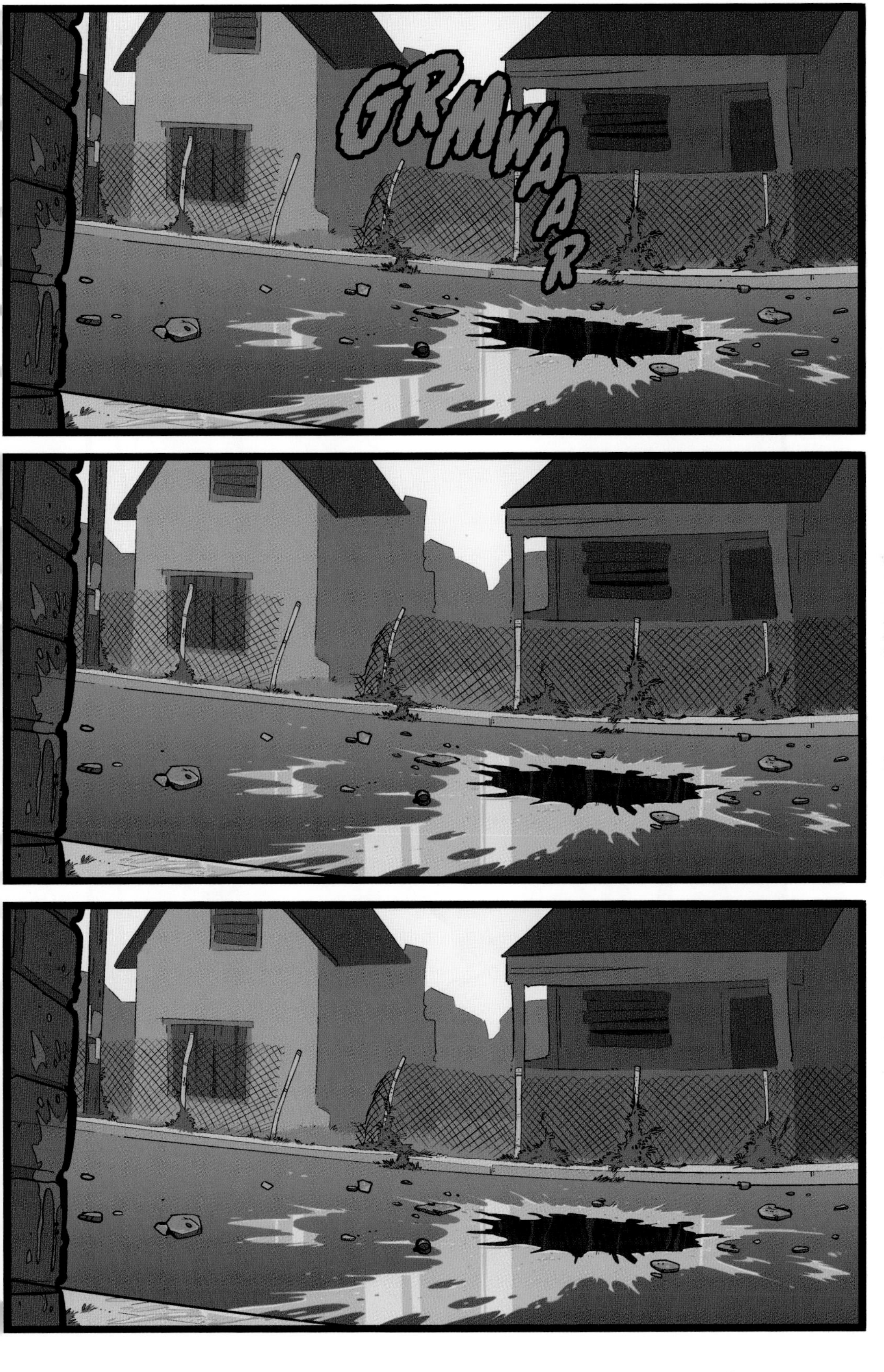
GRMWAAR

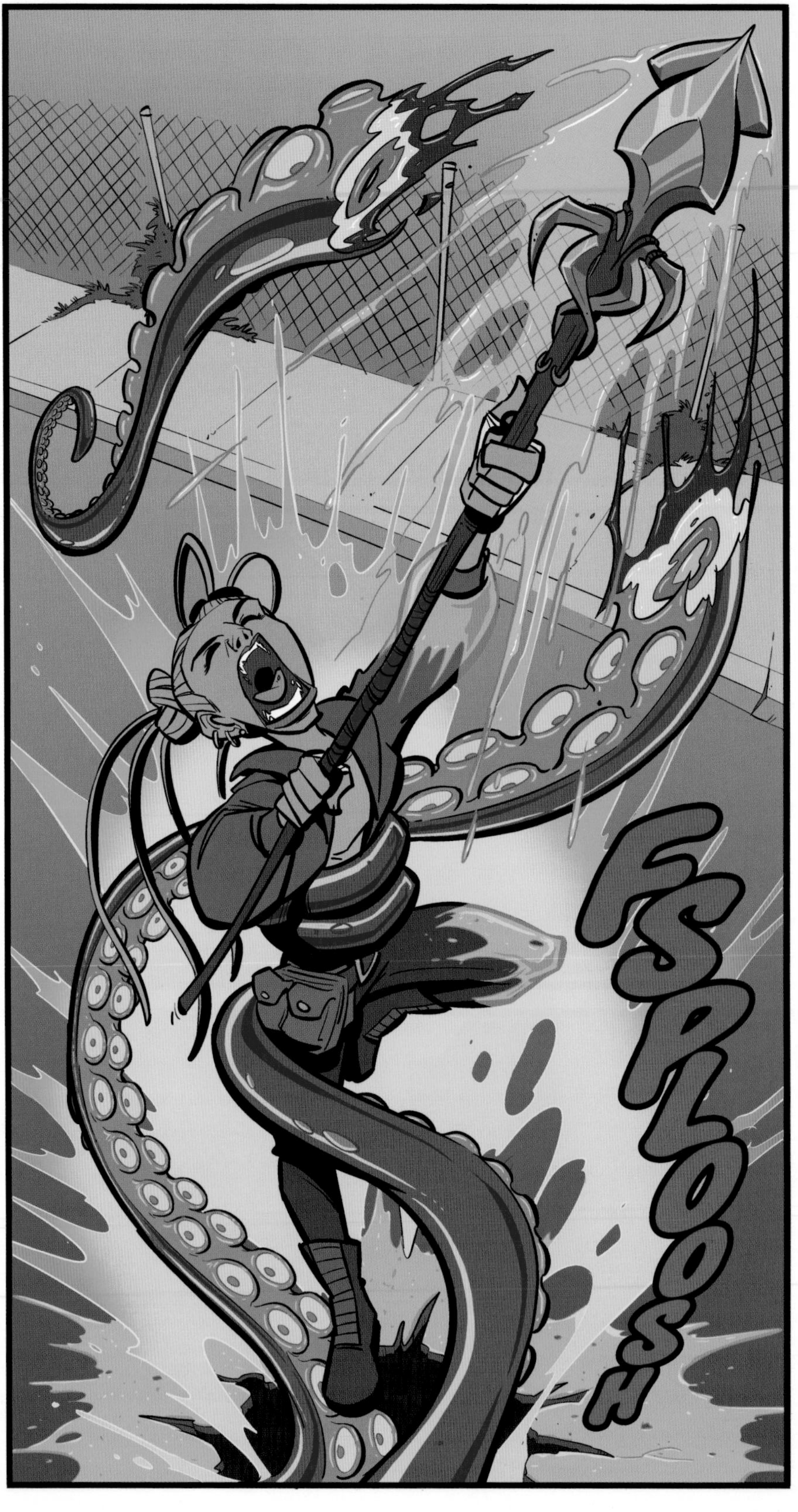
FSPLOOSH

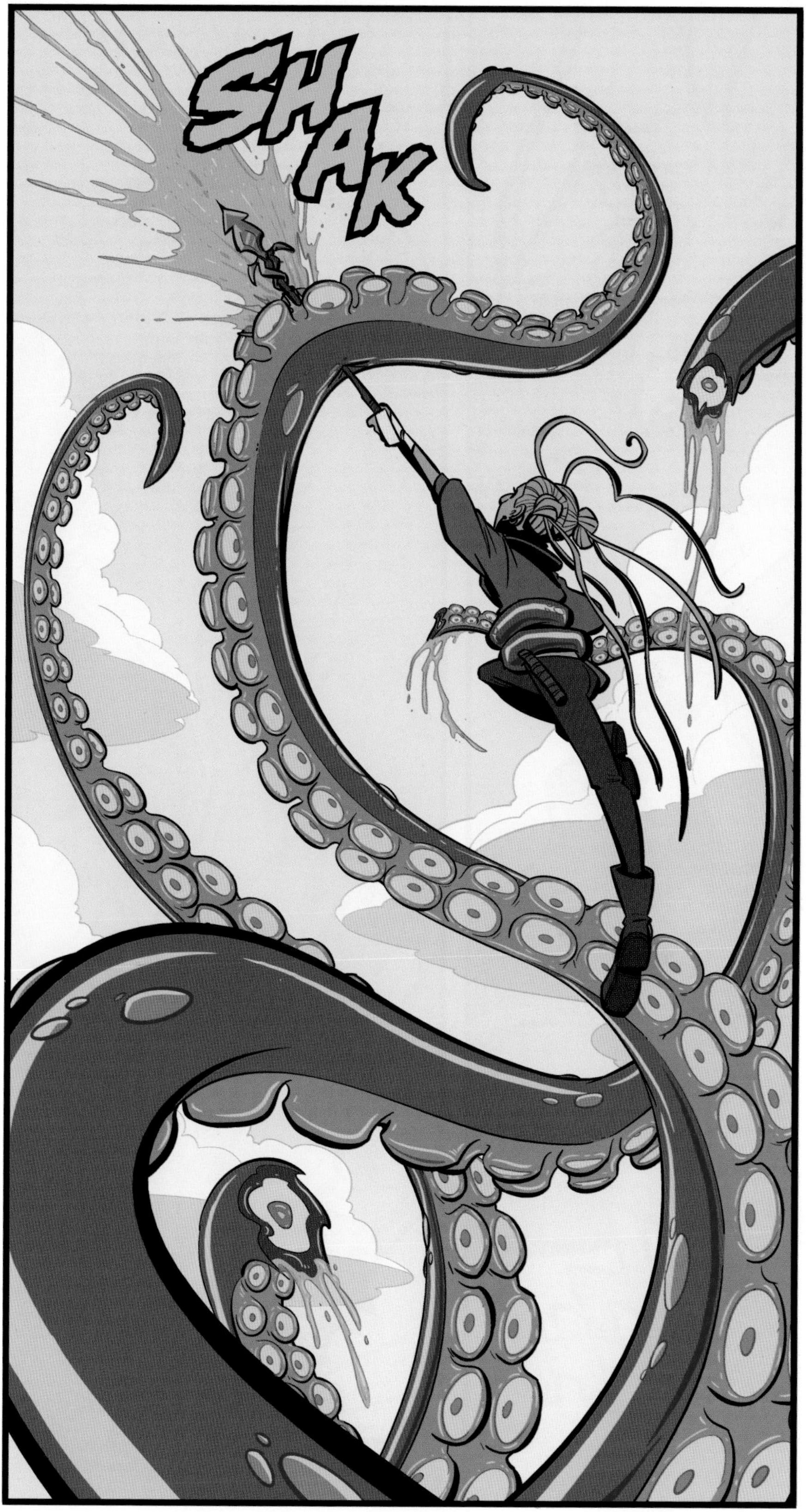
SHAK

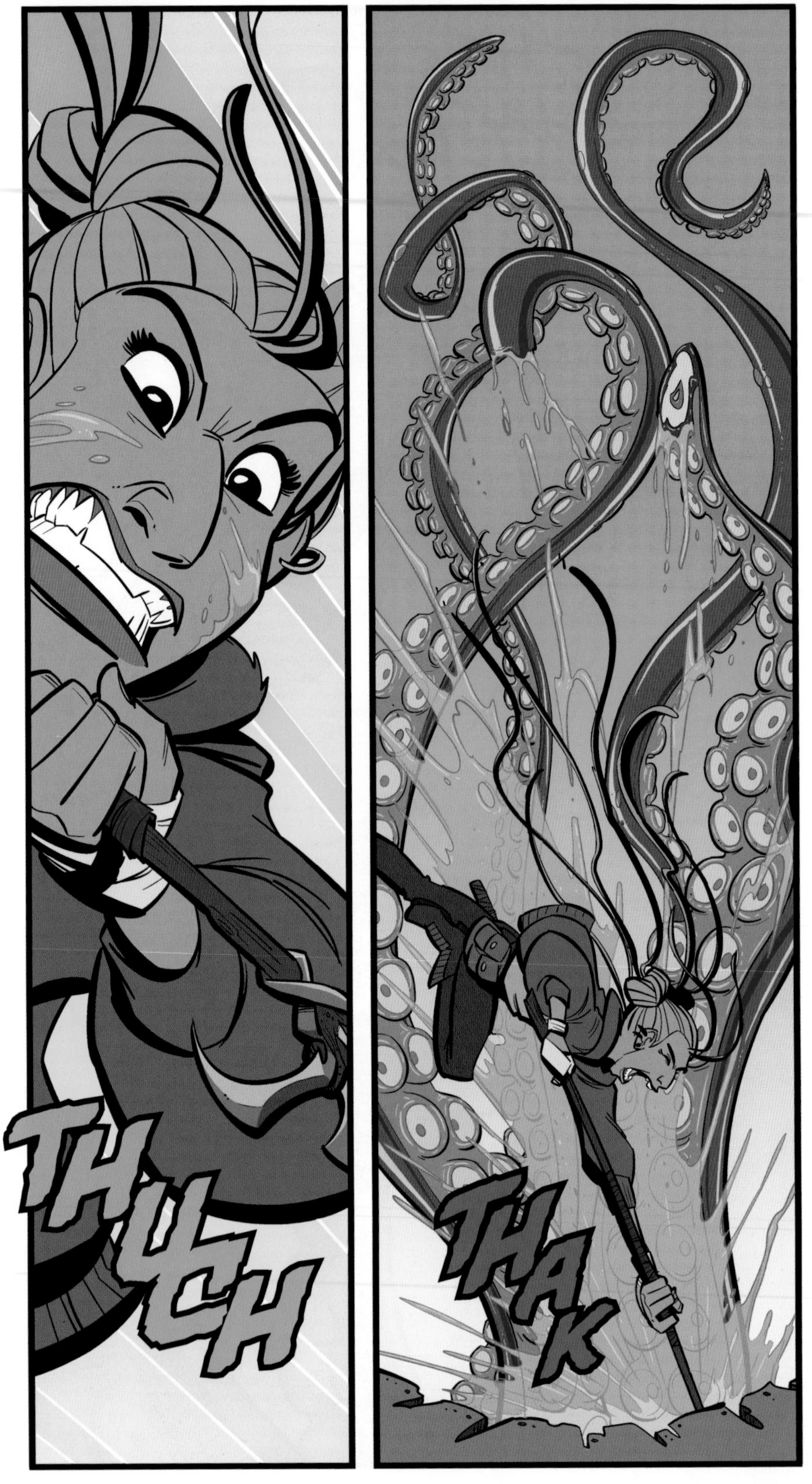
THUCH
THAK

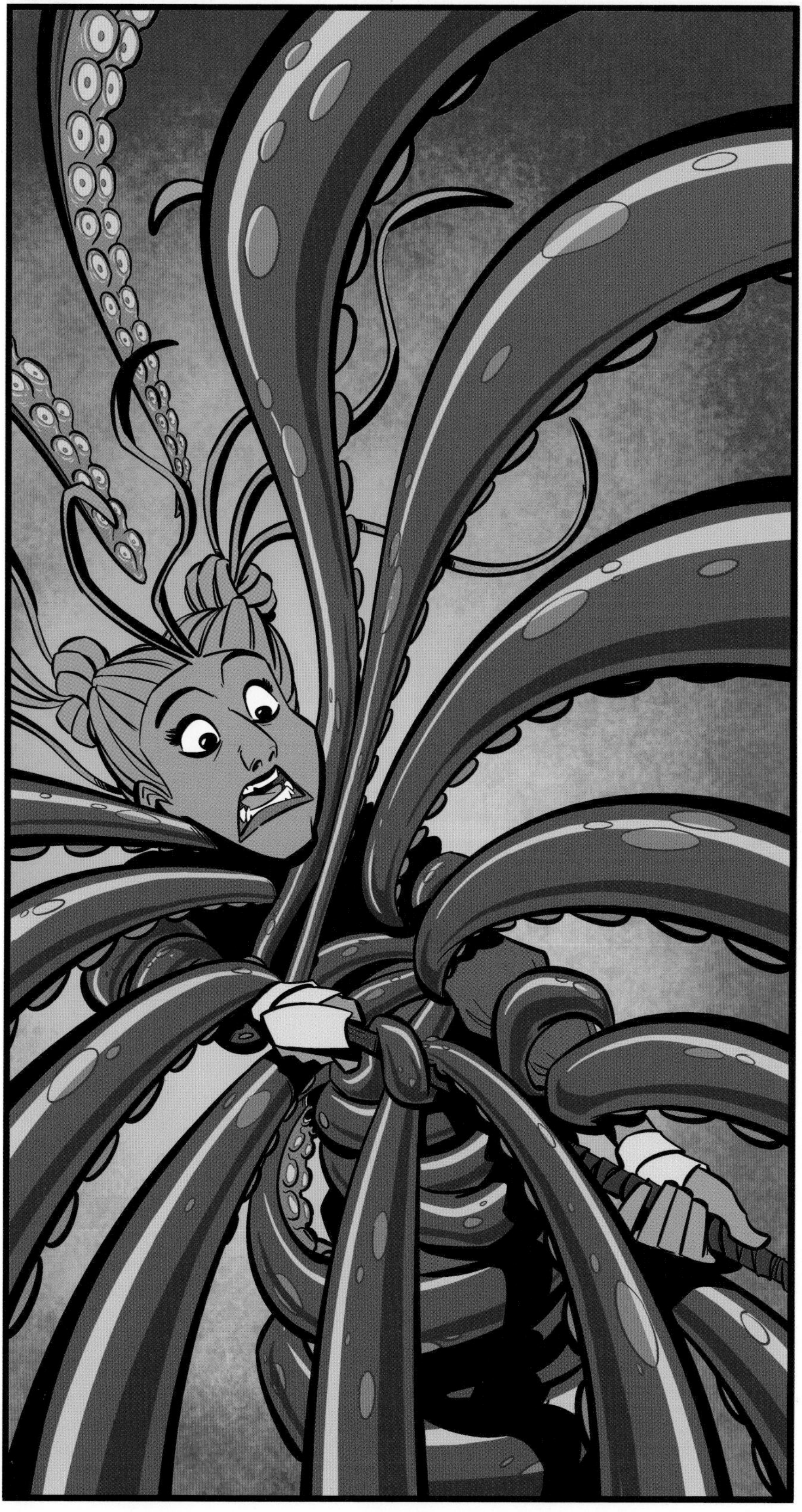

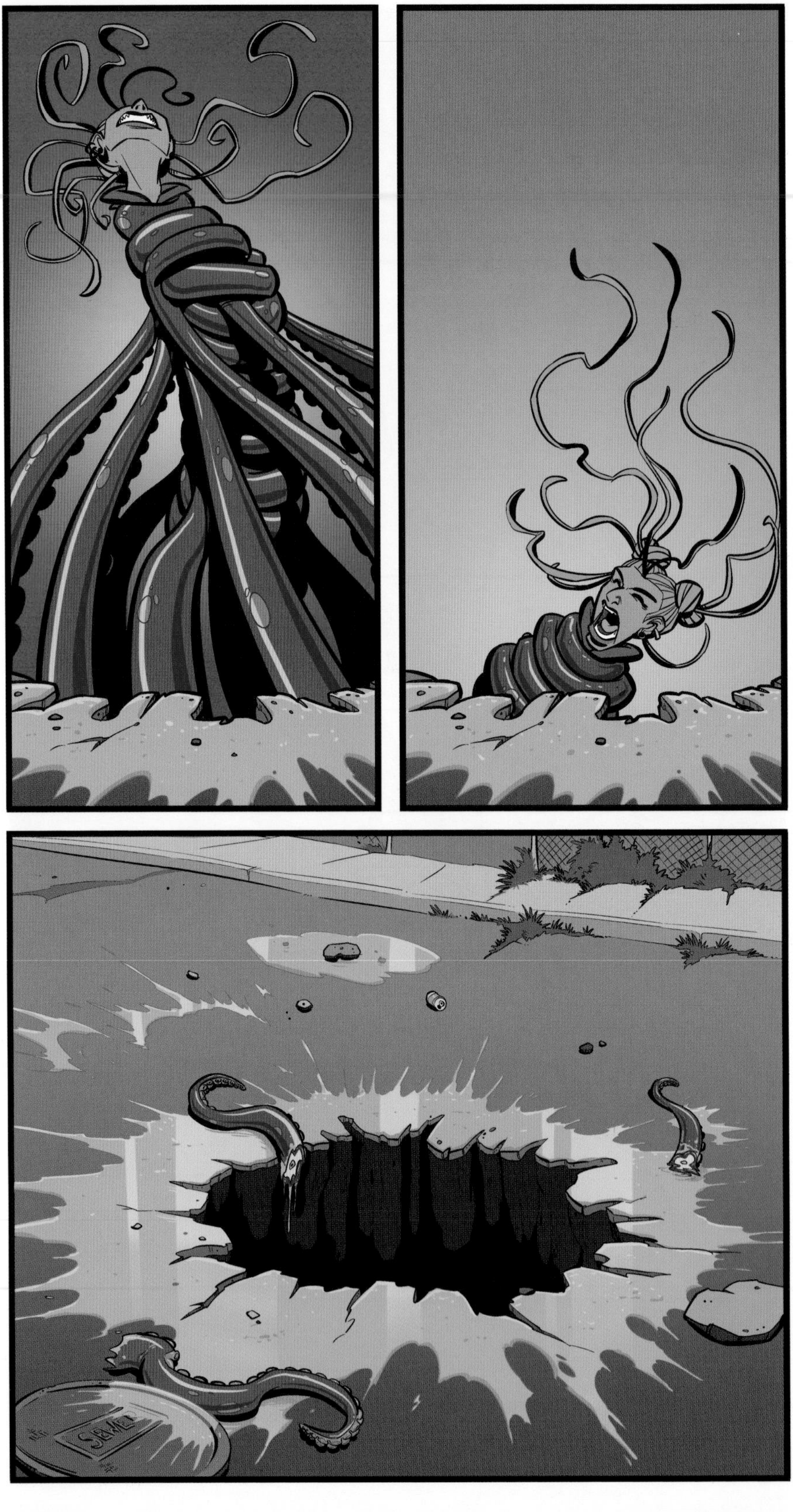

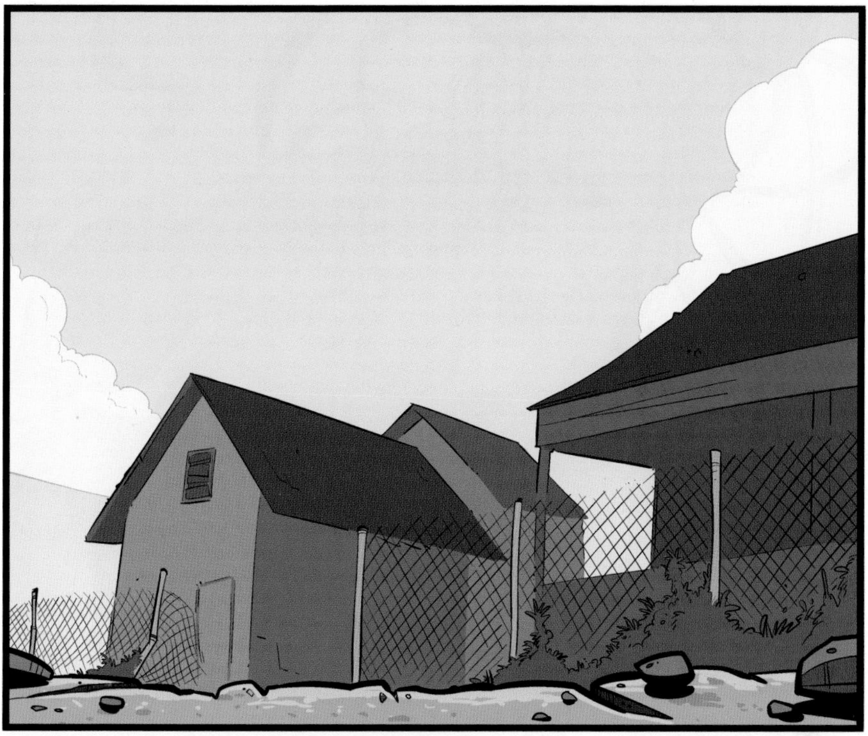

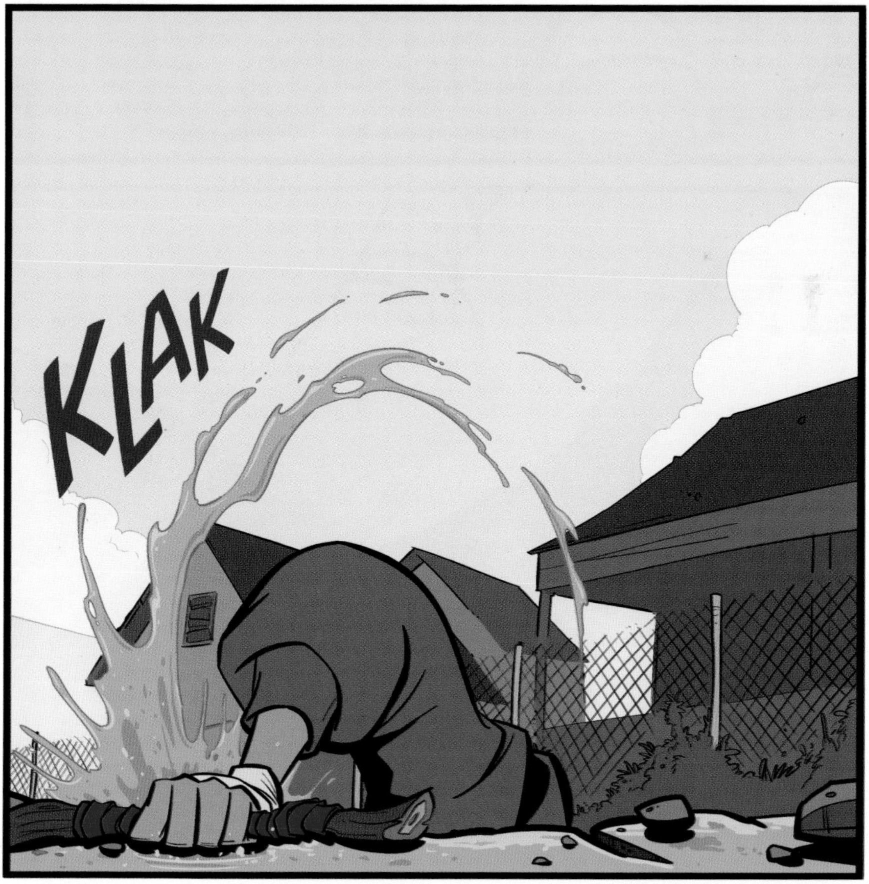
KLAK

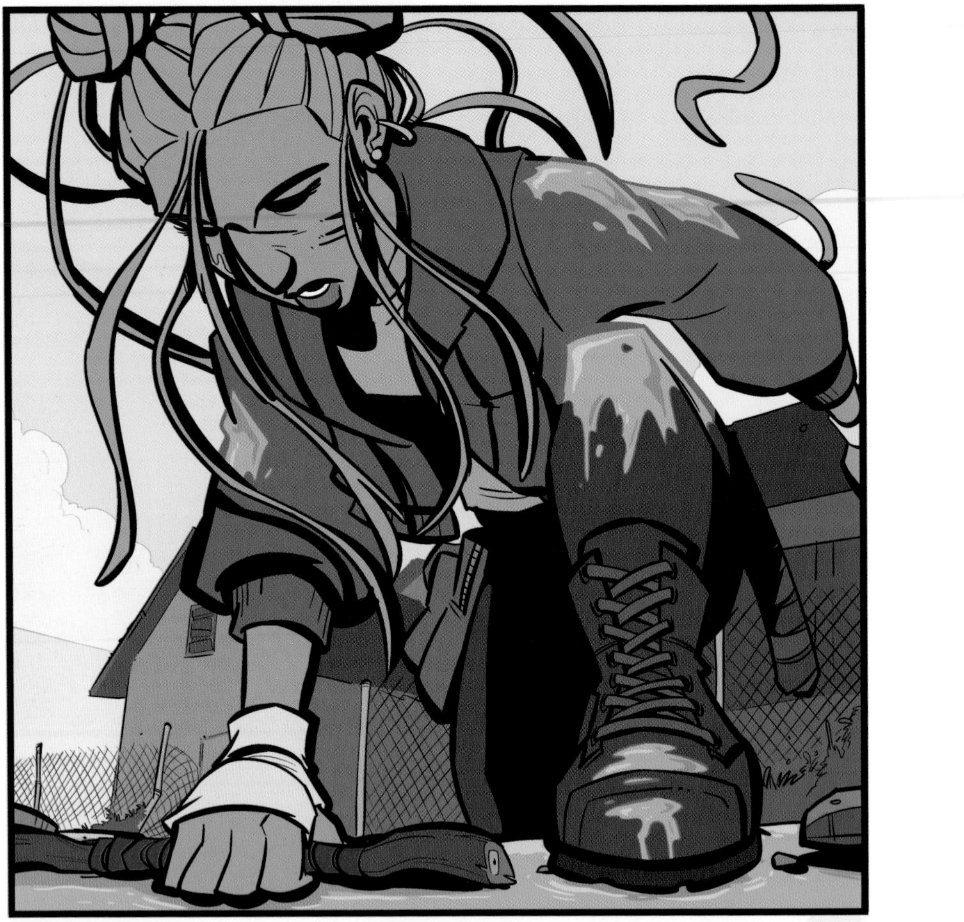

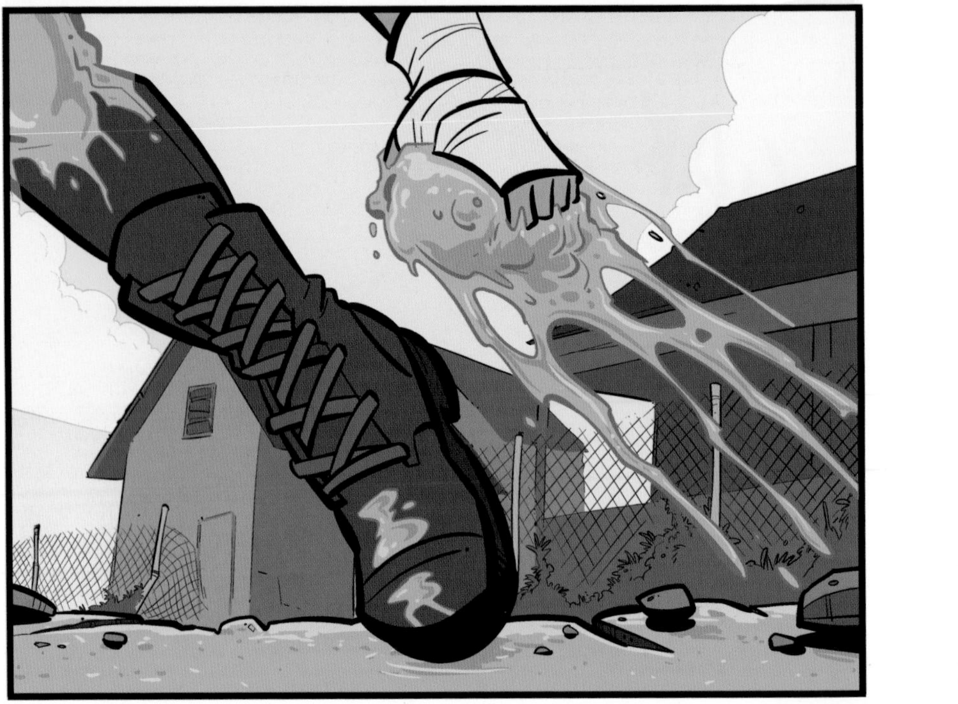

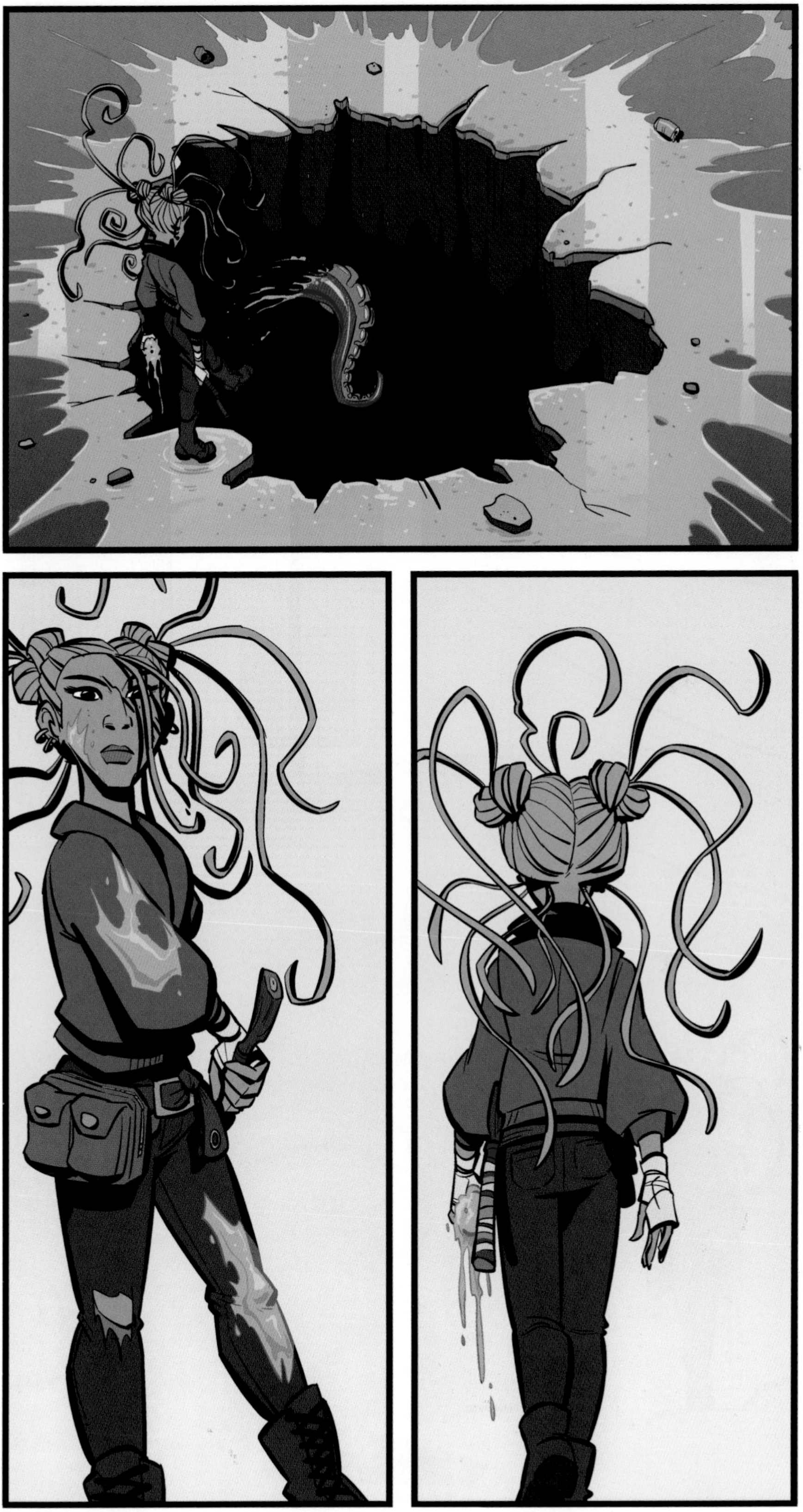

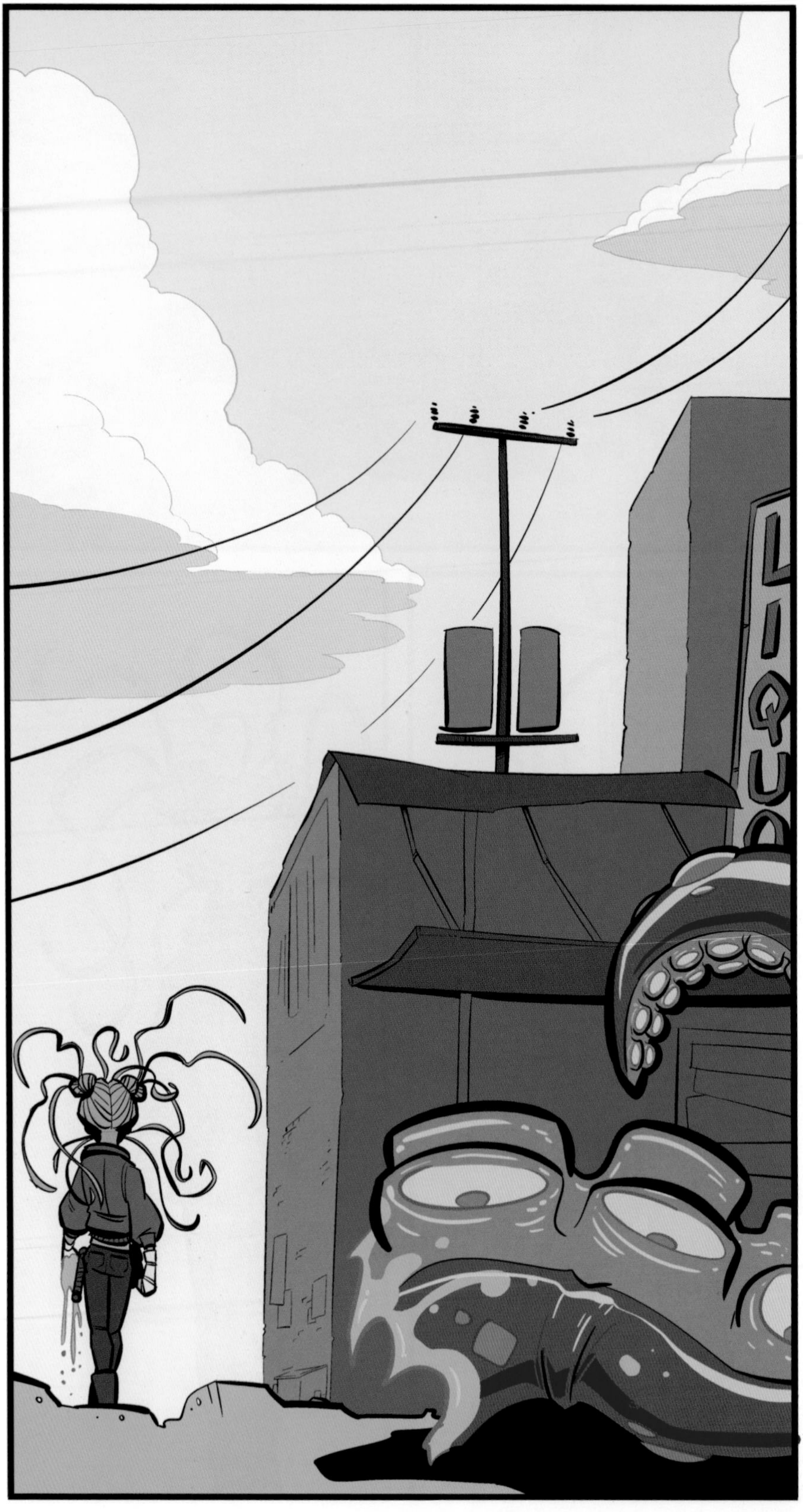

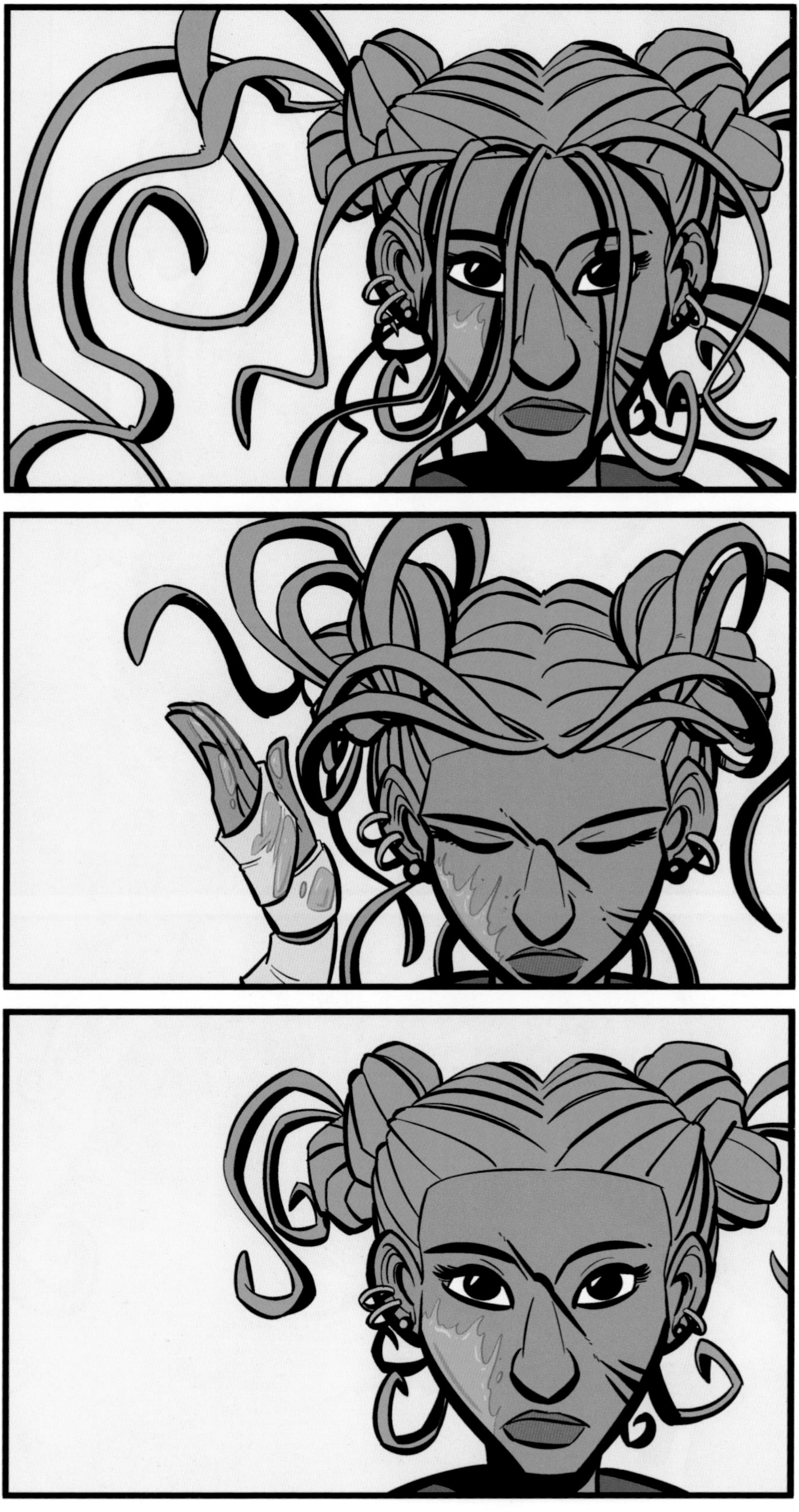

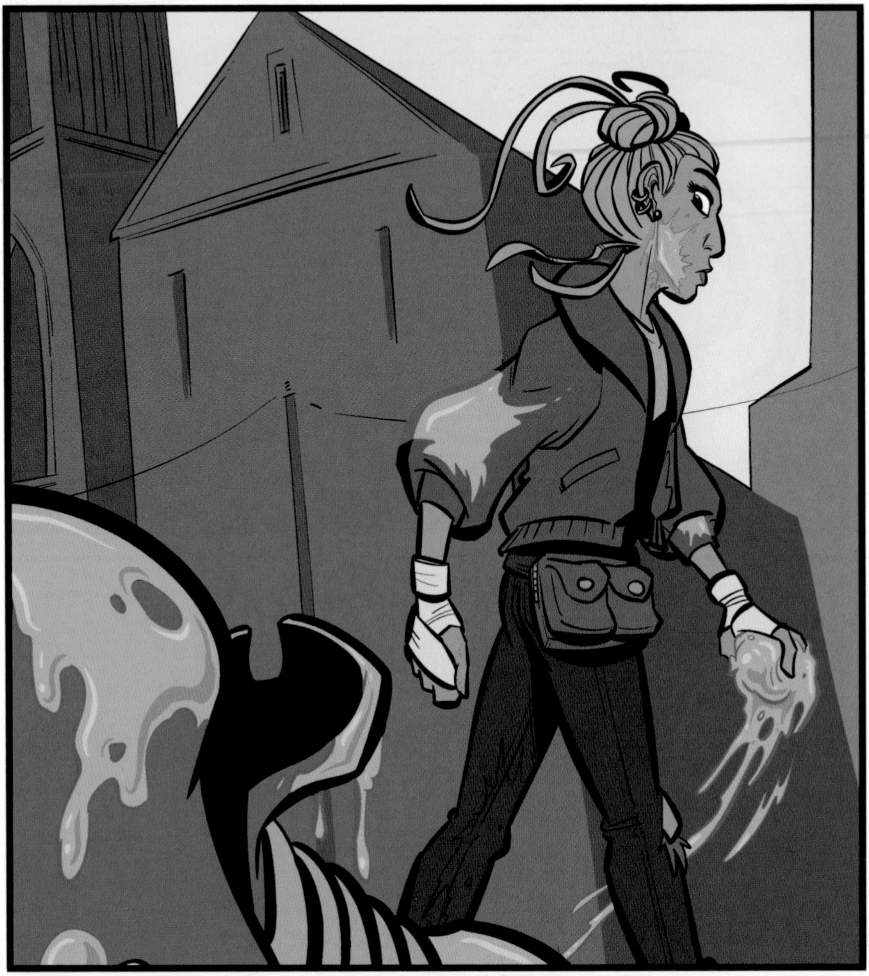

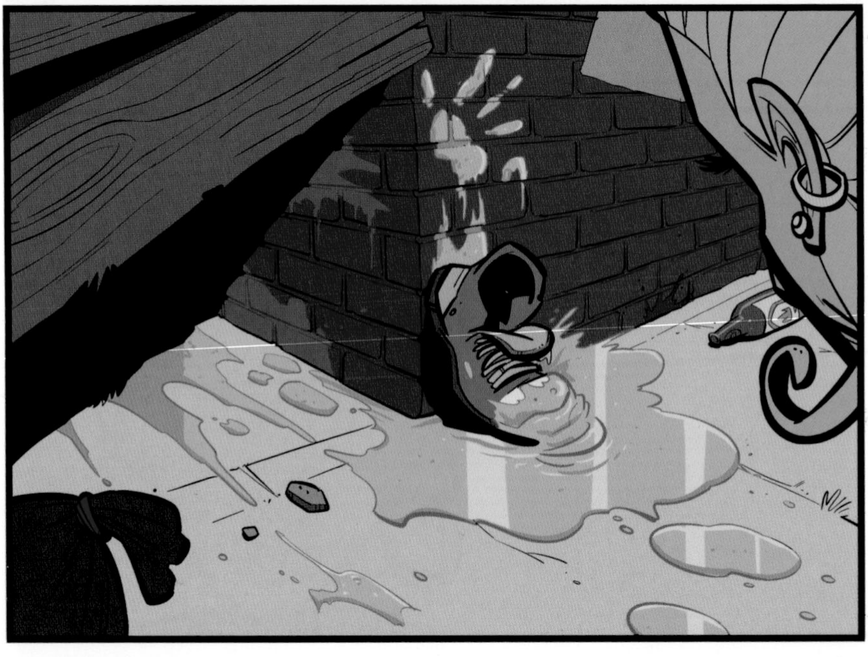

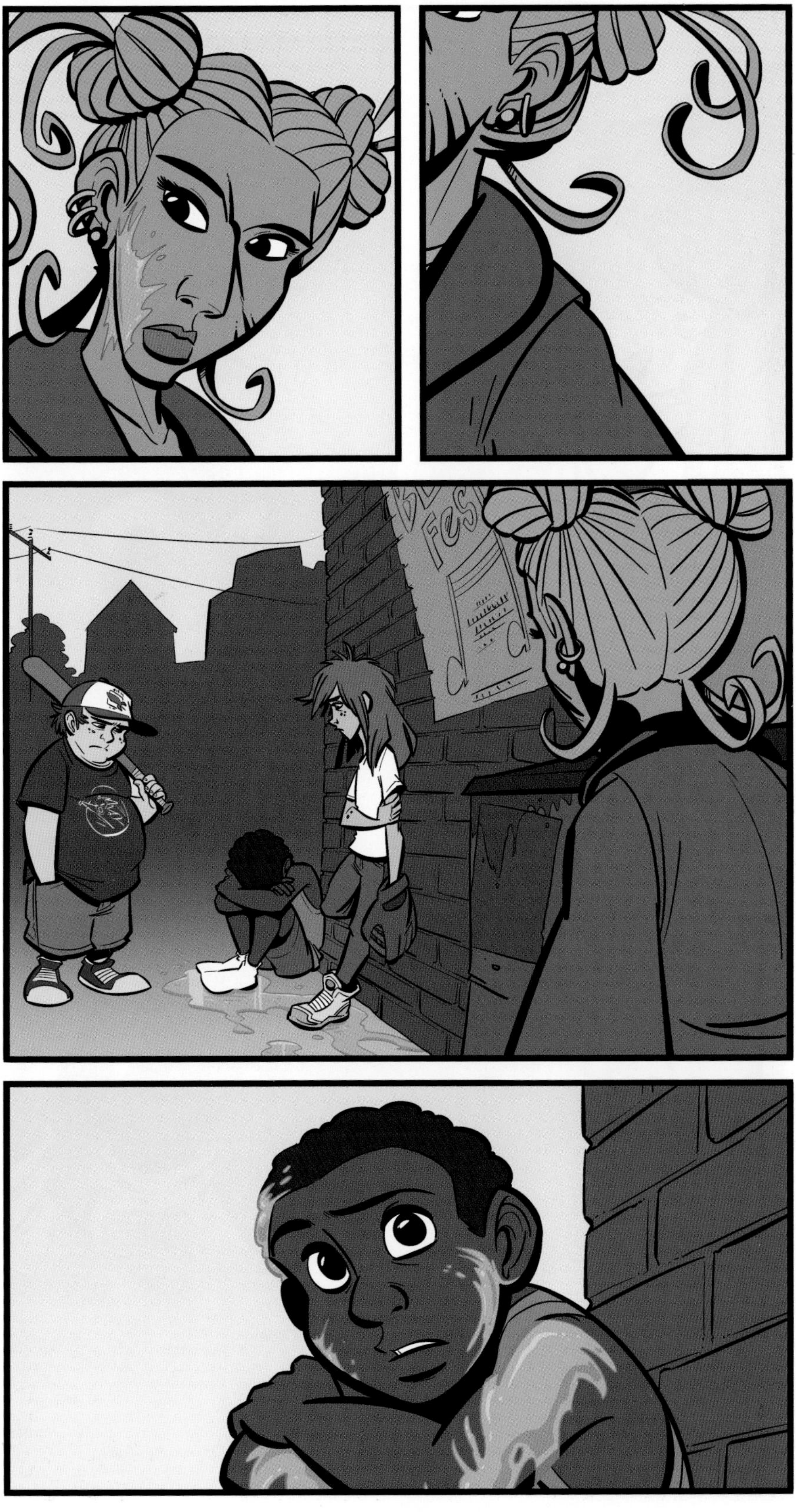

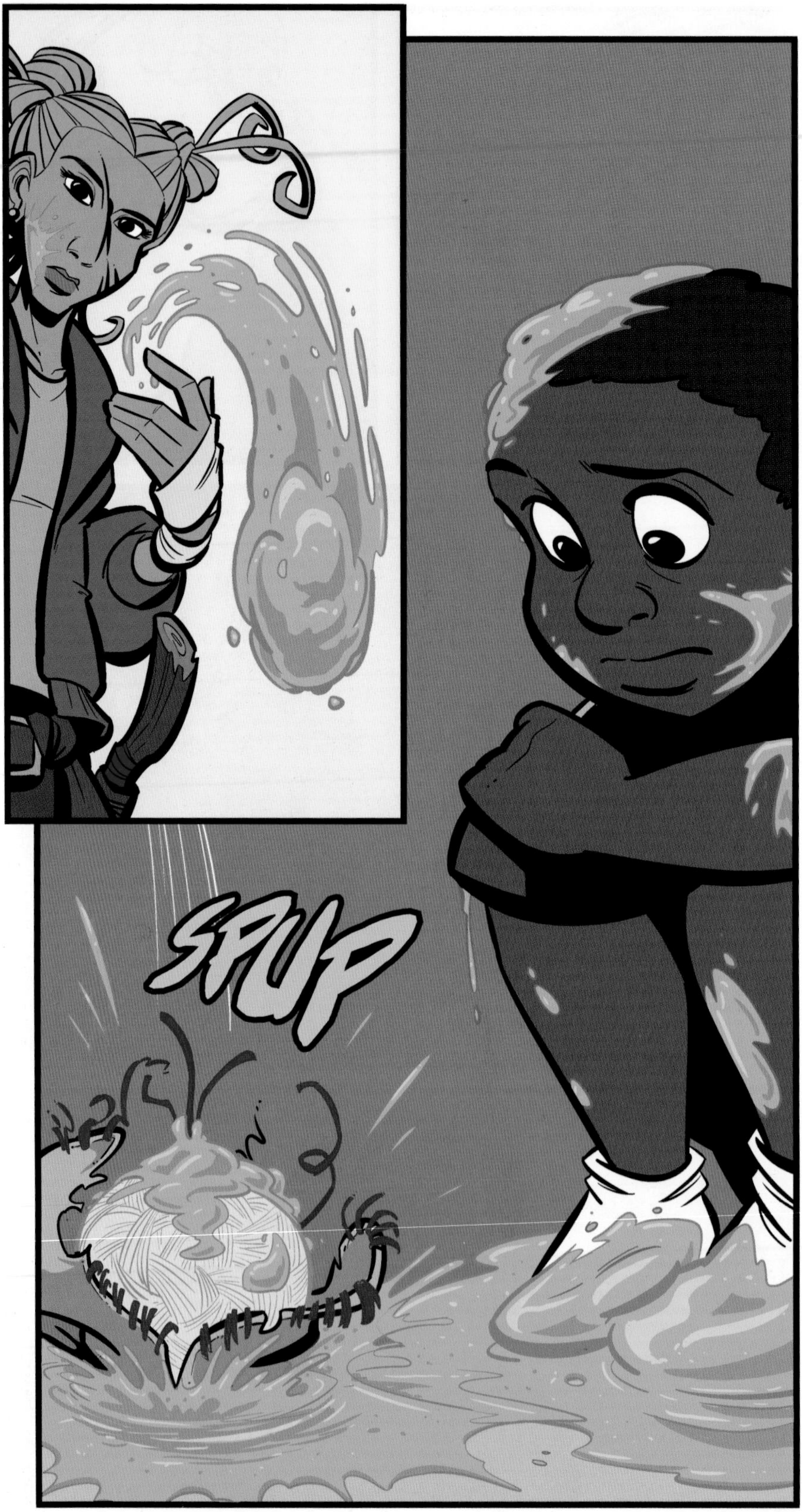
SPUP

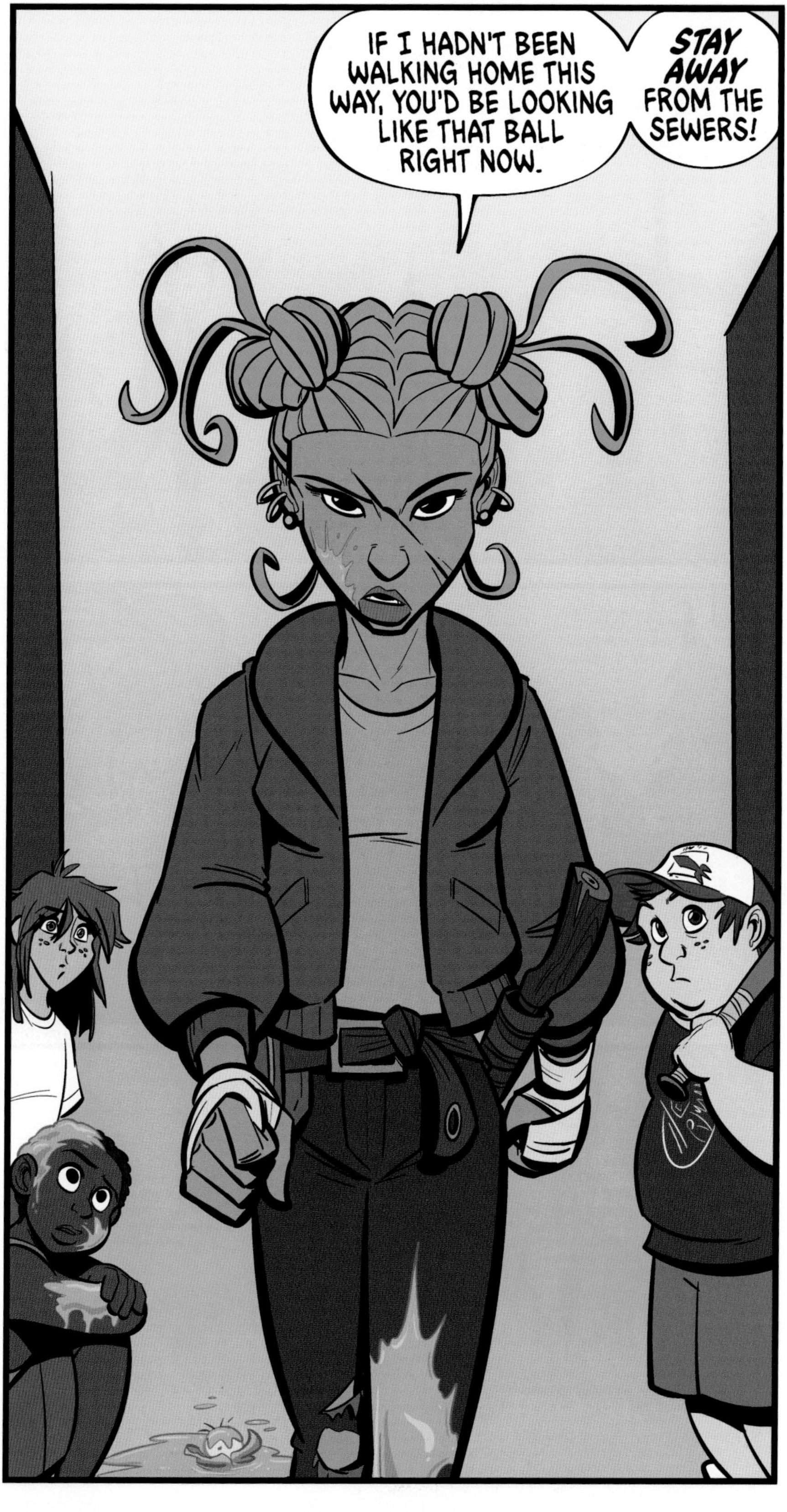
IF I HADN'T BEEN WALKING HOME THIS WAY, YOU'D BE LOOKING LIKE THAT BALL RIGHT NOW.
STAY AWAY FROM THE SEWERS!

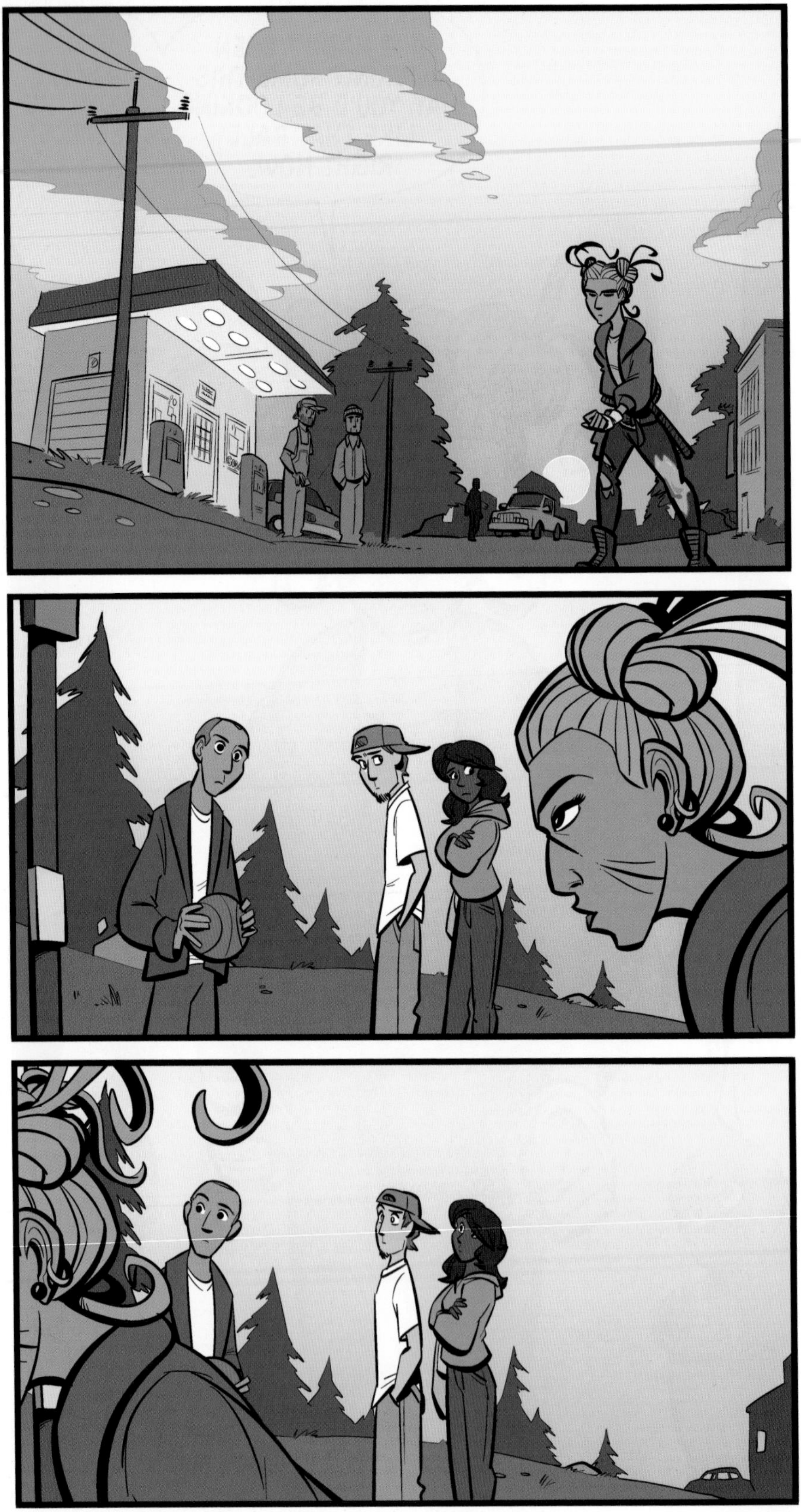

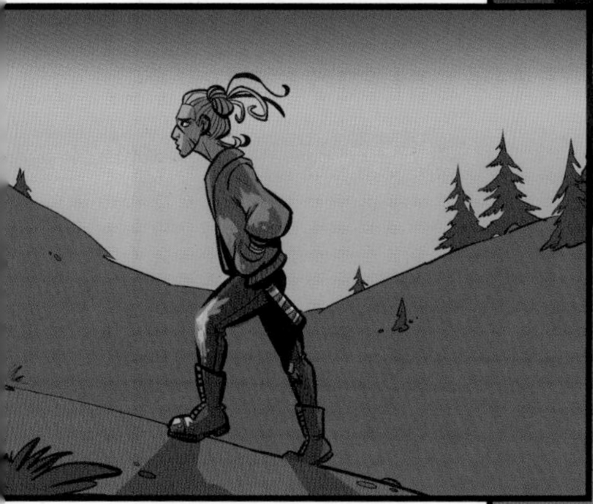

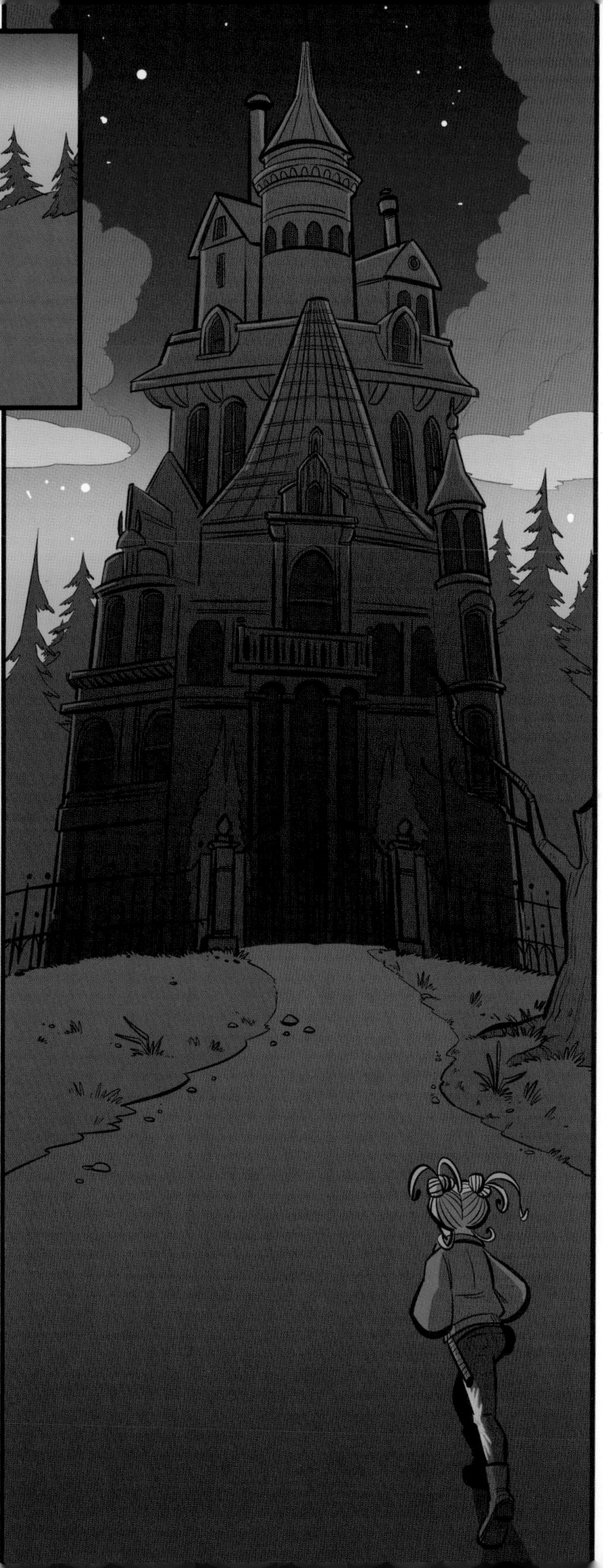

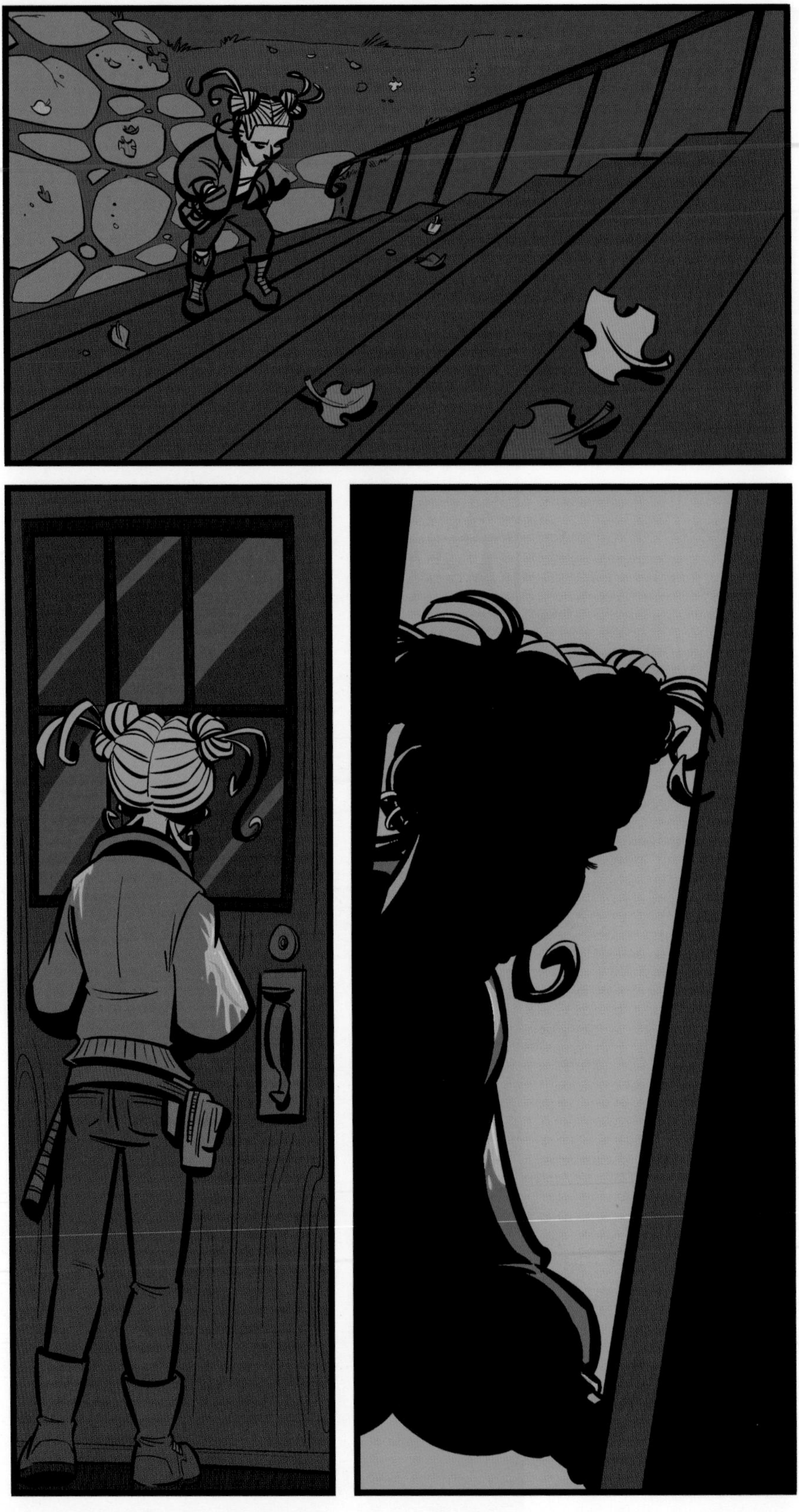

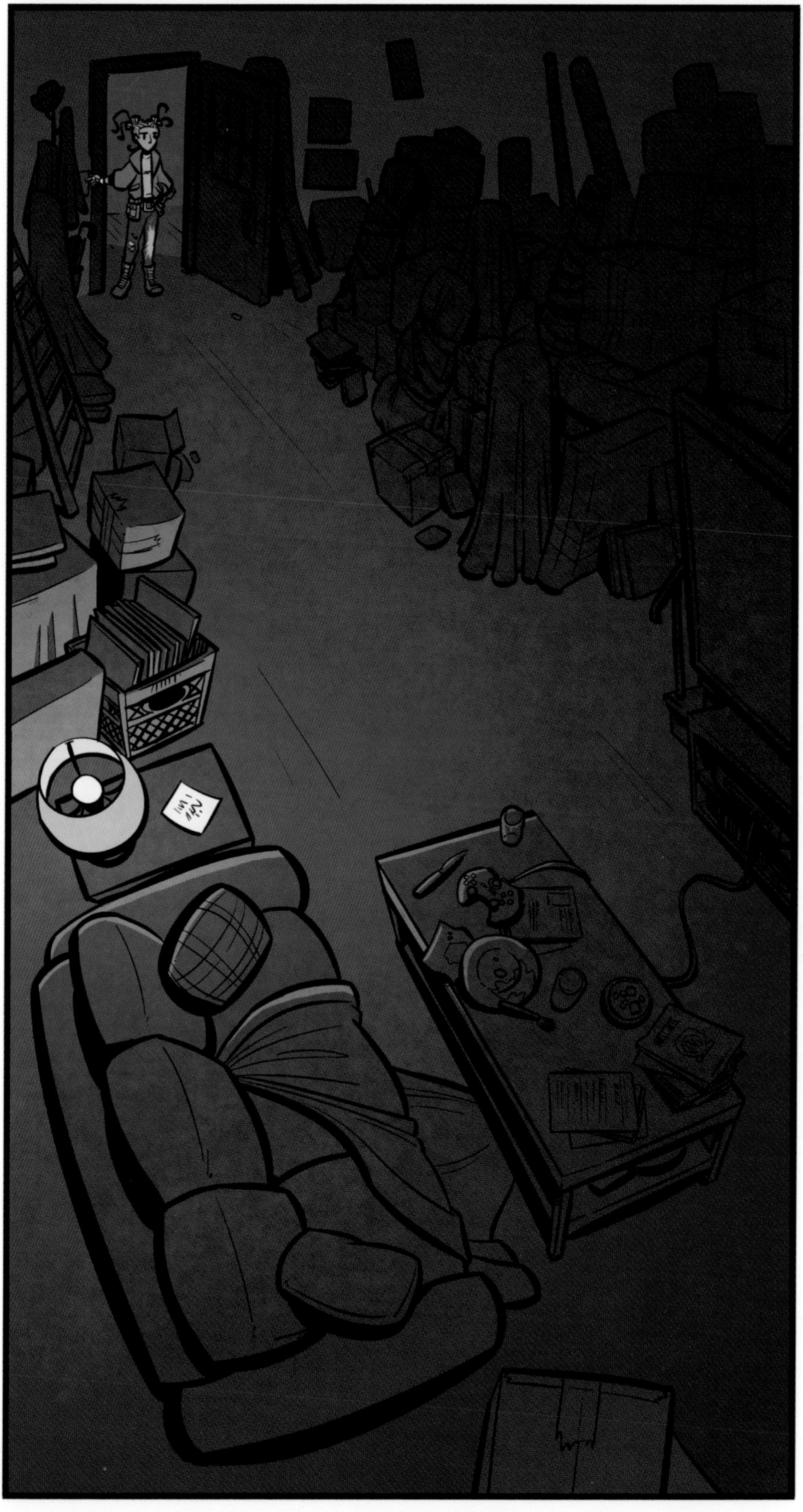

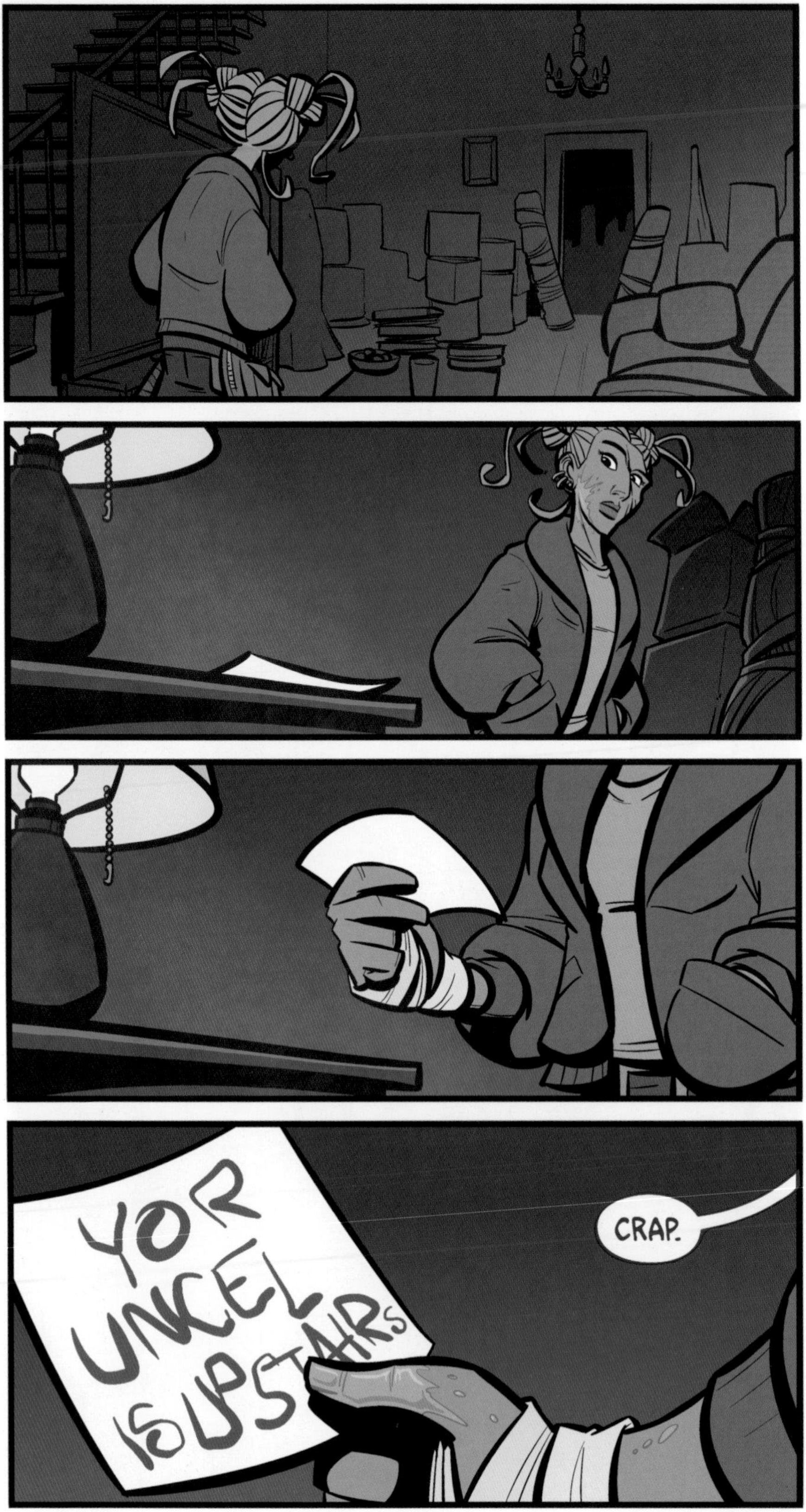
YOR UNCEL IS UPSTAIRS
CRAP.

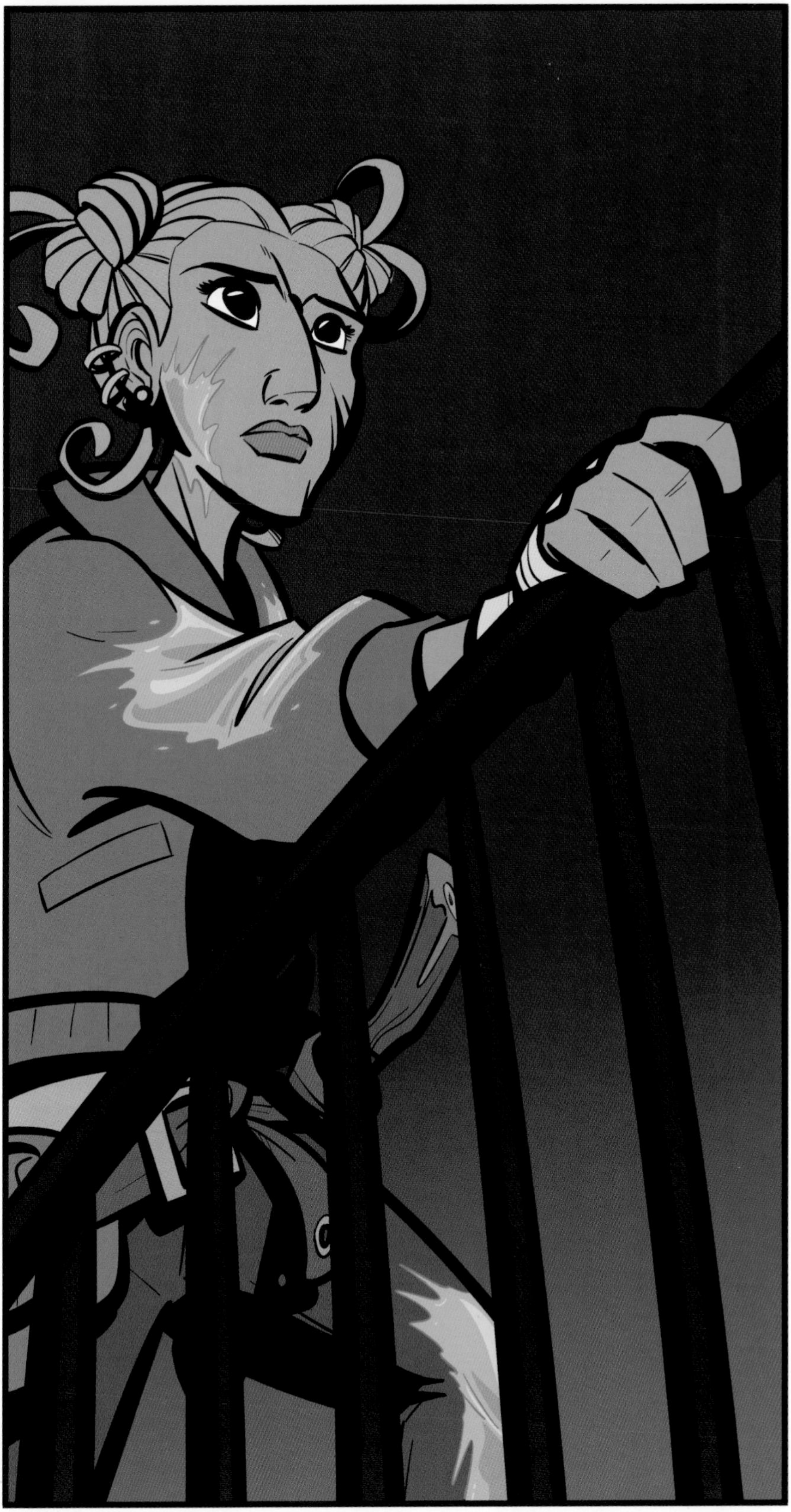

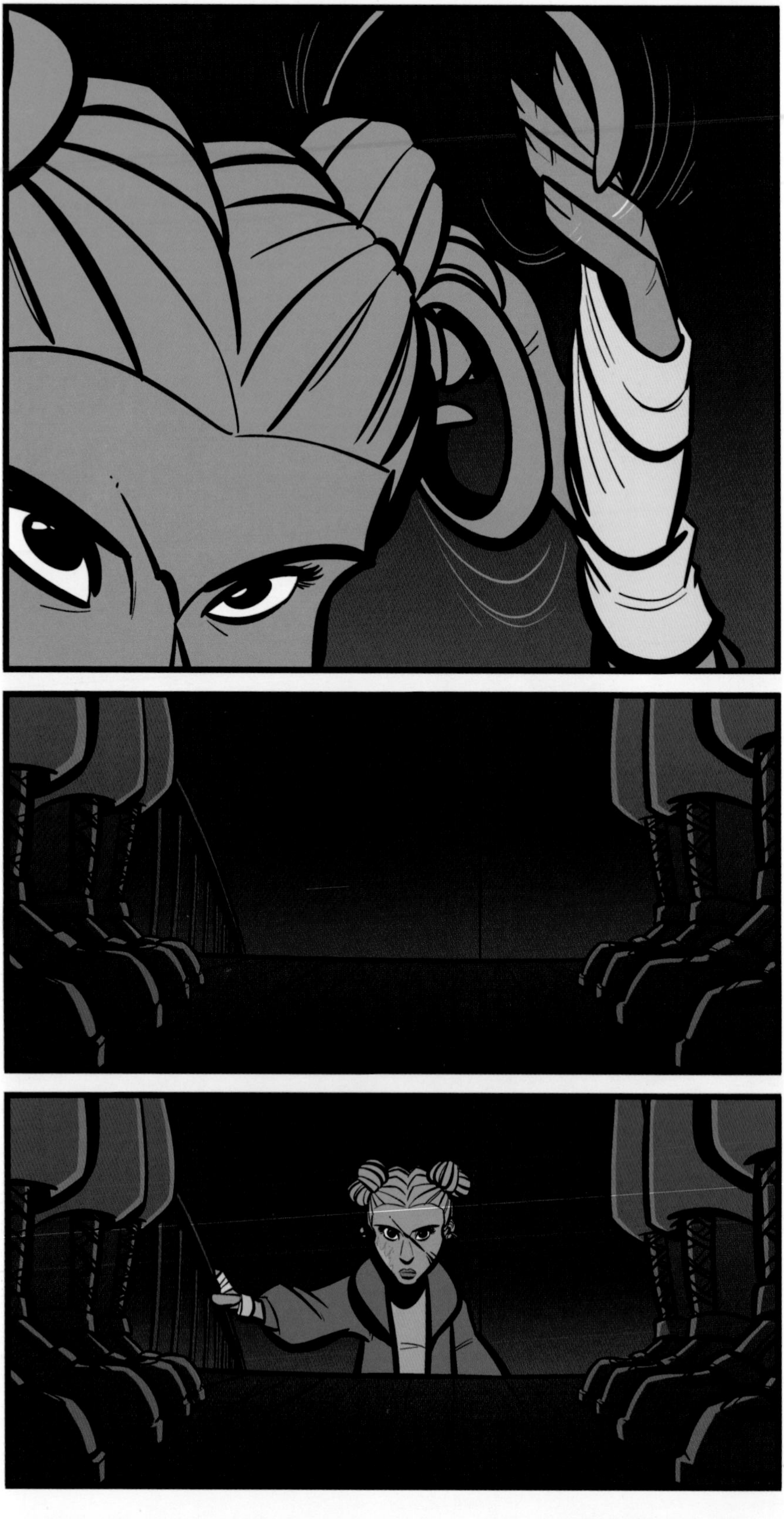

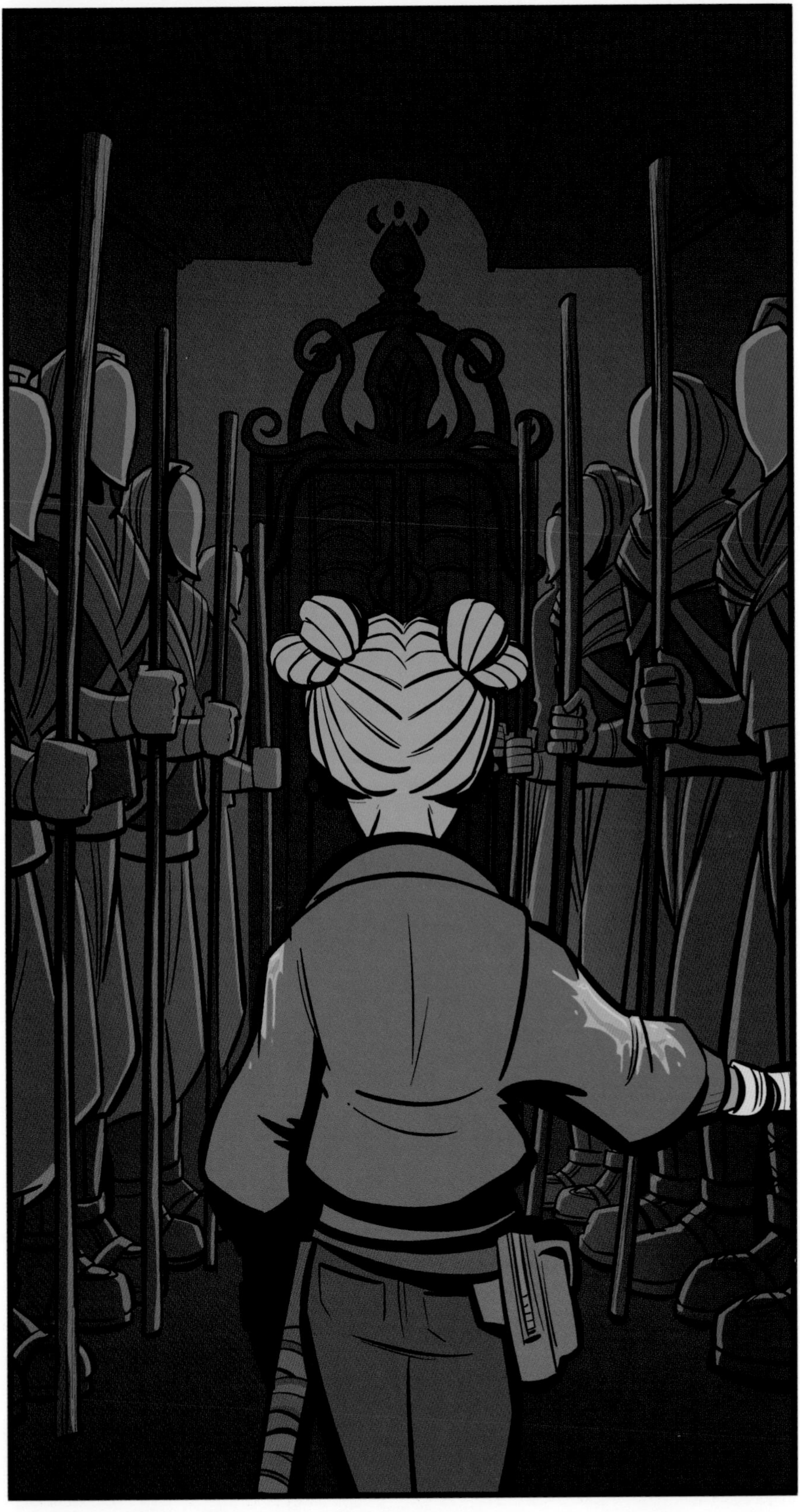

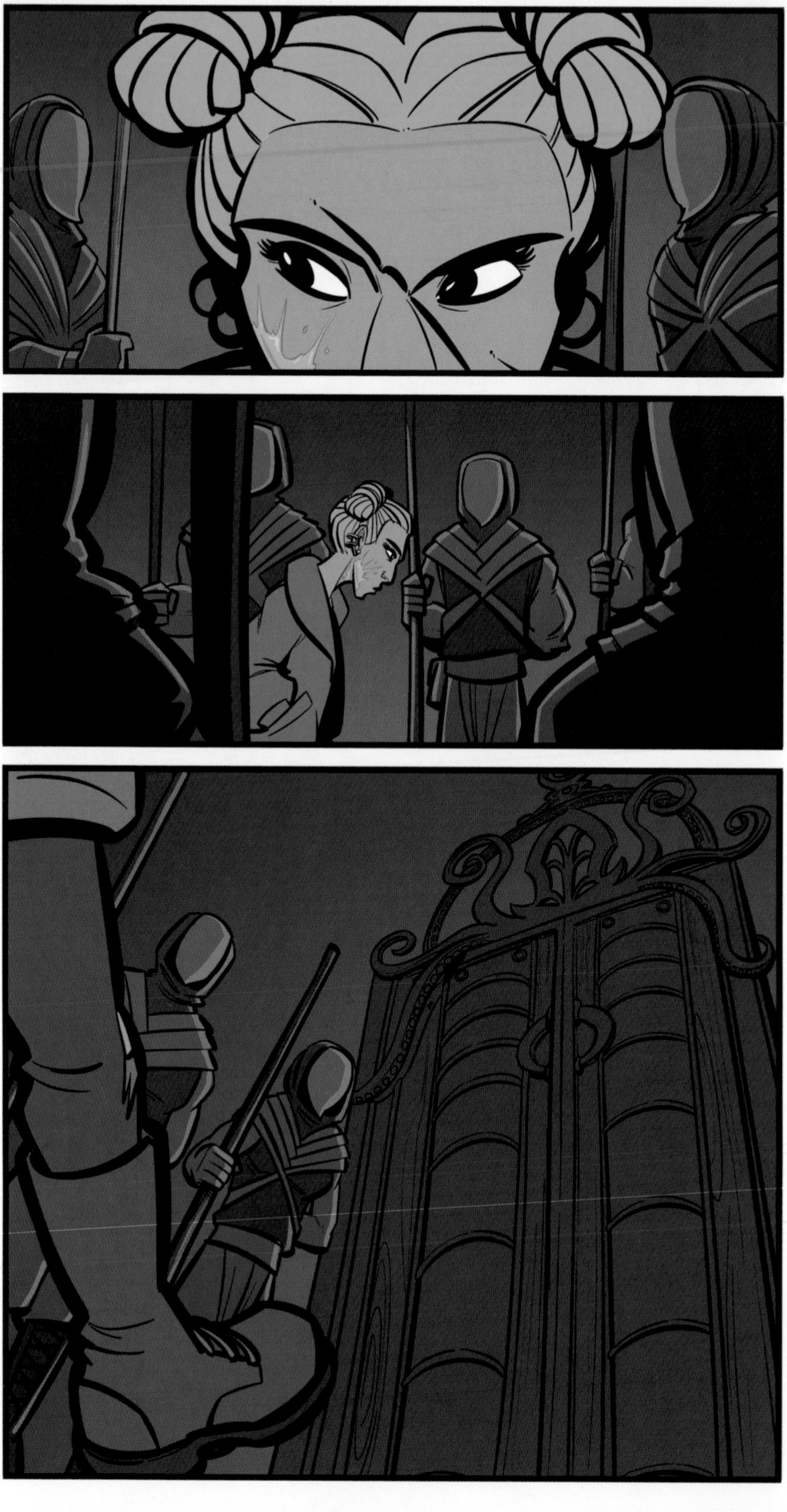

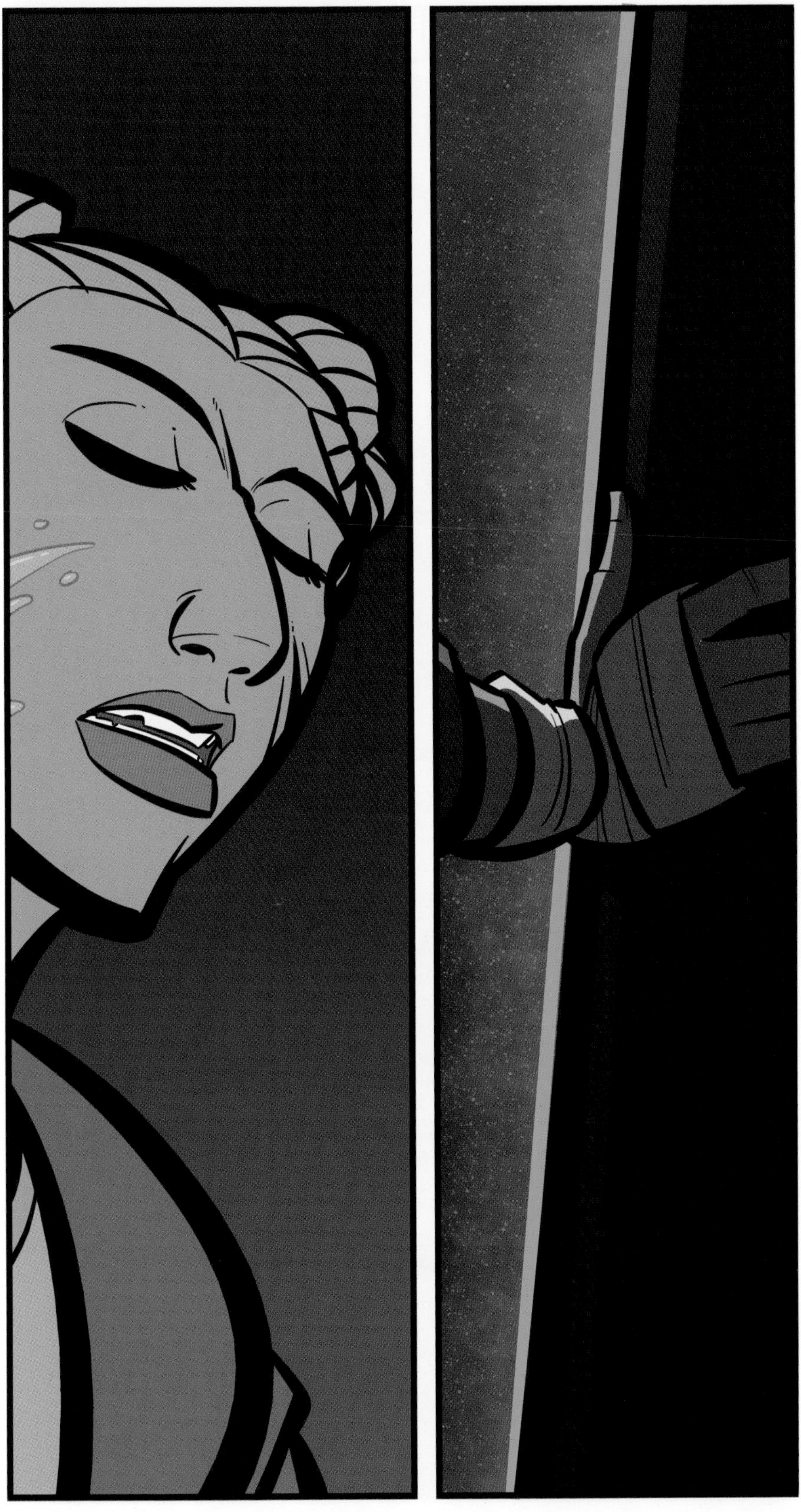

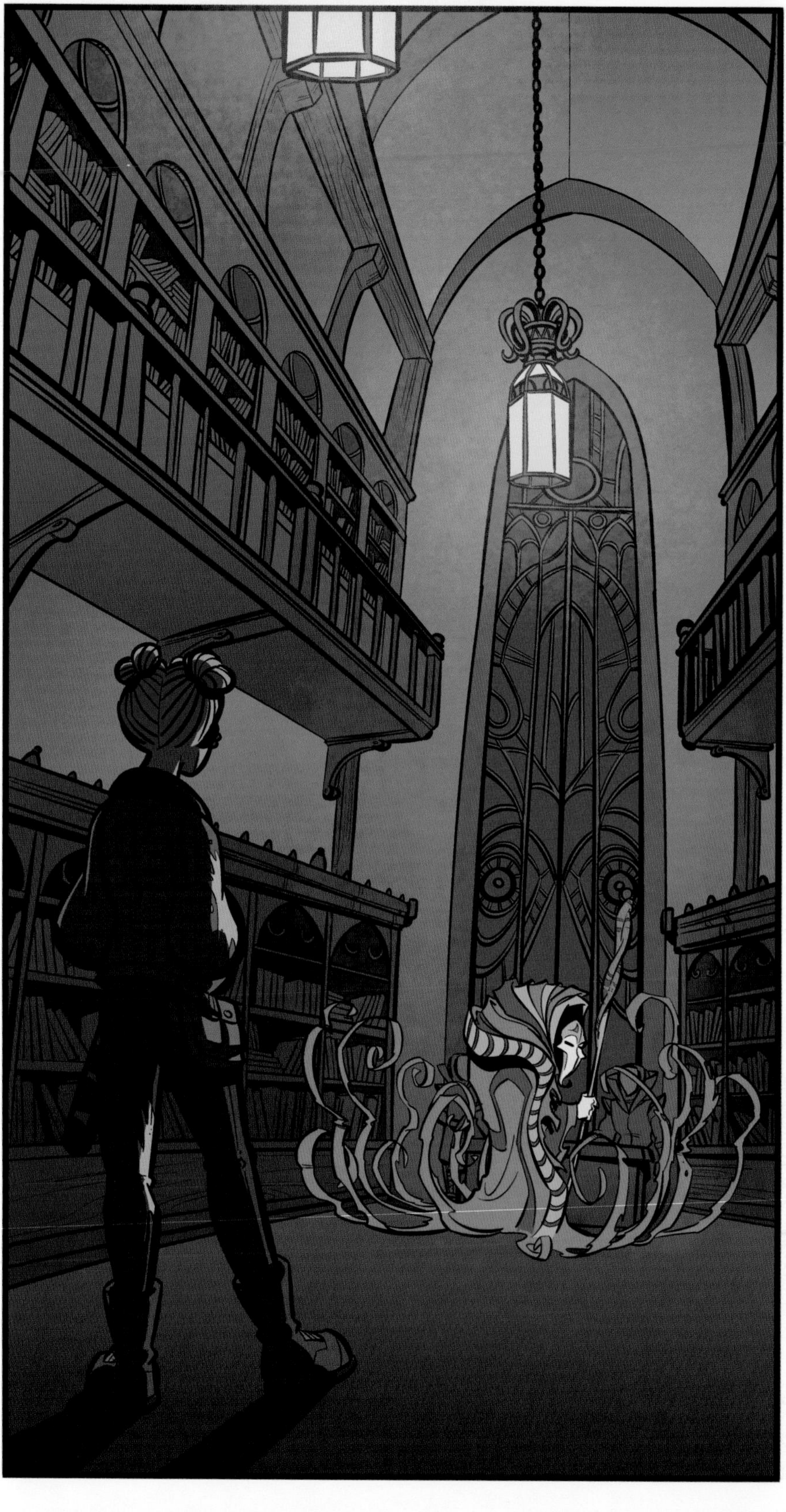

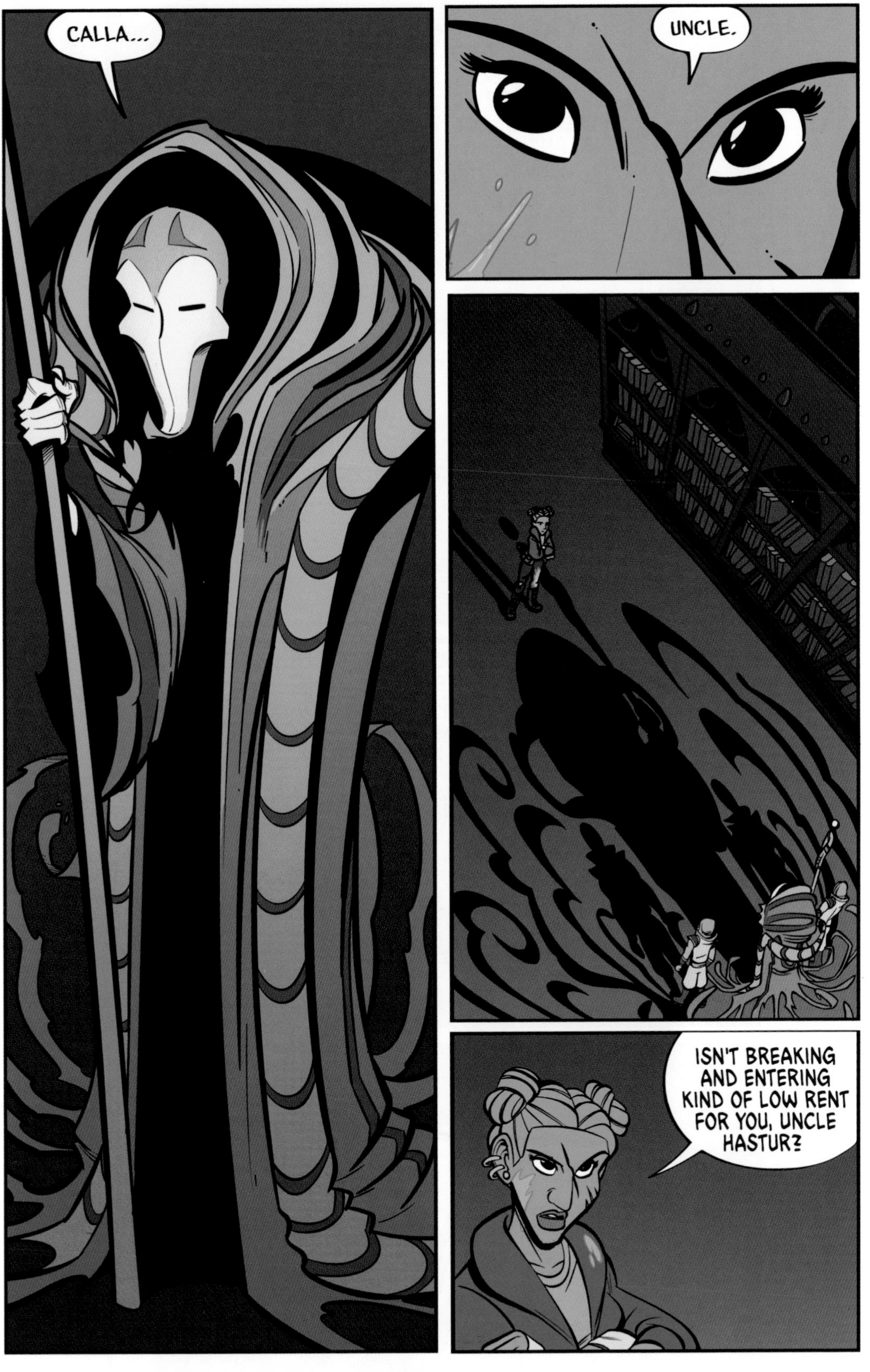
CALLA...
UNCLE.
ISN'T BREAKING AND ENTERING KIND OF LOW RENT FOR YOU, UNCLE HASTUR?

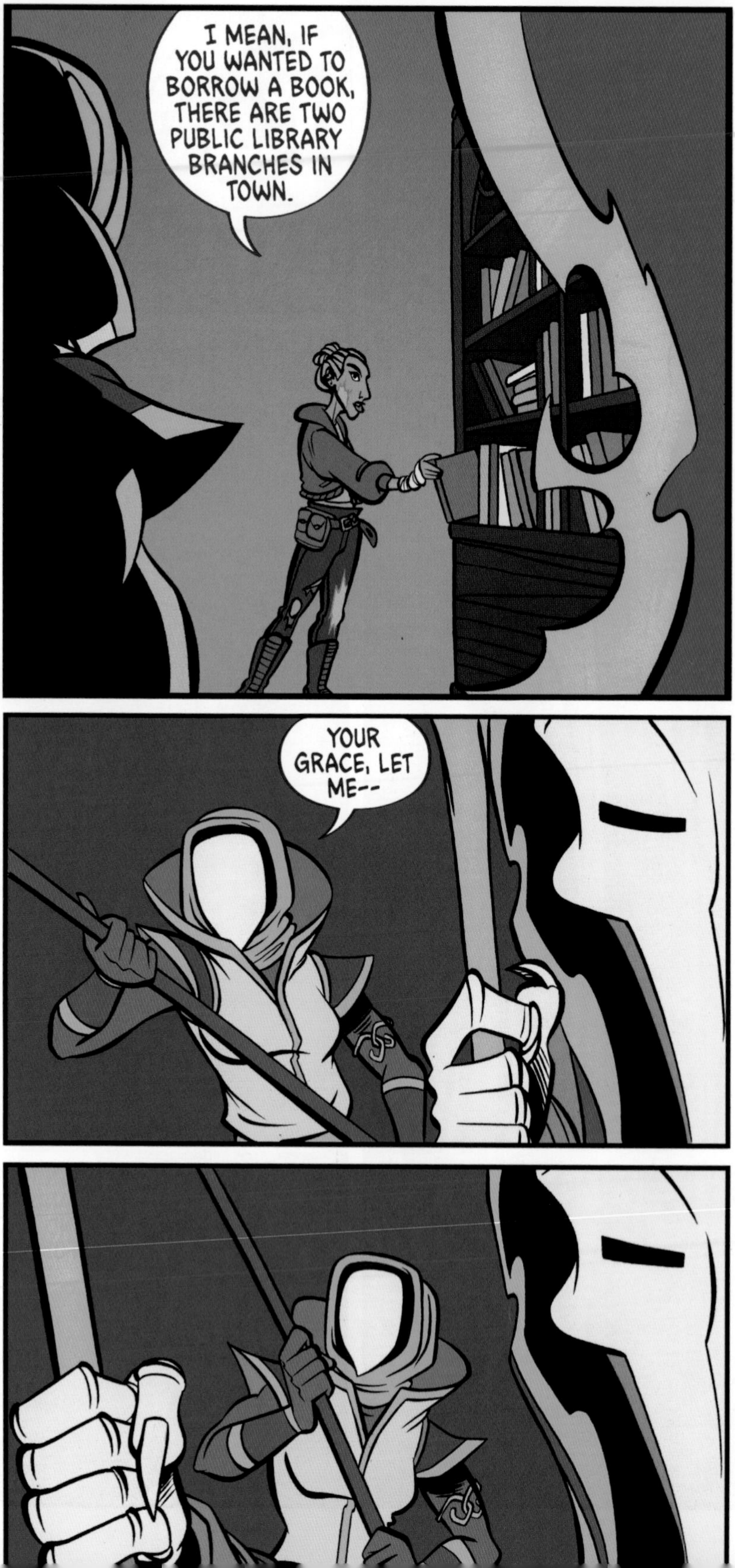
I MEAN, IF YOU WANTED TO BORROW A BOOK, THERE ARE TWO PUBLIC LIBRARY BRANCHES IN TOWN.
YOUR GRACE, LET ME--

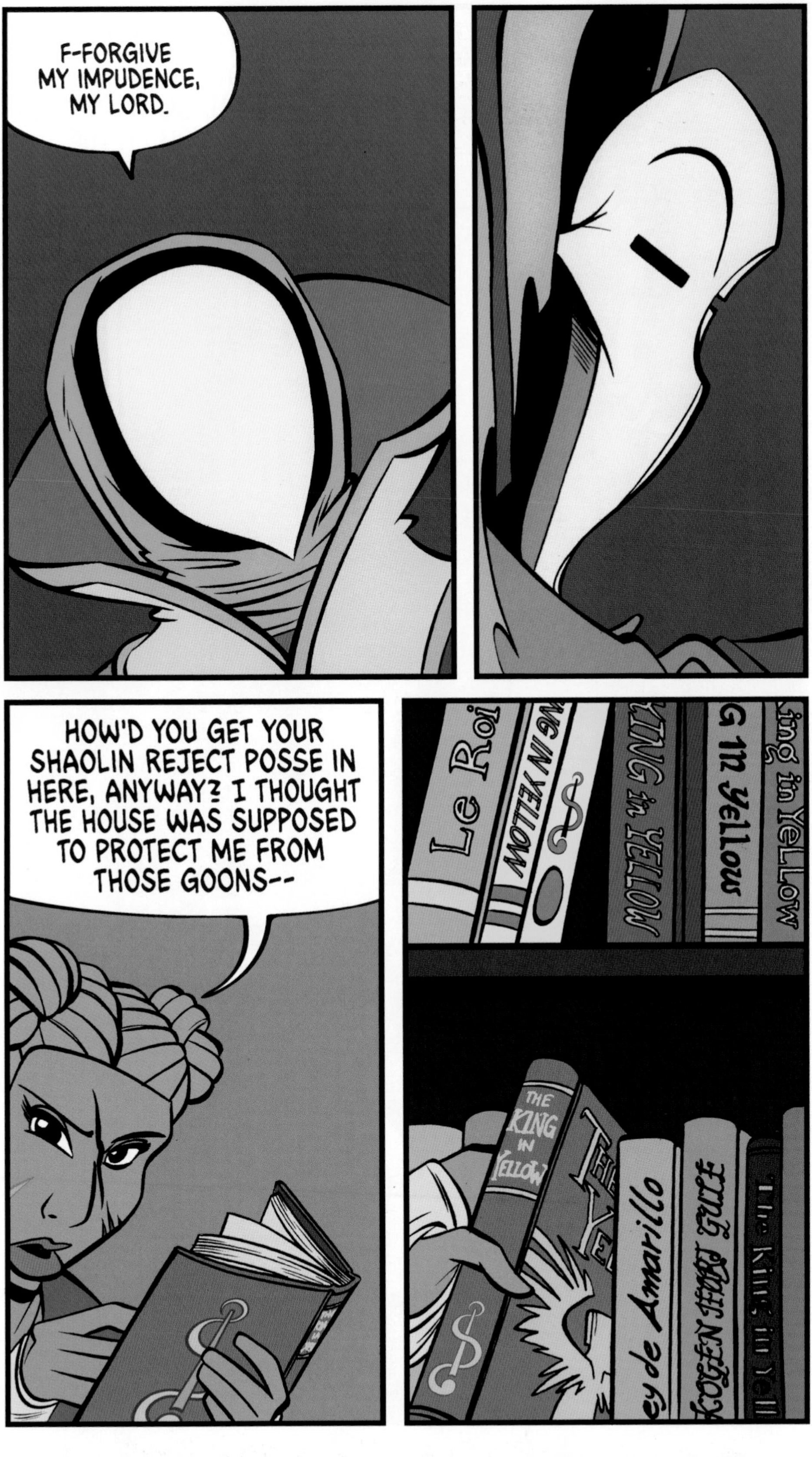
F-FORGIVE MY IMPUDENCE, MY LORD.
HOW'D YOU GET YOUR SHAOLIN REJECT POSSE IN HERE, ANYWAY? I THOUGHT THE HOUSE WAS SUPPOSED TO PROTECT ME FROM THOSE GOONS--
Le Roi
G in Yellow
ing in YeLLow
THE KING IN YELLOW
ey de Amarillo

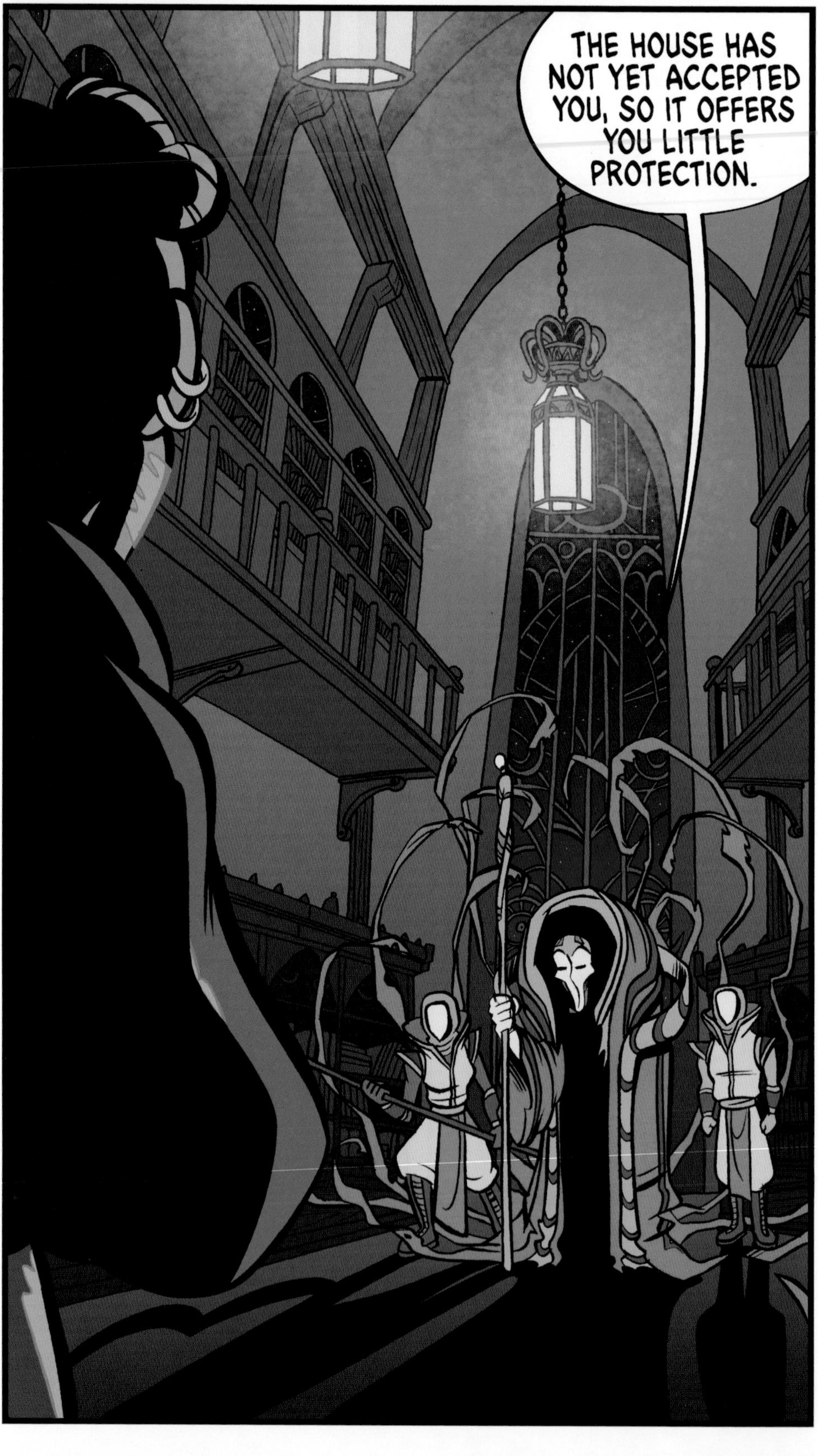
THE HOUSE HAS NOT YET ACCEPTED YOU, SO IT OFFERS YOU LITTLE PROTECTION.

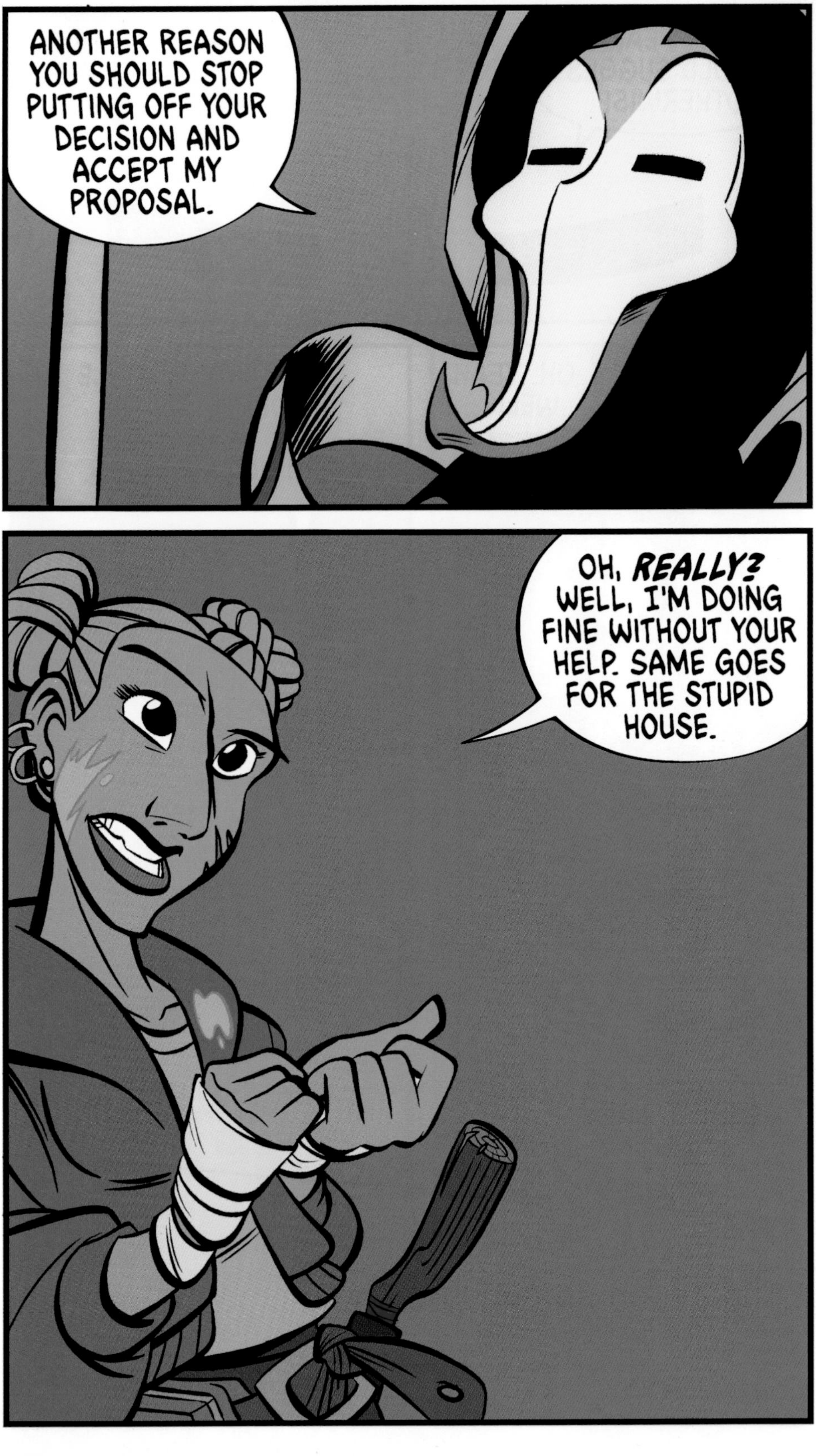
ANOTHER REASON YOU SHOULD STOP PUTTING OFF YOUR DECISION AND ACCEPT MY PROPOSAL.
OH, *REALLY?* WELL, I'M DOING FINE WITHOUT YOUR HELP. SAME GOES FOR THE STUPID HOUSE.

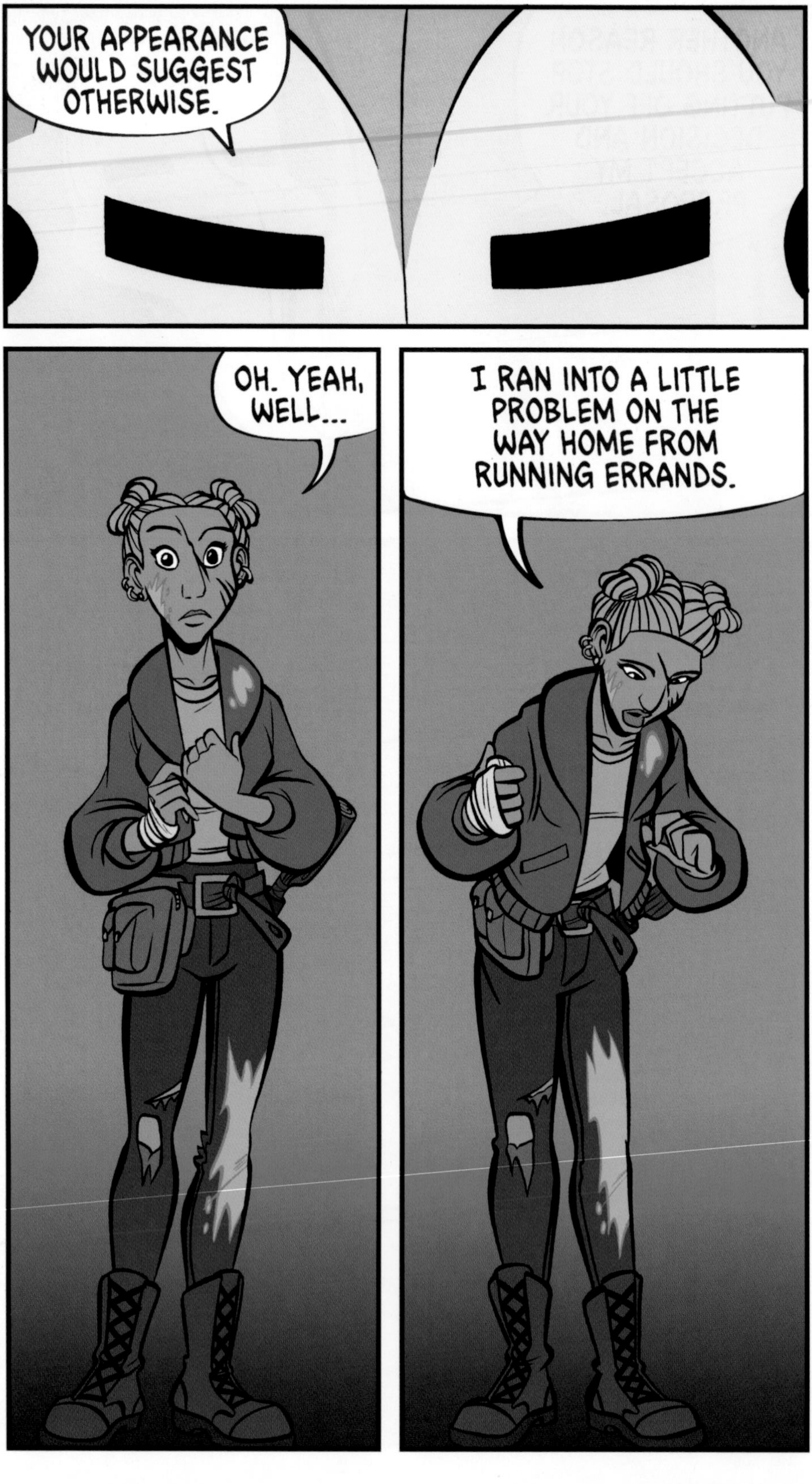
YOUR APPEARANCE WOULD SUGGEST OTHERWISE.
OH. YEAH, WELL...
I RAN INTO A LITTLE PROBLEM ON THE WAY HOME FROM RUNNING ERRANDS.

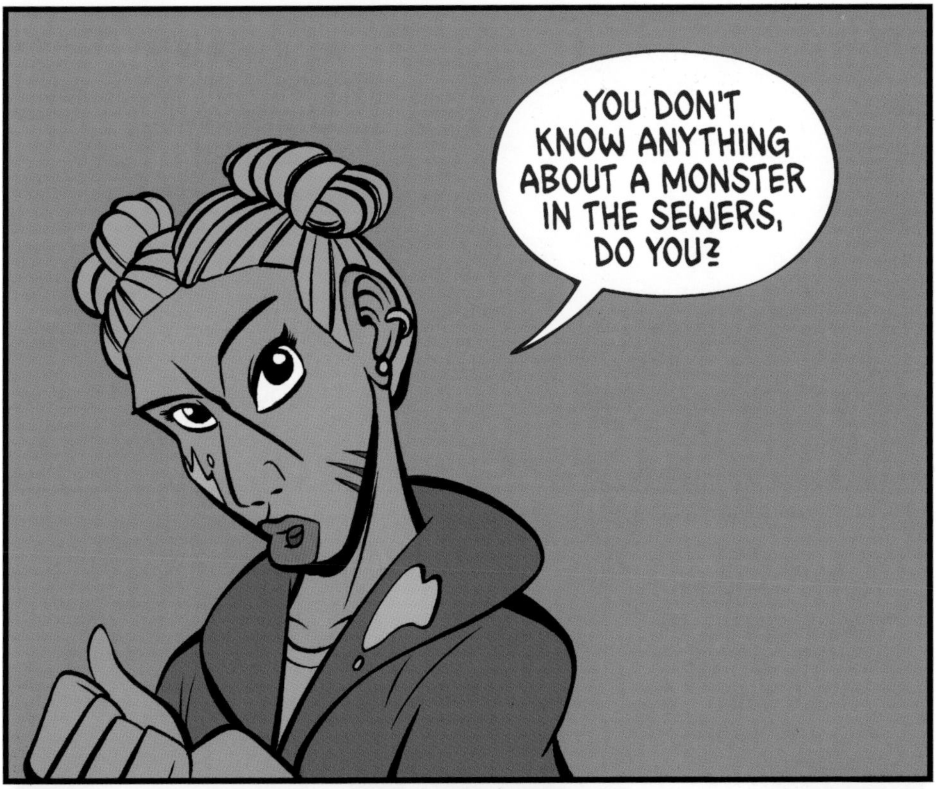
YOU DON'T KNOW ANYTHING ABOUT A MONSTER IN THE SEWERS, DO YOU?

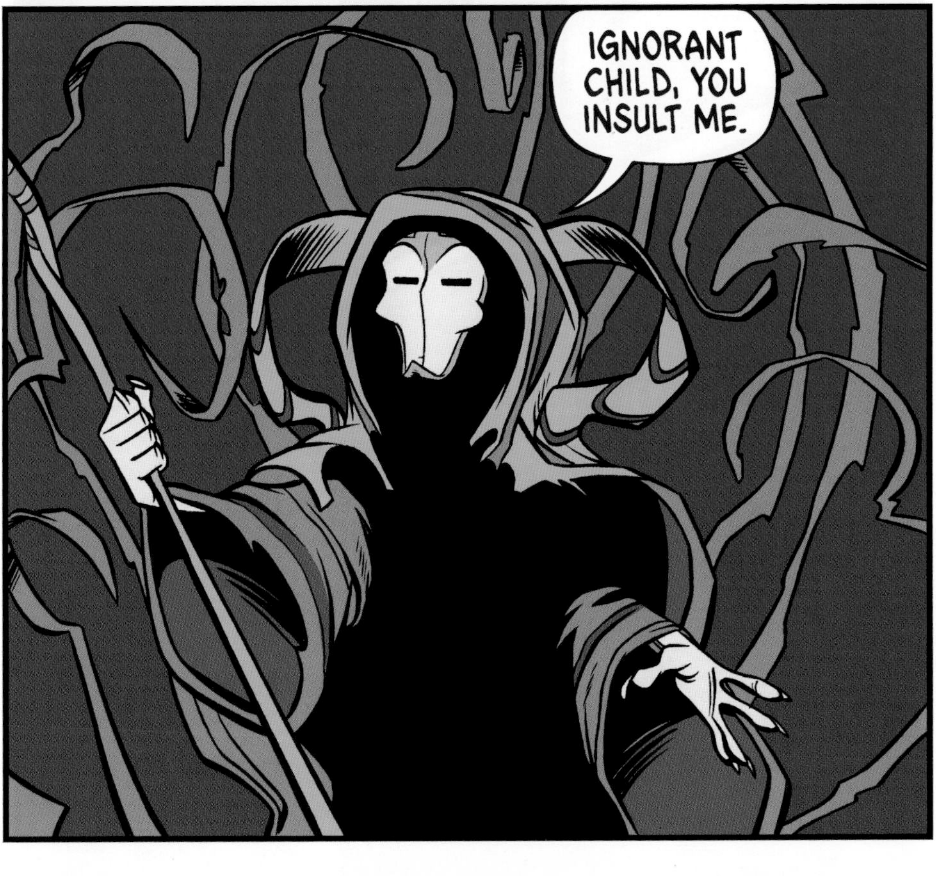
IGNORANT CHILD, YOU INSULT ME.

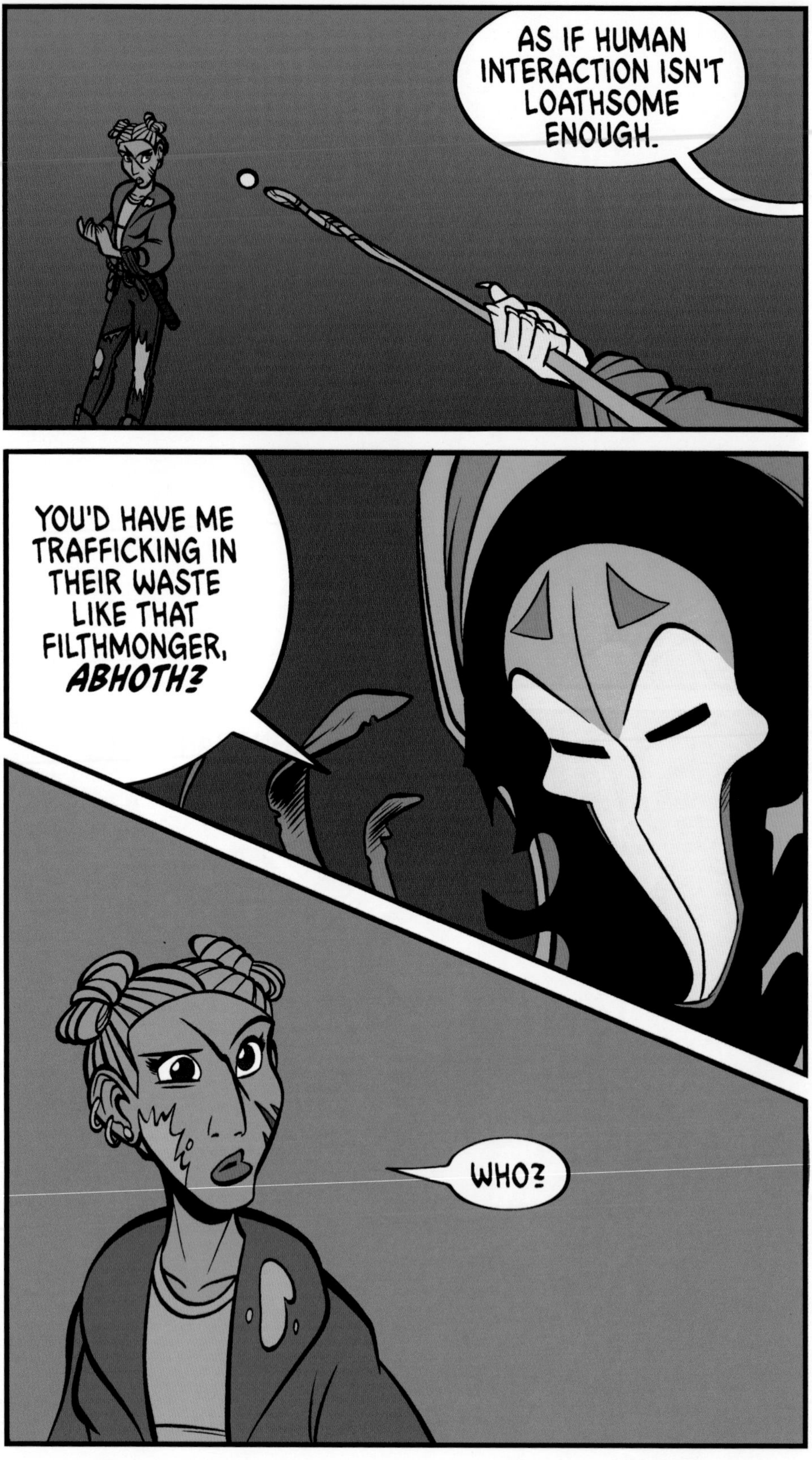
AS IF HUMAN INTERACTION ISN'T LOATHSOME ENOUGH.
YOU'D HAVE ME TRAFFICKING IN THEIR WASTE LIKE THAT FILTHMONGER, ABHOTH?
WHO?

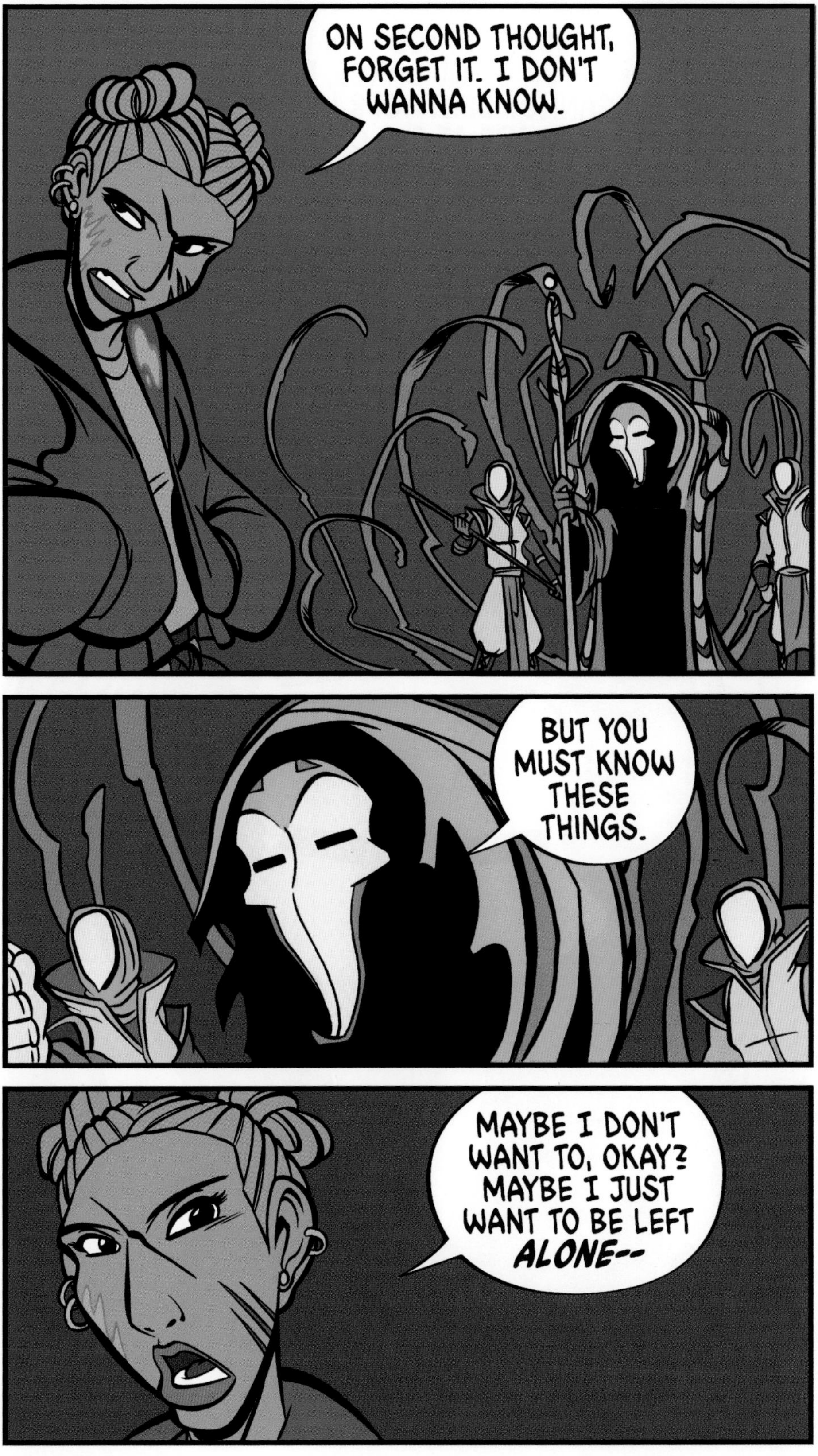
ON SECOND THOUGHT, FORGET IT. I DON'T WANNA KNOW.
BUT YOU MUST KNOW THESE THINGS.
MAYBE I DON'T WANT TO, OKAY? MAYBE I JUST WANT TO BE LEFT *ALONE--*

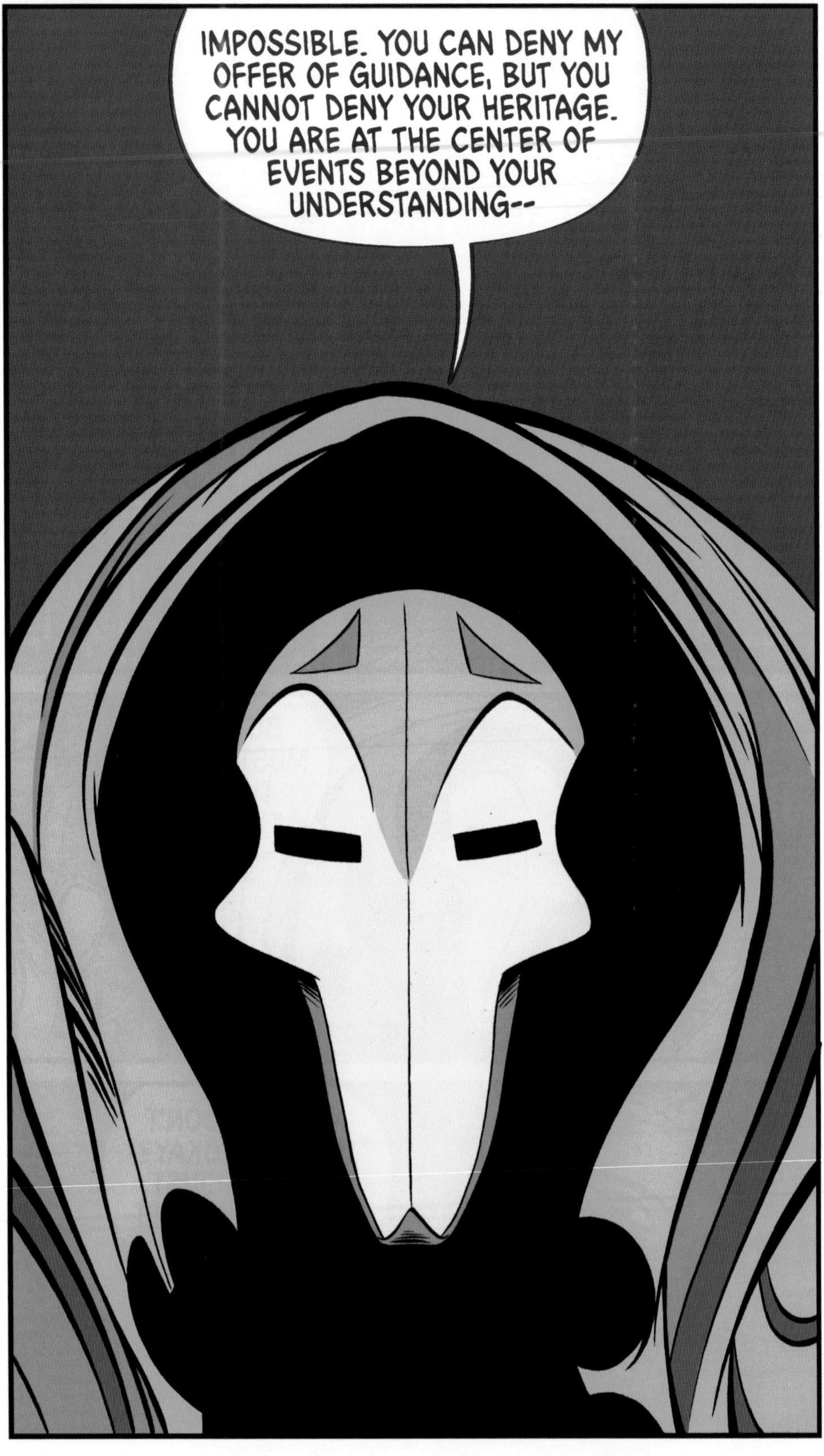
IMPOSSIBLE. YOU CAN DENY MY OFFER OF GUIDANCE, BUT YOU CANNOT DENY YOUR HERITAGE. YOU ARE AT THE CENTER OF EVENTS BEYOND YOUR UNDERSTANDING--

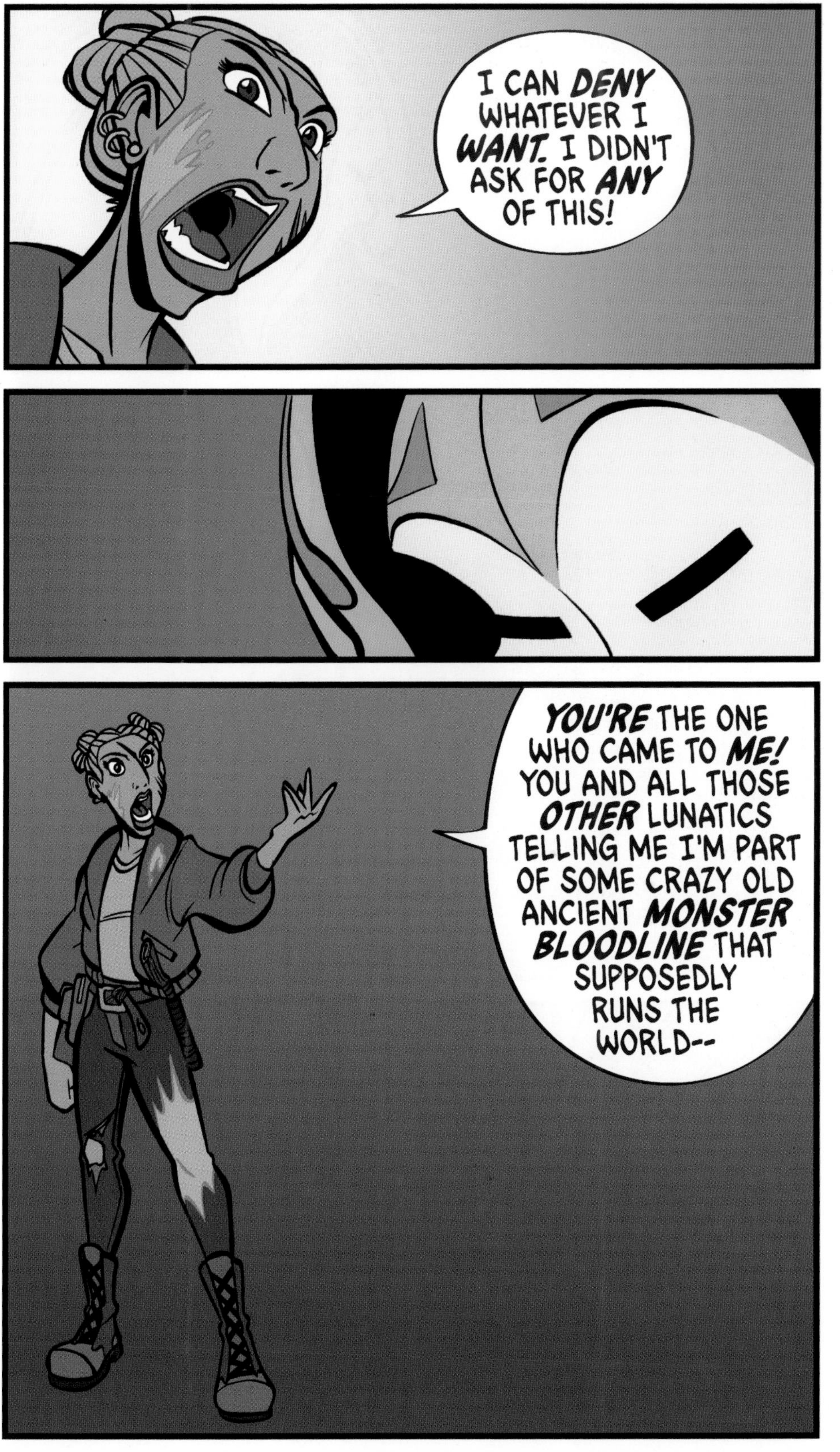
I CAN DENY WHATEVER I WANT. I DIDN'T ASK FOR ANY OF THIS!
YOU'RE THE ONE WHO CAME TO ME! YOU AND ALL THOSE OTHER LUNATICS TELLING ME I'M PART OF SOME CRAZY OLD ANCIENT MONSTER BLOODLINE THAT SUPPOSEDLY RUNS THE WORLD--

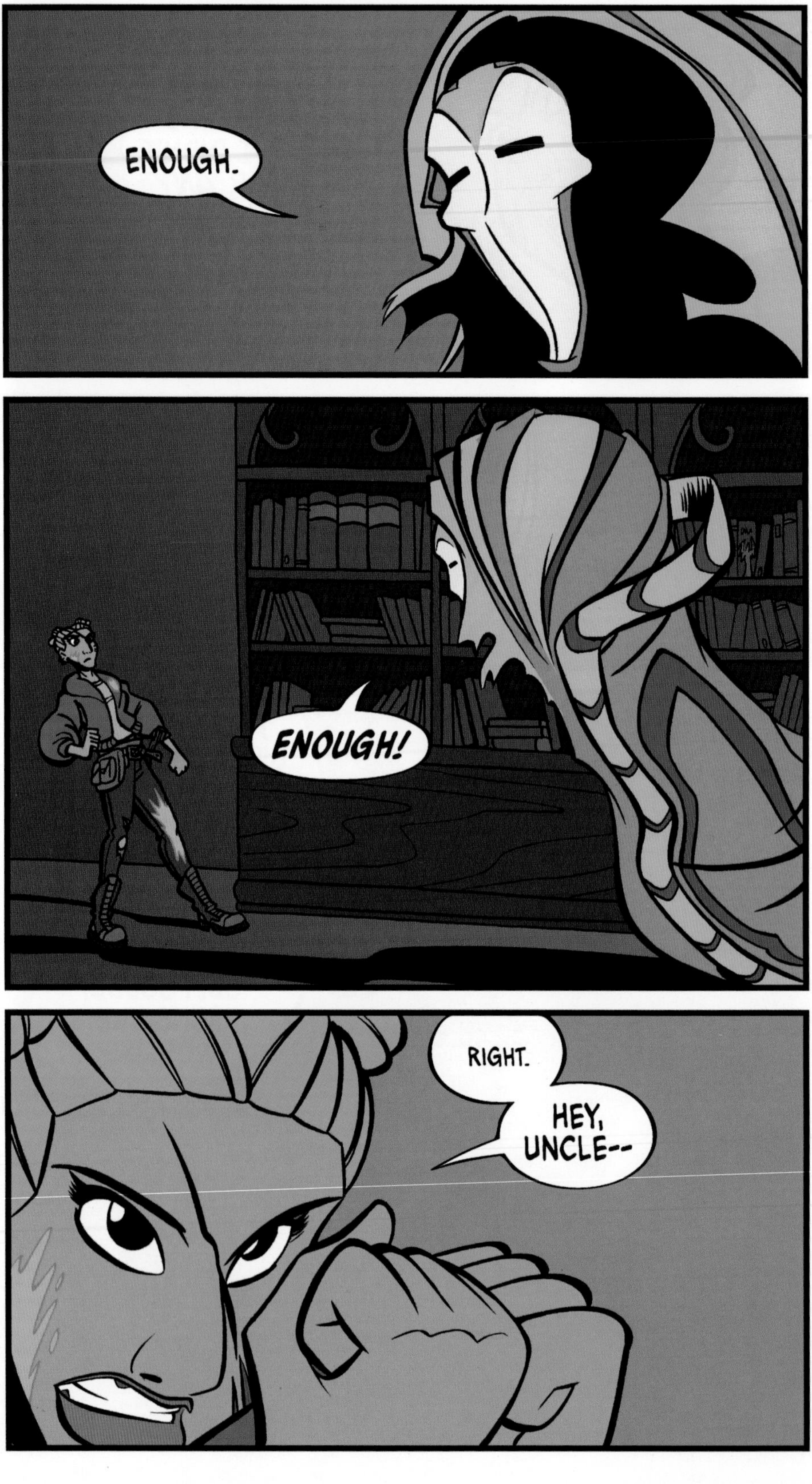
ENOUGH.
ENOUGH!
RIGHT.
HEY, UNCLE--

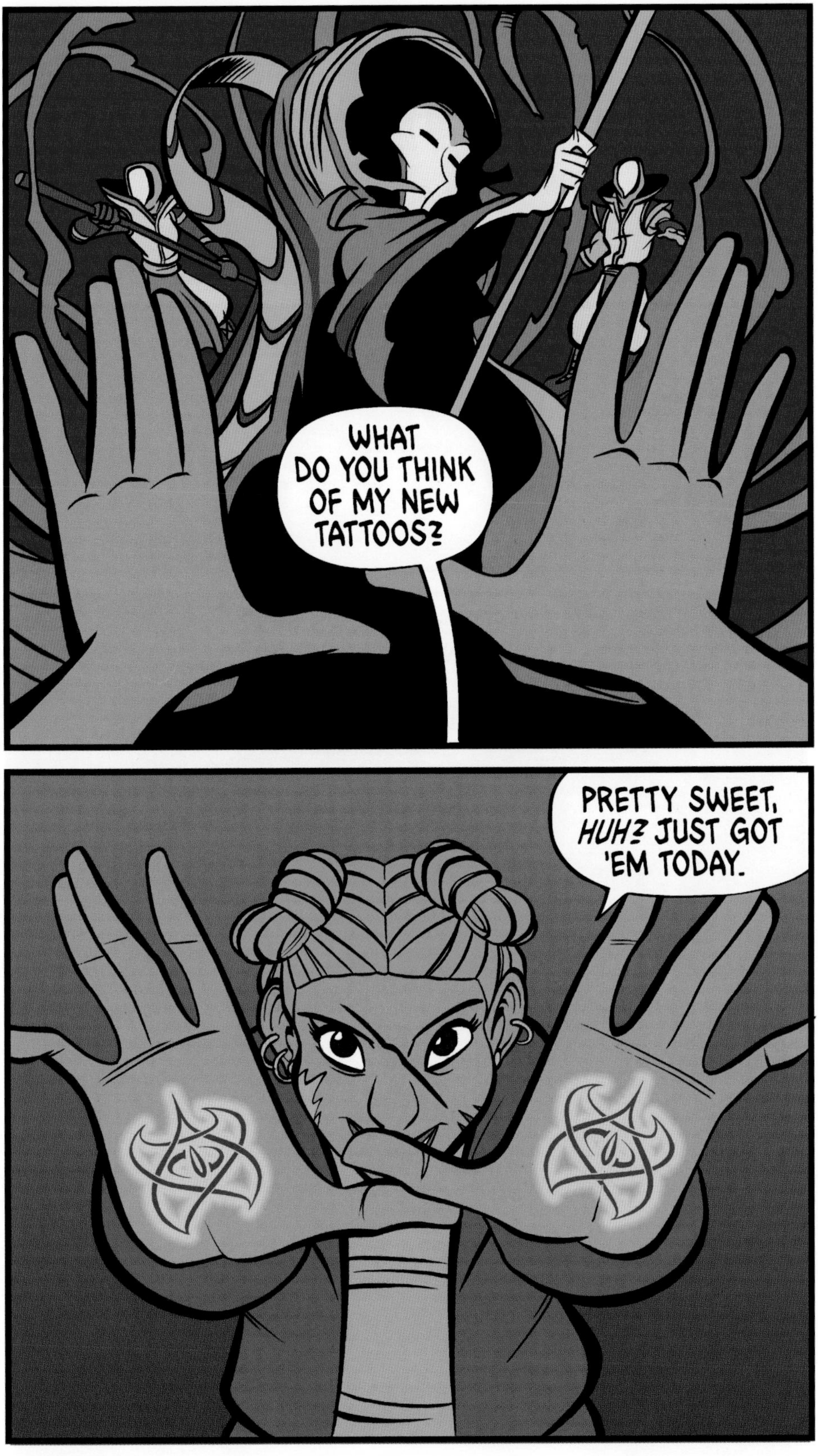
WHAT DO YOU THINK OF MY NEW TATTOOS?
PRETTY SWEET, *HUH?* JUST GOT 'EM TODAY.

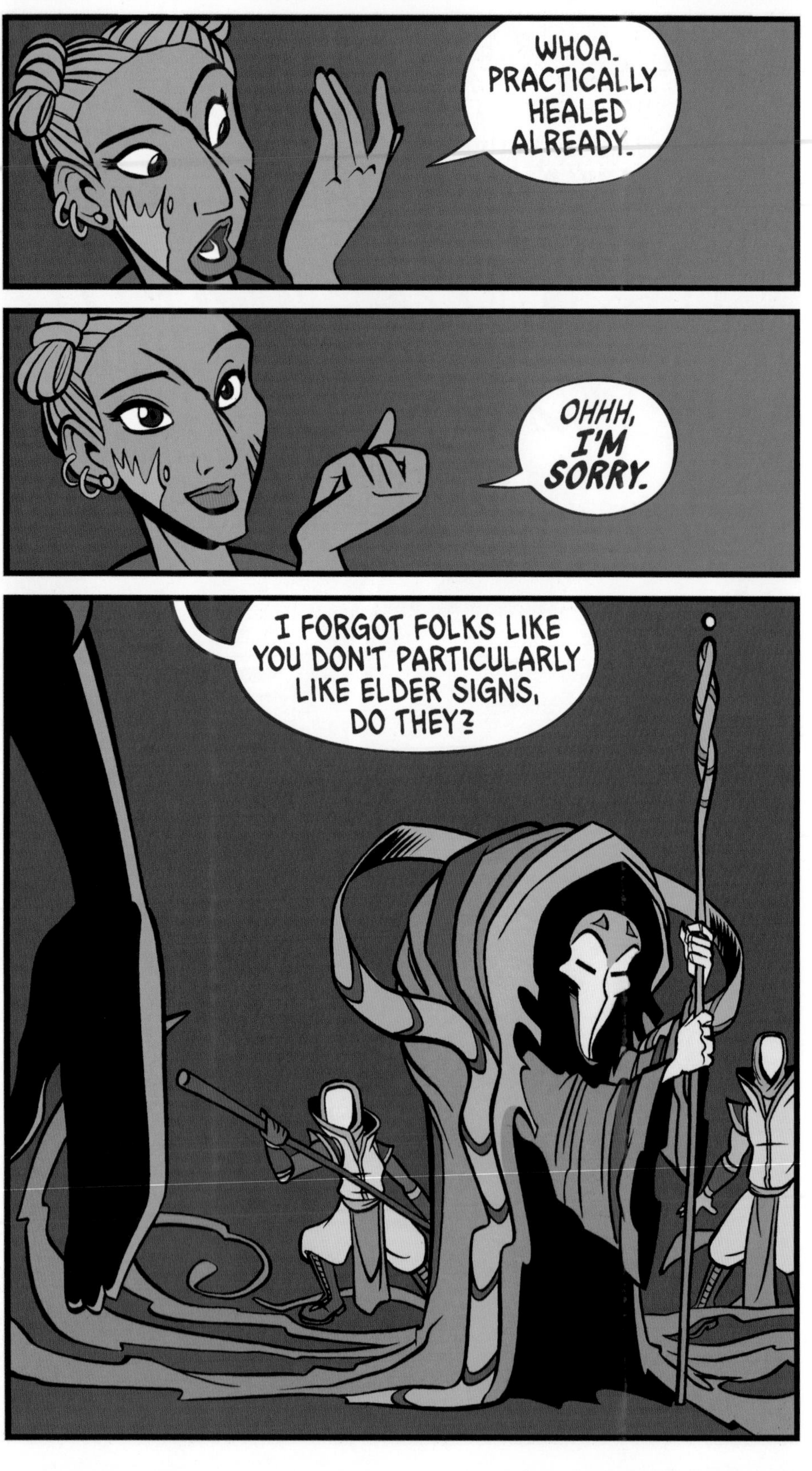
WHOA. PRACTICALLY HEALED ALREADY.
OHHH, I'M SORRY.
I FORGOT FOLKS LIKE YOU DON'T PARTICULARLY LIKE ELDER SIGNS, DO THEY?

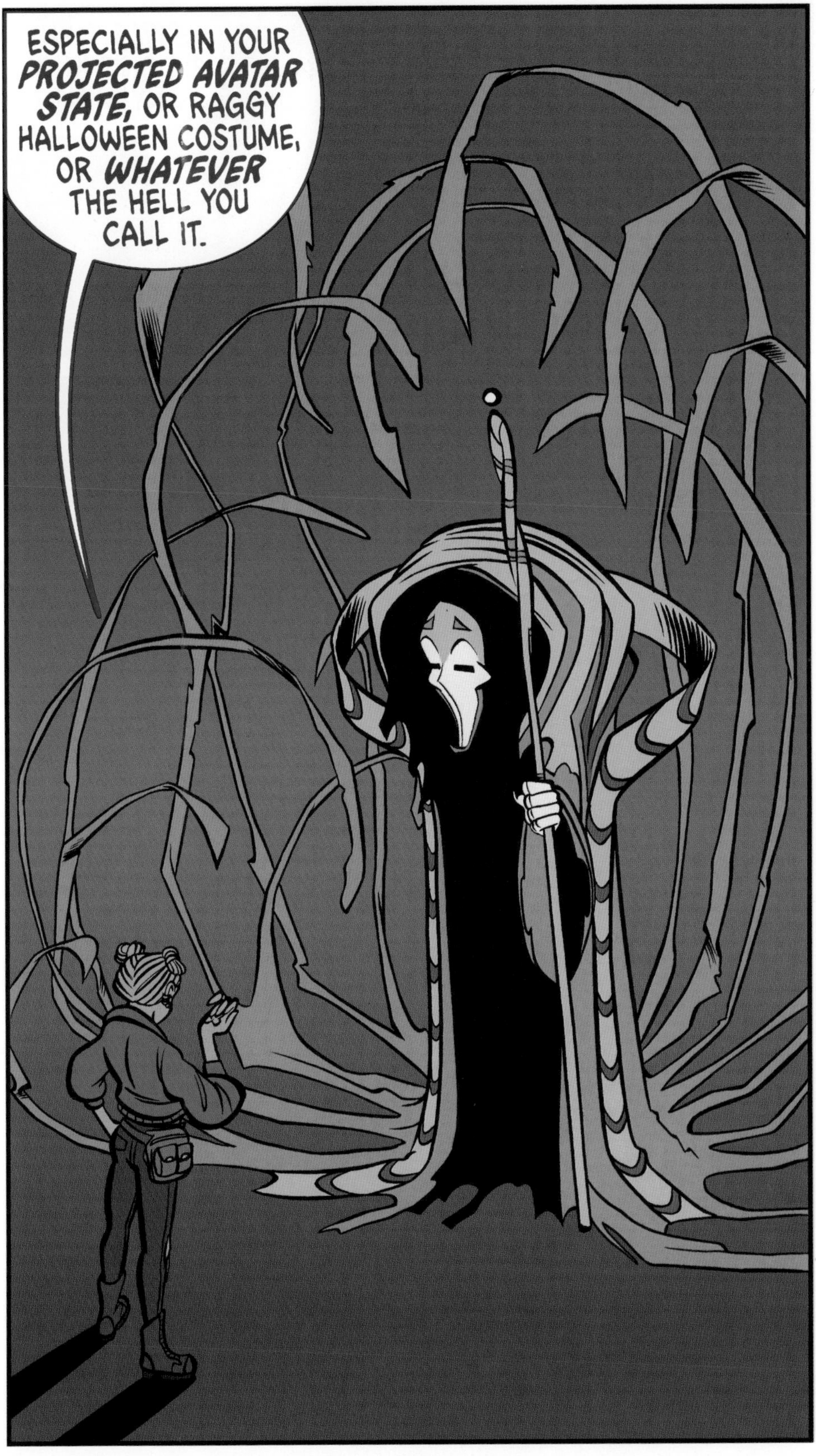
ESPECIALLY IN YOUR PROJECTED AVATAR STATE, OR RAGGY HALLOWEEN COSTUME, OR WHATEVER THE HELL YOU CALL IT.

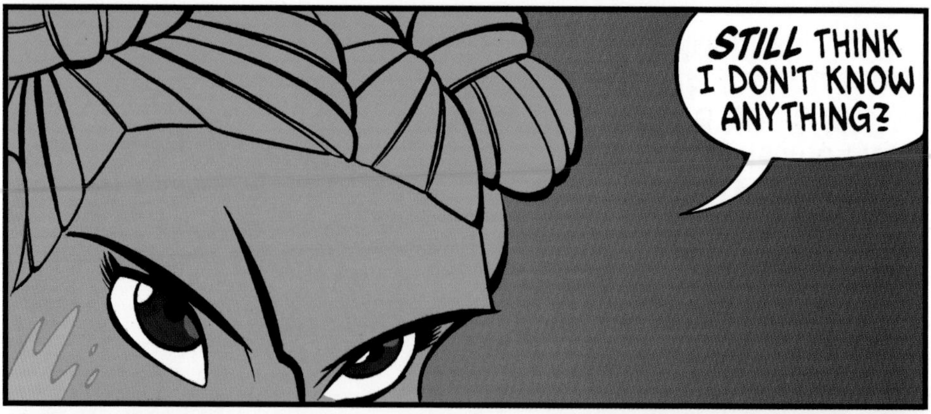
STILL THINK I DON'T KNOW ANYTHING?

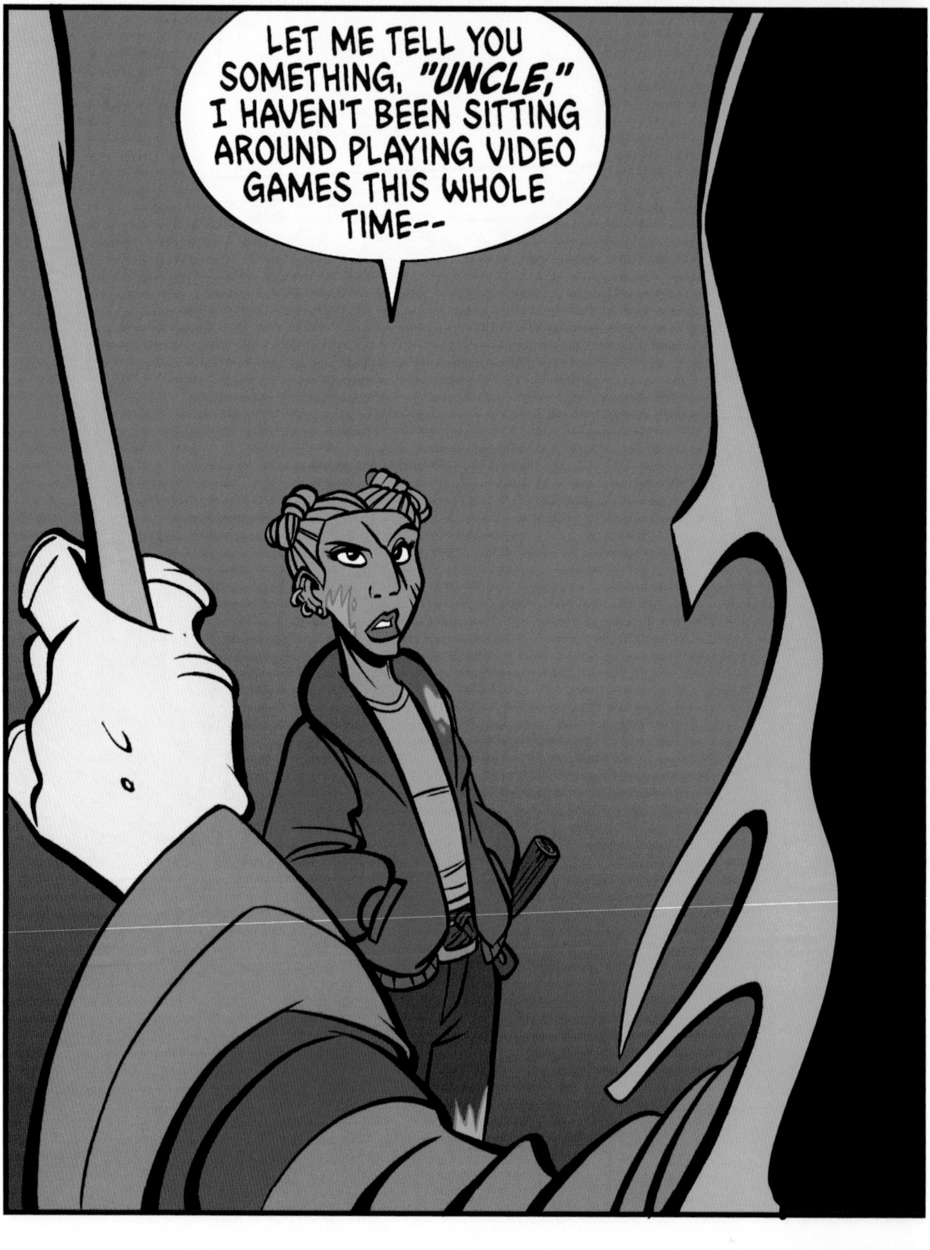
LET ME TELL YOU SOMETHING, "UNCLE," I HAVEN'T BEEN SITTING AROUND PLAYING VIDEO GAMES THIS WHOLE TIME--

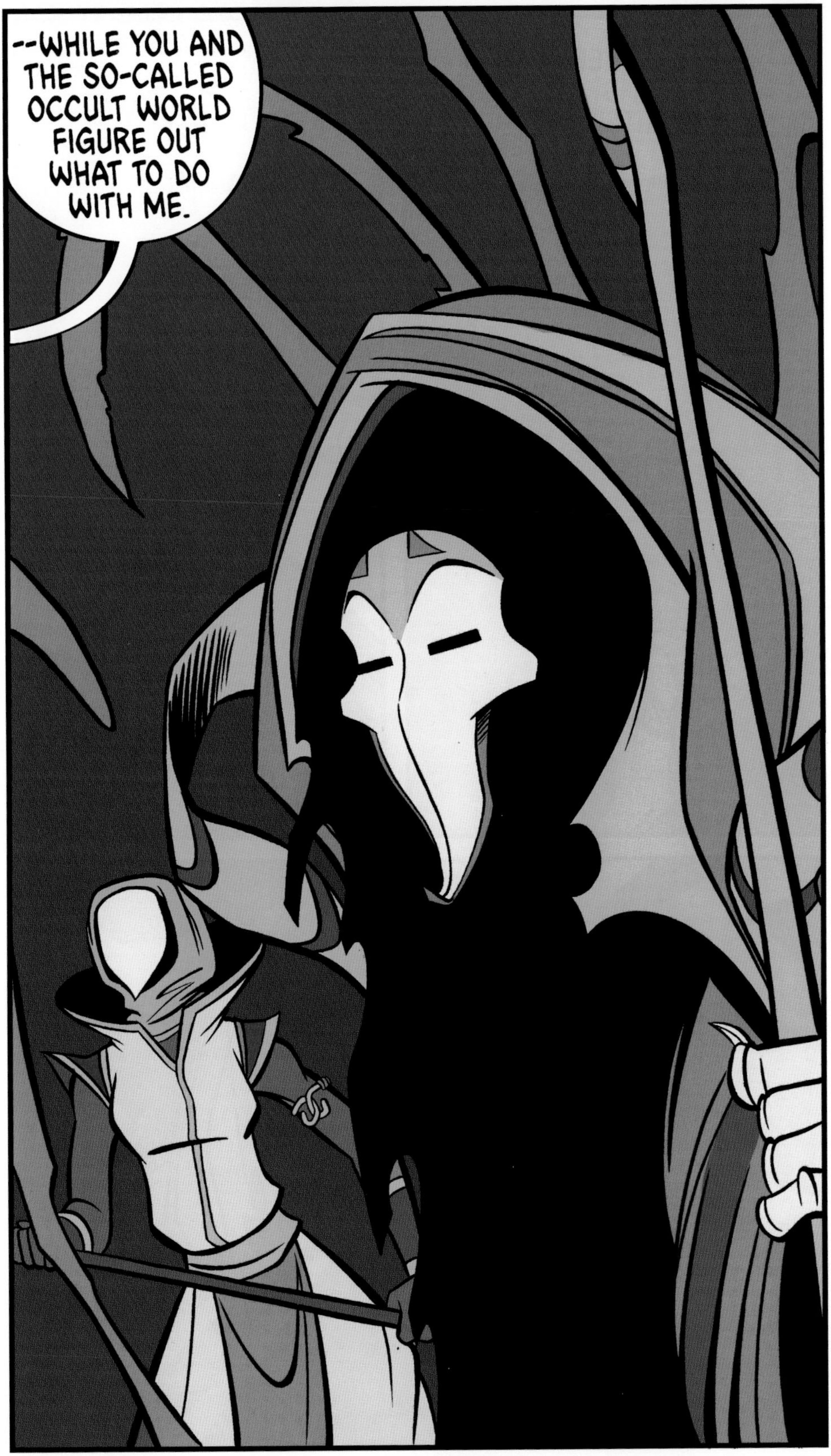
--WHILE YOU AND THE SO-CALLED OCCULT WORLD FIGURE OUT WHAT TO DO WITH ME.

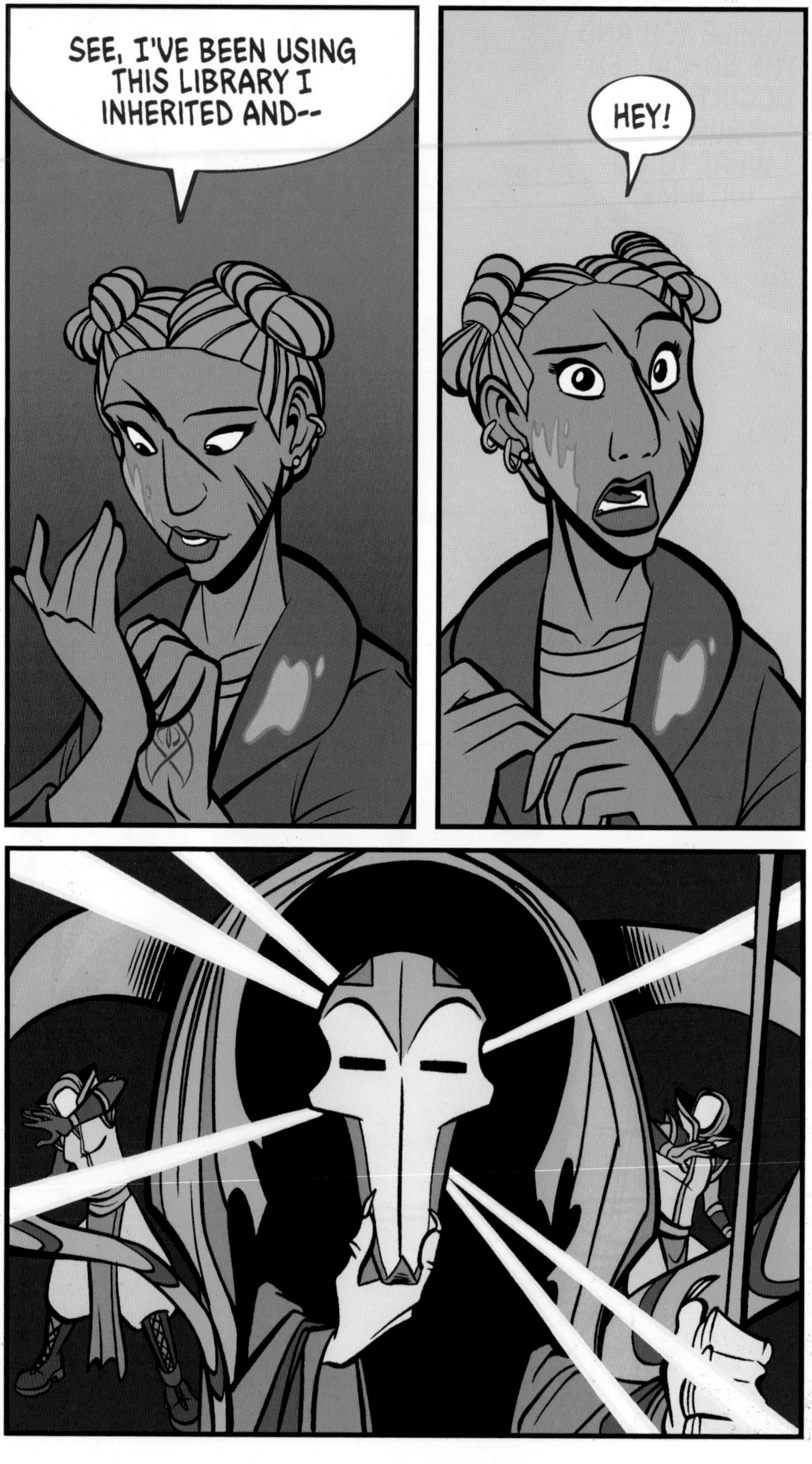
SEE, I'VE BEEN USING THIS LIBRARY I INHERITED AND--
HEY!

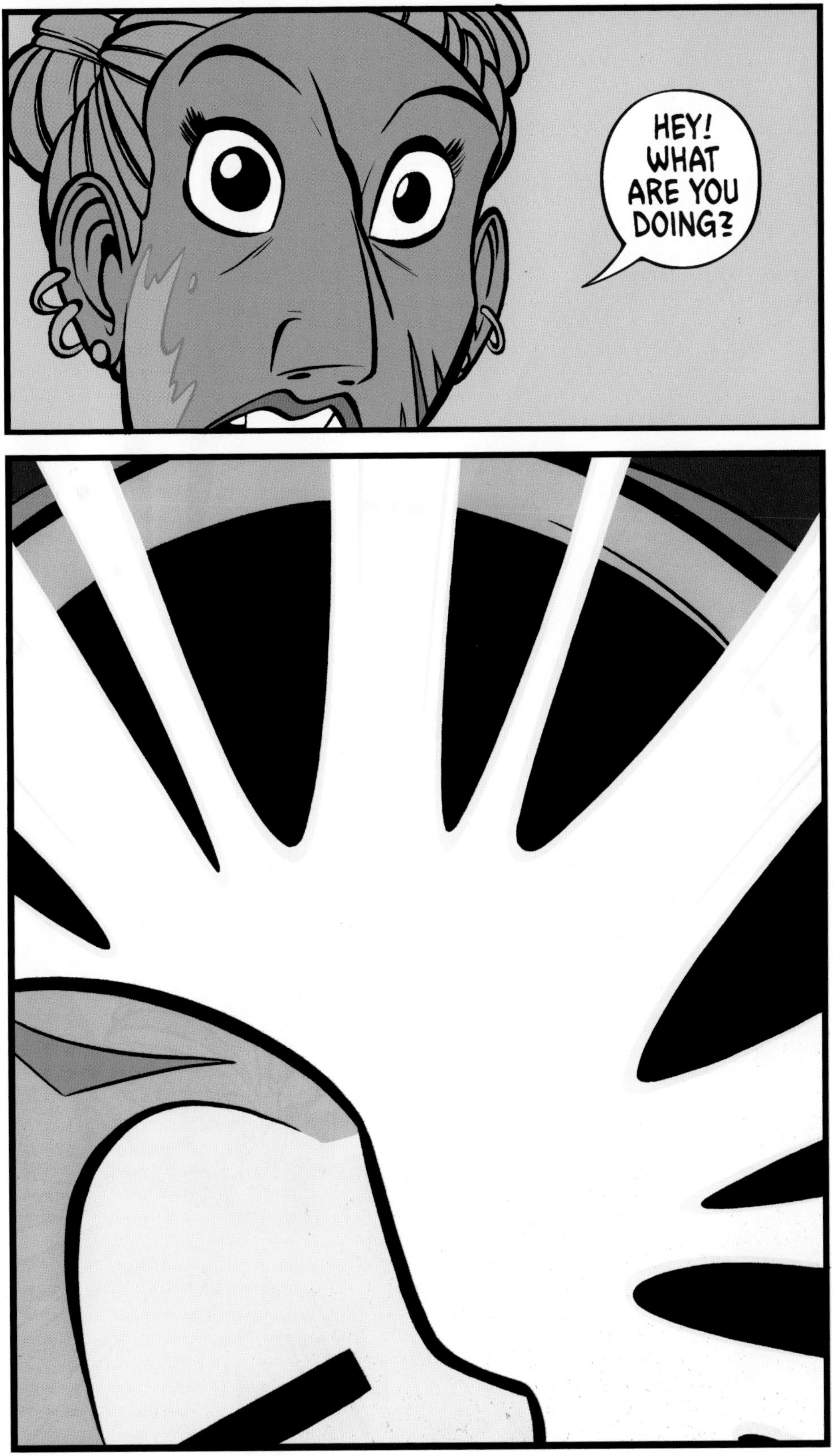
HEY! WHAT ARE YOU DOING?

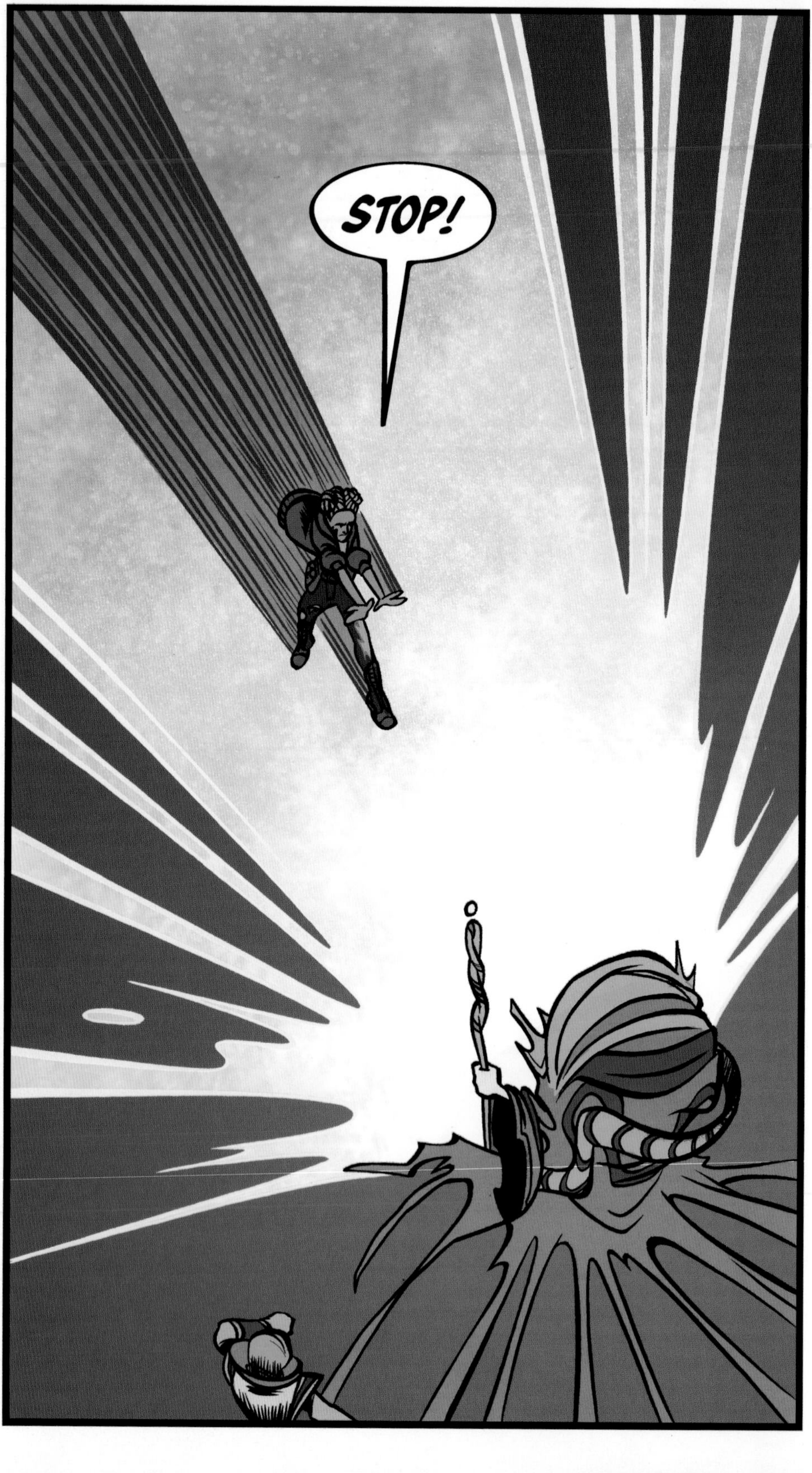
STOP!

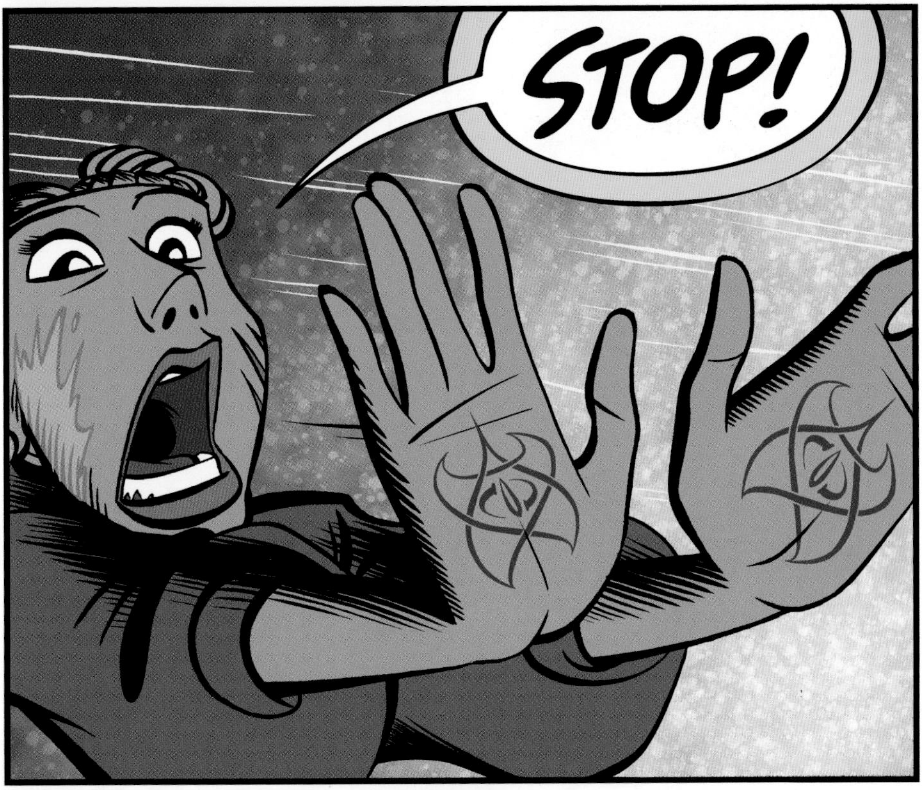
STOP!

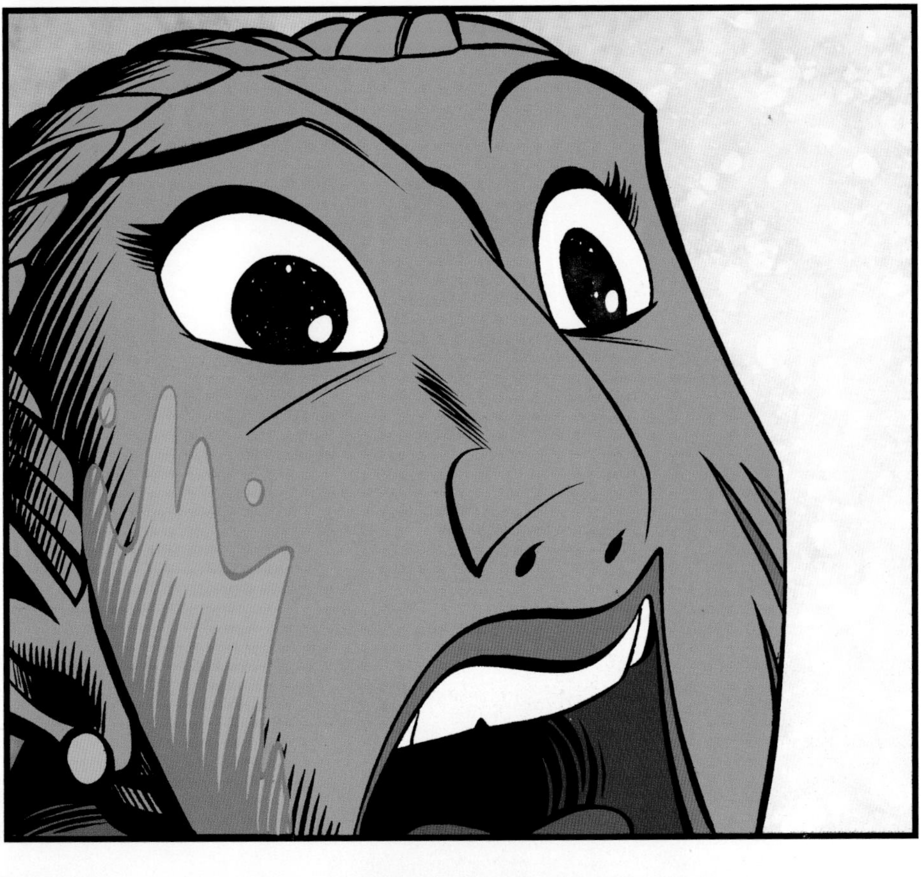

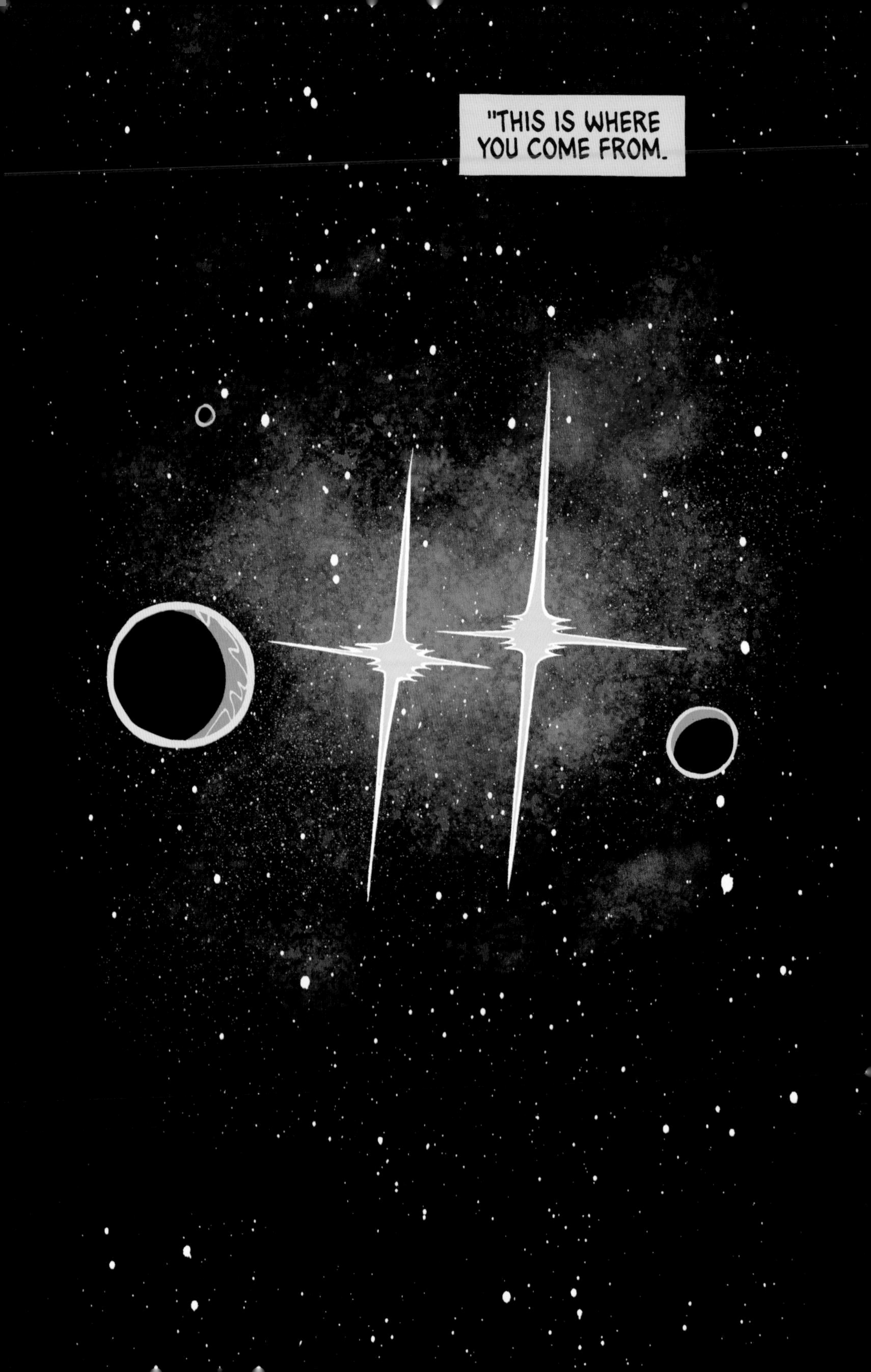
"THIS IS WHERE YOU COME FROM.

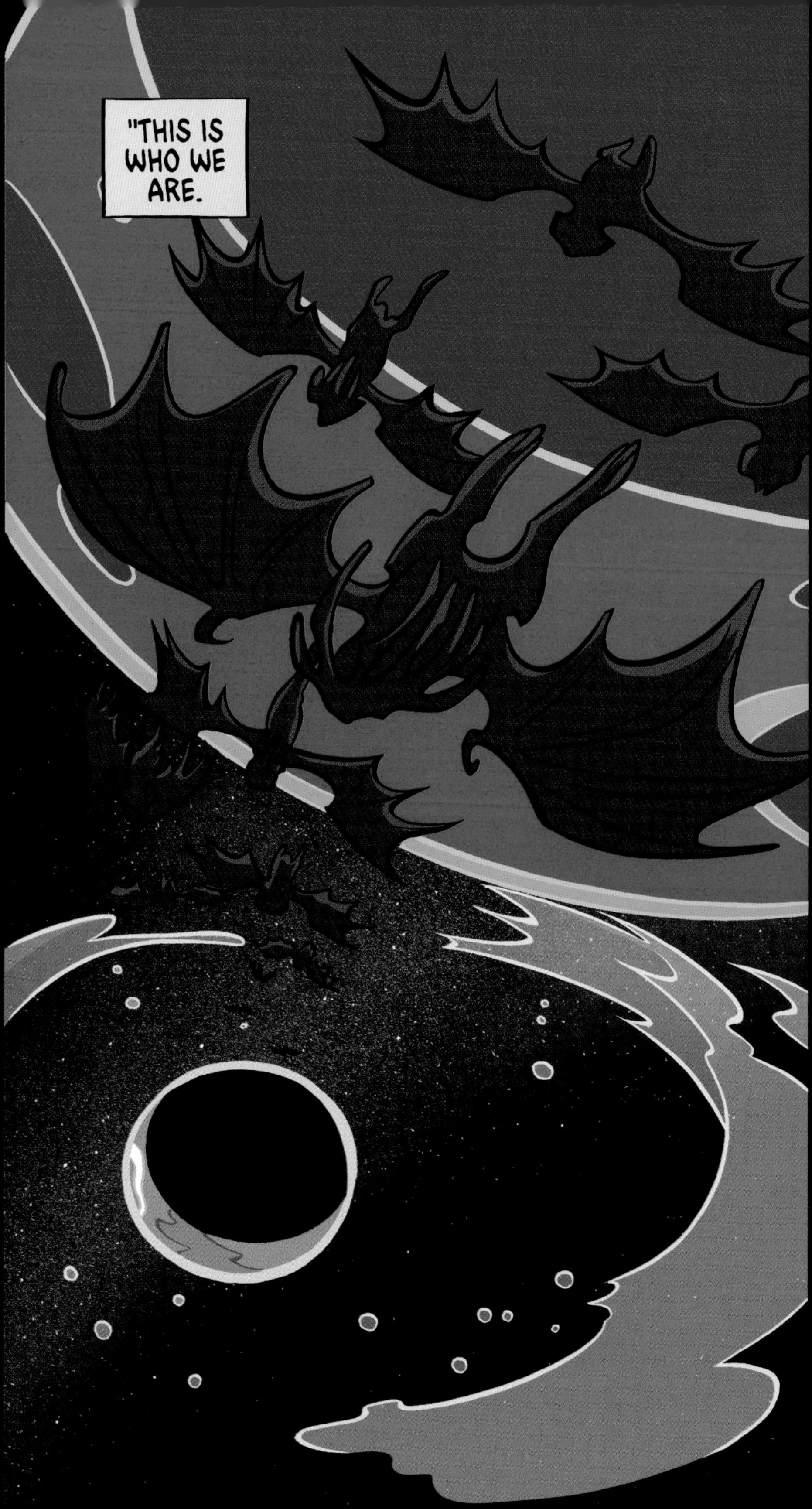
"THIS IS WHO WE ARE.

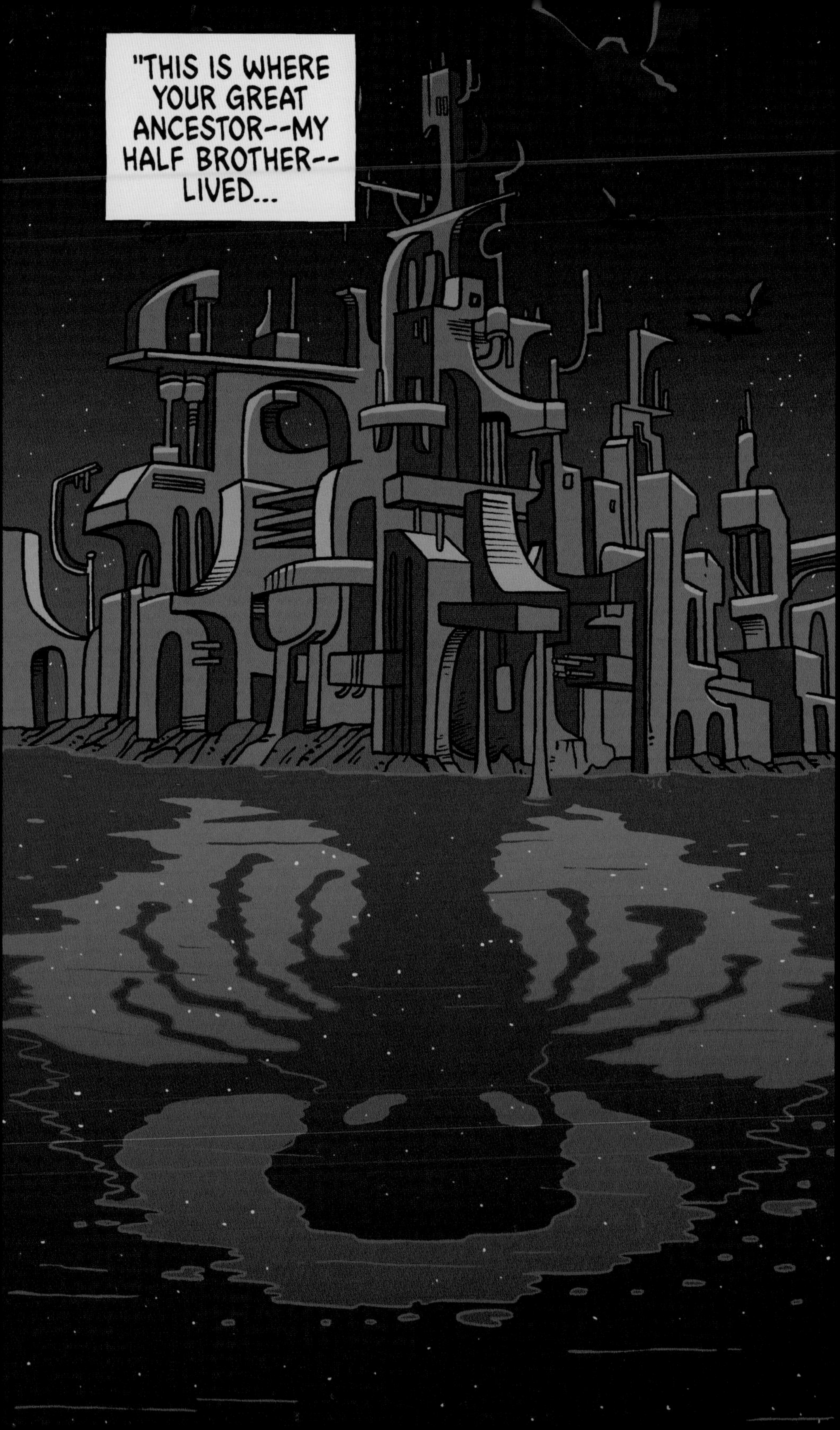
"THIS IS WHERE YOUR GREAT ANCESTOR--MY HALF BROTHER--LIVED...

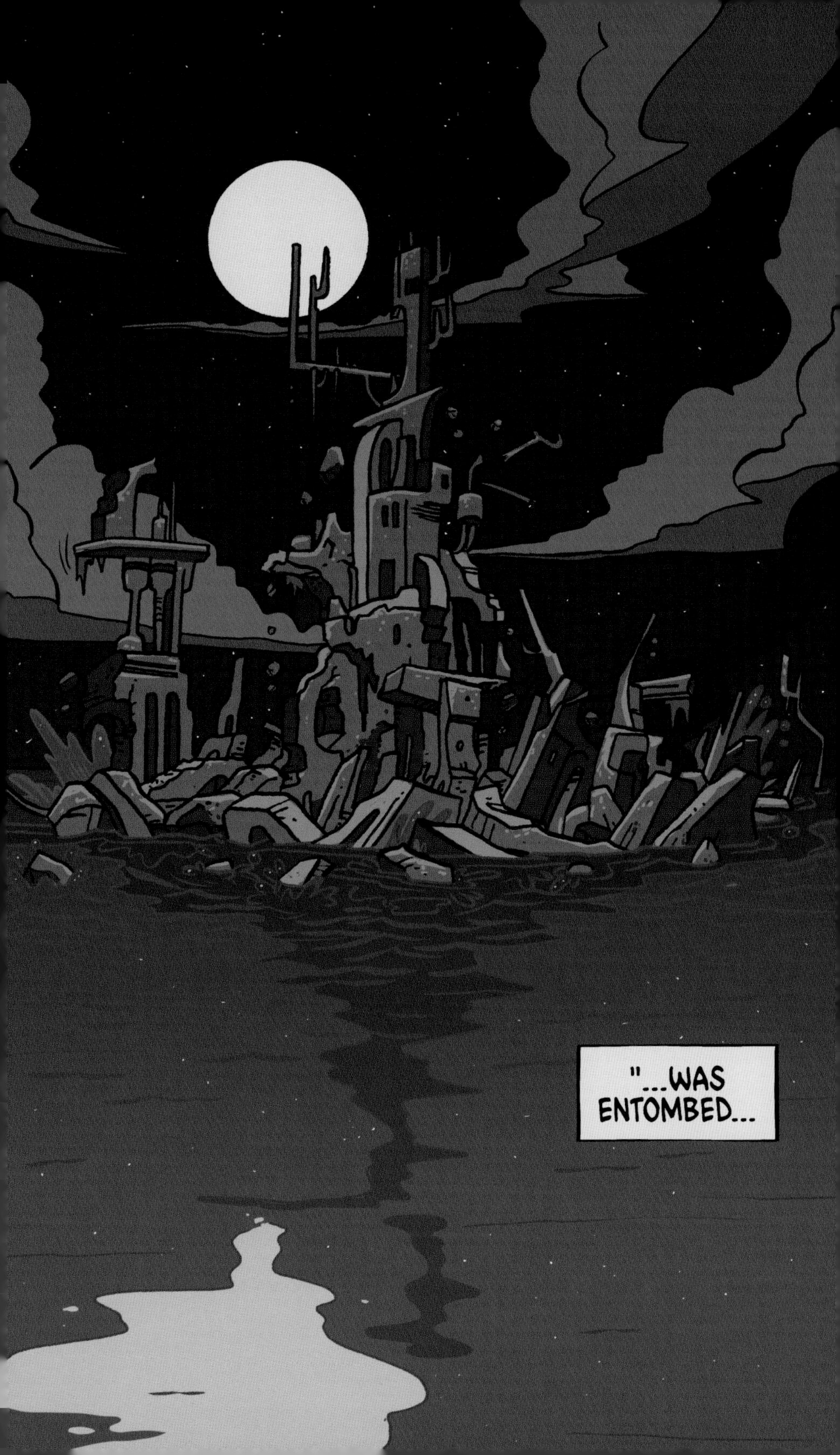
"...WAS
ENTOMBED...

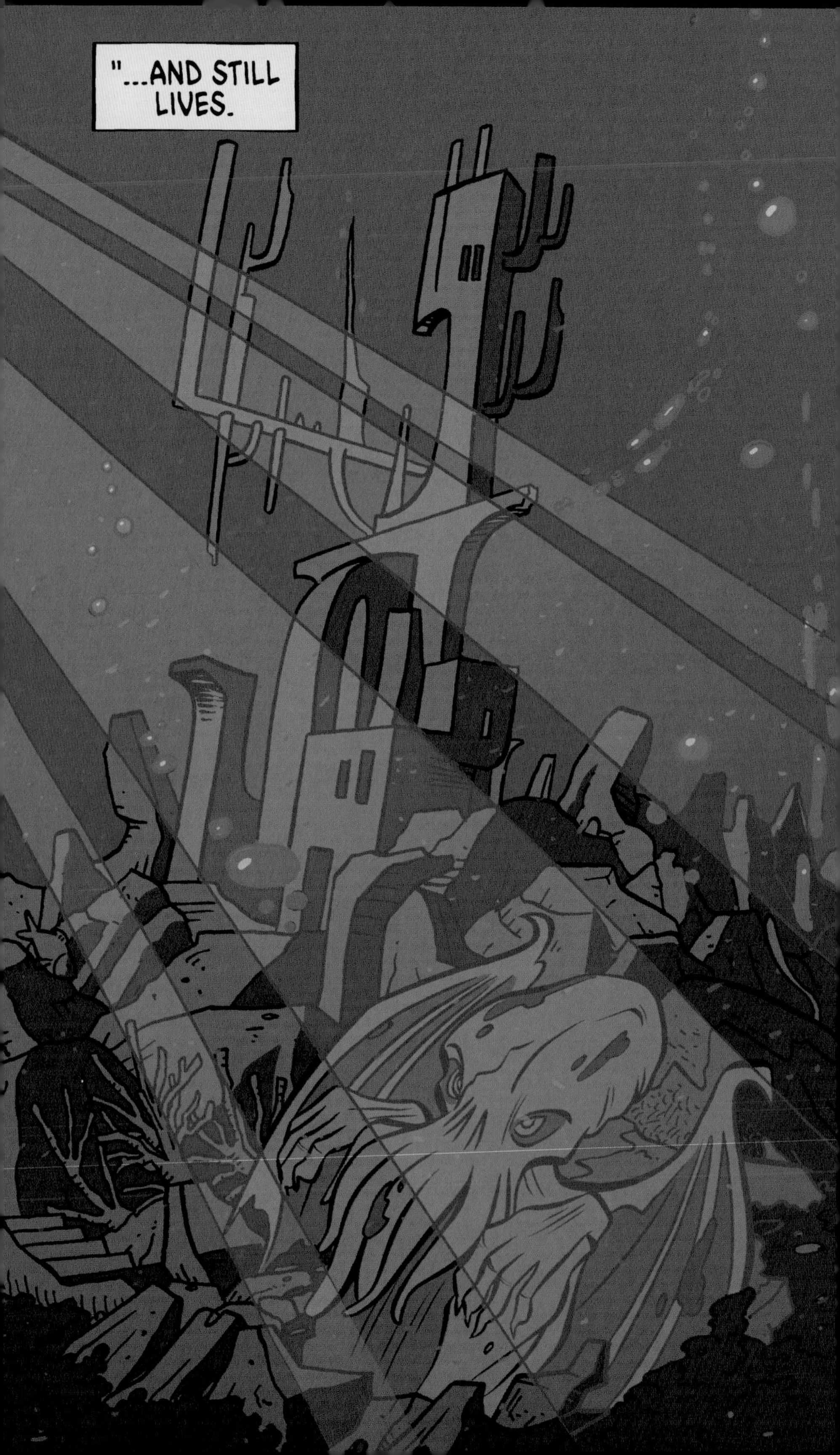
"...AND STILL LIVES.

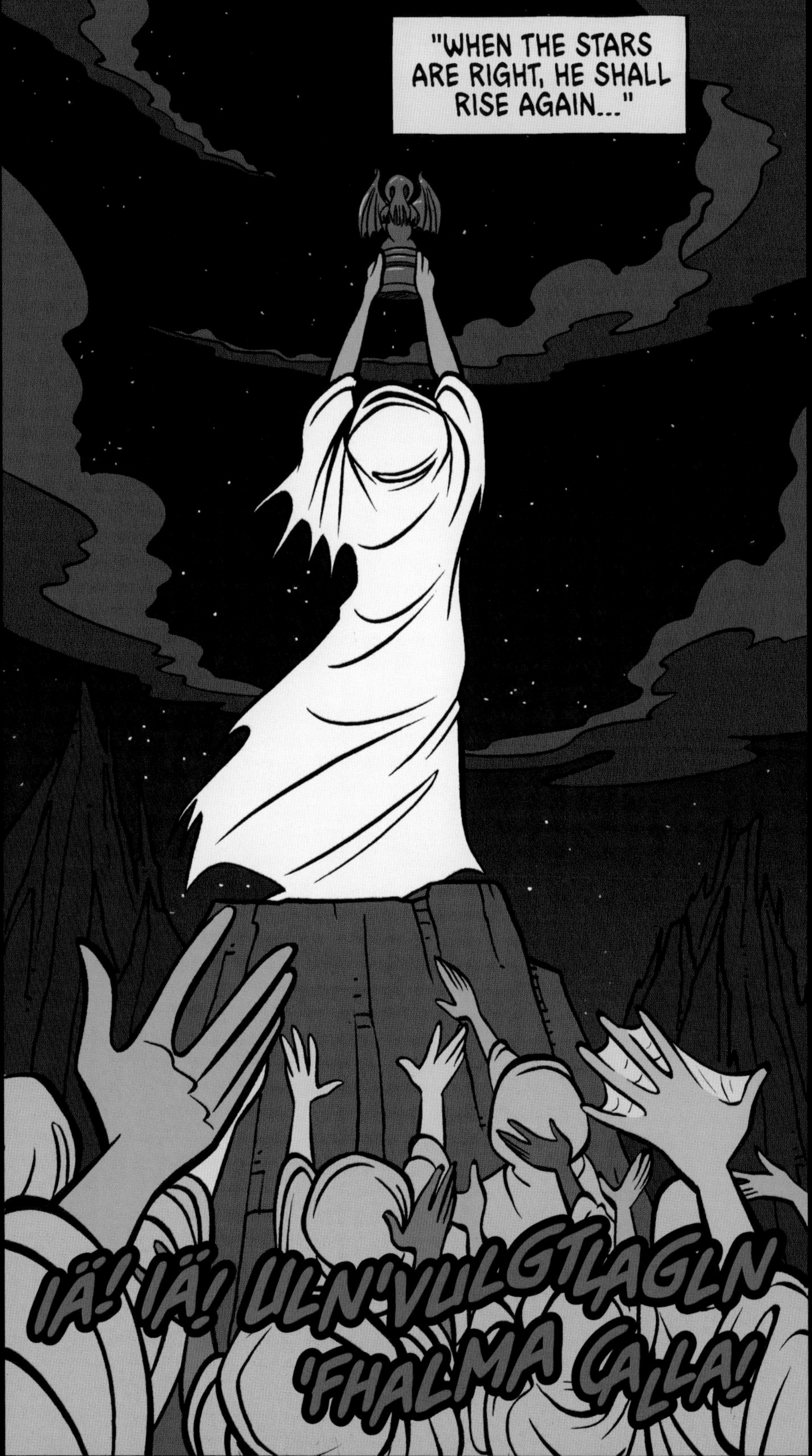
"WHEN THE STARS ARE RIGHT, HE SHALL RISE AGAIN..."
IÄ! IÄ! ULN'VULGTLAGLN 'FHALMA ÇALLA!

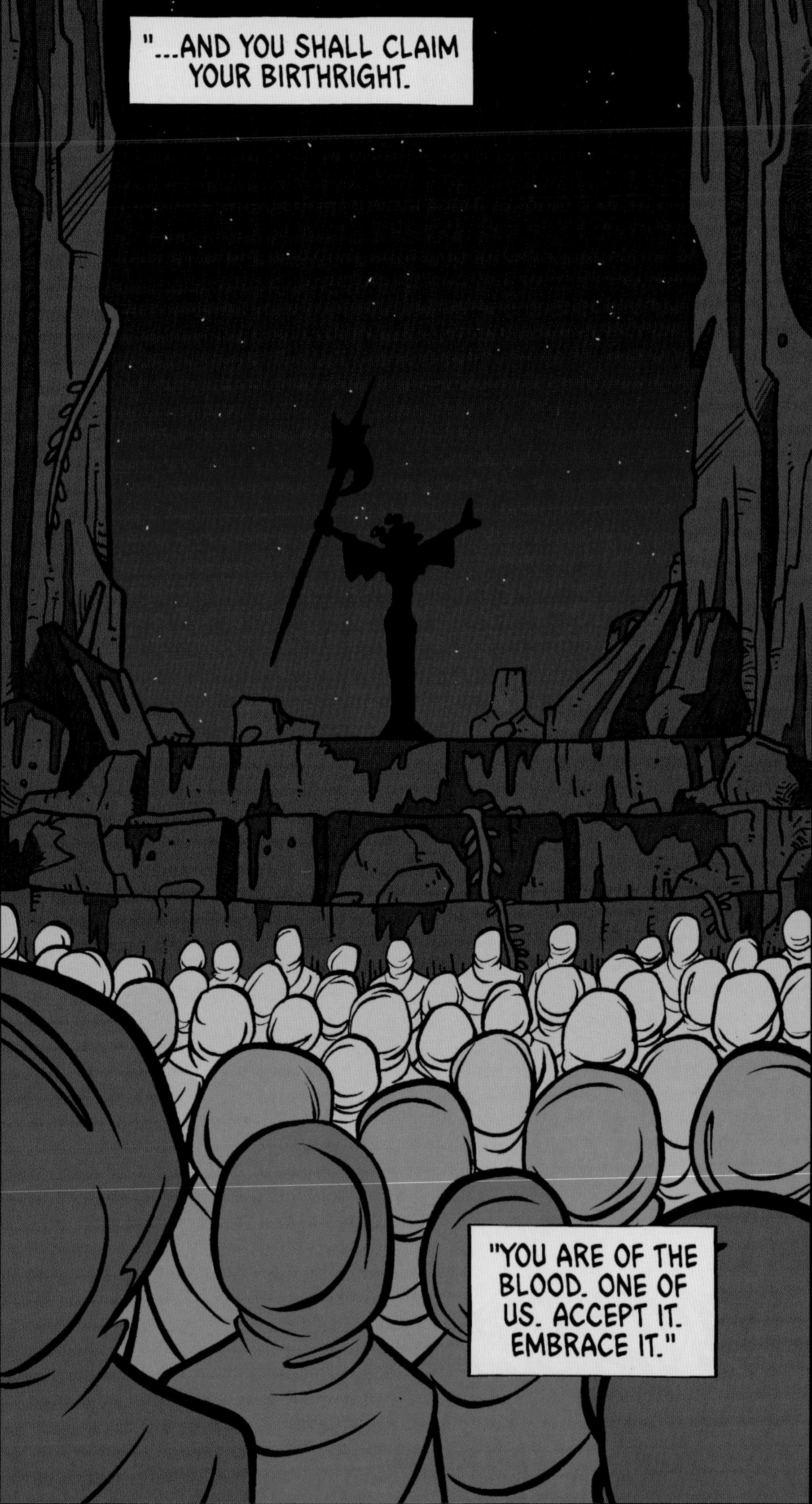
"...AND YOU SHALL CLAIM YOUR BIRTHRIGHT.
"YOU ARE OF THE BLOOD. ONE OF US. ACCEPT IT. EMBRACE IT."

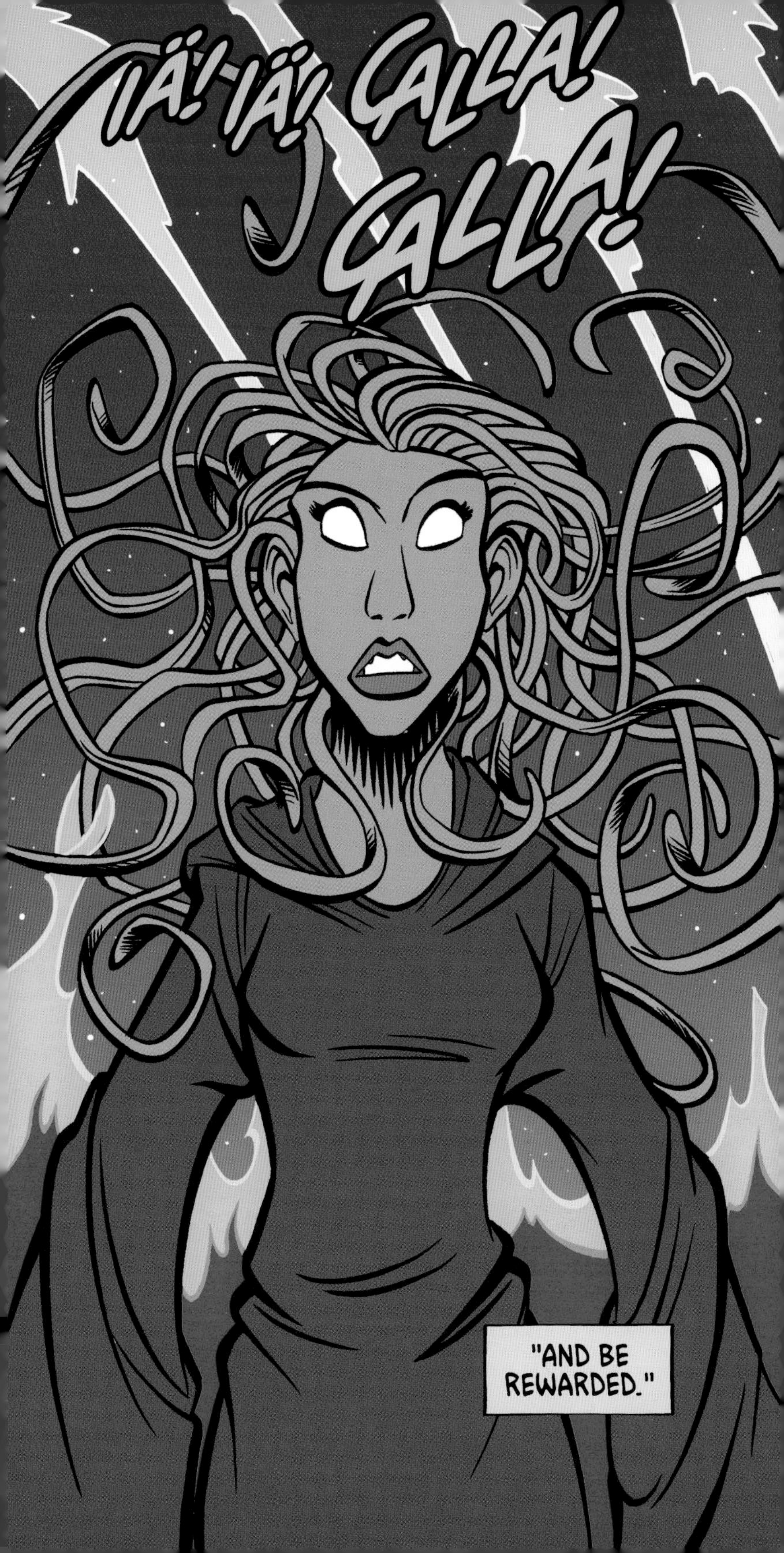
IÄ! IÄ! CALLA! CALLA!
"AND BE REWARDED."

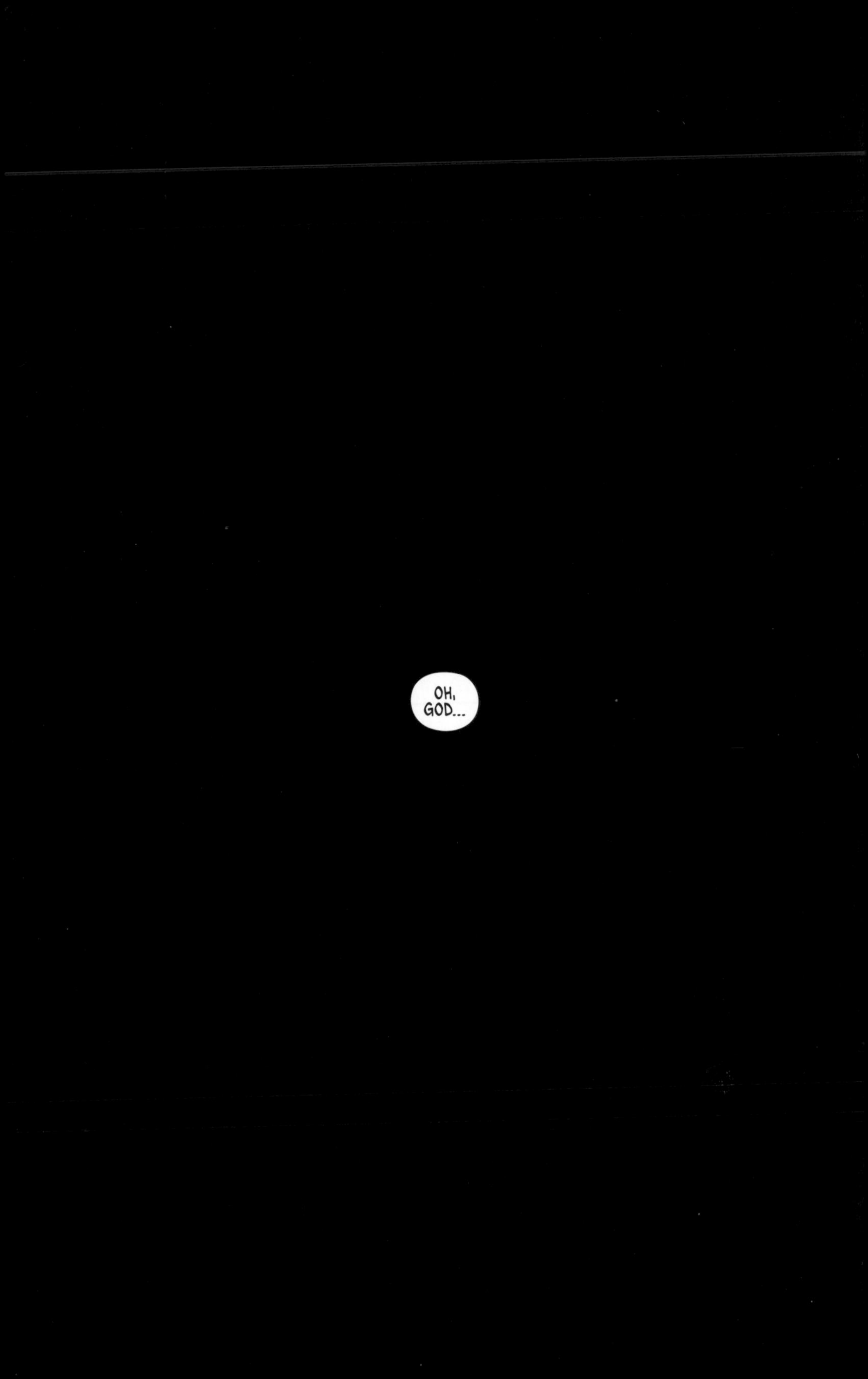
OH, GOD...

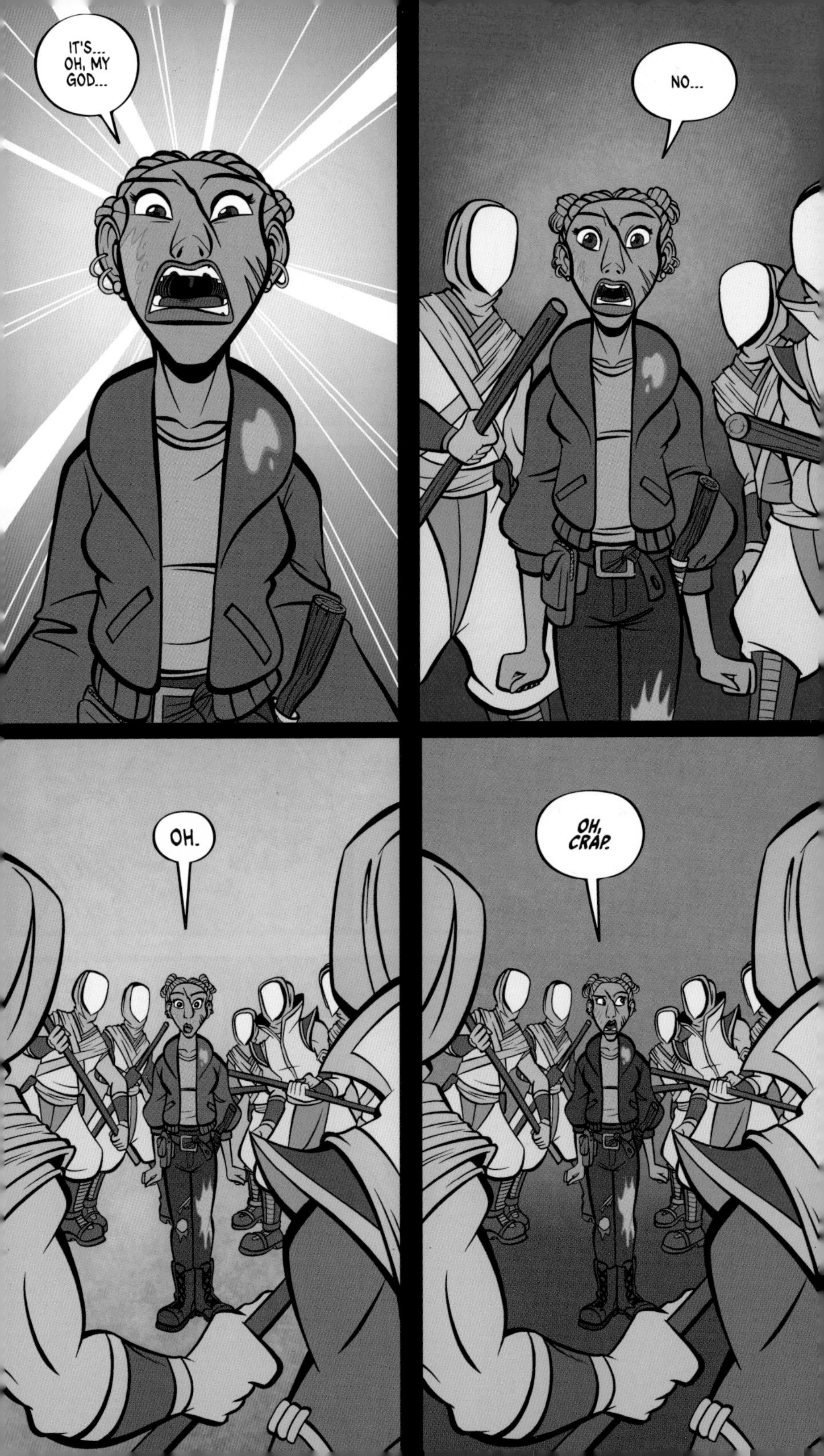
IT'S... OH, MY GOD...
NO...
OH.
OH, CRAP.

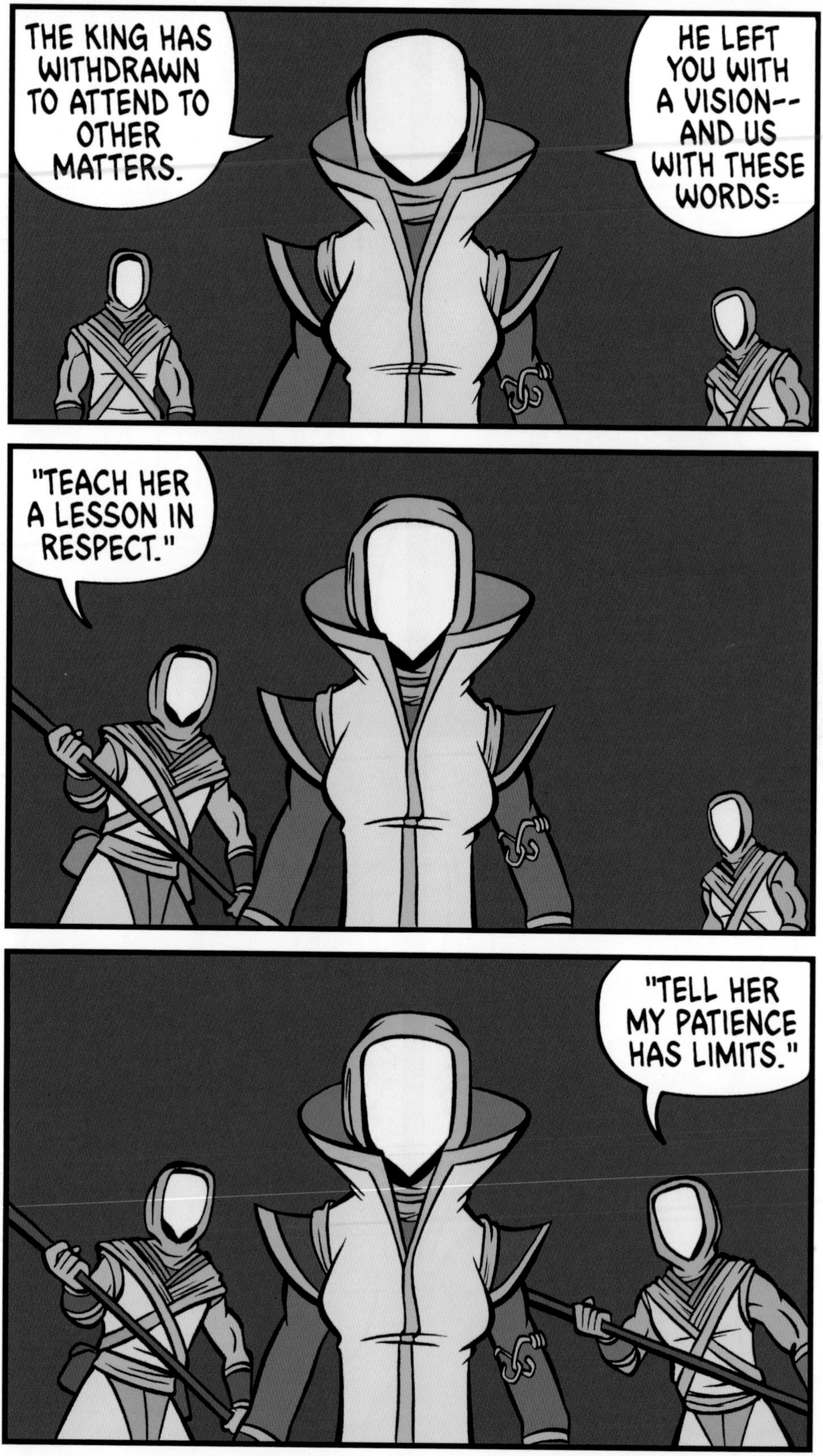
THE KING HAS WITHDRAWN TO ATTEND TO OTHER MATTERS.
HE LEFT YOU WITH A VISION-- AND US WITH THESE WORDS:
"TEACH HER A LESSON IN RESPECT."
"TELL HER MY PATIENCE HAS LIMITS."

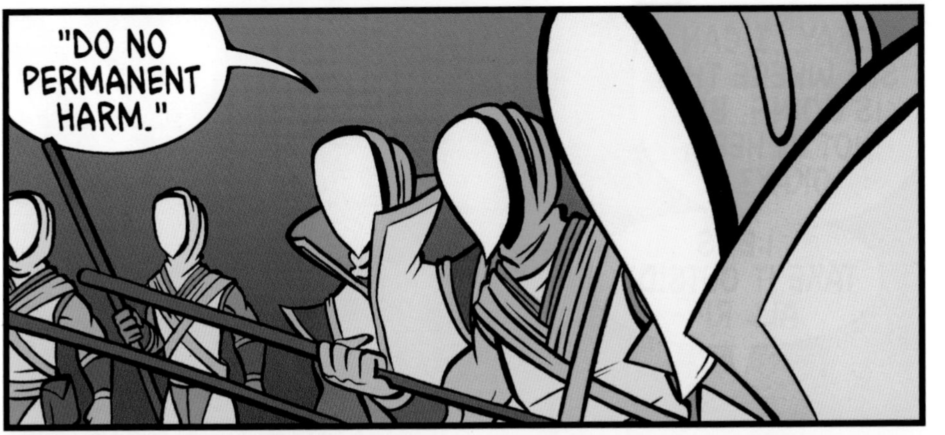
"DO NO PERMANENT HARM."

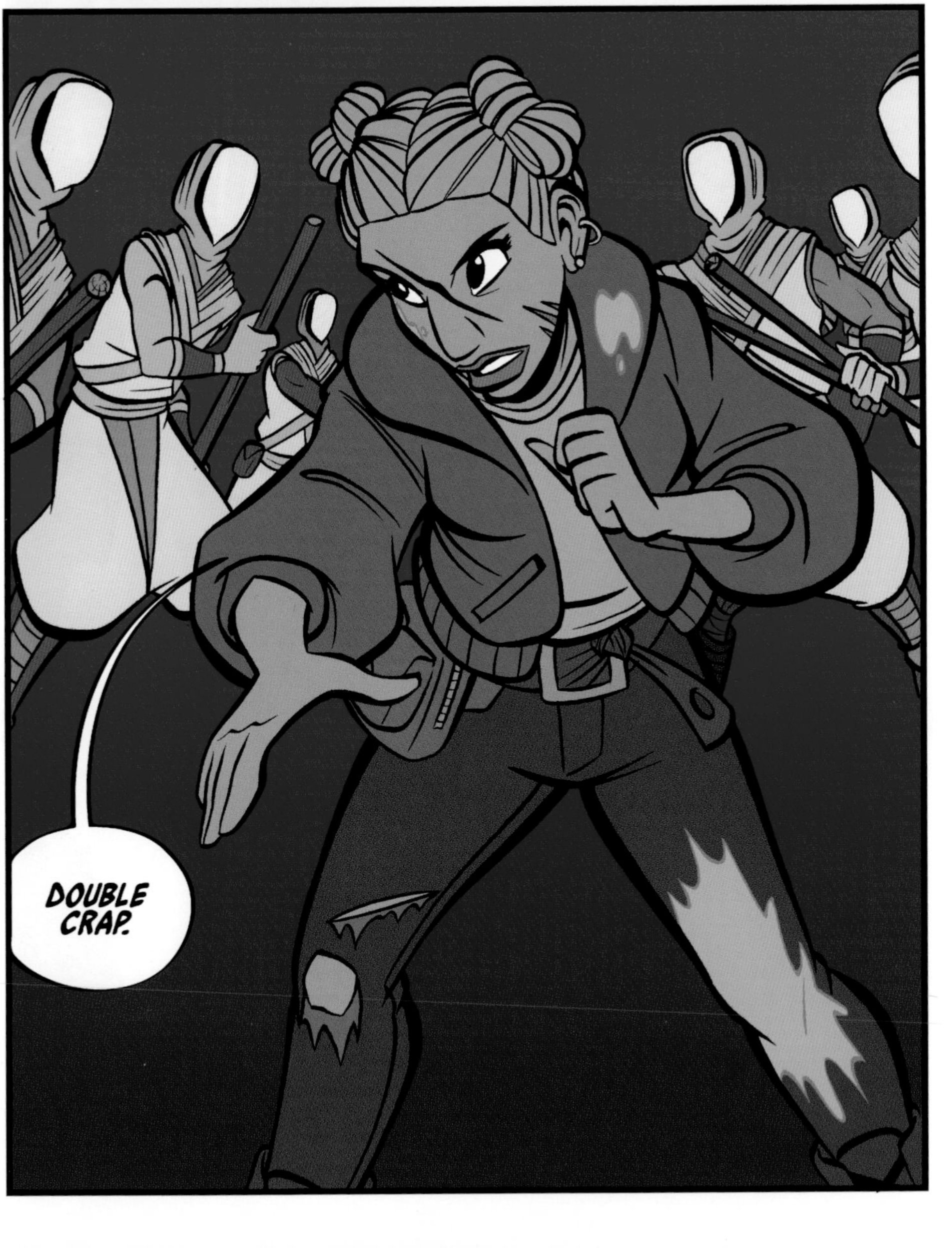
DOUBLE CRAP.

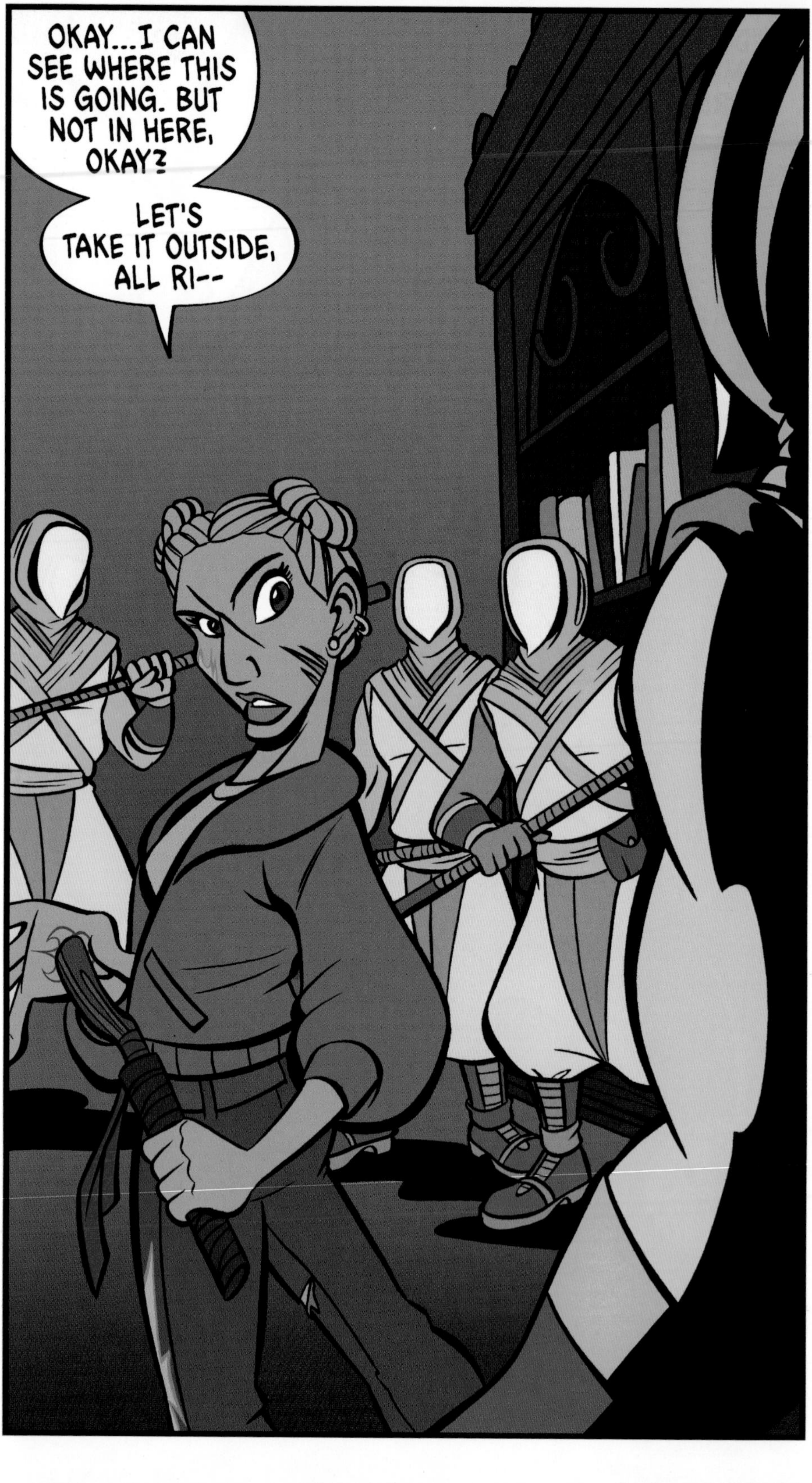
OKAY...I CAN SEE WHERE THIS IS GOING. BUT NOT IN HERE, OKAY?
LET'S TAKE IT OUTSIDE, ALL RI--

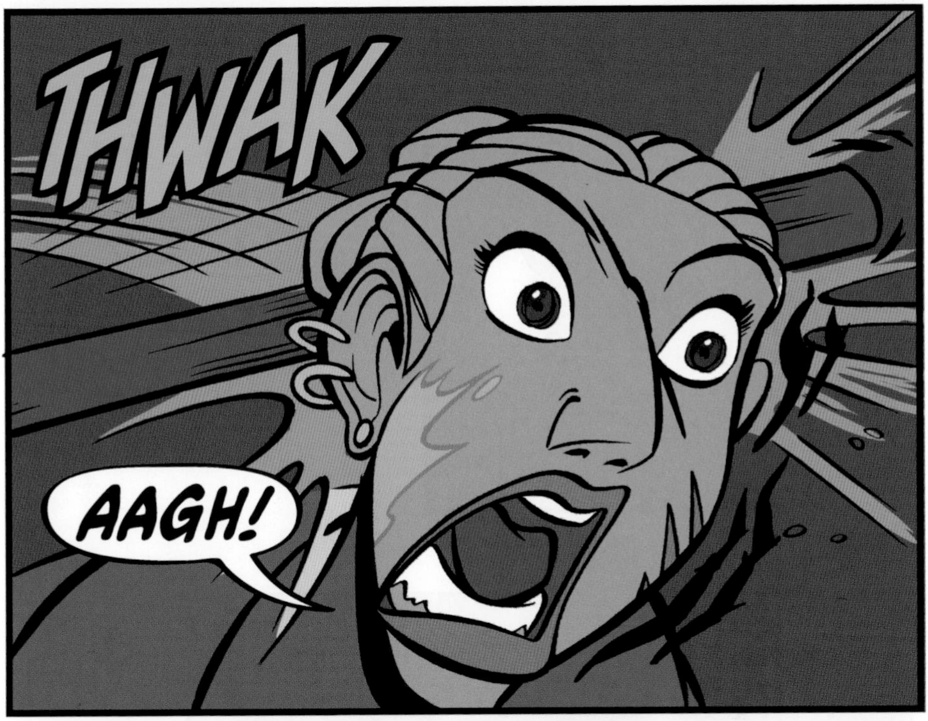
THWAK
AAGH!

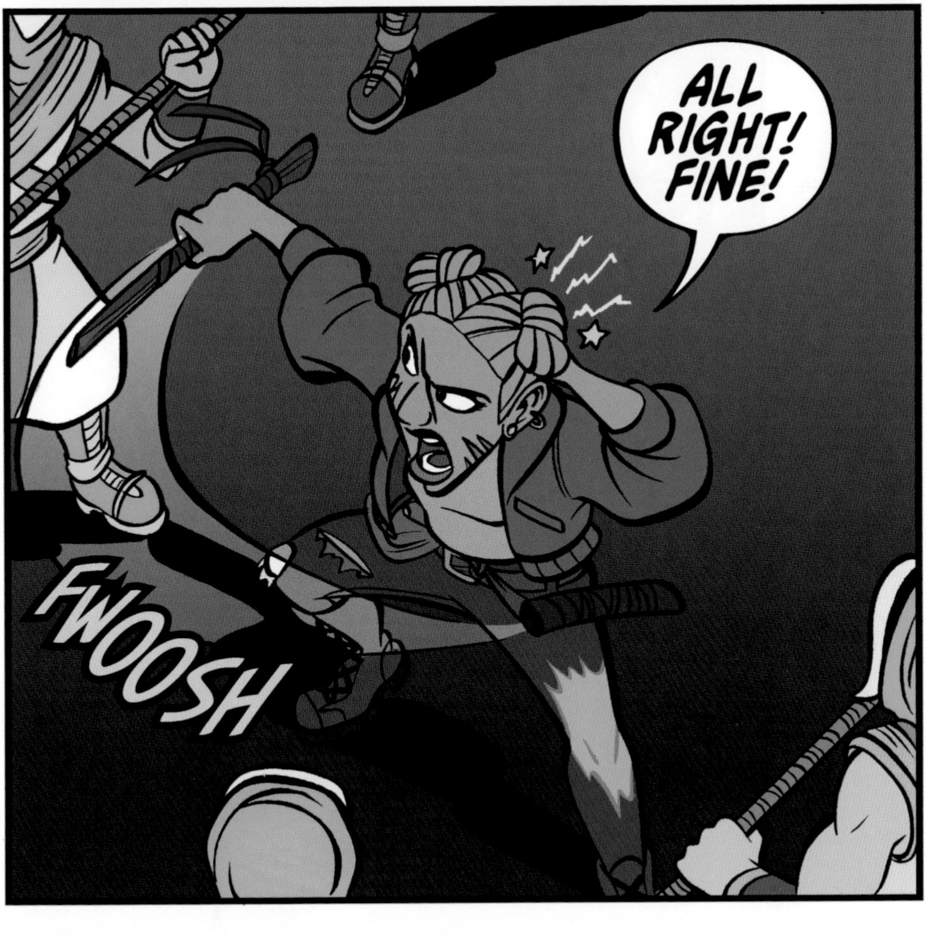
ALL RIGHT! FINE!
FWOOSH

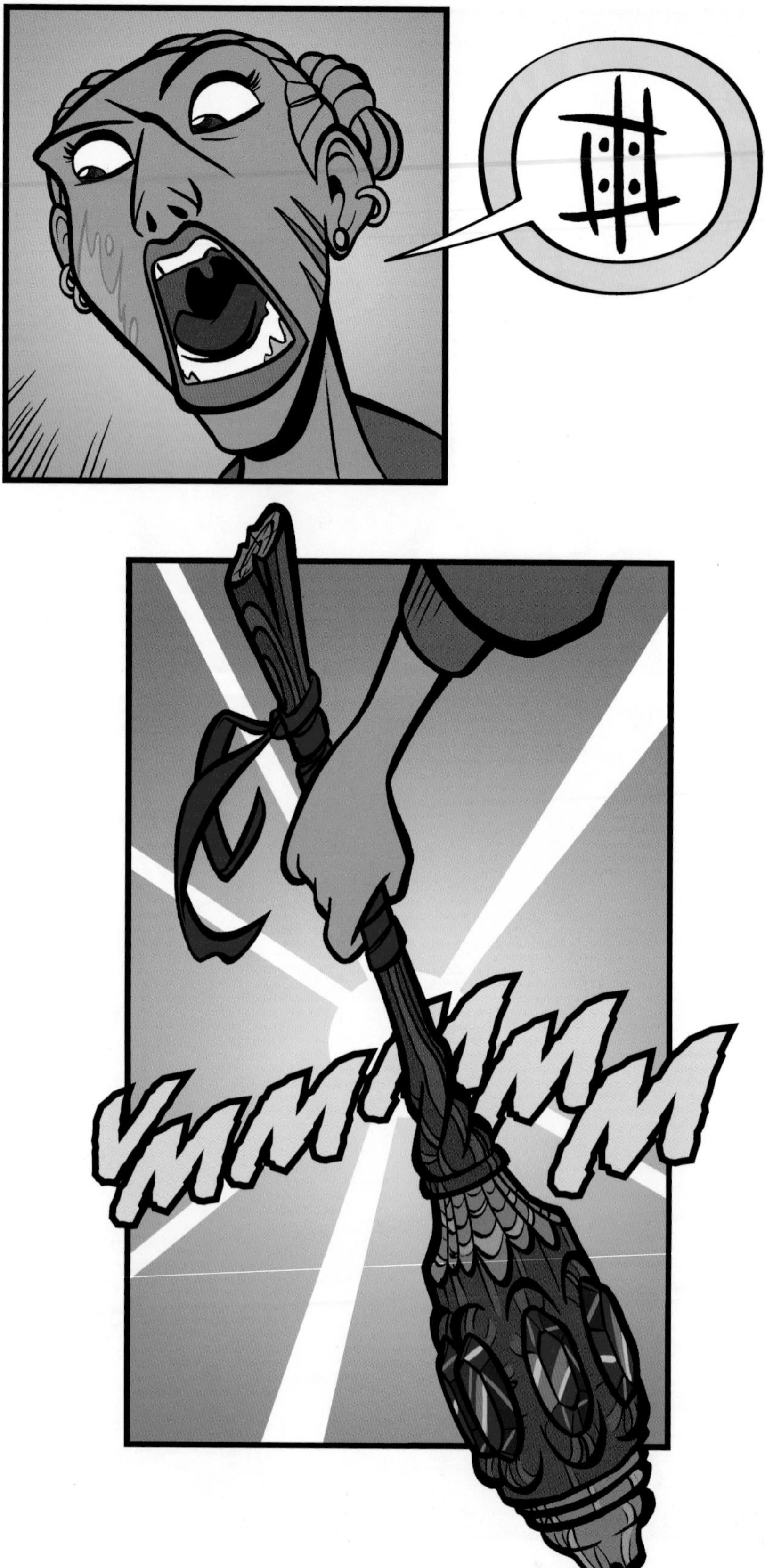
VMMMMM

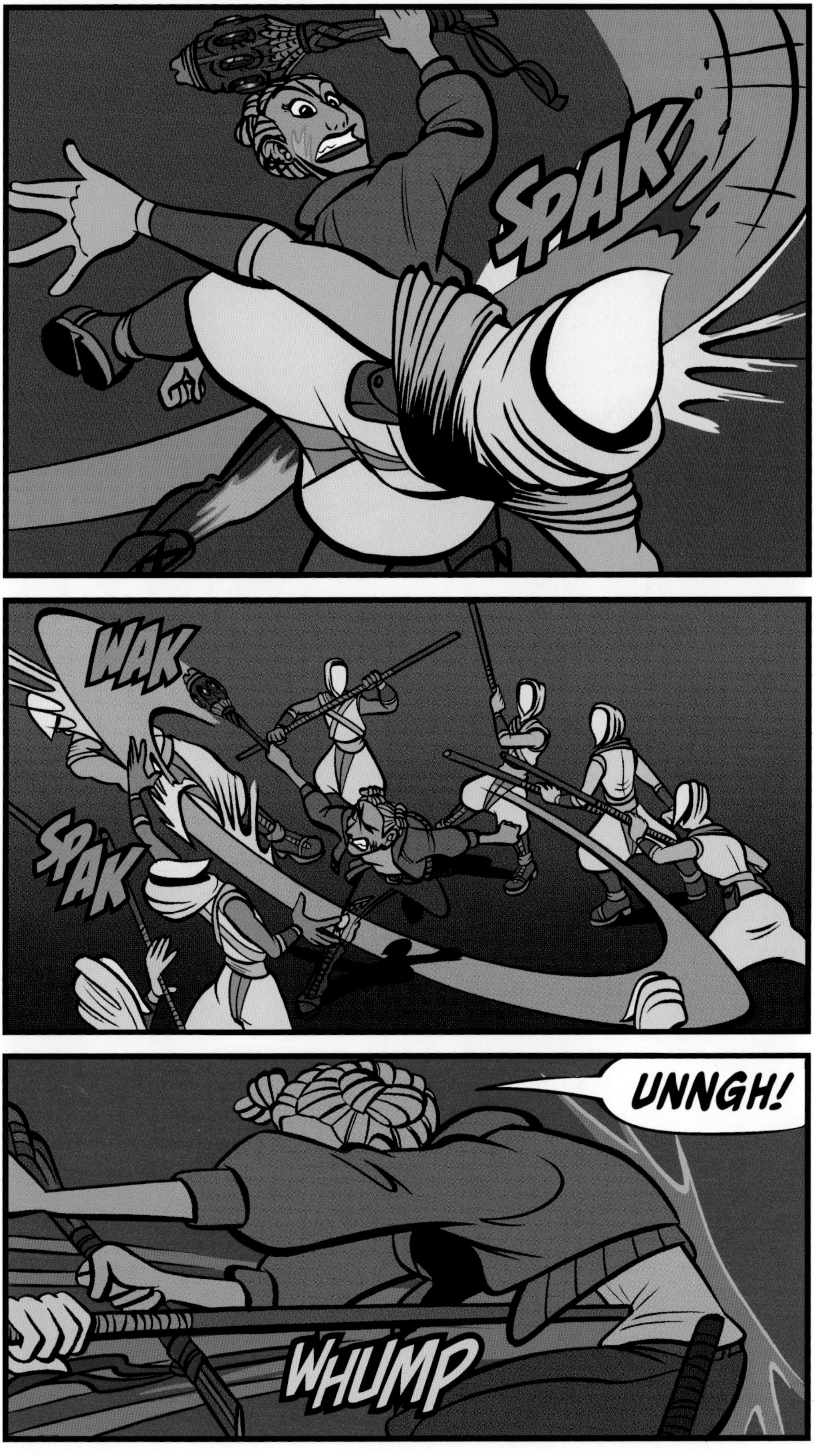
SPAK
WAK
SPAK
UNNGH!
WHUMP

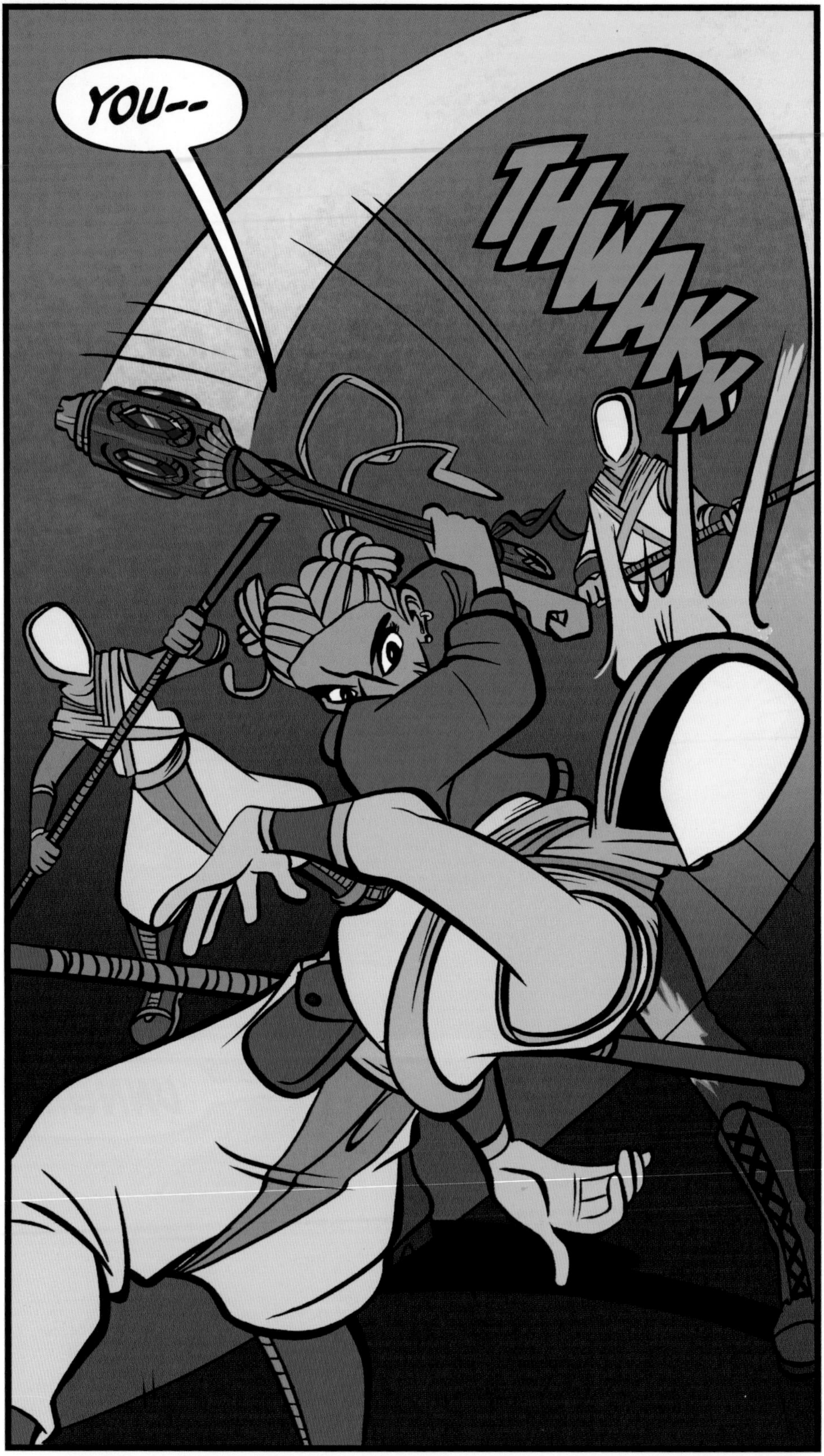
YOU--
THWAKK

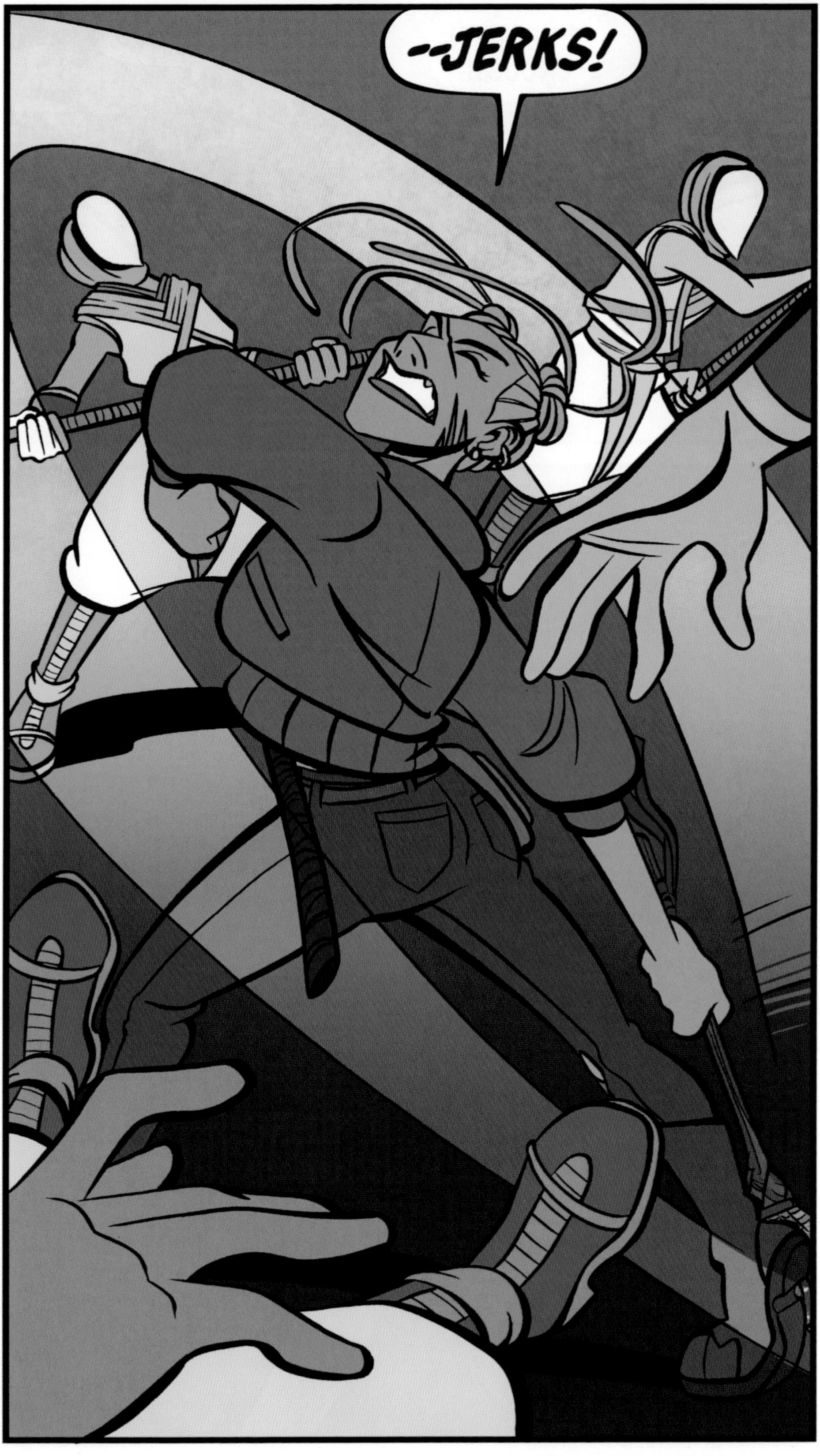
--JERKS!

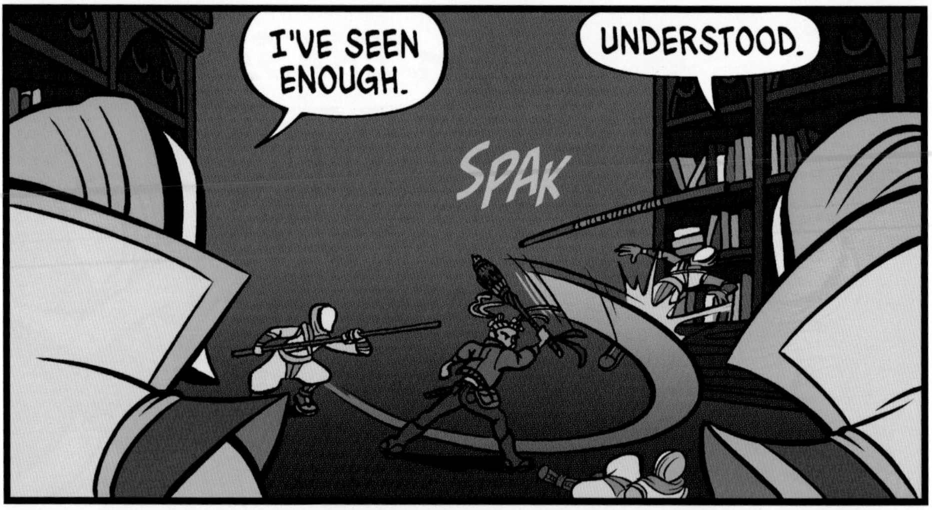
I'VE SEEN ENOUGH.
UNDERSTOOD.
SPAK

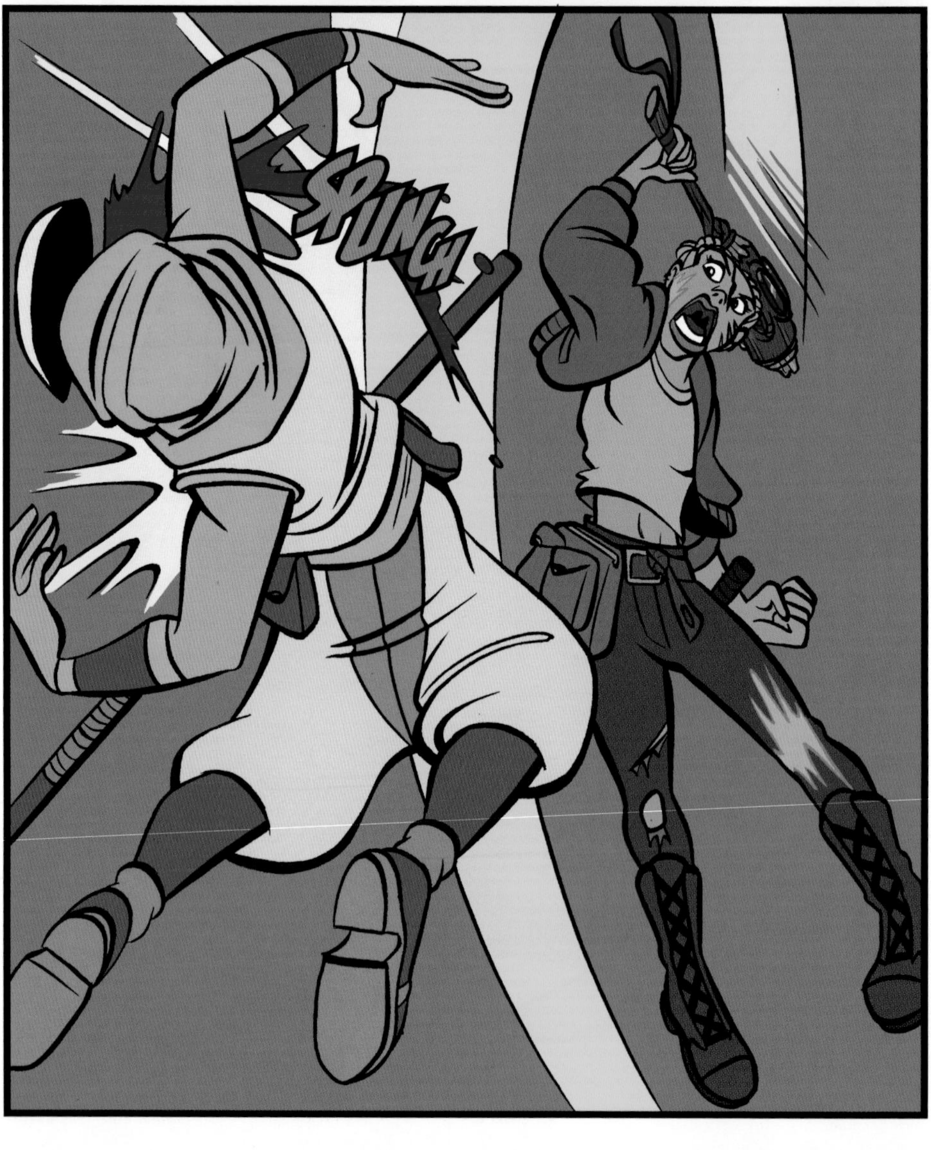
SPLUNCH

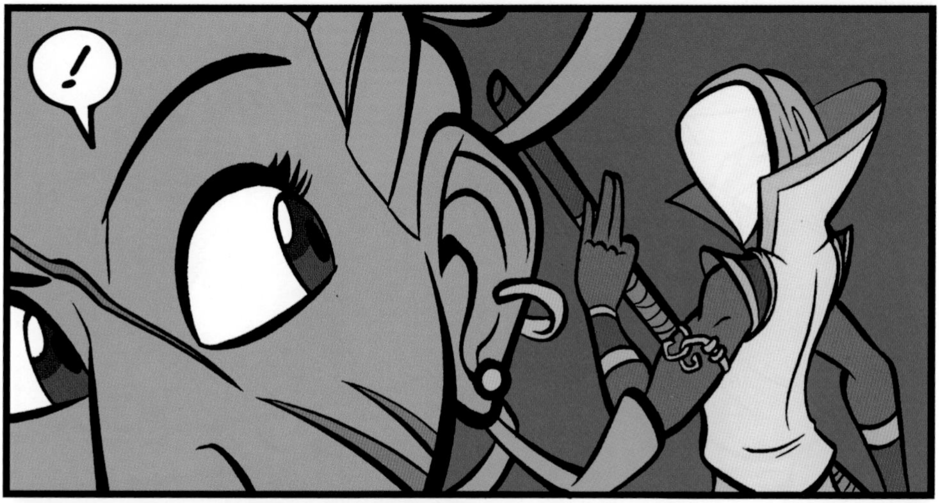
!

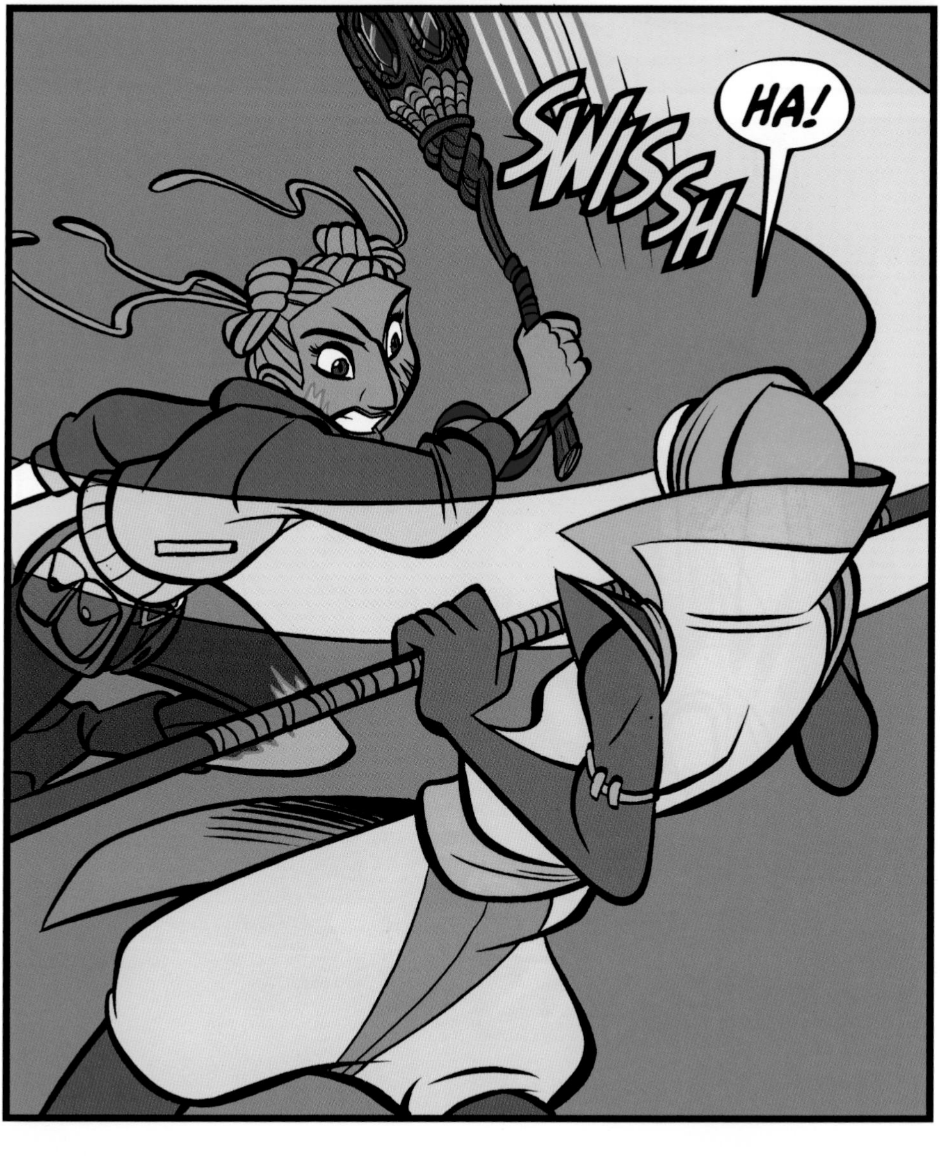
SWISSH
HA!

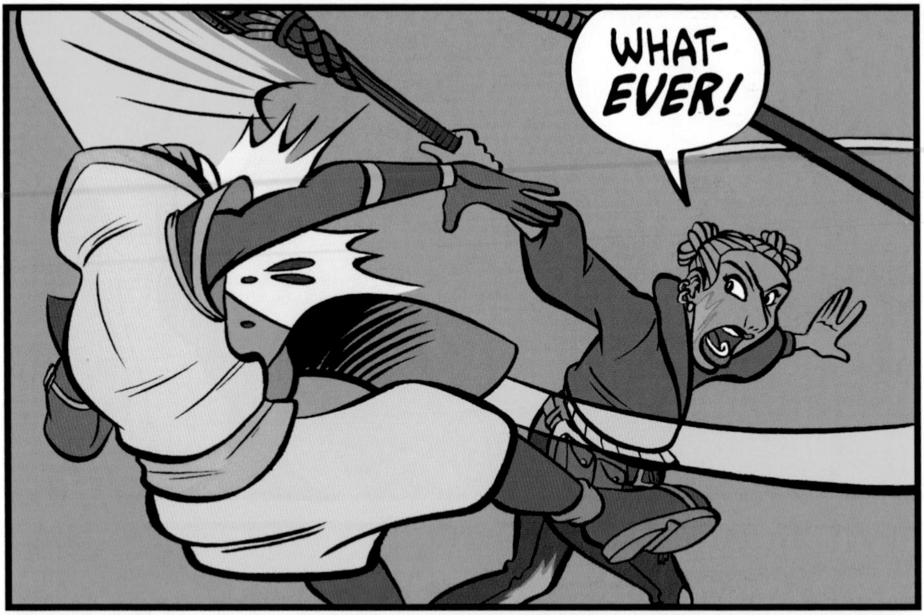
WHAT-
EVER!

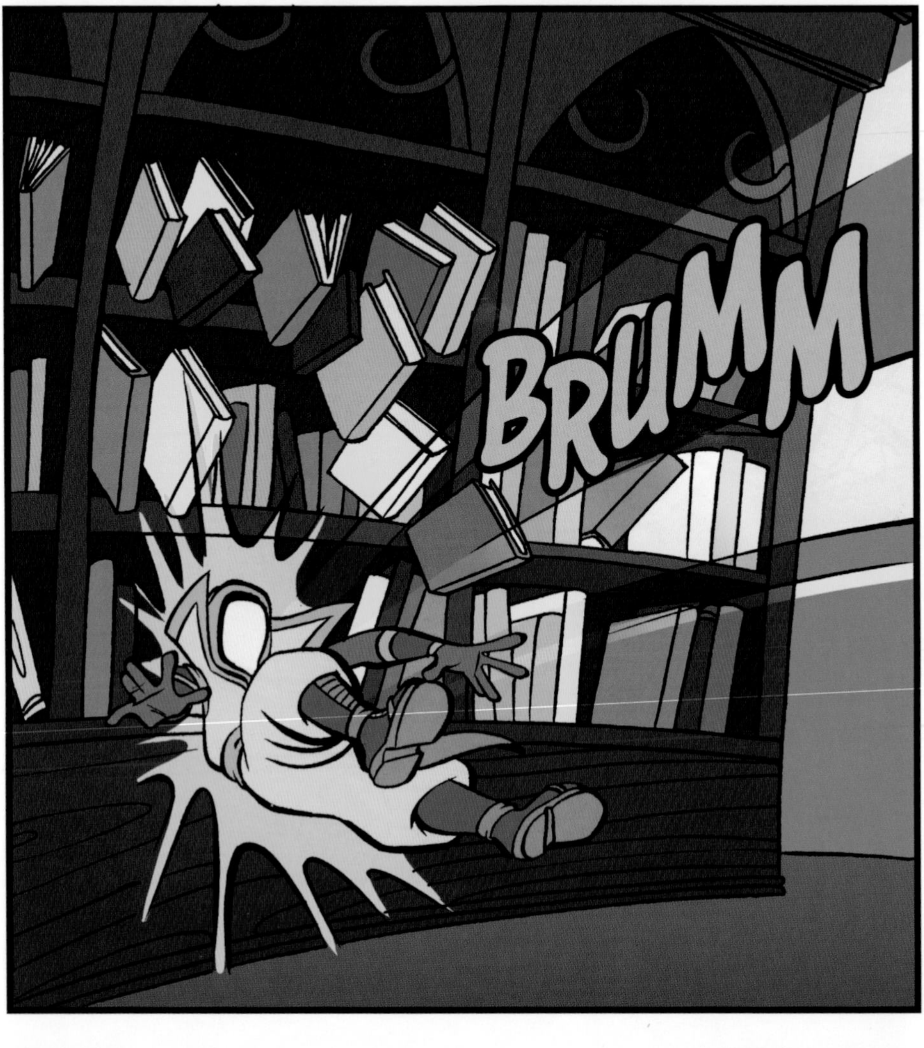
BRUMM

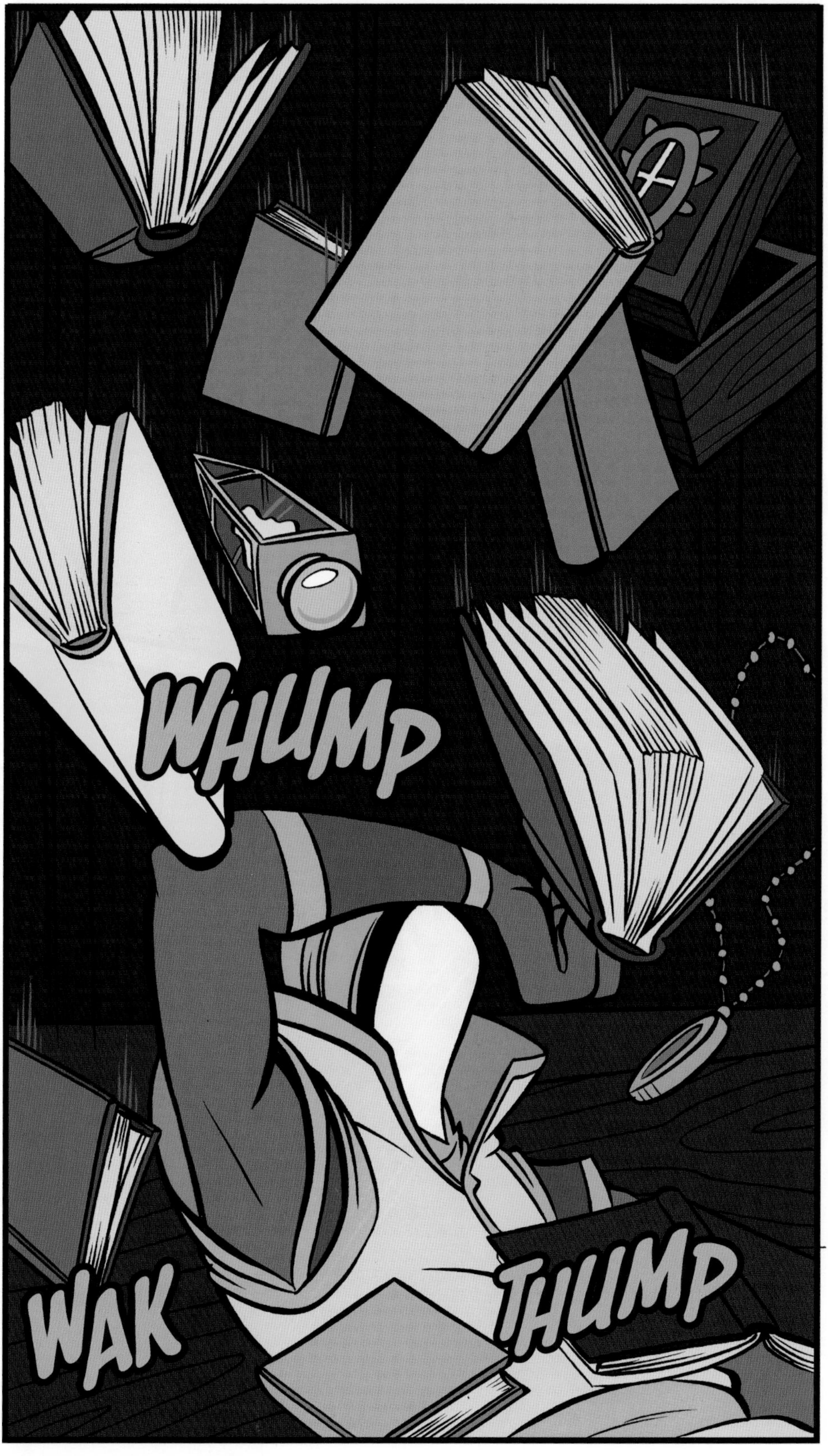
WHUMP
WAK
THUMP

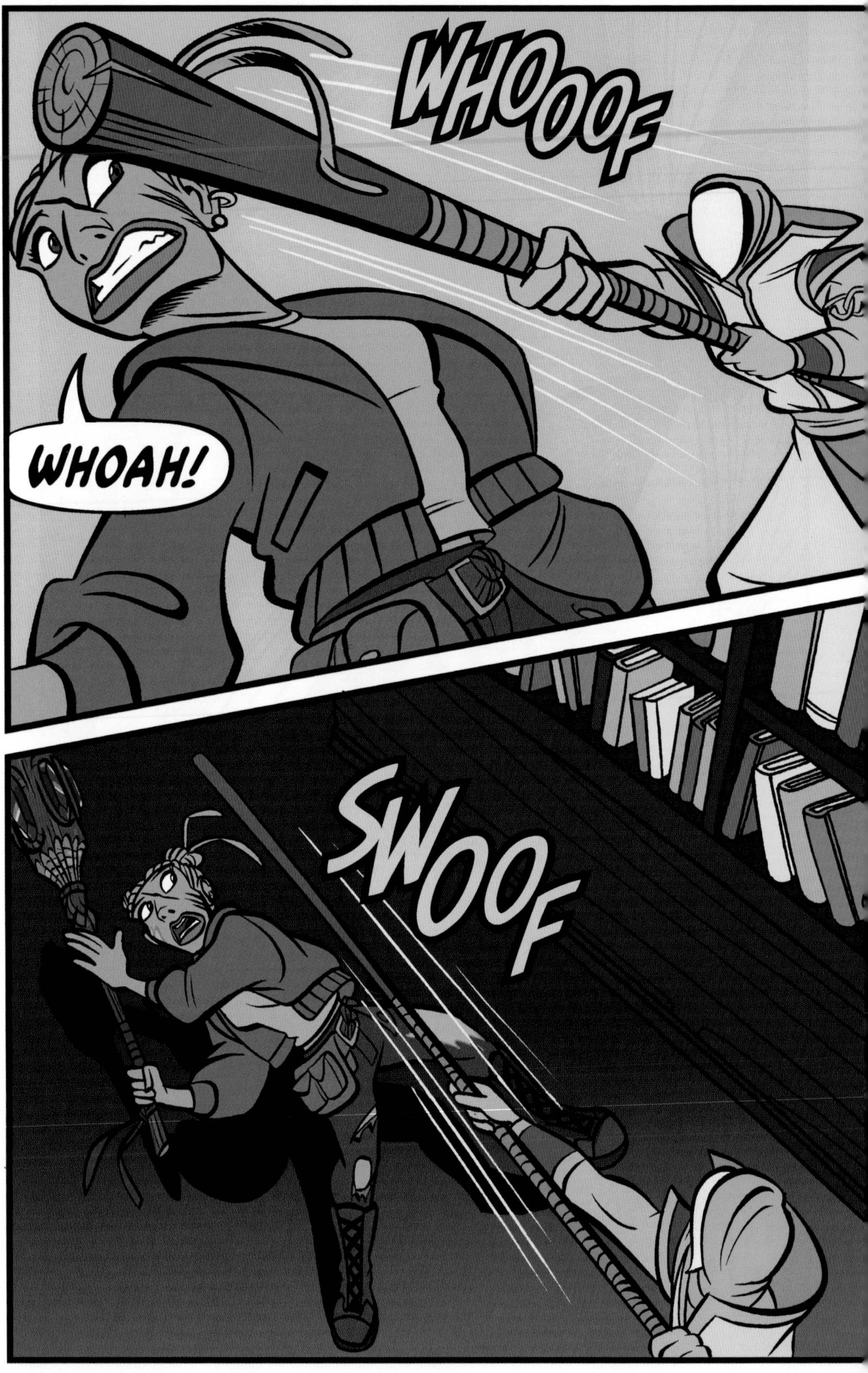
WHOOOF
WHOAH!
SWOOF

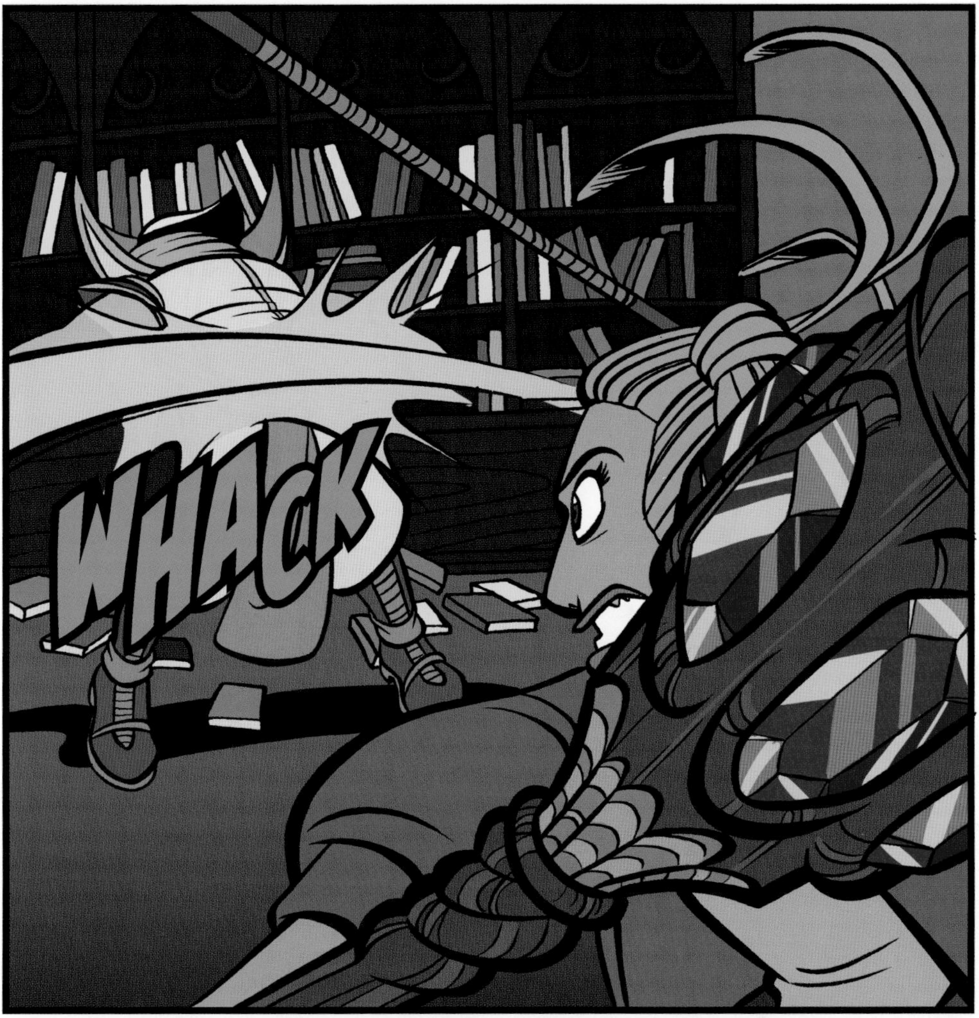
WHACK

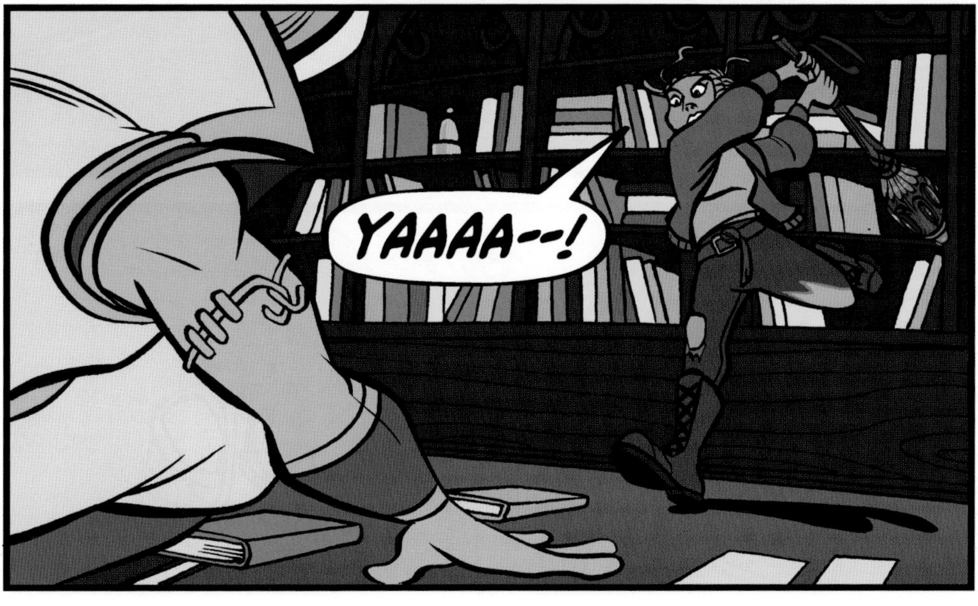
YAAAA--!

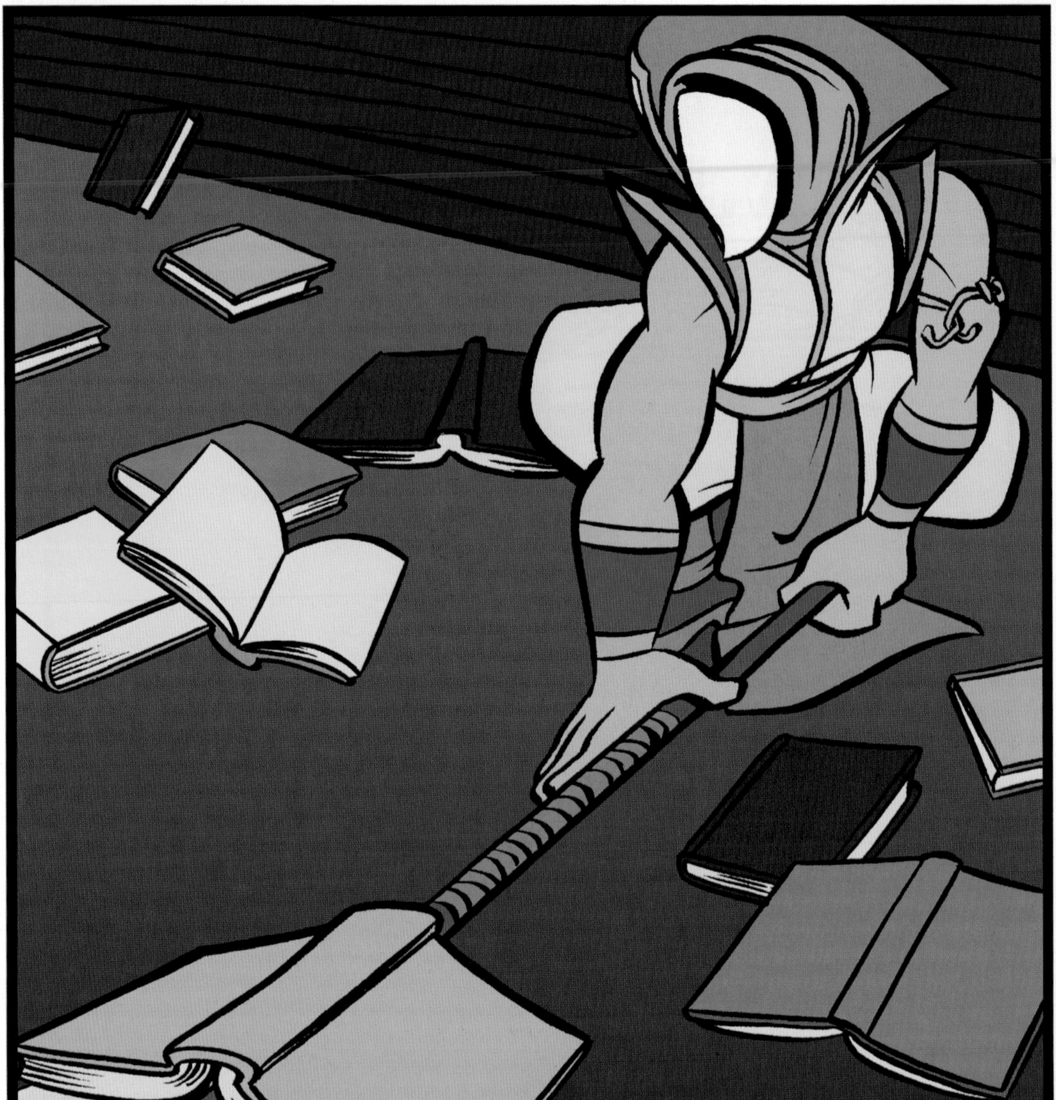

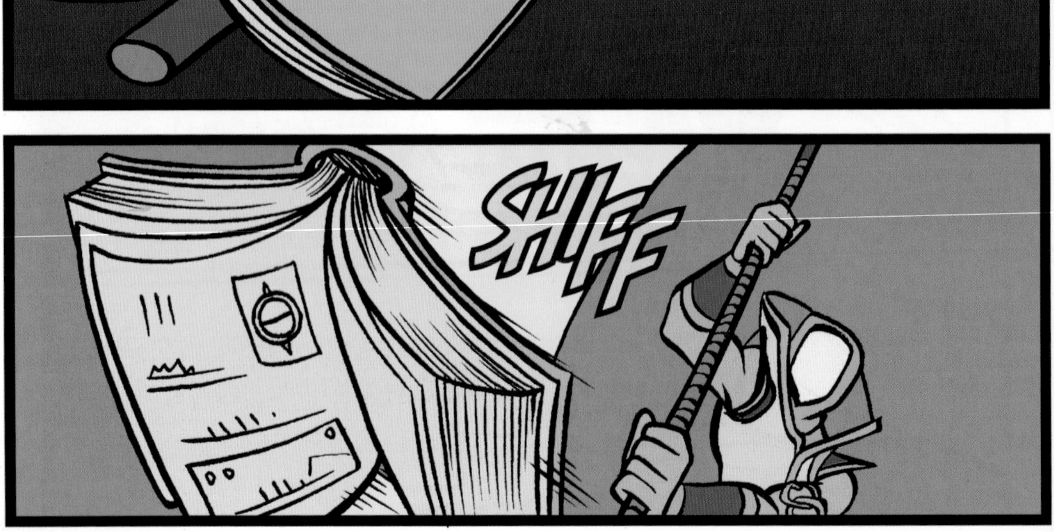
SHUFF

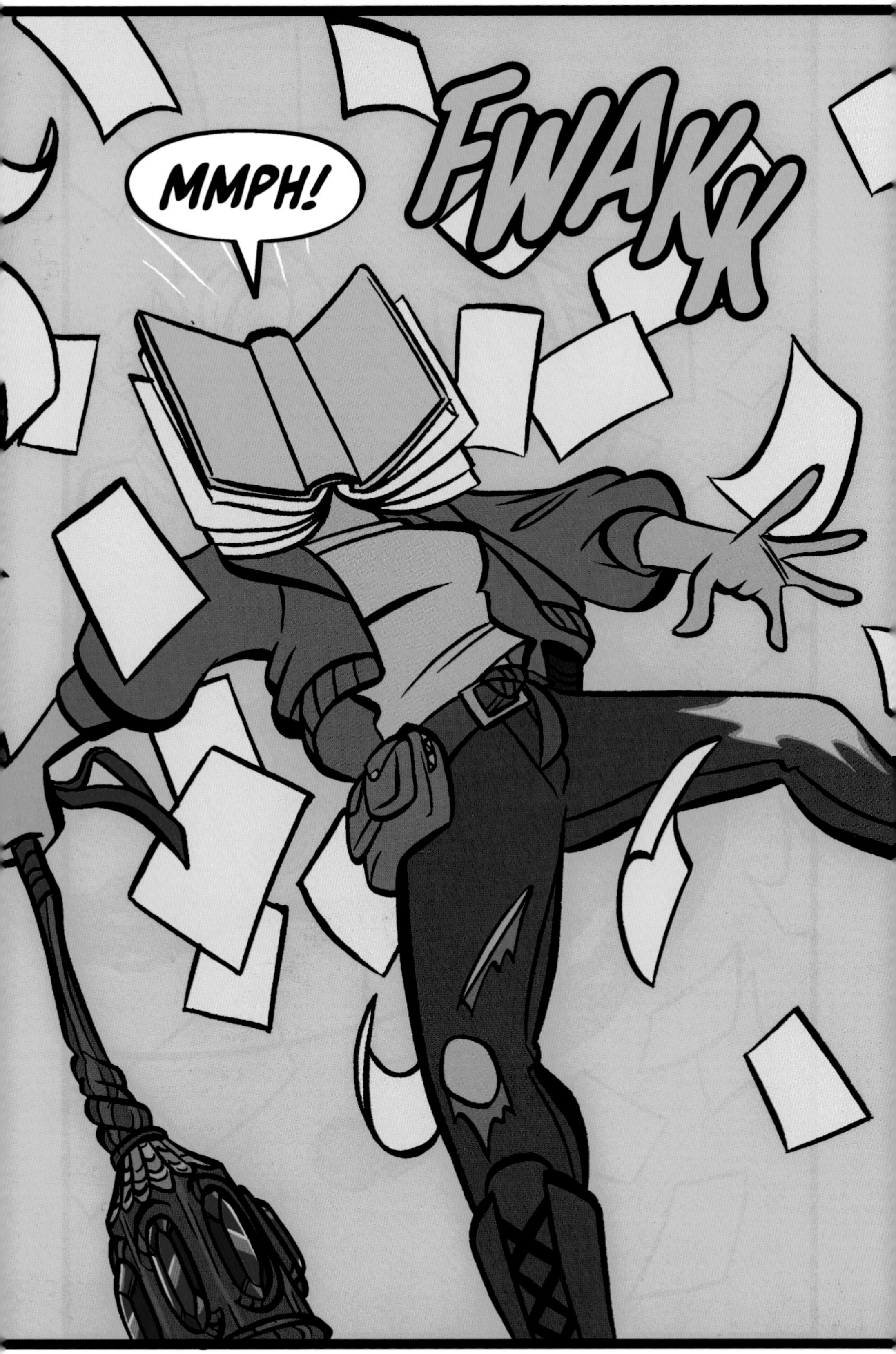
MMPH!
FWAKK

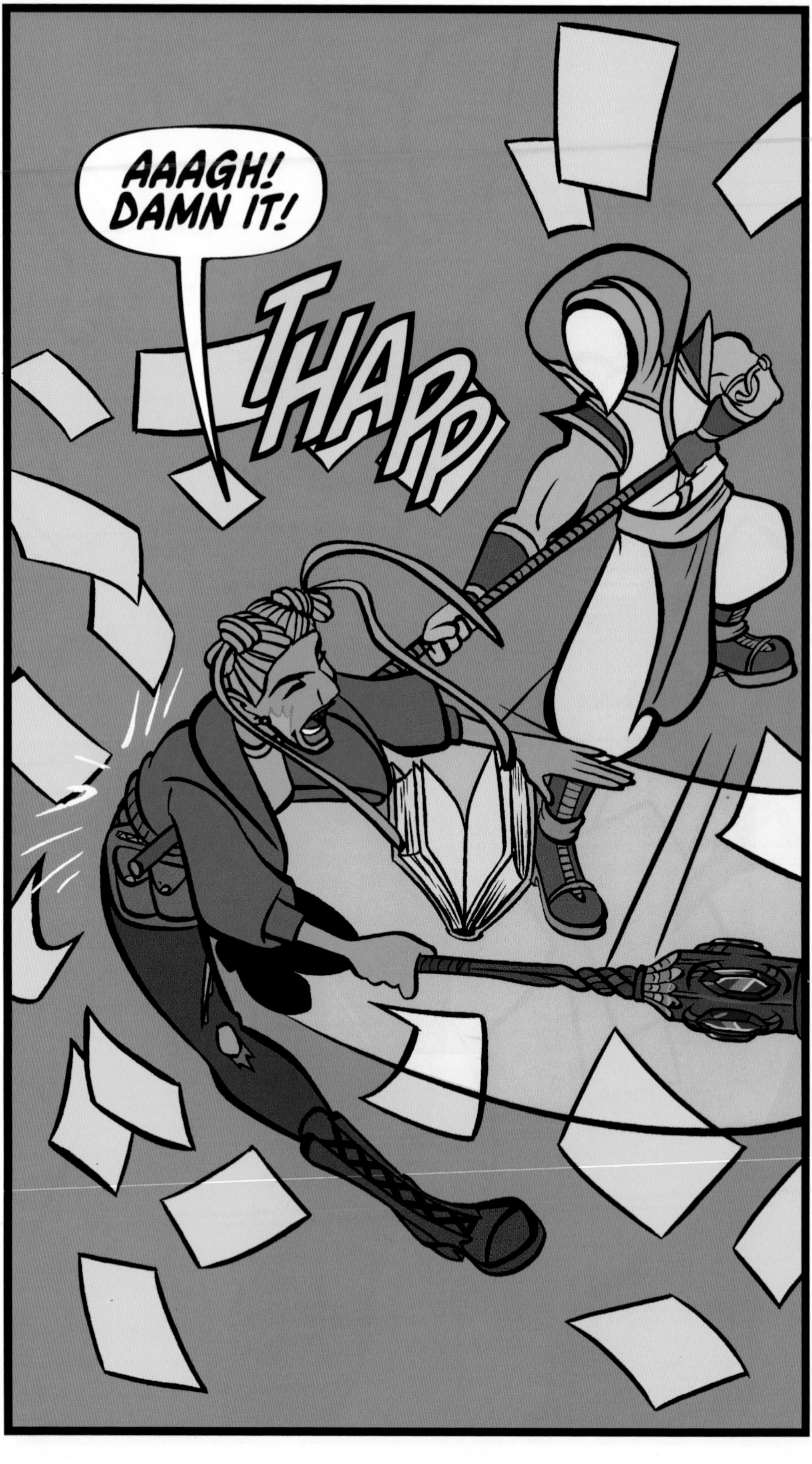
AAAGH! DAMN IT!
THAPP!

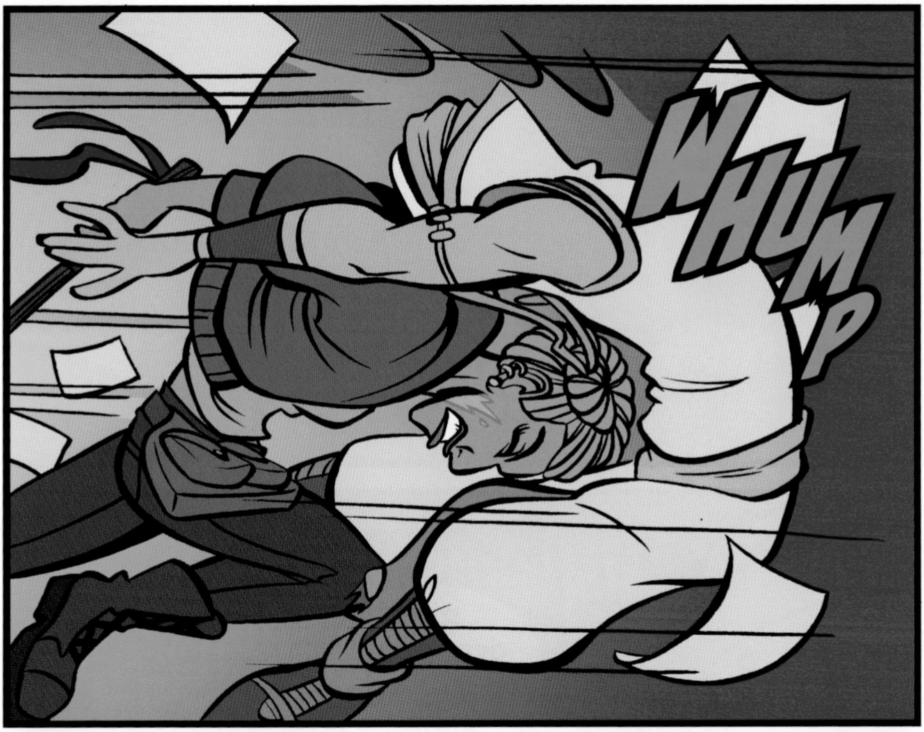
WHUMP

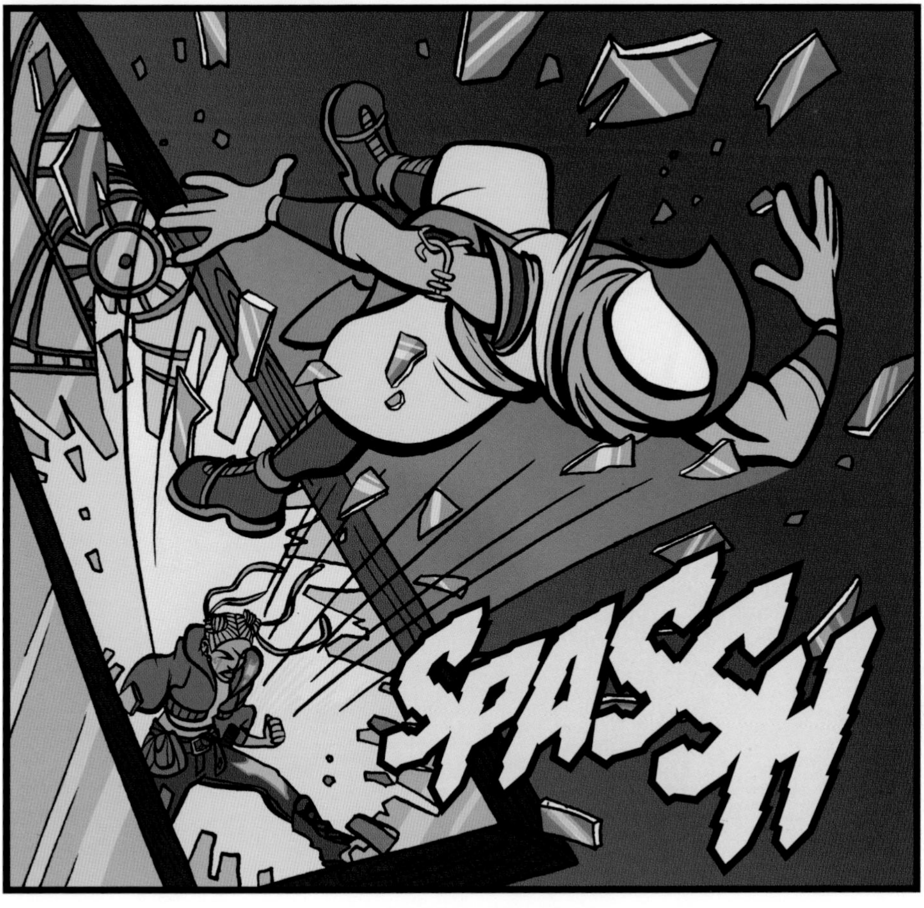
SPASSH

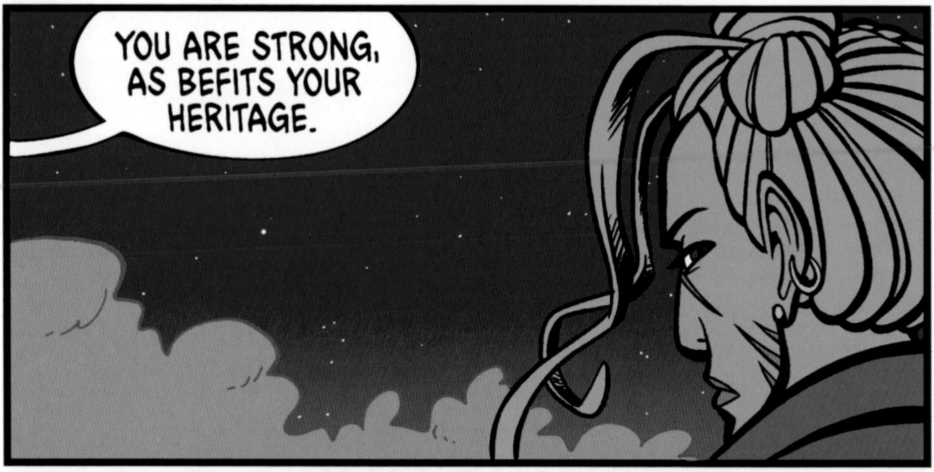
YOU ARE STRONG, AS BEFITS YOUR HERITAGE.

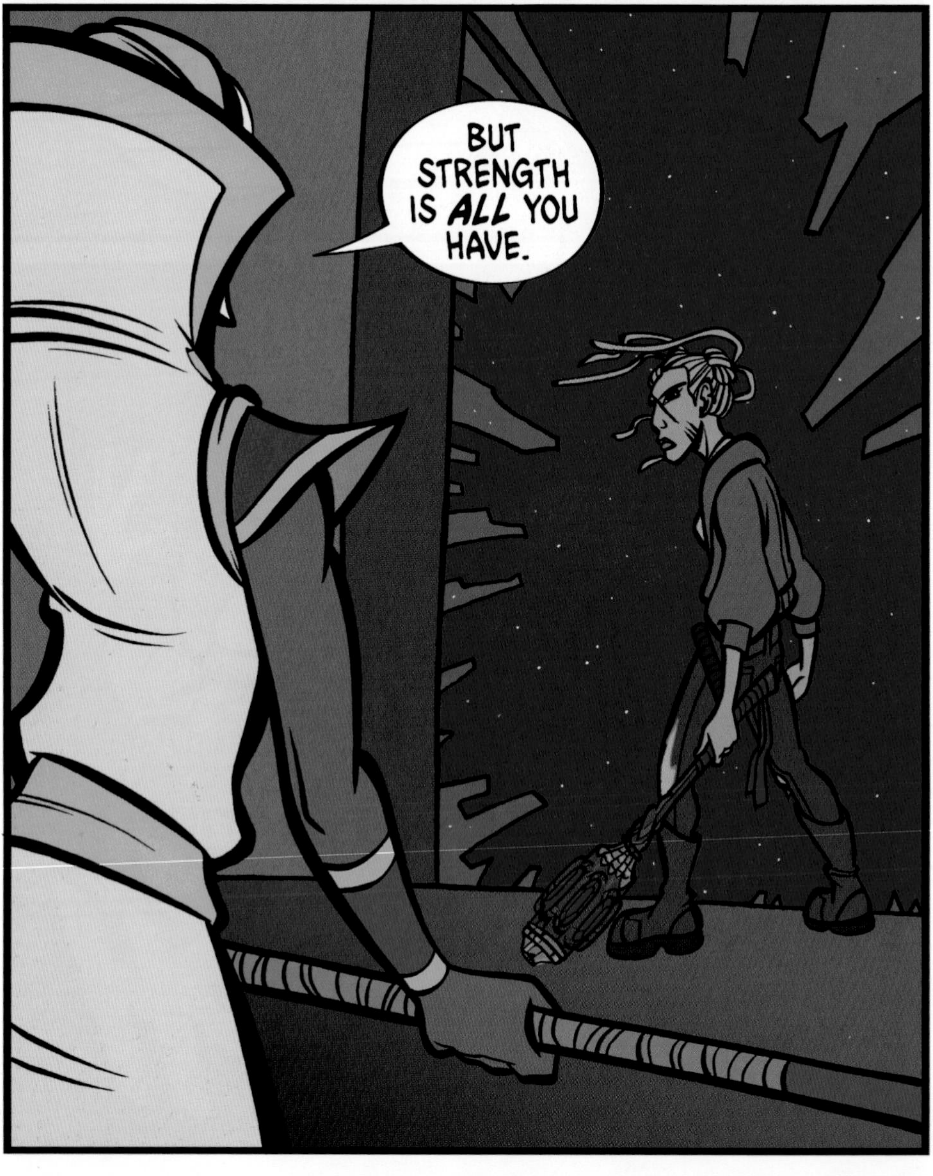
BUT STRENGTH IS *ALL* YOU HAVE.

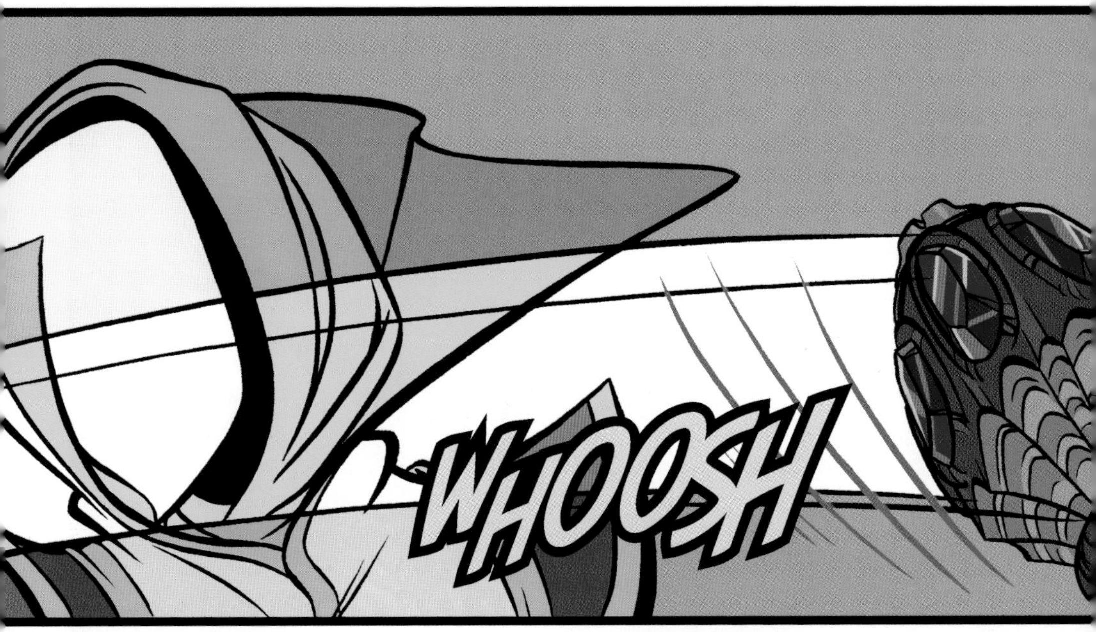
WHOOSH

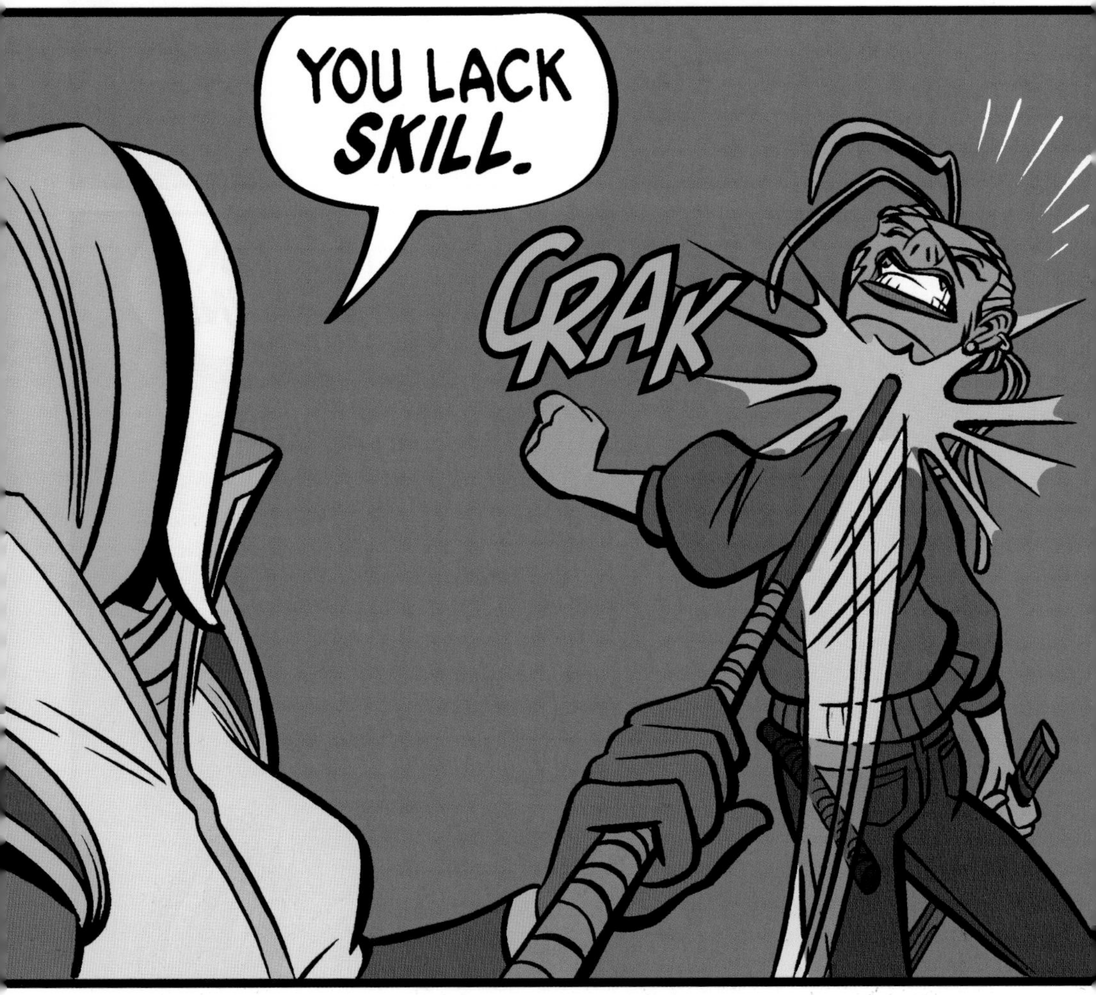
YOU LACK SKILL.
CRAK

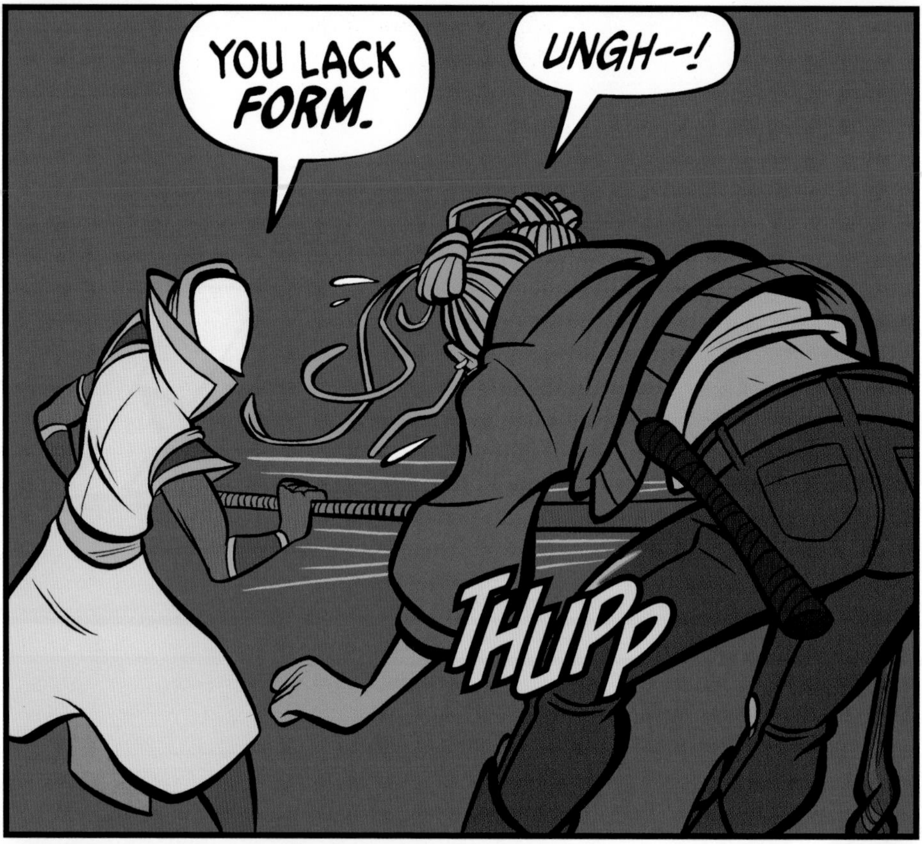
YOU LACK FORM.
UNGH--!
THUPP

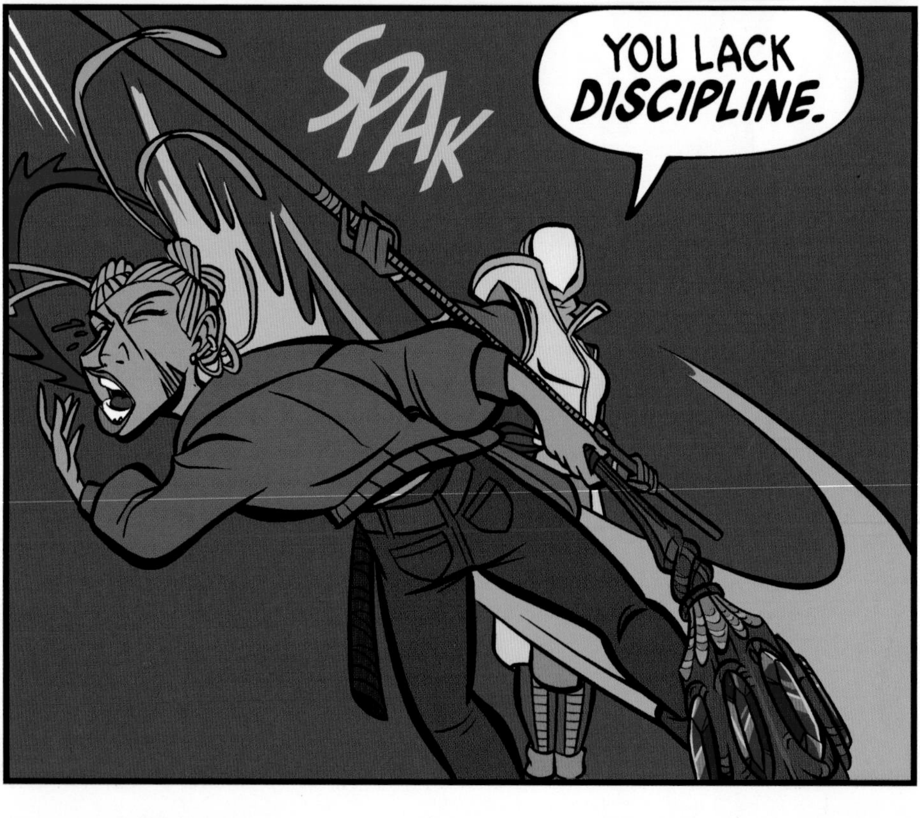
SPAK
YOU LACK DISCIPLINE.

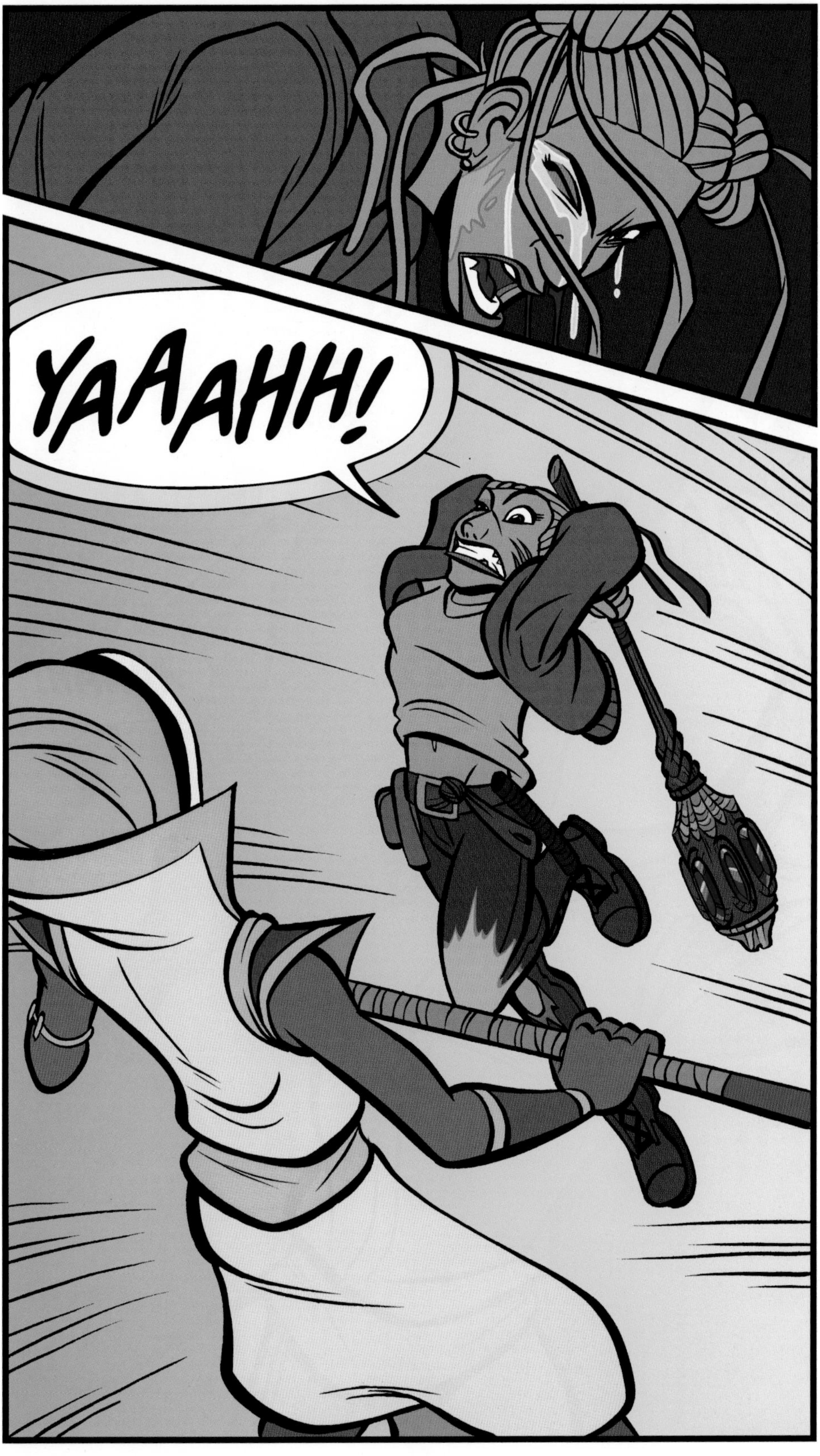
YAAAHH!

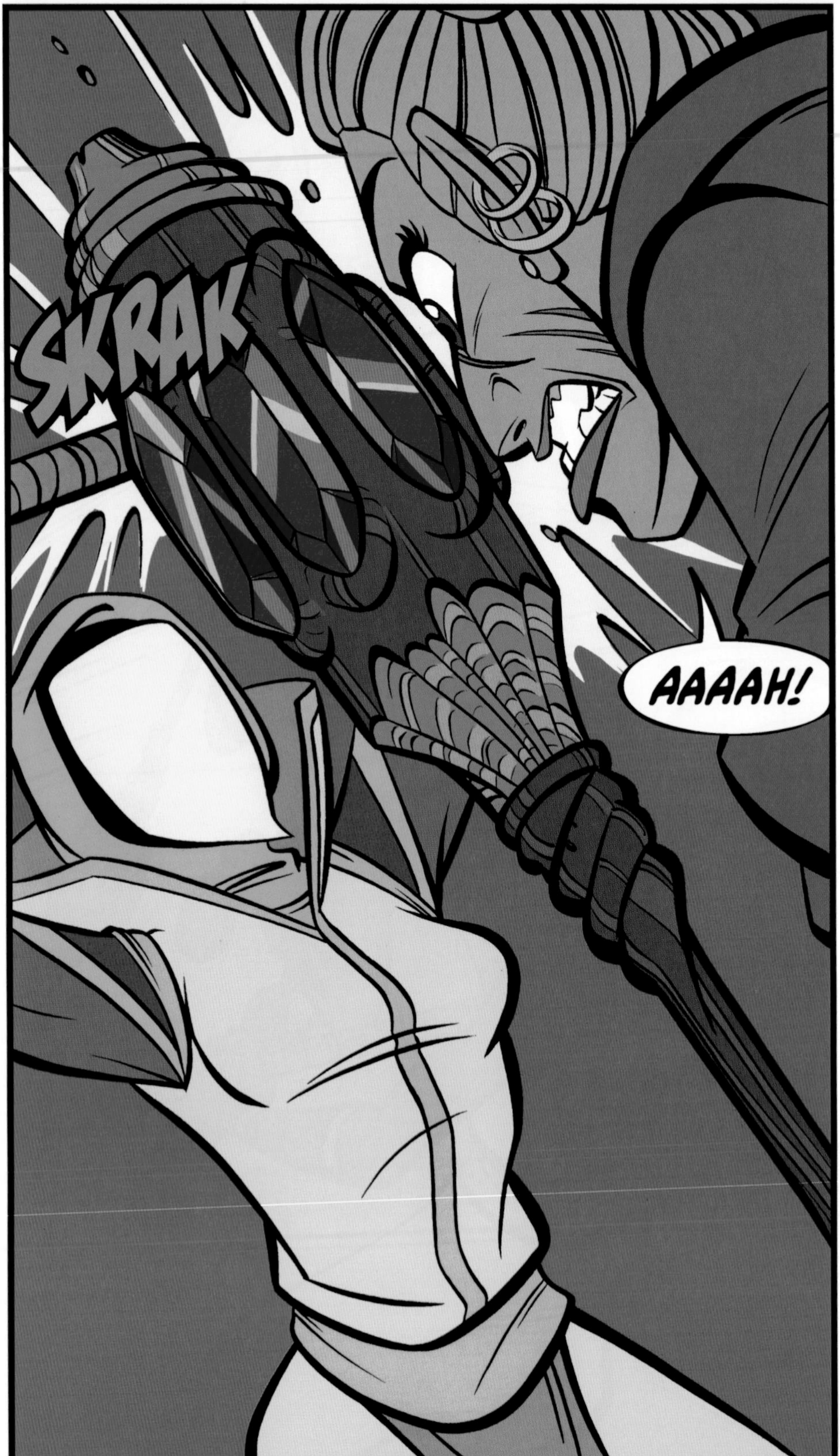
SKRAK
AAAAH!

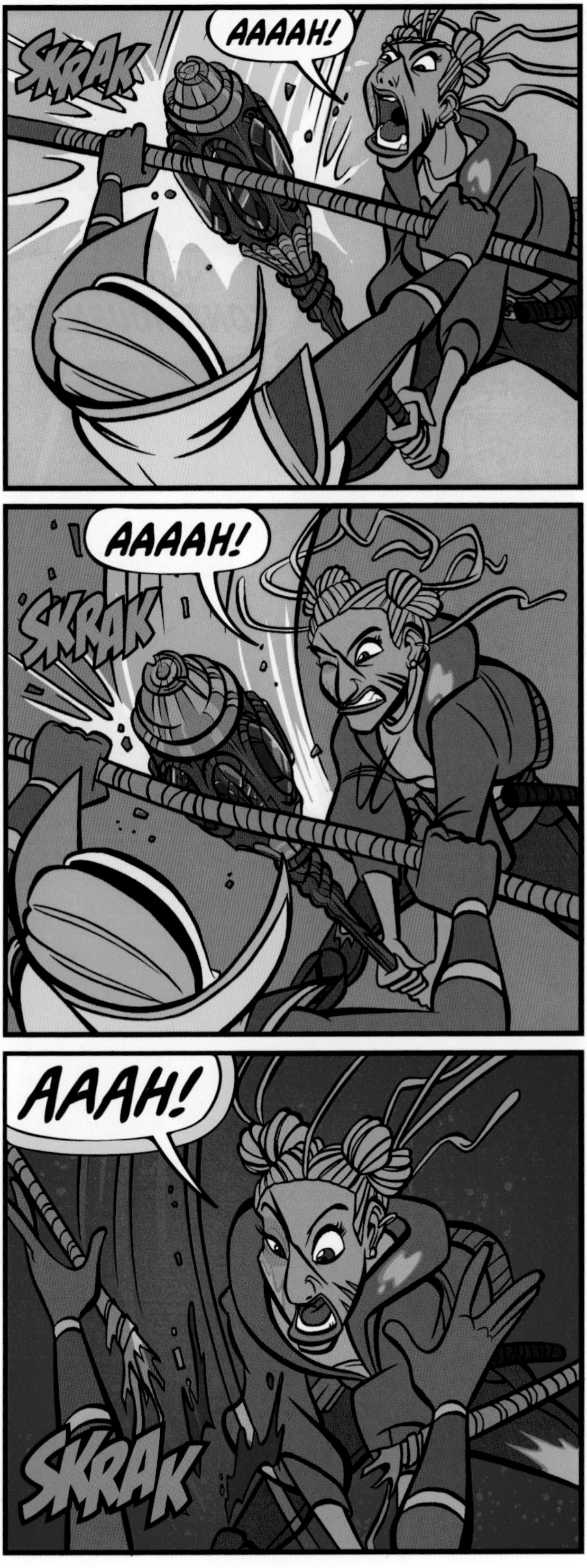
AAAAH!
SKRAK
AAAAH!
SKRAK
AAAH!
SKRAK

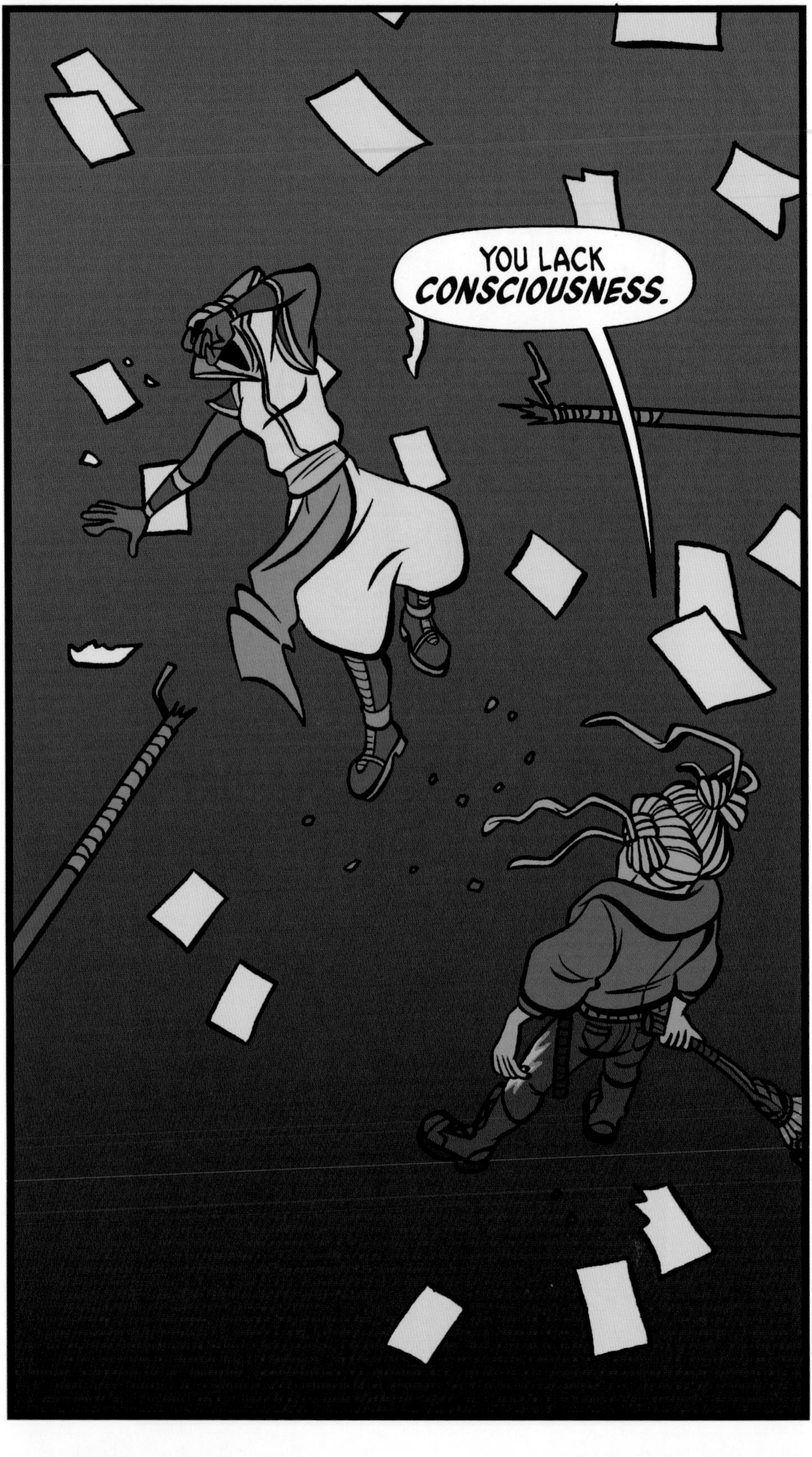
YOU LACK CONSCIOUSNESS.

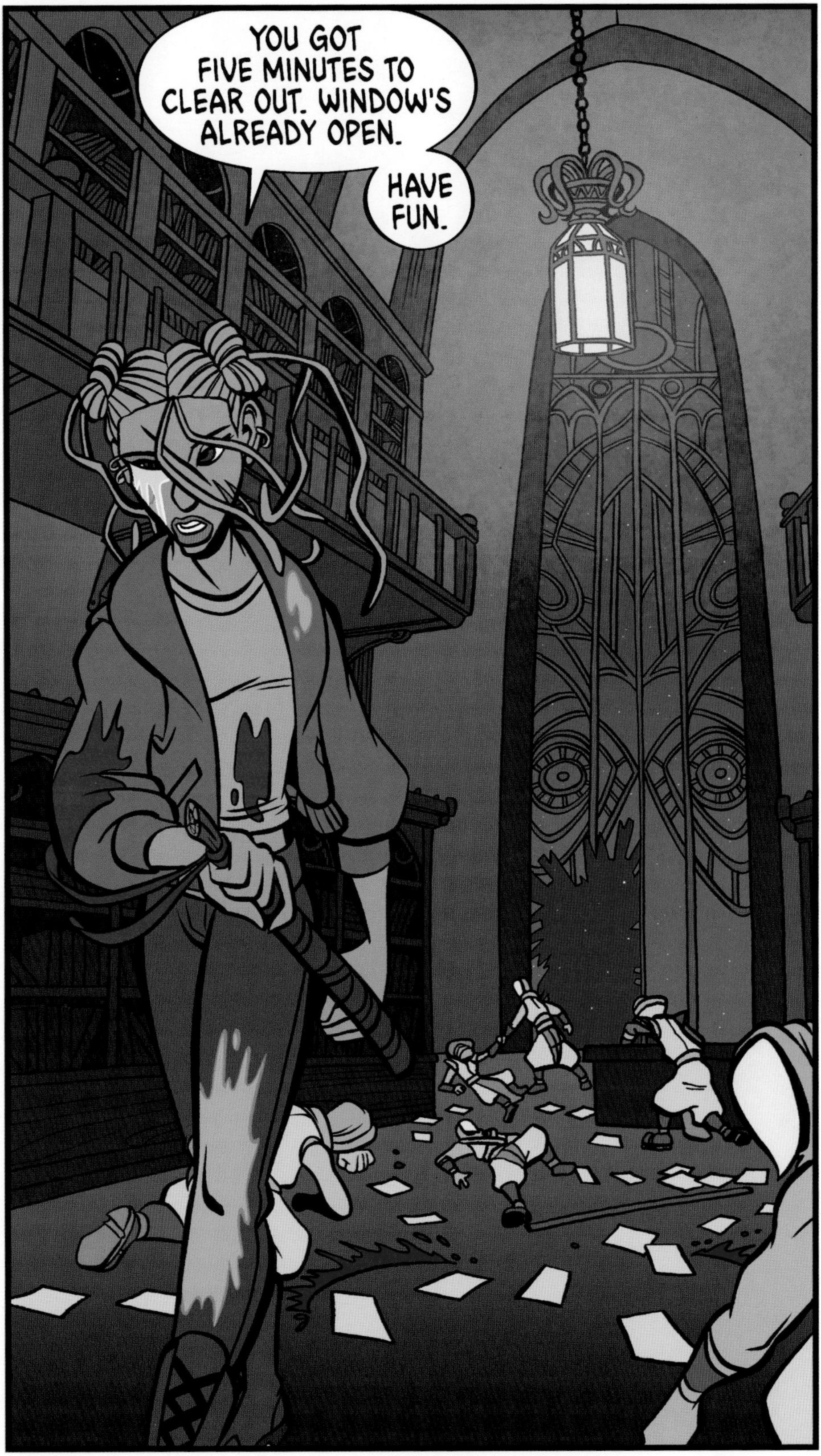
YOU GOT FIVE MINUTES TO CLEAR OUT. WINDOW'S ALREADY OPEN.
HAVE FUN.

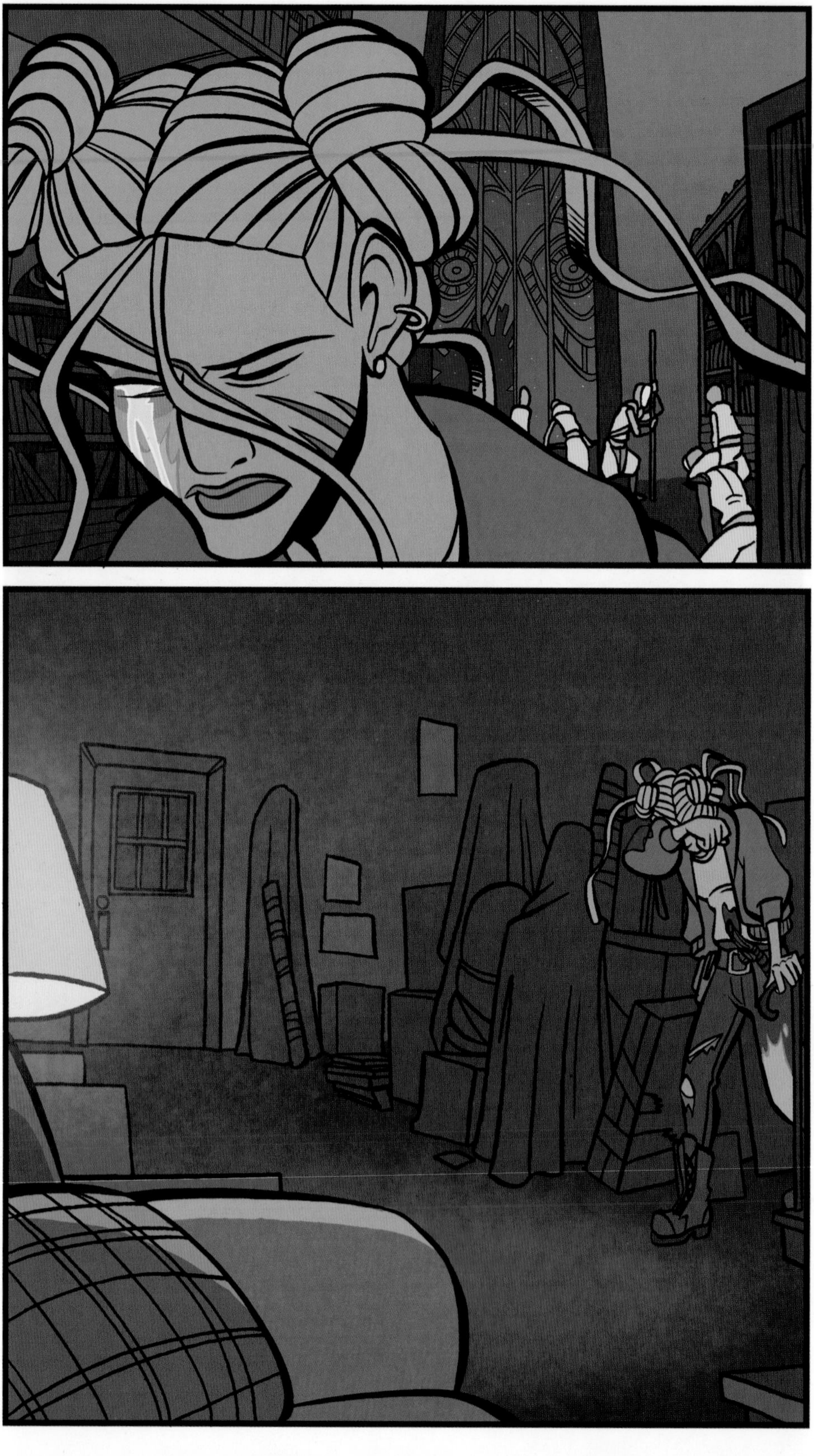

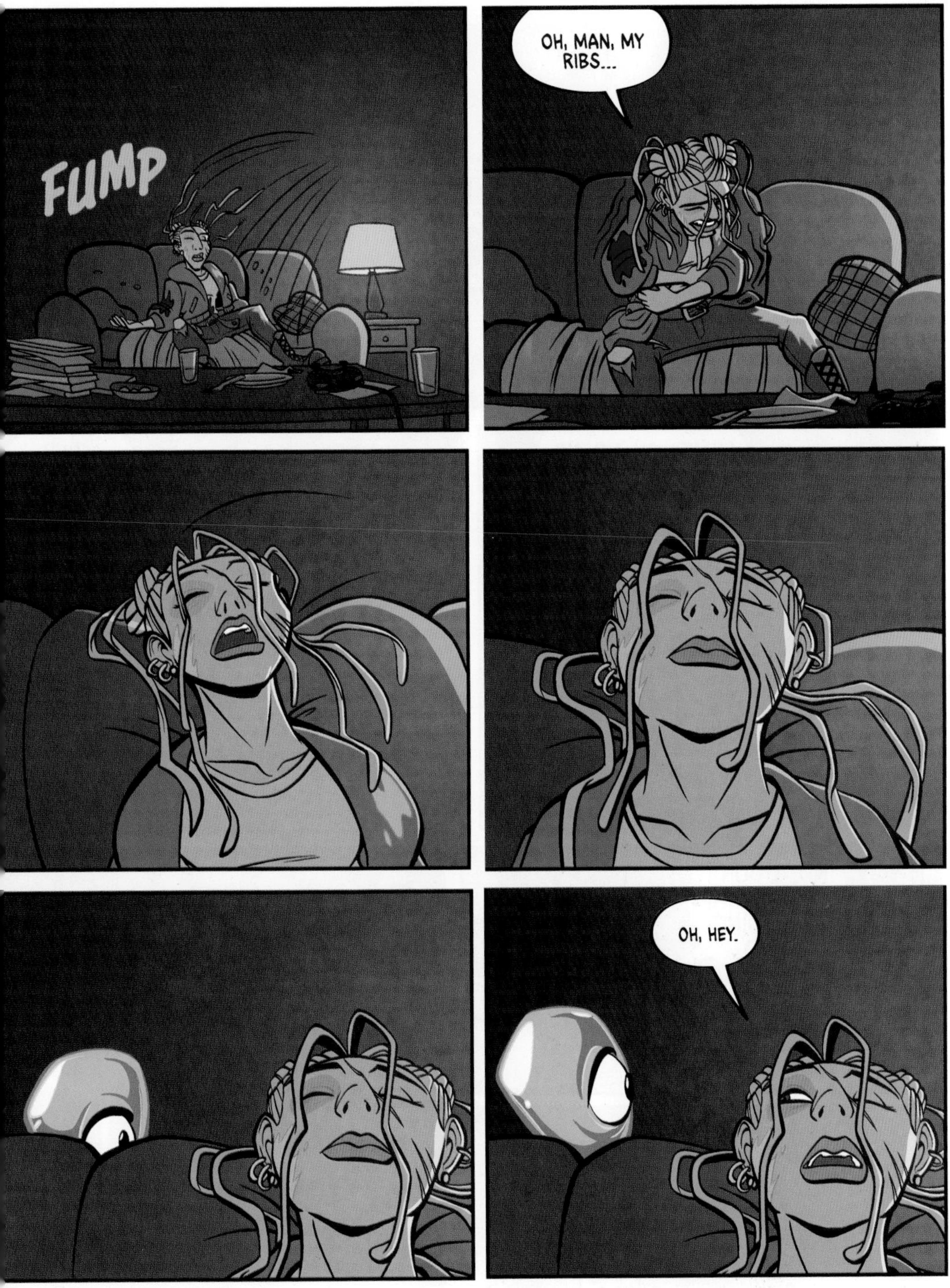
FUMP
OH, MAN, MY RIBS...
OH, HEY.

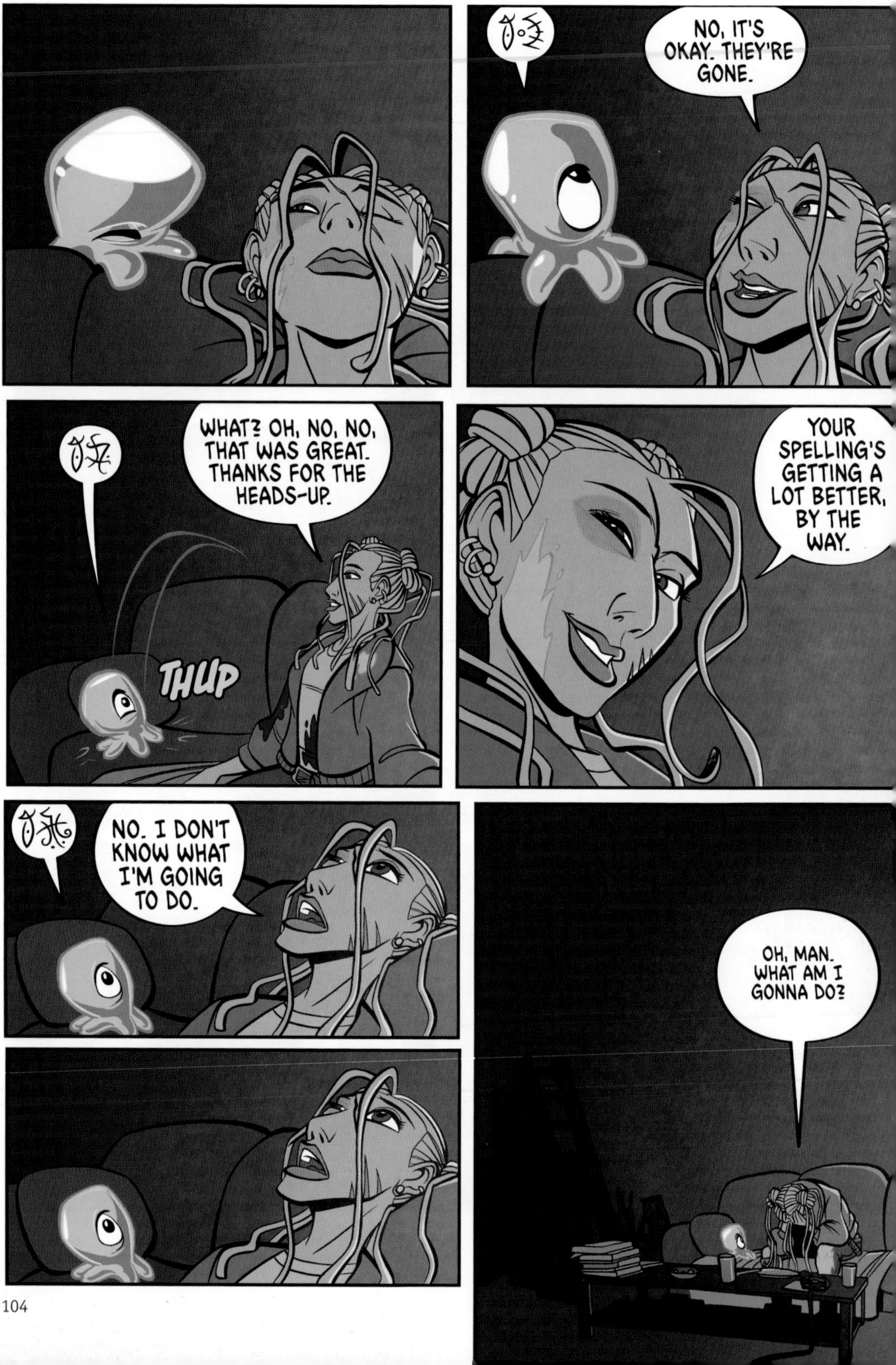
NO, IT'S OKAY. THEY'RE GONE.
WHAT? OH, NO, NO, THAT WAS GREAT. THANKS FOR THE HEADS-UP.
THUP
YOUR SPELLING'S GETTING A LOT BETTER, BY THE WAY.
NO. I DON'T KNOW WHAT I'M GOING TO DO.
OH, MAN. WHAT AM I GONNA DO?

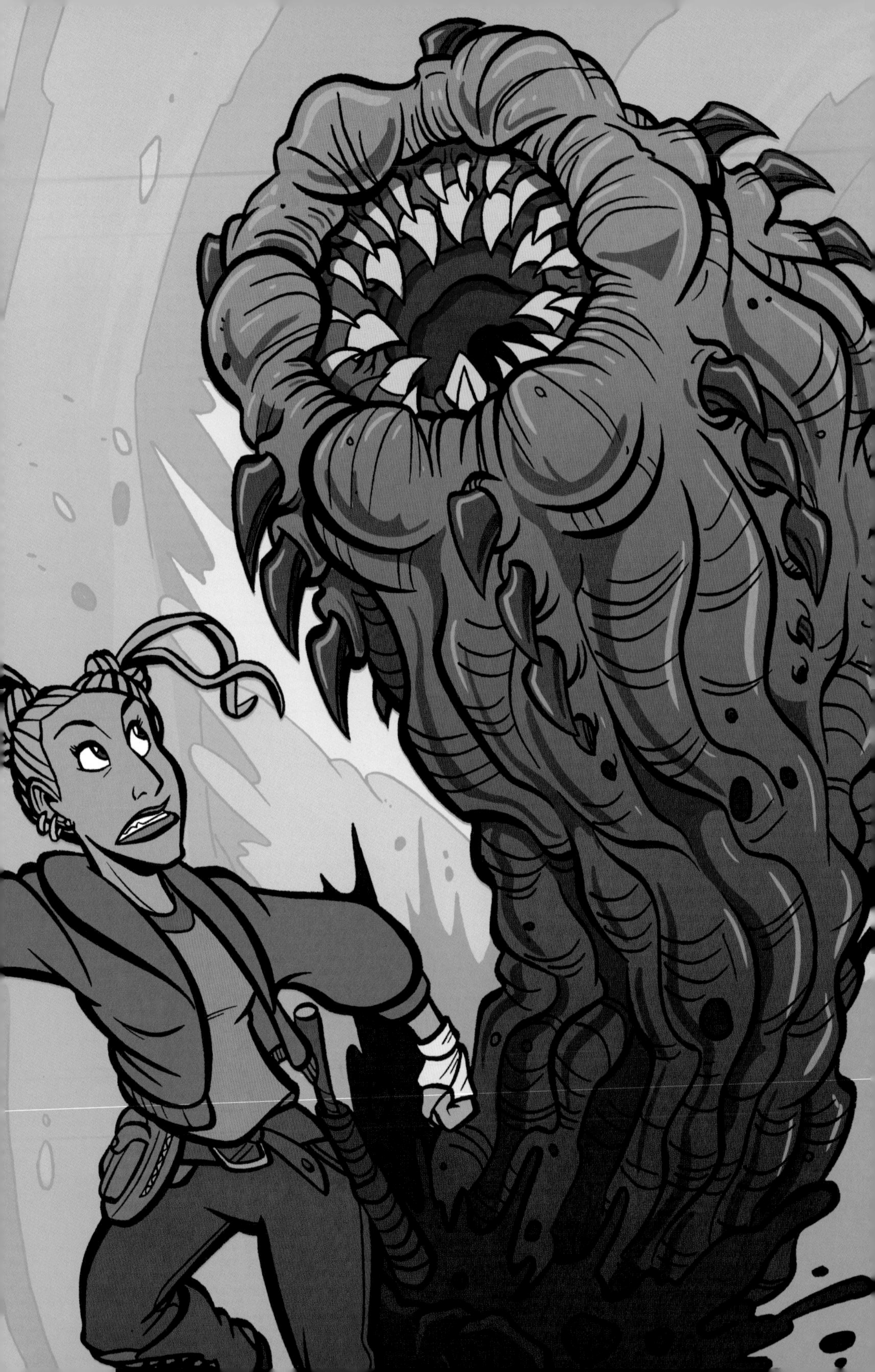

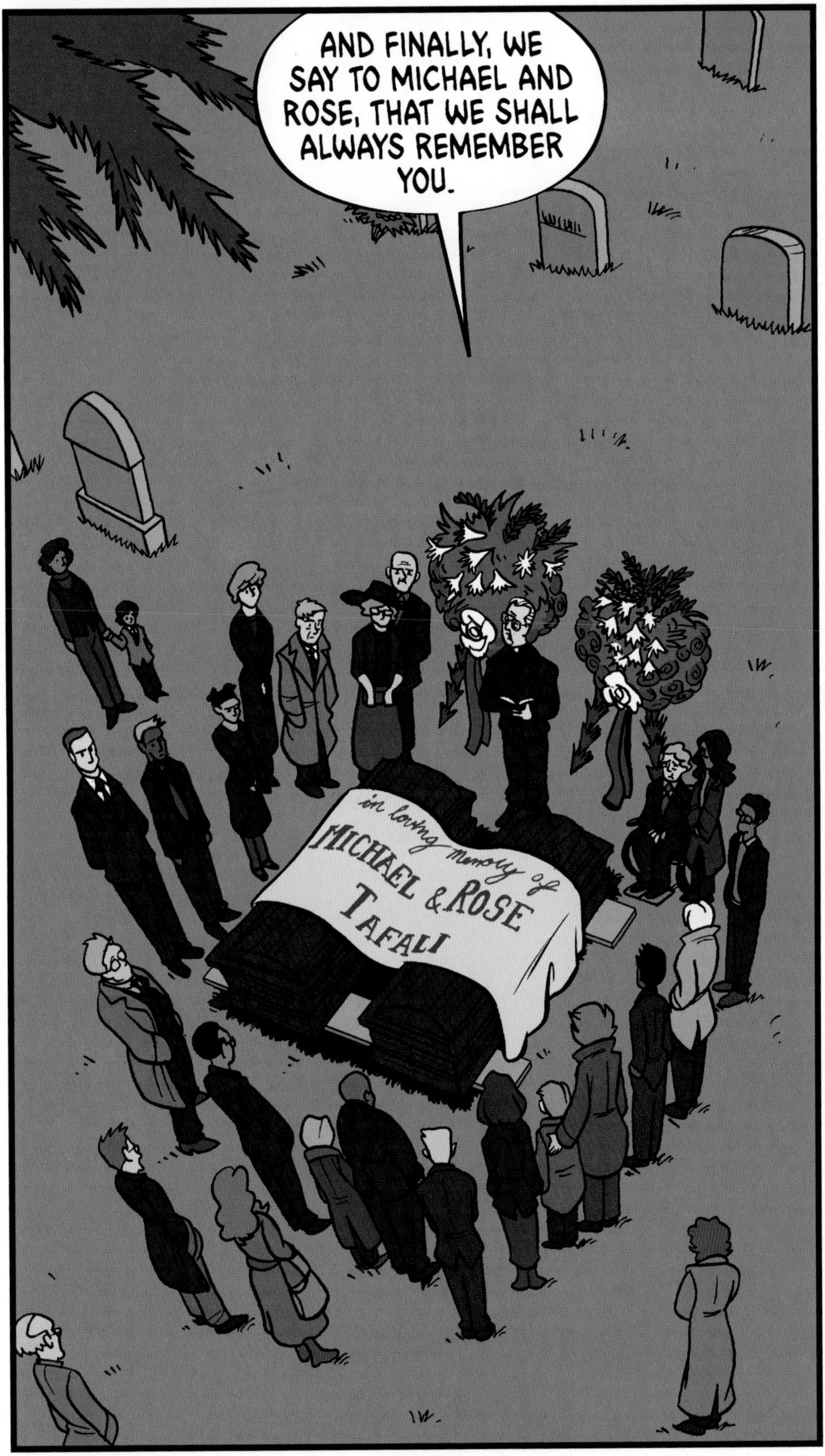
AND FINALLY, WE SAY TO MICHAEL AND ROSE, THAT WE SHALL ALWAYS REMEMBER YOU.
in loving memory of
MICHAEL & ROSE
TAFALI

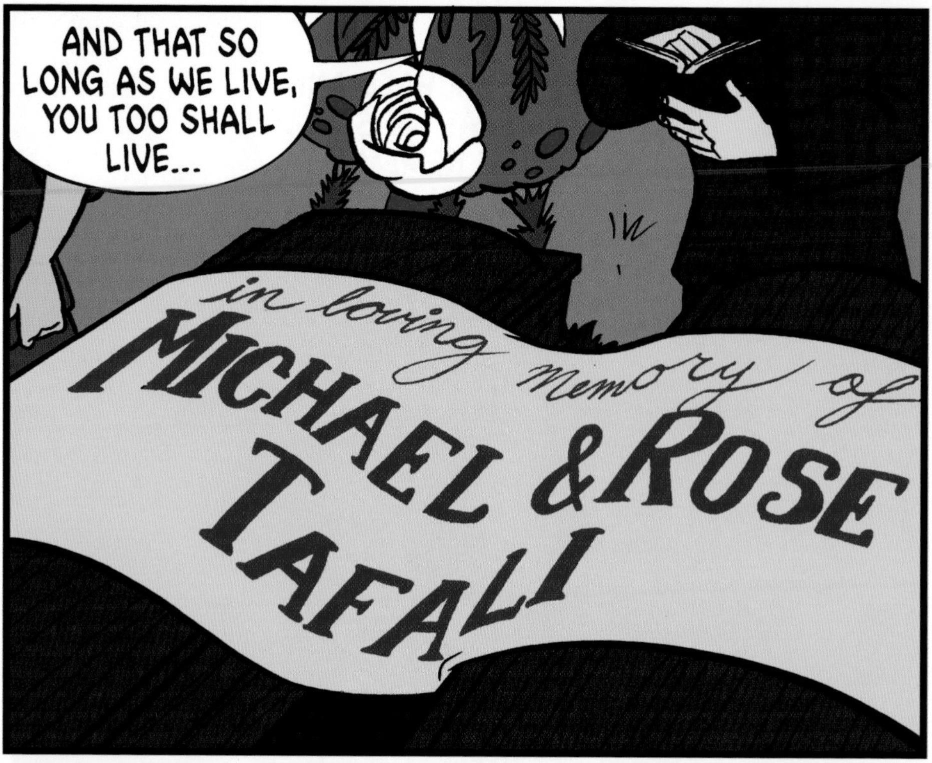
AND THAT SO LONG AS WE LIVE, YOU TOO SHALL LIVE...
in loving memory of
MICHAEL & ROSE
TAFALI

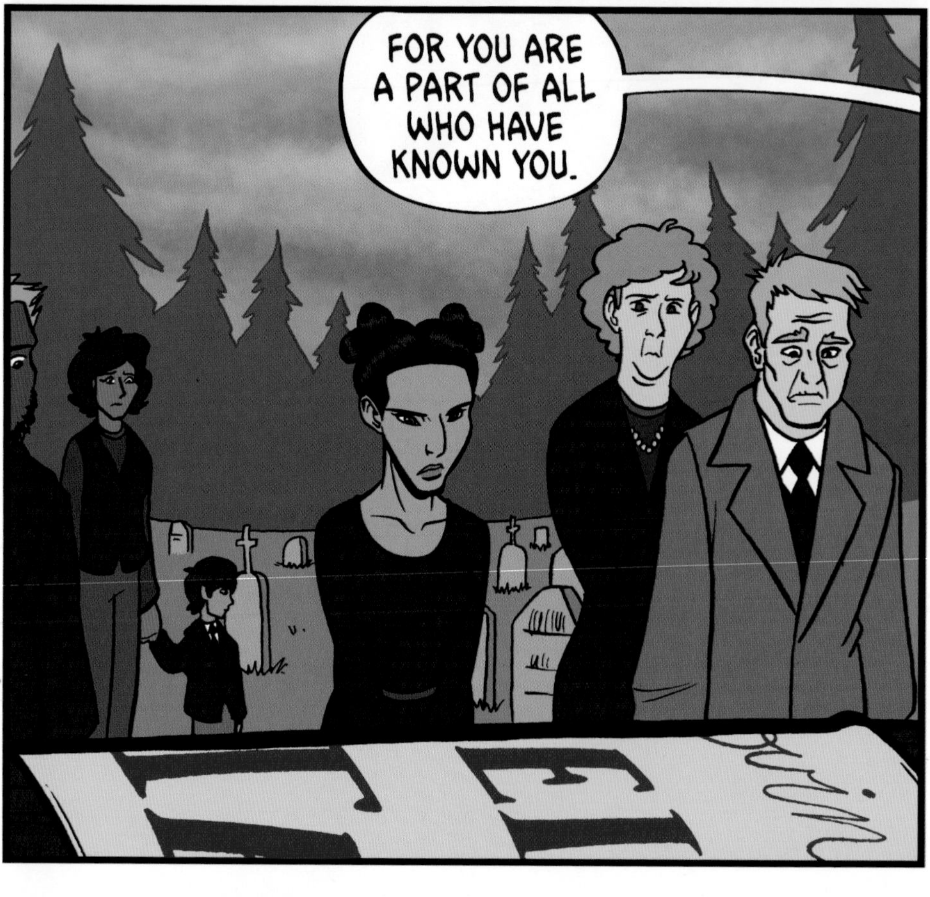
FOR YOU ARE A PART OF ALL WHO HAVE KNOWN YOU.

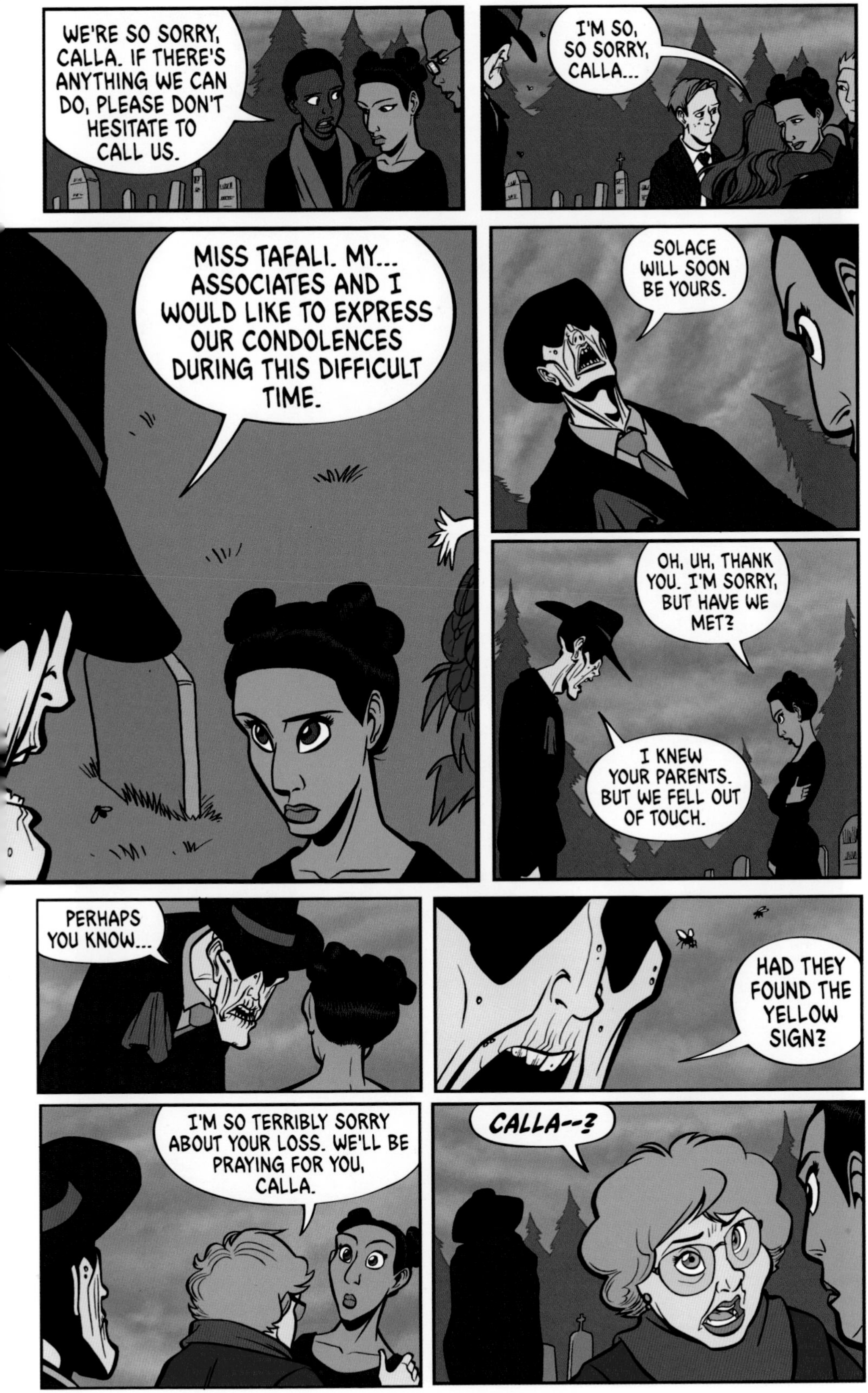
WE'RE SO SORRY, CALLA. IF THERE'S ANYTHING WE CAN DO, PLEASE DON'T HESITATE TO CALL US.
I'M SO, SO SORRY, CALLA...
MISS TAFALI. MY... ASSOCIATES AND I WOULD LIKE TO EXPRESS OUR CONDOLENCES DURING THIS DIFFICULT TIME.
SOLACE WILL SOON BE YOURS.
OH, UH, THANK YOU. I'M SORRY, BUT HAVE WE MET?
I KNEW YOUR PARENTS. BUT WE FELL OUT OF TOUCH.
PERHAPS YOU KNOW...
HAD THEY FOUND THE YELLOW SIGN?
I'M SO TERRIBLY SORRY ABOUT YOUR LOSS. WE'LL BE PRAYING FOR YOU, CALLA.
CALLA--?

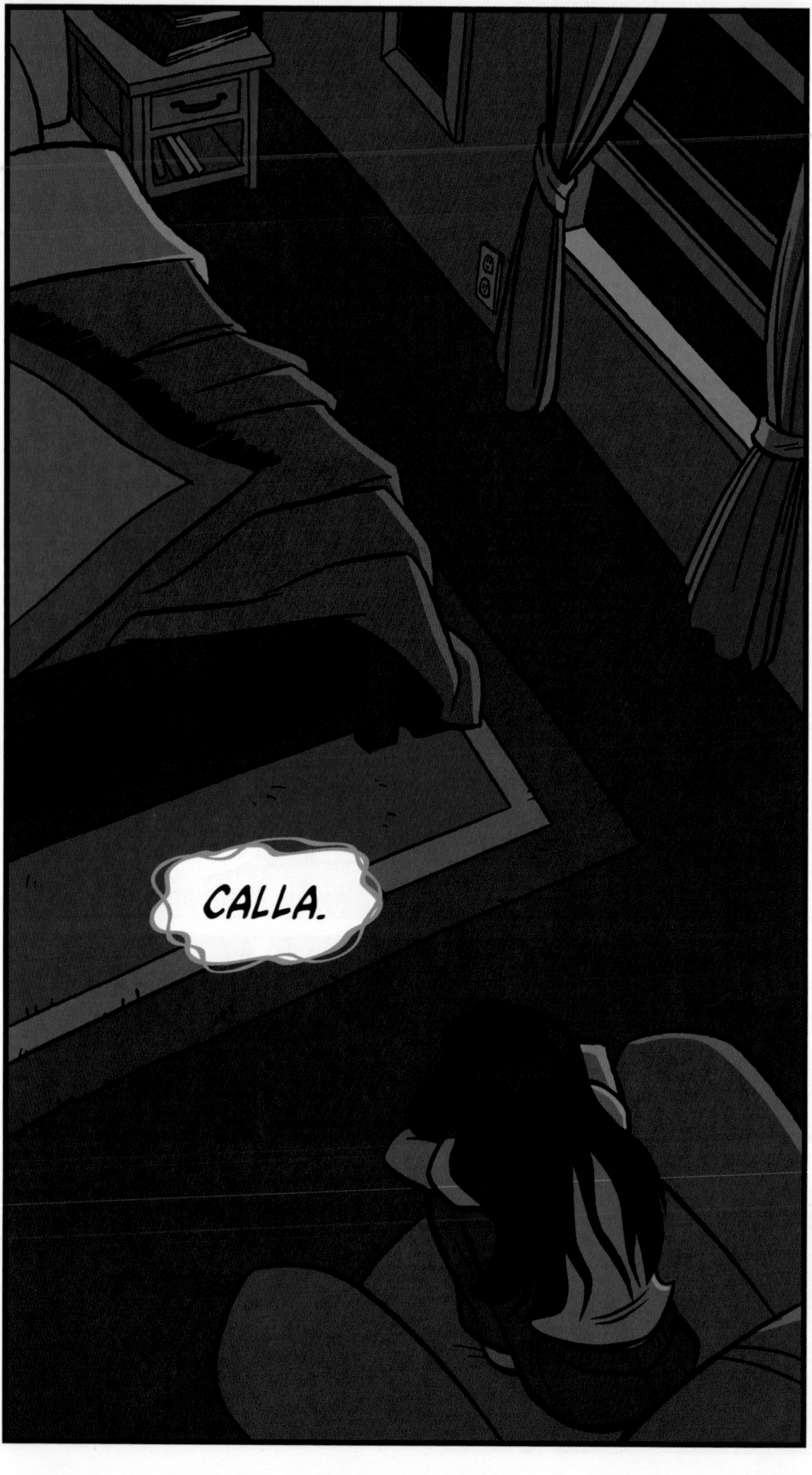
CALLA.

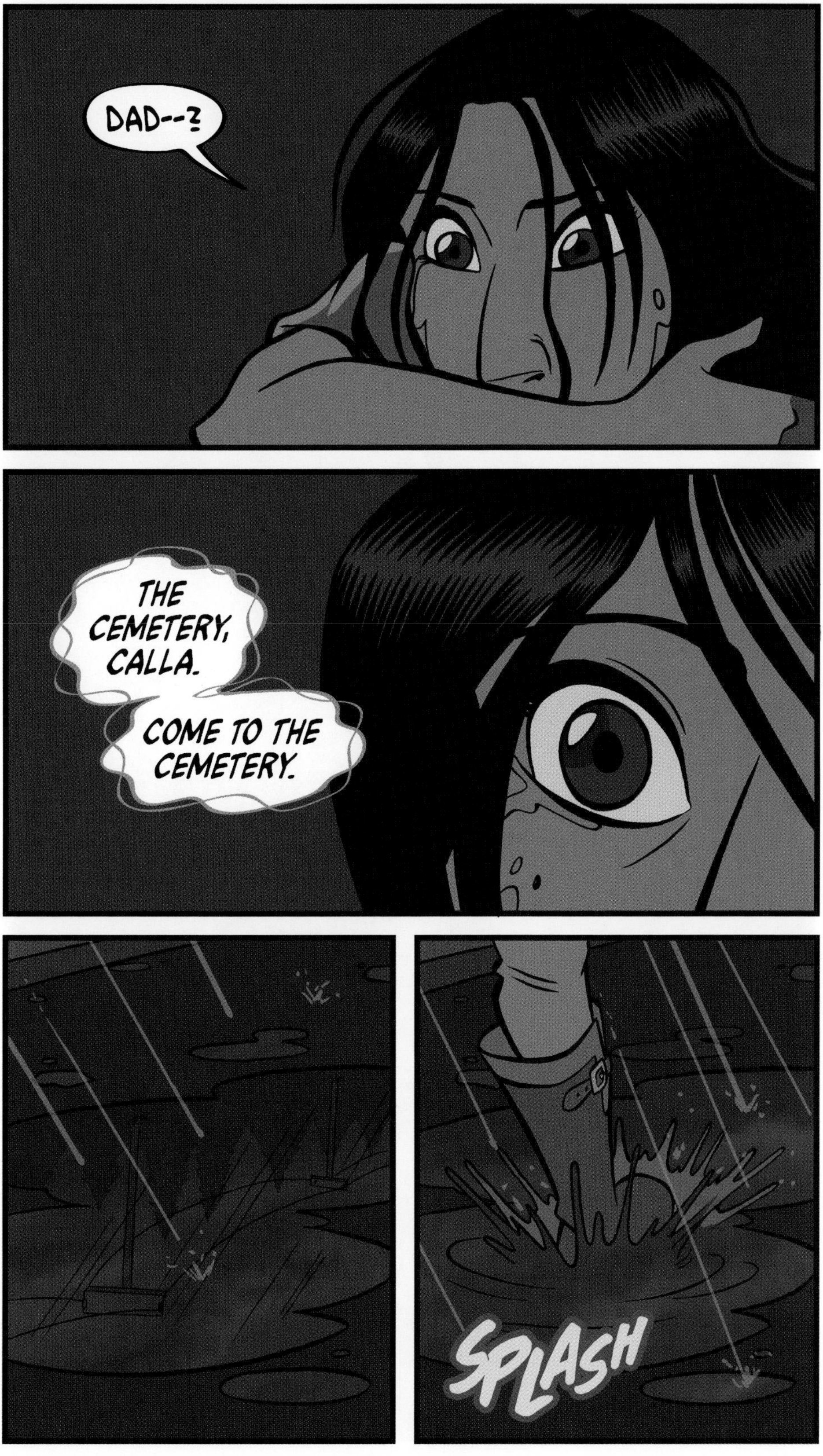
DAD--?
THE CEMETERY, CALLA.
COME TO THE CEMETERY.
SPLASH

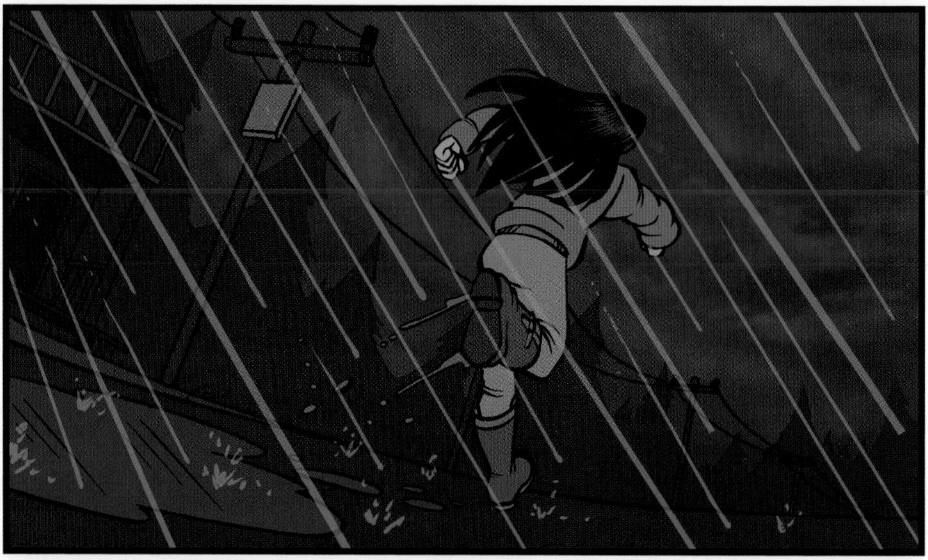

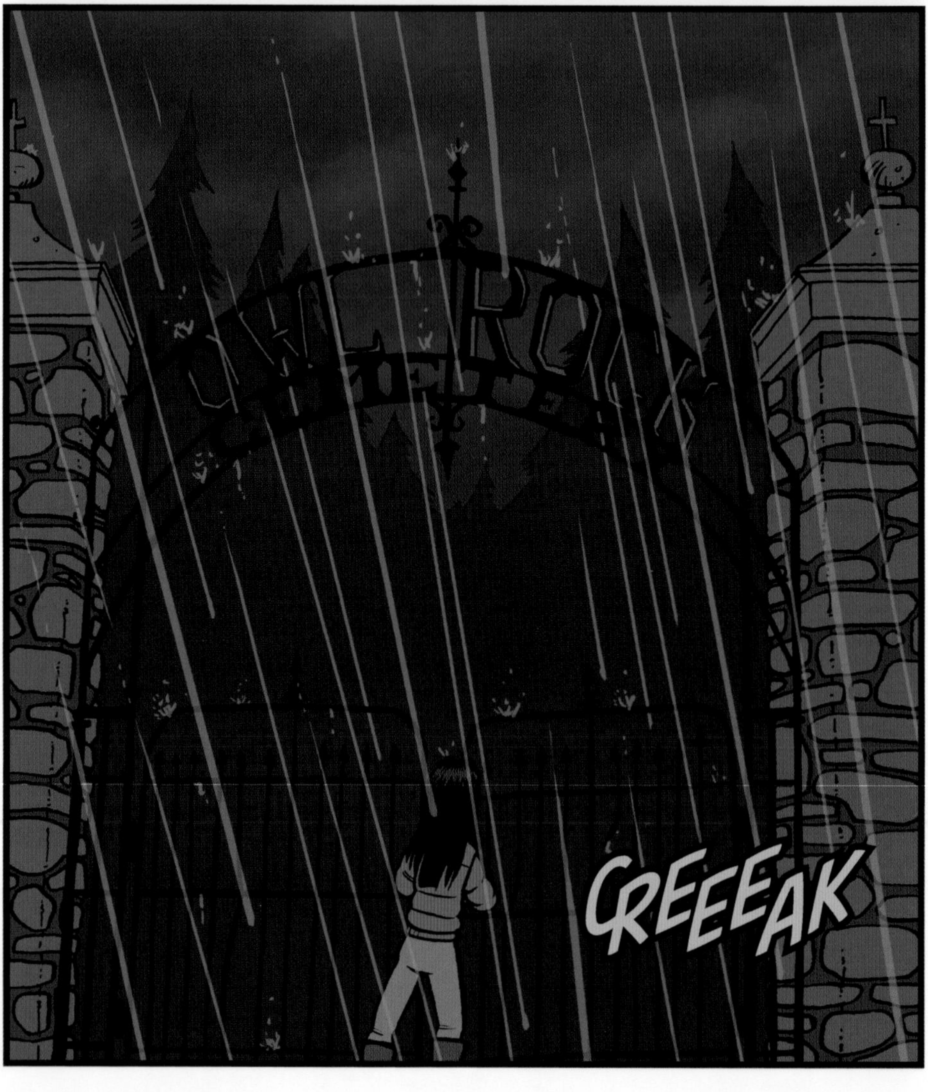
CREEEAK

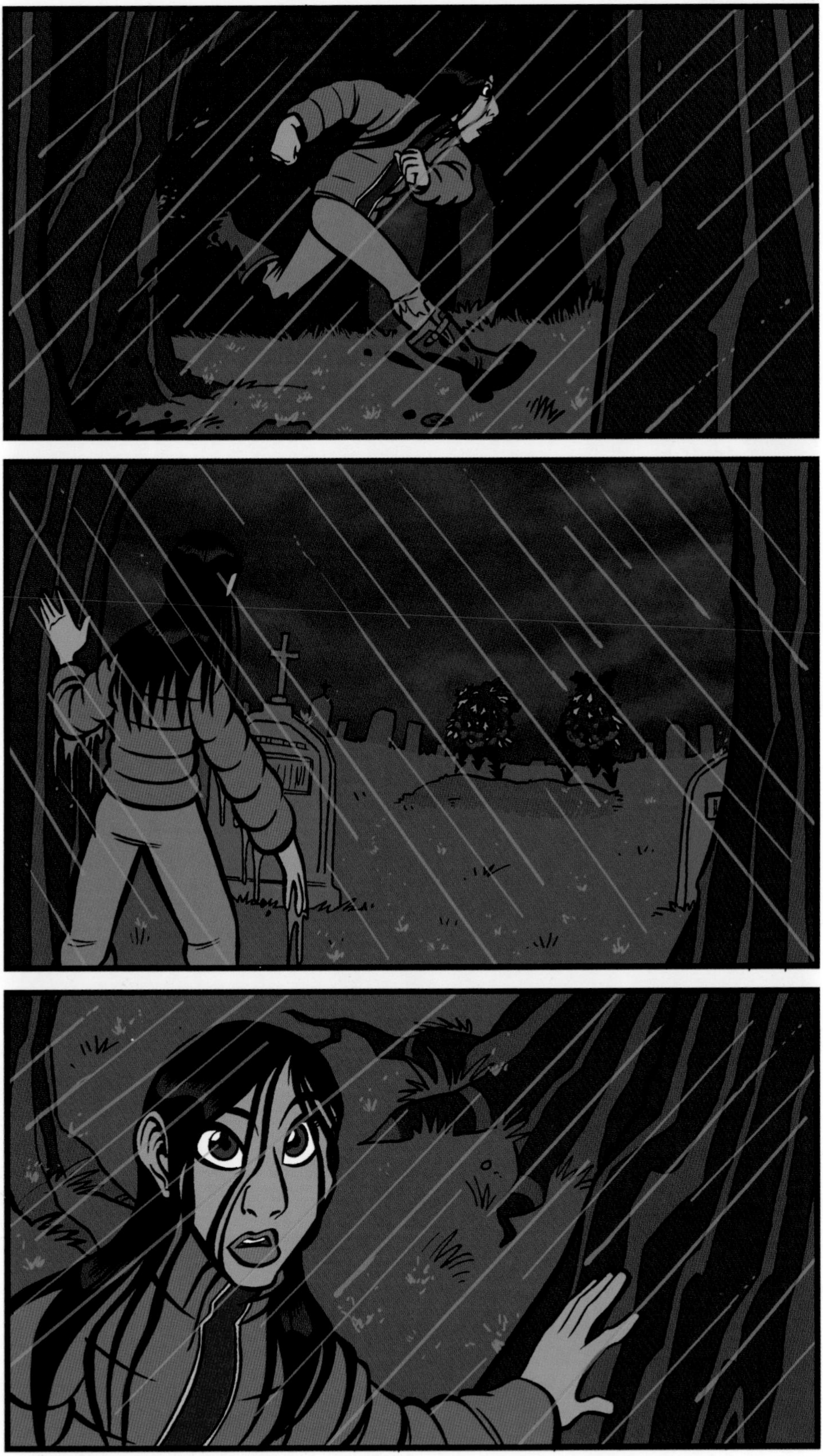

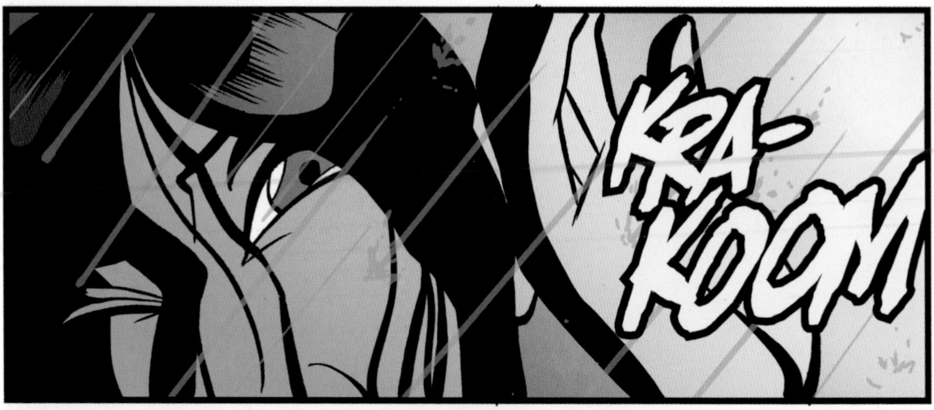
KRA-
KOOM

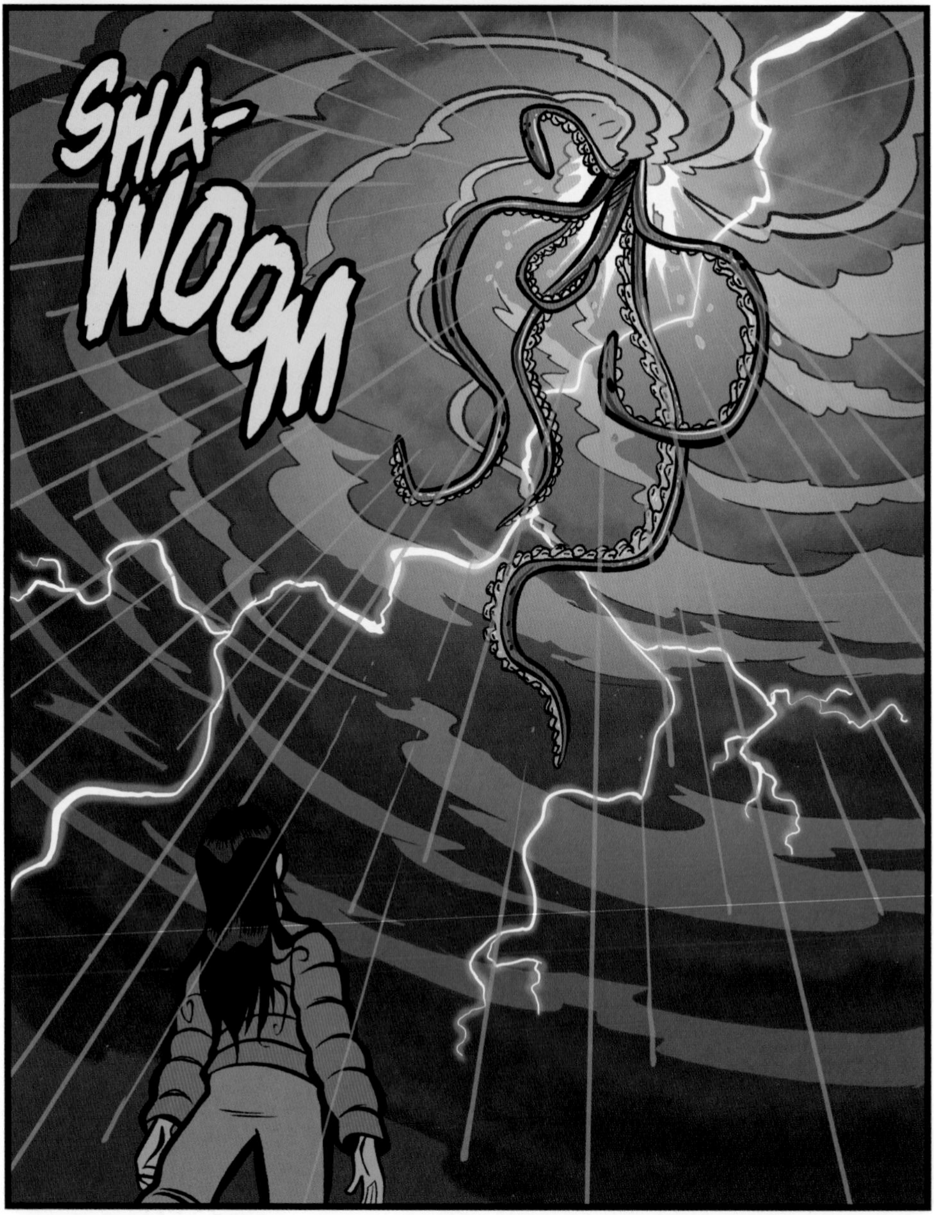
SHA-
WOOM

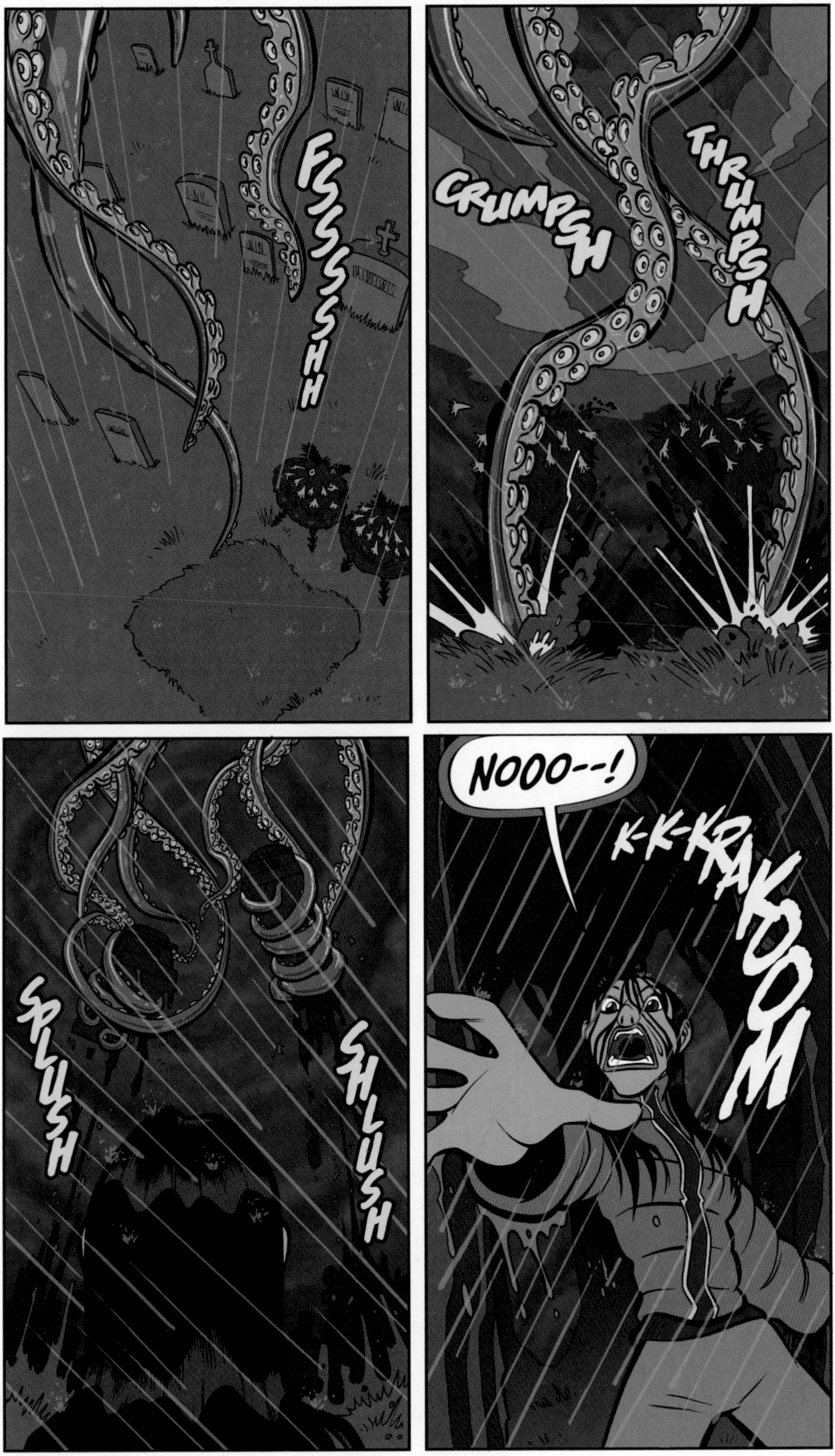
FSSSSSSHH
CRUMPSH
THRUMPSH
SPLUSH
SHLUSH
NOOO--!
K-K-KRAKOOM

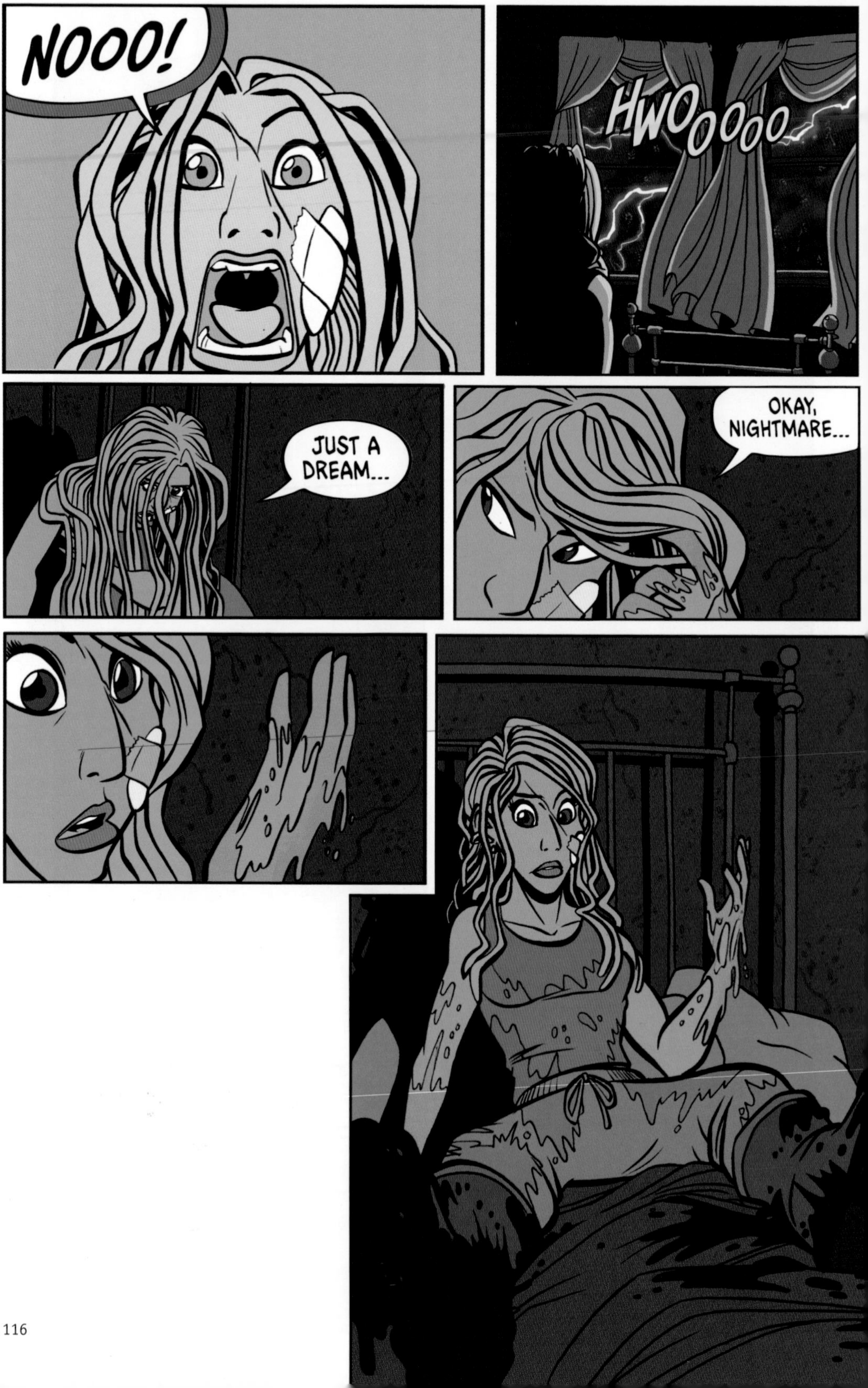
NOOO!
HWOOOOO
JUST A DREAM...
OKAY, NIGHTMARE...

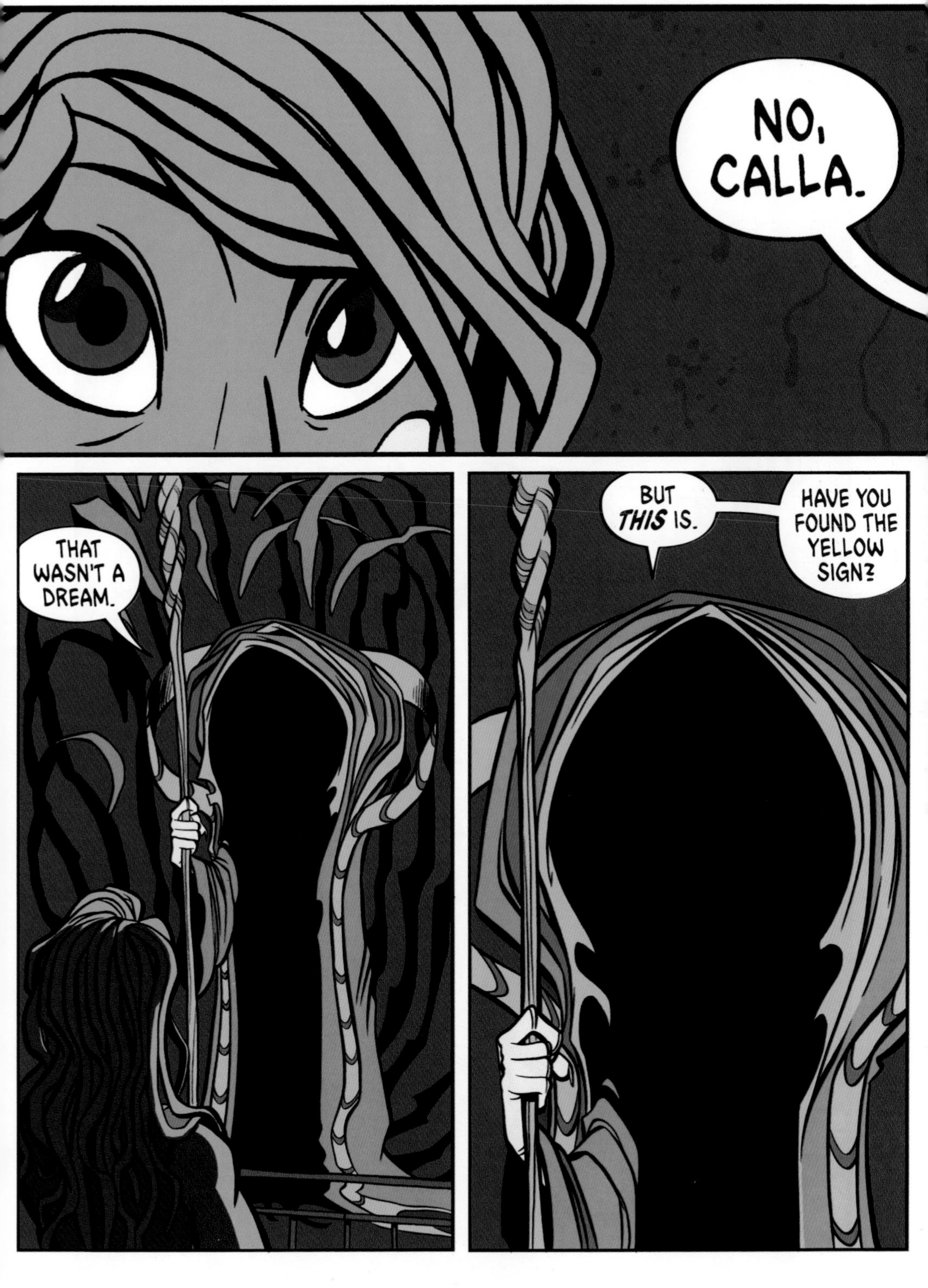
NO, CALLA.
THAT WASN'T A DREAM.
BUT *THIS* IS.
HAVE YOU FOUND THE YELLOW SIGN?

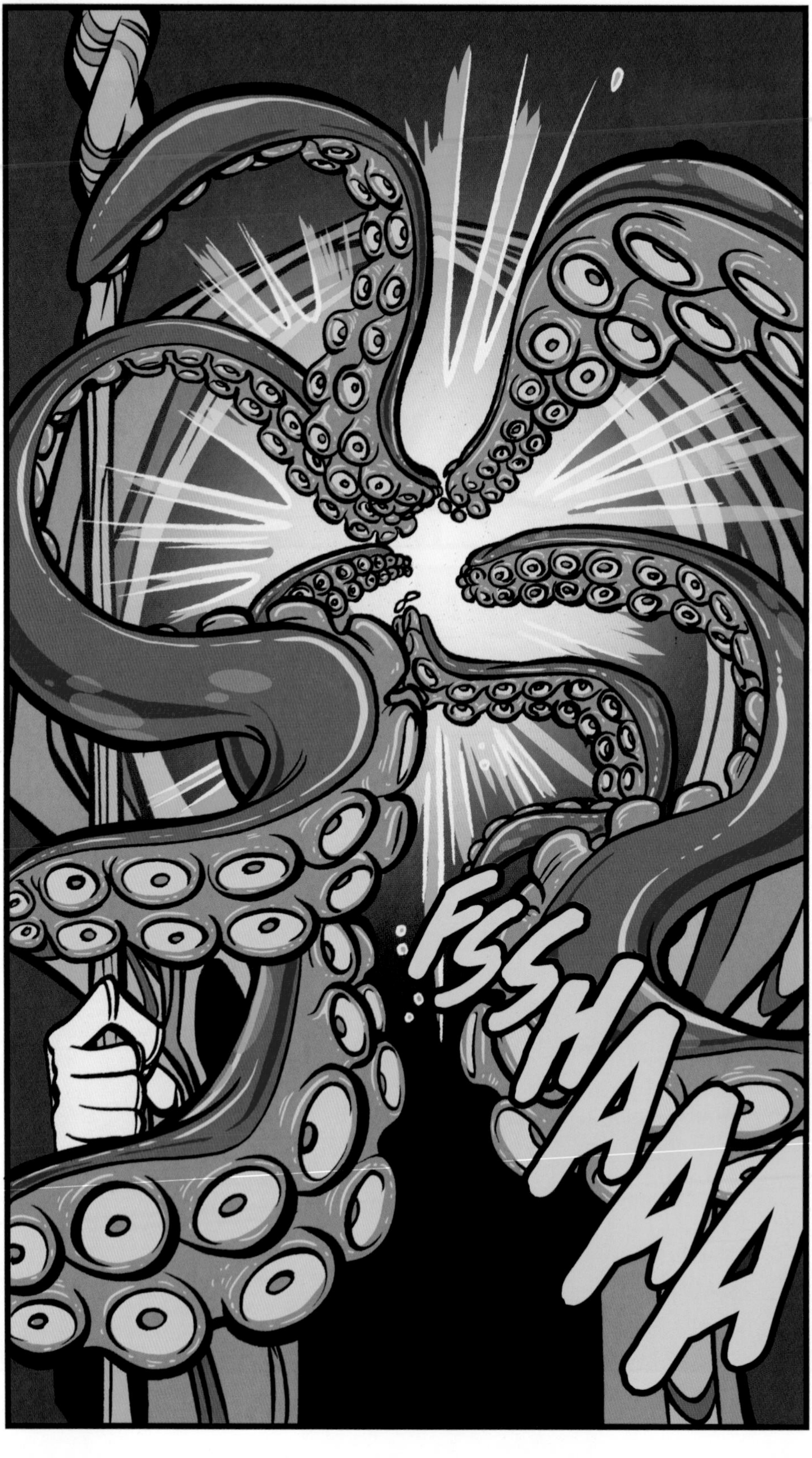
FSSHAAAA

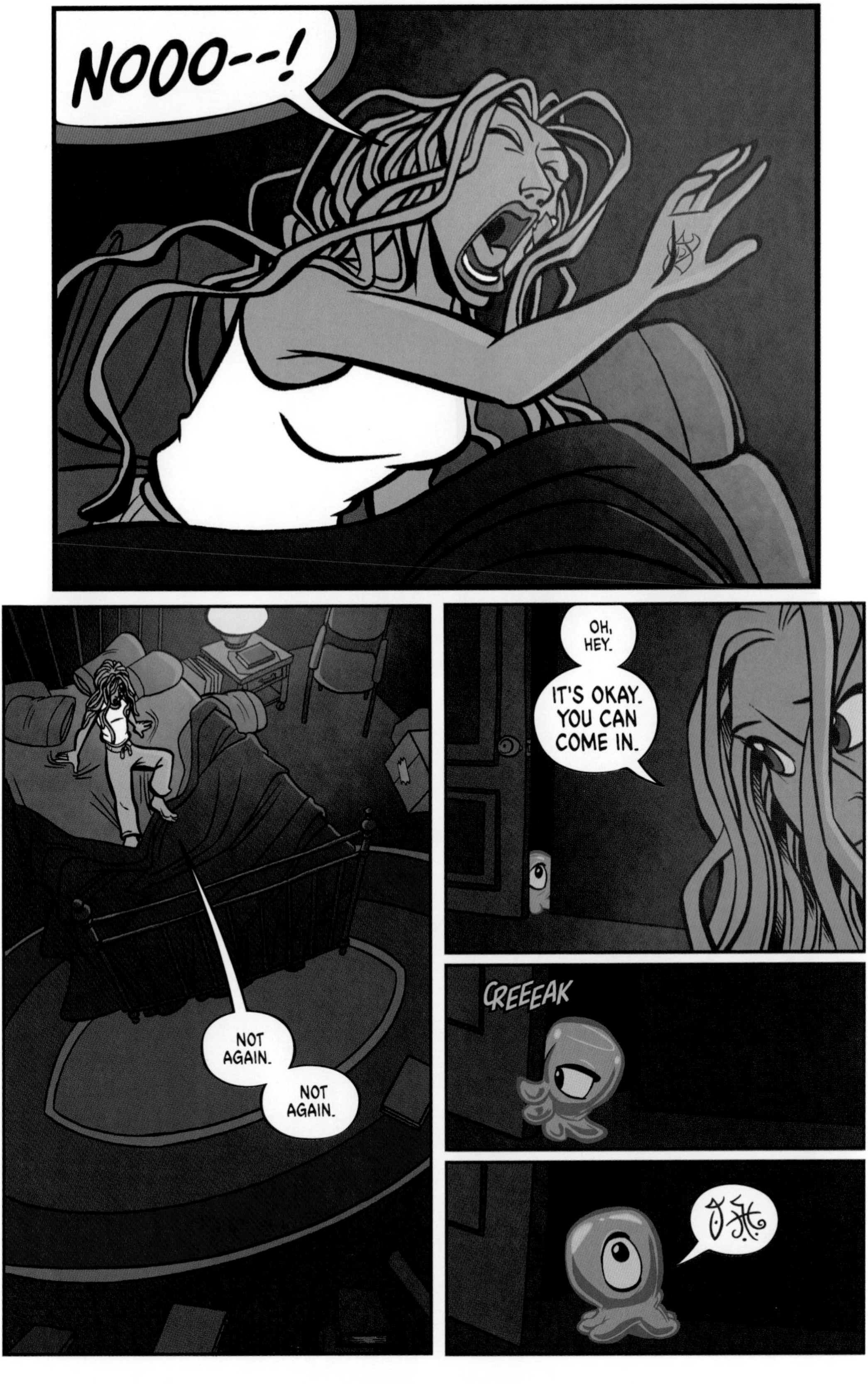
NOOO--!
NOT AGAIN.
NOT AGAIN.
OH, HEY.
IT'S OKAY. YOU CAN COME IN.
CREEEAK

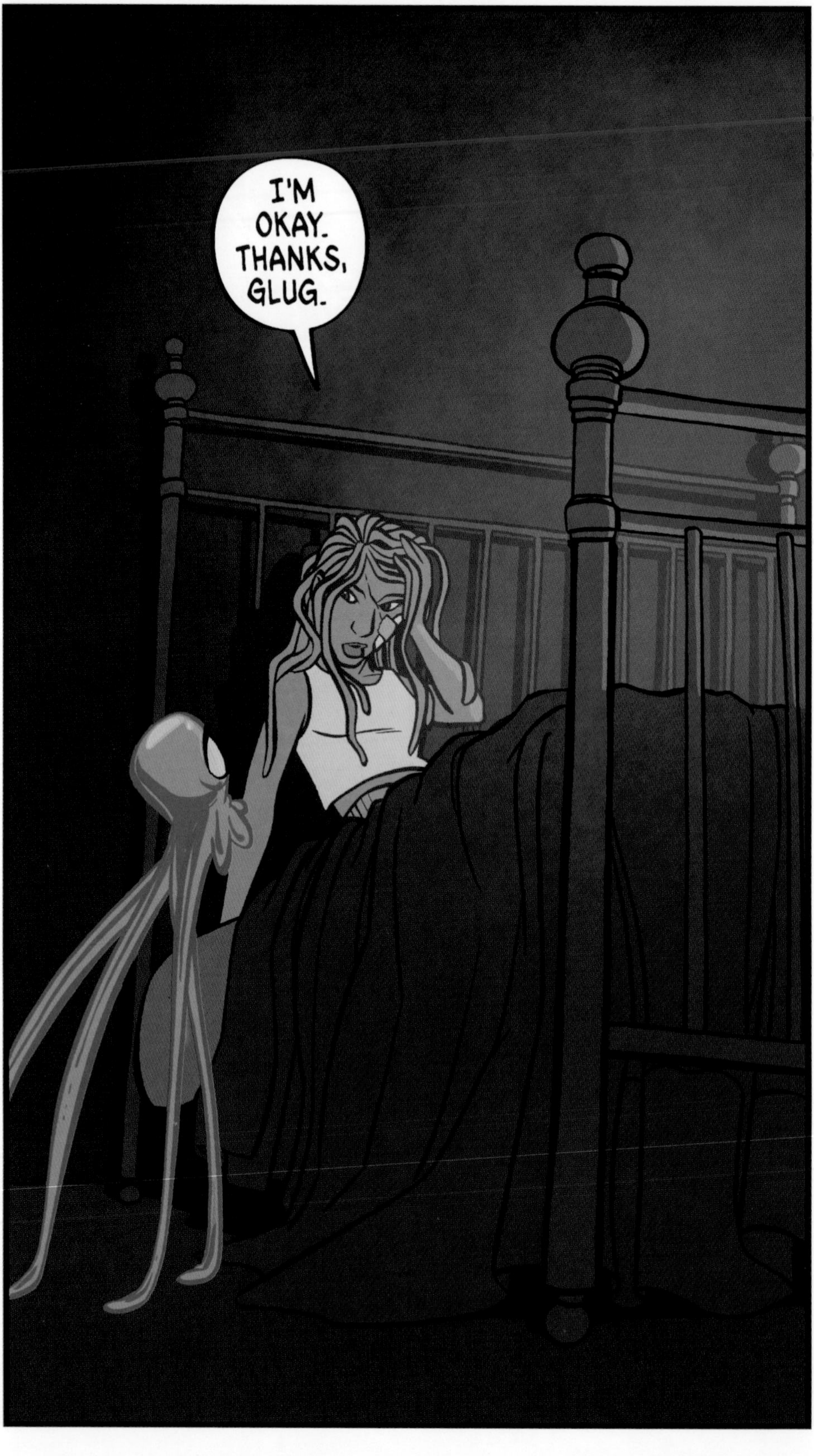
I'M OKAY. THANKS, GLUG.

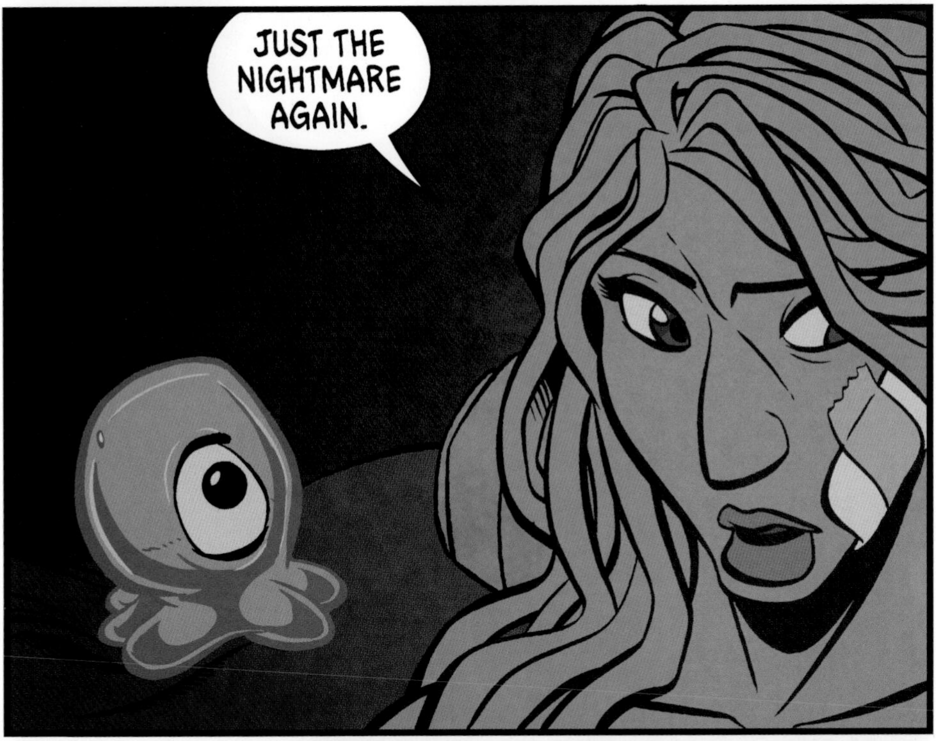
JUST THE NIGHTMARE AGAIN.

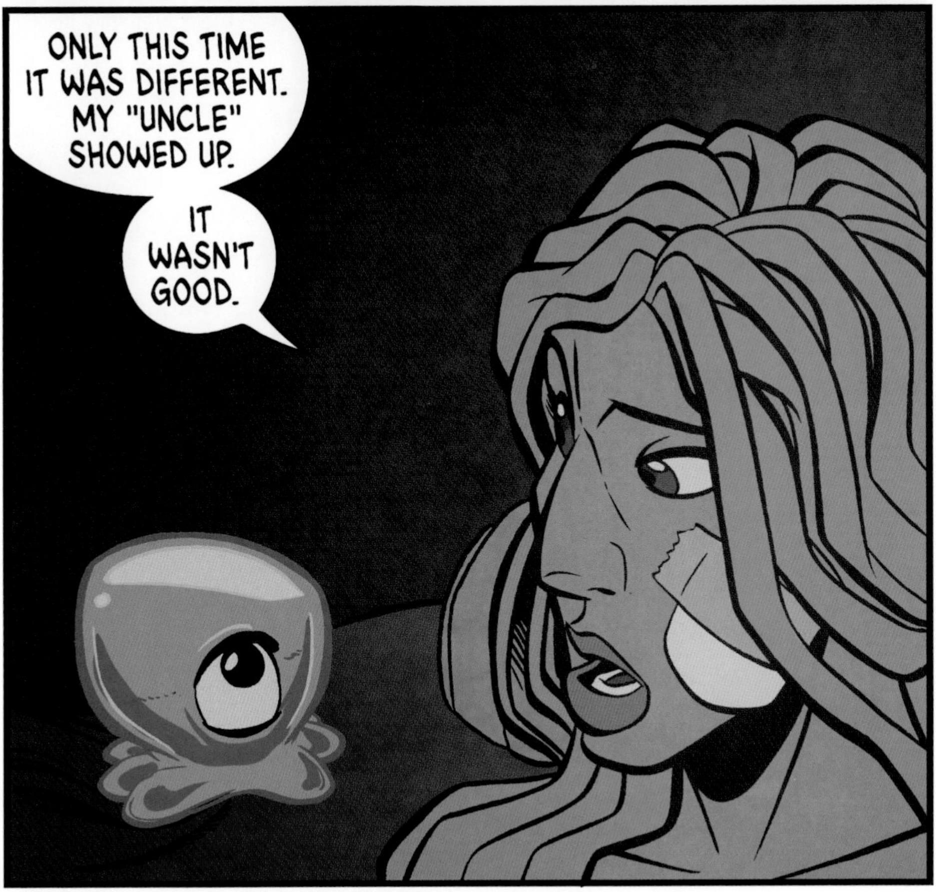
ONLY THIS TIME IT WAS DIFFERENT. MY "UNCLE" SHOWED UP.
IT WASN'T GOOD.

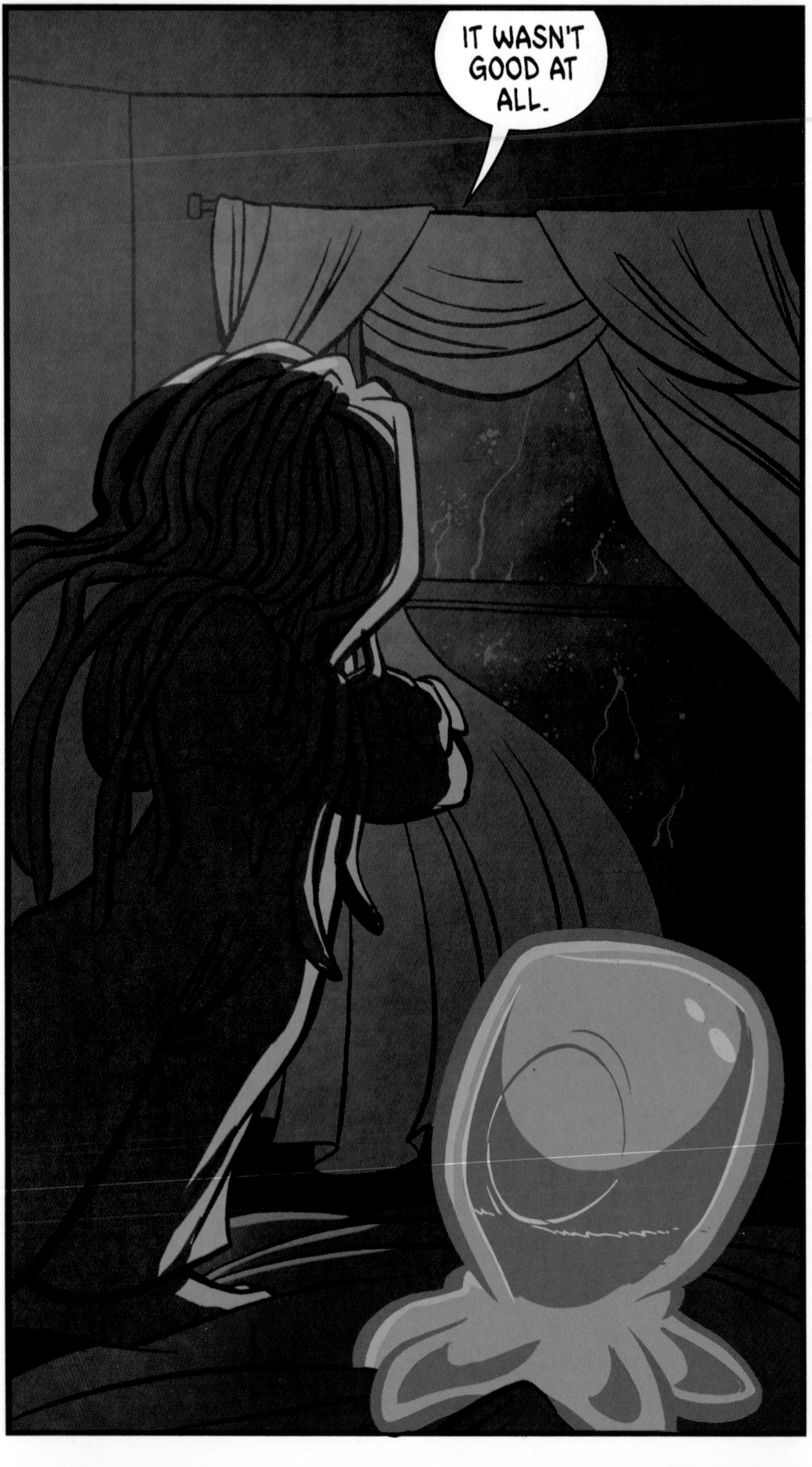
IT WASN'T GOOD AT ALL.

From: Calla T <callalily@myself.com>
To: TJ Rios <toofastTJ@gmail.com>

Subject: I'm alive

Hey! It's me! Sorry it's taken me so long to get in touch, but I haven't been able to get into my old email account. Please don't be mad - I know if you took off without a word I'd be totally freaking out, so I understand if you are. But I would have told you if I could, I swear.
First off, whatever my aunt is telling people, it's not true. She doesn't know where I am. And I can't tell you where I am, either. But I wanted you to know I was ok. Well, sort of ok, considering...

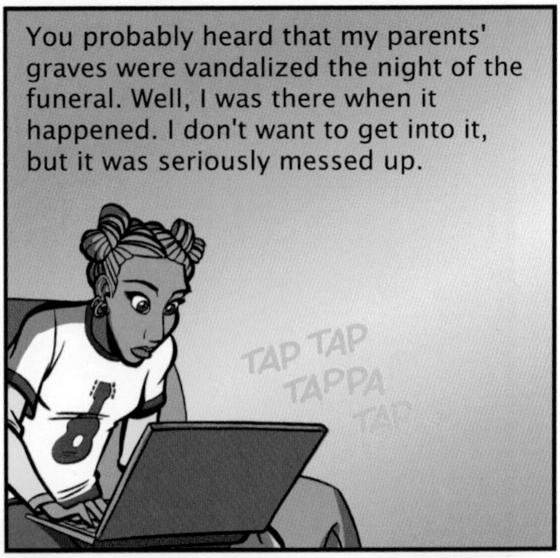

You probably heard that my parents' graves were vandalized the night of the funeral. Well, I was there when it happened. I don't want to get into it, but it was seriously messed up.
TAP TAP TAPPA TAP

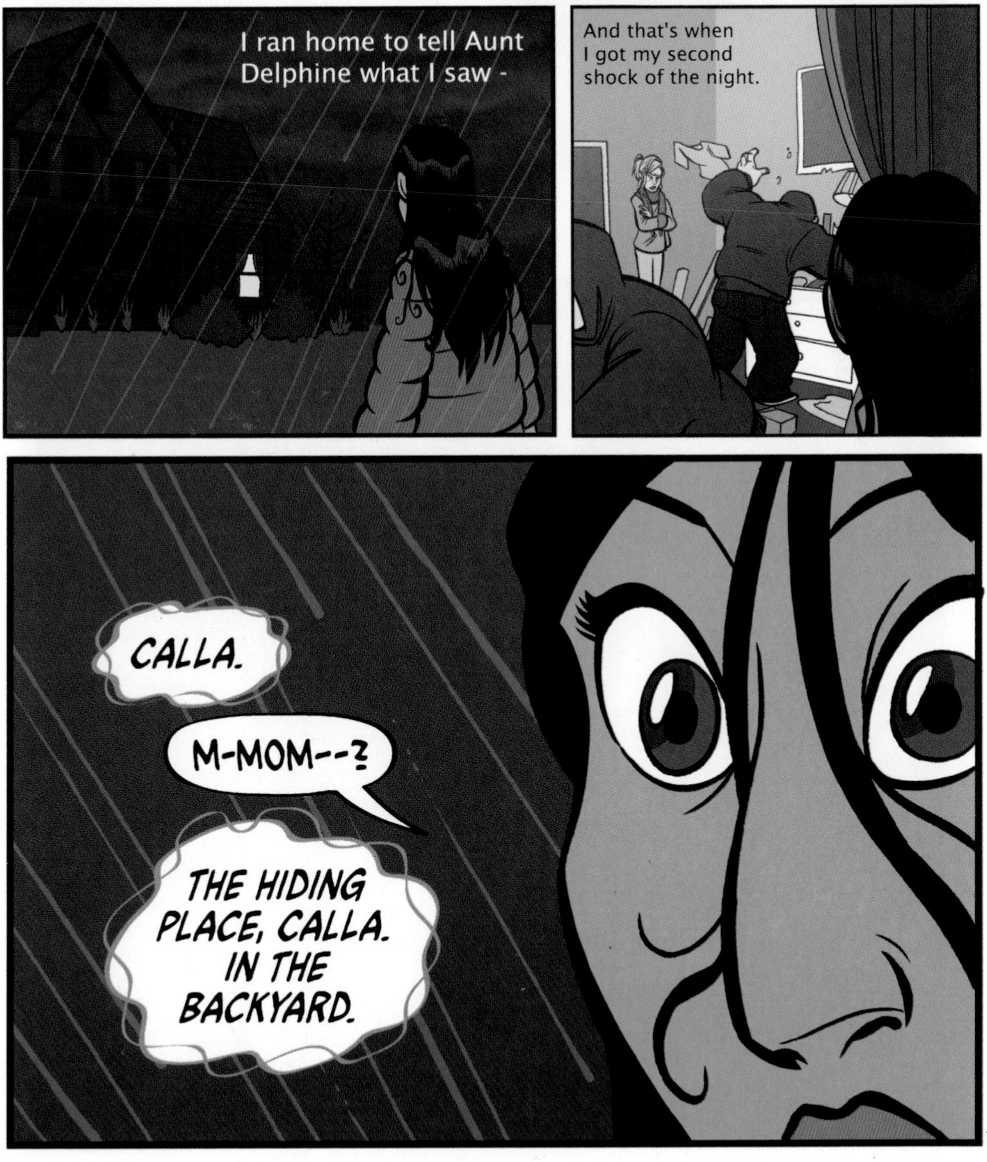

I ran home to tell Aunt Delphine what I saw -
And that's when I got my second shock of the night.
CALLA.
M-MOM--?
THE HIDING PLACE, CALLA. IN THE BACKYARD.

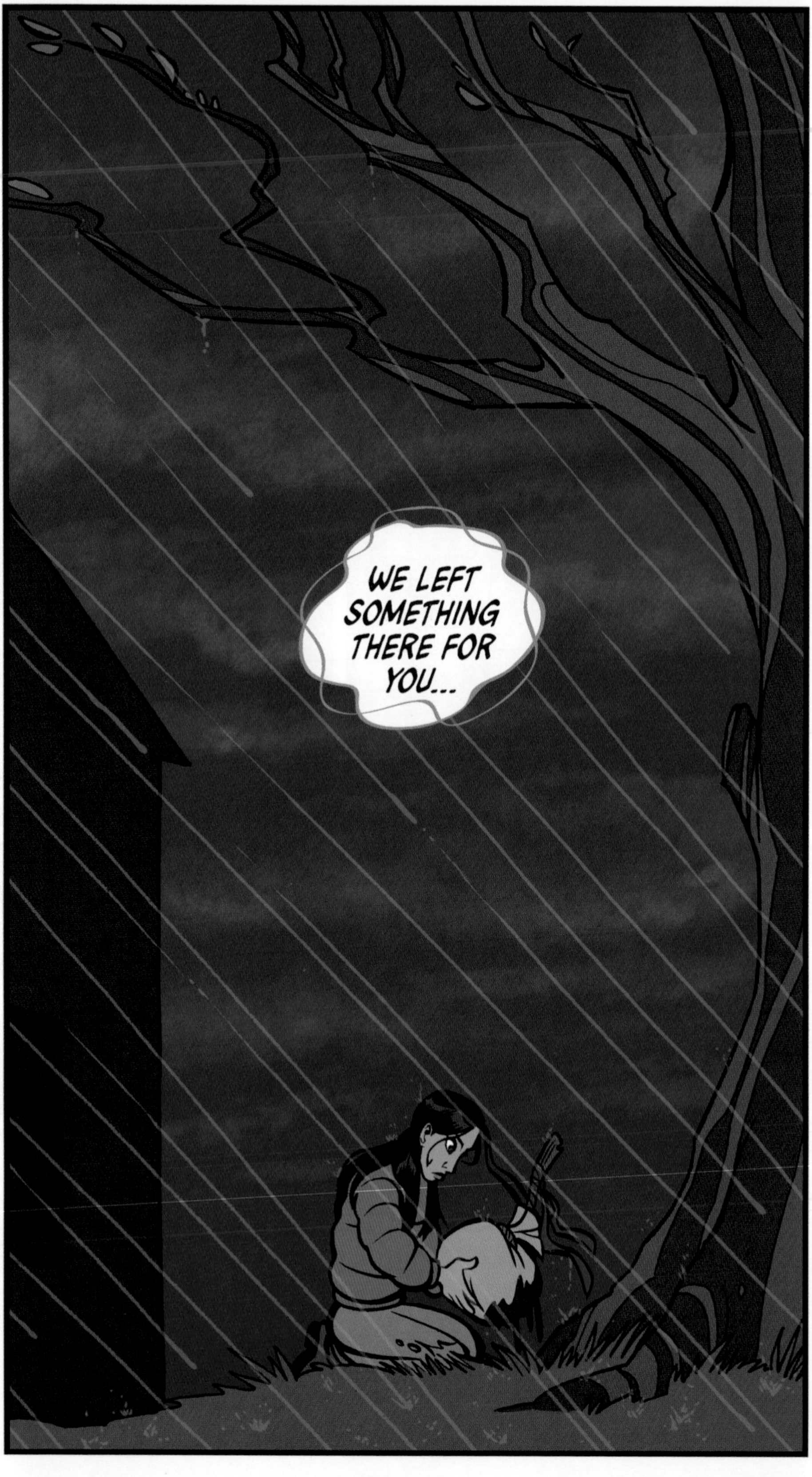
WE LEFT SOMETHING THERE FOR YOU...

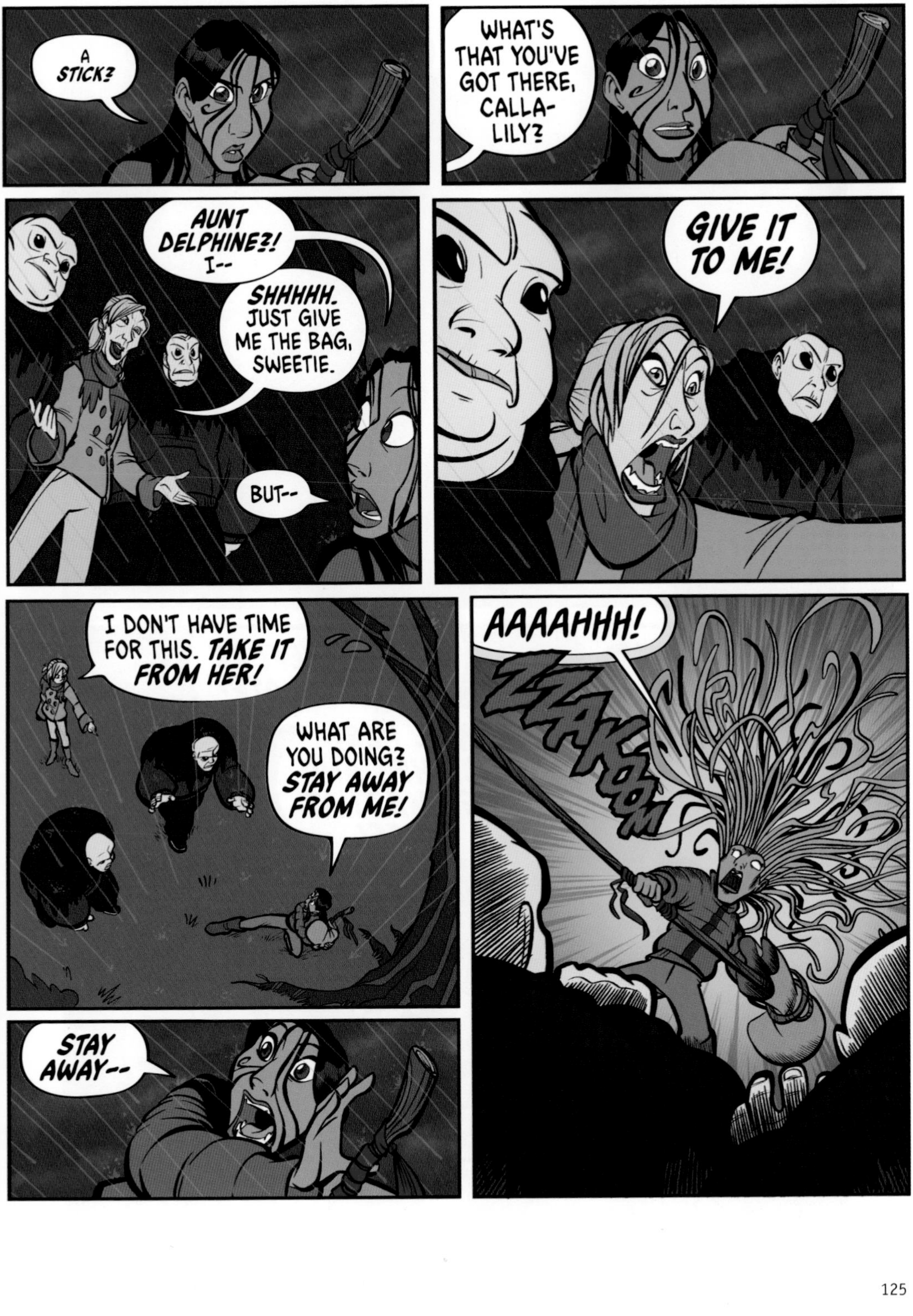
A STICK?
WHAT'S THAT YOU'VE GOT THERE, CALLA-LILY?
AUNT DELPHINE?! I--
SHHHHH. JUST GIVE ME THE BAG, SWEETIE.
BUT--
GIVE IT TO ME!
I DON'T HAVE TIME FOR THIS. TAKE IT FROM HER!
WHAT ARE YOU DOING? STAY AWAY FROM ME!
STAY AWAY--
AAAAHHH!
ZZAKOOM

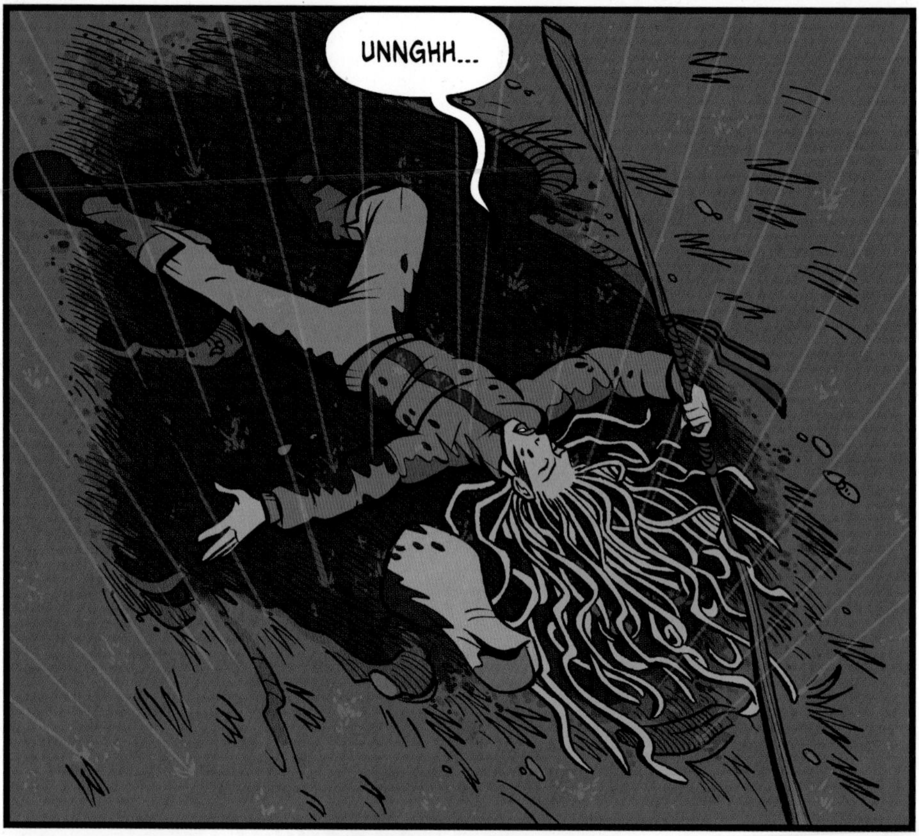
UNNGHH...

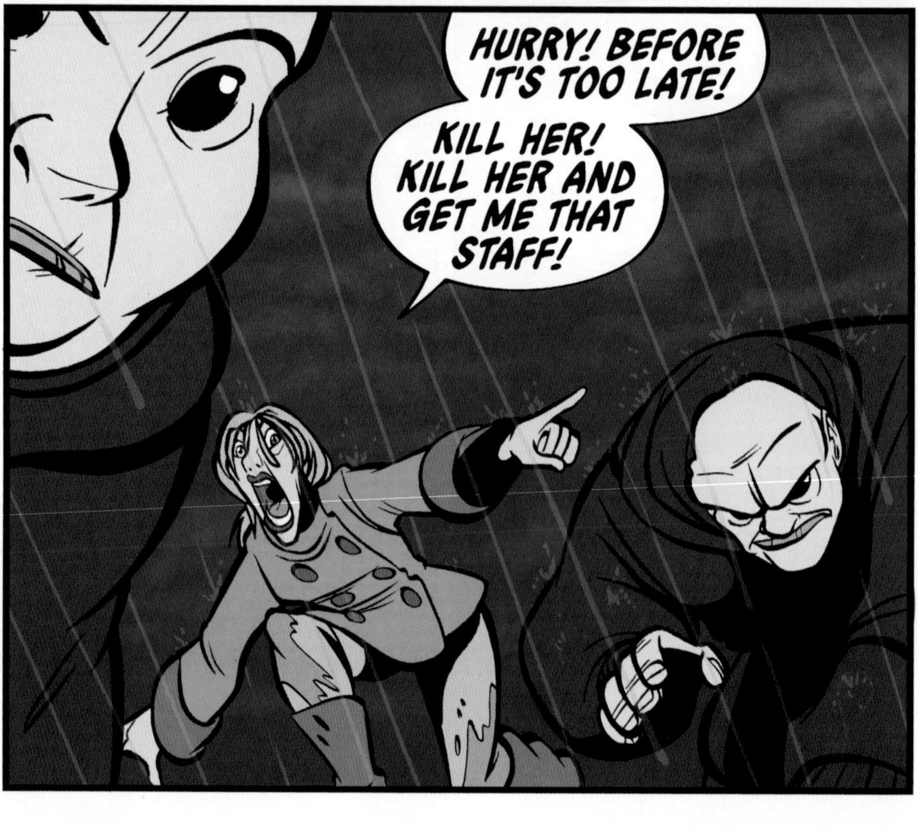
HURRY! BEFORE IT'S TOO LATE!
KILL HER! KILL HER AND GET ME THAT STAFF!

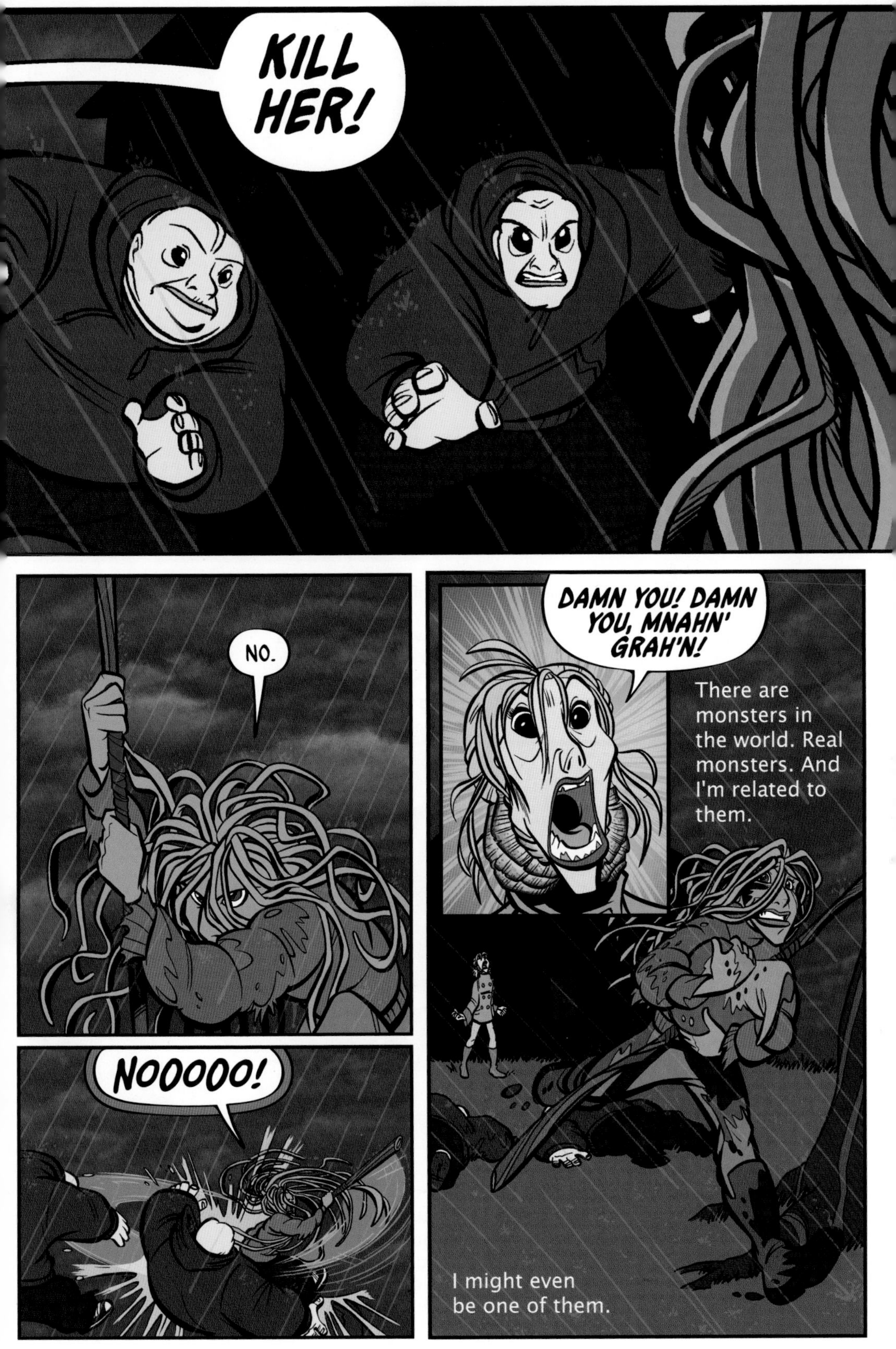
KILL HER!
NO.
NOOOOO!
DAMN YOU! DAMN YOU, MNAHN' GRAH'N!
There are monsters in the world. Real monsters. And I'm related to them.
I might even be one of them.

It's hard to explain what it felt like when I changed. It was like a light went on in my brain. Like I leveled up or something. It was amazing and terrible at the same time. And suddenly I could understand things that I never could before.

I ran for what seemed like forever. I slept in an alley when I couldn't run anymore. When I woke up, I looked through the bag I'd found – in it was an envelope full of cash, a key, and a letter from my parents. The letter was short, written quickly.

They said they were planning to tell me about all this – whatever "all this" is – but something went wrong. They said they were sorry. They said I was in terrible danger, and that the key was to a house where I could be safe.

And then they said, "Calla, you are a good person and we love you. We trust you will know right from wrong and do your best. The staff will protect you – keep it with you always. Be safe, be smart, be the girl we know and love.

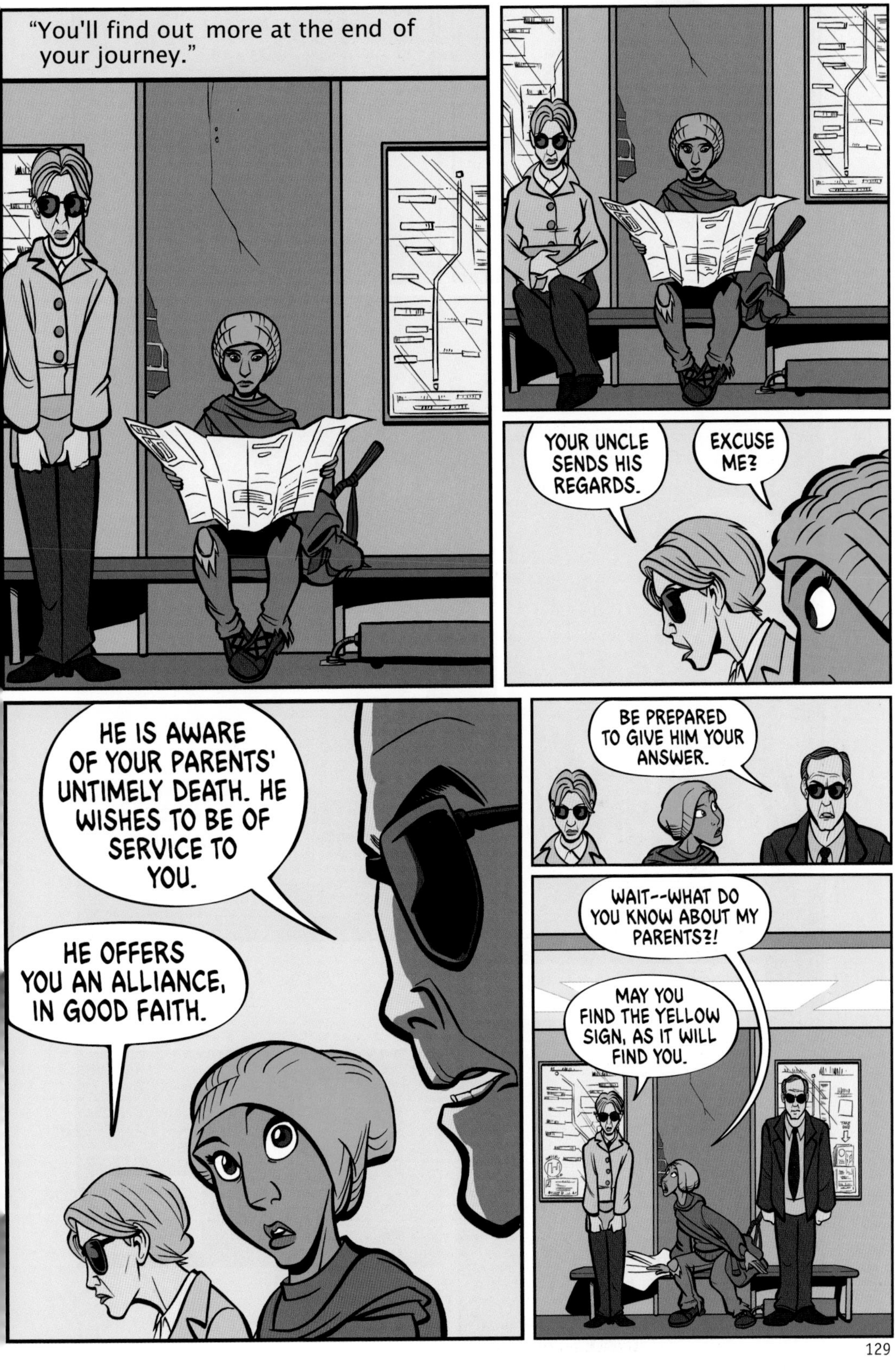
"You'll find out more at the end of your journey."
YOUR UNCLE SENDS HIS REGARDS.
EXCUSE ME?
HE IS AWARE OF YOUR PARENTS' UNTIMELY DEATH. HE WISHES TO BE OF SERVICE TO YOU.
HE OFFERS YOU AN ALLIANCE, IN GOOD FAITH.
BE PREPARED TO GIVE HIM YOUR ANSWER.
WAIT--WHAT DO YOU KNOW ABOUT MY PARENTS?!
MAY YOU FIND THE YELLOW SIGN, AS IT WILL FIND YOU.

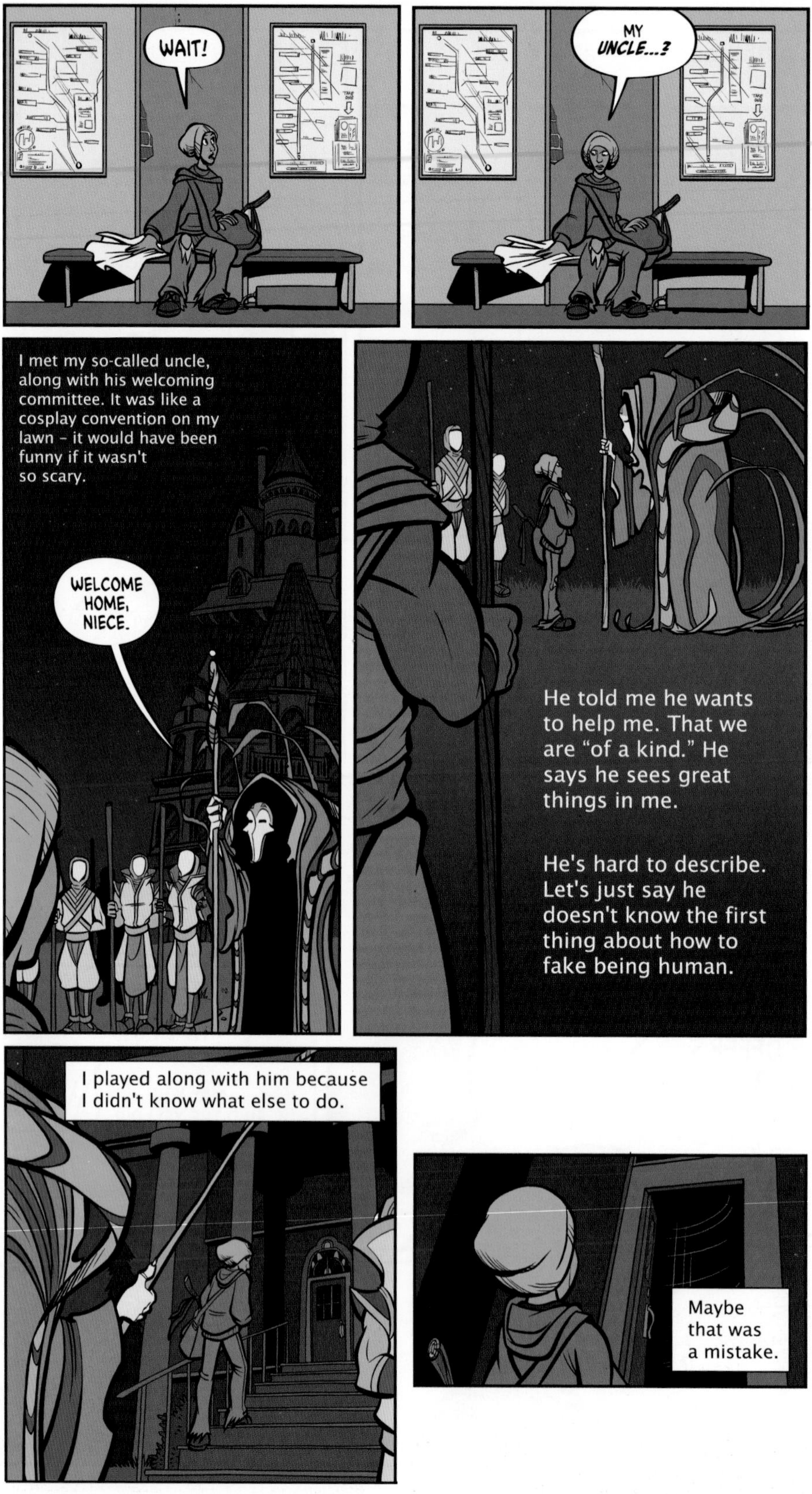
WAIT!
MY UNCLE...?
I met my so-called uncle, along with his welcoming committee. It was like a cosplay convention on my lawn – it would have been funny if it wasn't so scary.
WELCOME HOME, NIECE.
He told me he wants to help me. That we are "of a kind." He says he sees great things in me.
He's hard to describe. Let's just say he doesn't know the first thing about how to fake being human.
I played along with him because I didn't know what else to do.
Maybe that was a mistake.

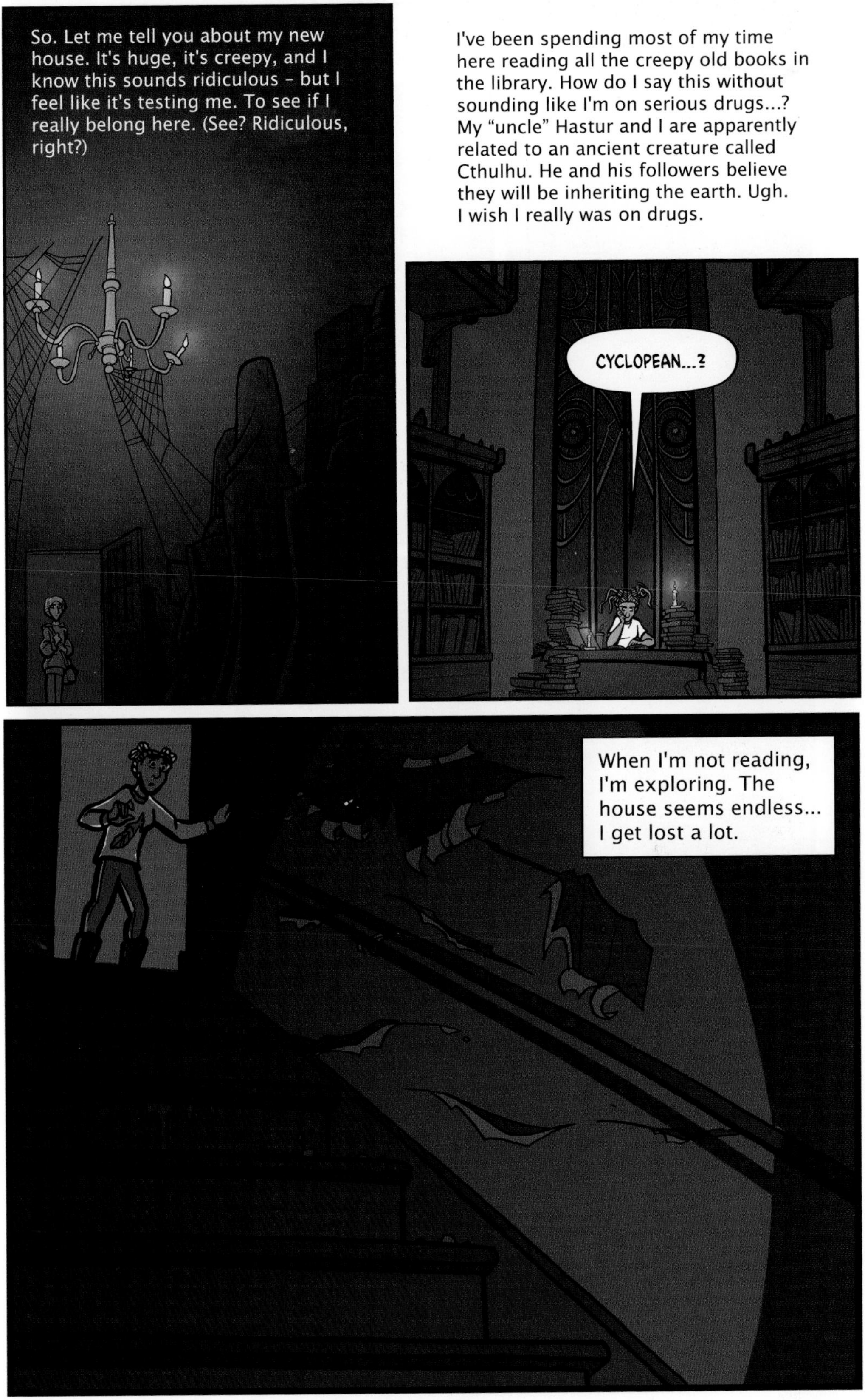
So. Let me tell you about my new house. It's huge, it's creepy, and I know this sounds ridiculous - but I feel like it's testing me. To see if I really belong here. (See? Ridiculous, right?)
I've been spending most of my time here reading all the creepy old books in the library. How do I say this without sounding like I'm on serious drugs...? My "uncle" Hastur and I are apparently related to an ancient creature called Cthulhu. He and his followers believe they will be inheriting the earth. Ugh. I wish I really was on drugs.
CYCLOPEAN...?
When I'm not reading, I'm exploring. The house seems endless... I get lost a lot.

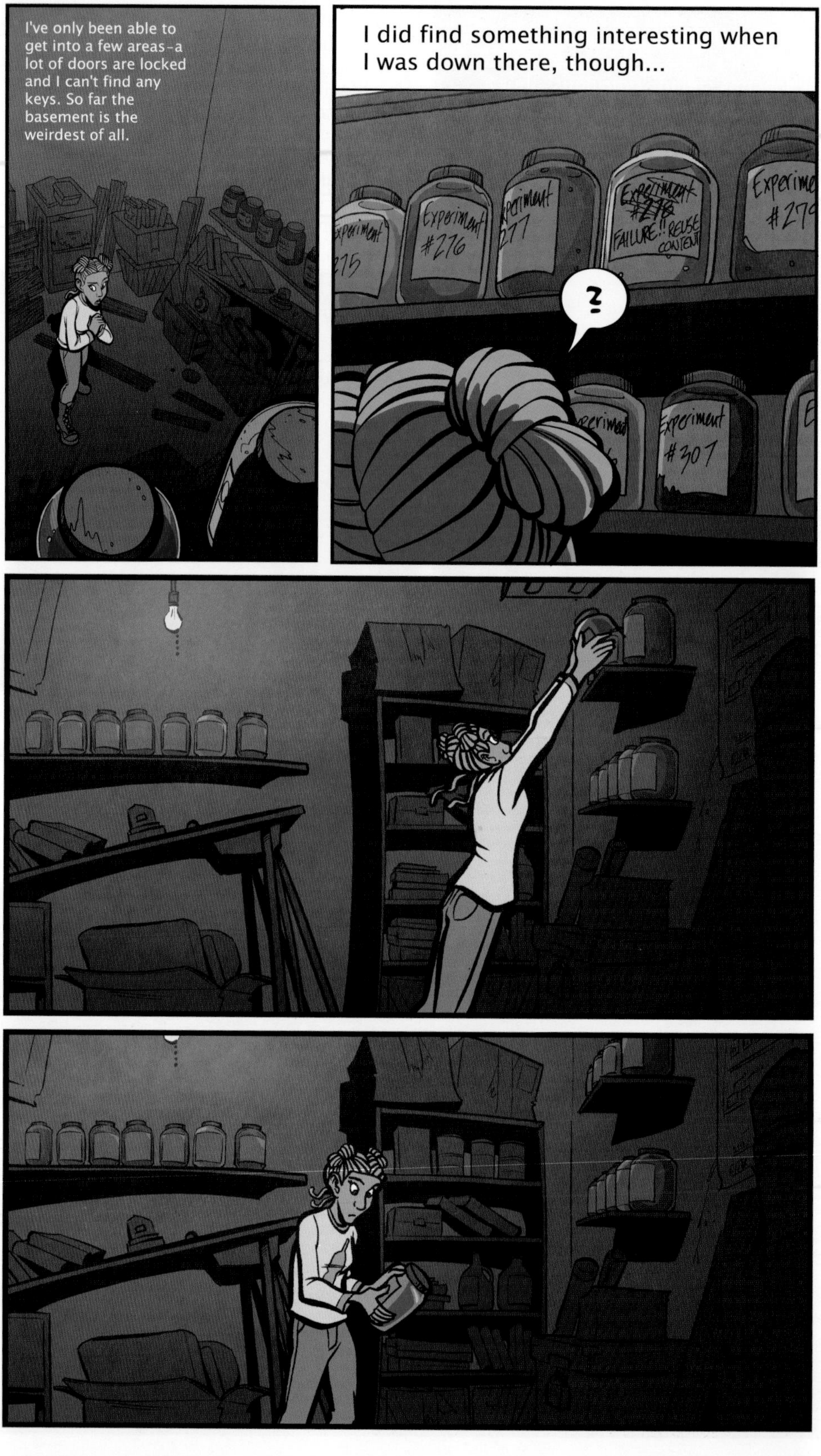
I've only been able to get into a few areas-a lot of doors are locked and I can't find any keys. So far the basement is the weirdest of all.
I did find something interesting when I was down there, though...
Experiment #276
Experiment 277
FAILURE!! REUSE CONTENT
Experiment #307
?

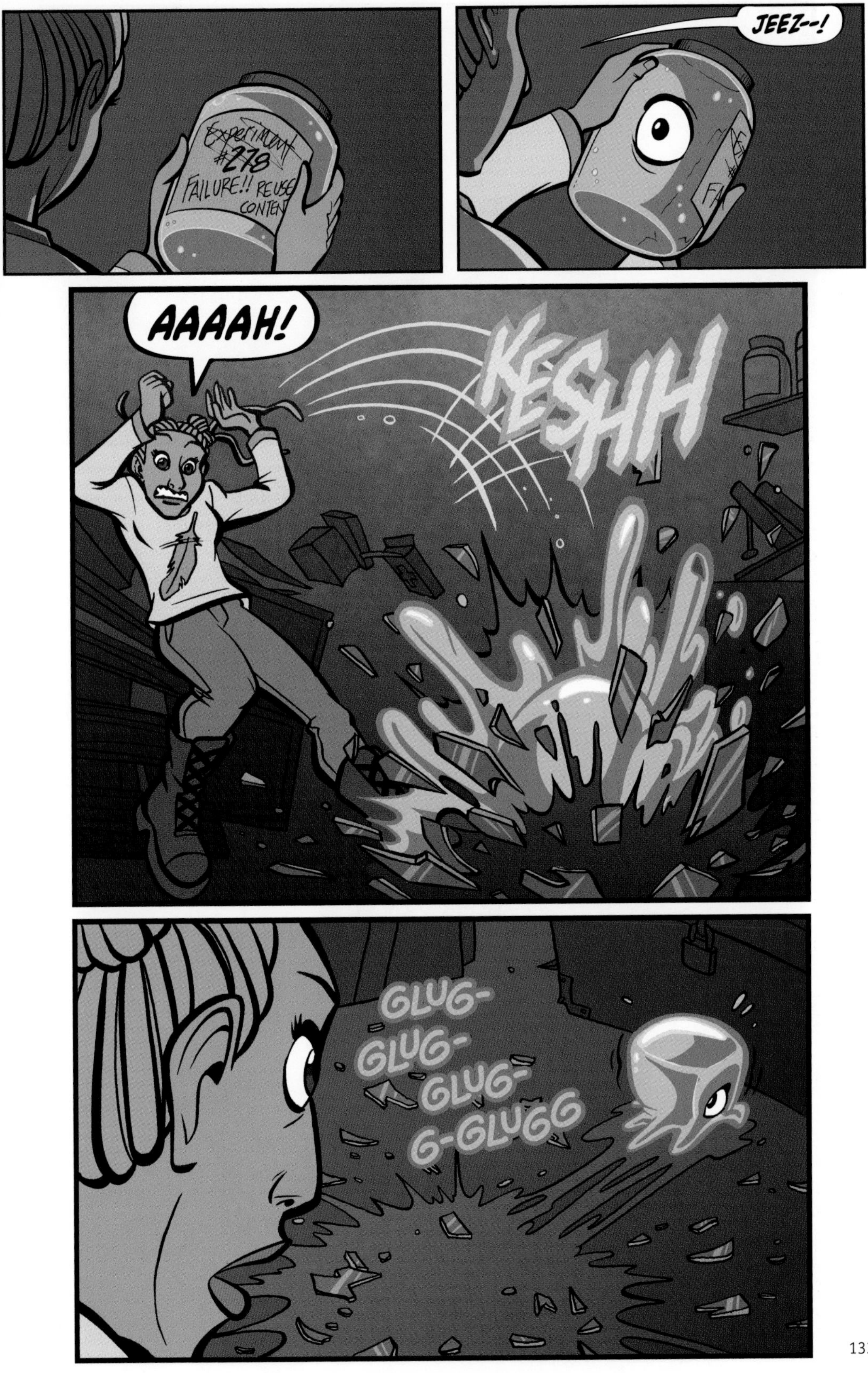
Experiment #278 FAILURE!! REUSE CONTEN
JEEZ--!
AAAAH!
KESHH
GLUG-
GLUG-
GLUG-
G-GLUGG

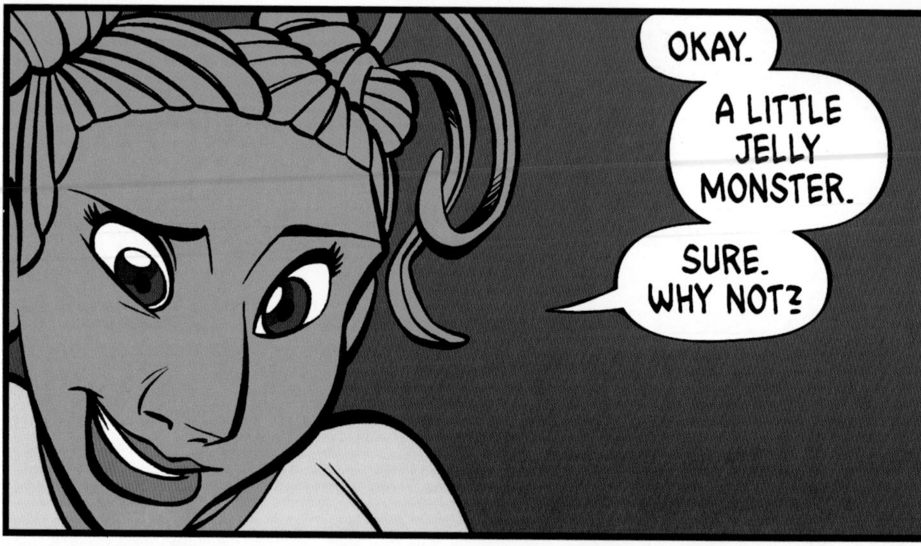
OKAY.
A LITTLE JELLY MONSTER.
SURE. WHY NOT?

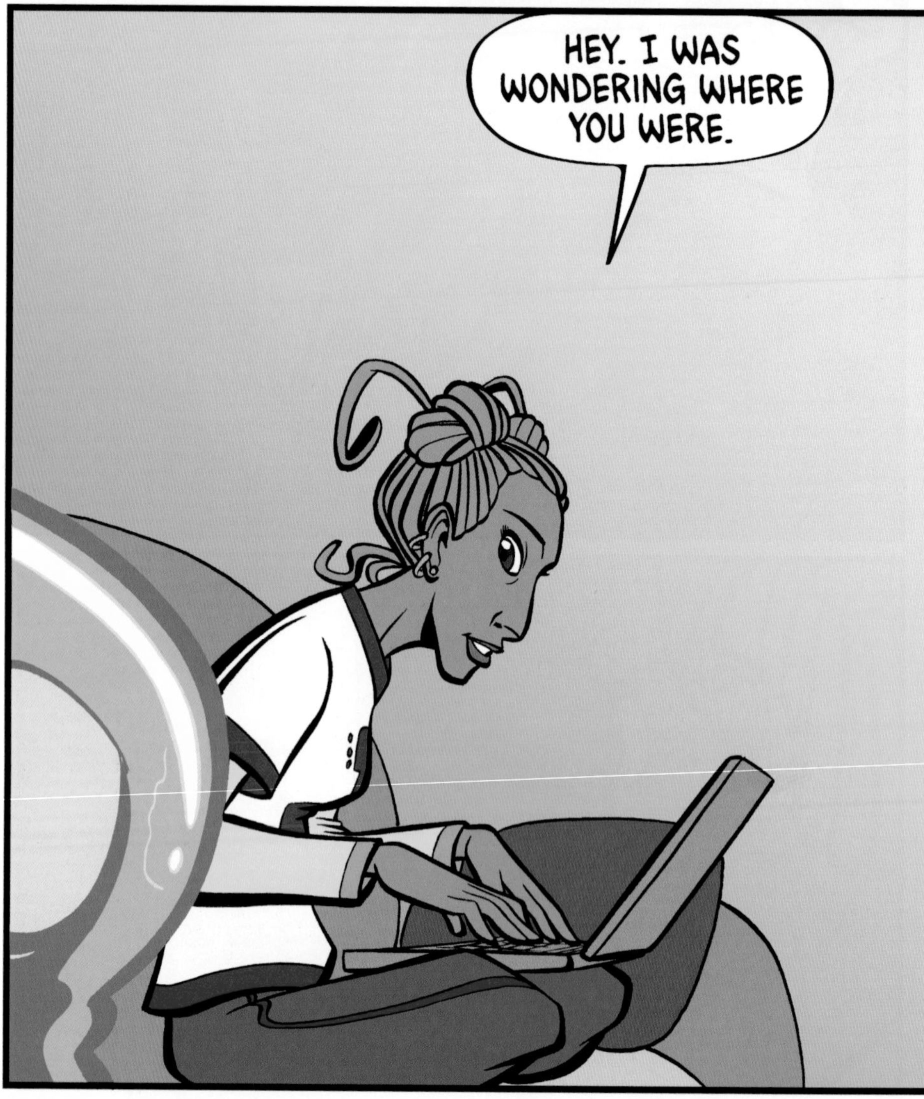
HEY. I WAS WONDERING WHERE YOU WERE.

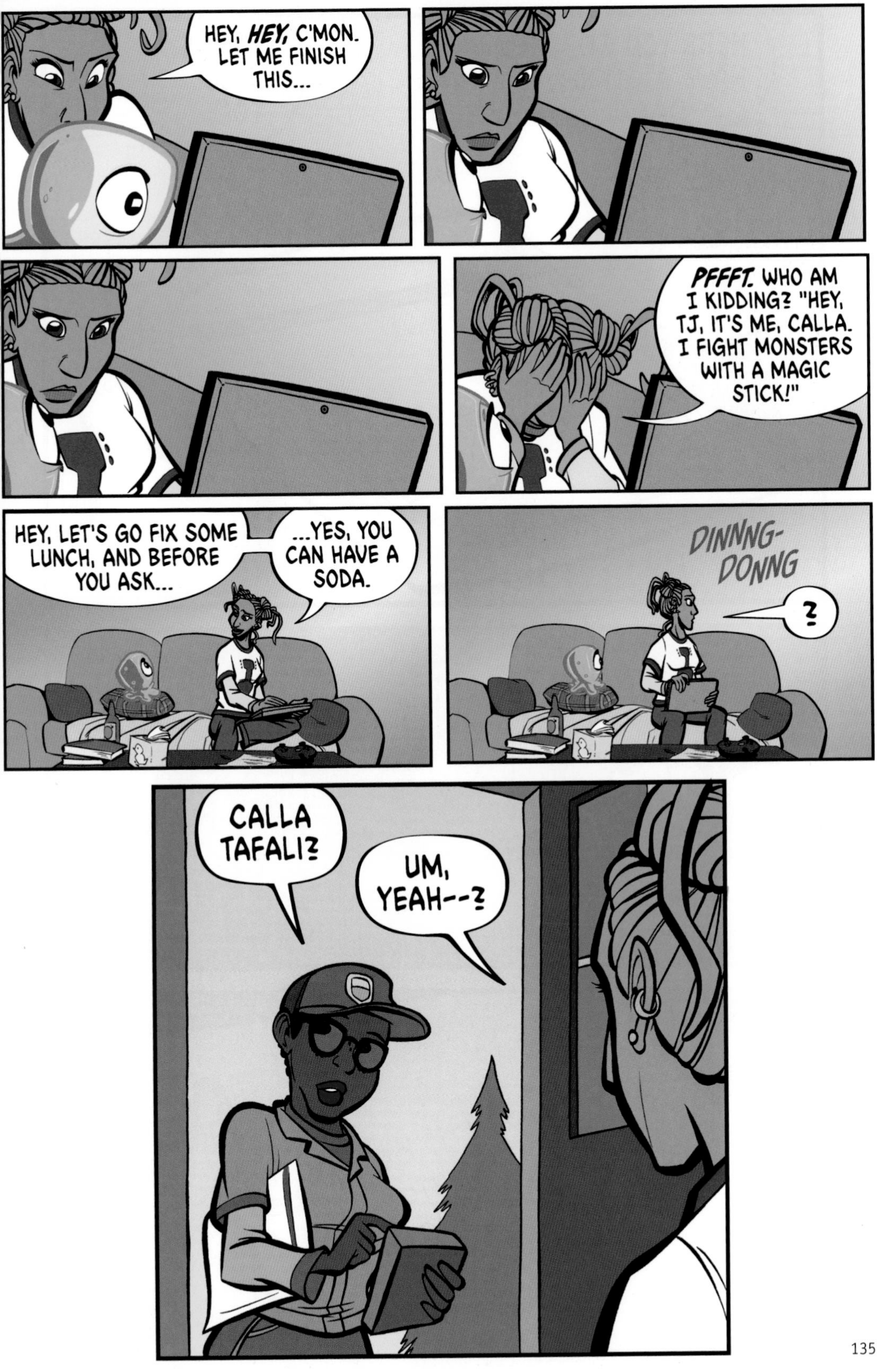
HEY, *HEY,* C'MON. LET ME FINISH THIS...
PFFFT. WHO AM I KIDDING? "HEY, TJ, IT'S ME, CALLA. I FIGHT MONSTERS WITH A MAGIC STICK!"
HEY, LET'S GO FIX SOME LUNCH, AND BEFORE YOU ASK...
...YES, YOU CAN HAVE A SODA.
DINNNG-DONNG
?
CALLA TAFALI?
UM, YEAH--?

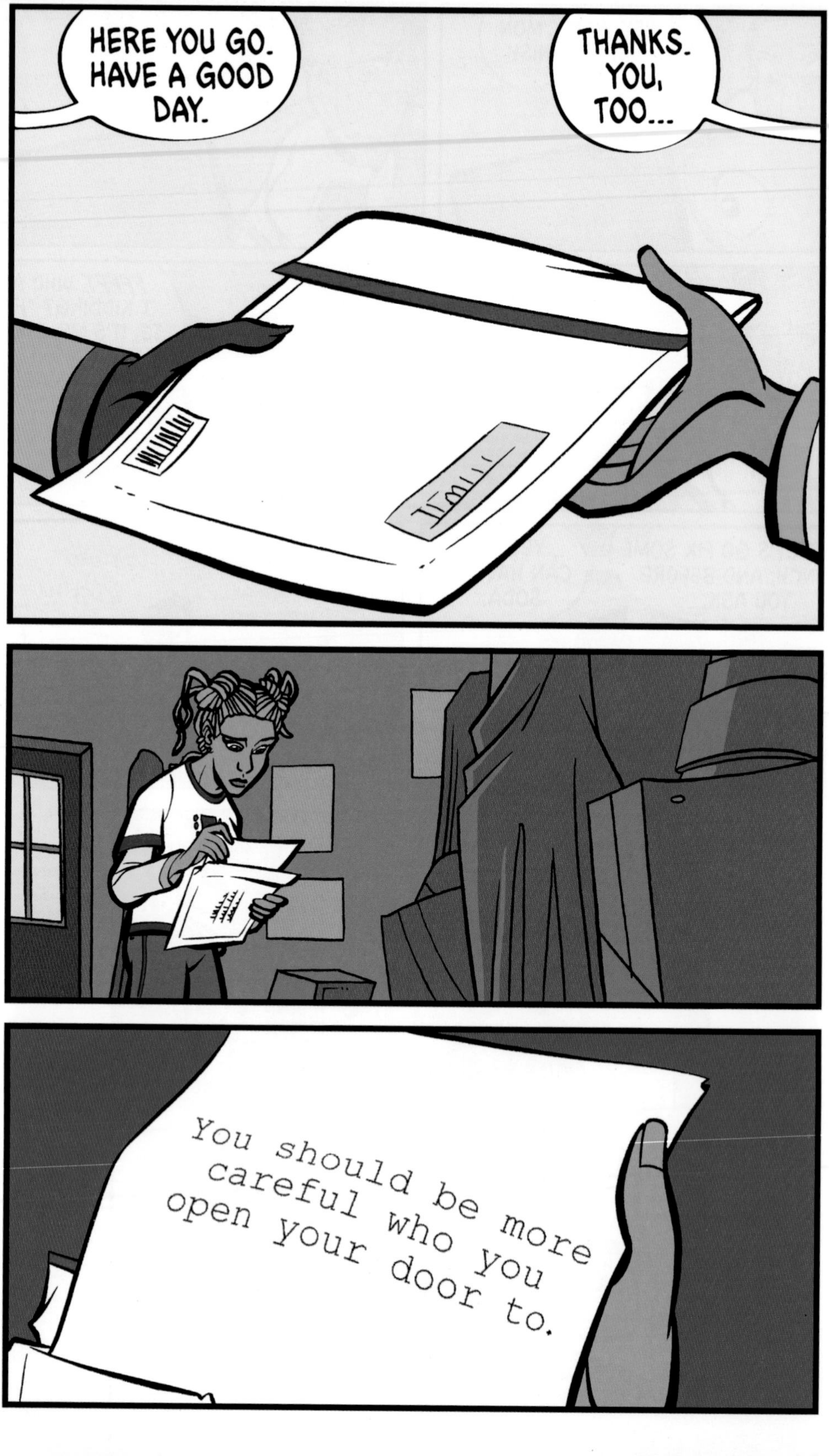
HERE YOU GO. HAVE A GOOD DAY.
THANKS. YOU, TOO...
You should be more careful who you open your door to.

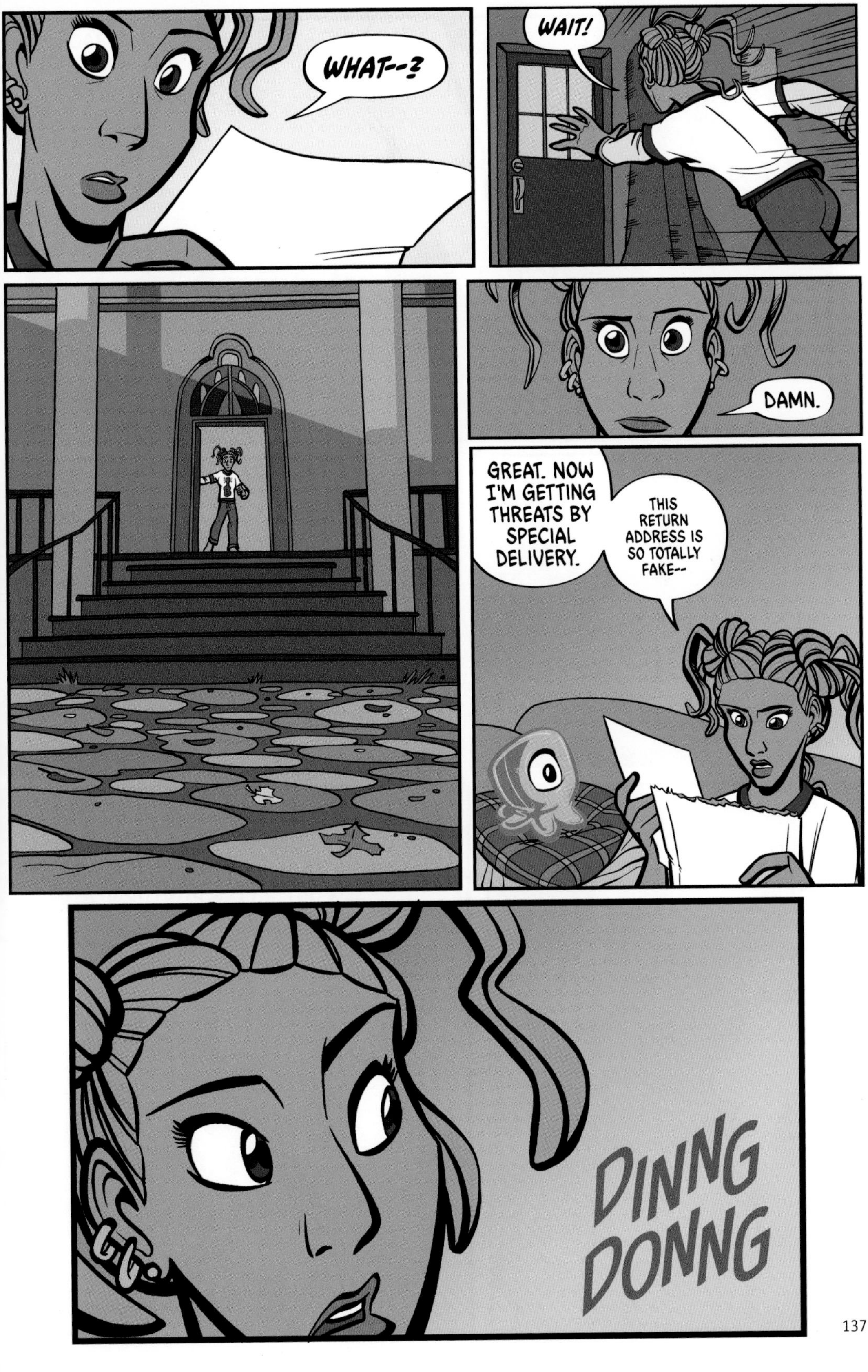
WHAT--?
WAIT!
DAMN.
GREAT. NOW I'M GETTING THREATS BY SPECIAL DELIVERY.
THIS RETURN ADDRESS IS SO TOTALLY FAKE--
DINNG DONNG

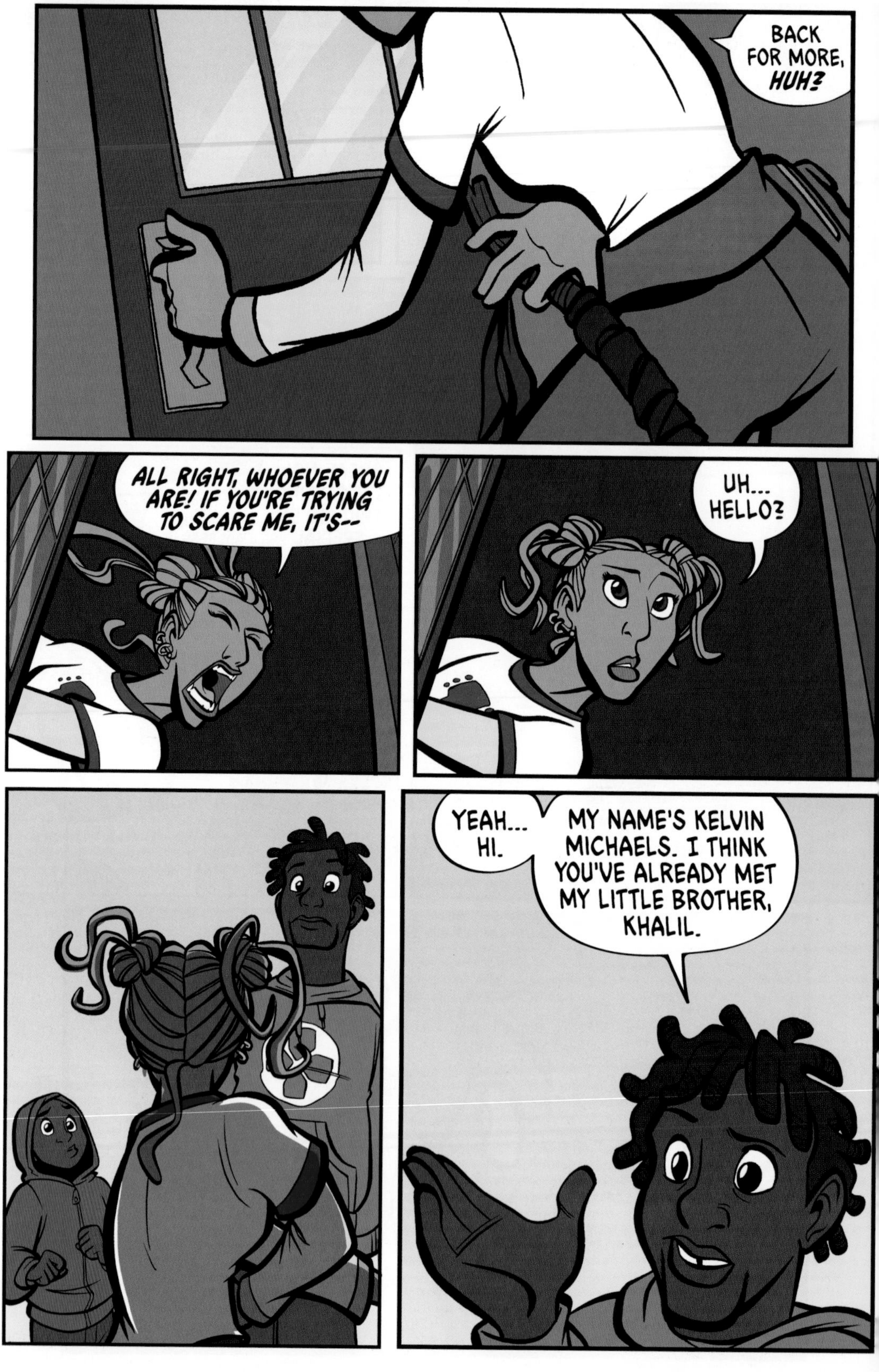
BACK FOR MORE, HUH?
ALL RIGHT, WHOEVER YOU ARE! IF YOU'RE TRYING TO SCARE ME, IT'S--
UH... HELLO?
YEAH... HI.
MY NAME'S KELVIN MICHAELS. I THINK YOU'VE ALREADY MET MY LITTLE BROTHER, KHALIL.

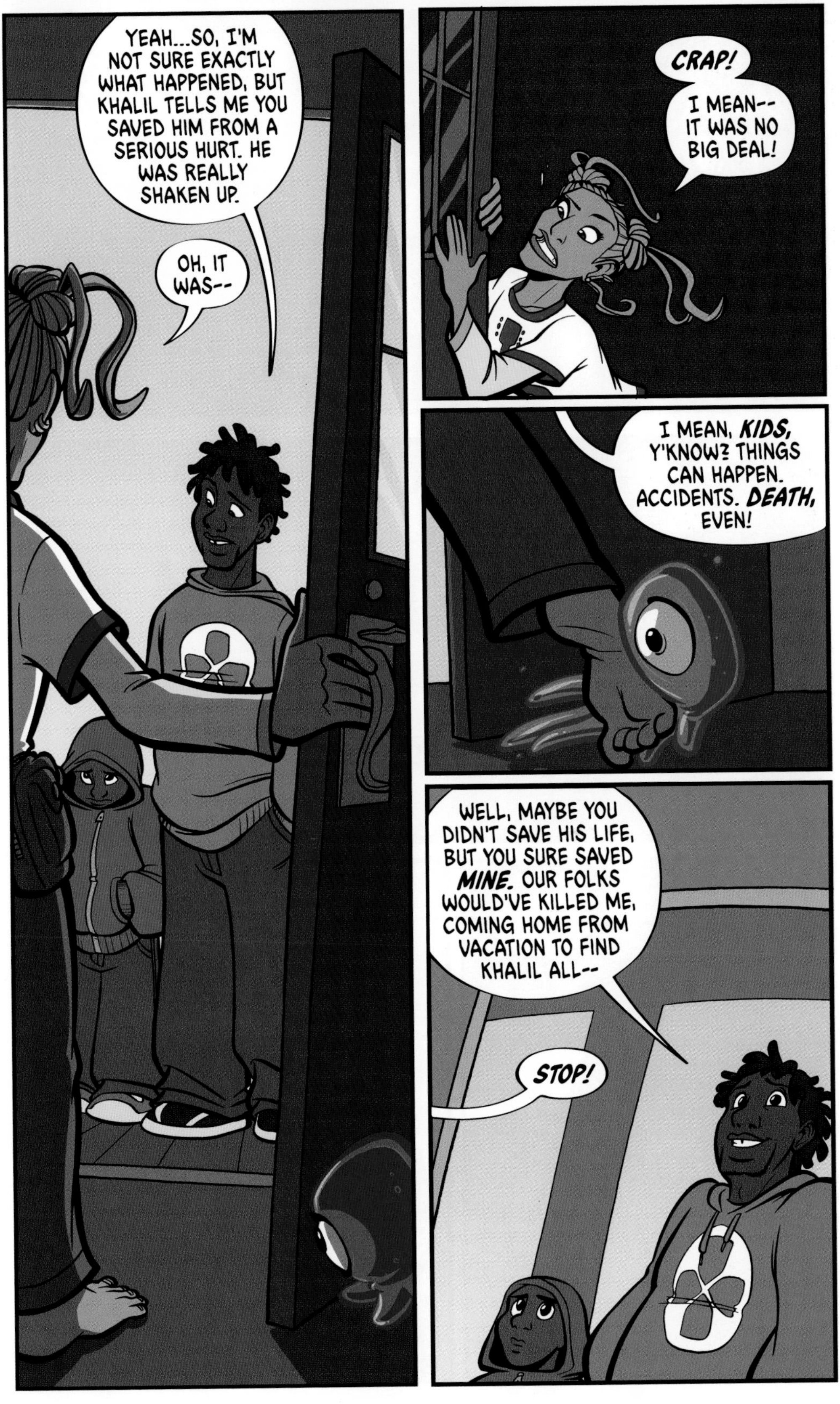
YEAH...SO, I'M NOT SURE EXACTLY WHAT HAPPENED, BUT KHALIL TELLS ME YOU SAVED HIM FROM A SERIOUS HURT. HE WAS REALLY SHAKEN UP.
OH, IT WAS--
CRAP!
I MEAN-- IT WAS NO BIG DEAL!
I MEAN, KIDS, Y'KNOW? THINGS CAN HAPPEN. ACCIDENTS. DEATH, EVEN!
WELL, MAYBE YOU DIDN'T SAVE HIS LIFE, BUT YOU SURE SAVED MINE. OUR FOLKS WOULD'VE KILLED ME, COMING HOME FROM VACATION TO FIND KHALIL ALL--
STOP!

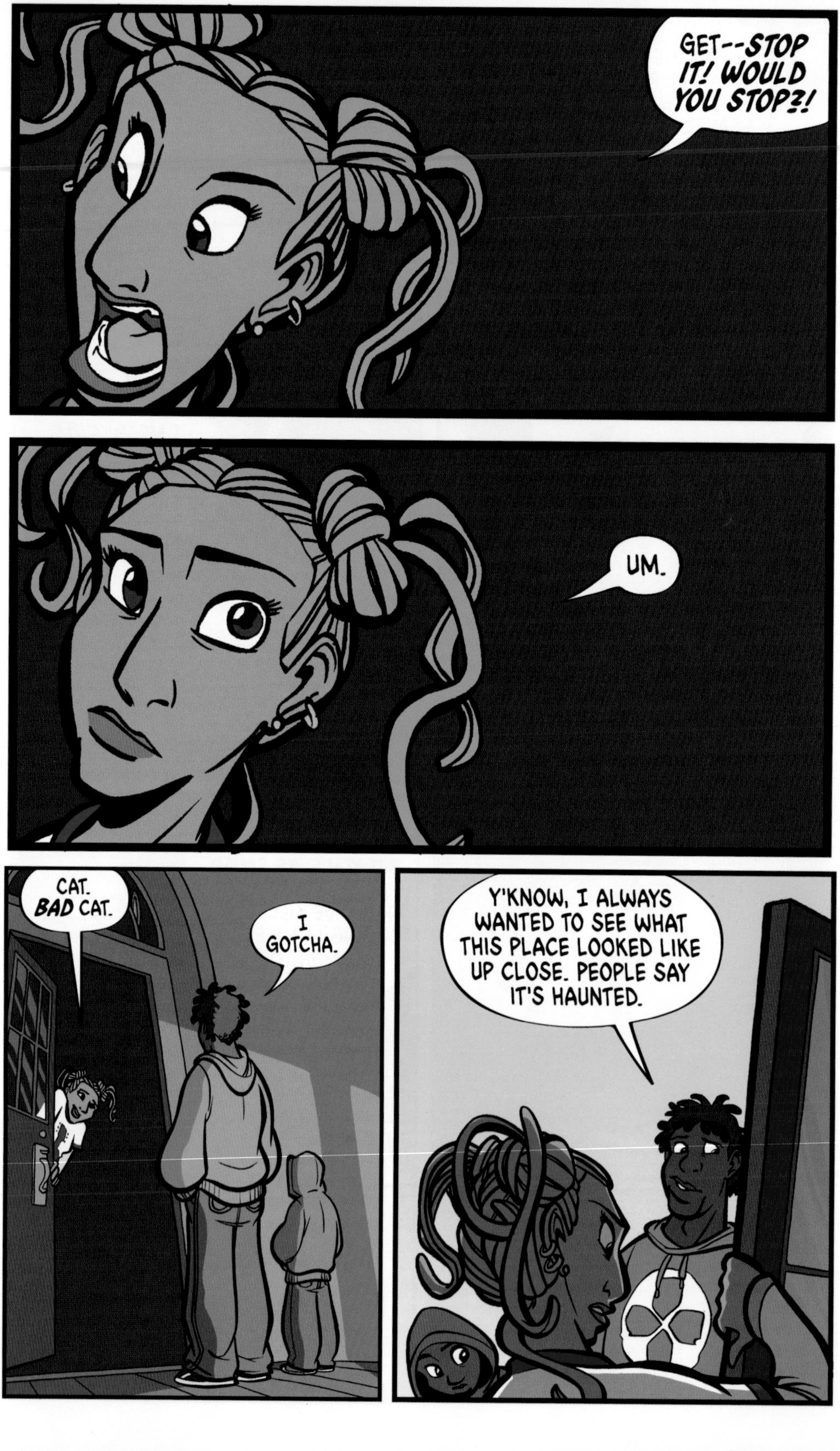
GET--STOP IT! WOULD YOU STOP?!
UM.
CAT. BAD CAT.
I GOTCHA.
Y'KNOW, I ALWAYS WANTED TO SEE WHAT THIS PLACE LOOKED LIKE UP CLOSE. PEOPLE SAY IT'S HAUNTED.

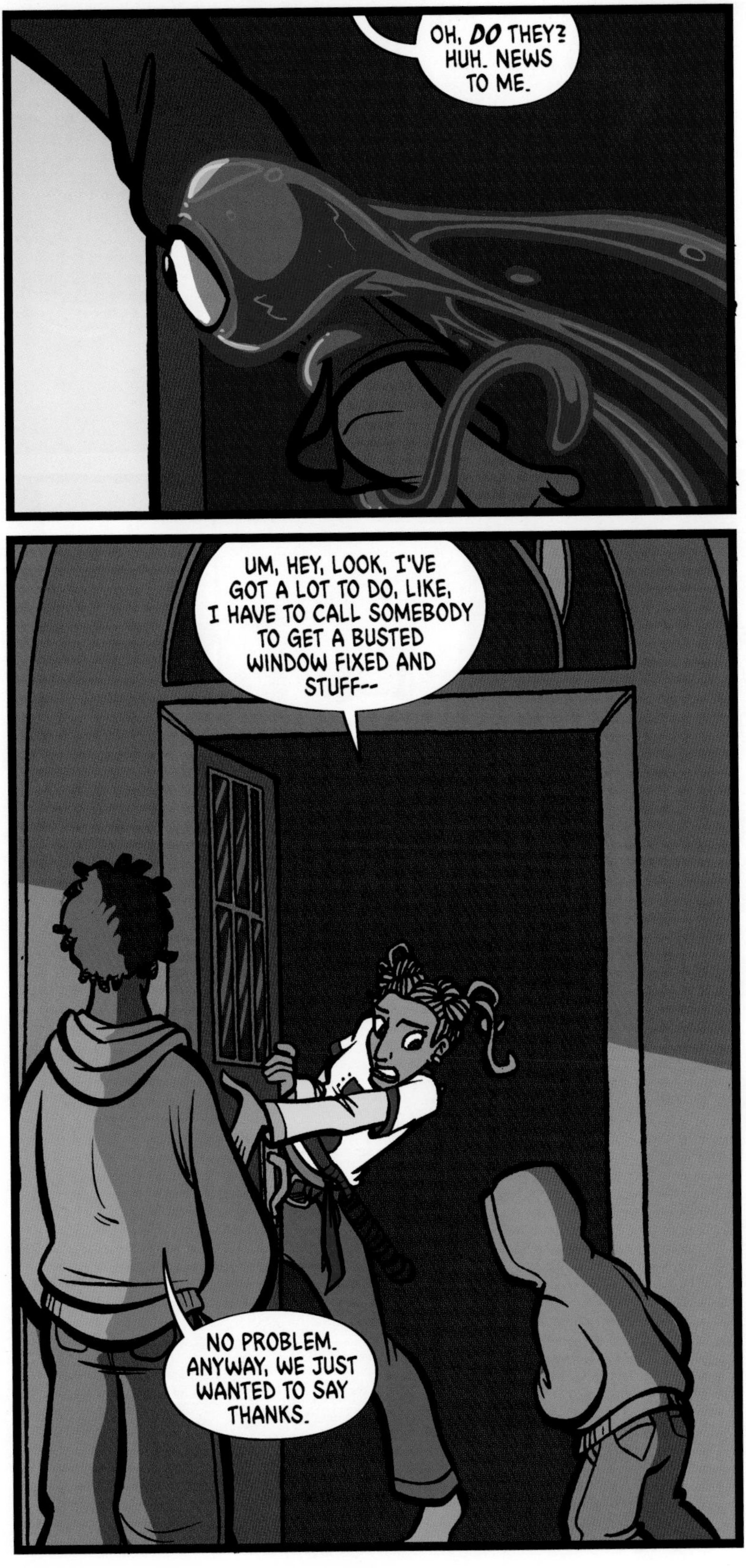
OH, DO THEY? HUH. NEWS TO ME.
UM, HEY, LOOK, I'VE GOT A LOT TO DO, LIKE, I HAVE TO CALL SOMEBODY TO GET A BUSTED WINDOW FIXED AND STUFF--
NO PROBLEM. ANYWAY, WE JUST WANTED TO SAY THANKS.

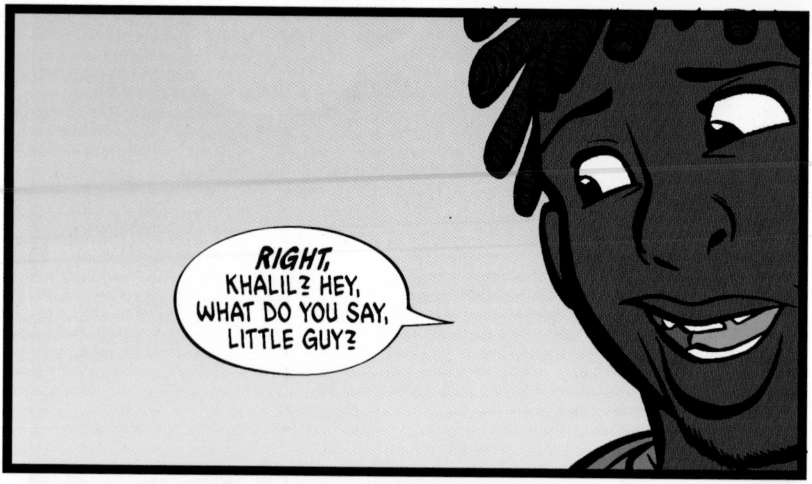
RIGHT, KHALIL? HEY, WHAT DO YOU SAY, LITTLE GUY?

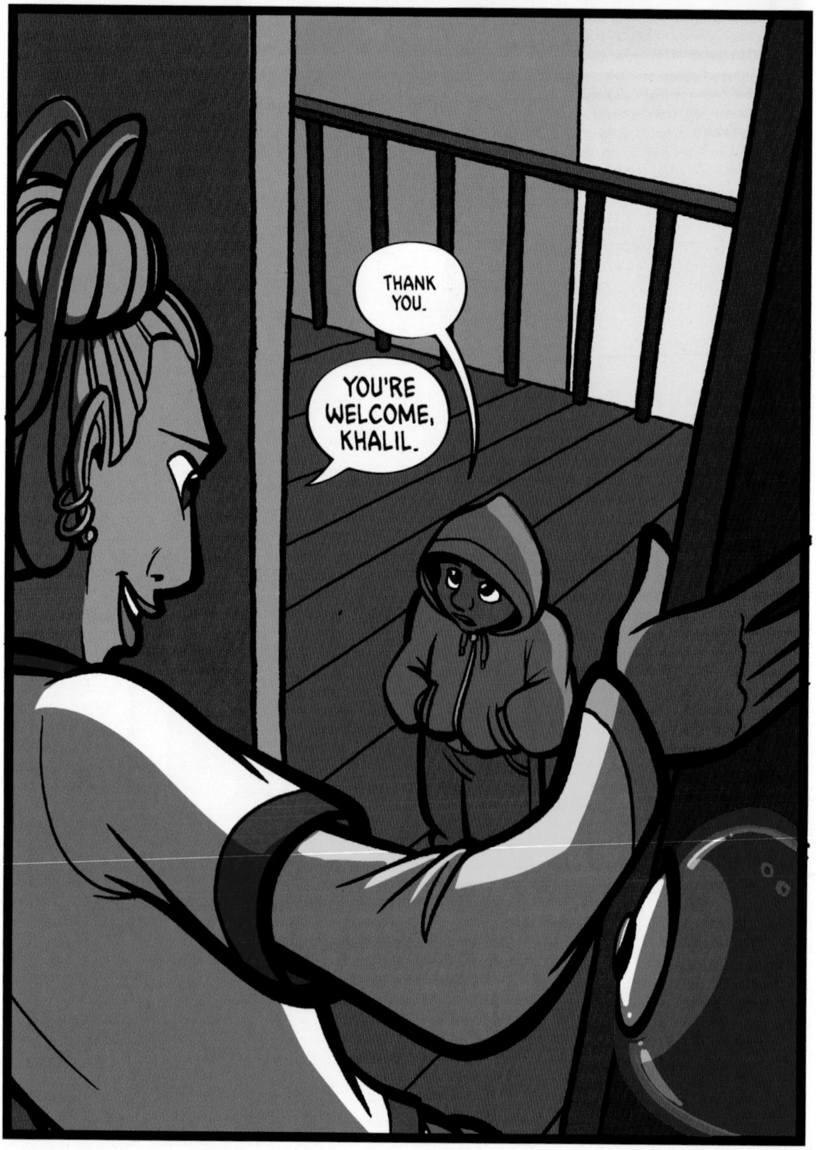
THANK YOU.
YOU'RE WELCOME, KHALIL.

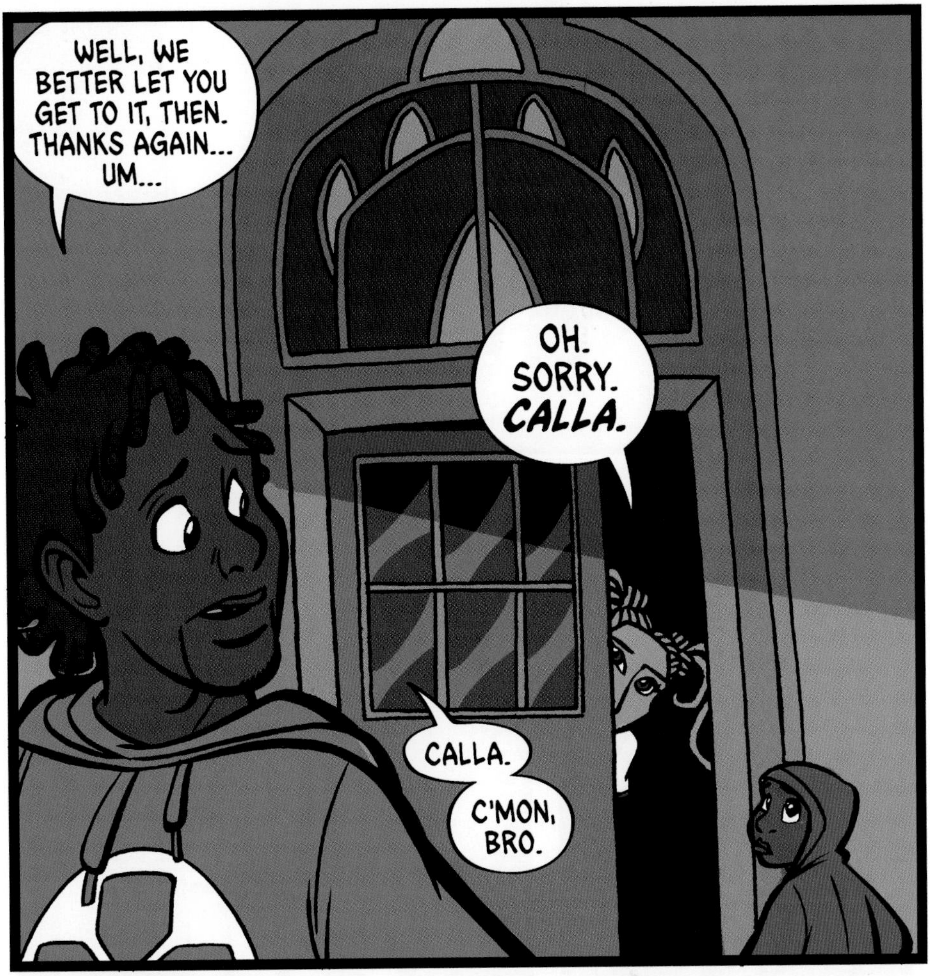
WELL, WE BETTER LET YOU GET TO IT, THEN. THANKS AGAIN... UM...
OH. SORRY. CALLA.
CALLA.
C'MON, BRO.

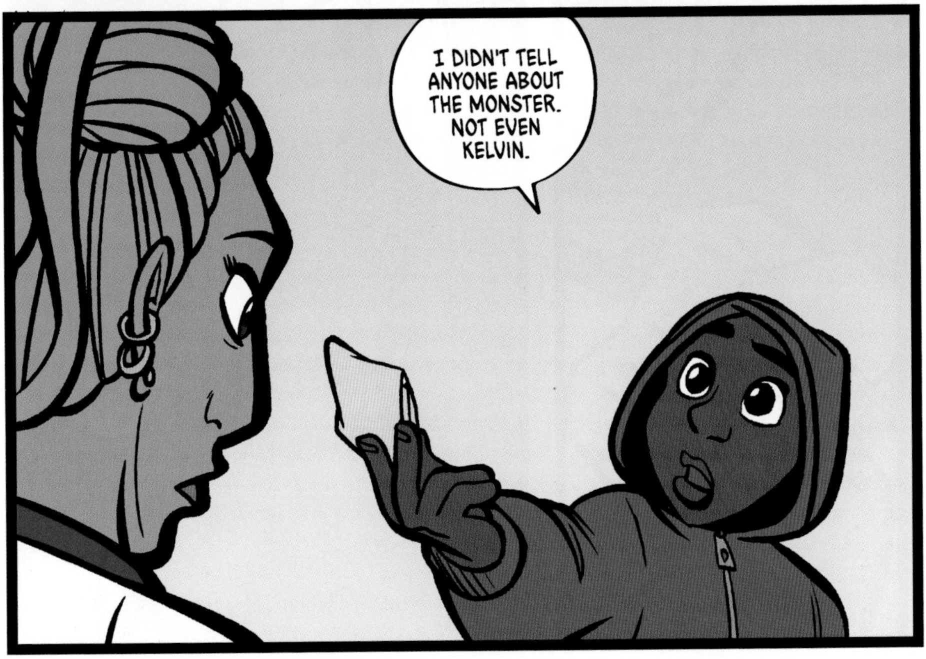
I DIDN'T TELL ANYONE ABOUT THE MONSTER. NOT EVEN KELVIN.

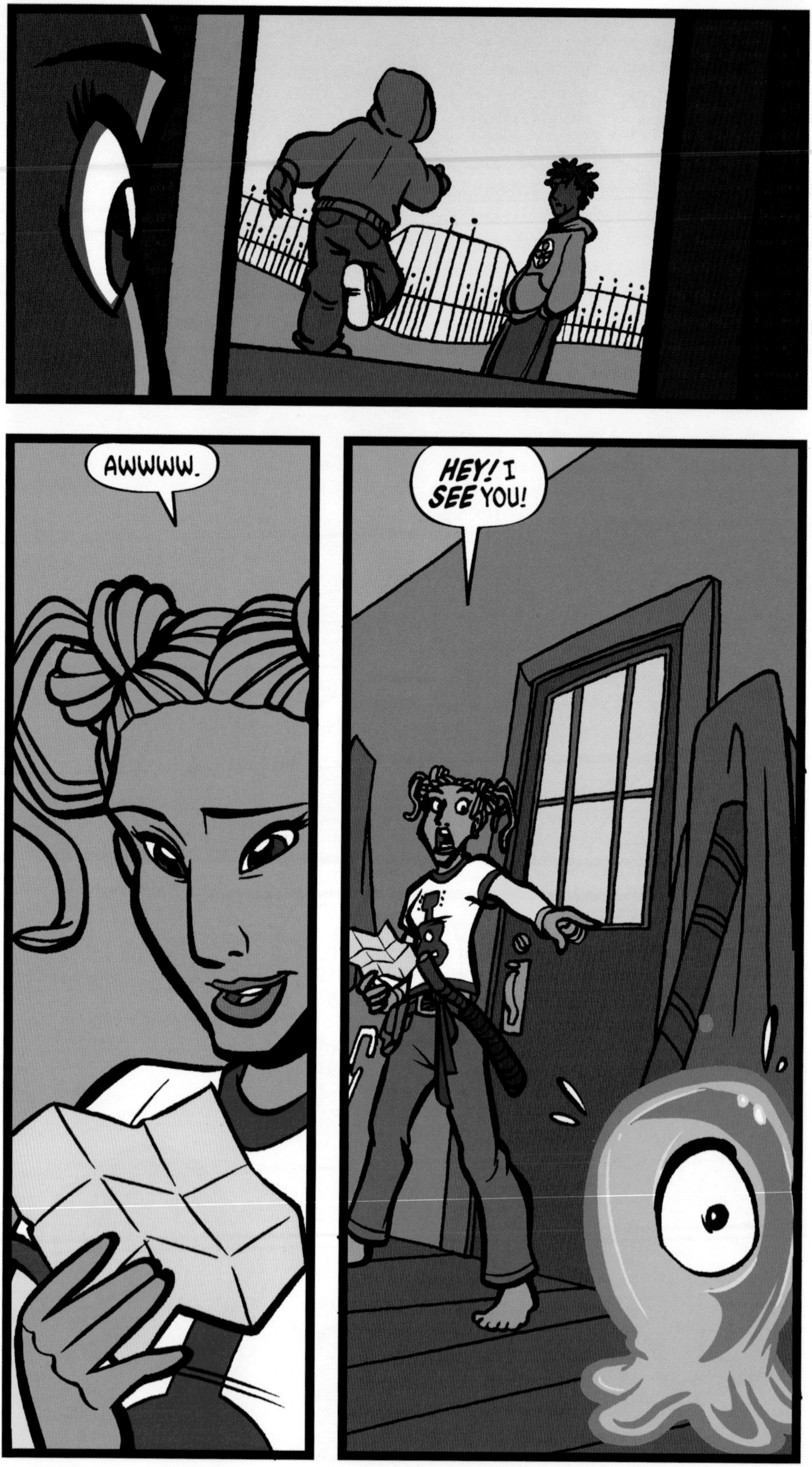
AWWWW.
HEY! I SEE YOU!

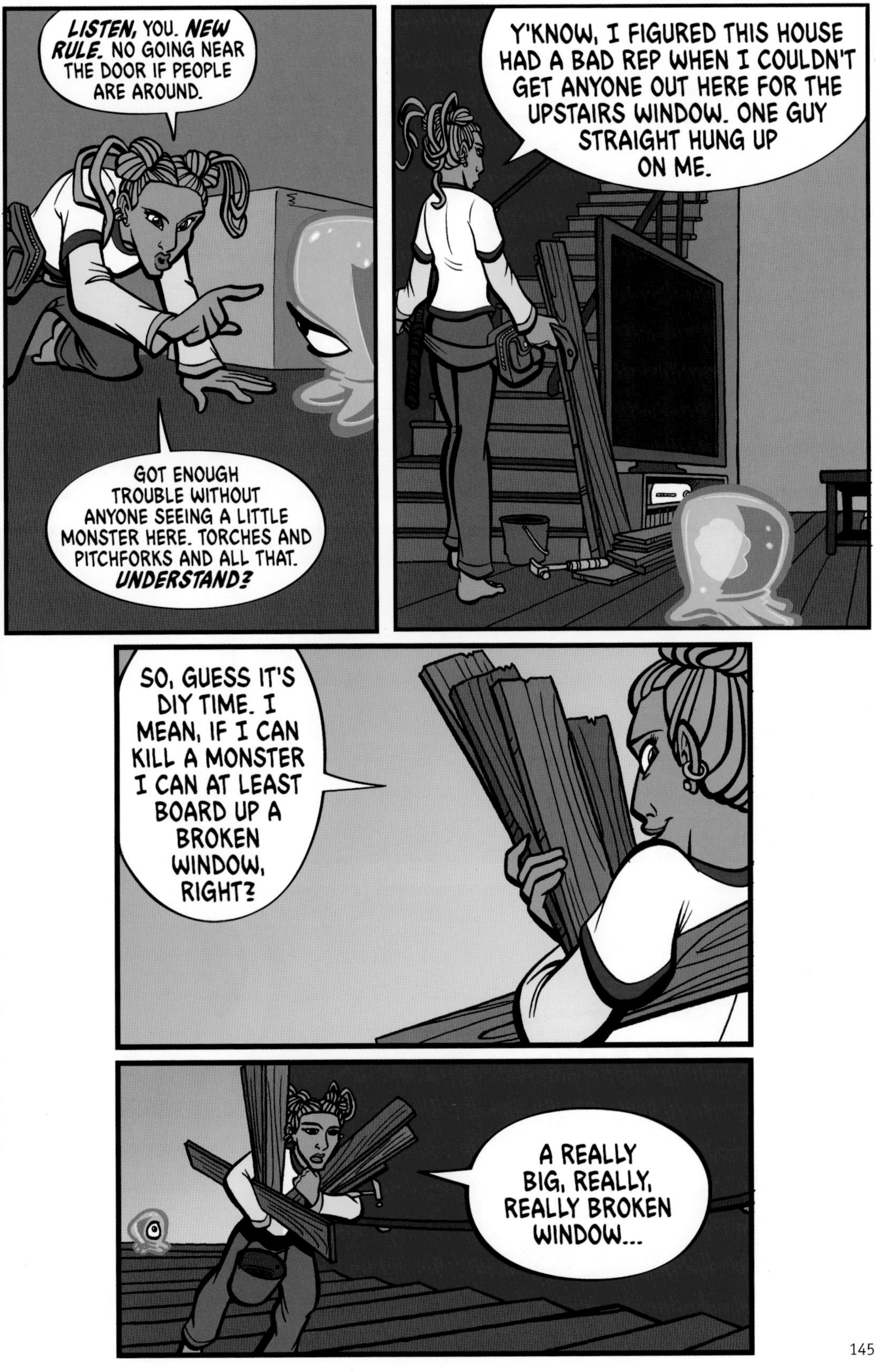
LISTEN, YOU. NEW RULE. NO GOING NEAR THE DOOR IF PEOPLE ARE AROUND.
GOT ENOUGH TROUBLE WITHOUT ANYONE SEEING A LITTLE MONSTER HERE. TORCHES AND PITCHFORKS AND ALL THAT. UNDERSTAND?
Y'KNOW, I FIGURED THIS HOUSE HAD A BAD REP WHEN I COULDN'T GET ANYONE OUT HERE FOR THE UPSTAIRS WINDOW. ONE GUY STRAIGHT HUNG UP ON ME.
SO, GUESS IT'S DIY TIME. I MEAN, IF I CAN KILL A MONSTER I CAN AT LEAST BOARD UP A BROKEN WINDOW, RIGHT?
A REALLY BIG, REALLY, REALLY BROKEN WINDOW...

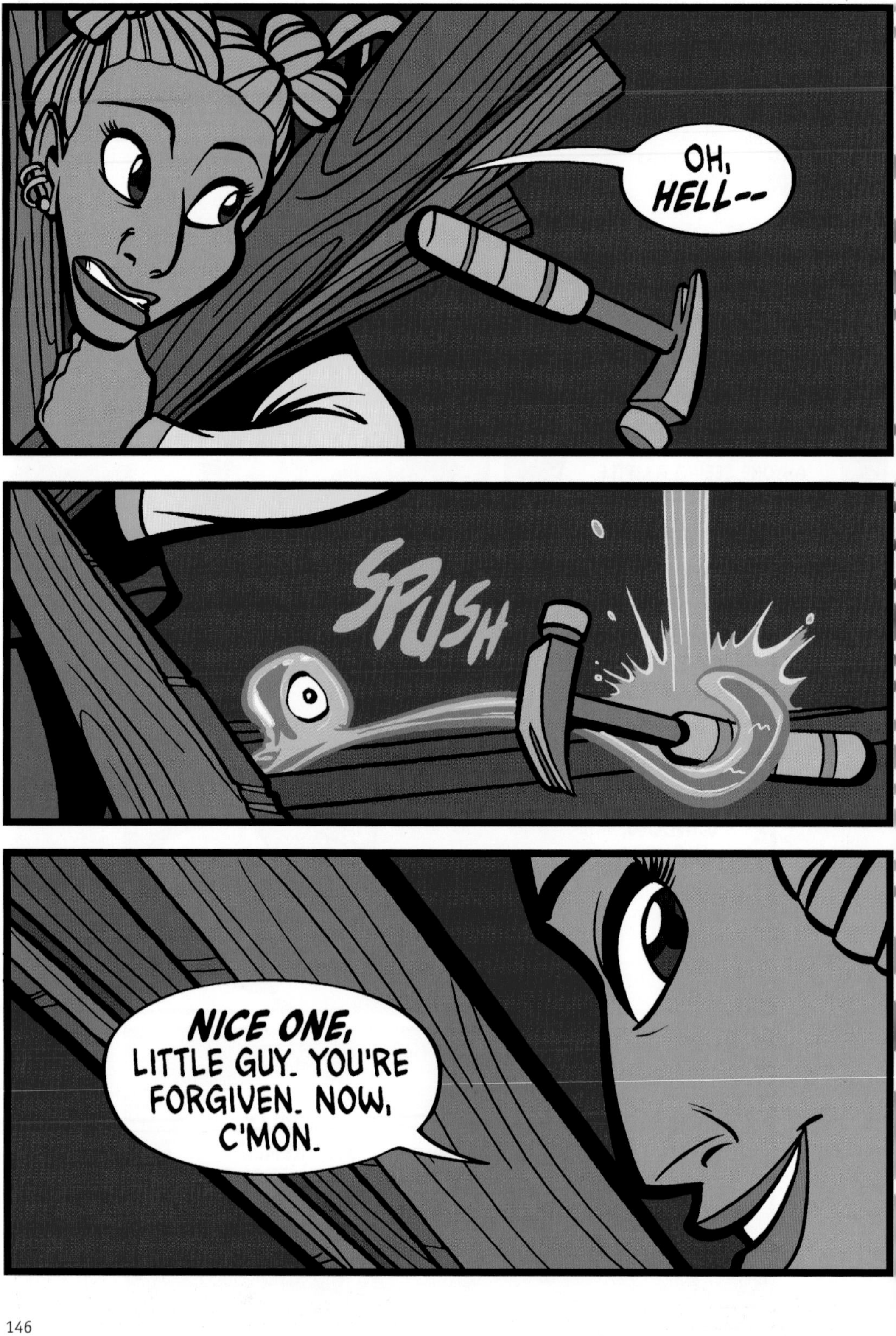
OH, HELL--
SPUSH
NICE ONE, LITTLE GUY. YOU'RE FORGIVEN. NOW, C'MON.

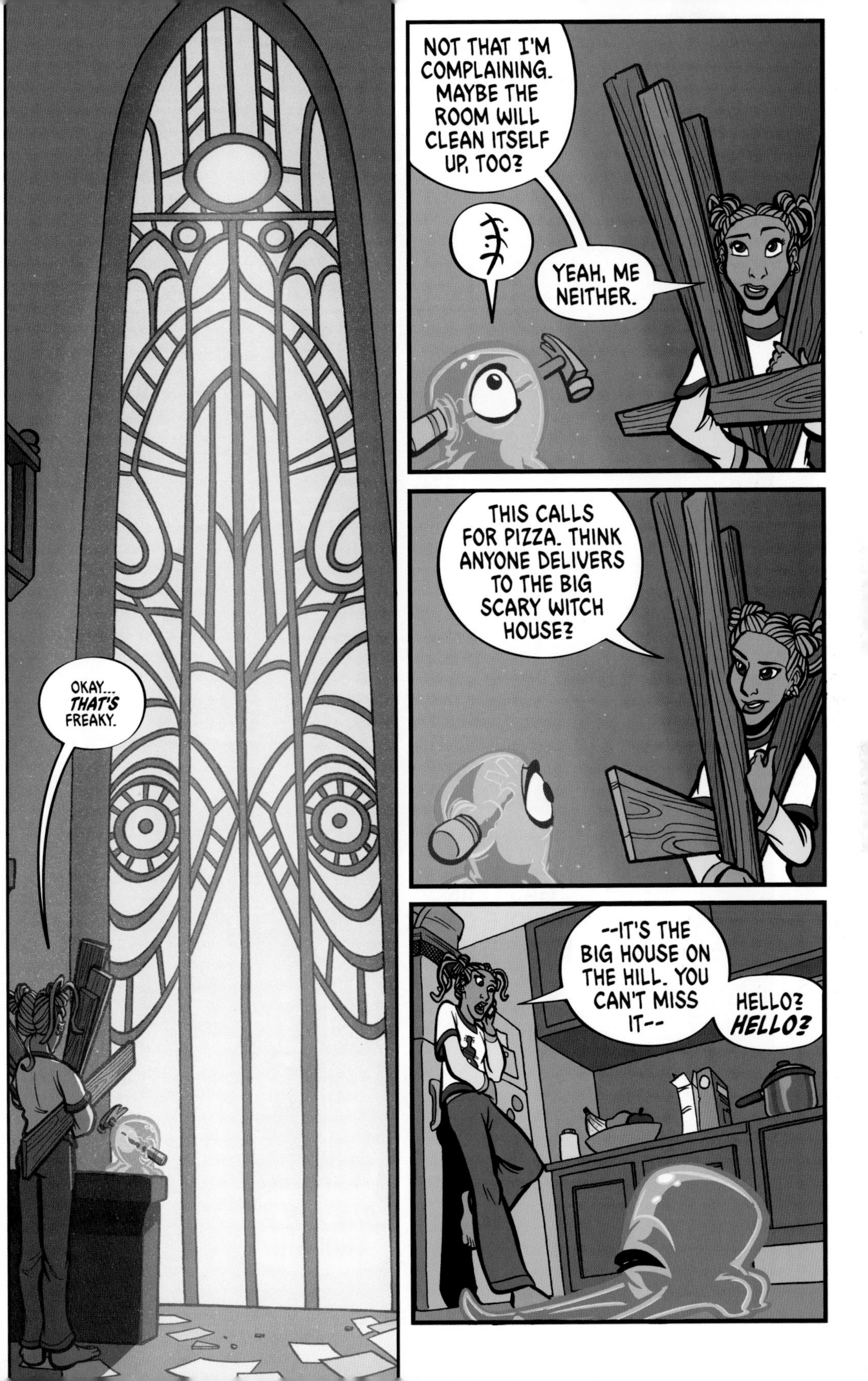
OKAY... *THAT'S* FREAKY.
NOT THAT I'M COMPLAINING. MAYBE THE ROOM WILL CLEAN ITSELF UP, TOO?
YEAH, ME NEITHER.
THIS CALLS FOR PIZZA. THINK ANYONE DELIVERS TO THE BIG SCARY WITCH HOUSE?
--IT'S THE BIG HOUSE ON THE HILL. YOU CAN'T MISS IT--
HELLO? *HELLO?*

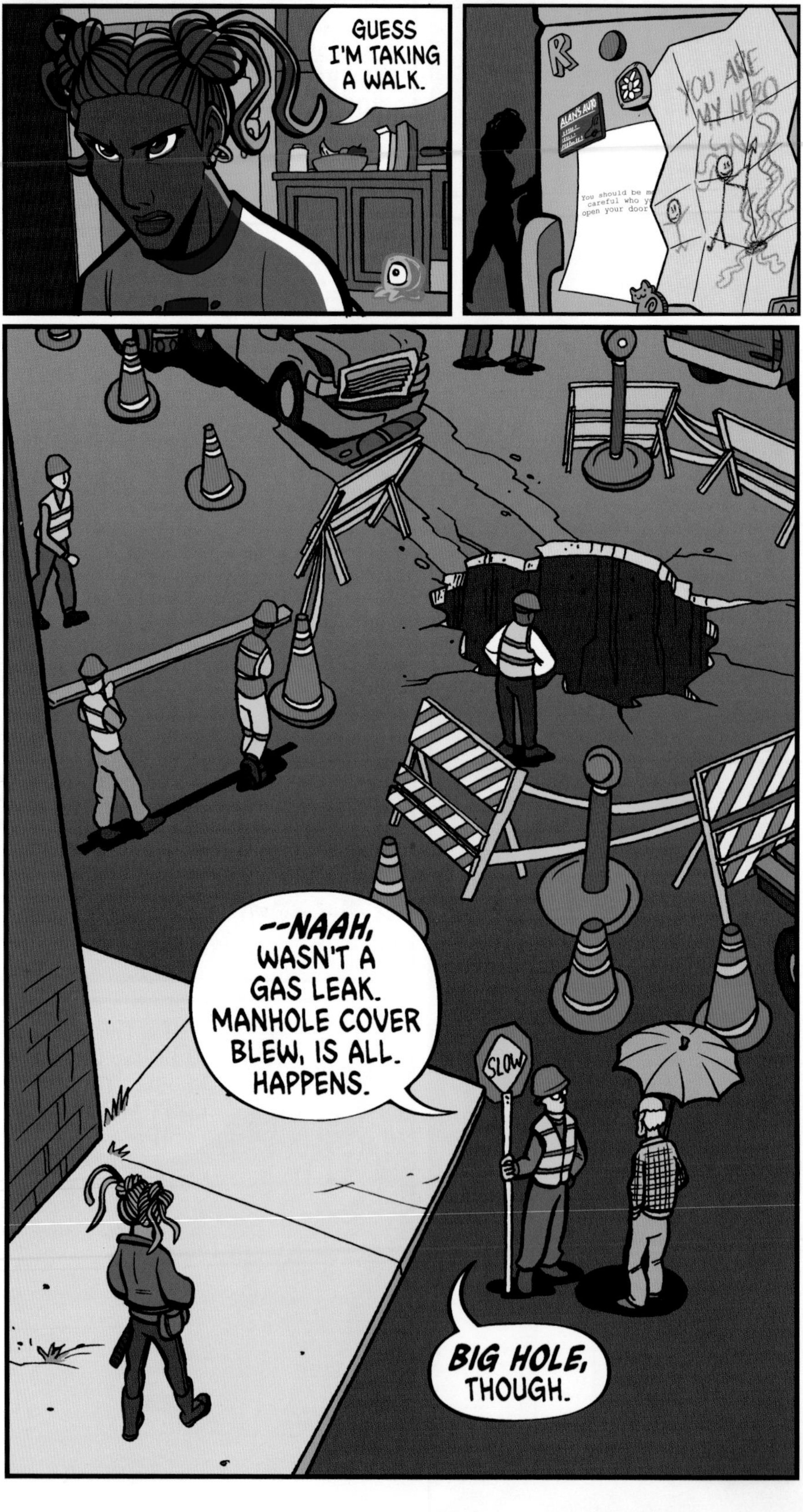
GUESS I'M TAKING A WALK.
ALAN'S AUTO
YOU ARE MY HERO
--NAAH, WASN'T A GAS LEAK. MANHOLE COVER BLEW, IS ALL. HAPPENS.
SLOW
BIG HOLE, THOUGH.

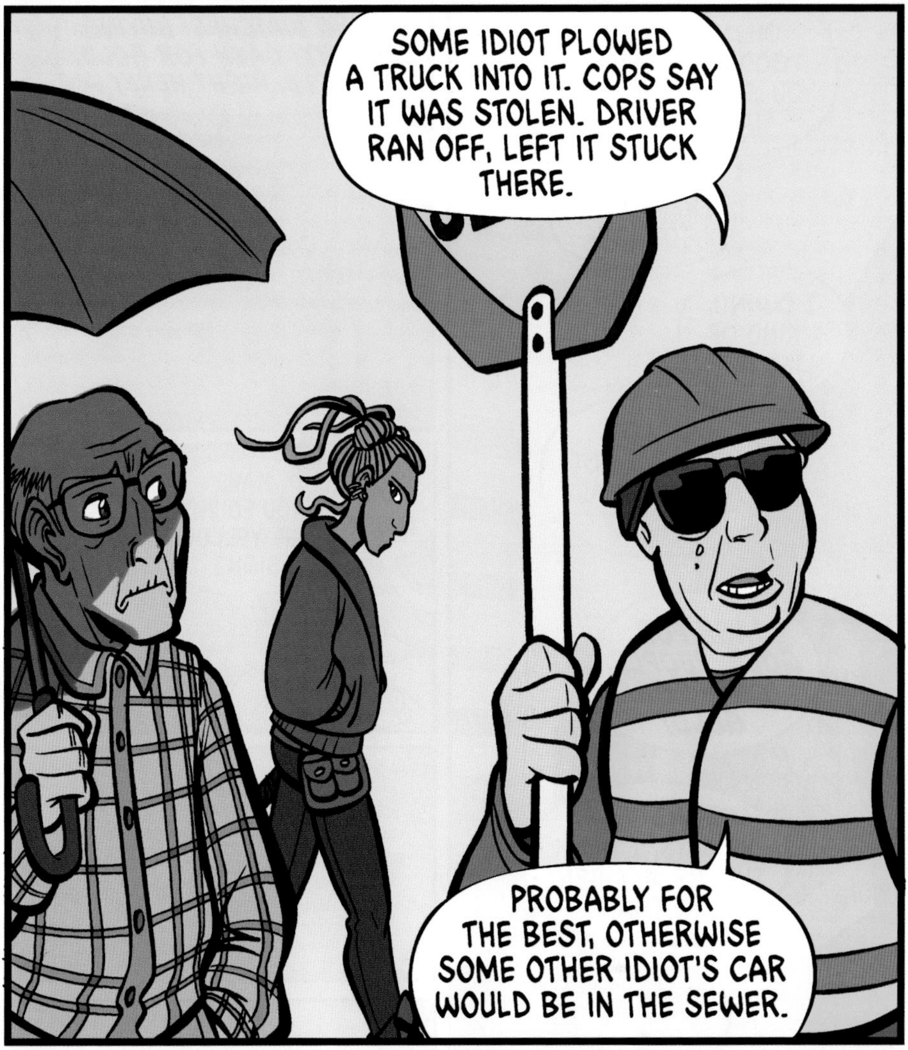
SOME IDIOT PLOWED A TRUCK INTO IT. COPS SAY IT WAS STOLEN. DRIVER RAN OFF, LEFT IT STUCK THERE.
PROBABLY FOR THE BEST, OTHERWISE SOME OTHER IDIOT'S CAR WOULD BE IN THE SEWER.

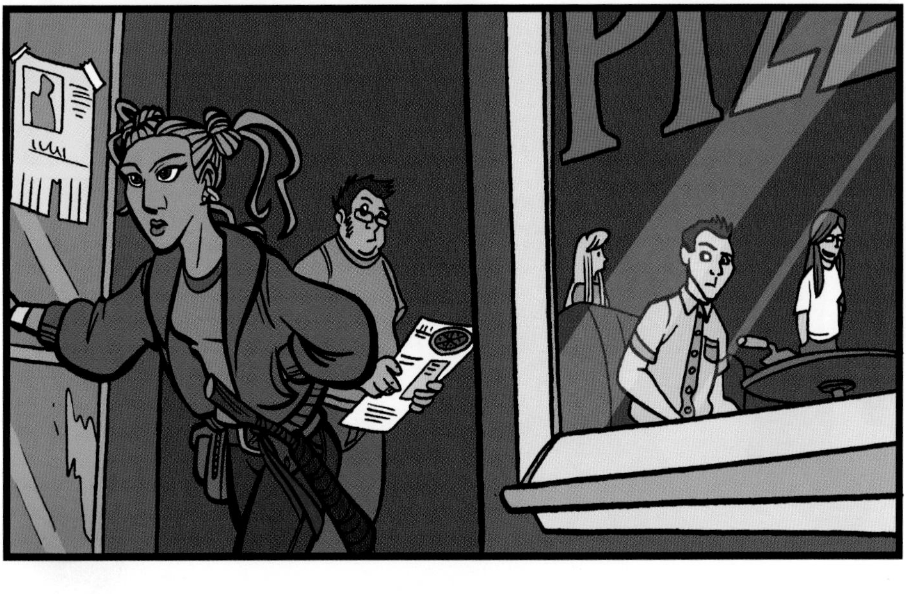

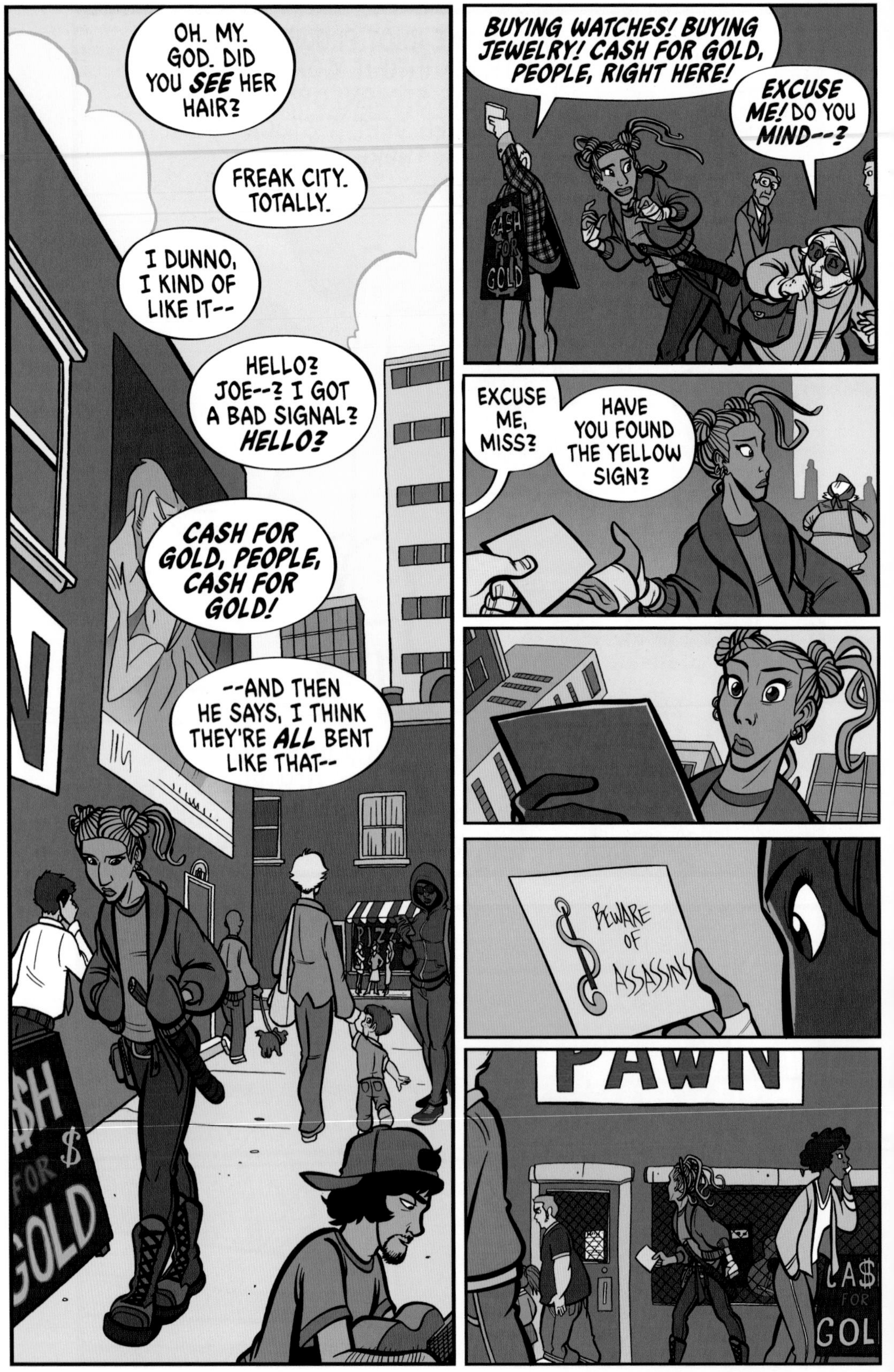
OH. MY. GOD. DID YOU *SEE* HER HAIR?
FREAK CITY. TOTALLY.
I DUNNO, I KIND OF LIKE IT--
HELLO? JOE--? I GOT A BAD SIGNAL? ***HELLO?***
CASH FOR GOLD, PEOPLE, CASH FOR GOLD!
--AND THEN HE SAYS, I THINK THEY'RE ***ALL*** BENT LIKE THAT--
BUYING WATCHES! BUYING JEWELRY! CASH FOR GOLD, PEOPLE, RIGHT HERE!
EXCUSE ME! DO YOU ***MIND--?***
CASH FOR GOLD
EXCUSE ME, MISS?
HAVE YOU FOUND THE YELLOW SIGN?
BEWARE OF ASSASSINS
PAWN

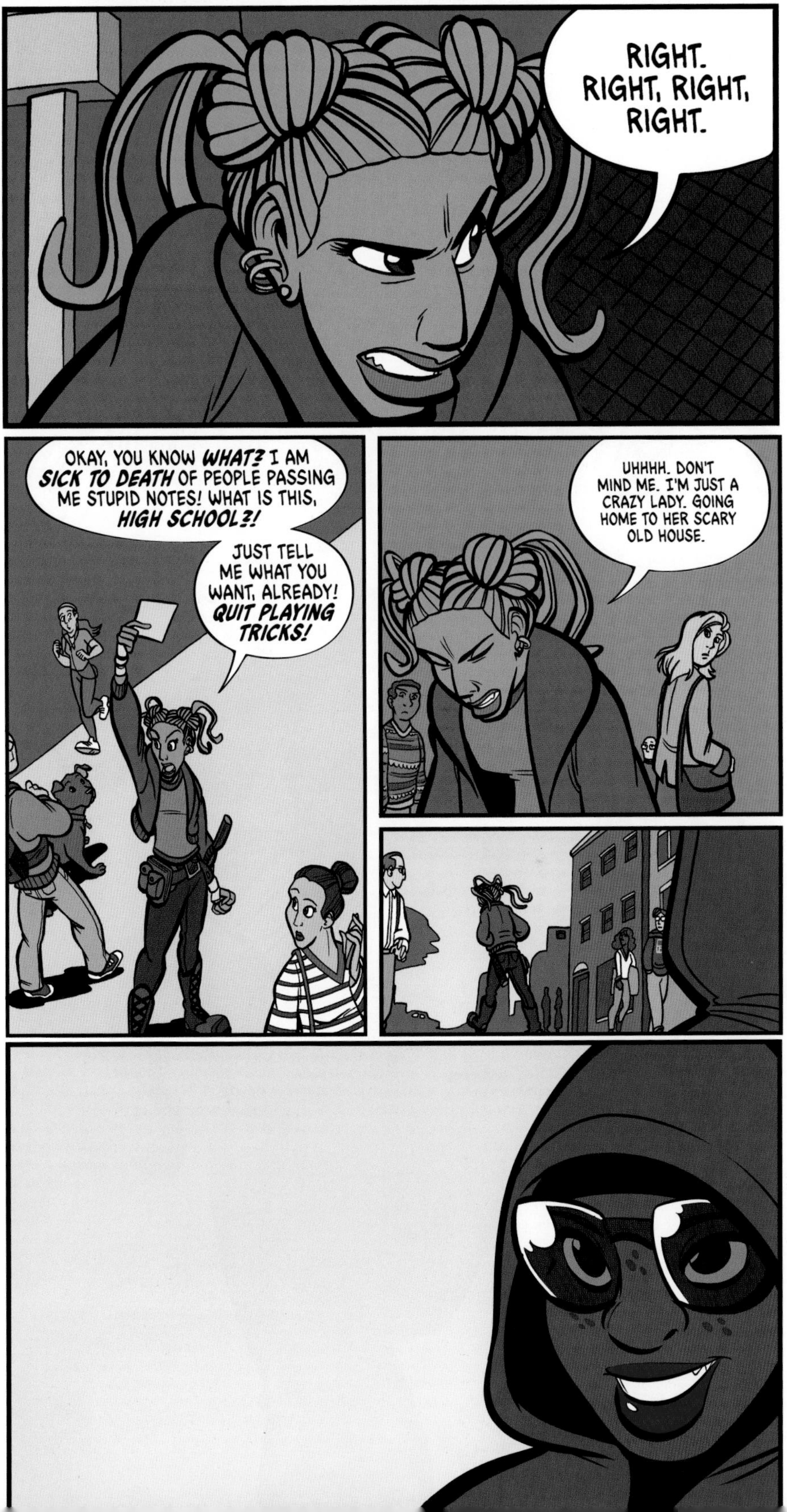
RIGHT. RIGHT, RIGHT, RIGHT.
OKAY, YOU KNOW WHAT? I AM SICK TO DEATH OF PEOPLE PASSING ME STUPID NOTES! WHAT IS THIS, HIGH SCHOOL?!
JUST TELL ME WHAT YOU WANT, ALREADY! QUIT PLAYING TRICKS!
UHHHH. DON'T MIND ME. I'M JUST A CRAZY LADY. GOING HOME TO HER SCARY OLD HOUSE.

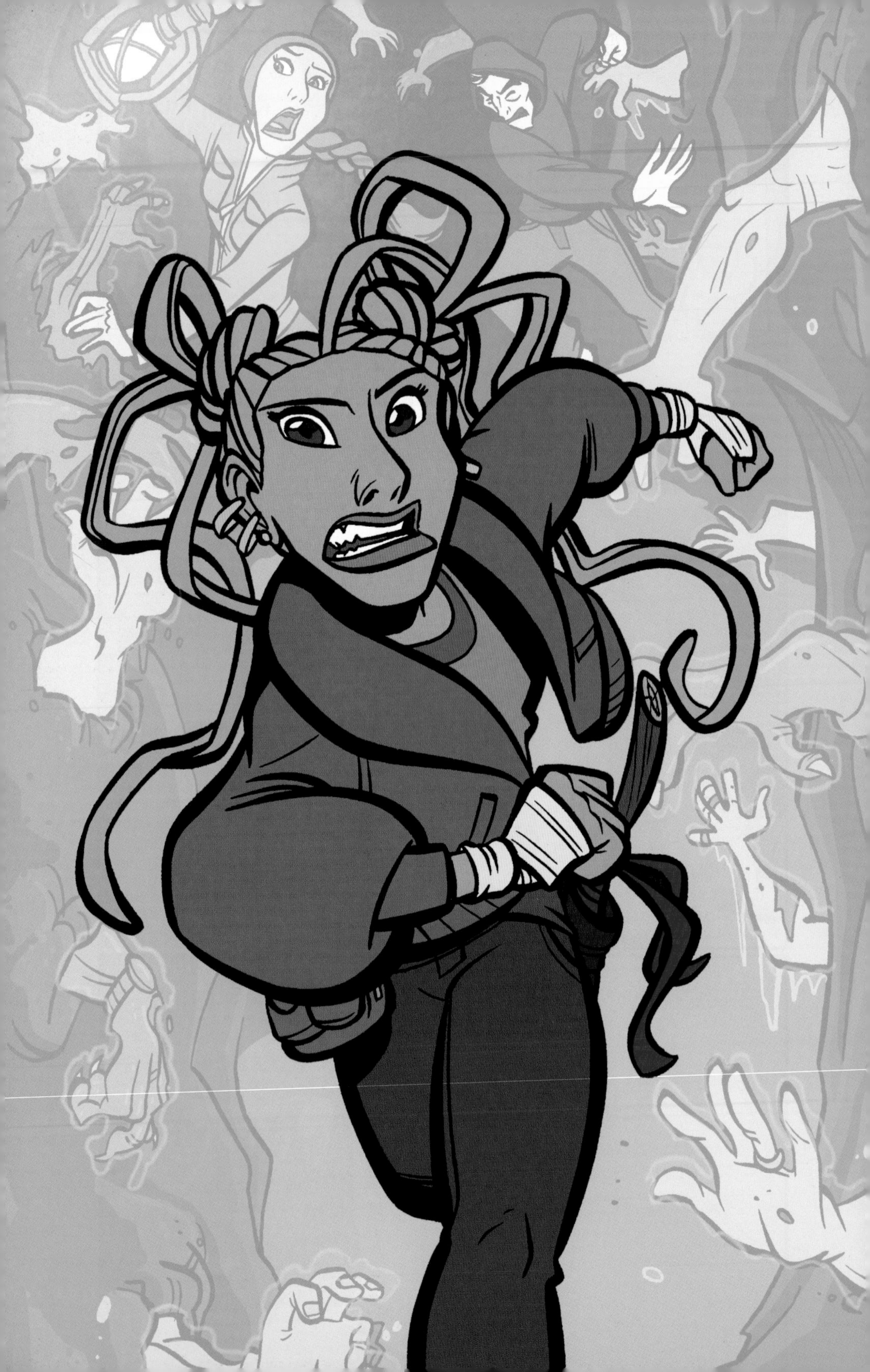

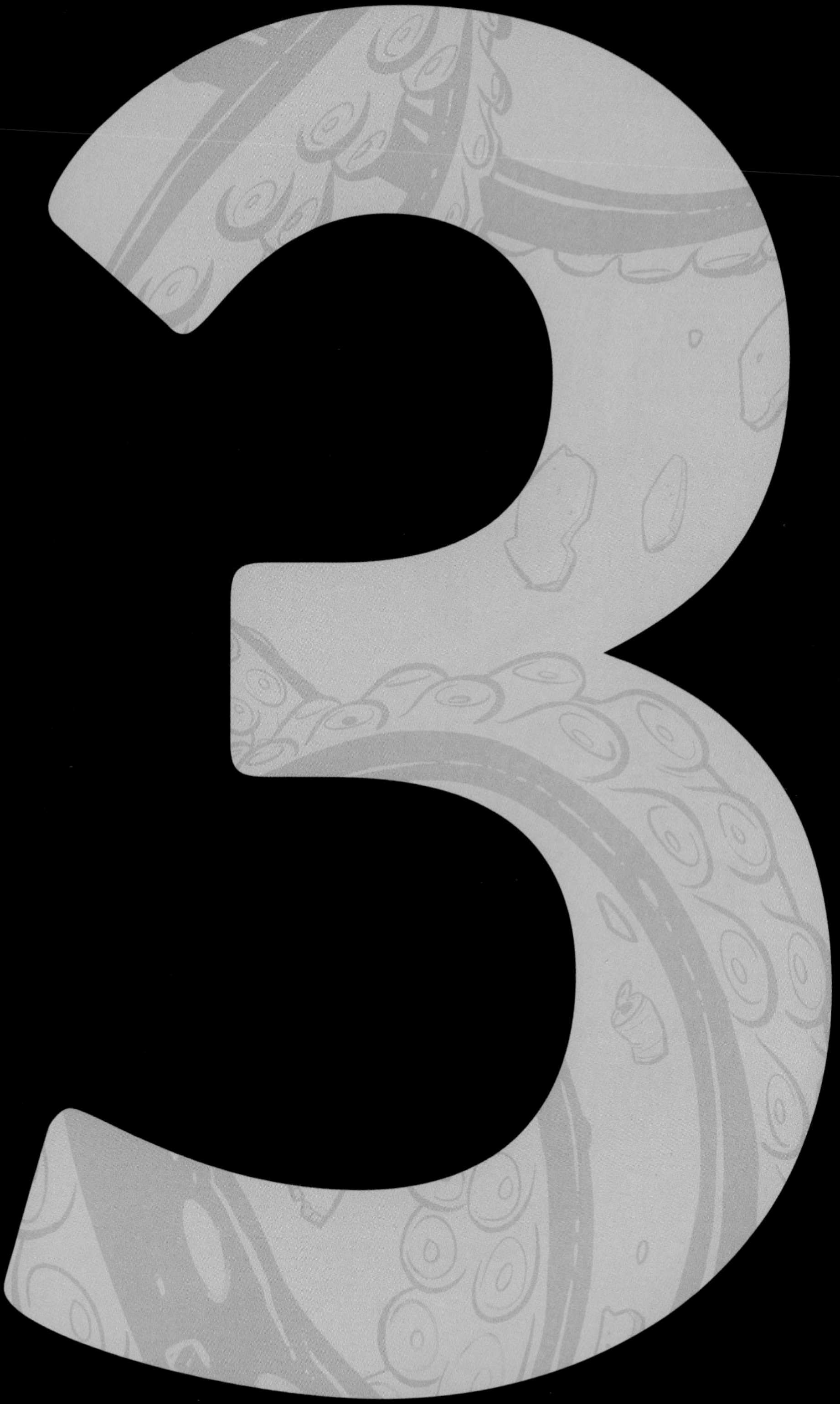
3

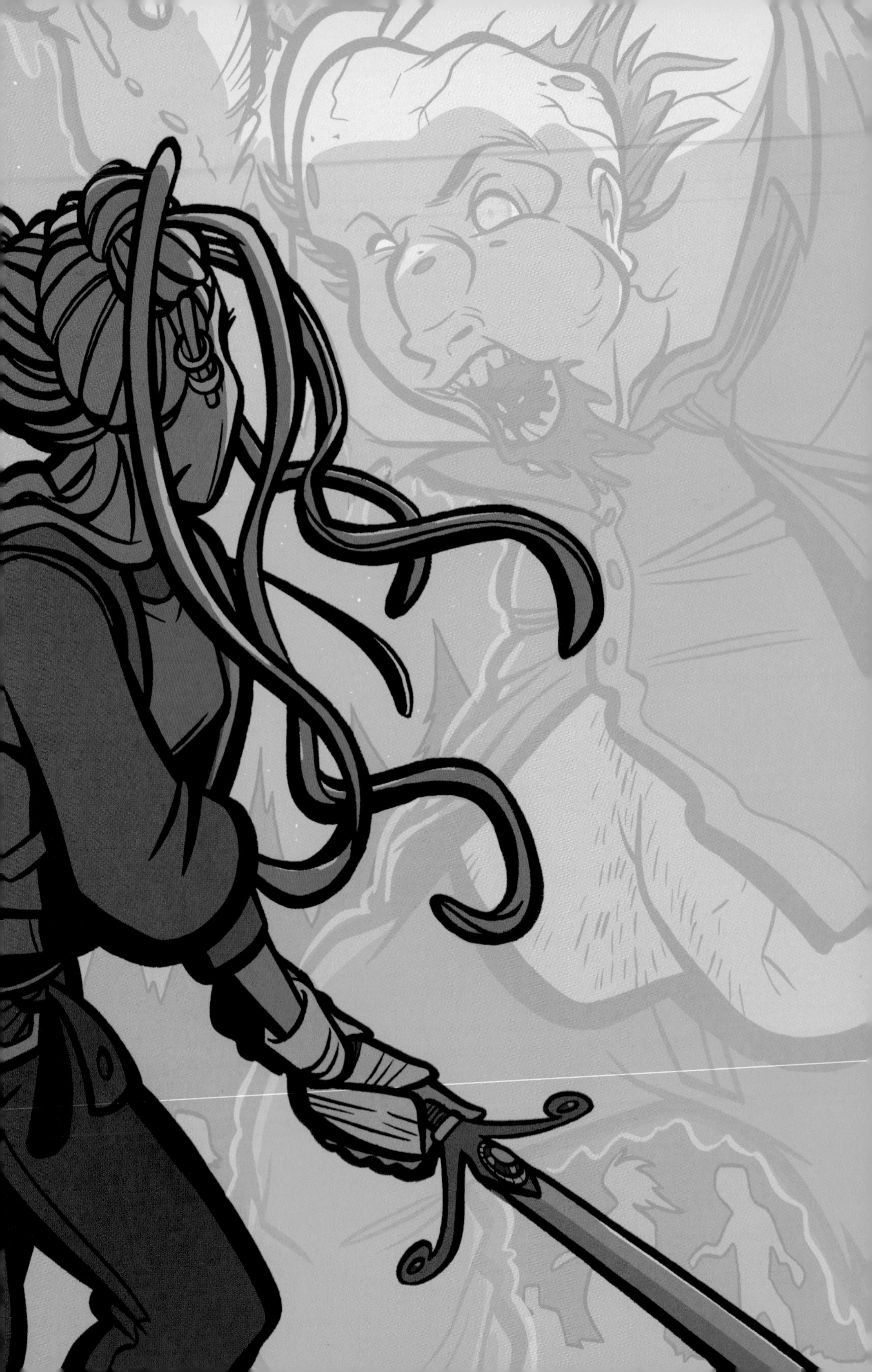

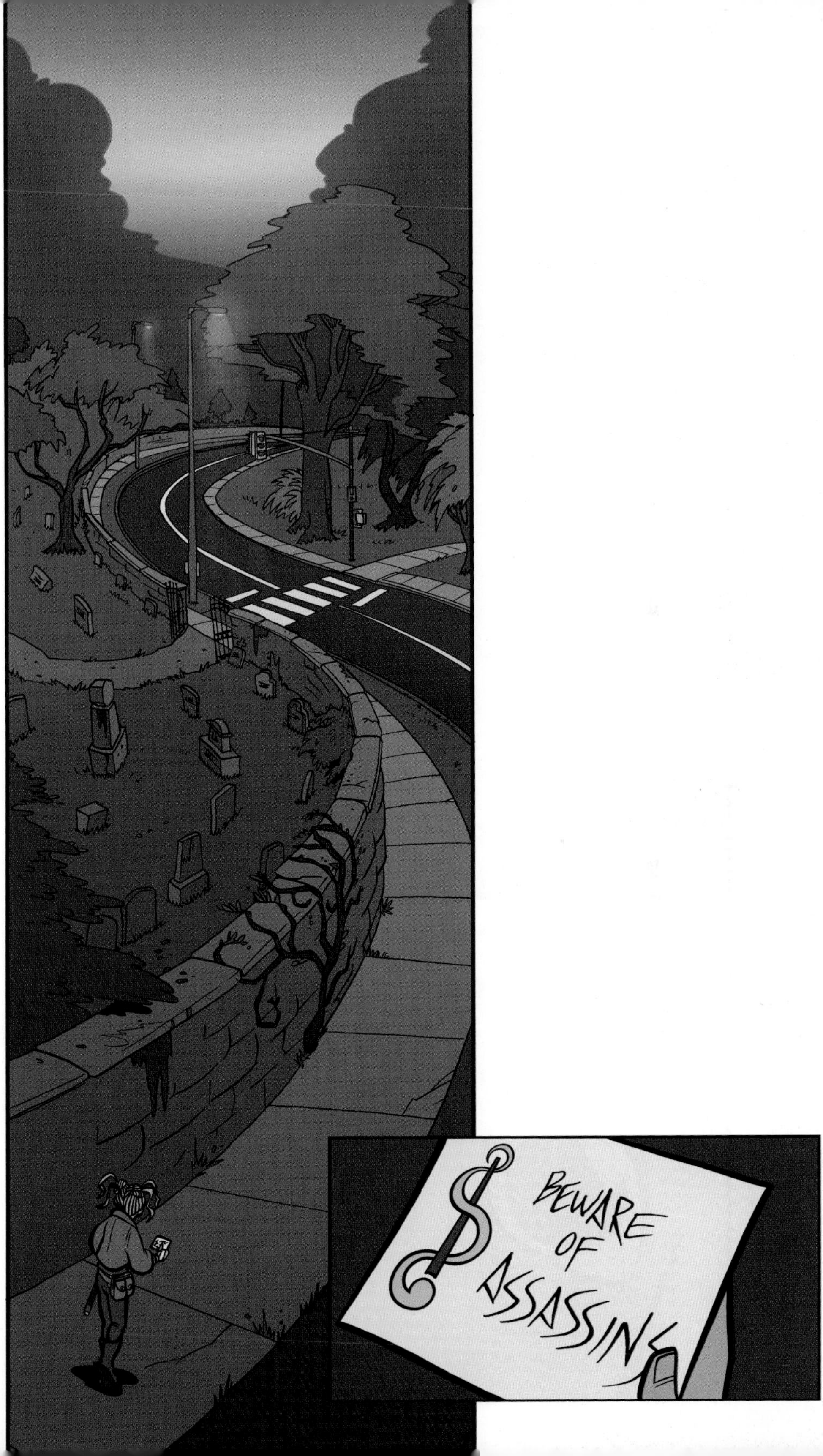
BEWARE OF ASSASSINS

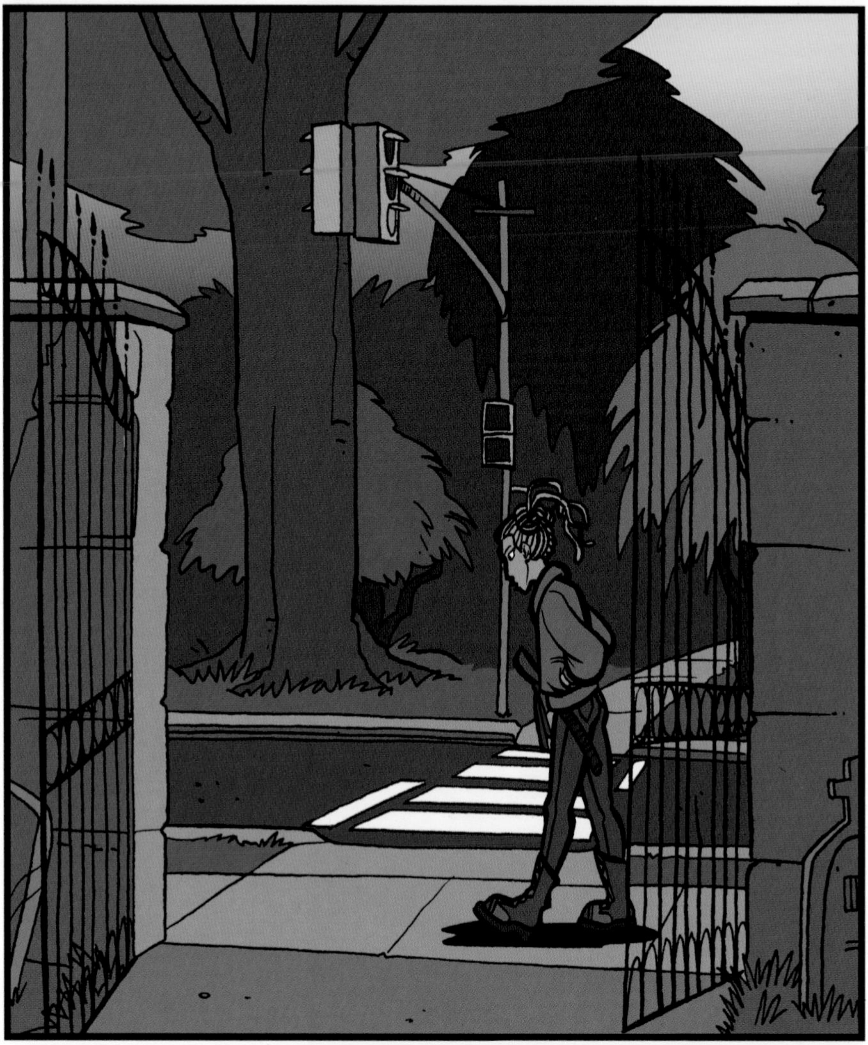

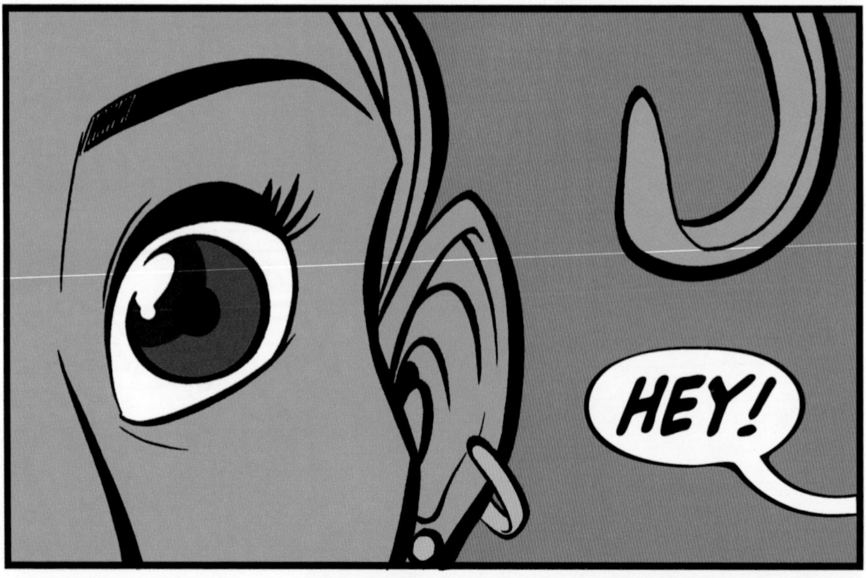
HEY!

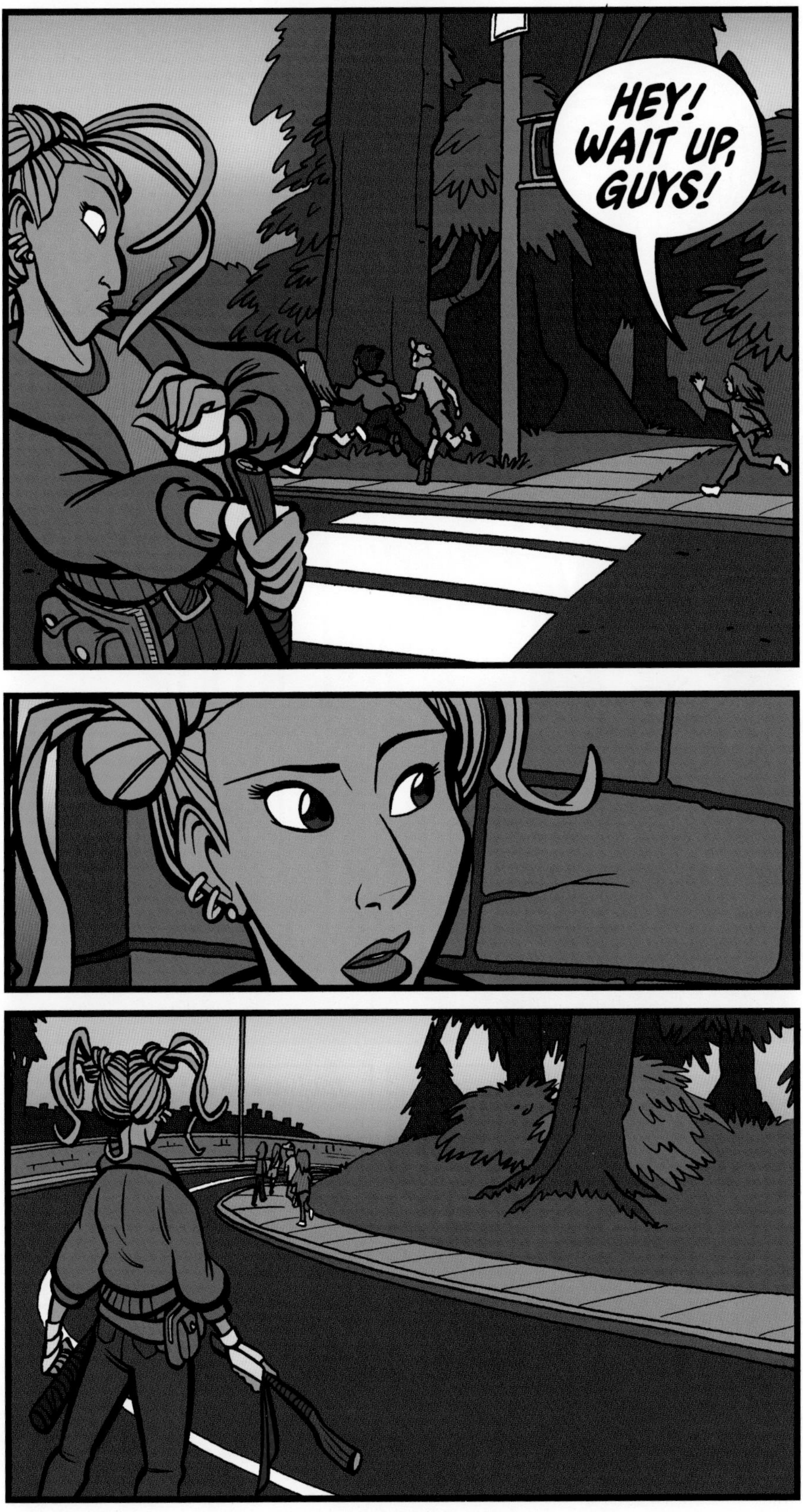
HEY! WAIT UP, GUYS!

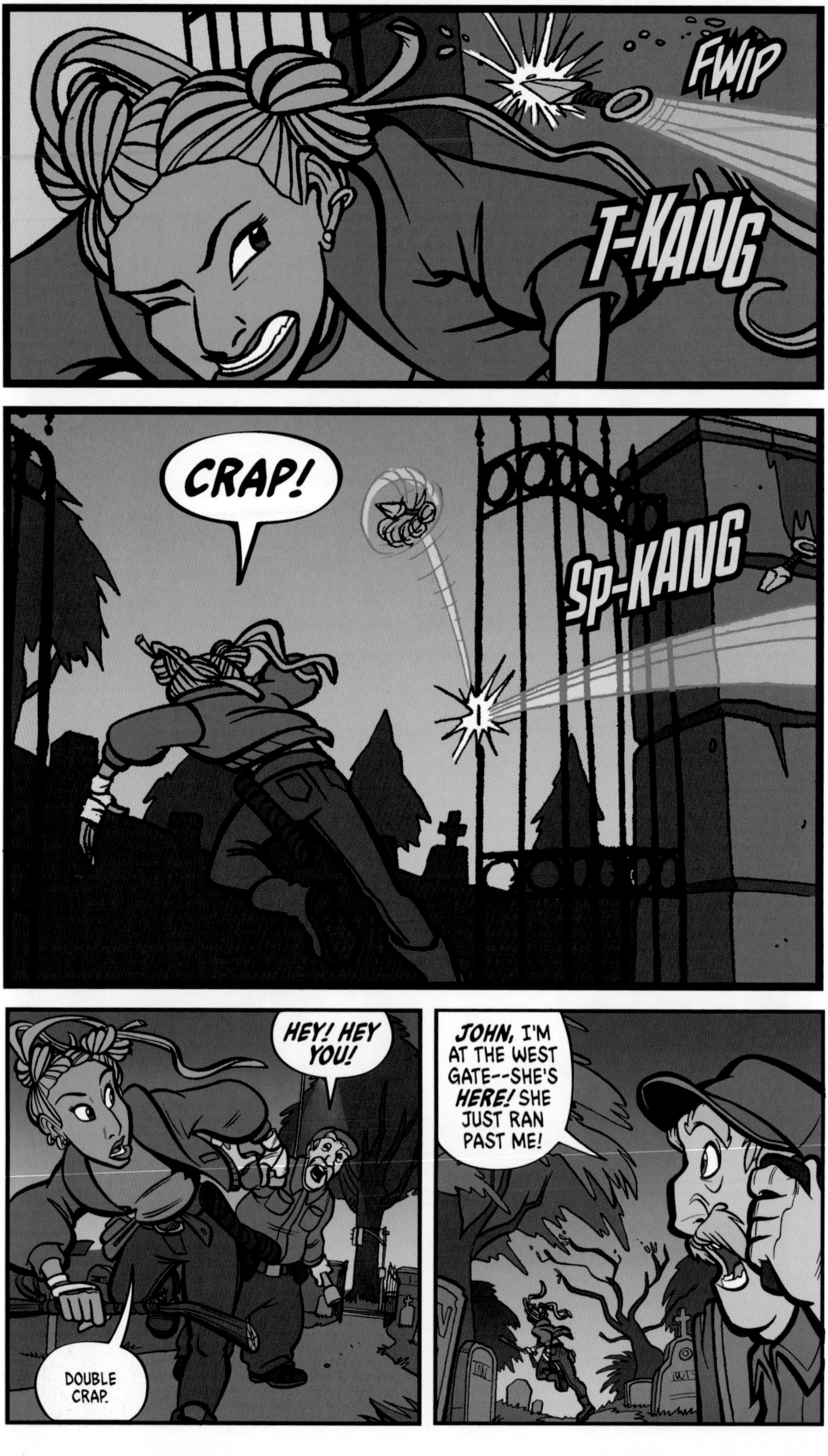
FWIP
T-KANG
CRAP!
Sp-KANG
HEY! HEY YOU!
DOUBLE CRAP.
JOHN, I'M AT THE WEST GATE--SHE'S HERE! SHE JUST RAN PAST ME!

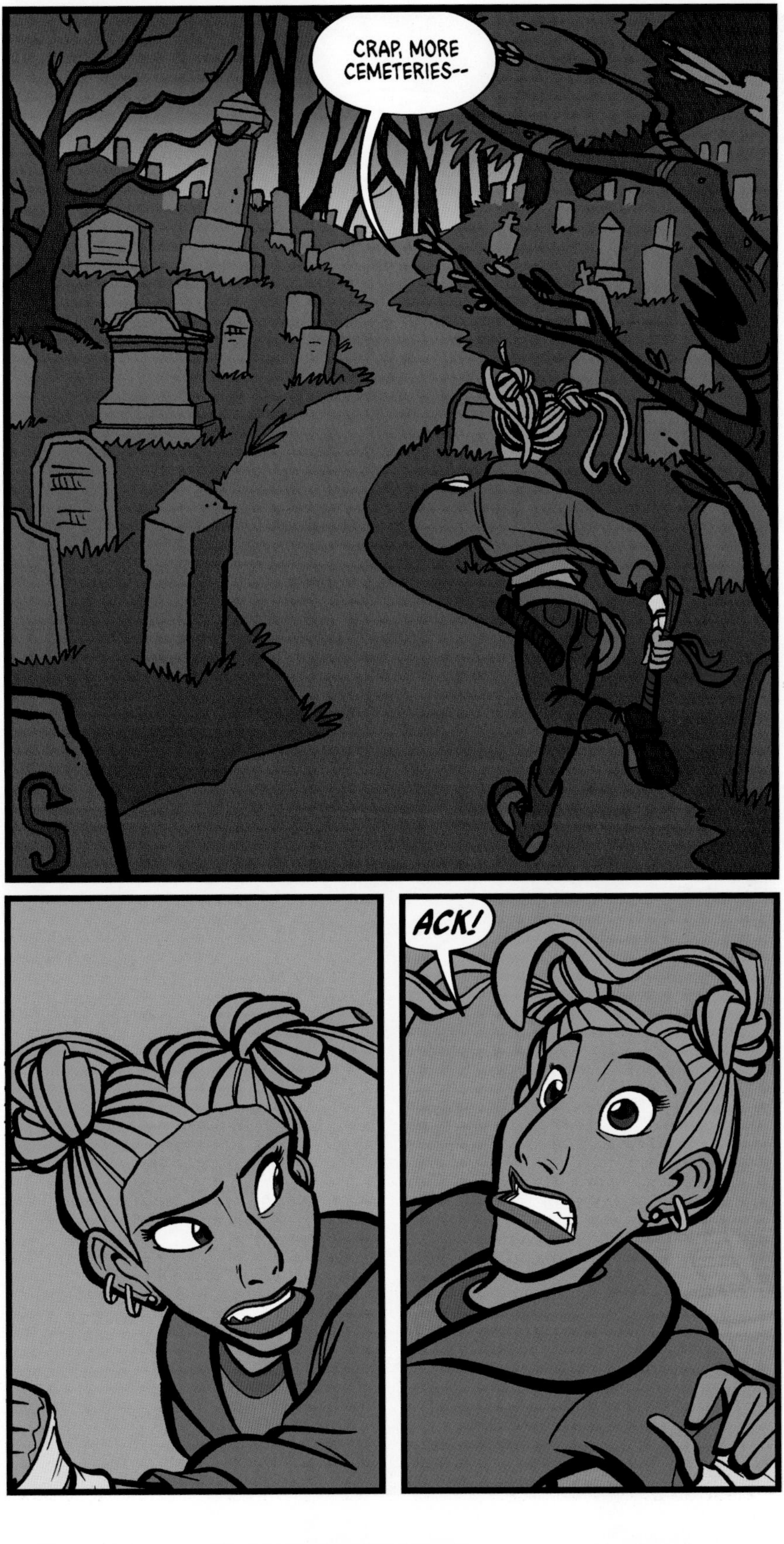
CRAP, MORE CEMETERIES--
ACK!

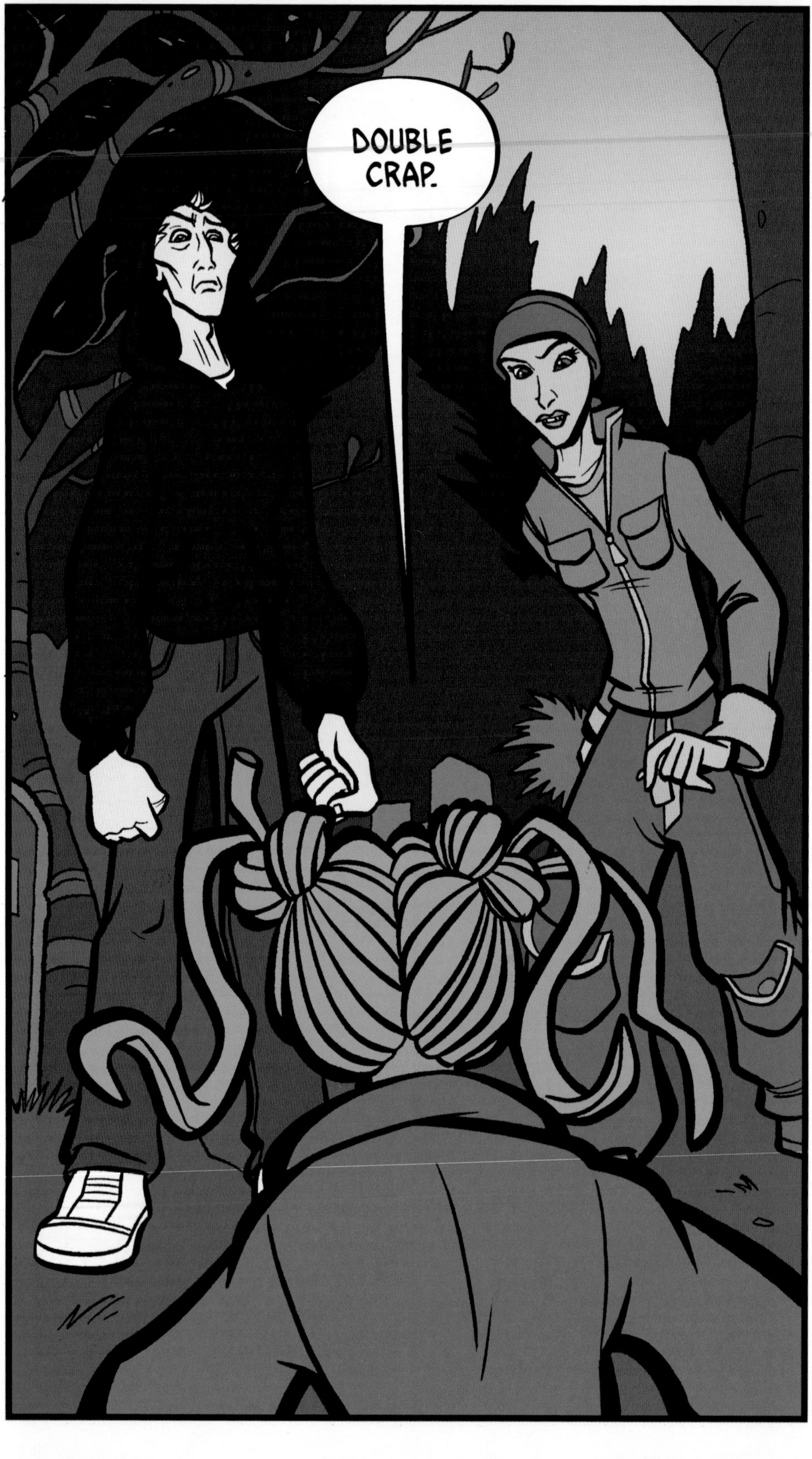
DOUBLE CRAP.

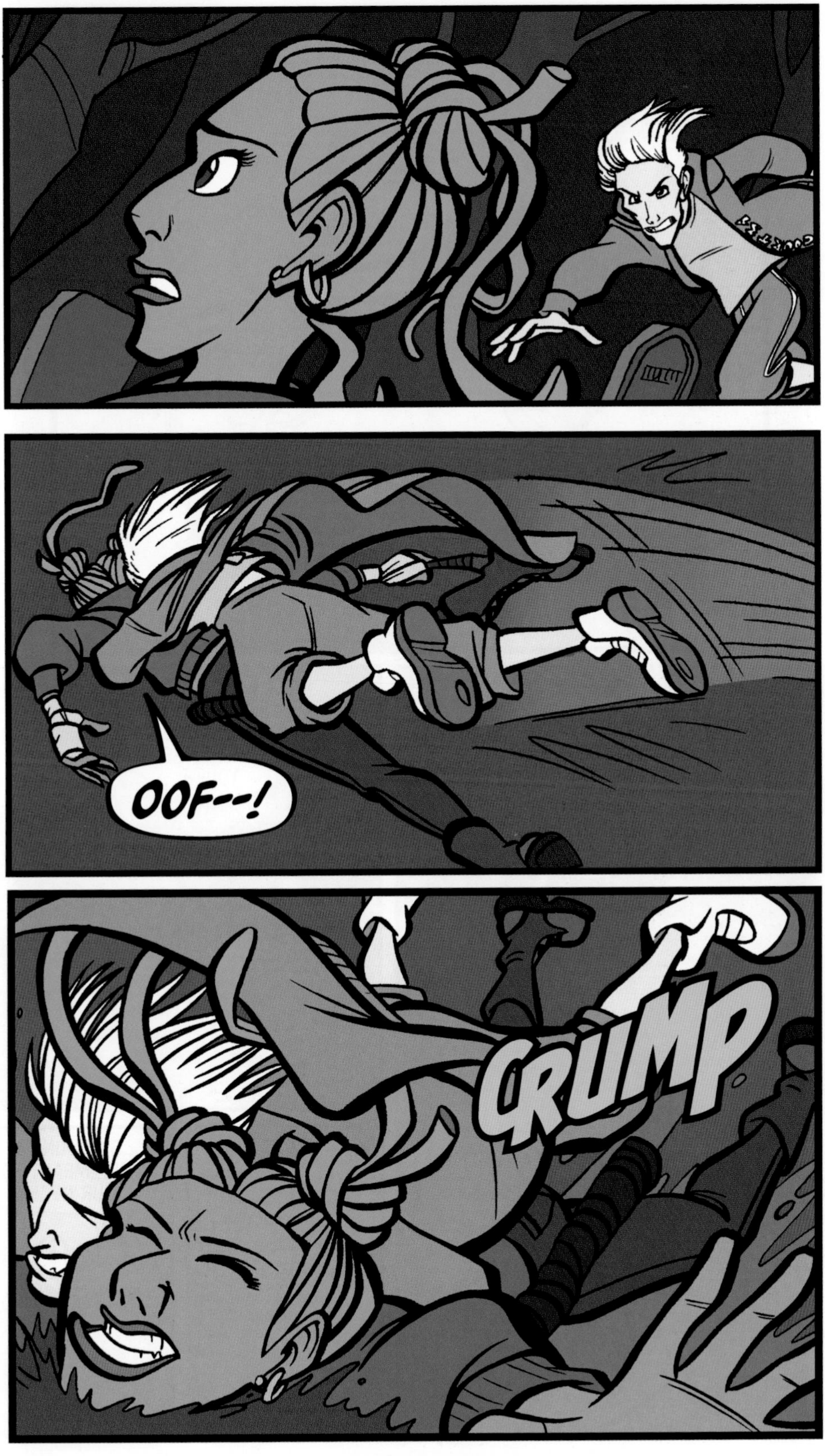
OOF--!
CRUMP

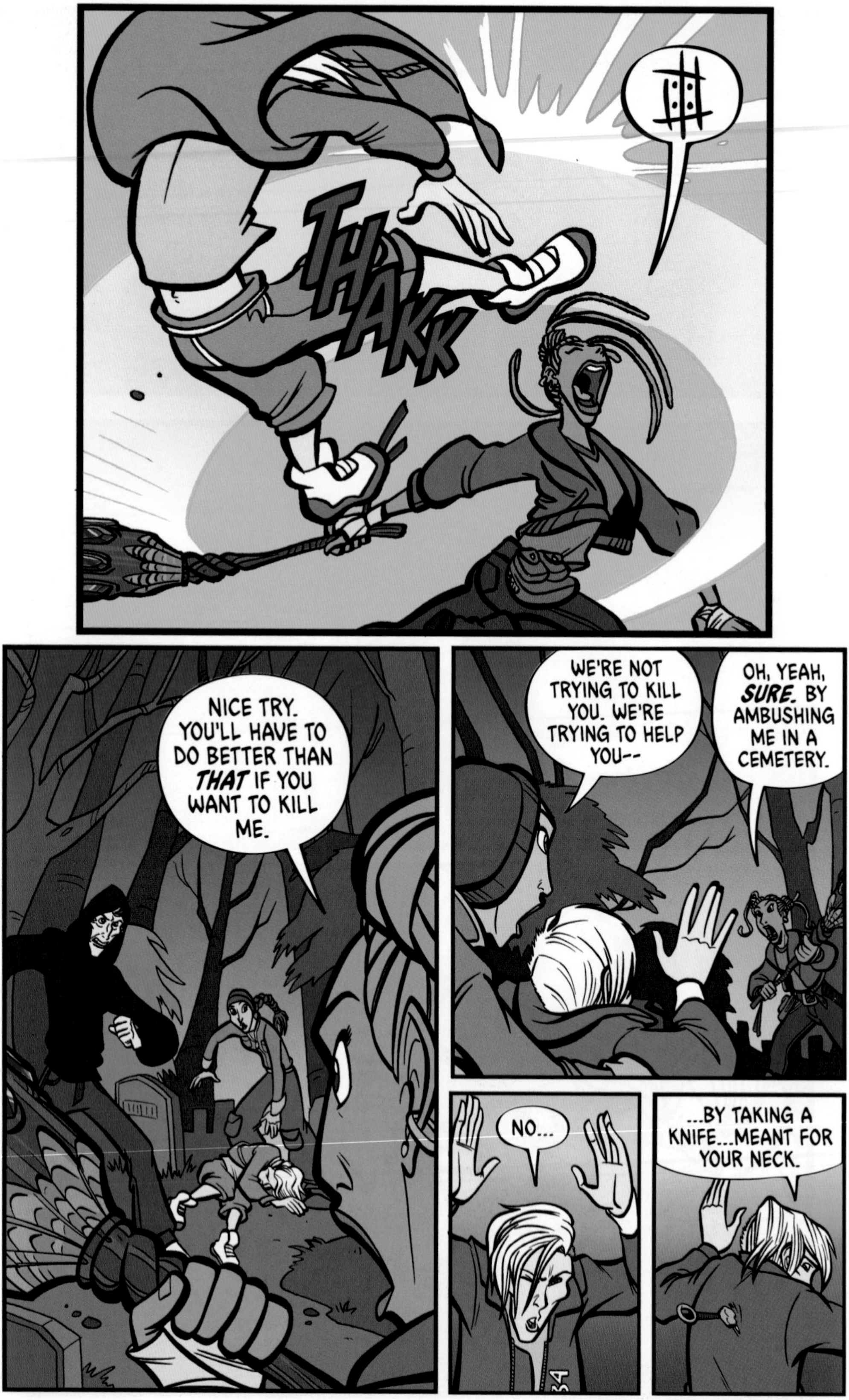
THAKK
NICE TRY. YOU'LL HAVE TO DO BETTER THAN *THAT* IF YOU WANT TO KILL ME.
WE'RE NOT TRYING TO KILL YOU. WE'RE TRYING TO HELP YOU--
OH, YEAH, *SURE.* BY AMBUSHING ME IN A CEMETERY.
NO...
...BY TAKING A KNIFE...MEANT FOR YOUR NECK.

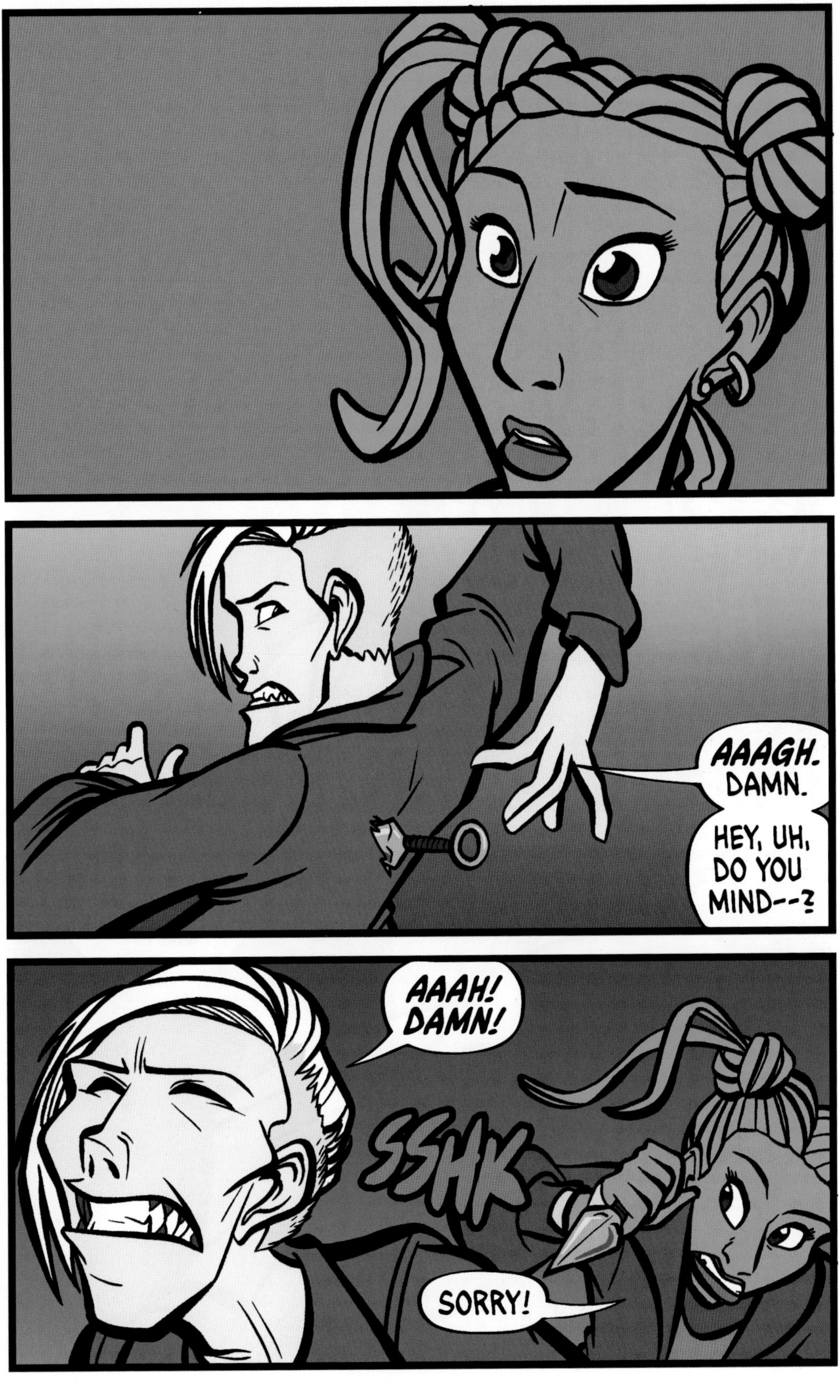
AAAGH. DAMN.
HEY, UH, DO YOU MIND--?
AAAH! DAMN!
SSHK
SORRY!

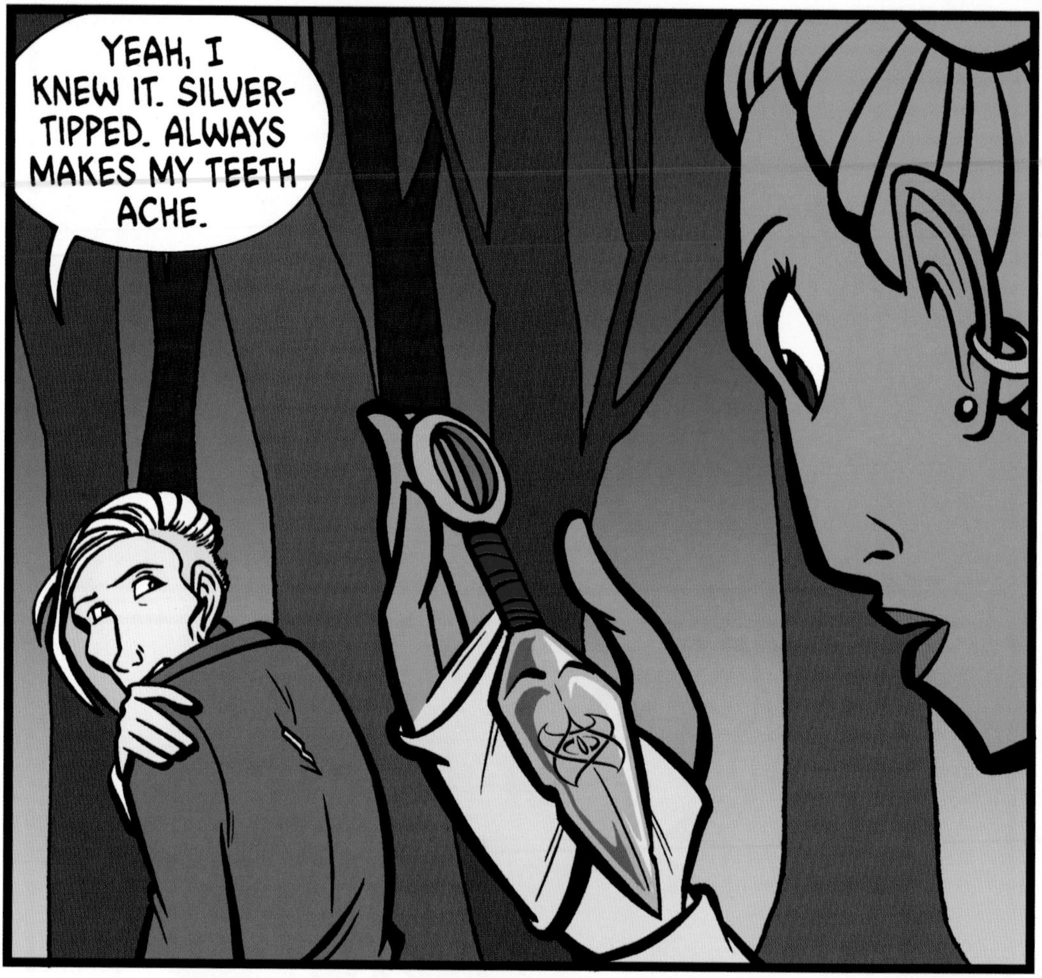
YEAH, I KNEW IT. SILVER-TIPPED. ALWAYS MAKES MY TEETH ACHE.

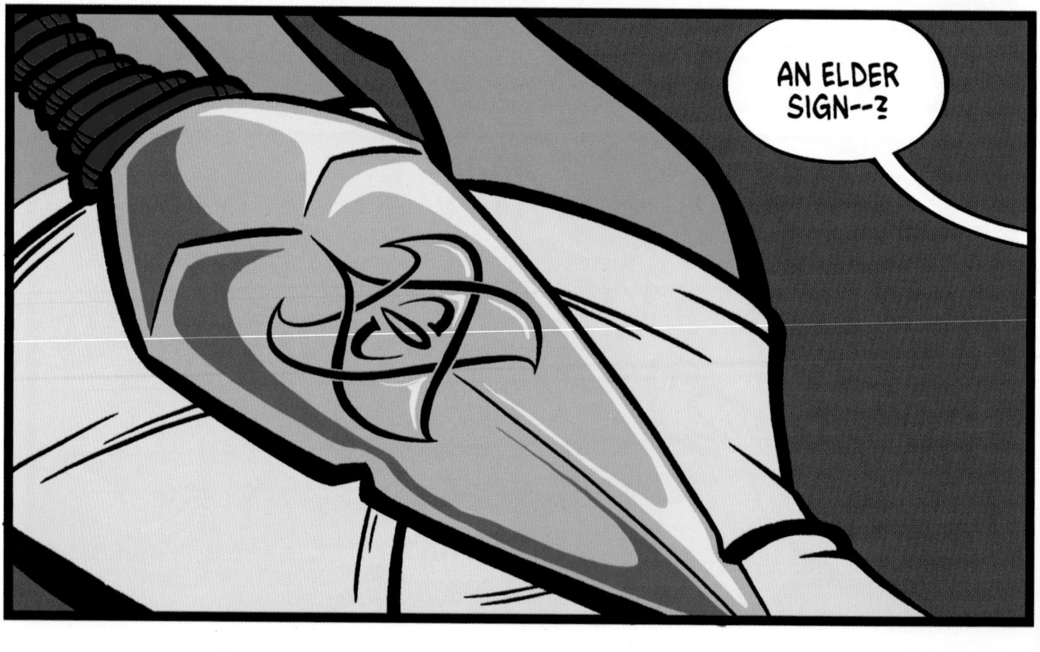
AN ELDER SIGN--?

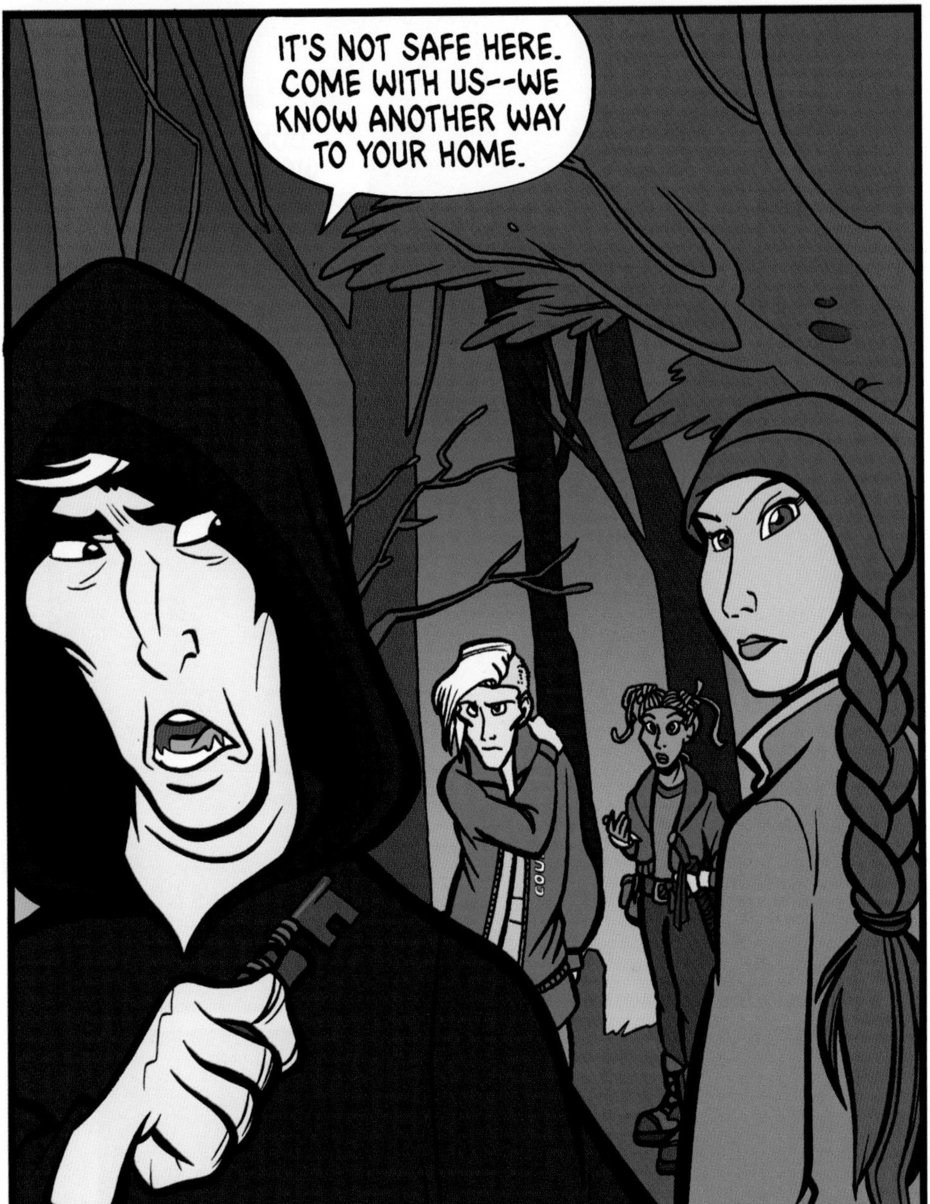
IT'S NOT SAFE HERE. COME WITH US--WE KNOW ANOTHER WAY TO YOUR HOME.

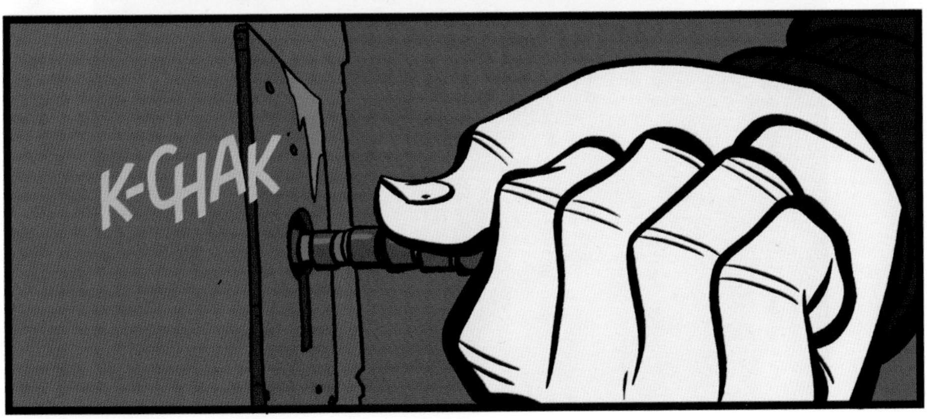
K-CHAK

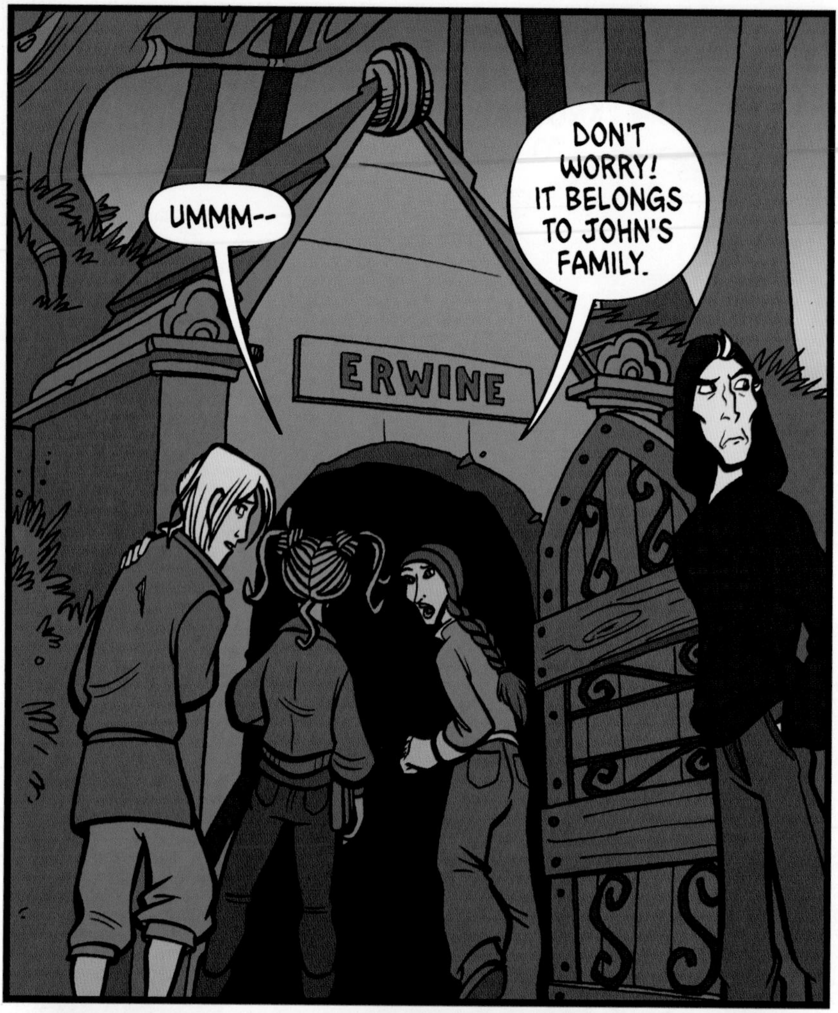
UMMM--
DON'T WORRY! IT BELONGS TO JOHN'S FAMILY.
ERWINE

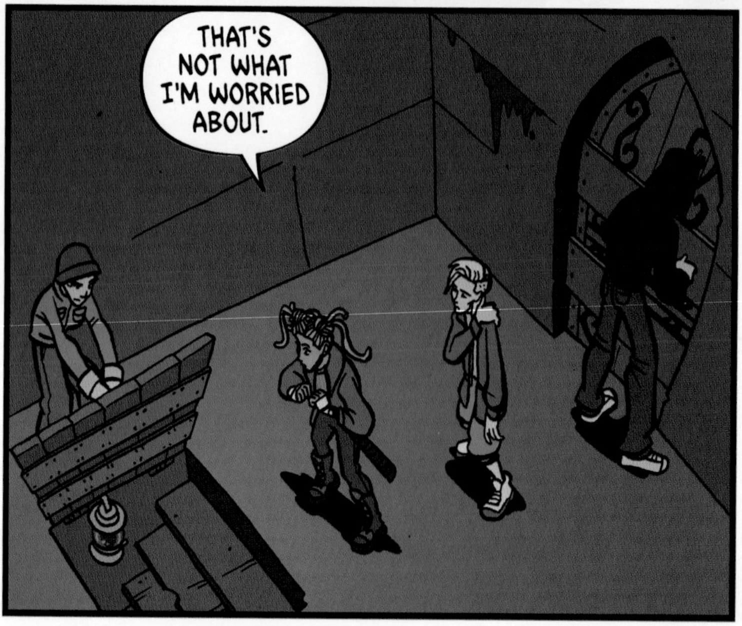
THAT'S NOT WHAT I'M WORRIED ABOUT.

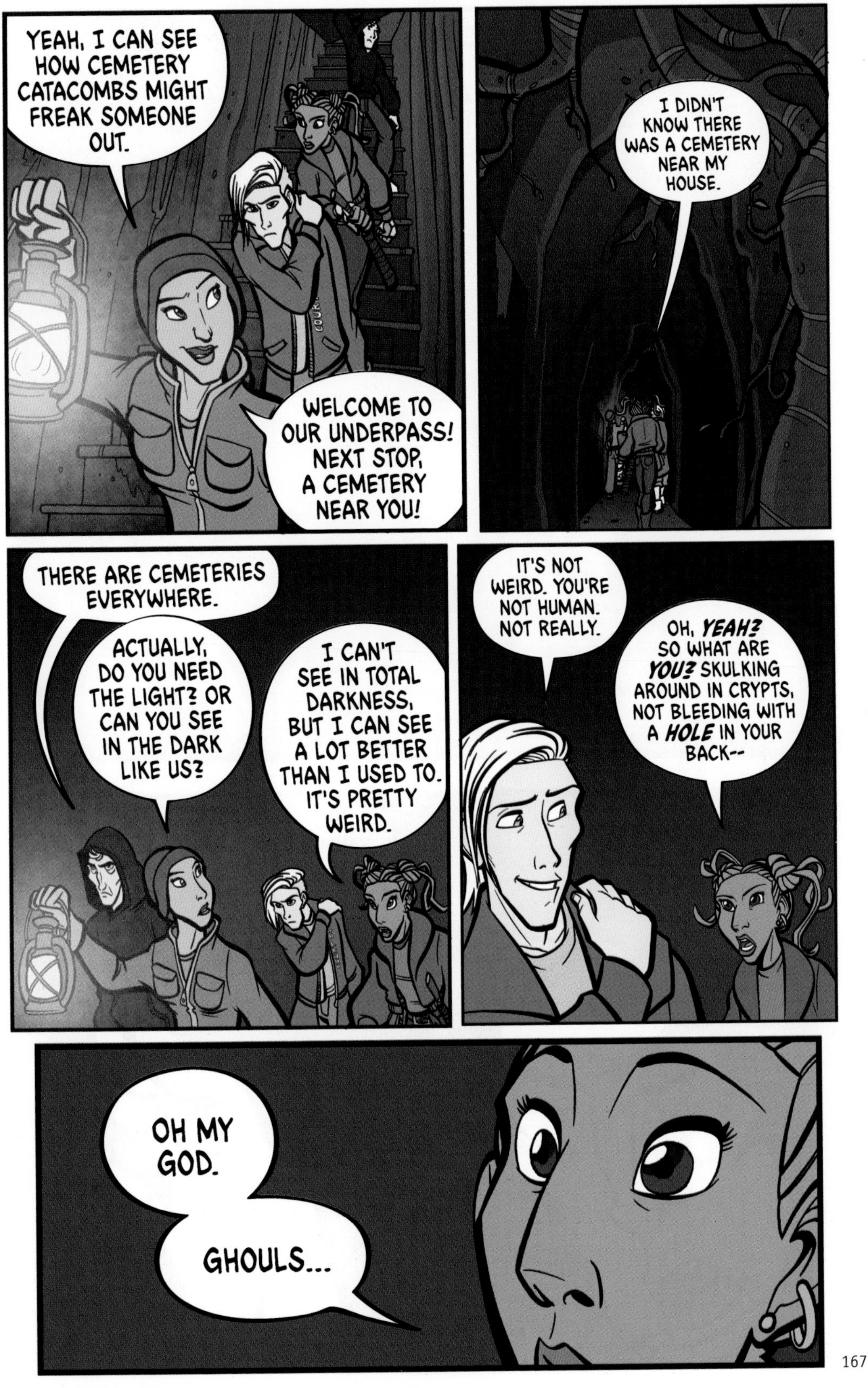
YEAH, I CAN SEE HOW CEMETERY CATACOMBS MIGHT FREAK SOMEONE OUT.
WELCOME TO OUR UNDERPASS! NEXT STOP, A CEMETERY NEAR YOU!
I DIDN'T KNOW THERE WAS A CEMETERY NEAR MY HOUSE.
THERE ARE CEMETERIES EVERYWHERE.
ACTUALLY, DO YOU NEED THE LIGHT? OR CAN YOU SEE IN THE DARK LIKE US?
I CAN'T SEE IN TOTAL DARKNESS, BUT I CAN SEE A LOT BETTER THAN I USED TO. IT'S PRETTY WEIRD.
IT'S NOT WEIRD. YOU'RE NOT HUMAN. NOT REALLY.
OH, *YEAH?* SO WHAT ARE *YOU?* SKULKING AROUND IN CRYPTS, NOT BLEEDING WITH A *HOLE* IN YOUR BACK--
OH MY GOD.
GHOULS...

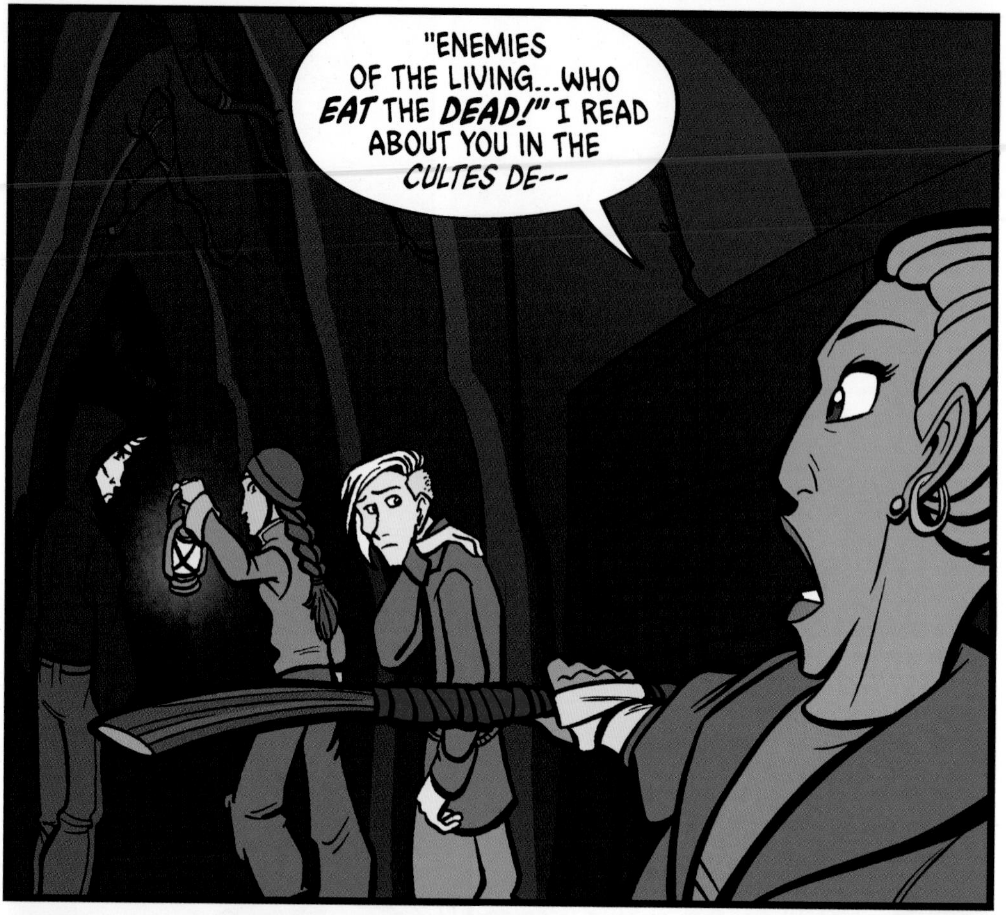
"ENEMIES OF THE LIVING...WHO EAT THE DEAD!" I READ ABOUT YOU IN THE CULTES DE--

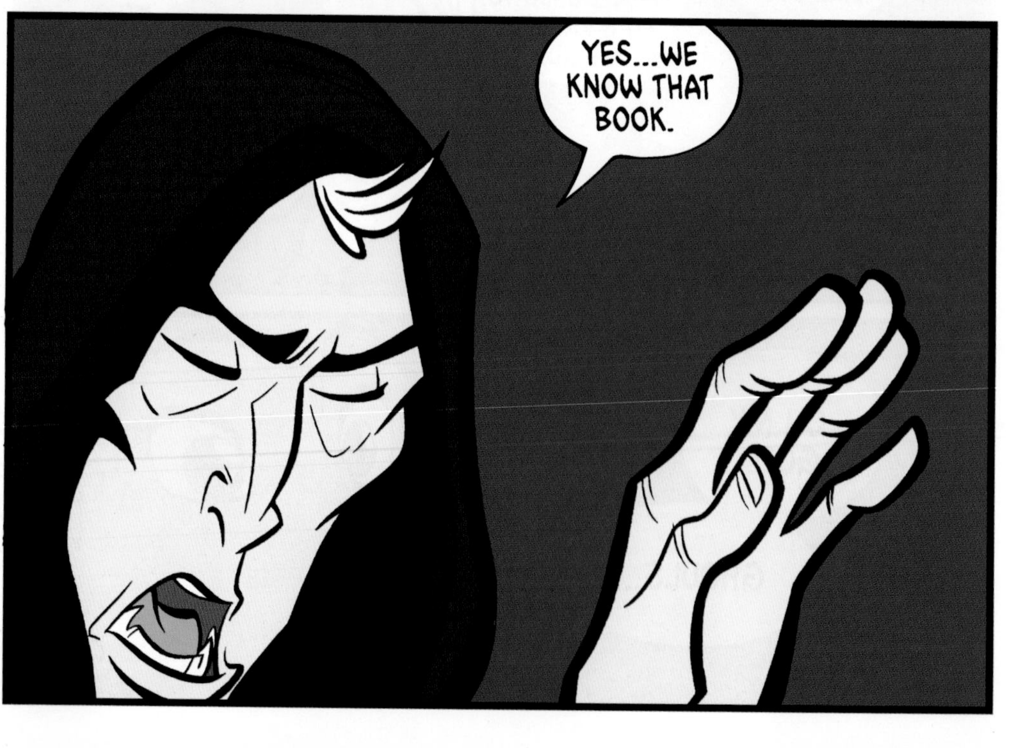
YES...WE KNOW THAT BOOK.

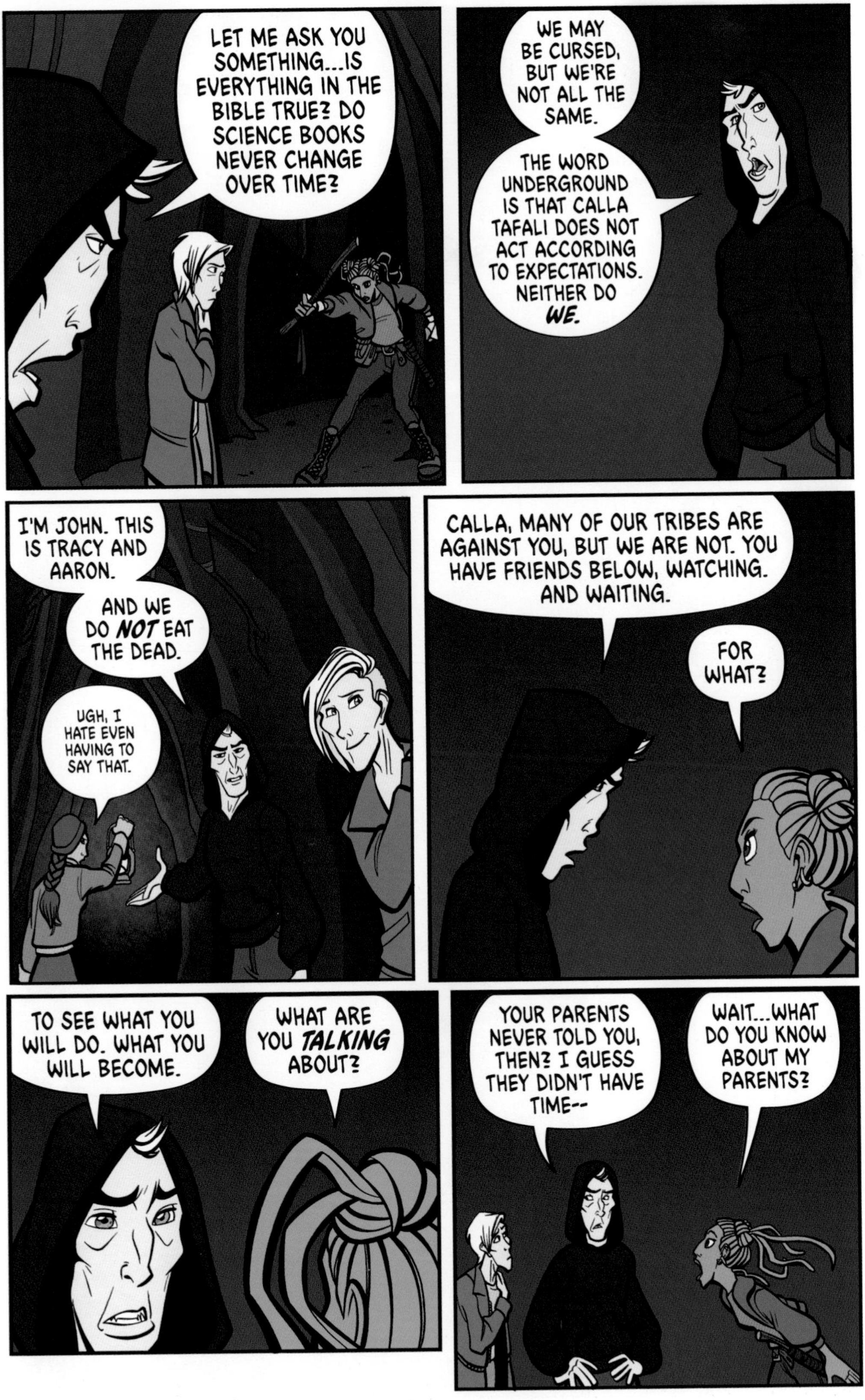
LET ME ASK YOU SOMETHING...IS EVERYTHING IN THE BIBLE TRUE? DO SCIENCE BOOKS NEVER CHANGE OVER TIME?
WE MAY BE CURSED, BUT WE'RE NOT ALL THE SAME.
THE WORD UNDERGROUND IS THAT CALLA TAFALI DOES NOT ACT ACCORDING TO EXPECTATIONS. NEITHER DO *WE.*
I'M JOHN. THIS IS TRACY AND AARON.
AND WE DO *NOT* EAT THE DEAD.
UGH, I HATE EVEN HAVING TO SAY THAT.
CALLA, MANY OF OUR TRIBES ARE AGAINST YOU, BUT WE ARE NOT. YOU HAVE FRIENDS BELOW, WATCHING. AND WAITING.
FOR WHAT?
TO SEE WHAT YOU WILL DO. WHAT YOU WILL BECOME.
WHAT ARE YOU *TALKING* ABOUT?
YOUR PARENTS NEVER TOLD YOU, THEN? I GUESS THEY DIDN'T HAVE TIME--
WAIT...WHAT DO YOU KNOW ABOUT MY PARENTS?

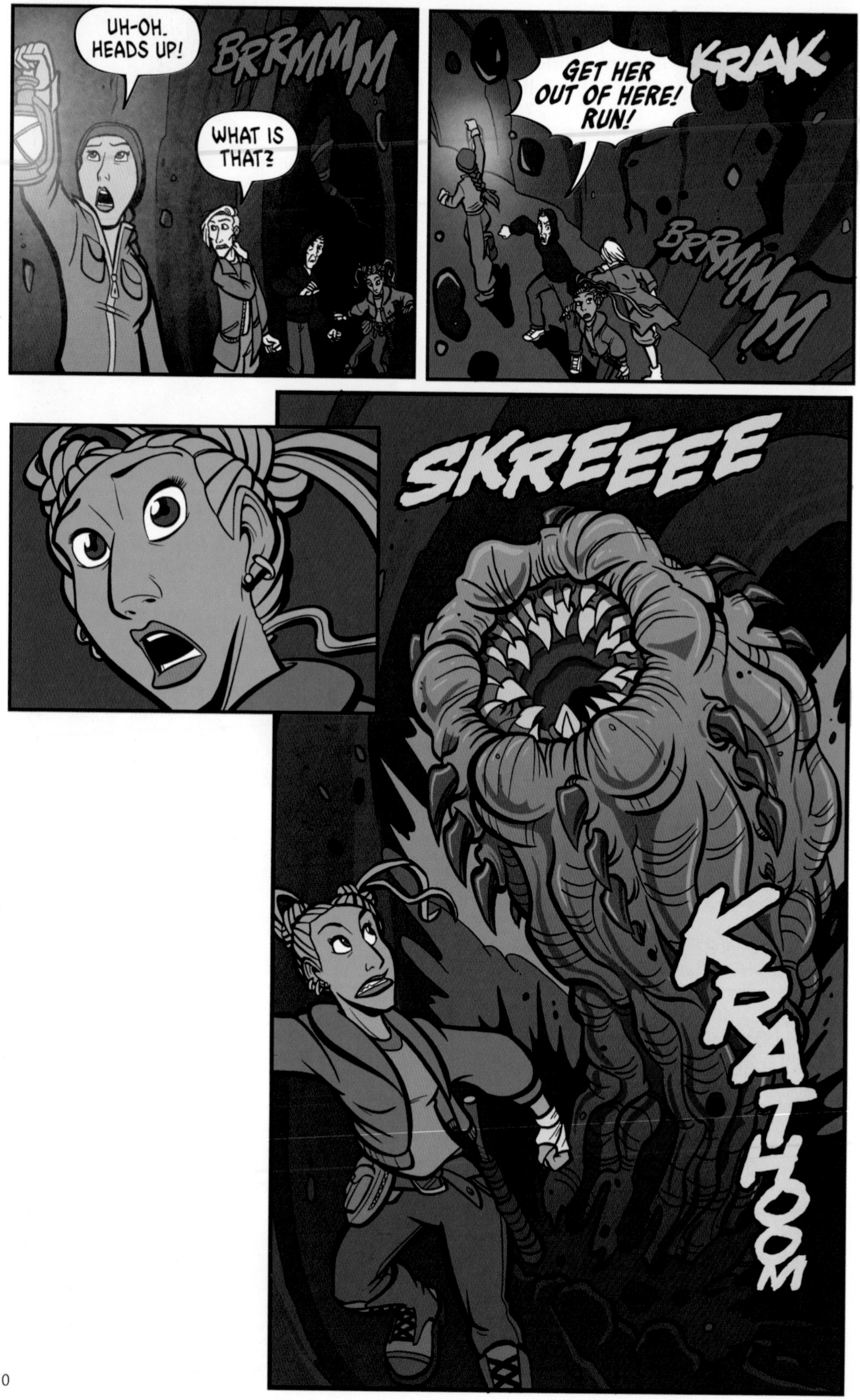
UH-OH. HEADS UP!
BRRMMM
WHAT IS THAT?
GET HER OUT OF HERE! RUN!
KRAK
BRRMMMM
SKREEEEE
KRATHOOM

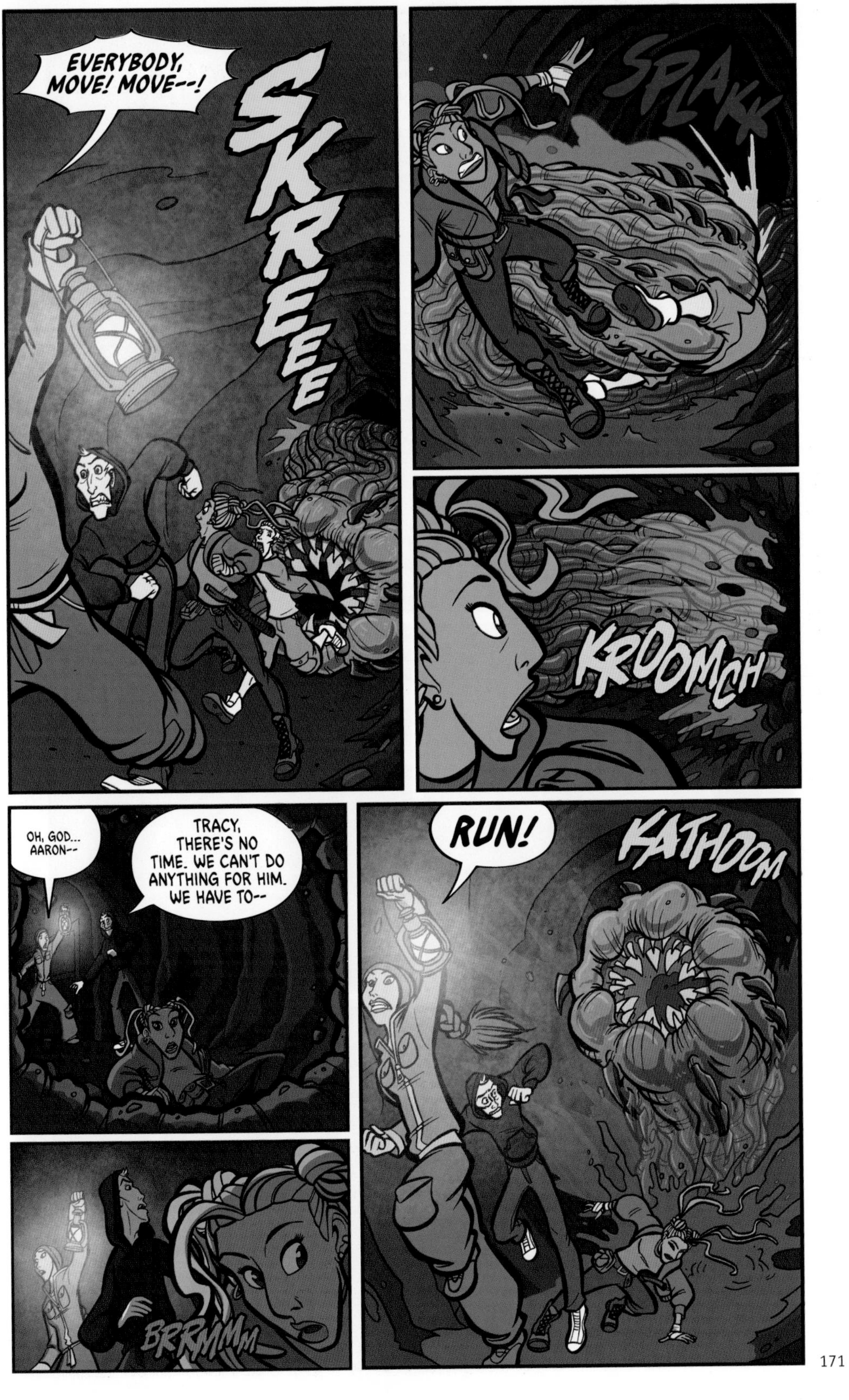
EVERYBODY, MOVE! MOVE--!
SKREEEE
SPLAKK
KROOMCH
OH, GOD... AARON--
TRACY, THERE'S NO TIME. WE CAN'T DO ANYTHING FOR HIM. WE HAVE TO--
BRRMMM
RUN!
KATHOOM

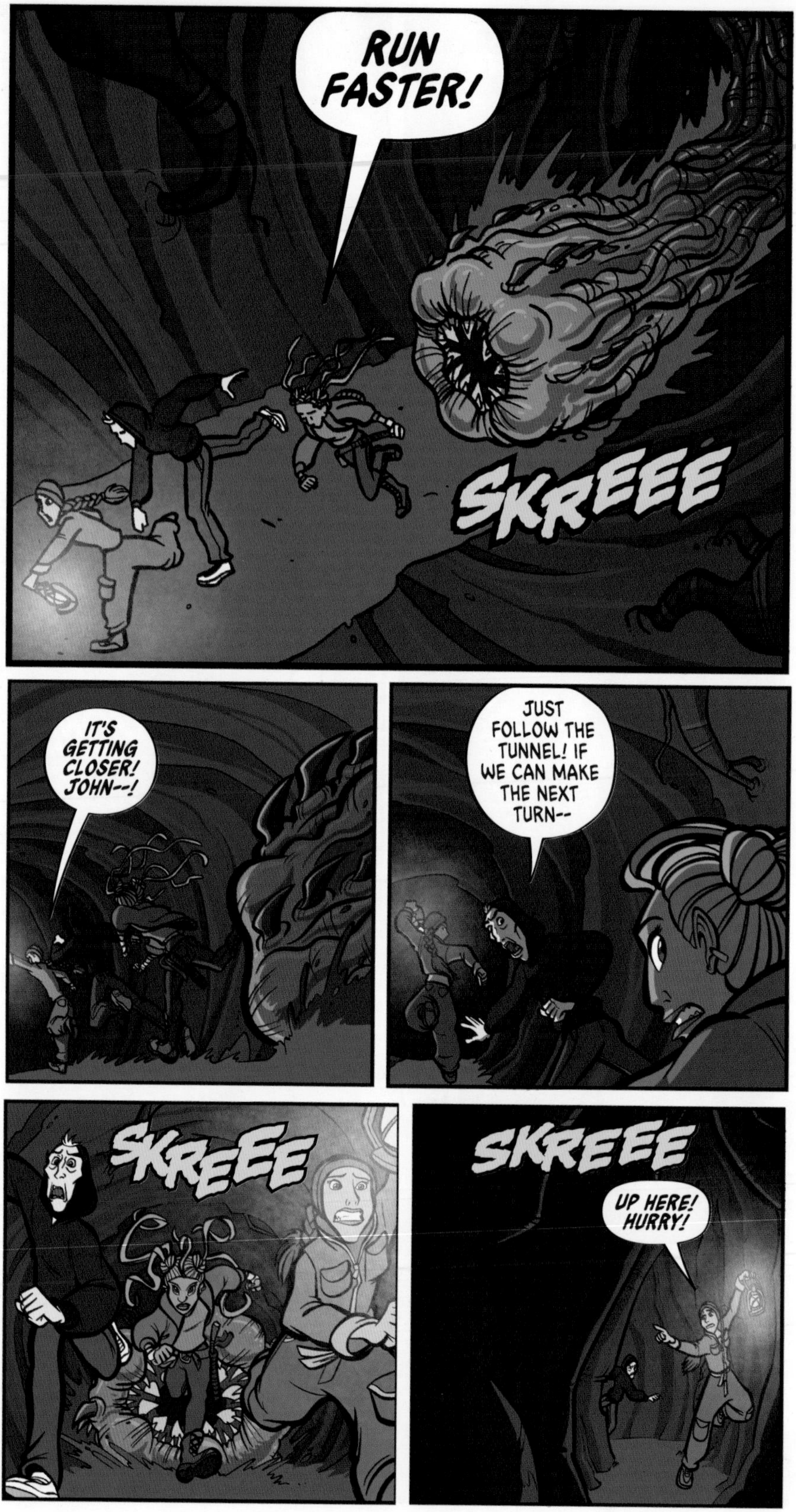
RUN FASTER!
SKREEE
IT'S GETTING CLOSER! JOHN--!
JUST FOLLOW THE TUNNEL! IF WE CAN MAKE THE NEXT TURN--
SKREEE
SKREEE
UP HERE! HURRY!

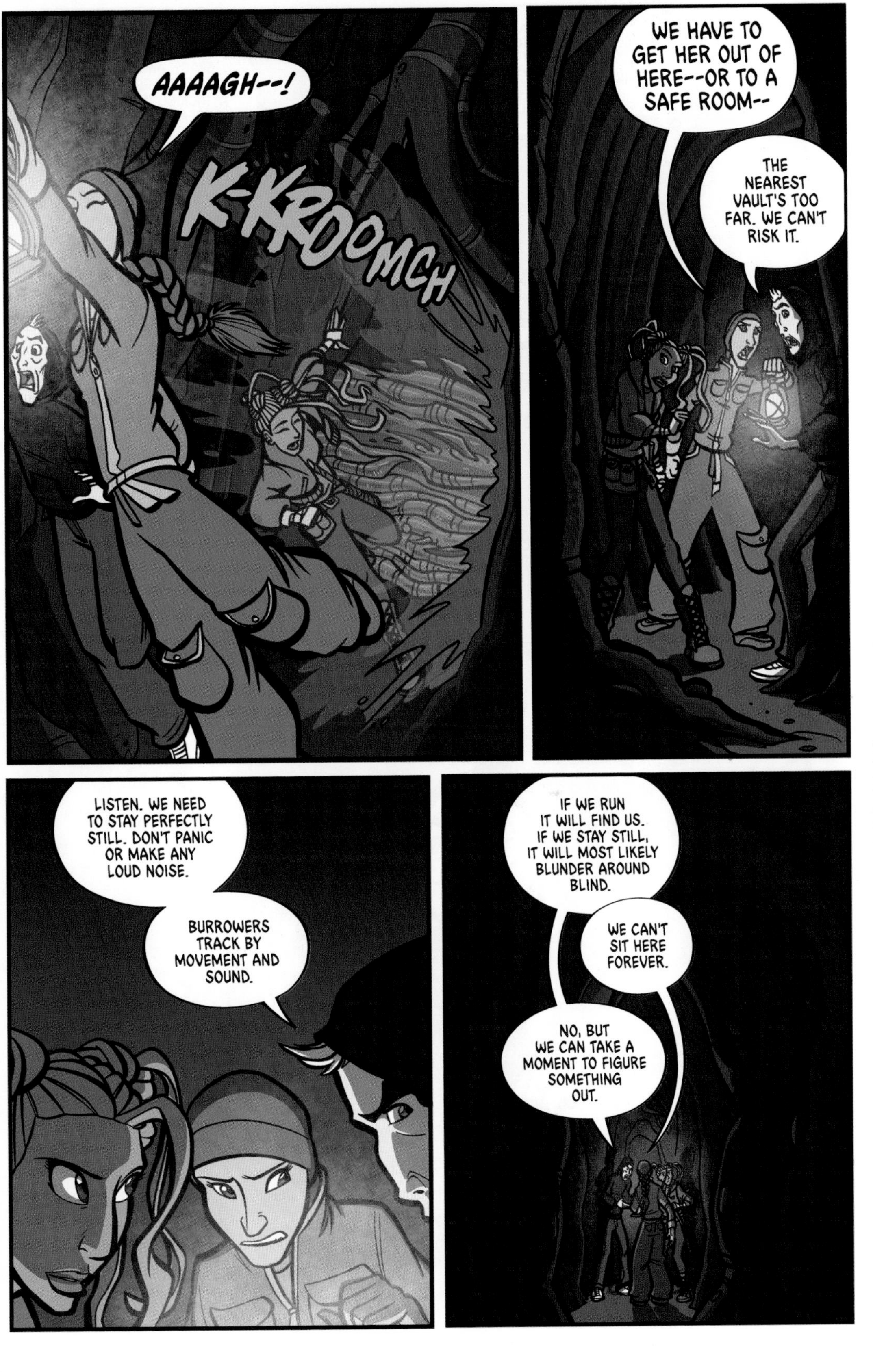
AAAAGH--!
K-KROOMCH
WE HAVE TO GET HER OUT OF HERE--OR TO A SAFE ROOM--
THE NEAREST VAULT'S TOO FAR. WE CAN'T RISK IT.
LISTEN. WE NEED TO STAY PERFECTLY STILL. DON'T PANIC OR MAKE ANY LOUD NOISE.
BURROWERS TRACK BY MOVEMENT AND SOUND.
IF WE RUN IT WILL FIND US. IF WE STAY STILL, IT WILL MOST LIKELY BLUNDER AROUND BLIND.
WE CAN'T SIT HERE FOREVER.
NO, BUT WE CAN TAKE A MOMENT TO FIGURE SOMETHING OUT.

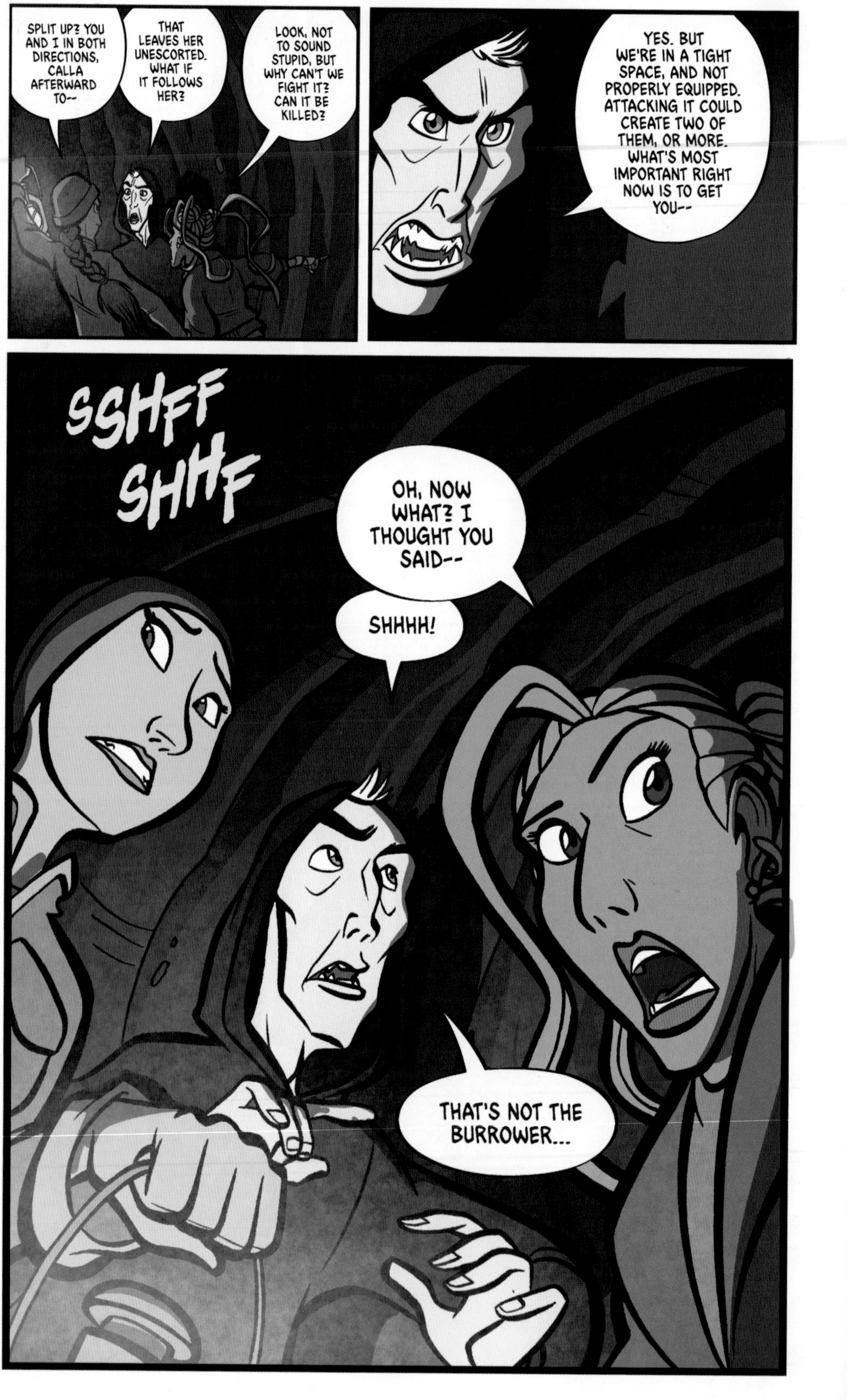
SPLIT UP? YOU AND I IN BOTH DIRECTIONS, CALLA AFTERWARD TO--
THAT LEAVES HER UNESCORTED. WHAT IF IT FOLLOWS HER?
LOOK, NOT TO SOUND STUPID, BUT WHY CAN'T WE FIGHT IT? CAN IT BE KILLED?
YES. BUT WE'RE IN A TIGHT SPACE, AND NOT PROPERLY EQUIPPED. ATTACKING IT COULD CREATE TWO OF THEM, OR MORE. WHAT'S MOST IMPORTANT RIGHT NOW IS TO GET YOU--
SSHFF SHHF
OH, NOW WHAT? I THOUGHT YOU SAID--
SHHHH!
THAT'S NOT THE BURROWER...

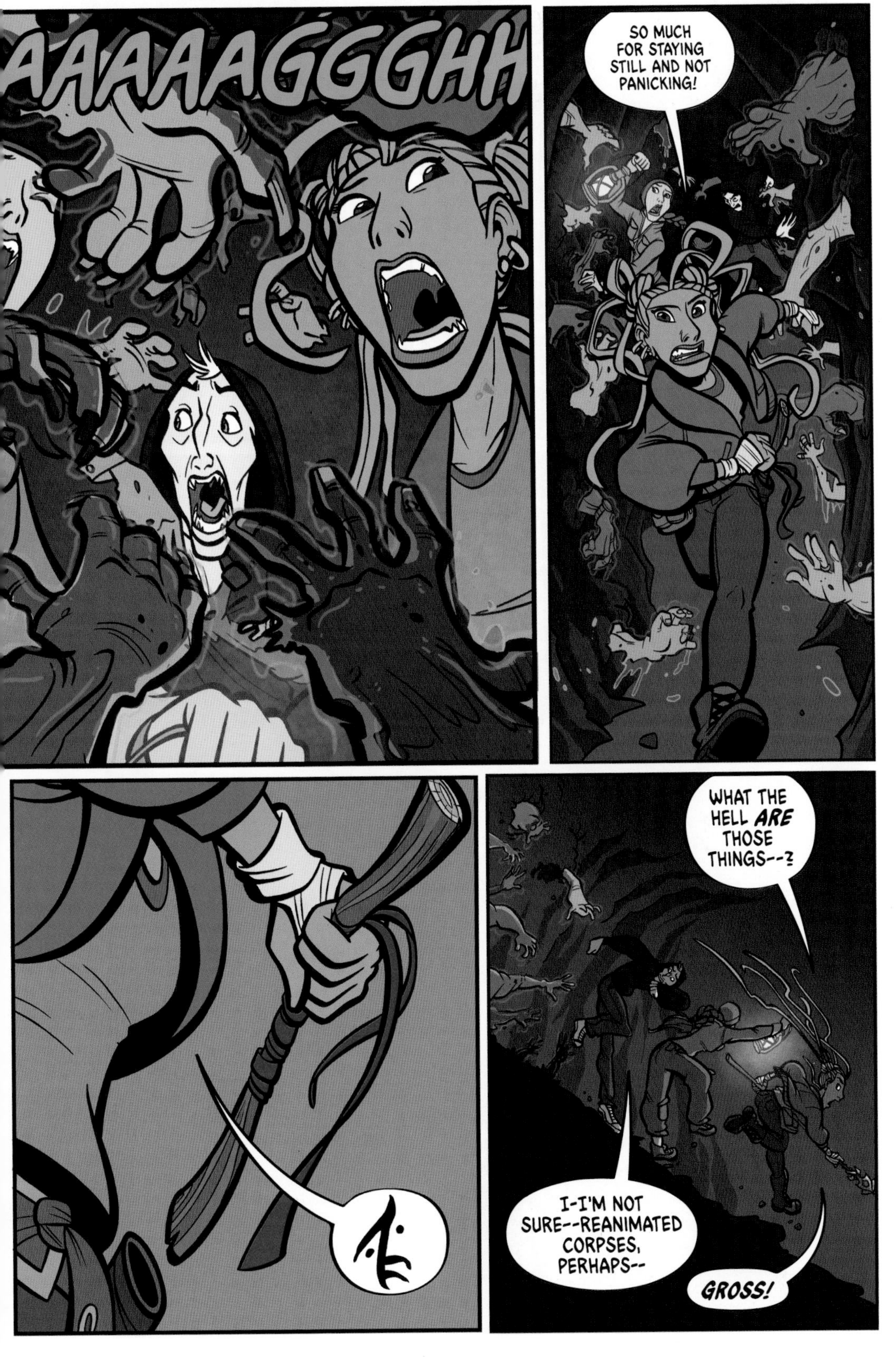
AAAAAAGGGGHH
SO MUCH FOR STAYING STILL AND NOT PANICKING!
WHAT THE HELL *ARE* THOSE THINGS--?
I-I'M NOT SURE--REANIMATED CORPSES, PERHAPS--
GROSS!

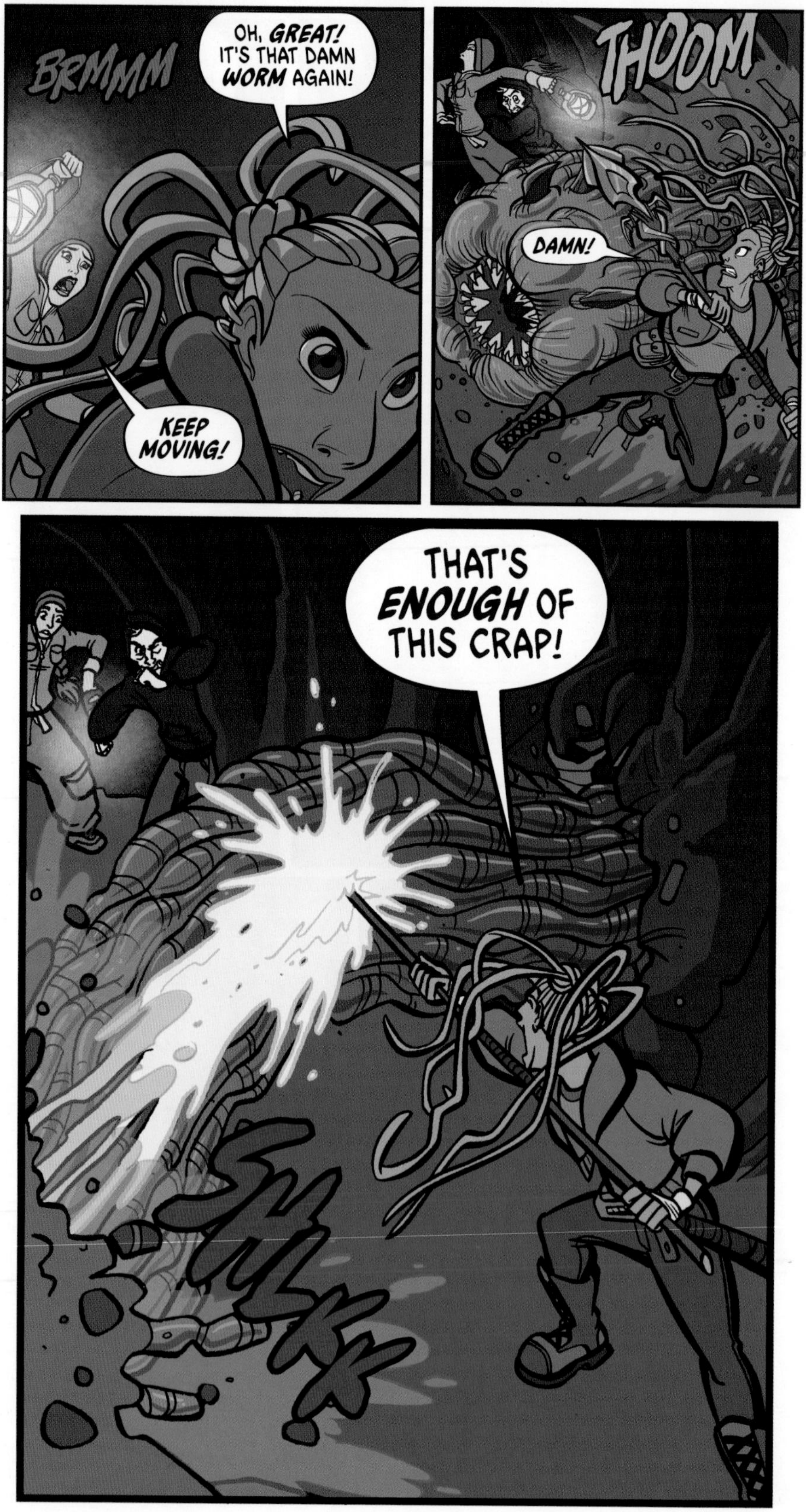
BRMMM
OH, GREAT! IT'S THAT DAMN WORM AGAIN!
KEEP MOVING!
THOOM
DAMN!
THAT'S ENOUGH OF THIS CRAP!
SHLKK

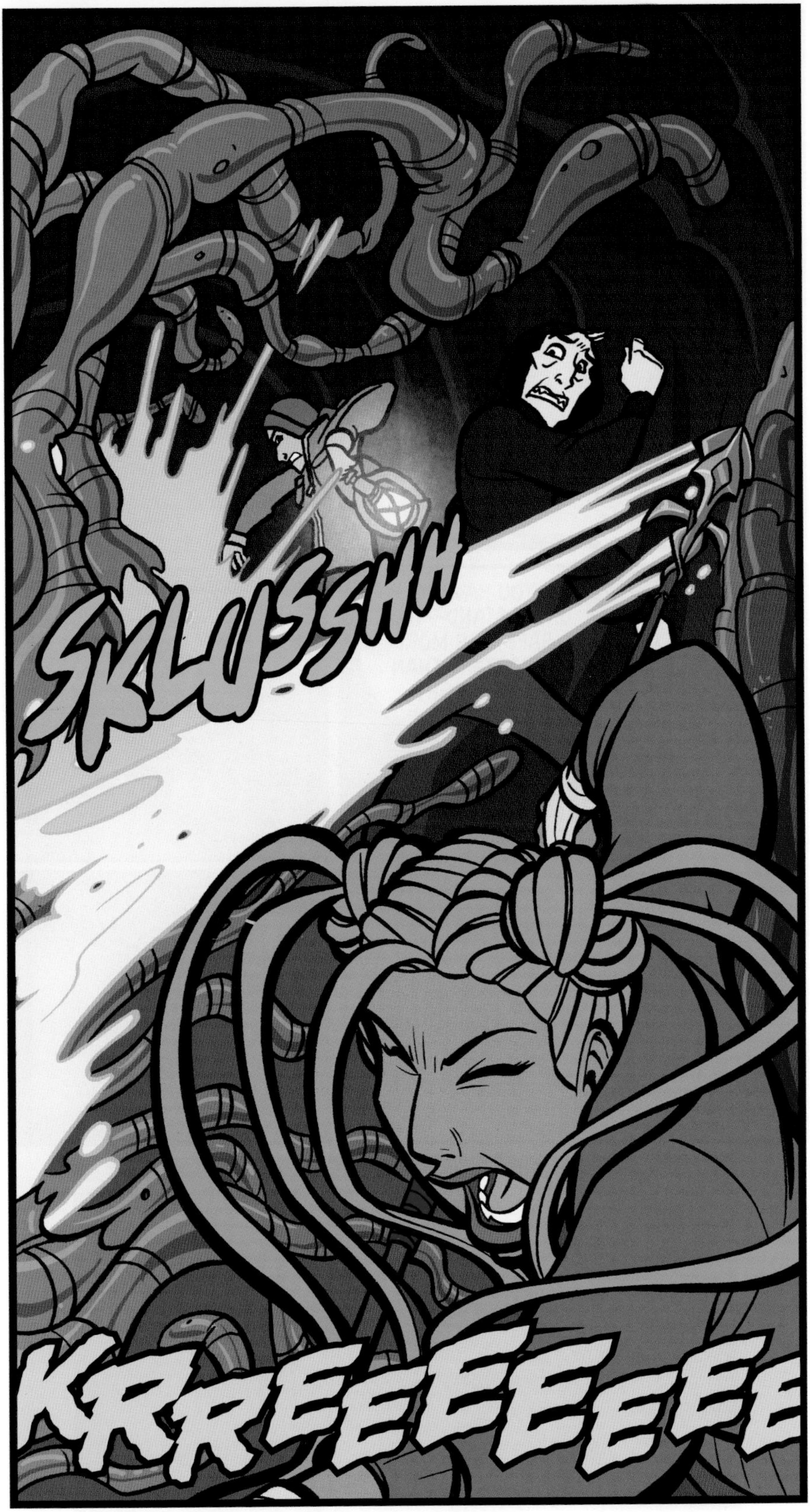
SKLUSSHH
KRREEEEEEEE

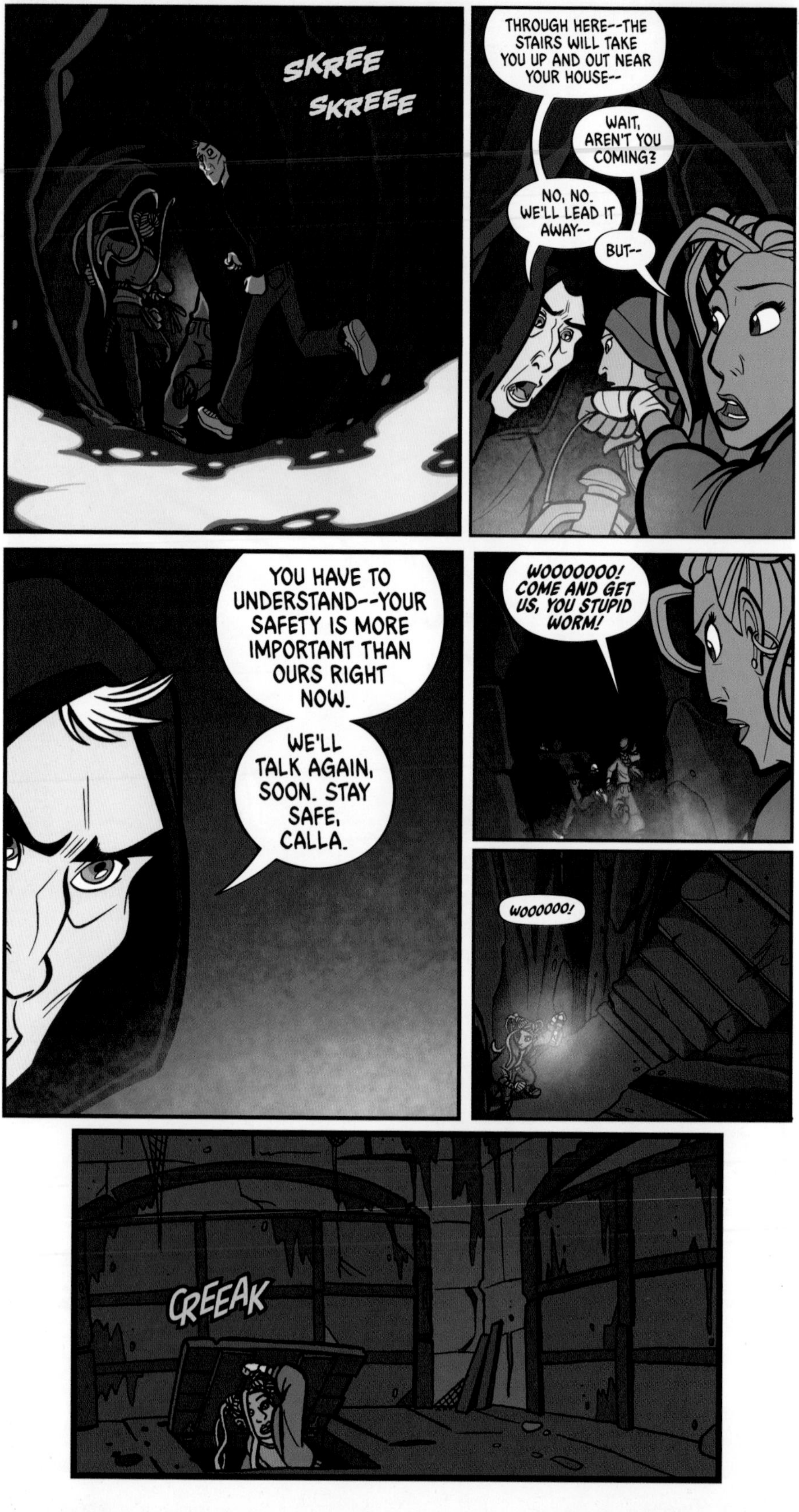
SKREE
SKREEE
THROUGH HERE--THE STAIRS WILL TAKE YOU UP AND OUT NEAR YOUR HOUSE--
WAIT, AREN'T YOU COMING?
NO, NO. WE'LL LEAD IT AWAY--
BUT--
YOU HAVE TO UNDERSTAND--YOUR SAFETY IS MORE IMPORTANT THAN OURS RIGHT NOW.
WE'LL TALK AGAIN, SOON. STAY SAFE, CALLA.
WOOOOOOO! COME AND GET US, YOU STUPID WORM!
WOOOOOO!
CREEAK

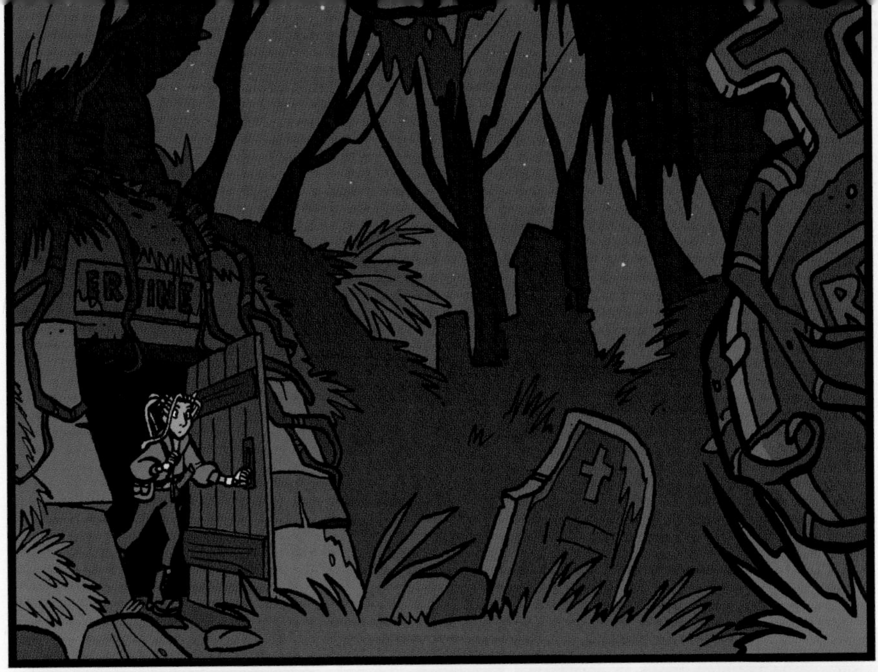

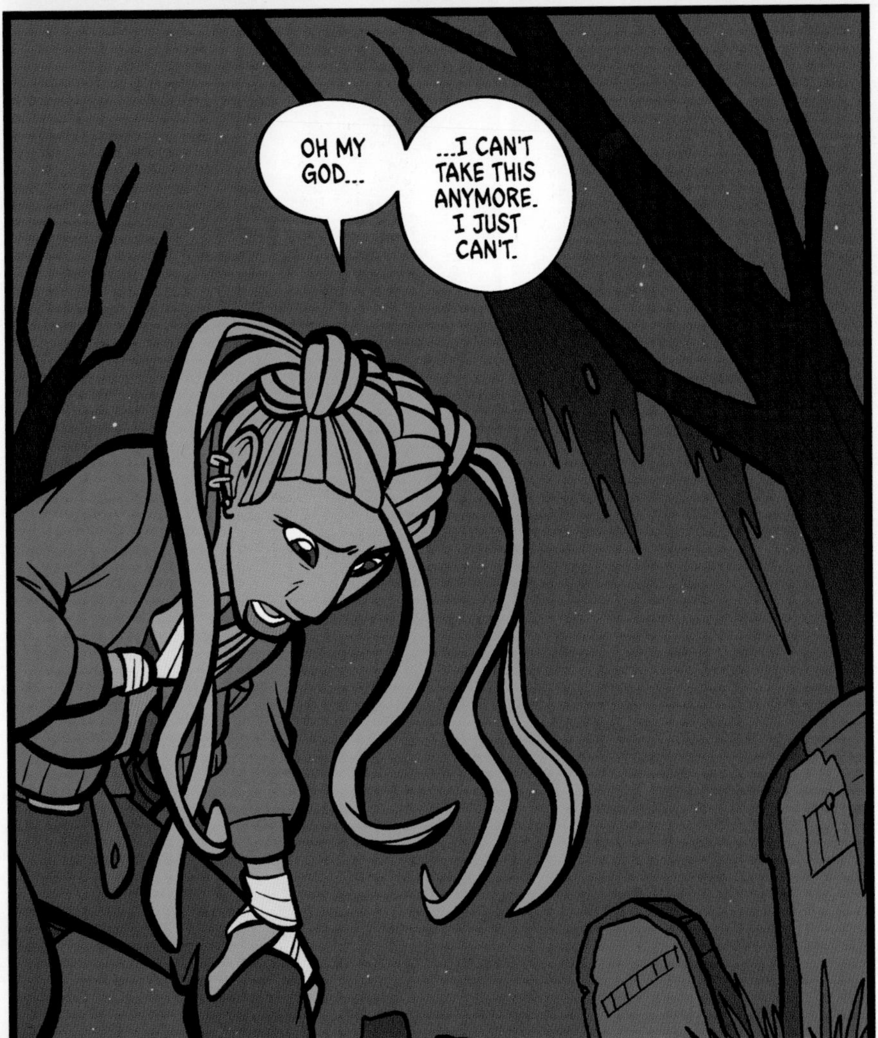
OH MY GOD...
...I CAN'T TAKE THIS ANYMORE. I JUST CAN'T.

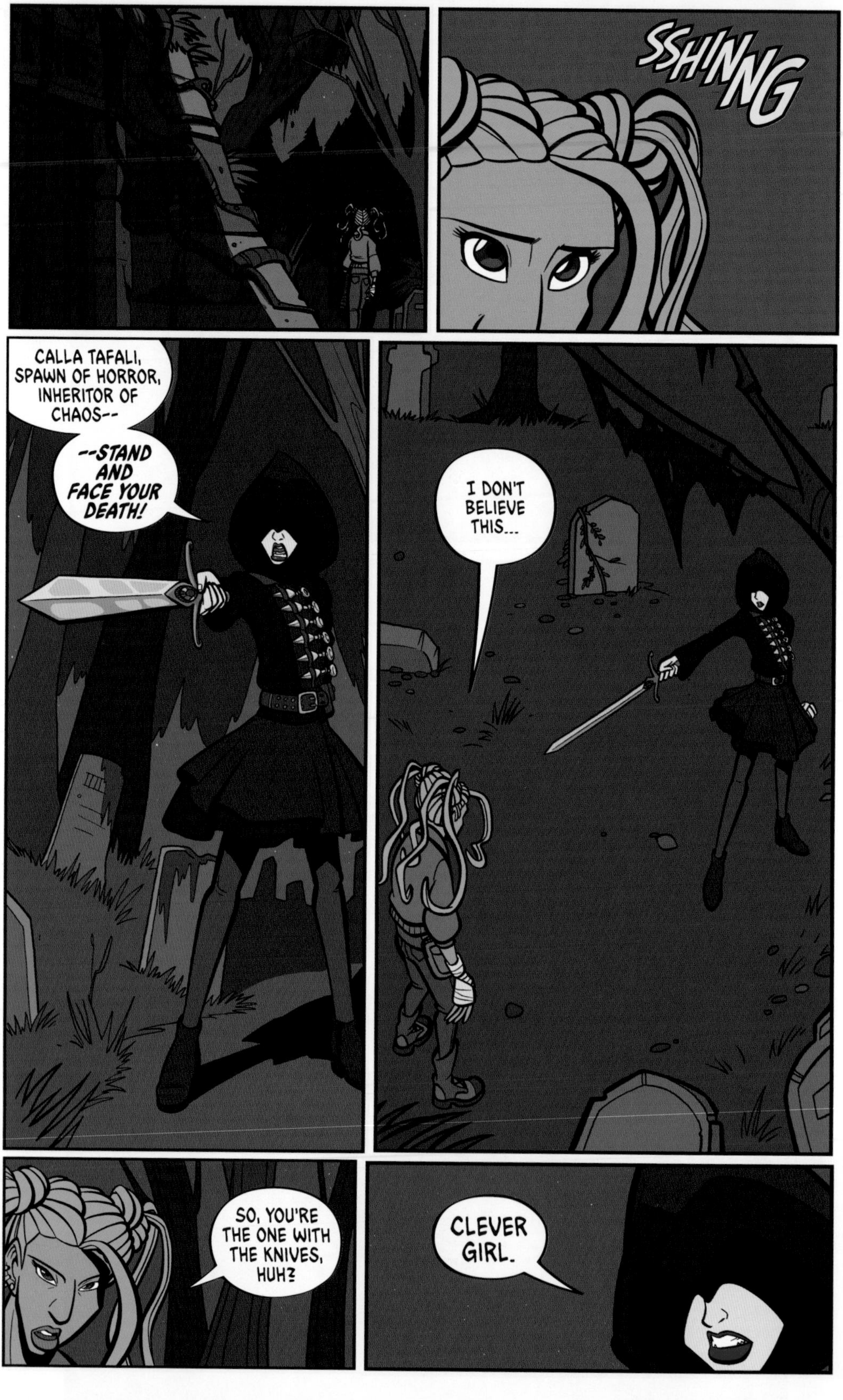
SSHINNG
CALLA TAFALI, SPAWN OF HORROR, INHERITOR OF CHAOS--
--STAND AND FACE YOUR DEATH!
I DON'T BELIEVE THIS...
SO, YOU'RE THE ONE WITH THE KNIVES, HUH?
CLEVER GIRL.

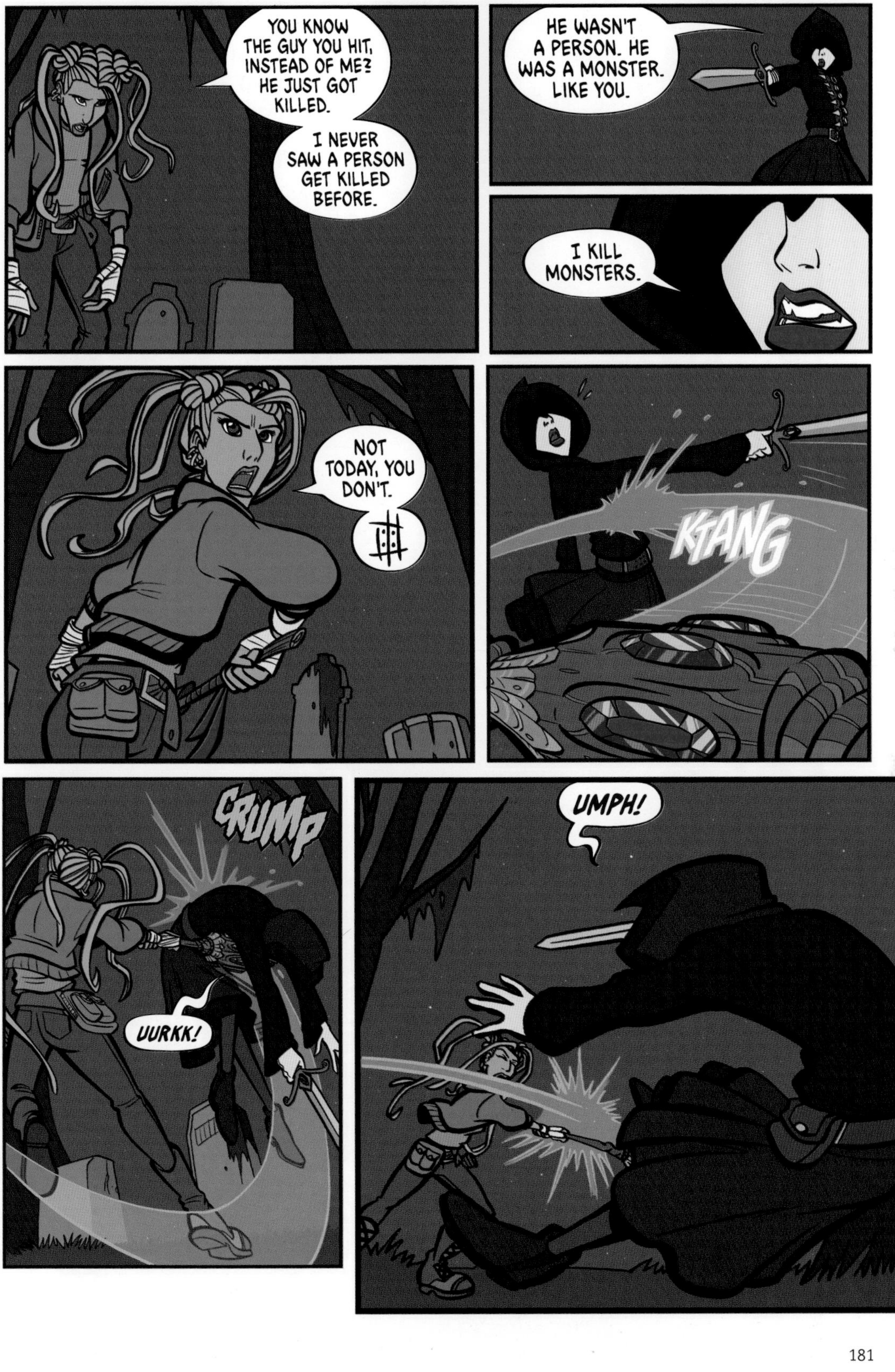
YOU KNOW THE GUY YOU HIT, INSTEAD OF ME? HE JUST GOT KILLED.
I NEVER SAW A PERSON GET KILLED BEFORE.
HE WASN'T A PERSON. HE WAS A MONSTER. LIKE YOU.
I KILL MONSTERS.
NOT TODAY, YOU DON'T.
KTANG
CRUMP
UURKK!
UMPH!

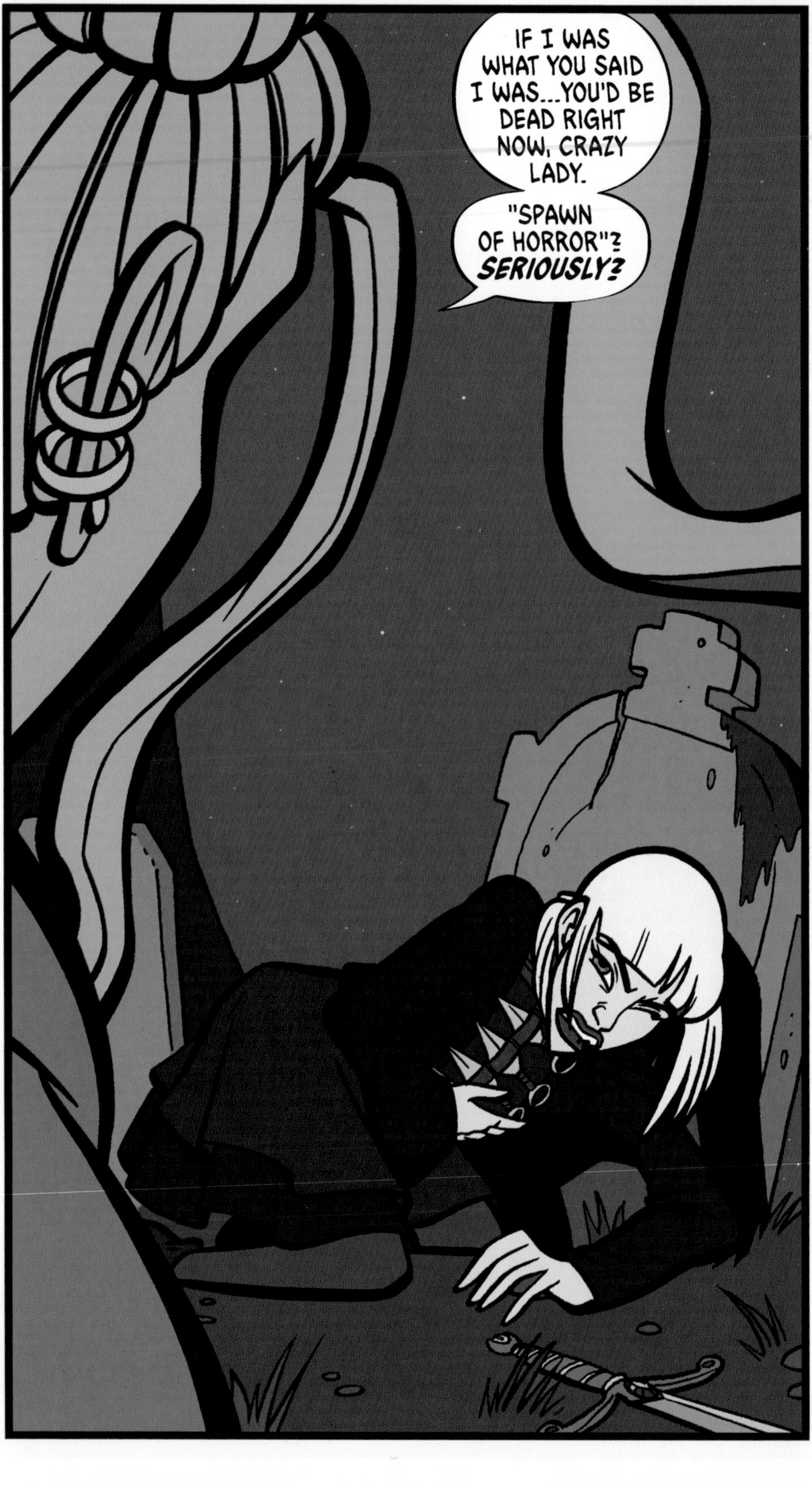
IF I WAS WHAT YOU SAID I WAS...YOU'D BE DEAD RIGHT NOW, CRAZY LADY.
"SPAWN OF HORROR"? SERIOUSLY?

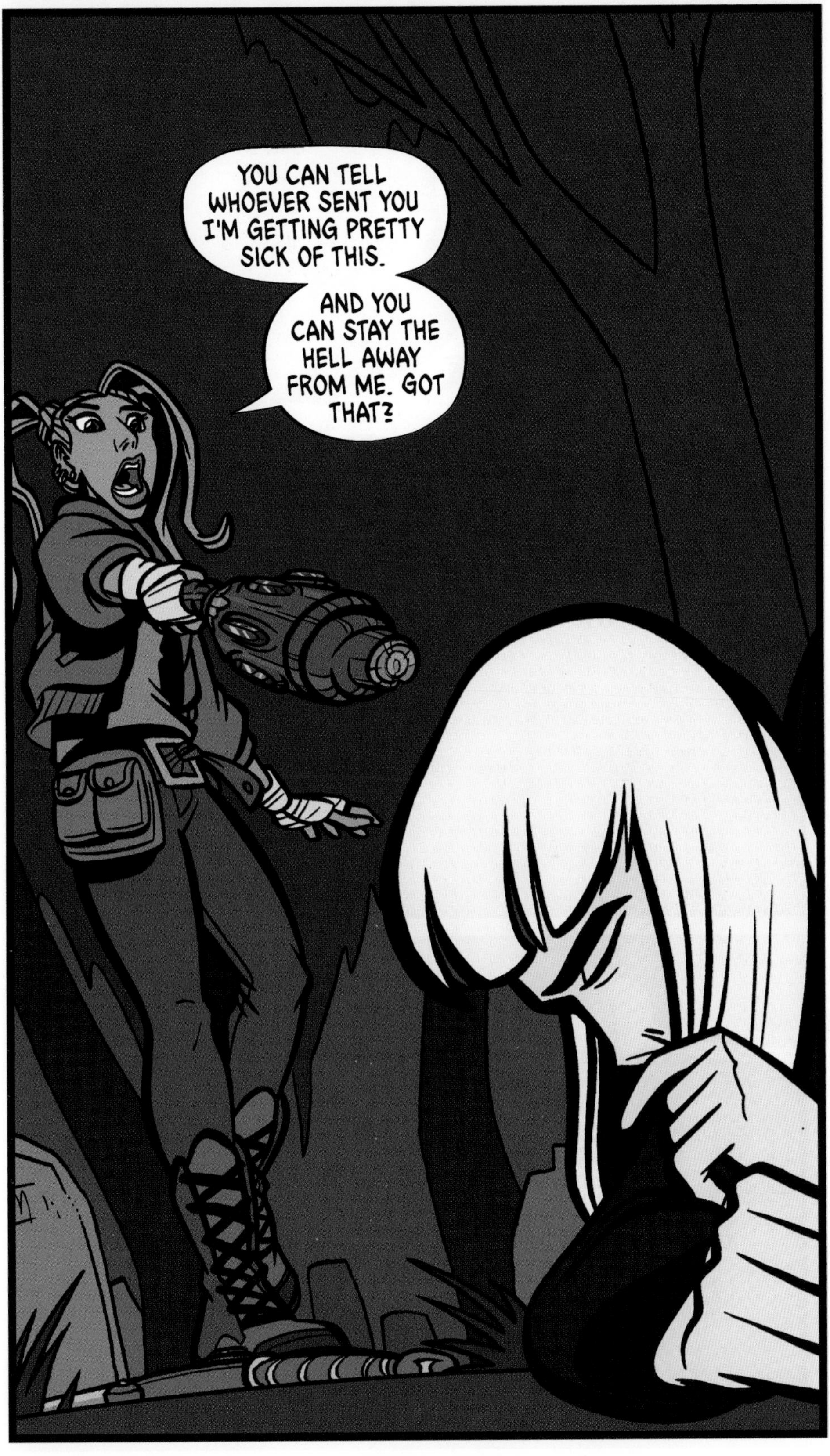
YOU CAN TELL WHOEVER SENT YOU I'M GETTING PRETTY SICK OF THIS.
AND YOU CAN STAY THE HELL AWAY FROM ME. GOT THAT?

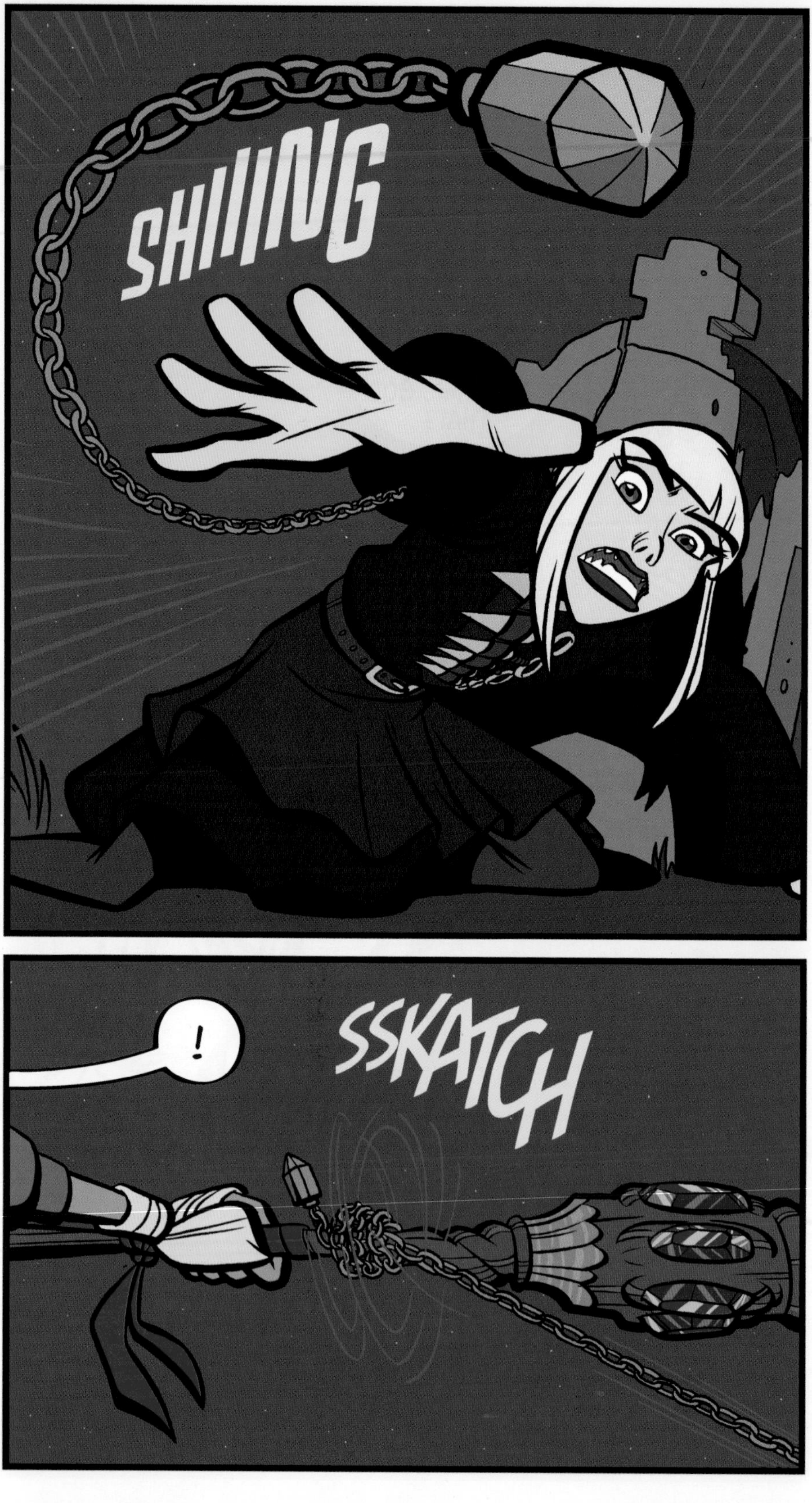
SHIIIING
!
SSKATCH

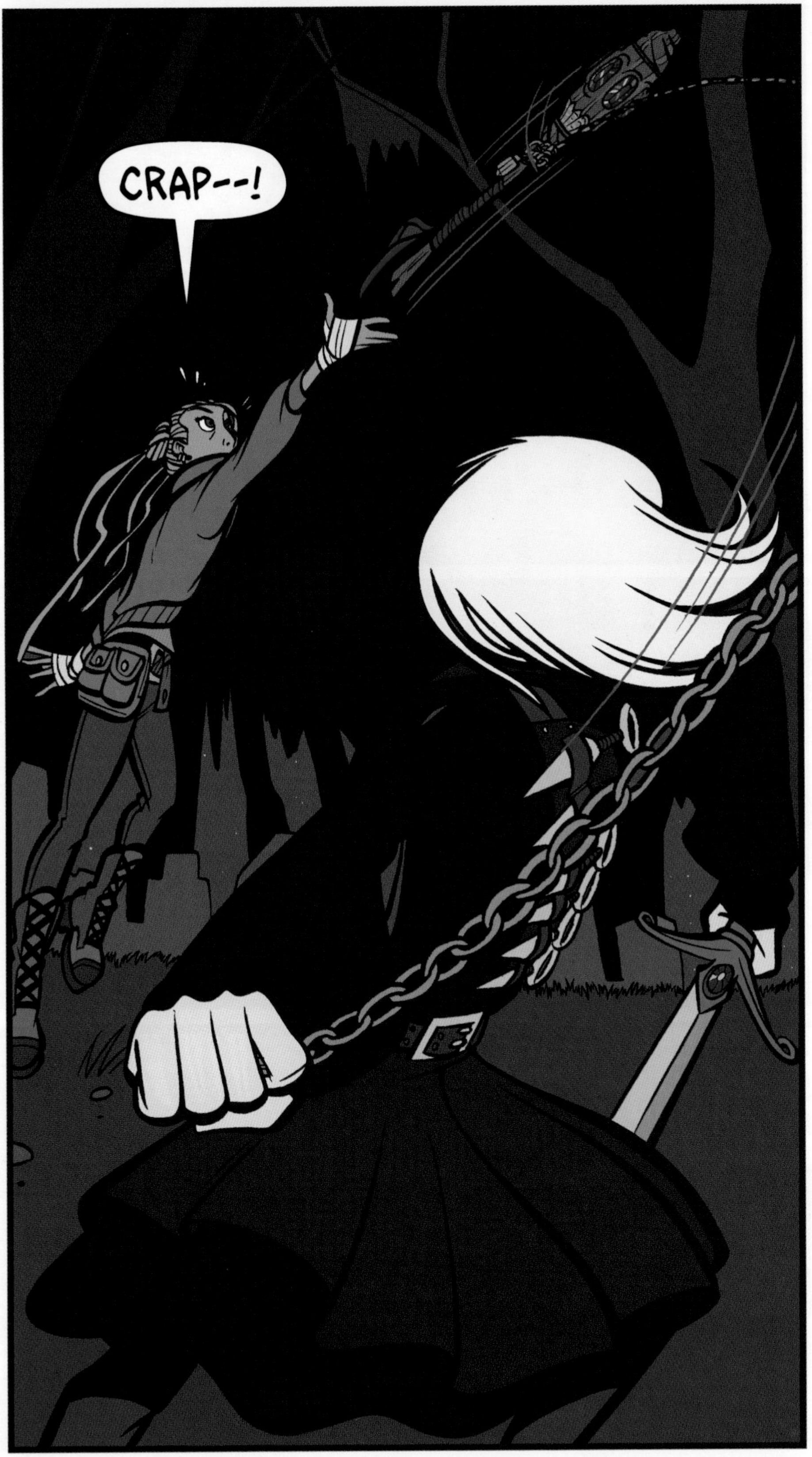
CRAP--!

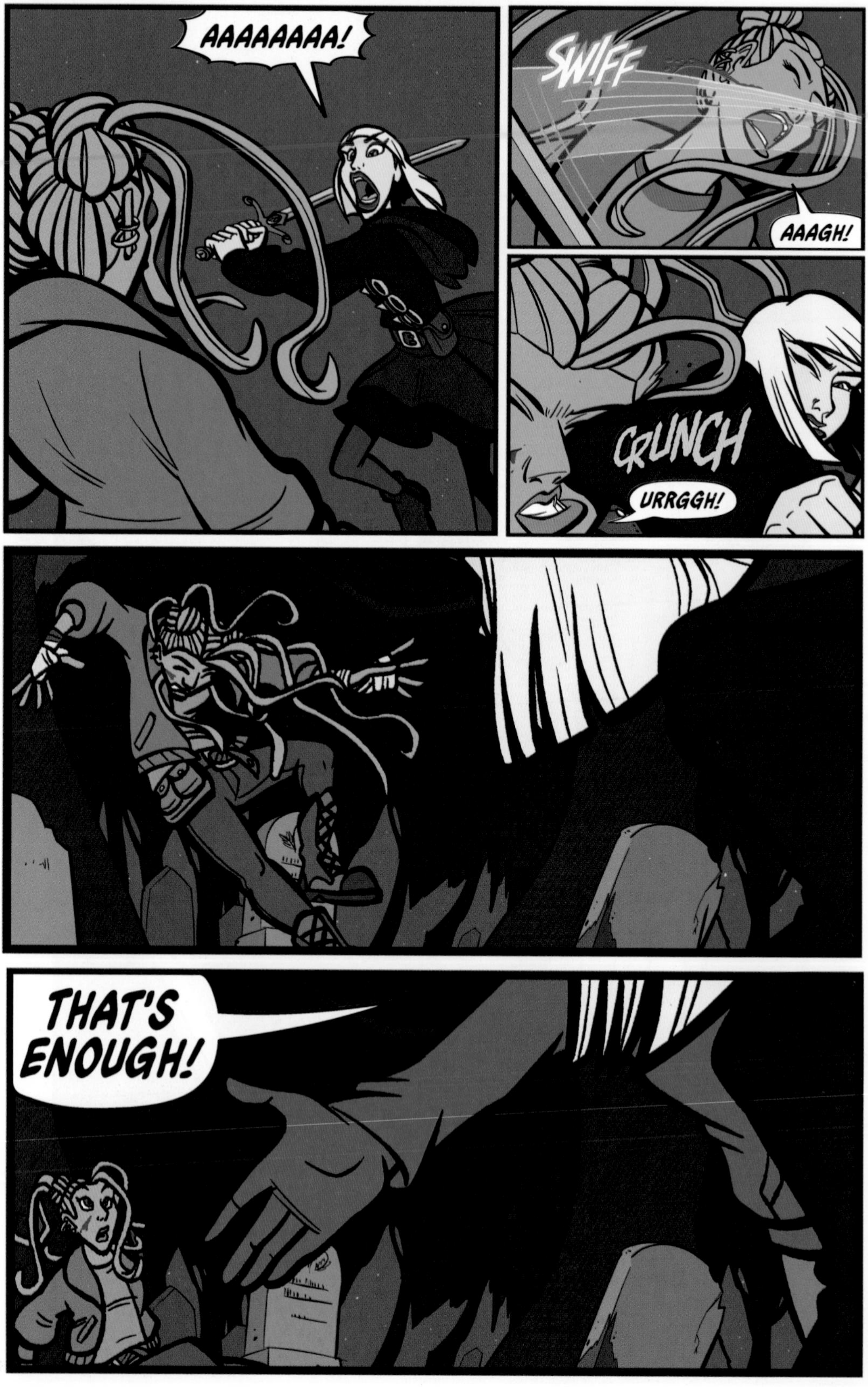
AAAAAAAA!
SWIFF
AAAGH!
CRUNCH
URRGGH!
THAT'S ENOUGH!

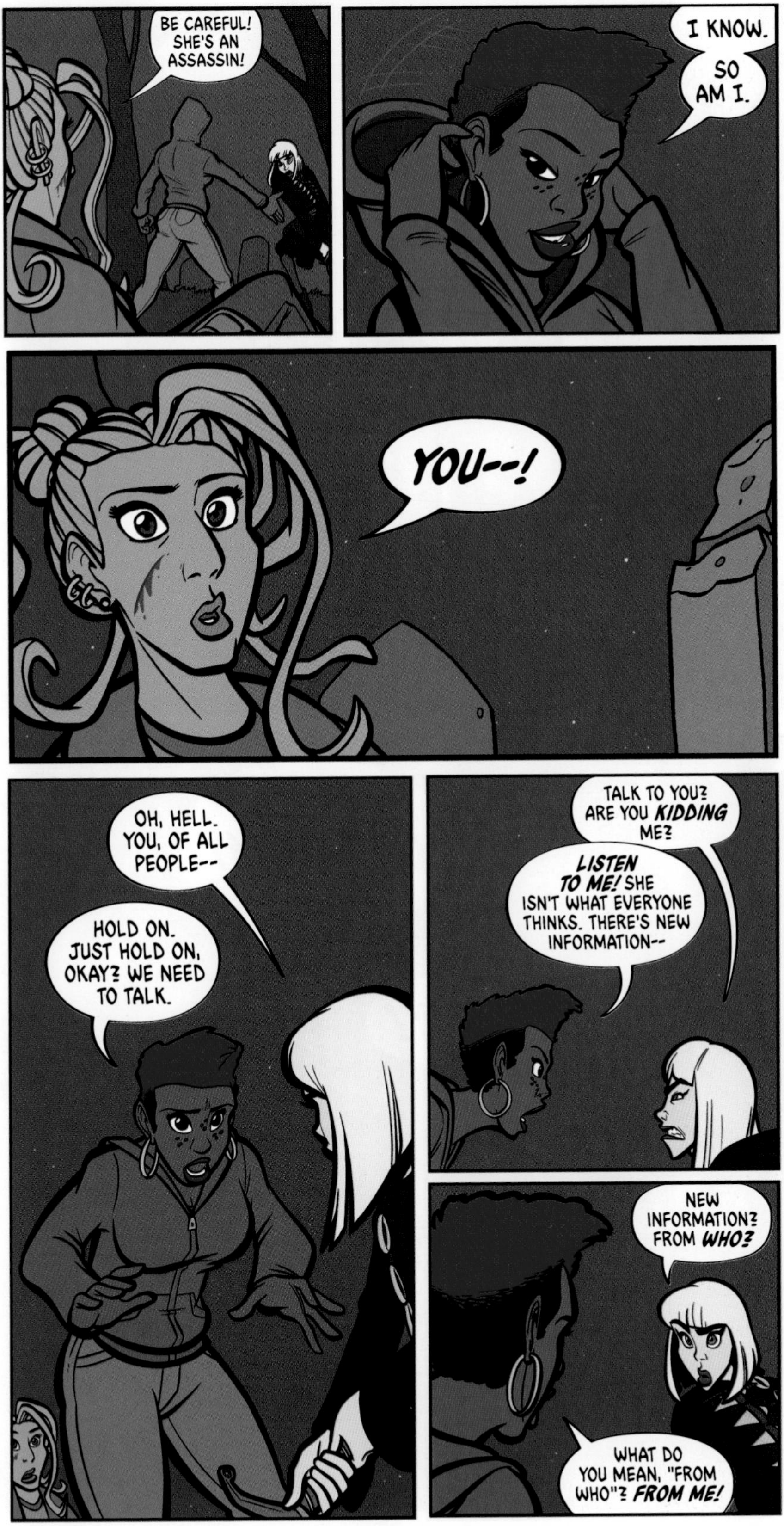
BE CAREFUL! SHE'S AN ASSASSIN!
I KNOW.
SO AM I.
YOU--!
OH, HELL. YOU, OF ALL PEOPLE--
HOLD ON. JUST HOLD ON, OKAY? WE NEED TO TALK.
TALK TO YOU? ARE YOU *KIDDING* ME?
LISTEN TO ME! SHE ISN'T WHAT EVERYONE THINKS. THERE'S NEW INFORMATION--
NEW INFORMATION? FROM *WHO?*
WHAT DO YOU MEAN, "FROM WHO"? *FROM ME!*

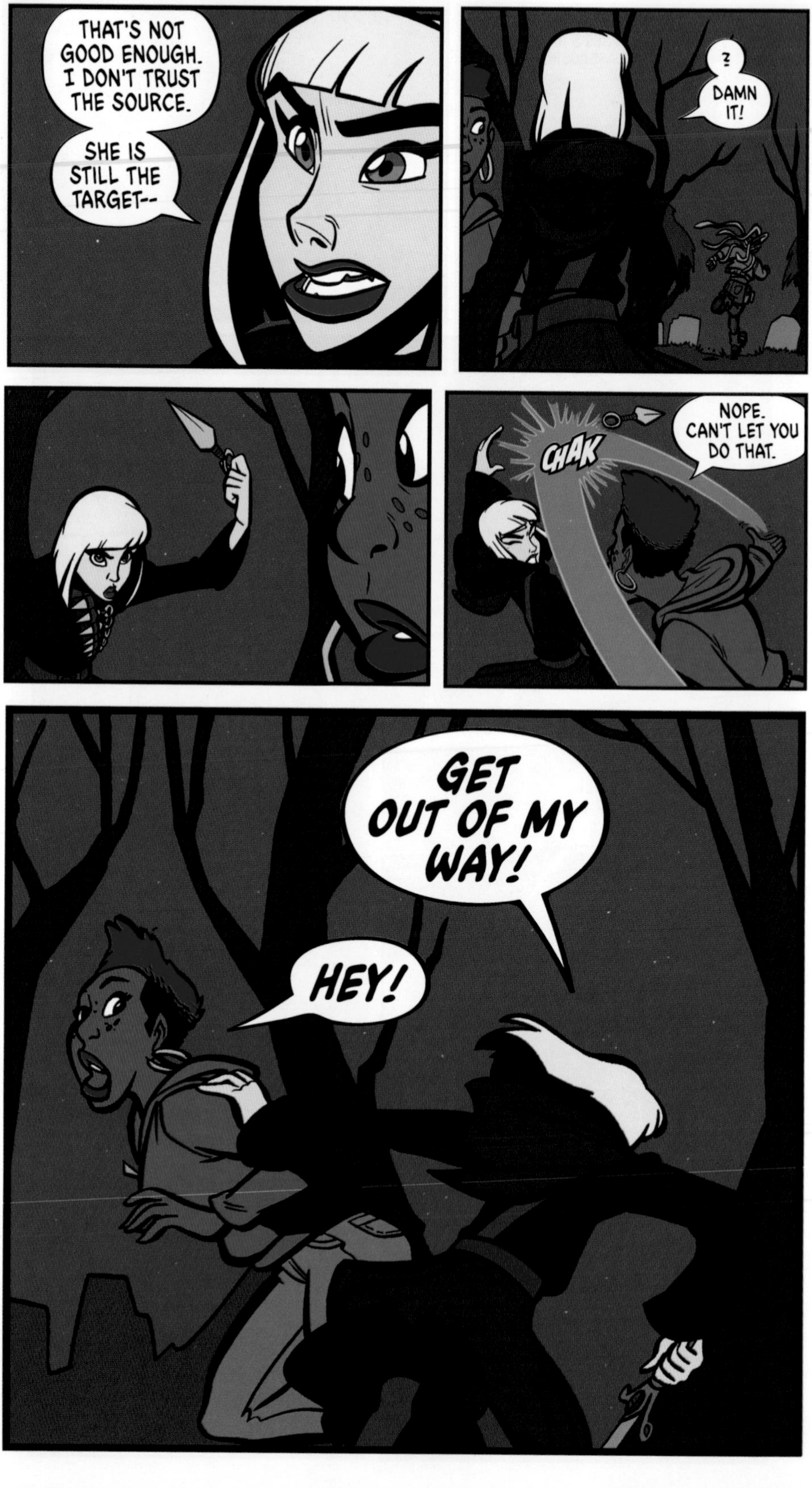
THAT'S NOT GOOD ENOUGH. I DON'T TRUST THE SOURCE.
SHE IS STILL THE TARGET--
?
DAMN IT!
CHAK
NOPE. CAN'T LET YOU DO THAT.
GET OUT OF MY WAY!
HEY!

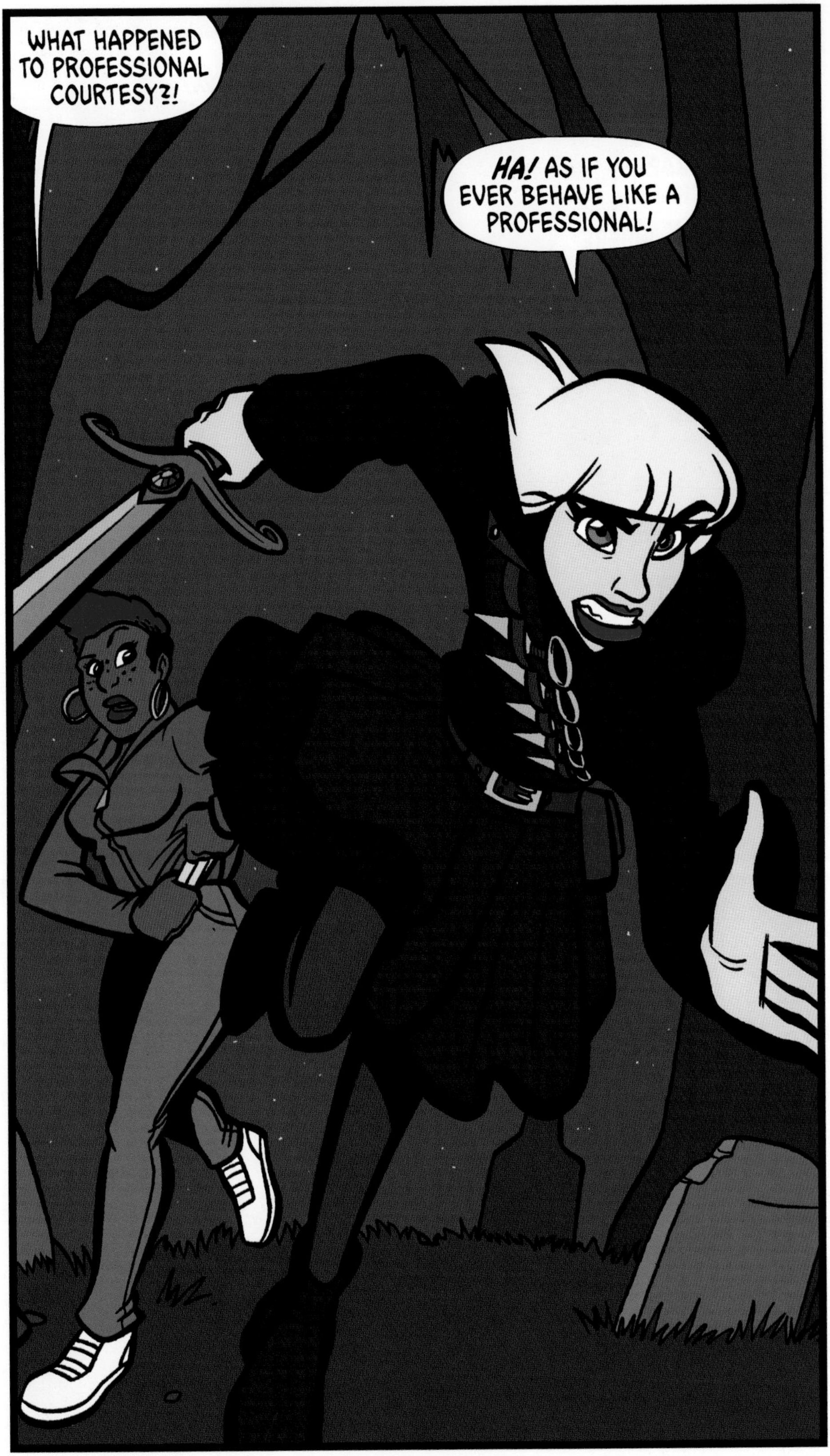
WHAT HAPPENED TO PROFESSIONAL COURTESY?!
HA! AS IF YOU EVER BEHAVE LIKE A PROFESSIONAL!

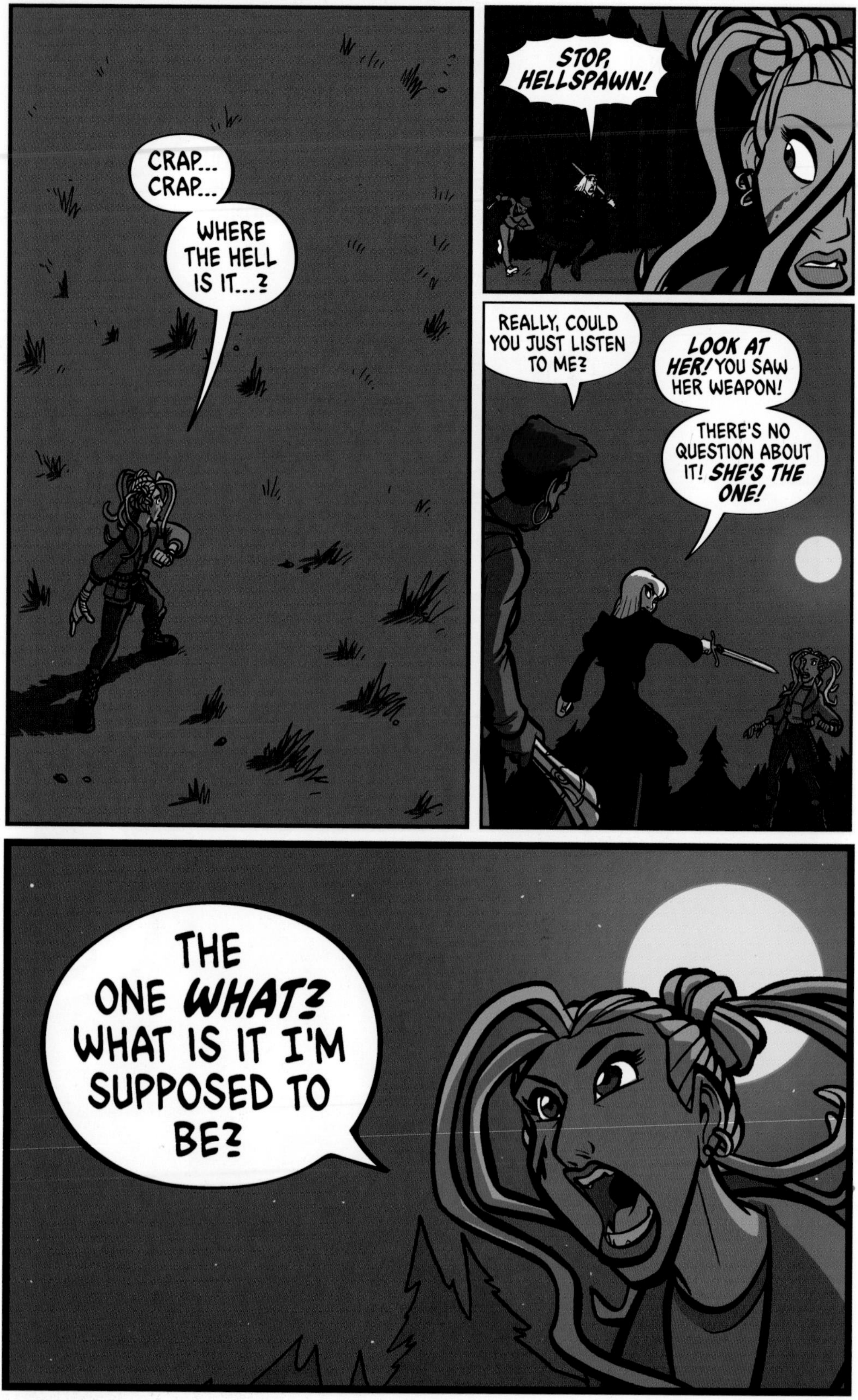
CRAP... CRAP...
WHERE THE HELL IS IT...?
STOP, HELLSPAWN!
REALLY, COULD YOU JUST LISTEN TO ME?
LOOK AT HER! YOU SAW HER WEAPON!
THERE'S NO QUESTION ABOUT IT! SHE'S THE ONE!
THE ONE WHAT? WHAT IS IT I'M SUPPOSED TO BE?

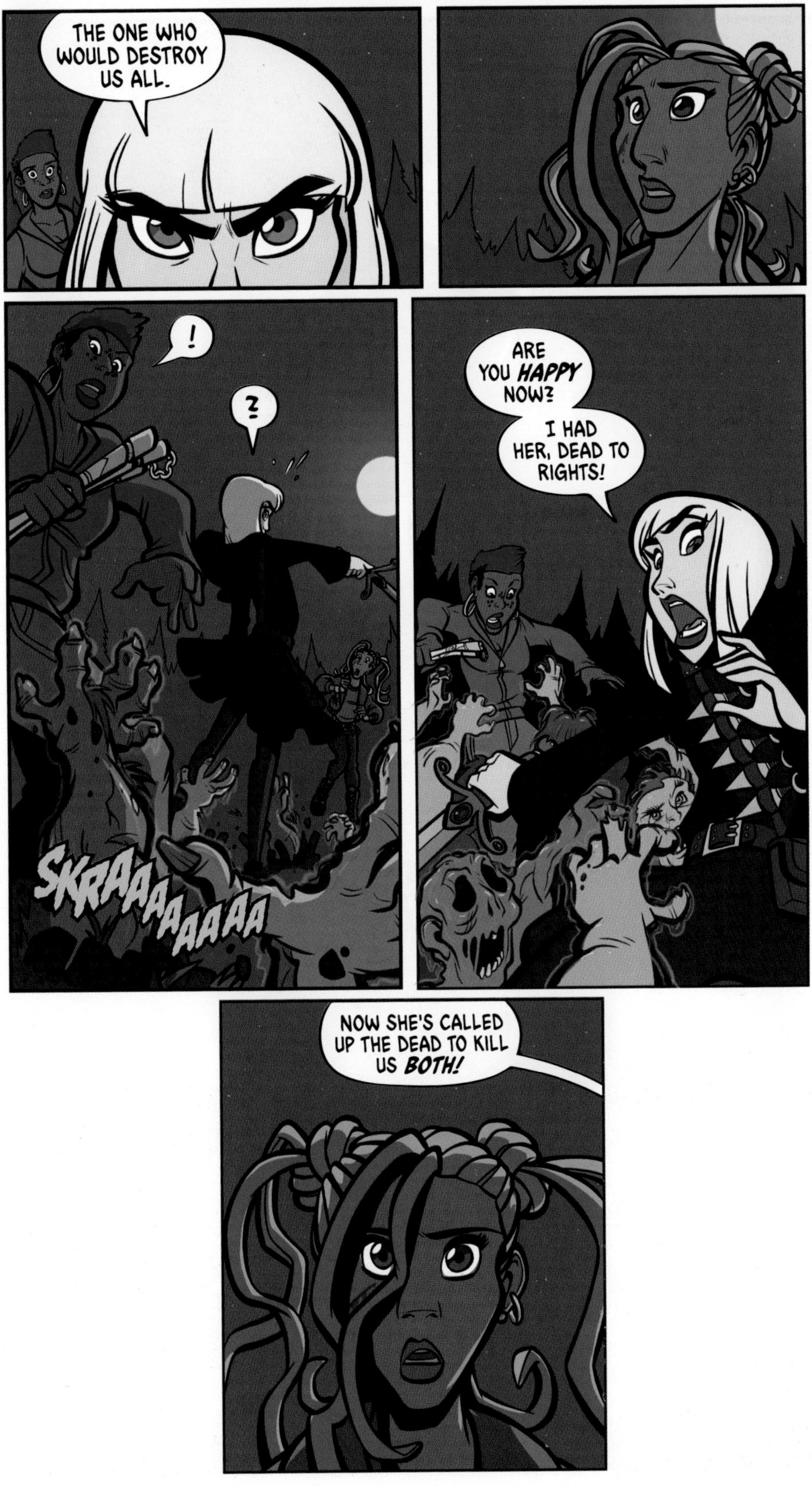
THE ONE WHO WOULD DESTROY US ALL.
!
?
SKRAAAAAAAAA
ARE YOU HAPPY NOW?
I HAD HER, DEAD TO RIGHTS!
NOW SHE'S CALLED UP THE DEAD TO KILL US BOTH!

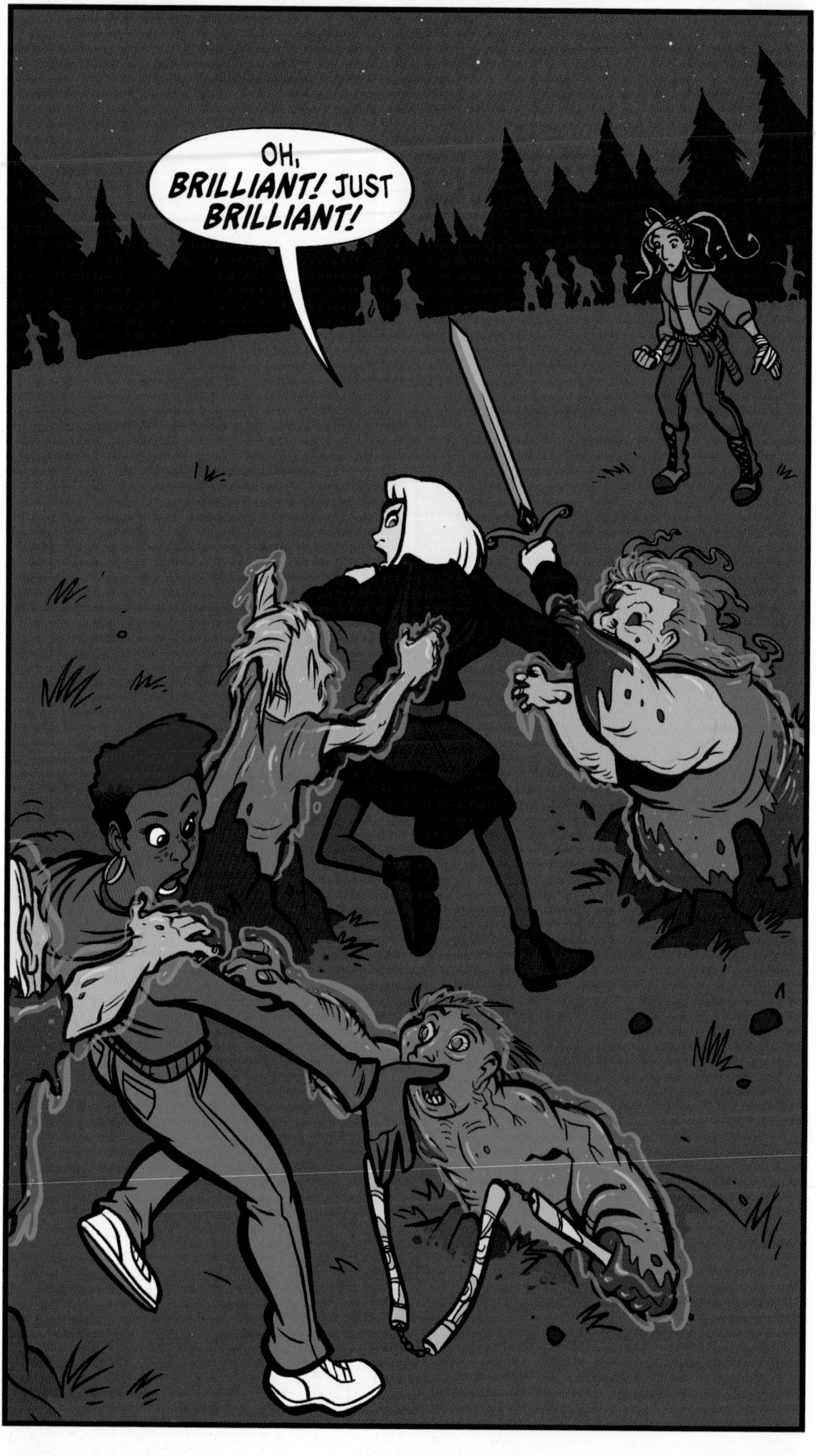
OH, BRILLIANT! JUST BRILLIANT!

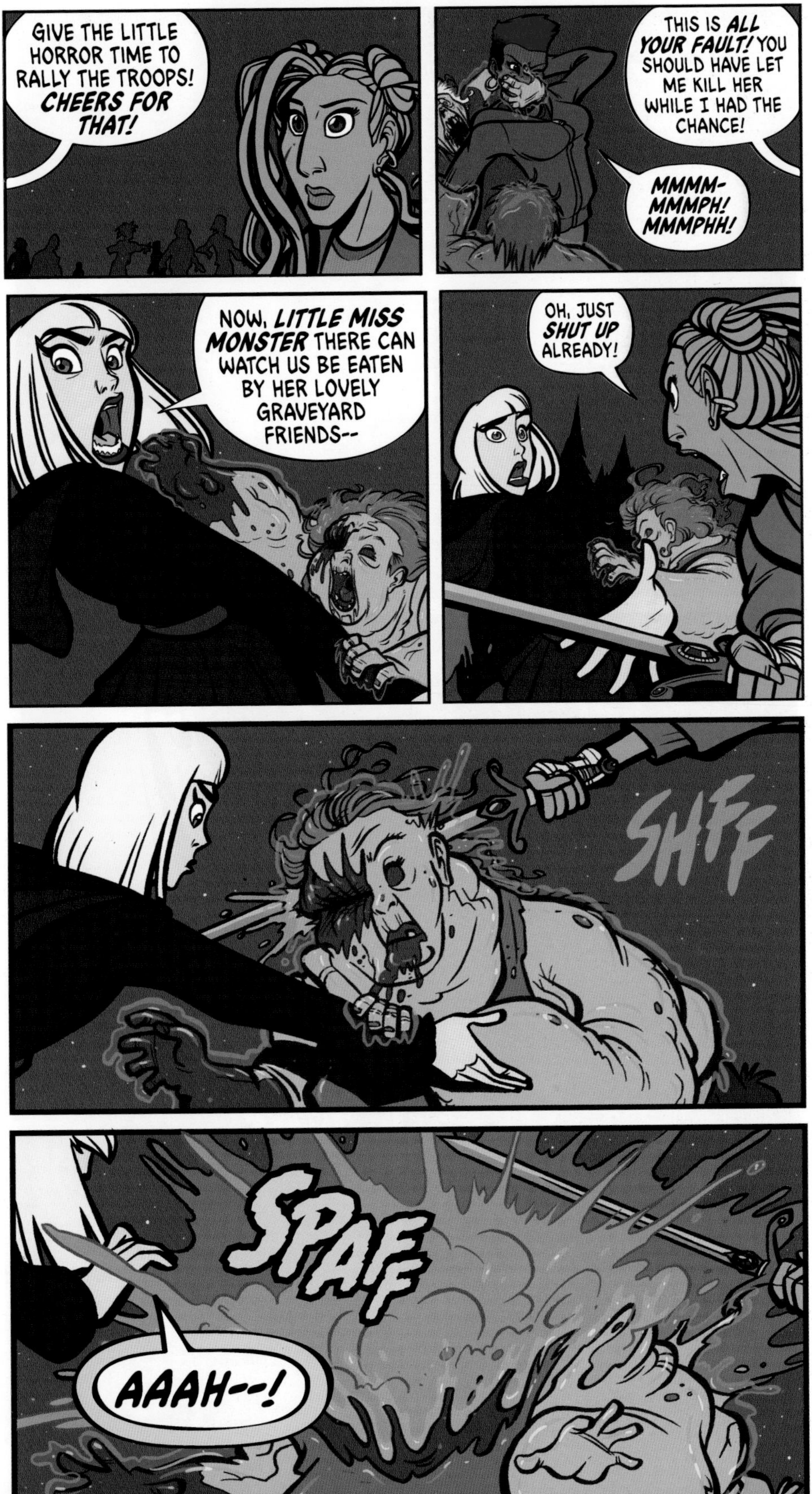
GIVE THE LITTLE HORROR TIME TO RALLY THE TROOPS! CHEERS FOR THAT!
THIS IS ALL YOUR FAULT! YOU SHOULD HAVE LET ME KILL HER WHILE I HAD THE CHANCE!
MMMM-MMMPH! MMMPHH!
NOW, LITTLE MISS MONSTER THERE CAN WATCH US BE EATEN BY HER LOVELY GRAVEYARD FRIENDS--
OH, JUST SHUT UP ALREADY!
SHFF
SPAFF
AAAH--!

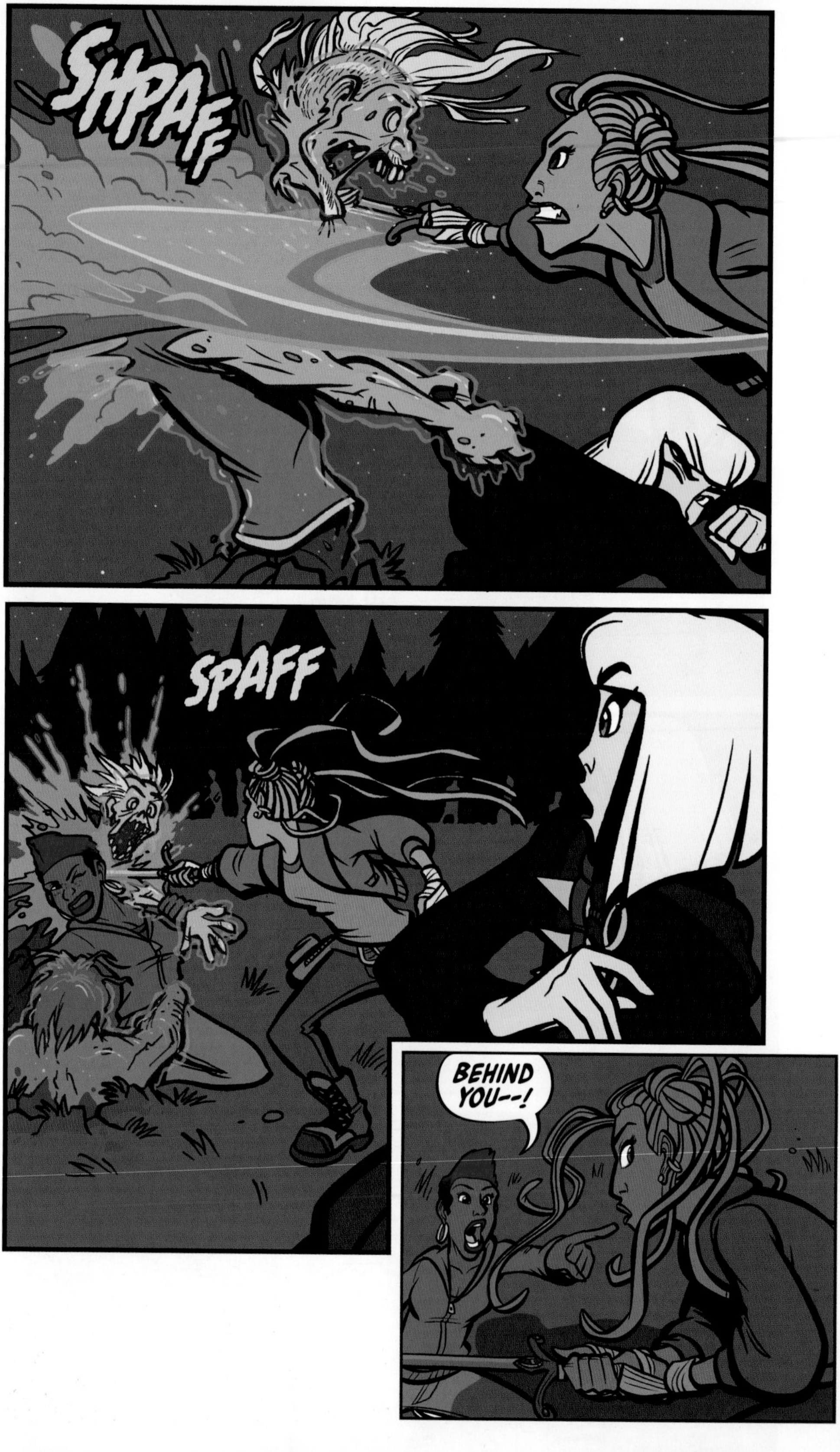
SHPAFF
SPAFF
BEHIND YOU--!

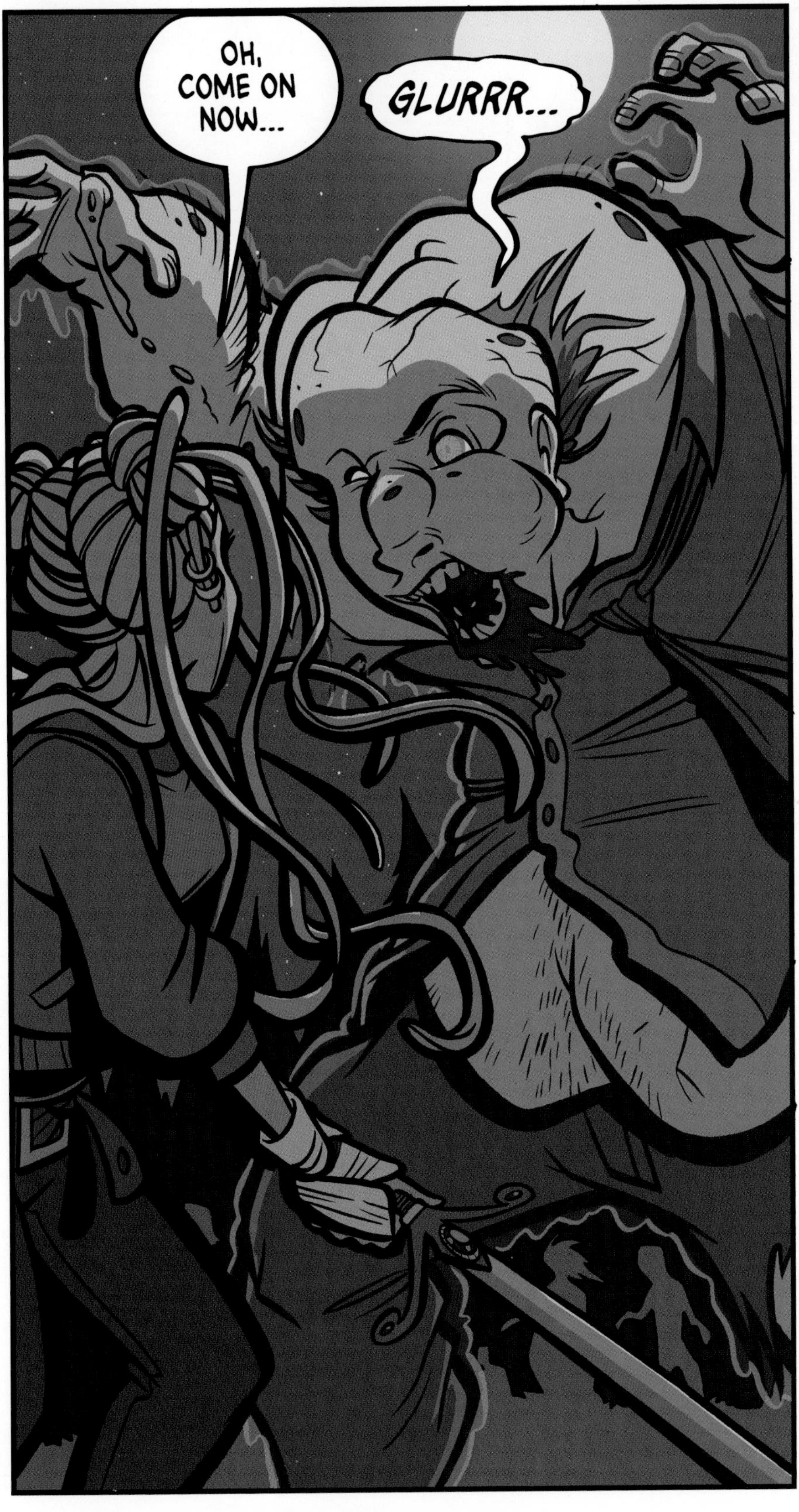
OH, COME ON NOW...
GLURRR...

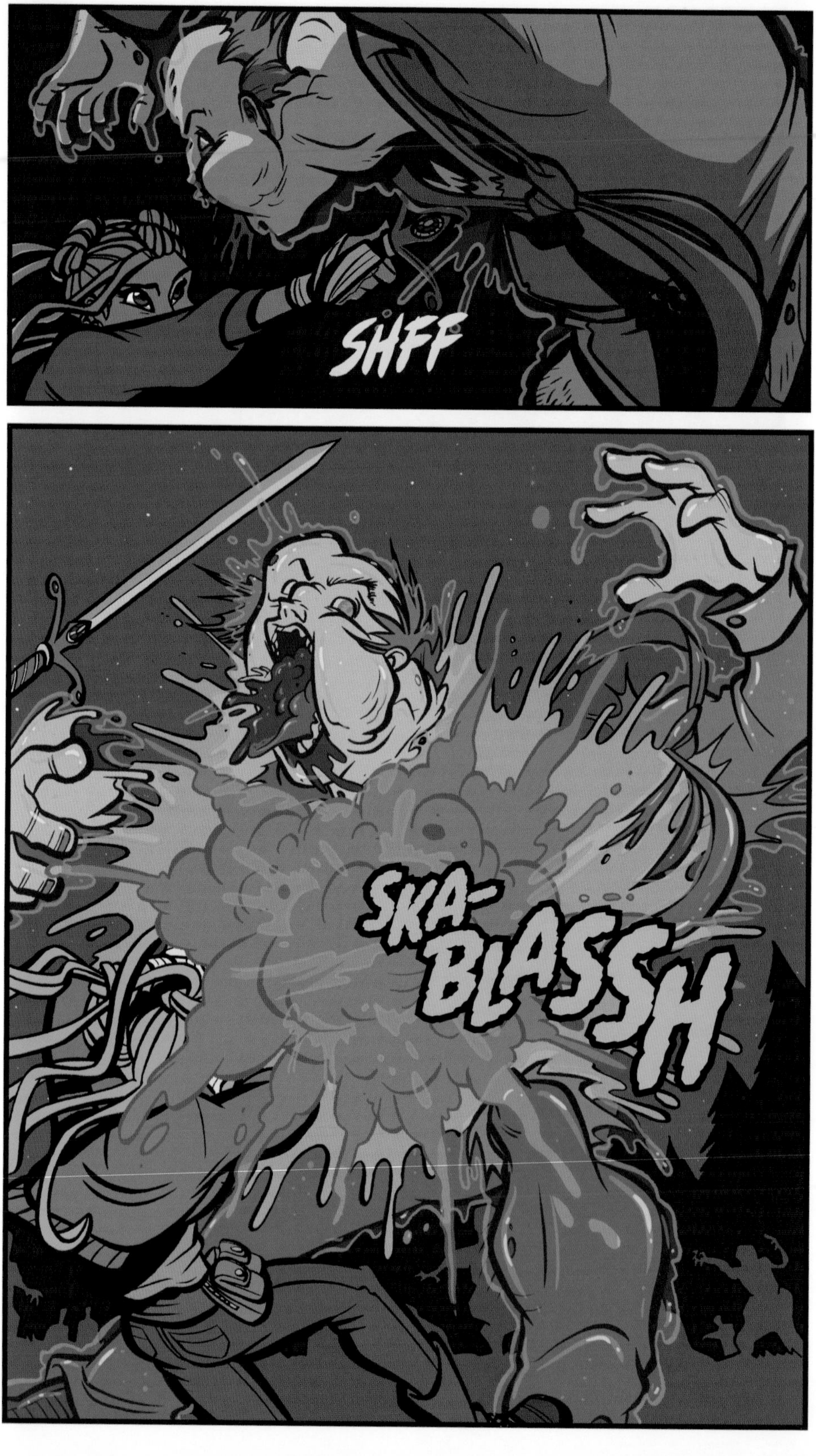
SHFF
SKA-
BLASSH

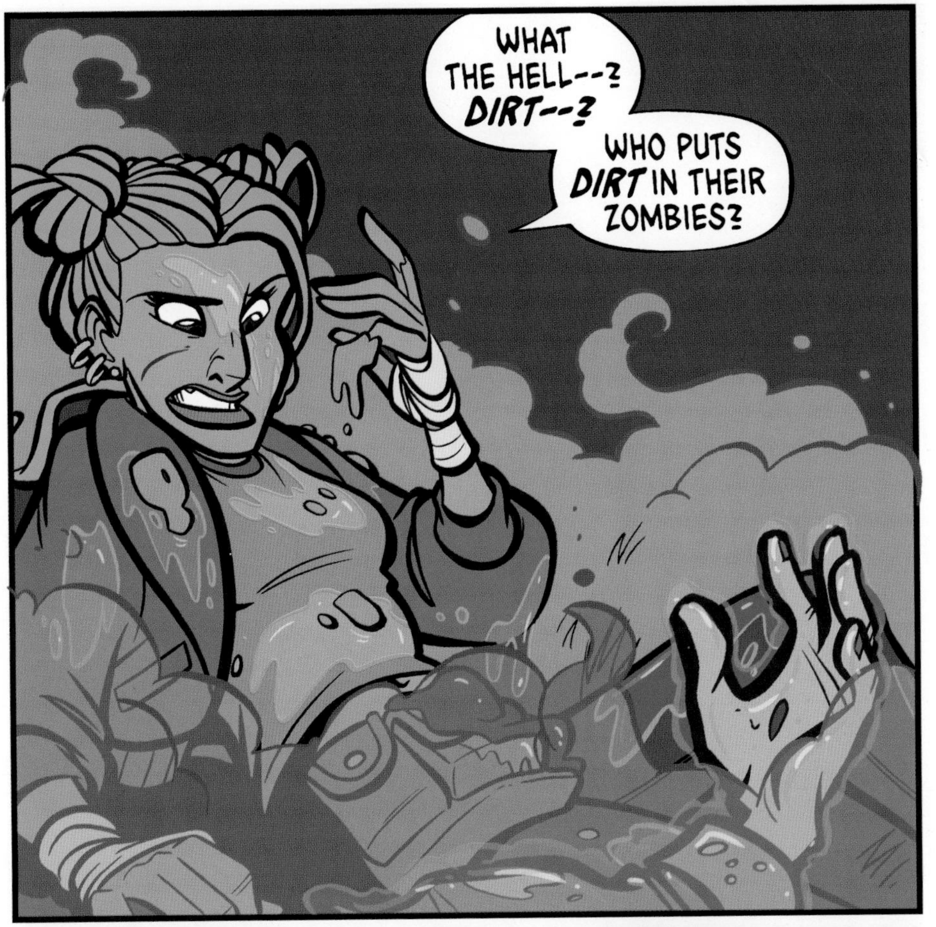
WHAT THE HELL--? DIRT--?
WHO PUTS DIRT IN THEIR ZOMBIES?

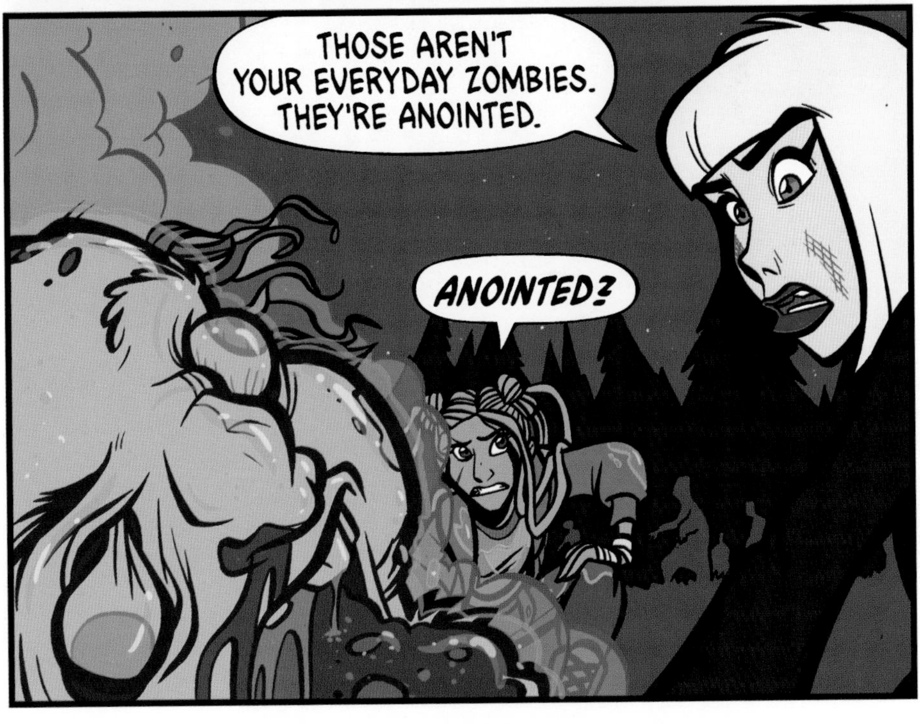
THOSE AREN'T YOUR EVERYDAY ZOMBIES. THEY'RE ANOINTED.
ANOINTED?

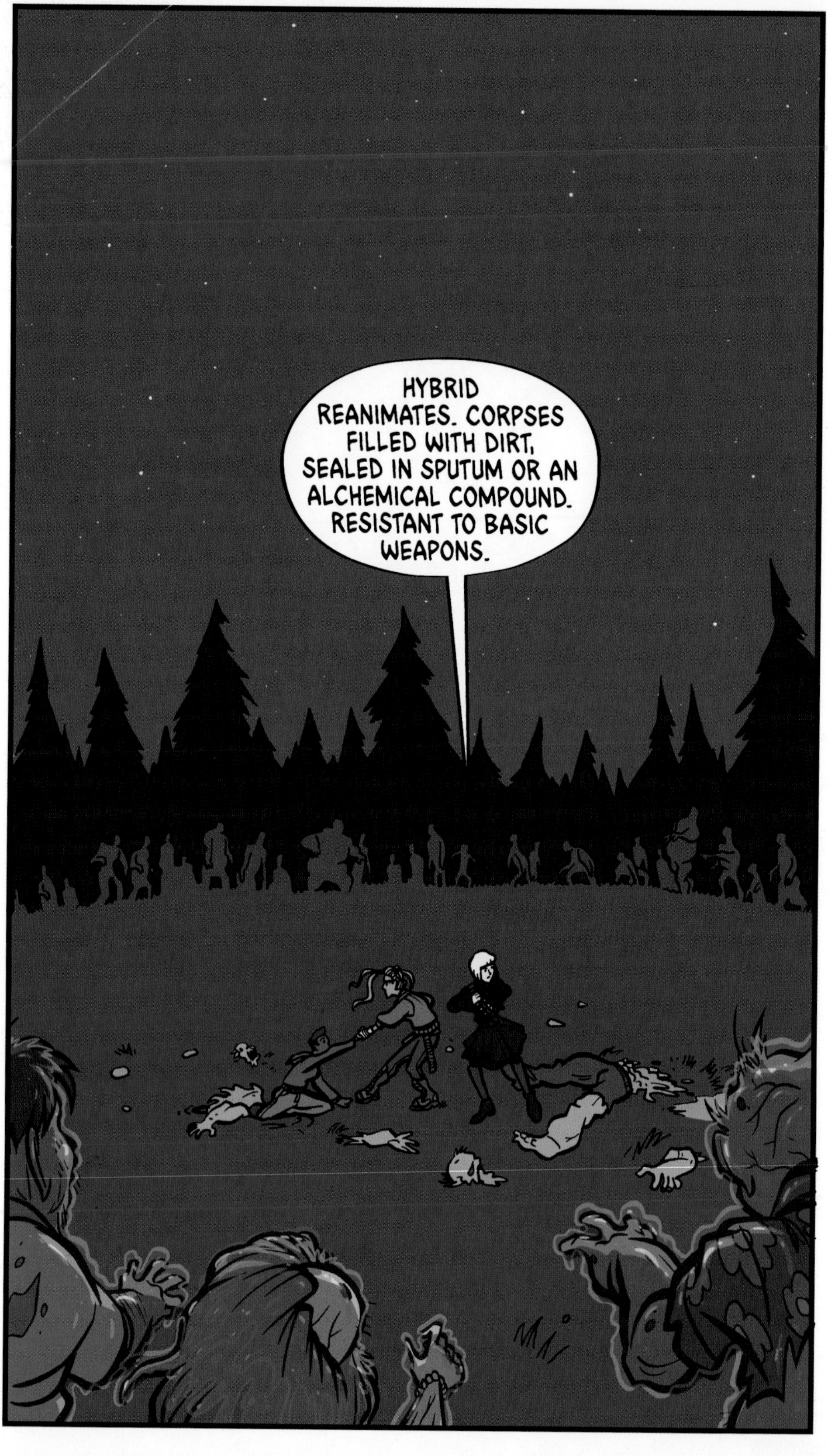
HYBRID REANIMATES. CORPSES FILLED WITH DIRT, SEALED IN SPUTUM OR AN ALCHEMICAL COMPOUND. RESISTANT TO BASIC WEAPONS.

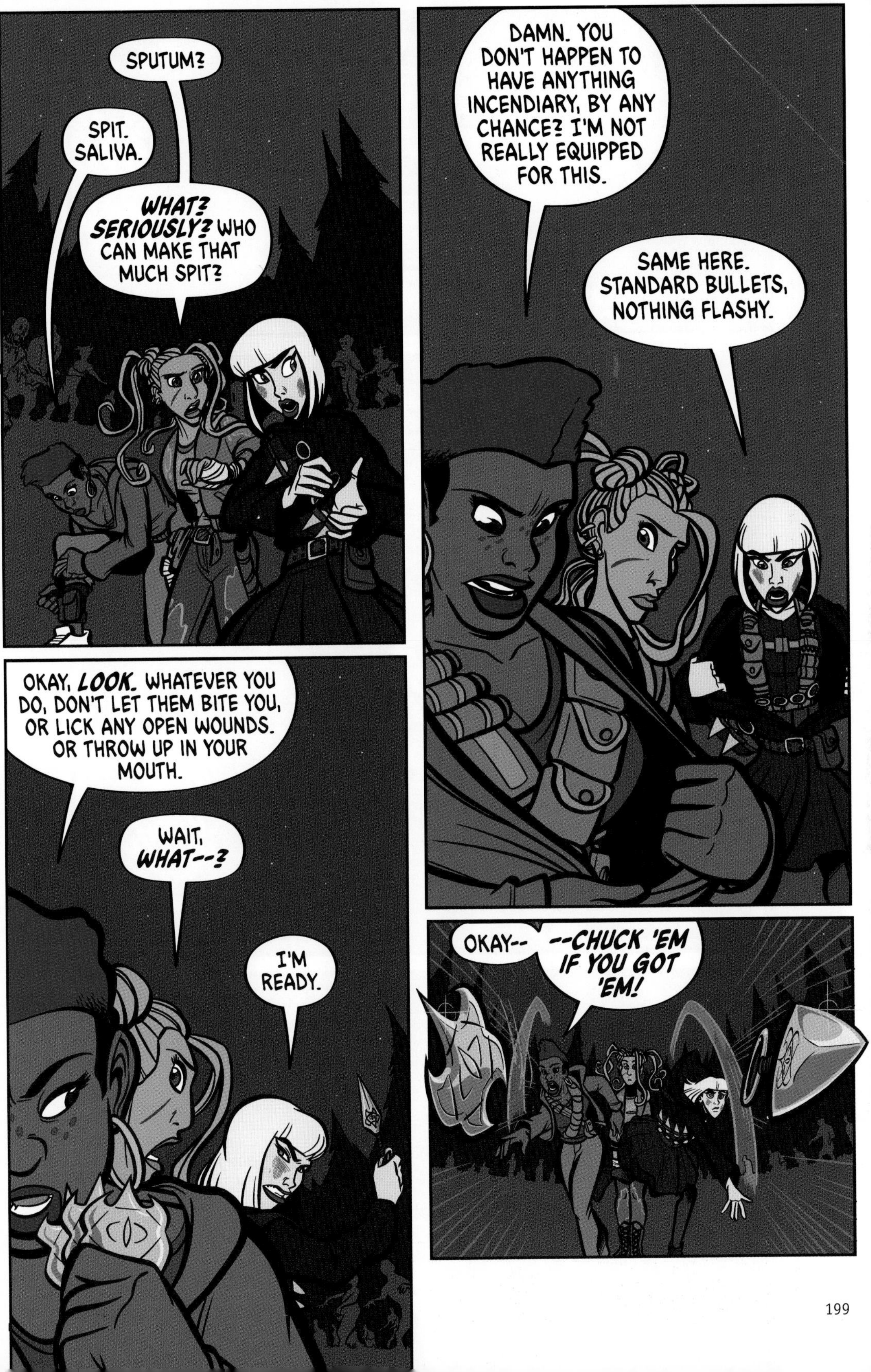
SPUTUM?
SPIT. SALIVA.
WHAT? SERIOUSLY? WHO CAN MAKE THAT MUCH SPIT?
DAMN. YOU DON'T HAPPEN TO HAVE ANYTHING INCENDIARY, BY ANY CHANCE? I'M NOT REALLY EQUIPPED FOR THIS.
SAME HERE. STANDARD BULLETS, NOTHING FLASHY.
OKAY, LOOK. WHATEVER YOU DO, DON'T LET THEM BITE YOU, OR LICK ANY OPEN WOUNDS. OR THROW UP IN YOUR MOUTH.
WAIT, WHAT--?
I'M READY.
OKAY--
--CHUCK 'EM IF YOU GOT 'EM!

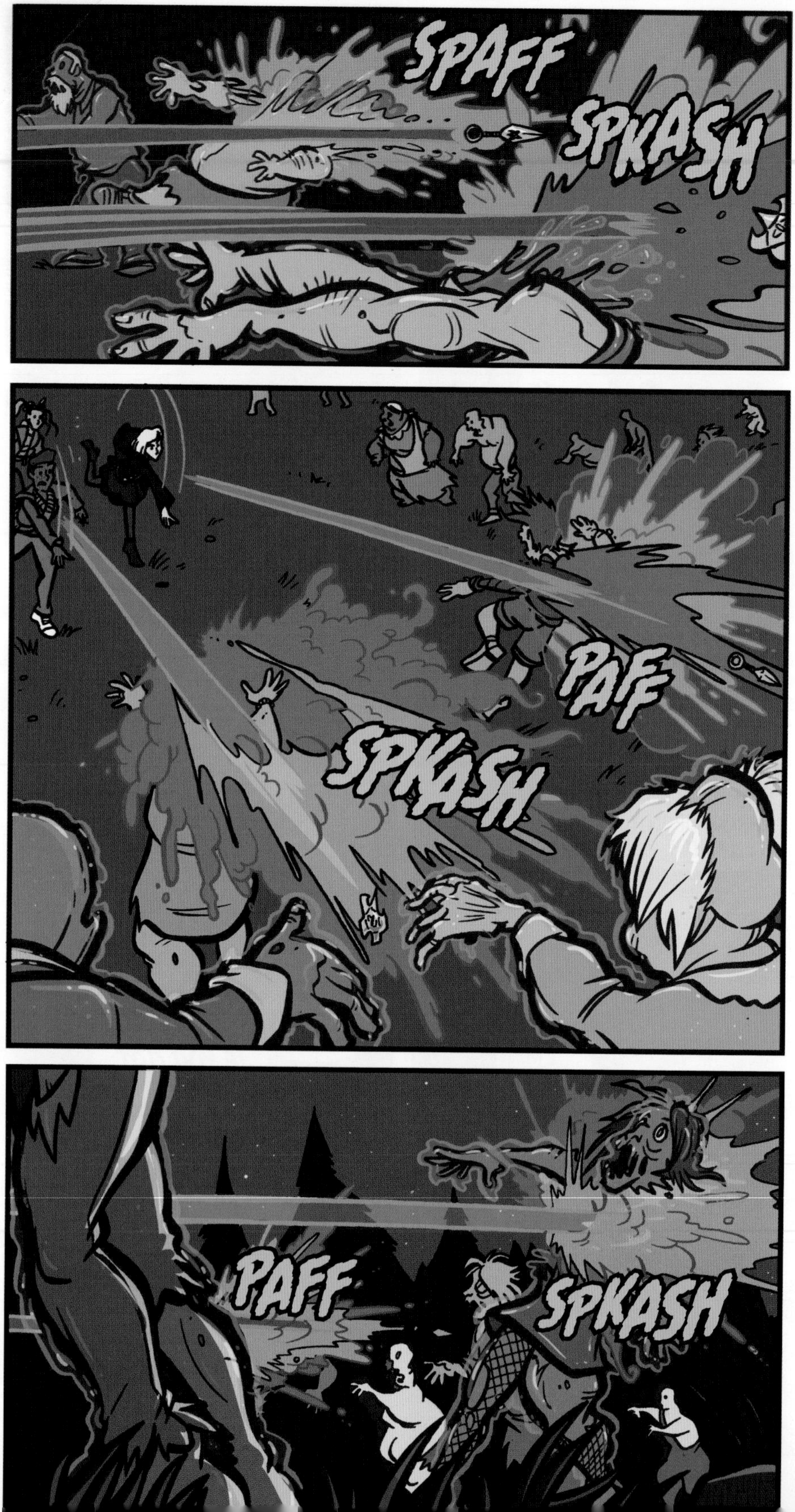
SPAFF
SPKASH
PAFF
SPKASH
PAFF
SPKASH

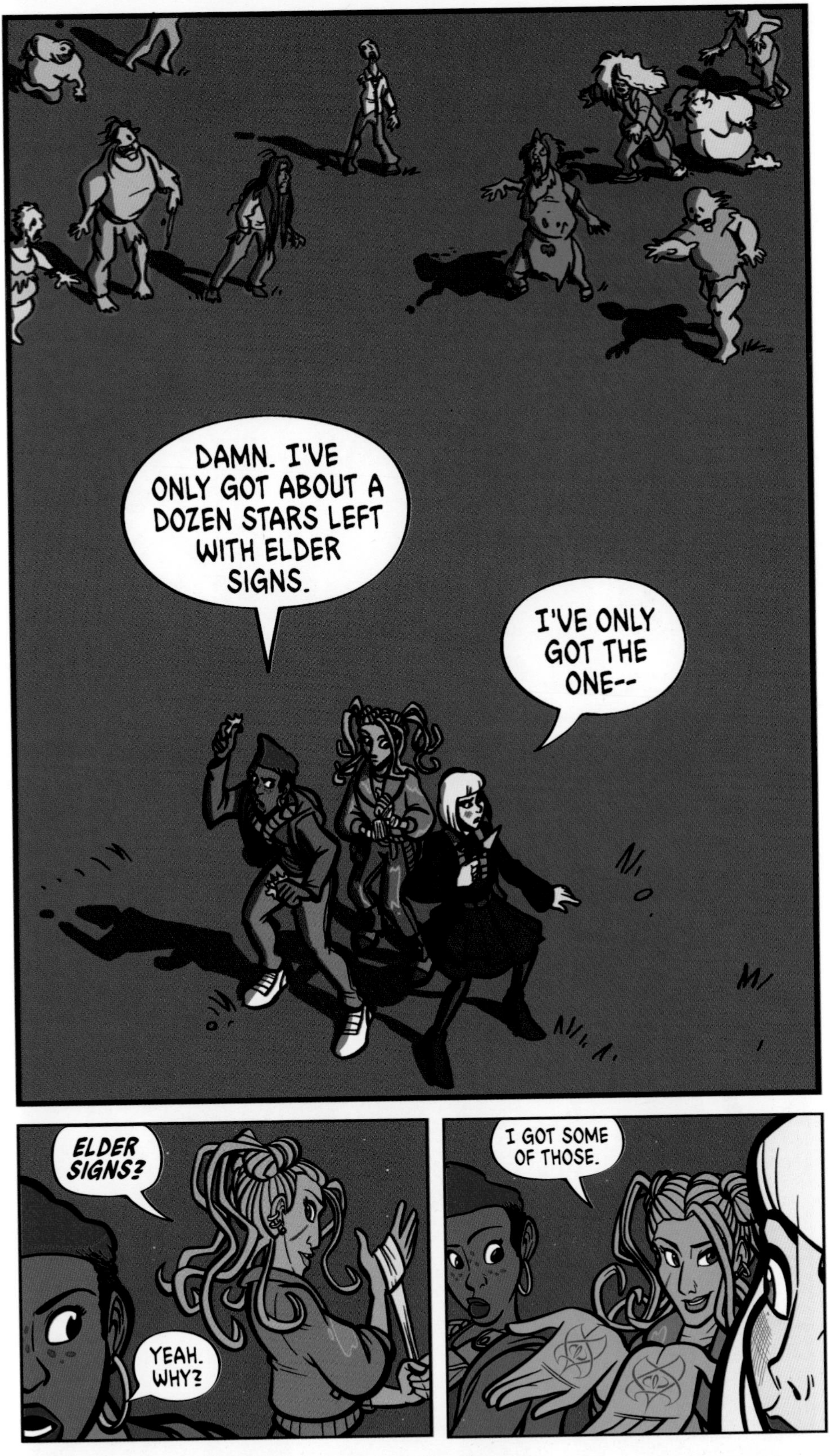
DAMN. I'VE ONLY GOT ABOUT A DOZEN STARS LEFT WITH ELDER SIGNS.
I'VE ONLY GOT THE ONE--
ELDER SIGNS?
YEAH. WHY?
I GOT SOME OF THOSE.

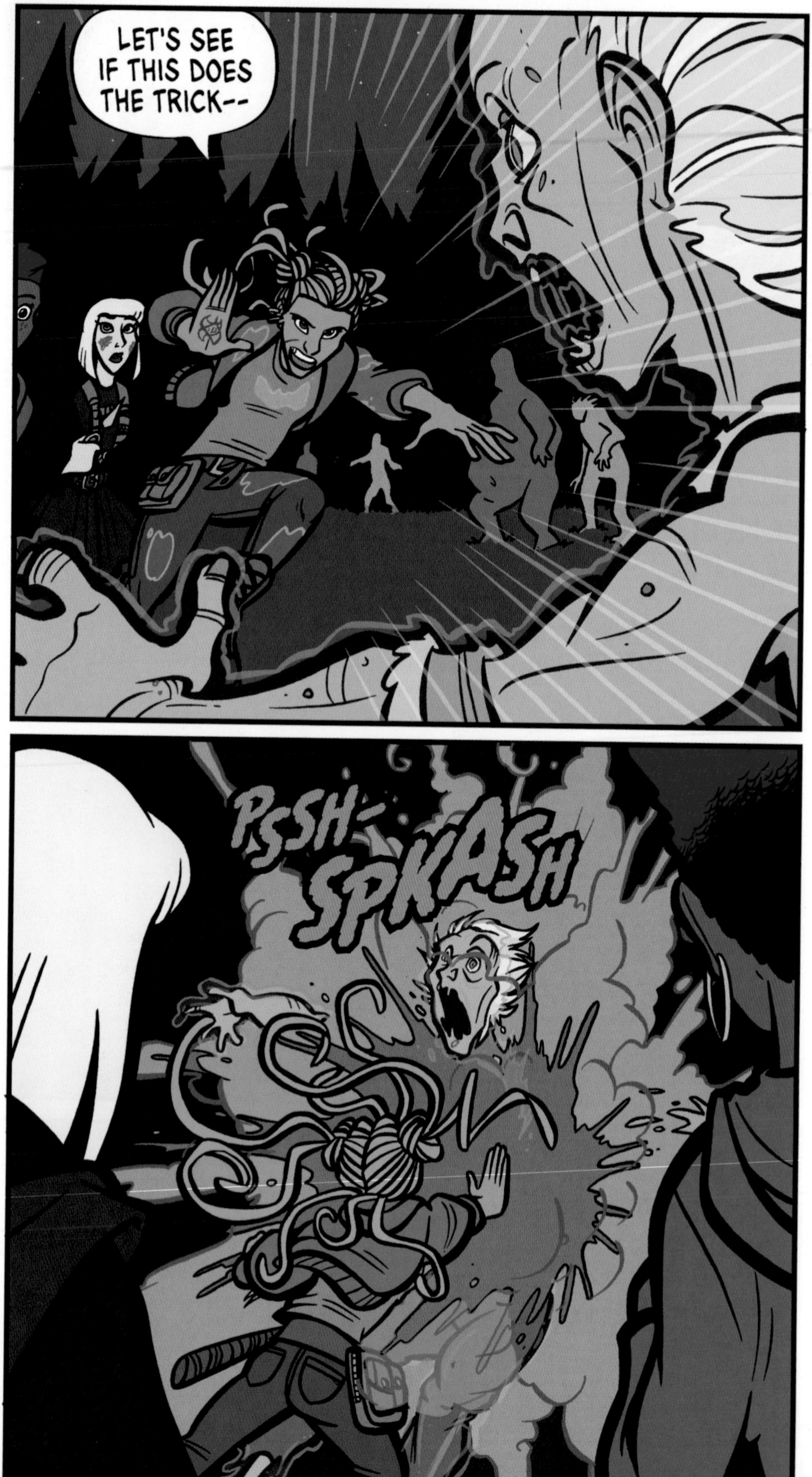
LET'S SEE IF THIS DOES THE TRICK--
PSSH-
SPKASH

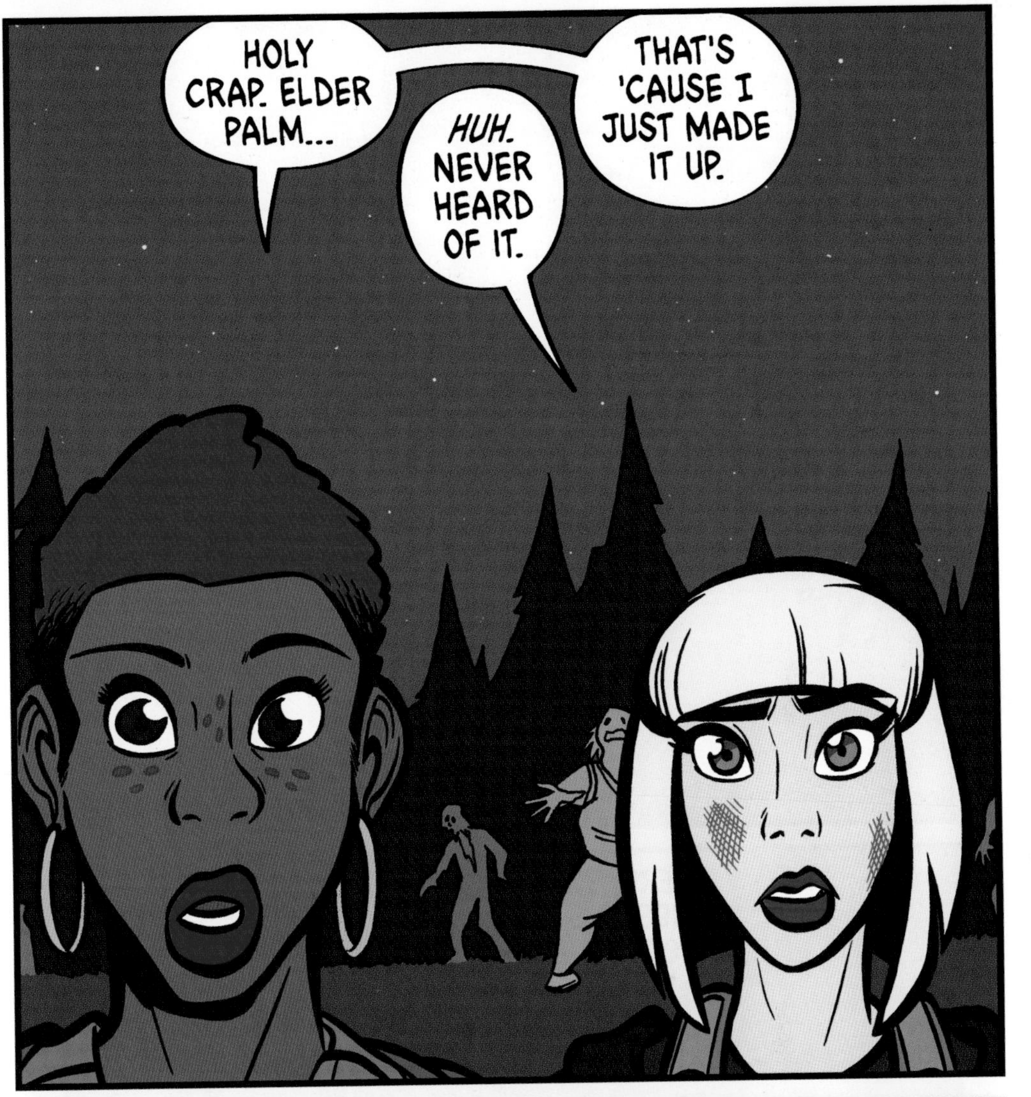
HOLY CRAP. ELDER PALM...
HUH. NEVER HEARD OF IT.
THAT'S 'CAUSE I JUST MADE IT UP.

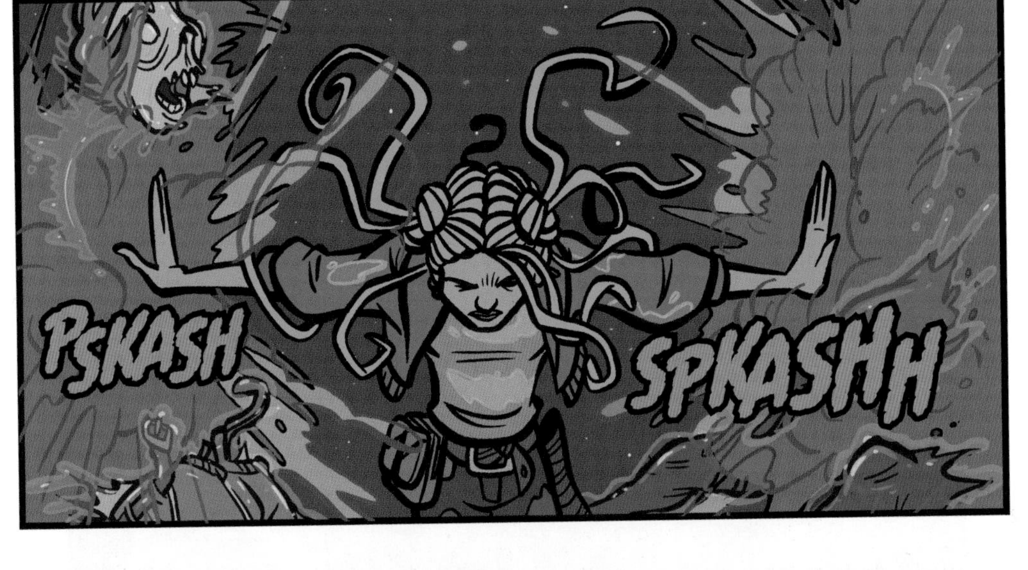
PSKASH
SPKASHH

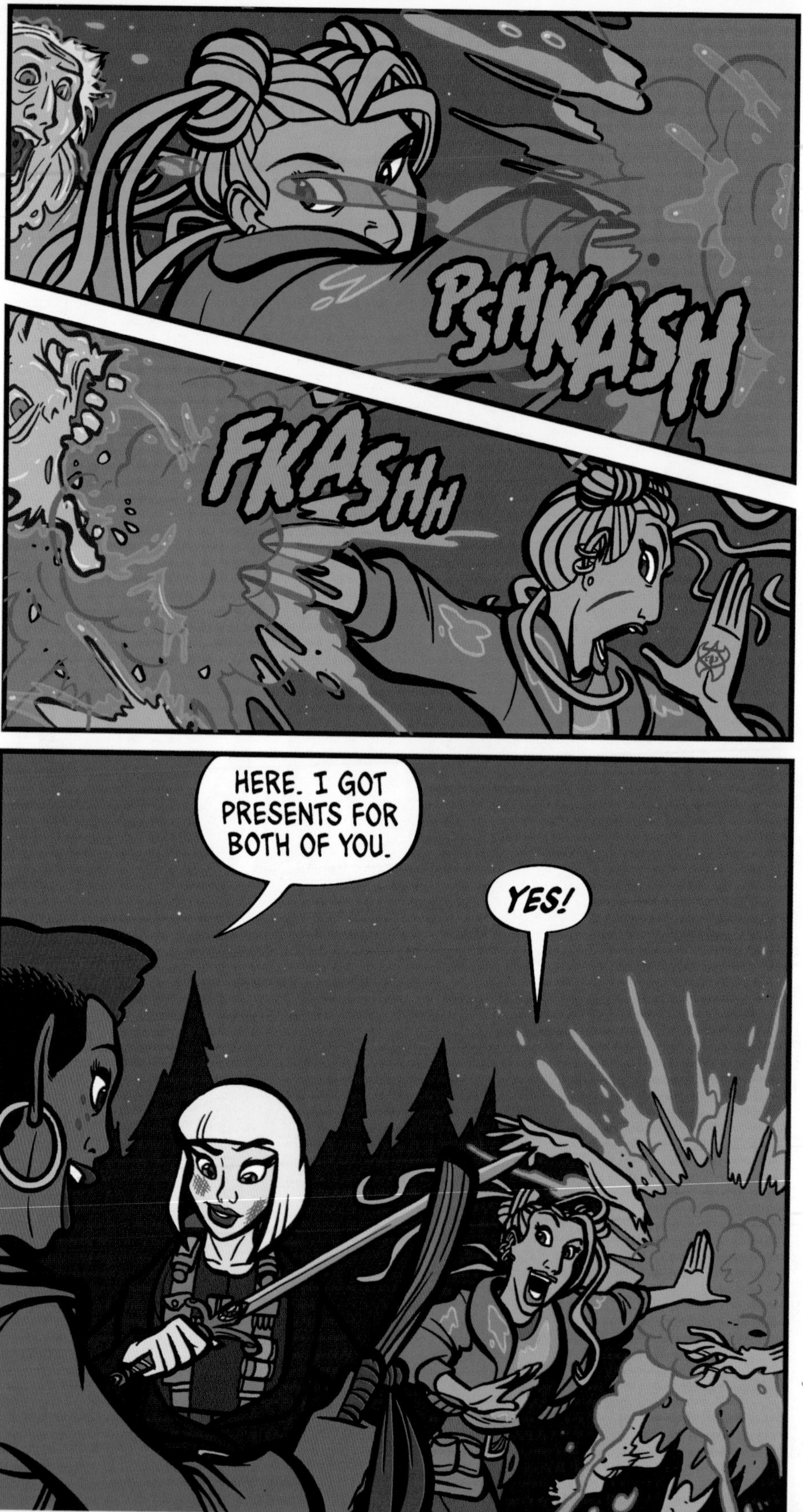
PSHKASH
FKASHH
HERE. I GOT PRESENTS FOR BOTH OF YOU.
YES!

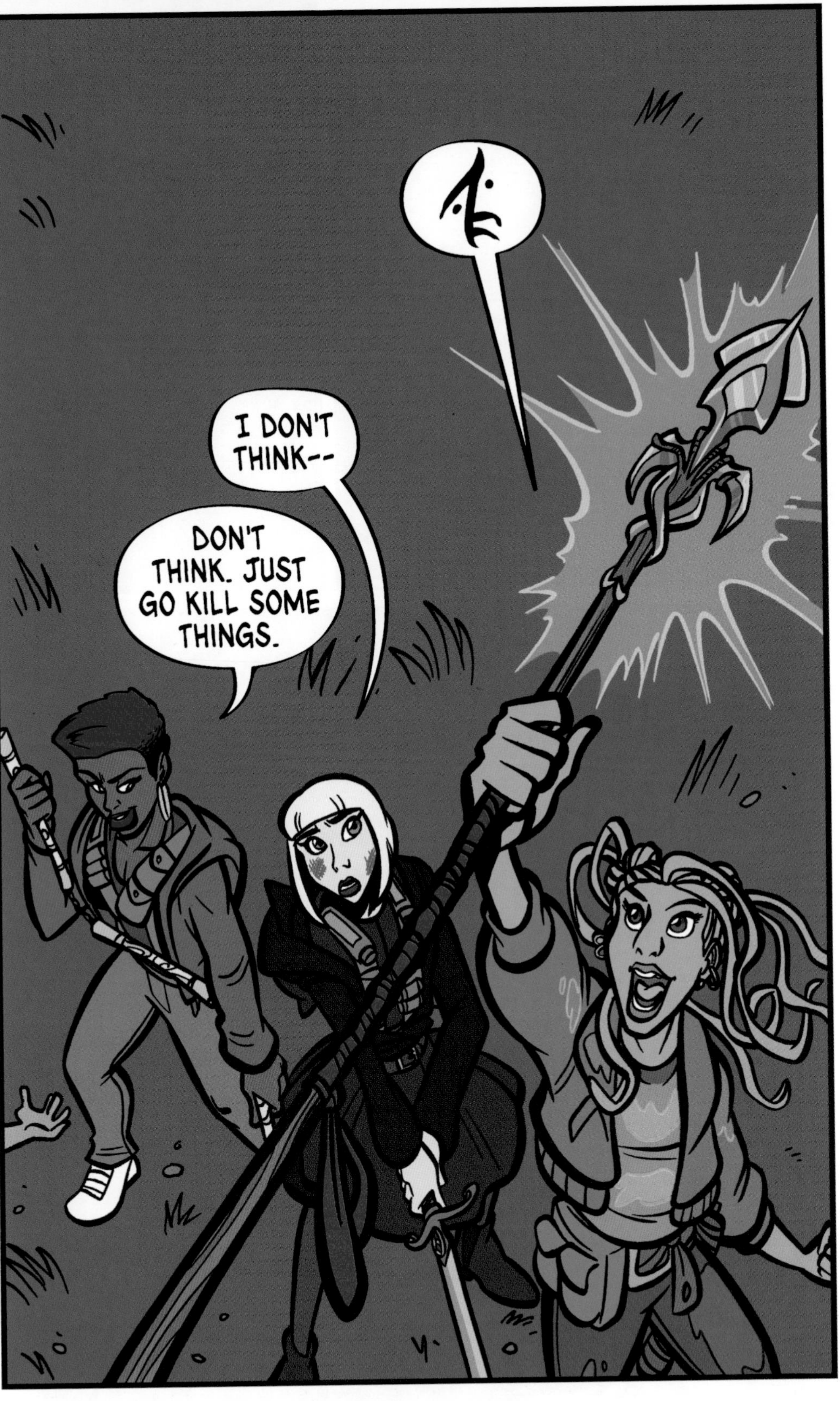
I DON'T THINK--
DON'T THINK. JUST GO KILL SOME THINGS.

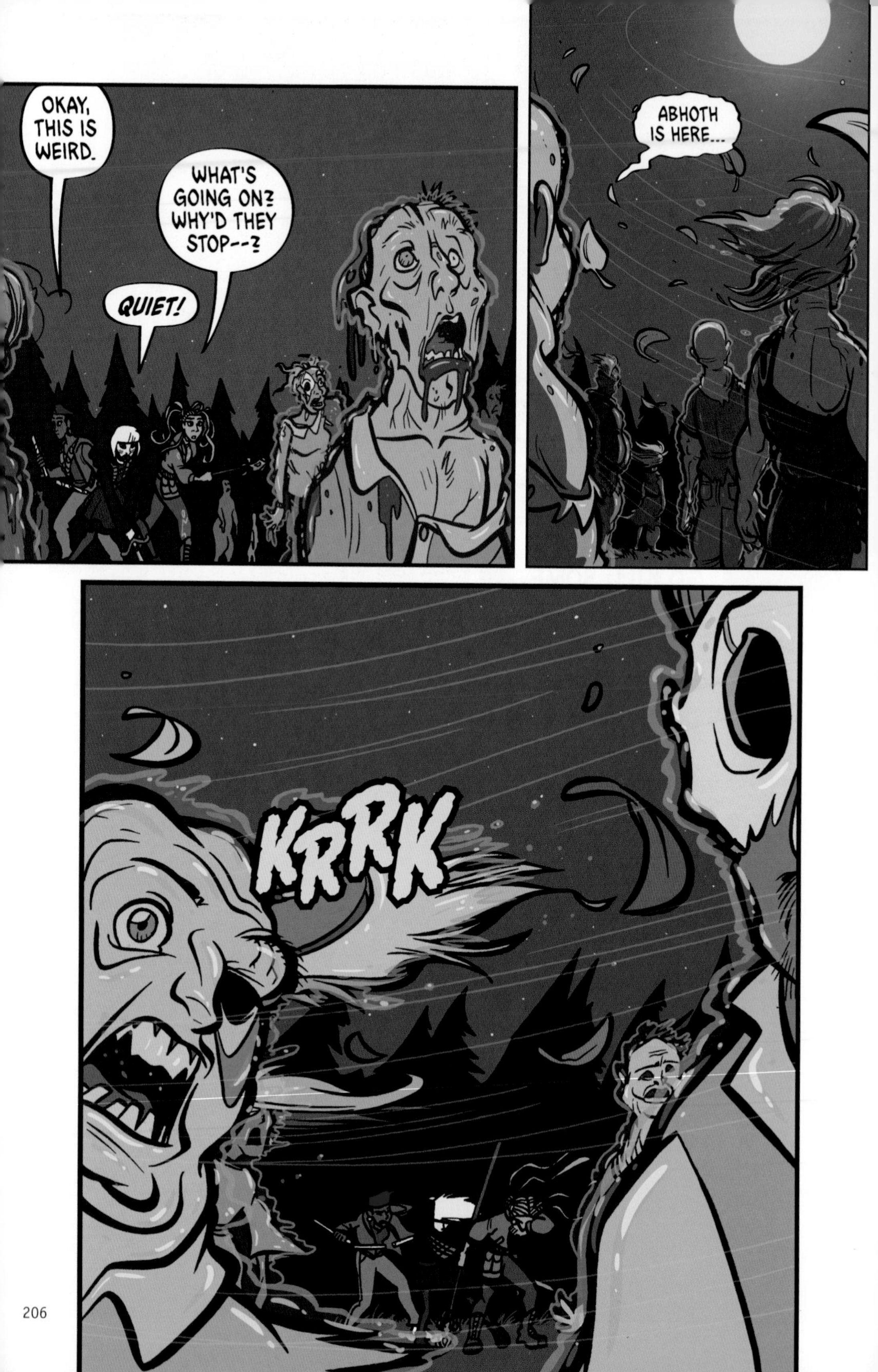
OKAY, THIS IS WEIRD.
WHAT'S GOING ON? WHY'D THEY STOP--?
QUIET!
ABHOTH IS HERE...
KRRK

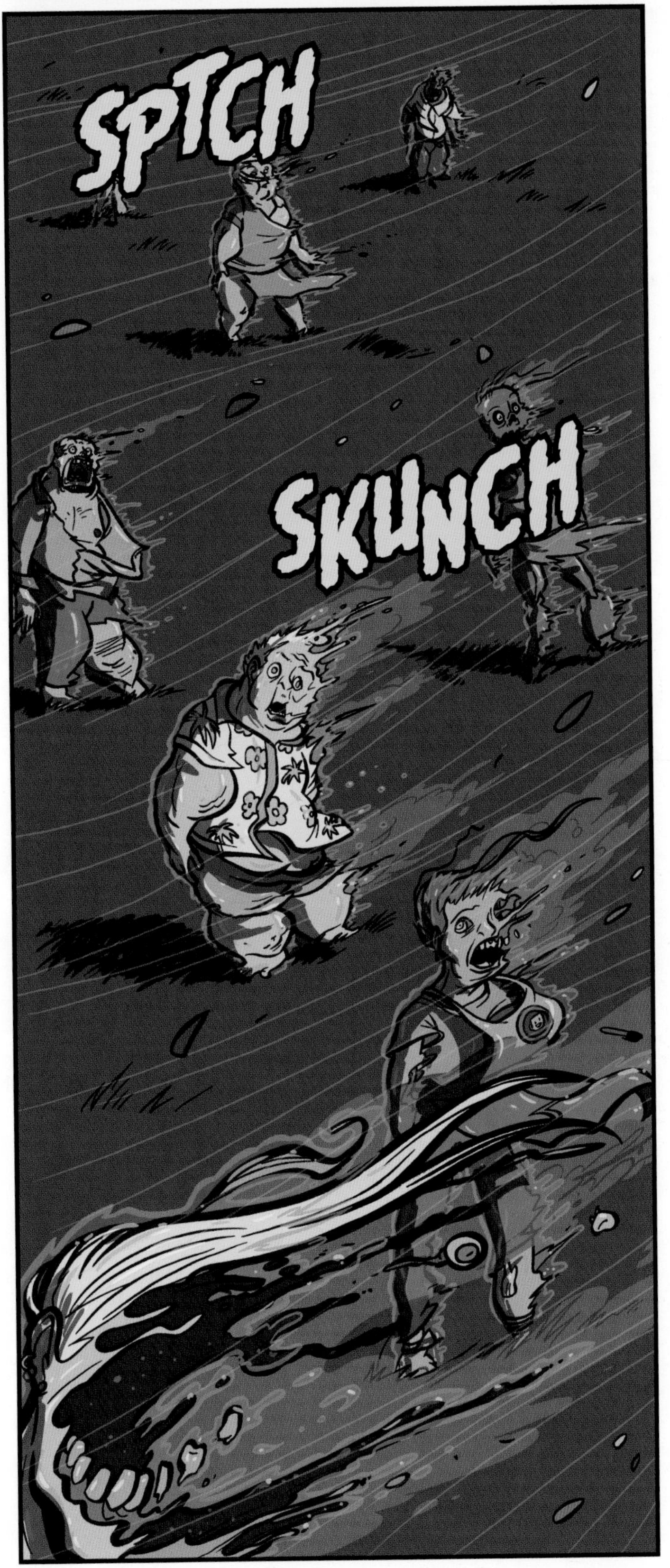
SPTCH
SKUNCH

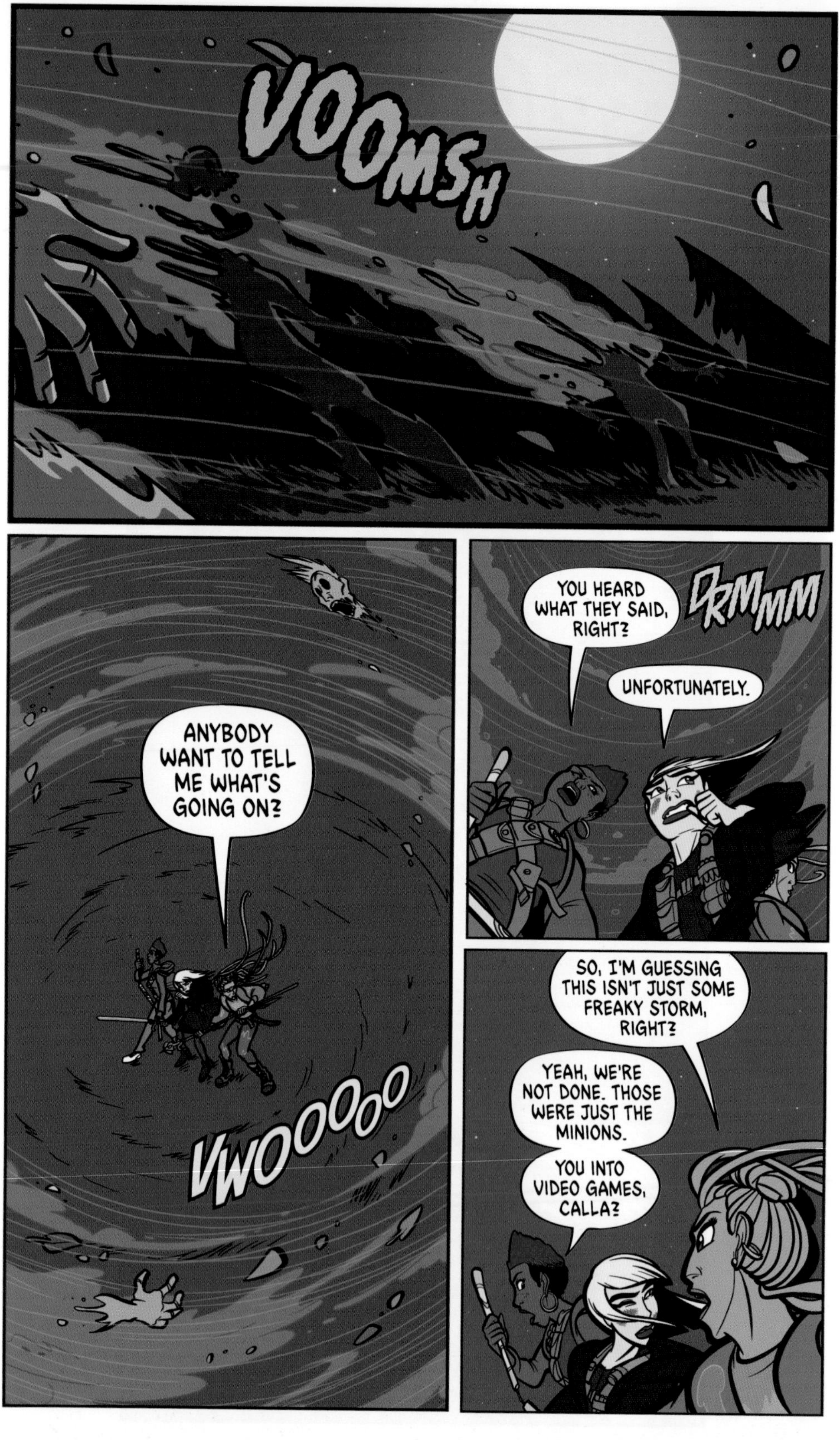
VOOMSH
ANYBODY WANT TO TELL ME WHAT'S GOING ON?
VWOOOOO
YOU HEARD WHAT THEY SAID, RIGHT?
DRMMM
UNFORTUNATELY.
SO, I'M GUESSING THIS ISN'T JUST SOME FREAKY STORM, RIGHT?
YEAH, WE'RE NOT DONE. THOSE WERE JUST THE MINIONS.
YOU INTO VIDEO GAMES, CALLA?

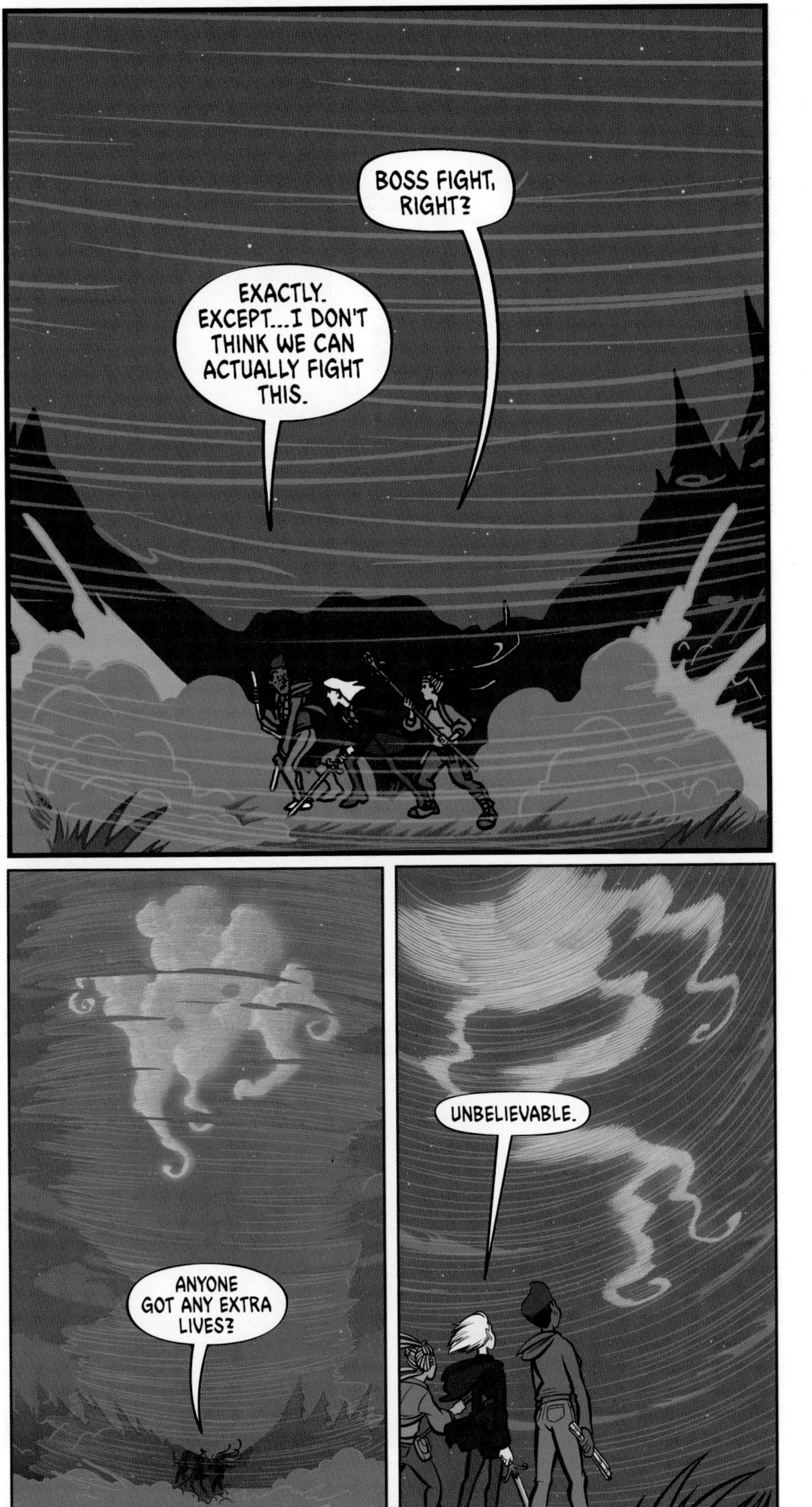
BOSS FIGHT, RIGHT?
EXACTLY. EXCEPT...I DON'T THINK WE CAN ACTUALLY FIGHT THIS.
ANYONE GOT ANY EXTRA LIVES?
UNBELIEVABLE.

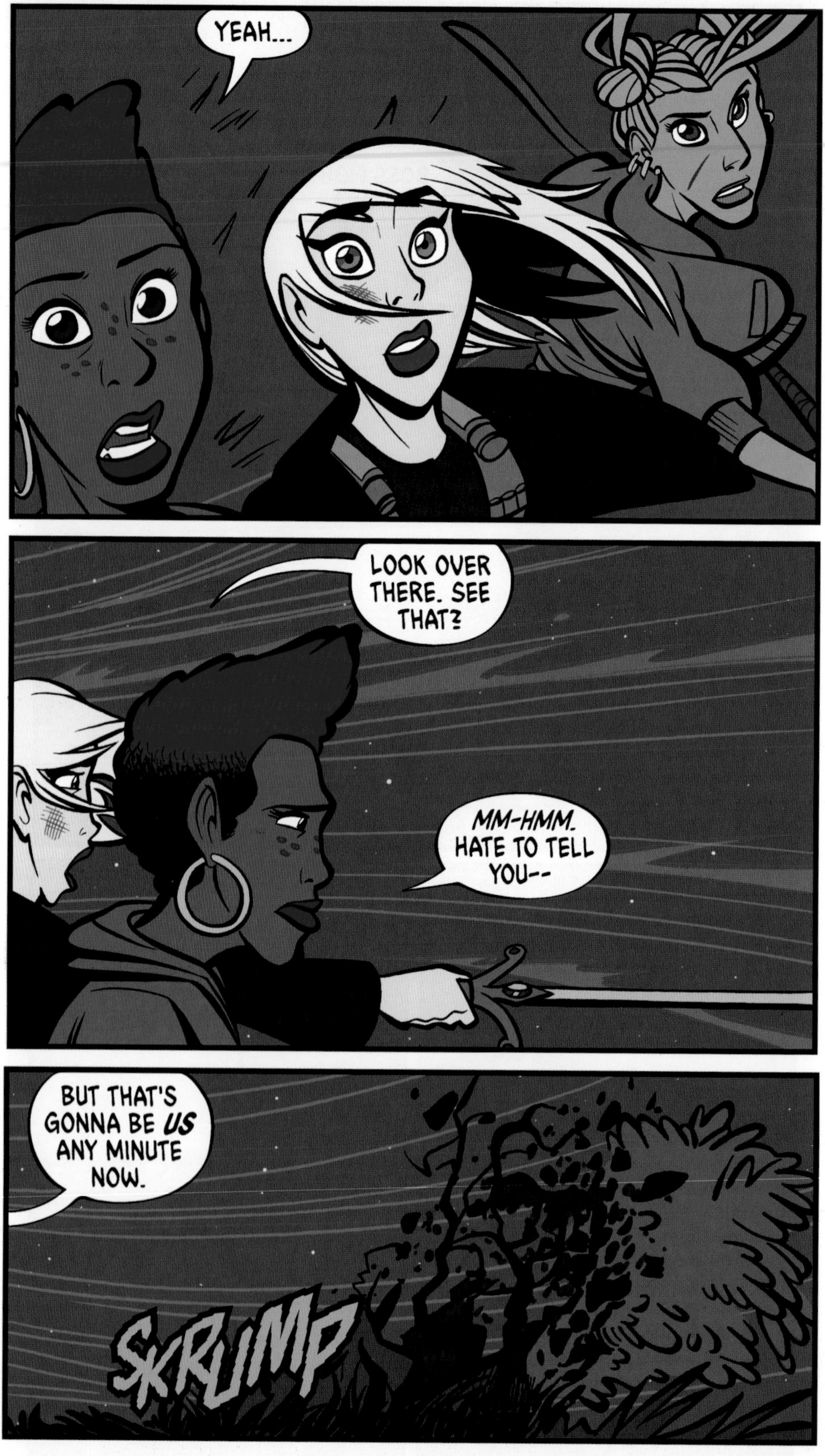
YEAH...
LOOK OVER THERE. SEE THAT?
MM-HMM. HATE TO TELL YOU--
BUT THAT'S GONNA BE US ANY MINUTE NOW.
SKRUMP

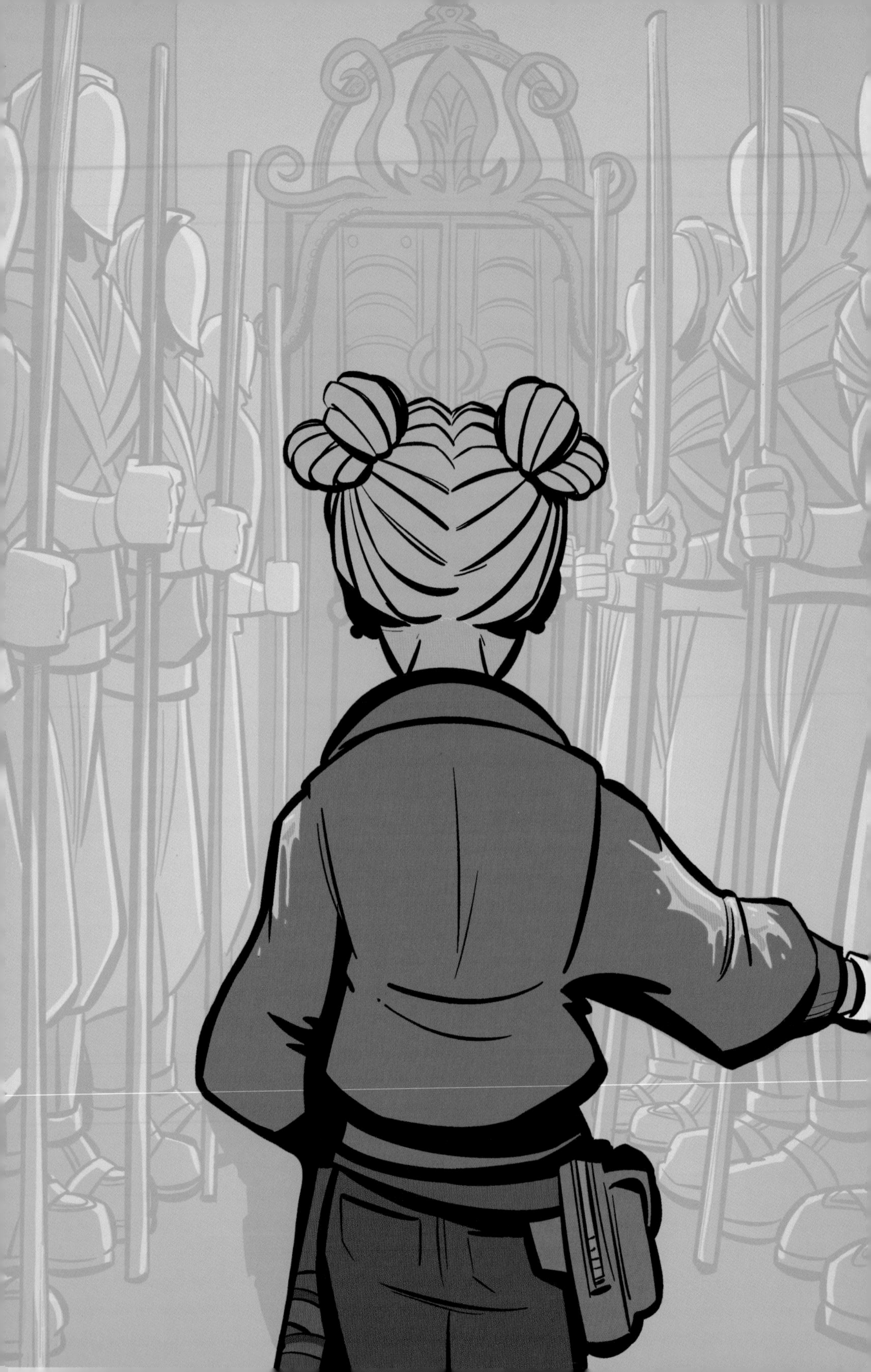

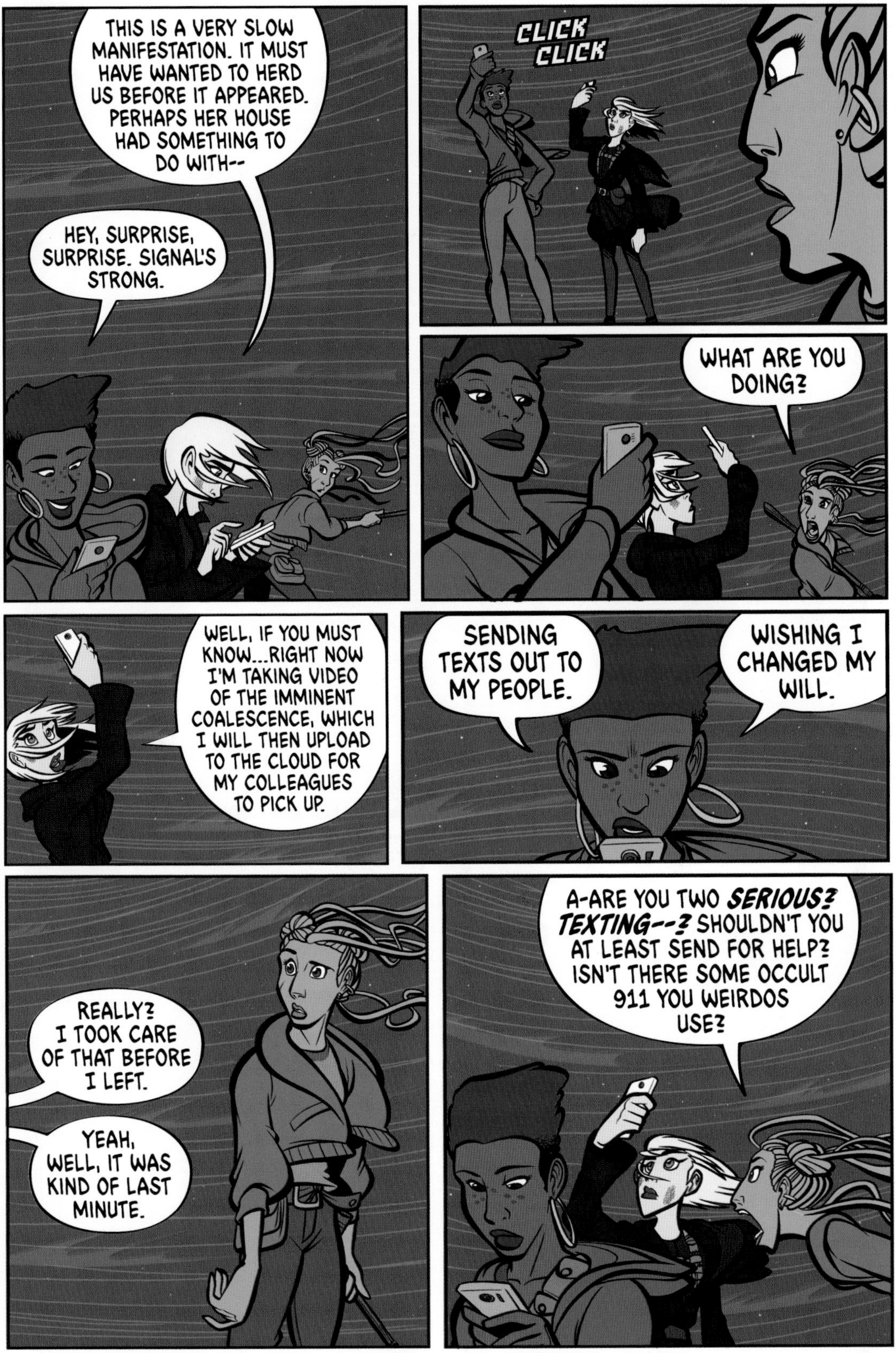
THIS IS A VERY SLOW MANIFESTATION. IT MUST HAVE WANTED TO HERD US BEFORE IT APPEARED. PERHAPS HER HOUSE HAD SOMETHING TO DO WITH--
HEY, SURPRISE, SURPRISE. SIGNAL'S STRONG.
CLICK CLICK
WHAT ARE YOU DOING?
WELL, IF YOU MUST KNOW...RIGHT NOW I'M TAKING VIDEO OF THE IMMINENT COALESCENCE, WHICH I WILL THEN UPLOAD TO THE CLOUD FOR MY COLLEAGUES TO PICK UP.
SENDING TEXTS OUT TO MY PEOPLE.
WISHING I CHANGED MY WILL.
REALLY? I TOOK CARE OF THAT BEFORE I LEFT.
YEAH, WELL, IT WAS KIND OF LAST MINUTE.
A-ARE YOU TWO SERIOUS? TEXTING--? SHOULDN'T YOU AT LEAST SEND FOR HELP? ISN'T THERE SOME OCCULT 911 YOU WEIRDOS USE?

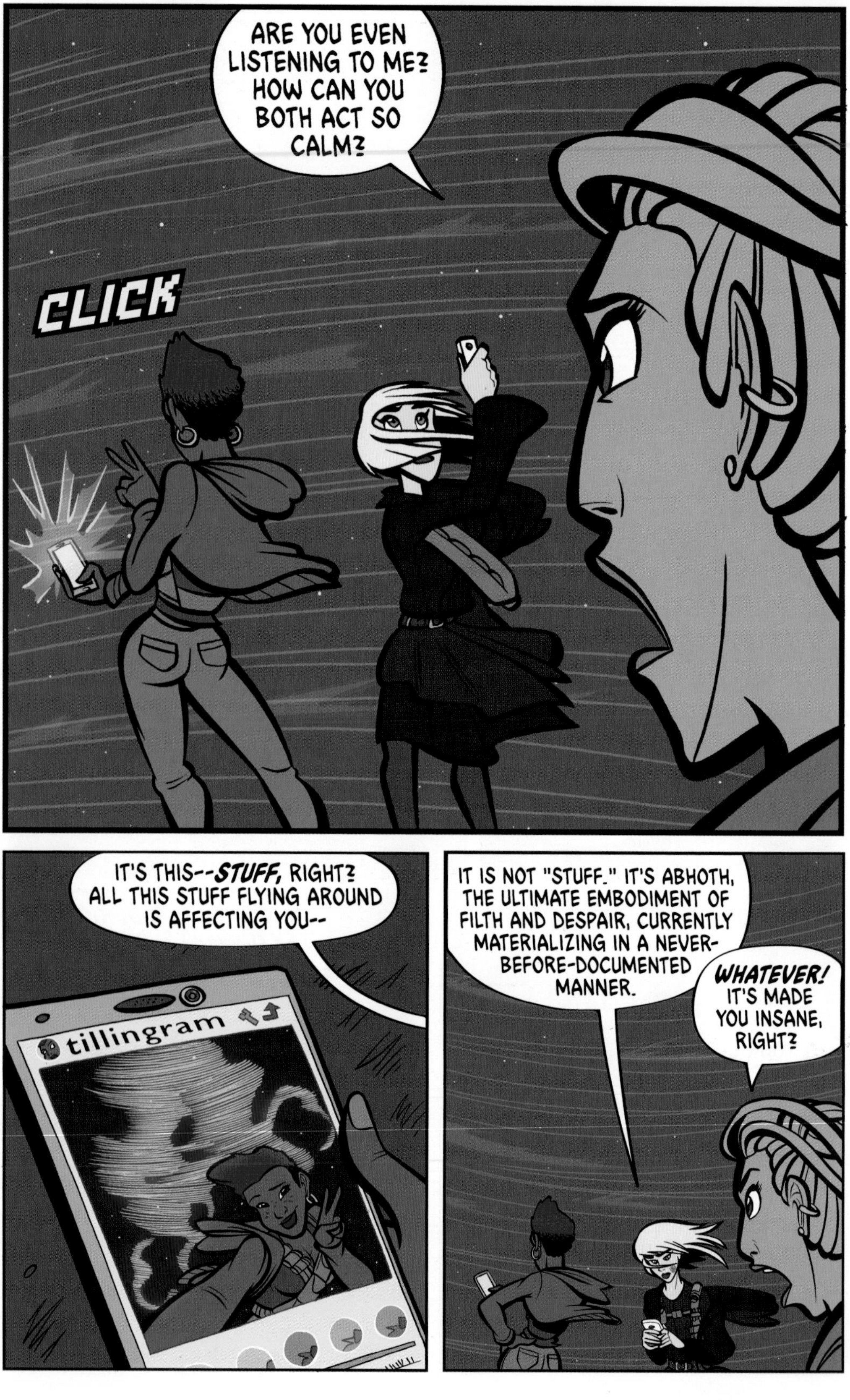
ARE YOU EVEN LISTENING TO ME? HOW CAN YOU BOTH ACT SO CALM?
CLICK
IT'S THIS--*STUFF,* RIGHT? ALL THIS STUFF FLYING AROUND IS AFFECTING YOU--
tillingram
IT IS NOT "STUFF." IT'S ABHOTH, THE ULTIMATE EMBODIMENT OF FILTH AND DESPAIR, CURRENTLY MATERIALIZING IN A NEVER-BEFORE-DOCUMENTED MANNER.
WHATEVER! IT'S MADE YOU INSANE, RIGHT?

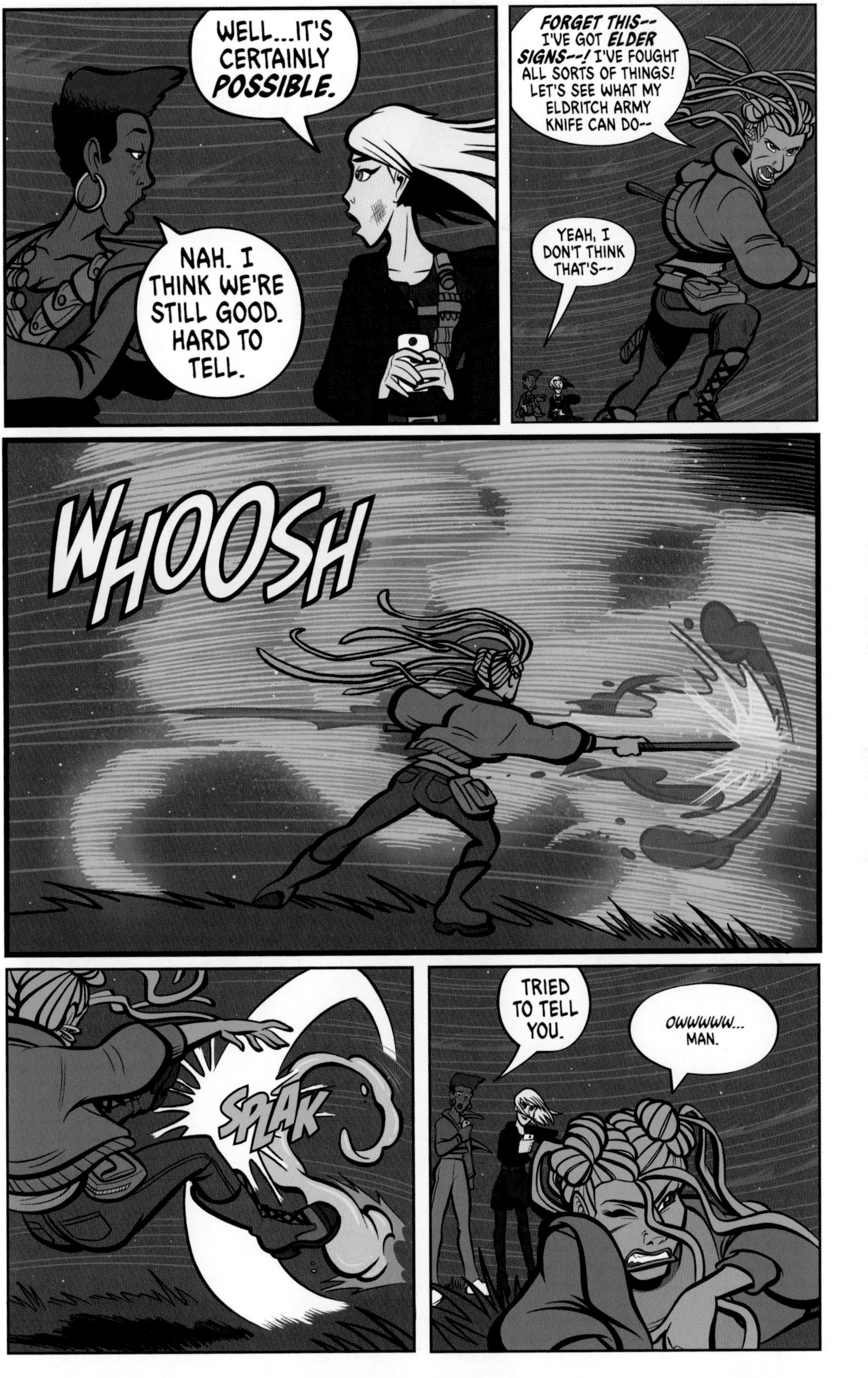
WELL...IT'S CERTAINLY POSSIBLE.
NAH. I THINK WE'RE STILL GOOD. HARD TO TELL.
FORGET THIS-- I'VE GOT ELDER SIGNS--! I'VE FOUGHT ALL SORTS OF THINGS! LET'S SEE WHAT MY ELDRITCH ARMY KNIFE CAN DO--
YEAH, I DON'T THINK THAT'S--
WHOOSH
SPLAK
TRIED TO TELL YOU.
OWWWWW... MAN.

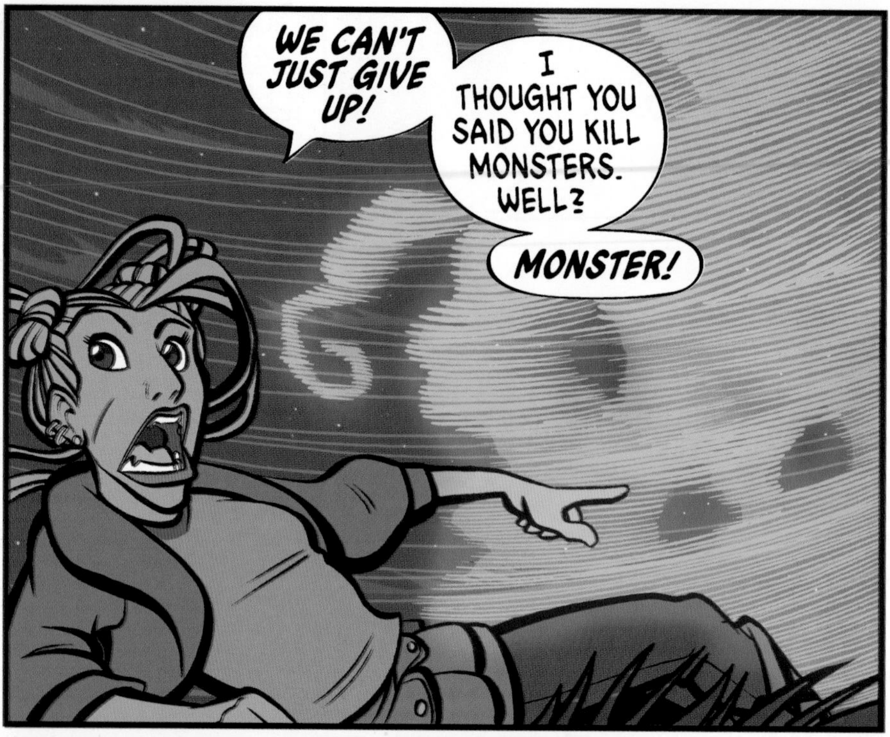
WE CAN'T JUST GIVE UP!
I THOUGHT YOU SAID YOU KILL MONSTERS. WELL?
MONSTER!

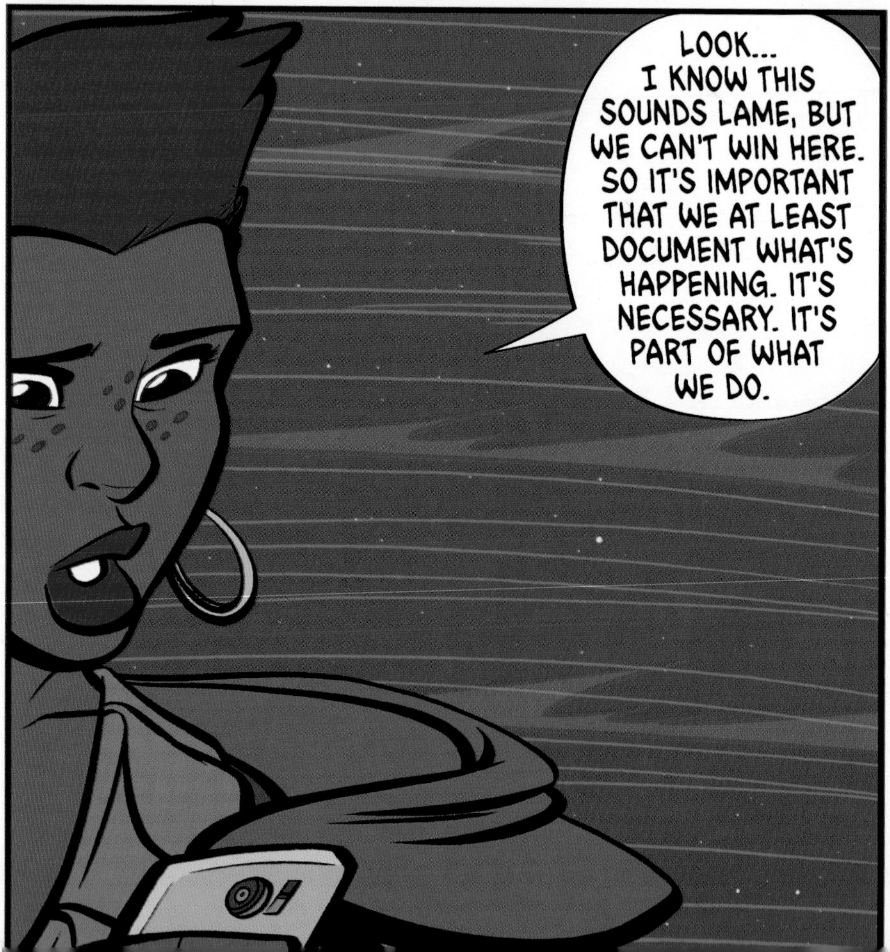
LOOK... I KNOW THIS SOUNDS LAME, BUT WE CAN'T WIN HERE. SO IT'S IMPORTANT THAT WE AT LEAST DOCUMENT WHAT'S HAPPENING. IT'S NECESSARY. IT'S PART OF WHAT WE DO.

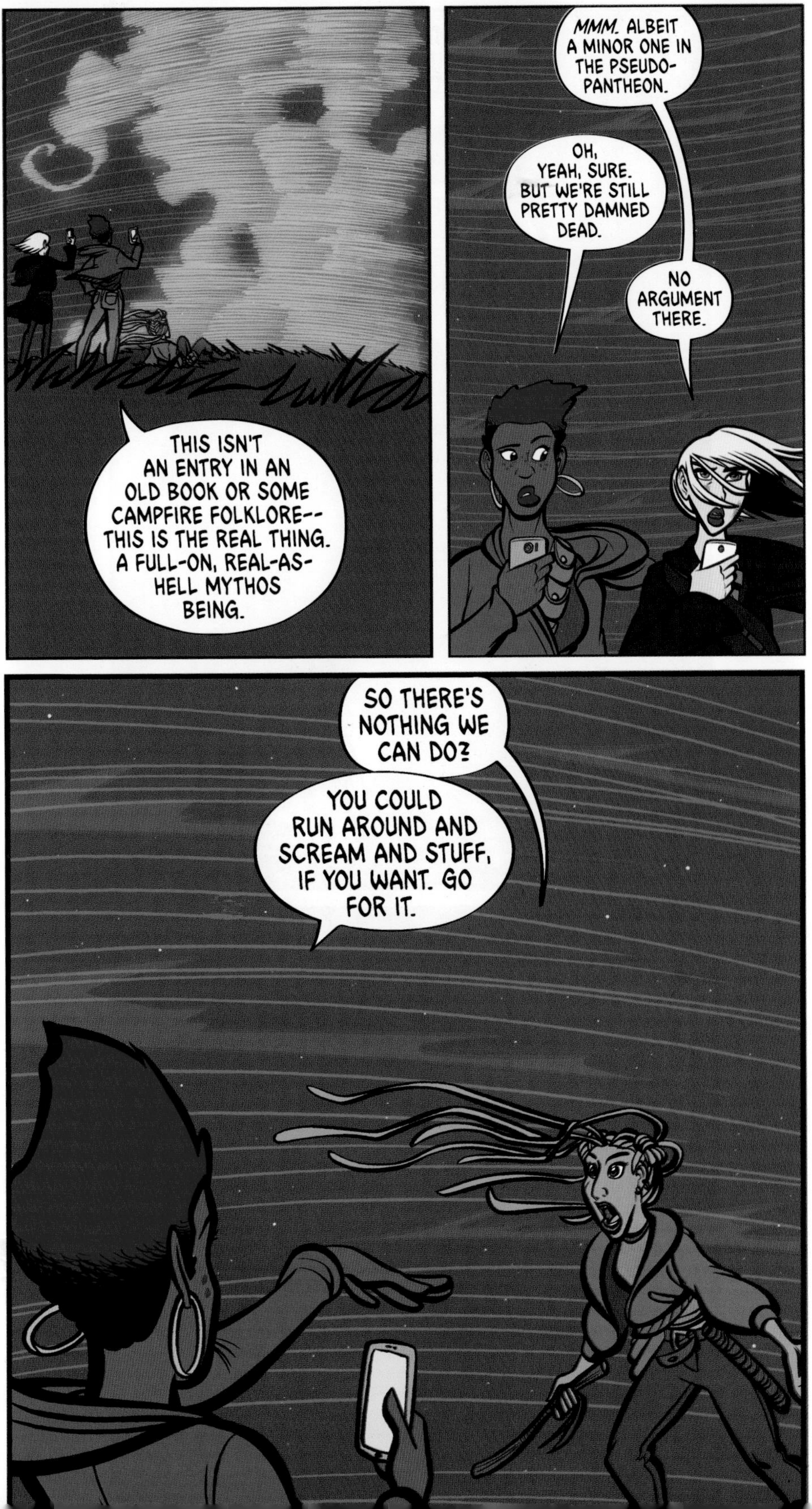
THIS ISN'T AN ENTRY IN AN OLD BOOK OR SOME CAMPFIRE FOLKLORE--THIS IS THE REAL THING. A FULL-ON, REAL-AS-HELL MYTHOS BEING.
MMM. ALBEIT A MINOR ONE IN THE PSEUDO-PANTHEON.
OH, YEAH, SURE. BUT WE'RE STILL PRETTY DAMNED DEAD.
NO ARGUMENT THERE.
SO THERE'S NOTHING WE CAN DO?
YOU COULD RUN AROUND AND SCREAM AND STUFF, IF YOU WANT. GO FOR IT.

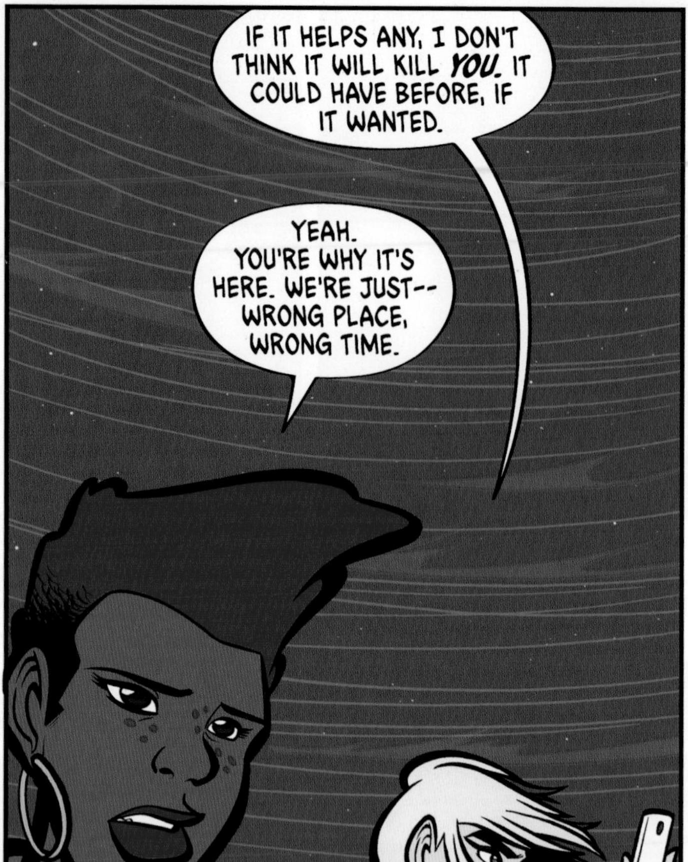
IF IT HELPS ANY, I DON'T THINK IT WILL KILL *YOU.* IT COULD HAVE BEFORE, IF IT WANTED.
YEAH. YOU'RE WHY IT'S HERE. WE'RE JUST-- WRONG PLACE, WRONG TIME.

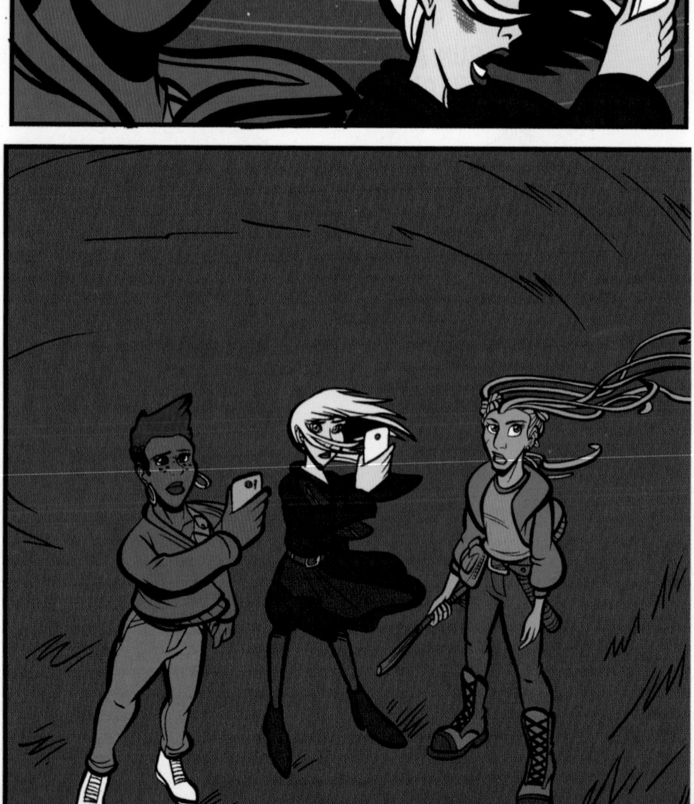

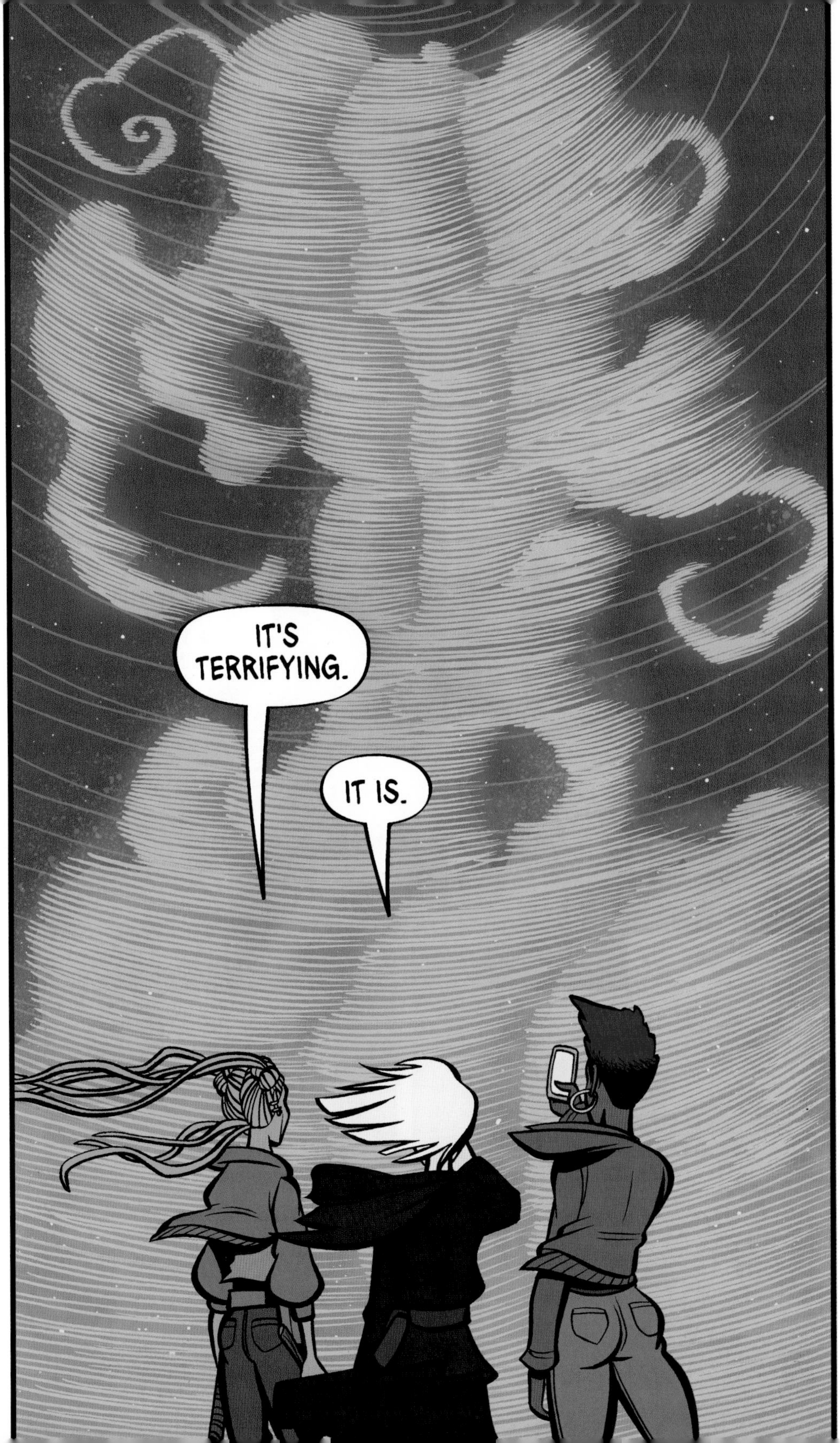
IT'S TERRIFYING.
IT IS.

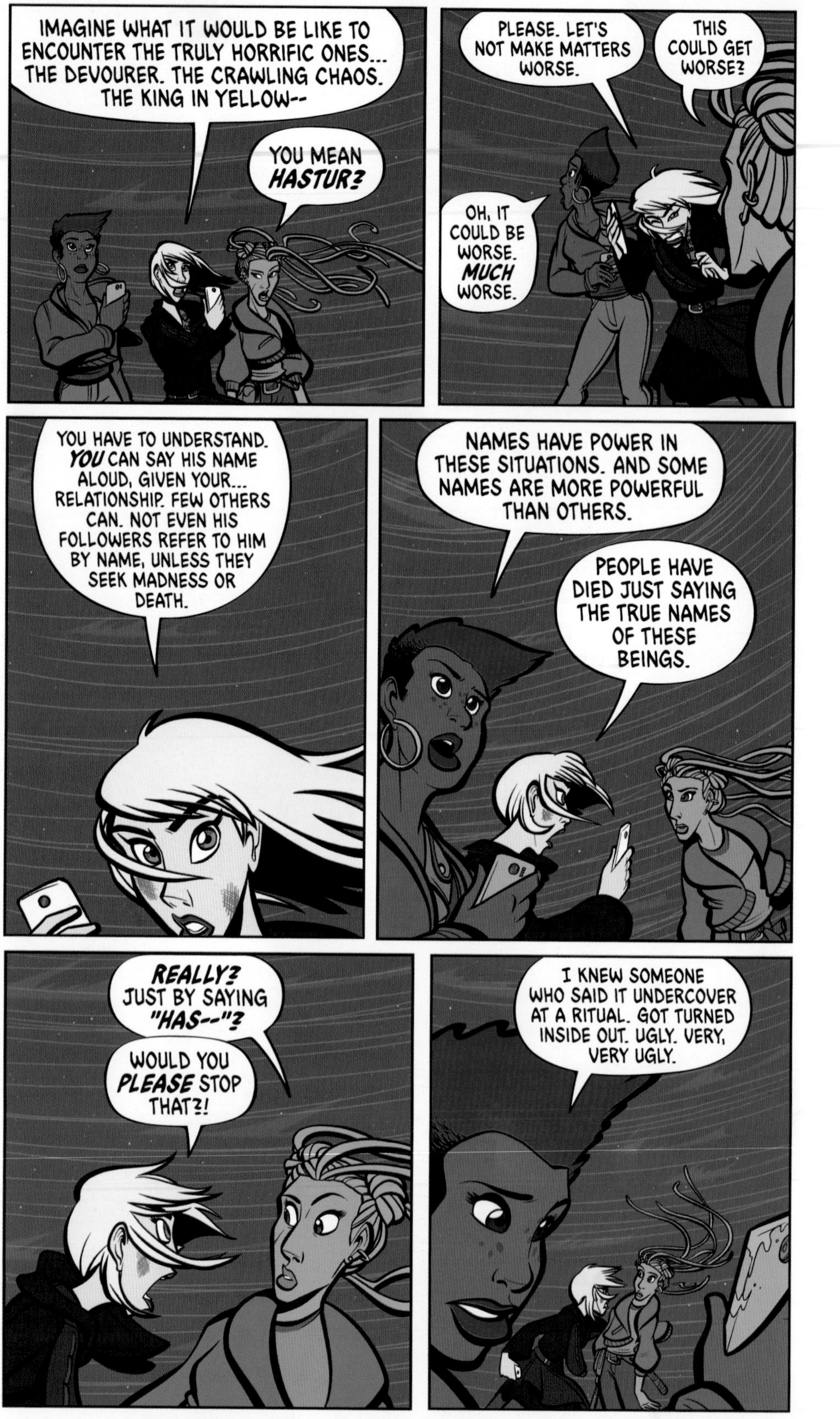
IMAGINE WHAT IT WOULD BE LIKE TO ENCOUNTER THE TRULY HORRIFIC ONES... THE DEVOURER. THE CRAWLING CHAOS. THE KING IN YELLOW--
YOU MEAN *HASTUR?*
PLEASE. LET'S NOT MAKE MATTERS WORSE.
THIS COULD GET WORSE?
OH, IT COULD BE WORSE. *MUCH* WORSE.
YOU HAVE TO UNDERSTAND. *YOU* CAN SAY HIS NAME ALOUD, GIVEN YOUR... RELATIONSHIP. FEW OTHERS CAN. NOT EVEN HIS FOLLOWERS REFER TO HIM BY NAME, UNLESS THEY SEEK MADNESS OR DEATH.
NAMES HAVE POWER IN THESE SITUATIONS. AND SOME NAMES ARE MORE POWERFUL THAN OTHERS.
PEOPLE HAVE DIED JUST SAYING THE TRUE NAMES OF THESE BEINGS.
REALLY? JUST BY SAYING *"HAS--"?*
WOULD YOU *PLEASE* STOP THAT?!
I KNEW SOMEONE WHO SAID IT UNDERCOVER AT A RITUAL. GOT TURNED INSIDE OUT. UGLY. VERY, VERY UGLY.

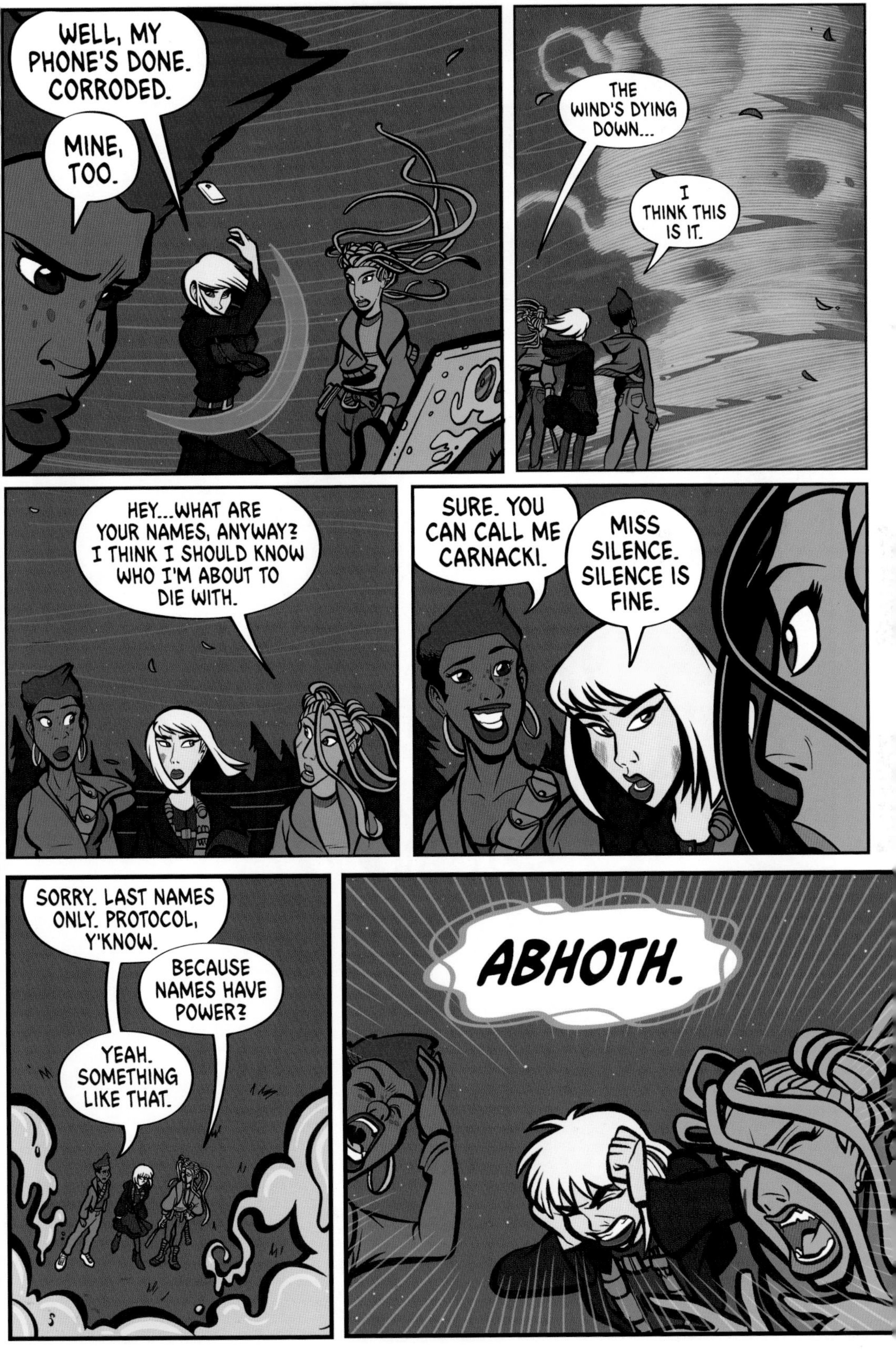

WELL, MY PHONE'S DONE. CORRODED.
MINE, TOO.
THE WIND'S DYING DOWN...
I THINK THIS IS IT.
HEY...WHAT ARE YOUR NAMES, ANYWAY? I THINK I SHOULD KNOW WHO I'M ABOUT TO DIE WITH.
SURE. YOU CAN CALL ME CARNACKI.
MISS SILENCE. SILENCE IS FINE.
SORRY. LAST NAMES ONLY. PROTOCOL, Y'KNOW.
BECAUSE NAMES HAVE POWER?
YEAH. SOMETHING LIKE THAT.
ABHOTH.

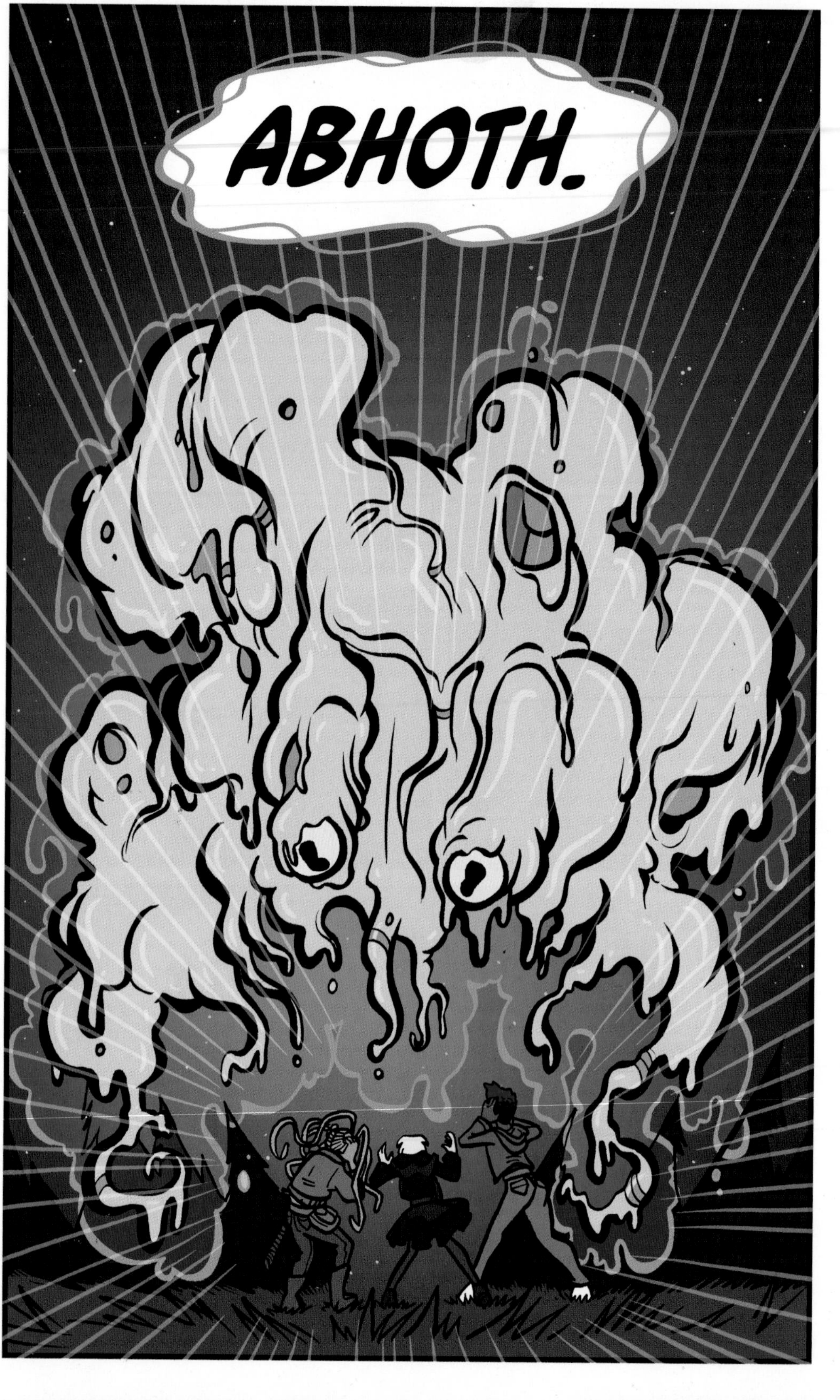
ABHOTH.

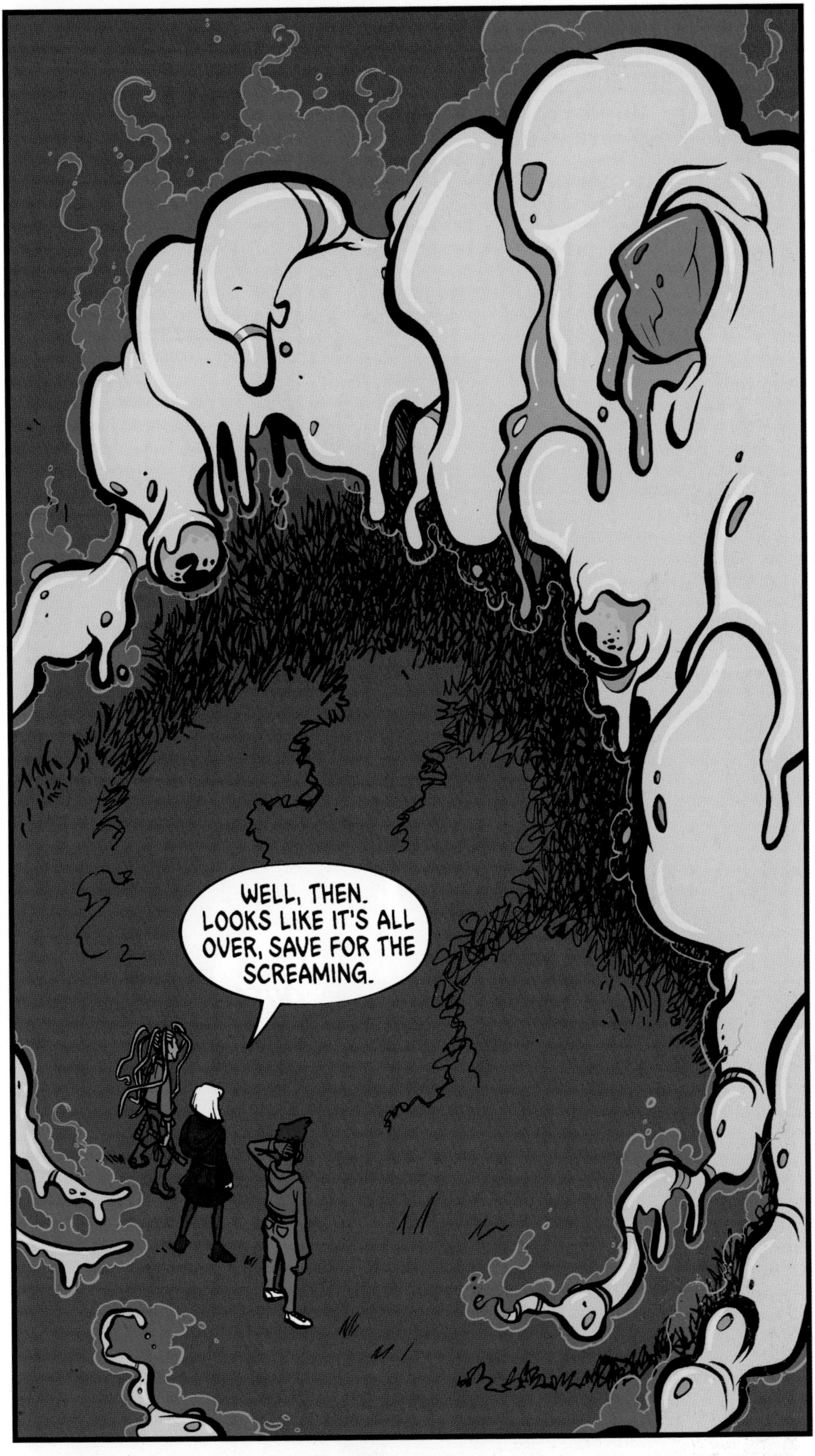
WELL, THEN. LOOKS LIKE IT'S ALL OVER, SAVE FOR THE SCREAMING.

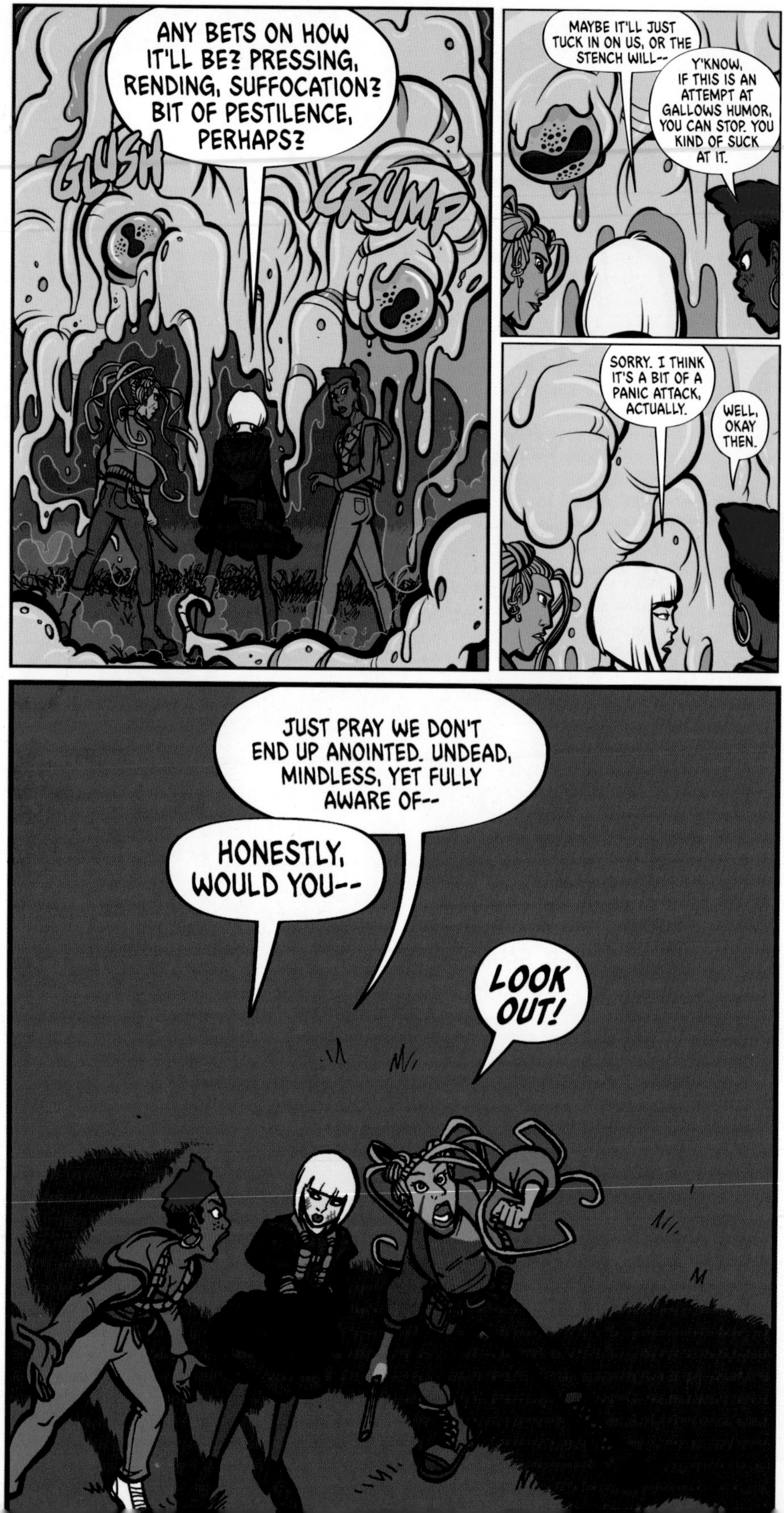
ANY BETS ON HOW IT'LL BE? PRESSING, RENDING, SUFFOCATION? BIT OF PESTILENCE, PERHAPS?
GLUSH
CRUMP
MAYBE IT'LL JUST TUCK IN ON US, OR THE STENCH WILL--
Y'KNOW, IF THIS IS AN ATTEMPT AT GALLOWS HUMOR, YOU CAN STOP. YOU KIND OF SUCK AT IT.
SORRY. I THINK IT'S A BIT OF A PANIC ATTACK, ACTUALLY.
WELL, OKAY THEN.
JUST PRAY WE DON'T END UP ANOINTED. UNDEAD, MINDLESS, YET FULLY AWARE OF--
HONESTLY, WOULD YOU--
LOOK OUT!

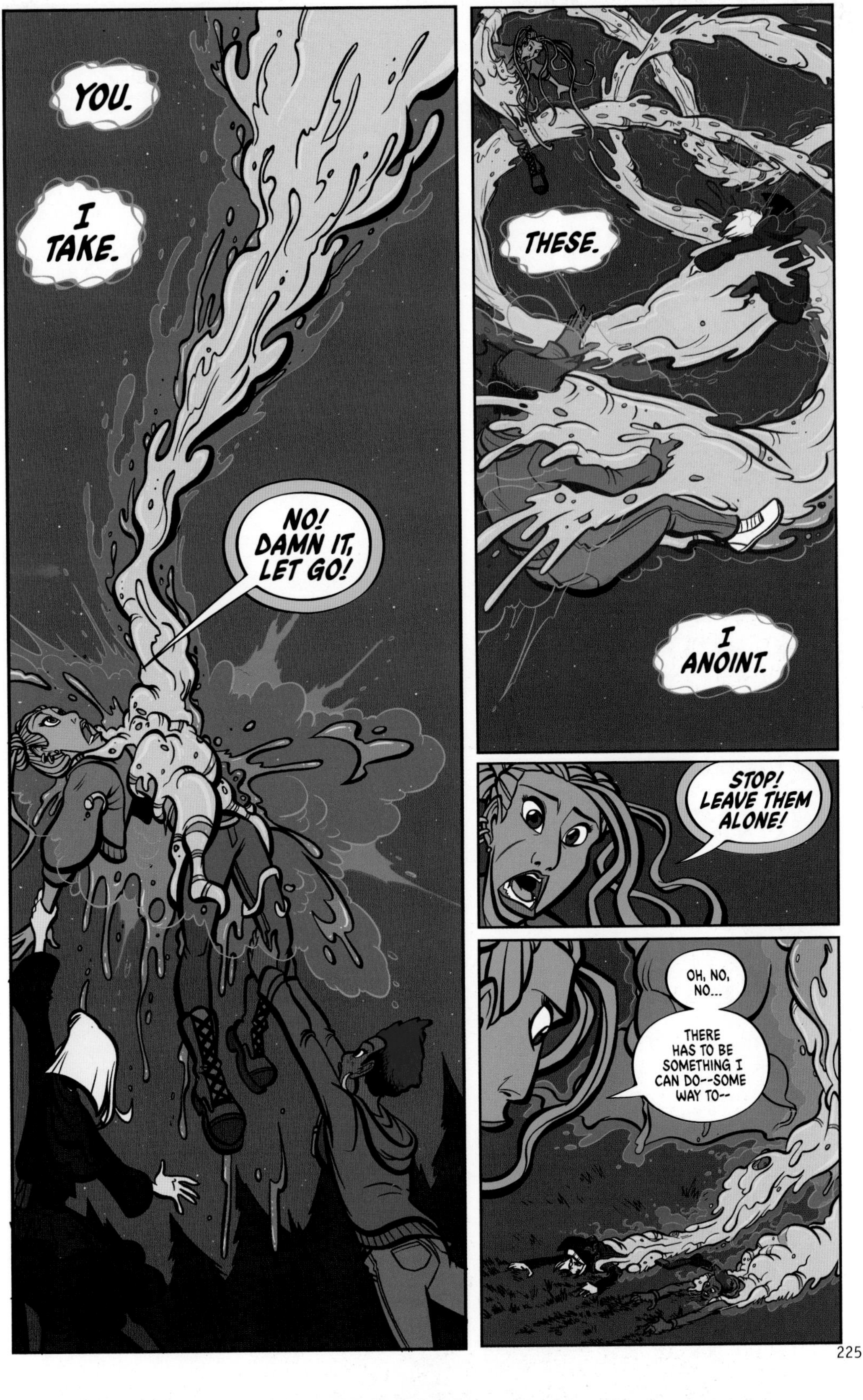
YOU.
I TAKE.
NO! DAMN IT, LET GO!
THESE.
I ANOINT.
STOP! LEAVE THEM ALONE!
OH, NO, NO...
THERE HAS TO BE SOMETHING I CAN DO--SOME WAY TO--

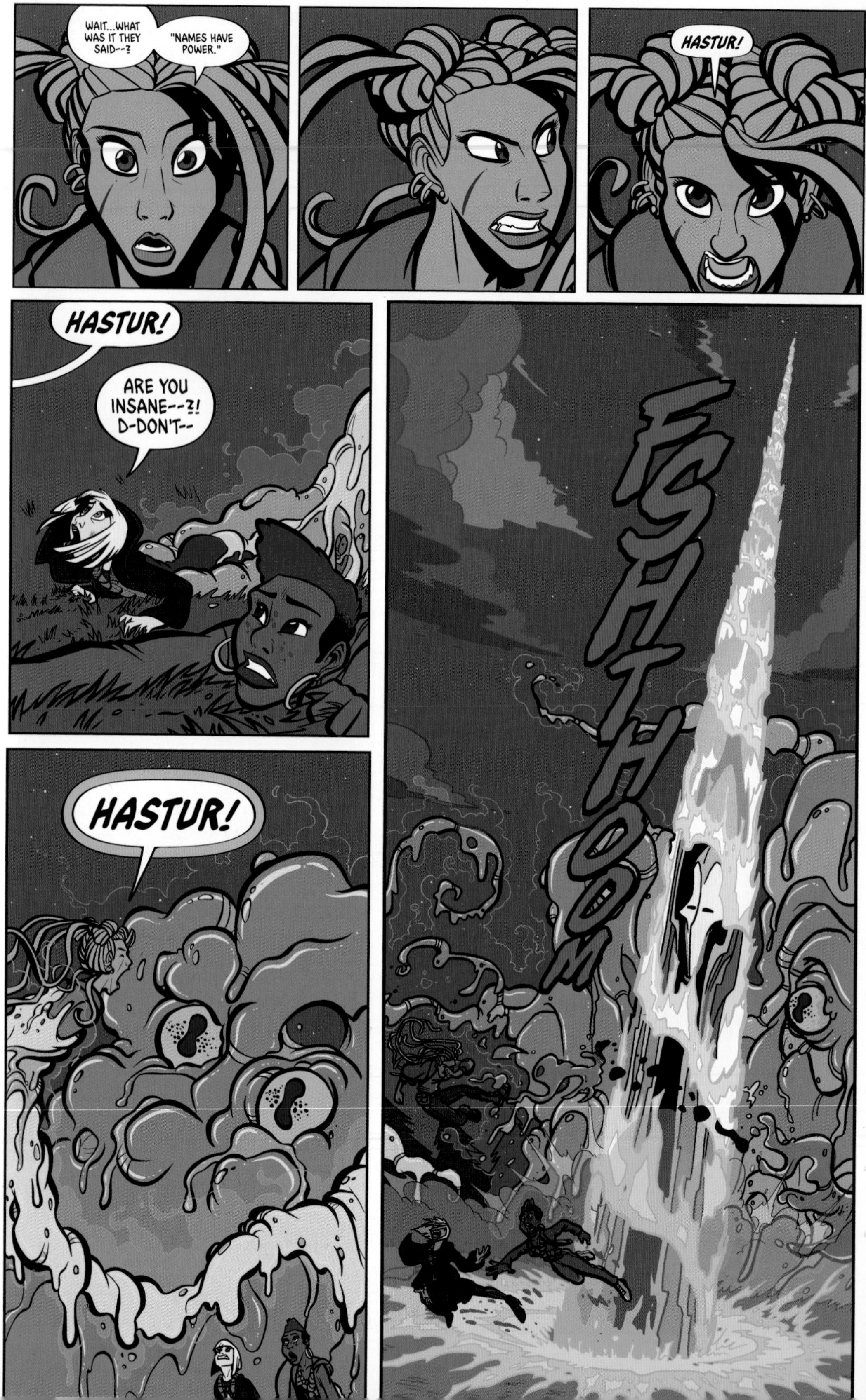
WAIT...WHAT WAS IT THEY SAID--?
"NAMES HAVE POWER."
HASTUR!
HASTUR!
ARE YOU INSANE--?! D-DON'T--
HASTUR!
FSHHHOOOM

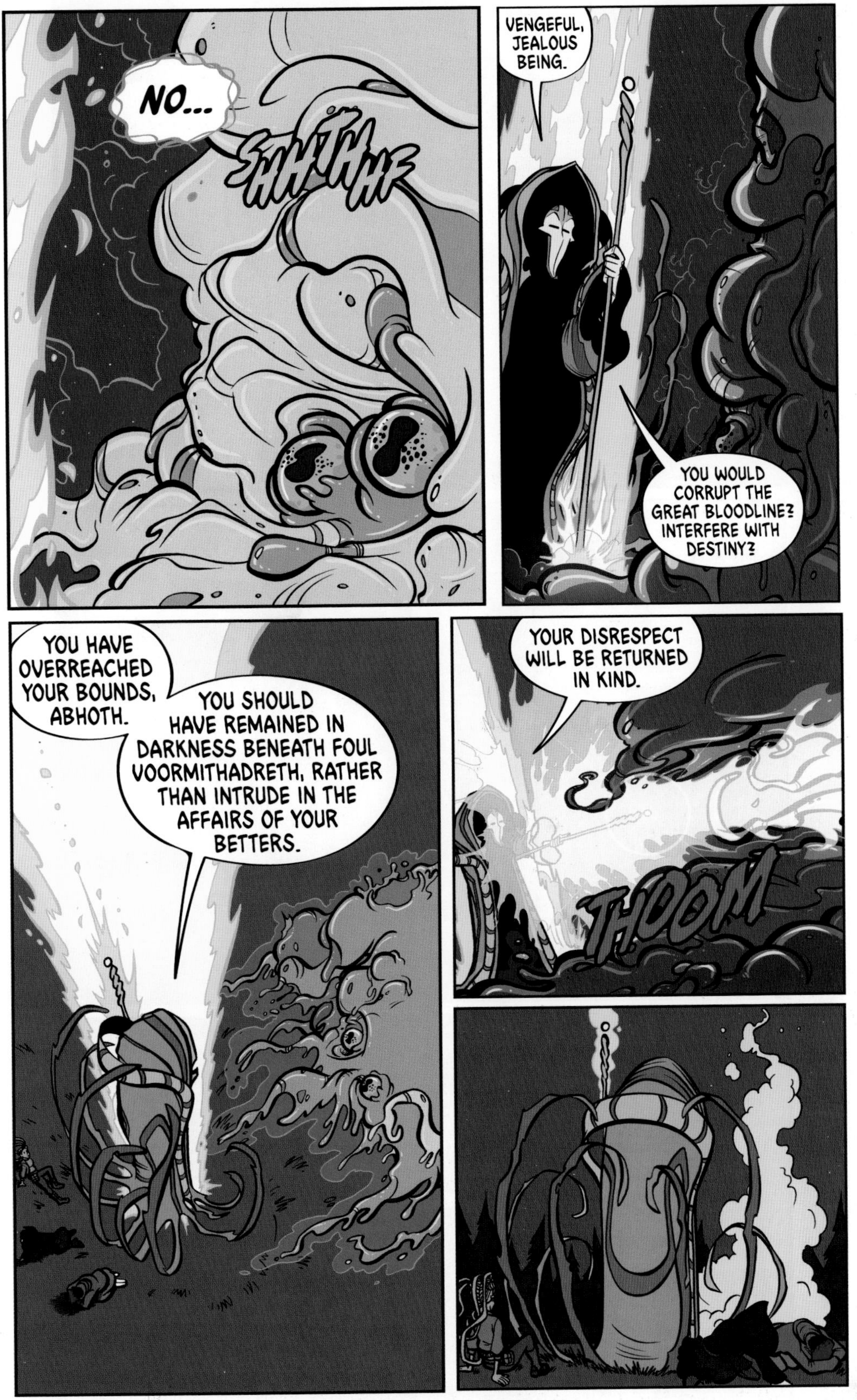
NO...
SHHTHHF
VENGEFUL, JEALOUS BEING.
YOU WOULD CORRUPT THE GREAT BLOODLINE? INTERFERE WITH DESTINY?
YOU HAVE OVERREACHED YOUR BOUNDS, ABHOTH.
YOU SHOULD HAVE REMAINED IN DARKNESS BENEATH FOUL VOORMITHADRETH, RATHER THAN INTRUDE IN THE AFFAIRS OF YOUR BETTERS.
YOUR DISRESPECT WILL BE RETURNED IN KIND.
THOOM

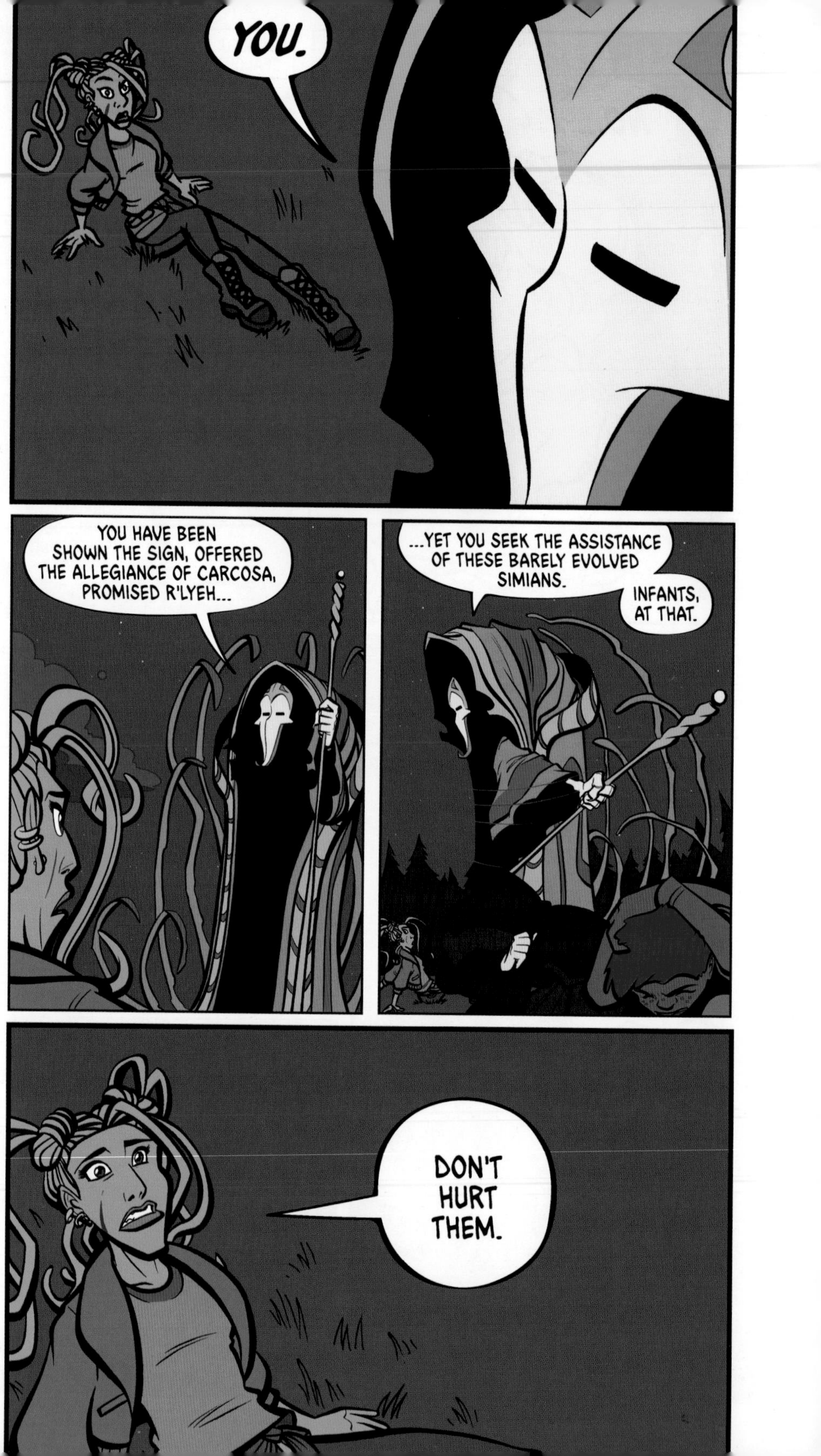
YOU.
YOU HAVE BEEN SHOWN THE SIGN, OFFERED THE ALLEGIANCE OF CARCOSA, PROMISED R'LYEH...
...YET YOU SEEK THE ASSISTANCE OF THESE BARELY EVOLVED SIMIANS.
INFANTS, AT THAT.
DON'T HURT THEM.

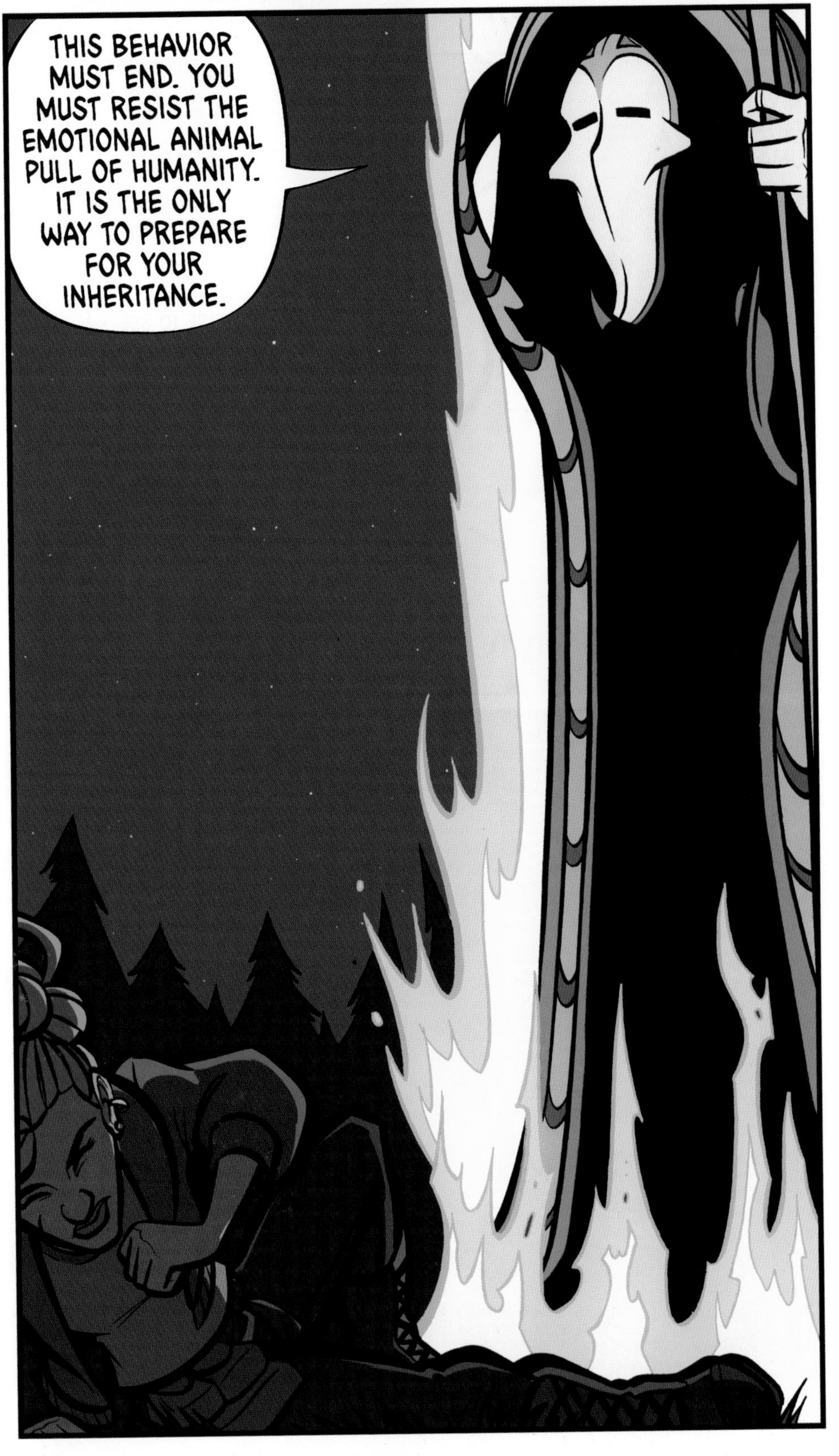
THIS BEHAVIOR MUST END. YOU MUST RESIST THE EMOTIONAL ANIMAL PULL OF HUMANITY. IT IS THE ONLY WAY TO PREPARE FOR YOUR INHERITANCE.

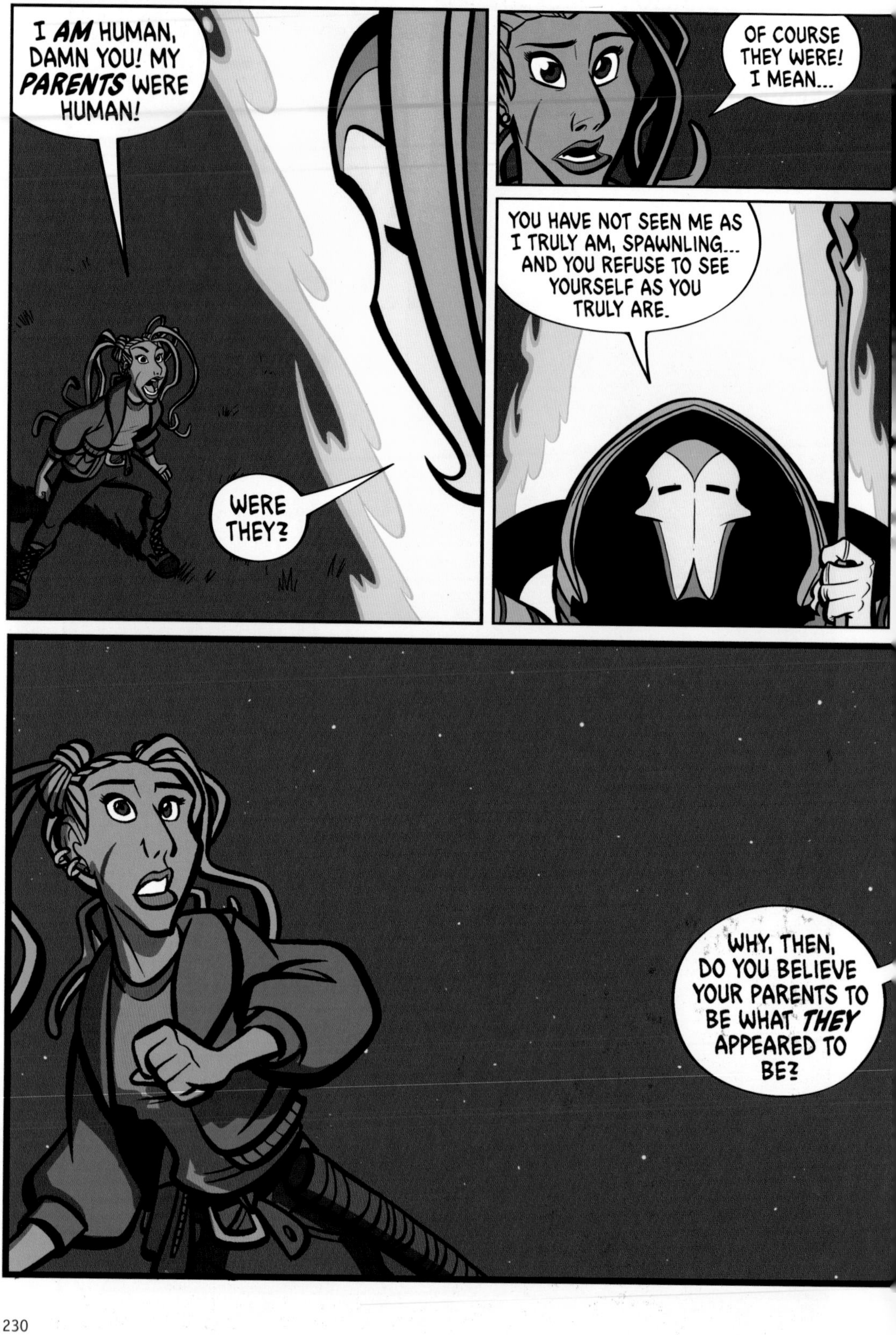
I AM HUMAN, DAMN YOU! MY PARENTS WERE HUMAN!
WERE THEY?
OF COURSE THEY WERE! I MEAN...
YOU HAVE NOT SEEN ME AS I TRULY AM, SPAWNLING... AND YOU REFUSE TO SEE YOURSELF AS YOU TRULY ARE.
WHY, THEN, DO YOU BELIEVE YOUR PARENTS TO BE WHAT THEY APPEARED TO BE?

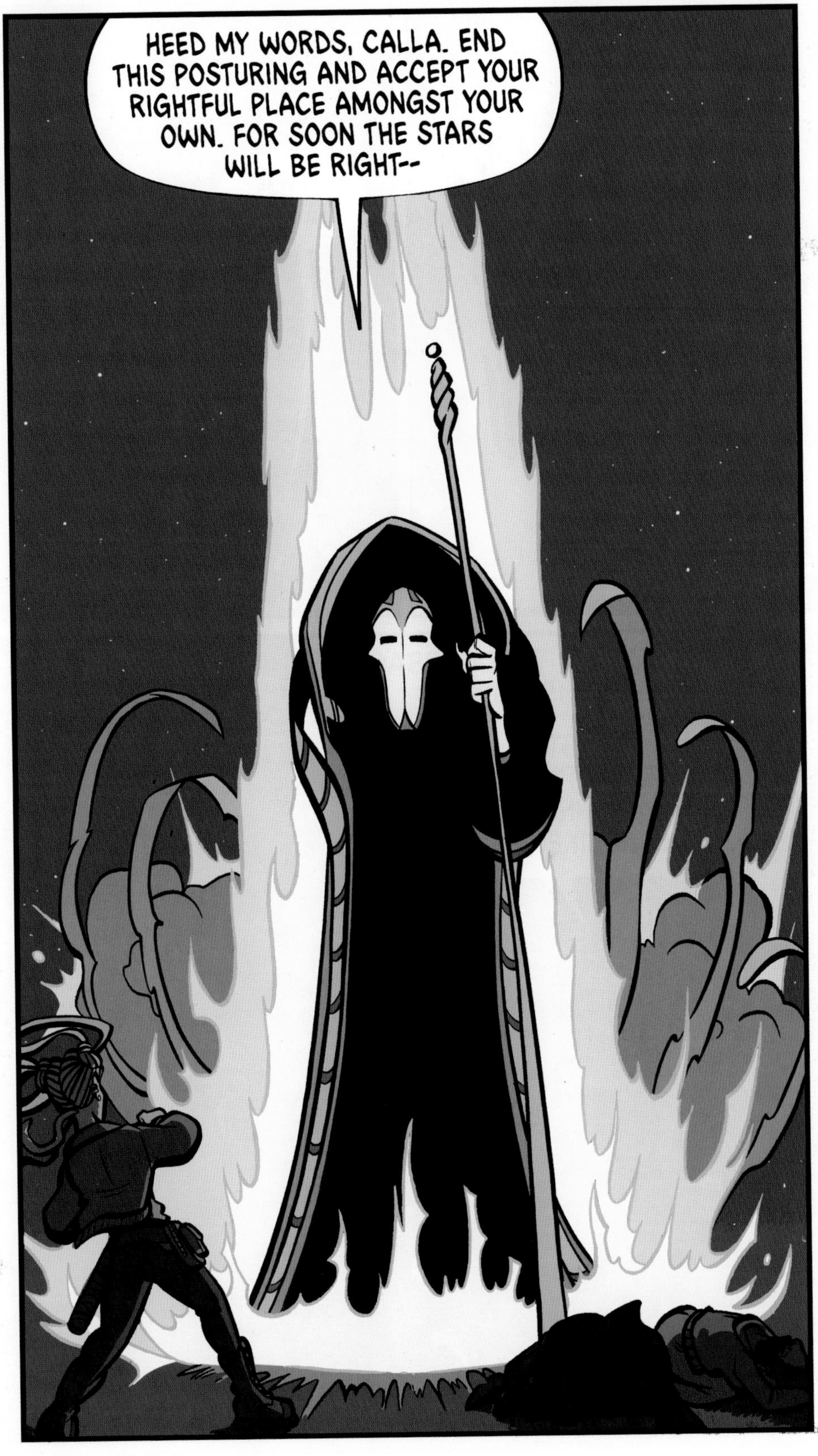
HEED MY WORDS, CALLA. END THIS POSTURING AND ACCEPT YOUR RIGHTFUL PLACE AMONGST YOUR OWN. FOR SOON THE STARS WILL BE RIGHT--

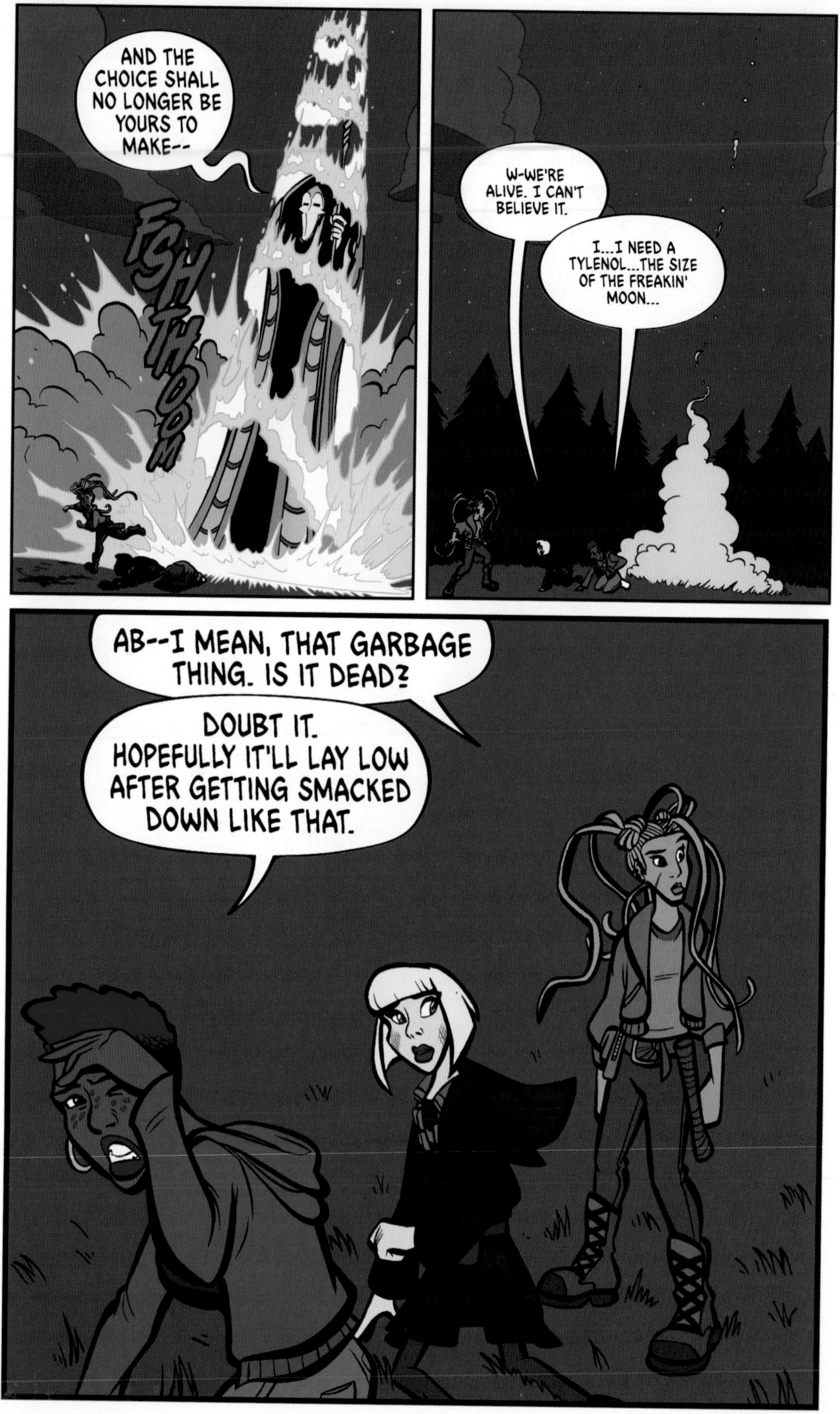
AND THE CHOICE SHALL NO LONGER BE YOURS TO MAKE--
FSHTHOOM
W-WE'RE ALIVE. I CAN'T BELIEVE IT.
I...I NEED A TYLENOL...THE SIZE OF THE FREAKIN' MOON...
AB--I MEAN, THAT GARBAGE THING. IS IT DEAD?
DOUBT IT. HOPEFULLY IT'LL LAY LOW AFTER GETTING SMACKED DOWN LIKE THAT.

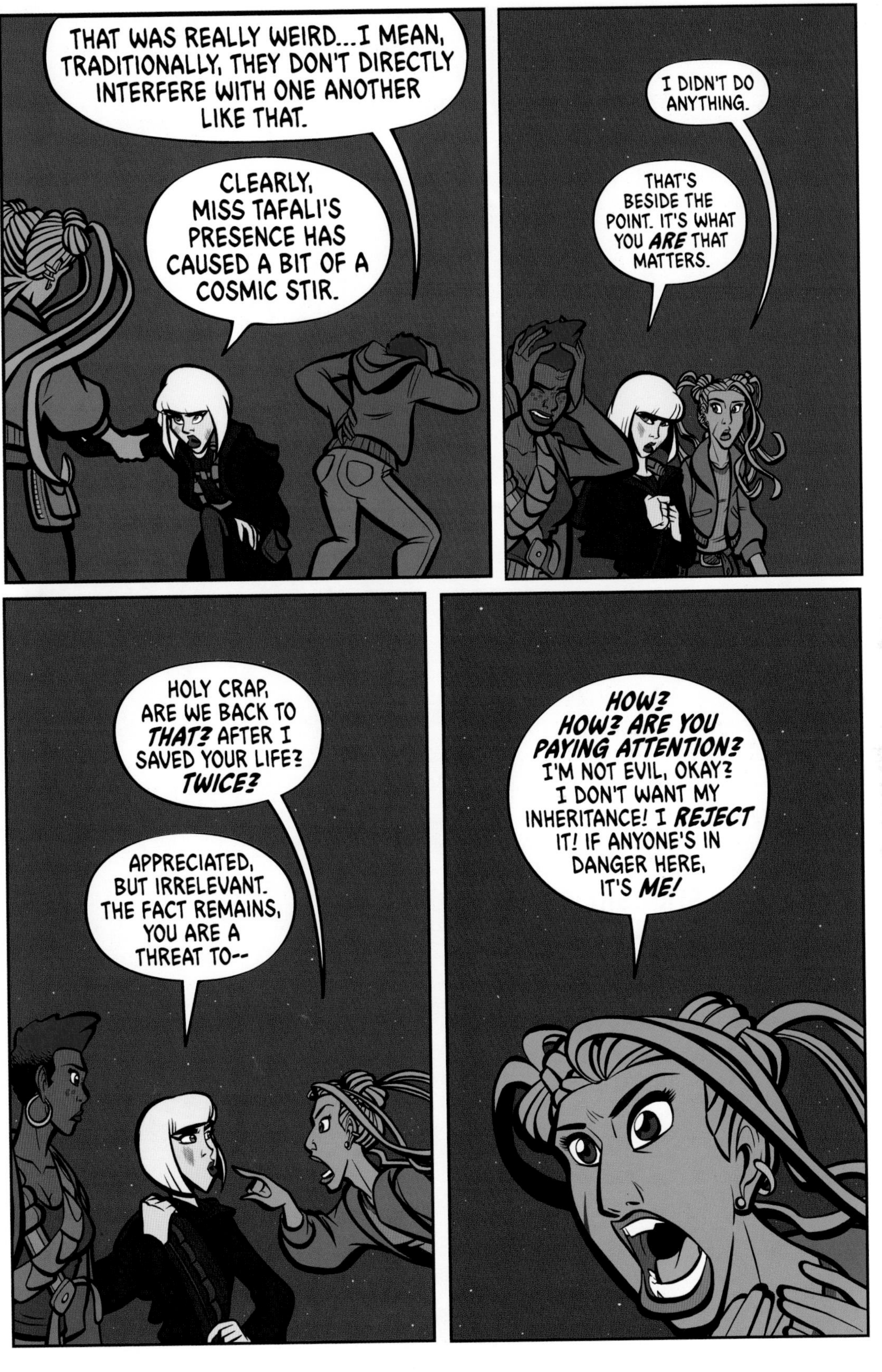
THAT WAS REALLY WEIRD...I MEAN, TRADITIONALLY, THEY DON'T DIRECTLY INTERFERE WITH ONE ANOTHER LIKE THAT.
CLEARLY, MISS TAFALI'S PRESENCE HAS CAUSED A BIT OF A COSMIC STIR.
I DIDN'T DO ANYTHING.
THAT'S BESIDE THE POINT. IT'S WHAT YOU *ARE* THAT MATTERS.
HOLY CRAP, ARE WE BACK TO *THAT?* AFTER I SAVED YOUR LIFE? *TWICE?*
APPRECIATED, BUT IRRELEVANT. THE FACT REMAINS, YOU ARE A THREAT TO--
HOW? HOW? ARE YOU PAYING ATTENTION? I'M NOT EVIL, OKAY? I DON'T WANT MY INHERITANCE! I *REJECT* IT! IF ANYONE'S IN DANGER HERE, IT'S *ME!*

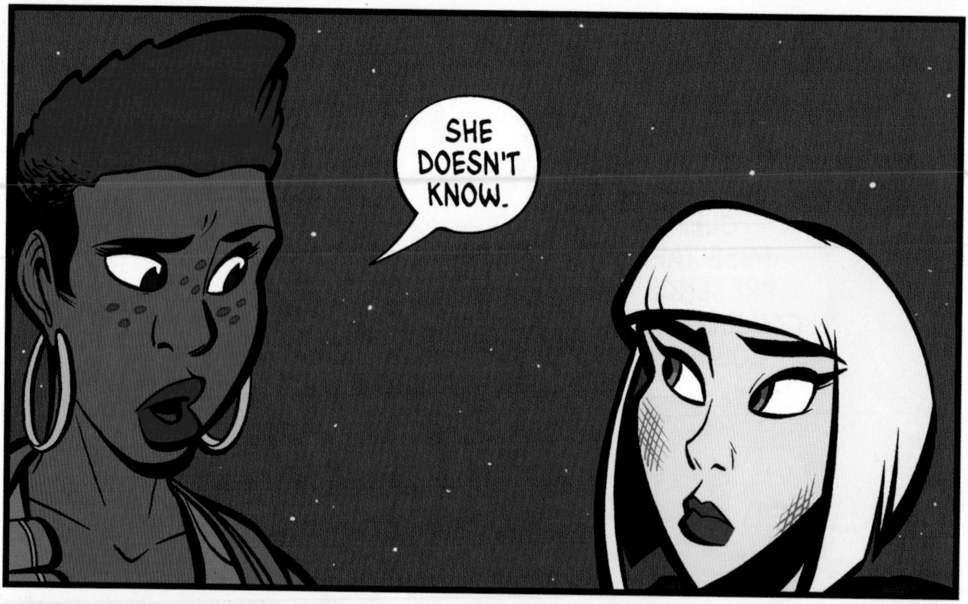
SHE DOESN'T KNOW.

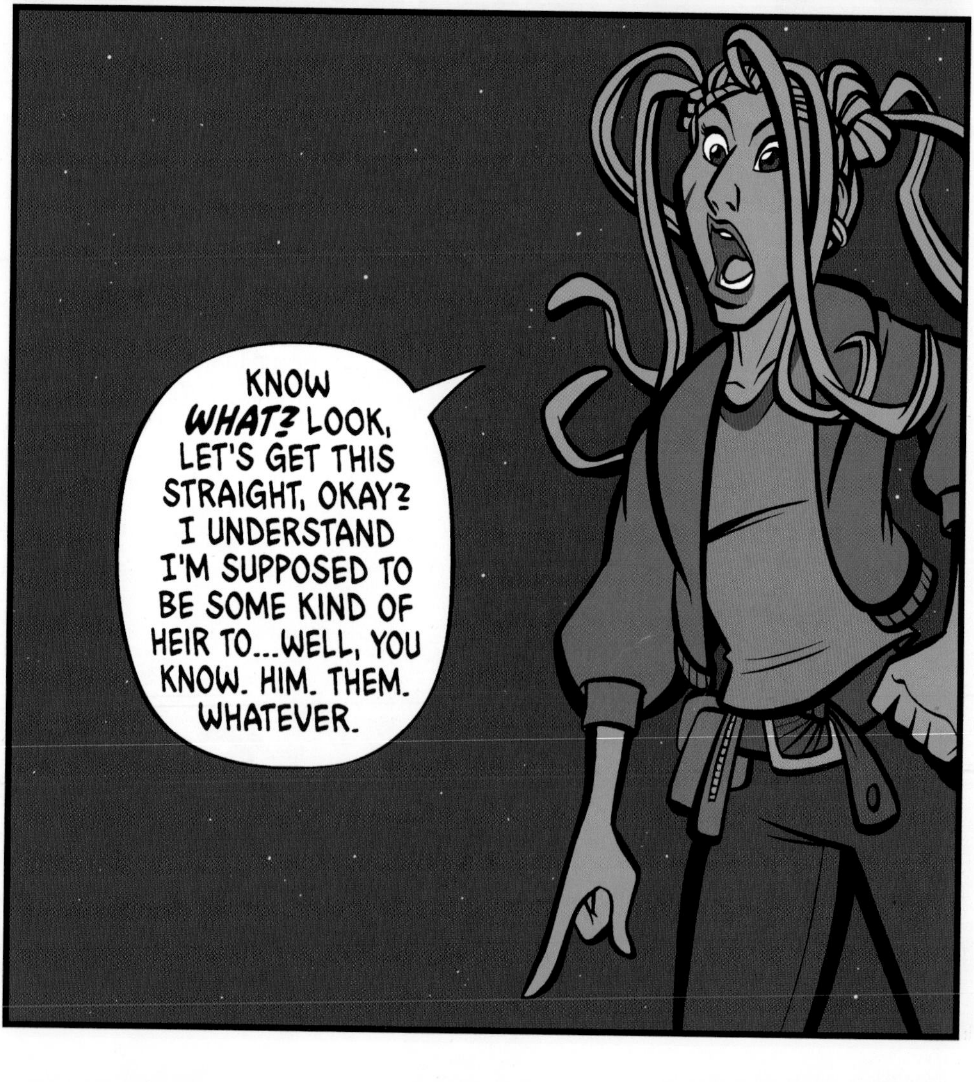
KNOW ***WHAT?*** LOOK, LET'S GET THIS STRAIGHT, OKAY? I UNDERSTAND I'M SUPPOSED TO BE SOME KIND OF HEIR TO...WELL, YOU KNOW. HIM. THEM. WHATEVER.

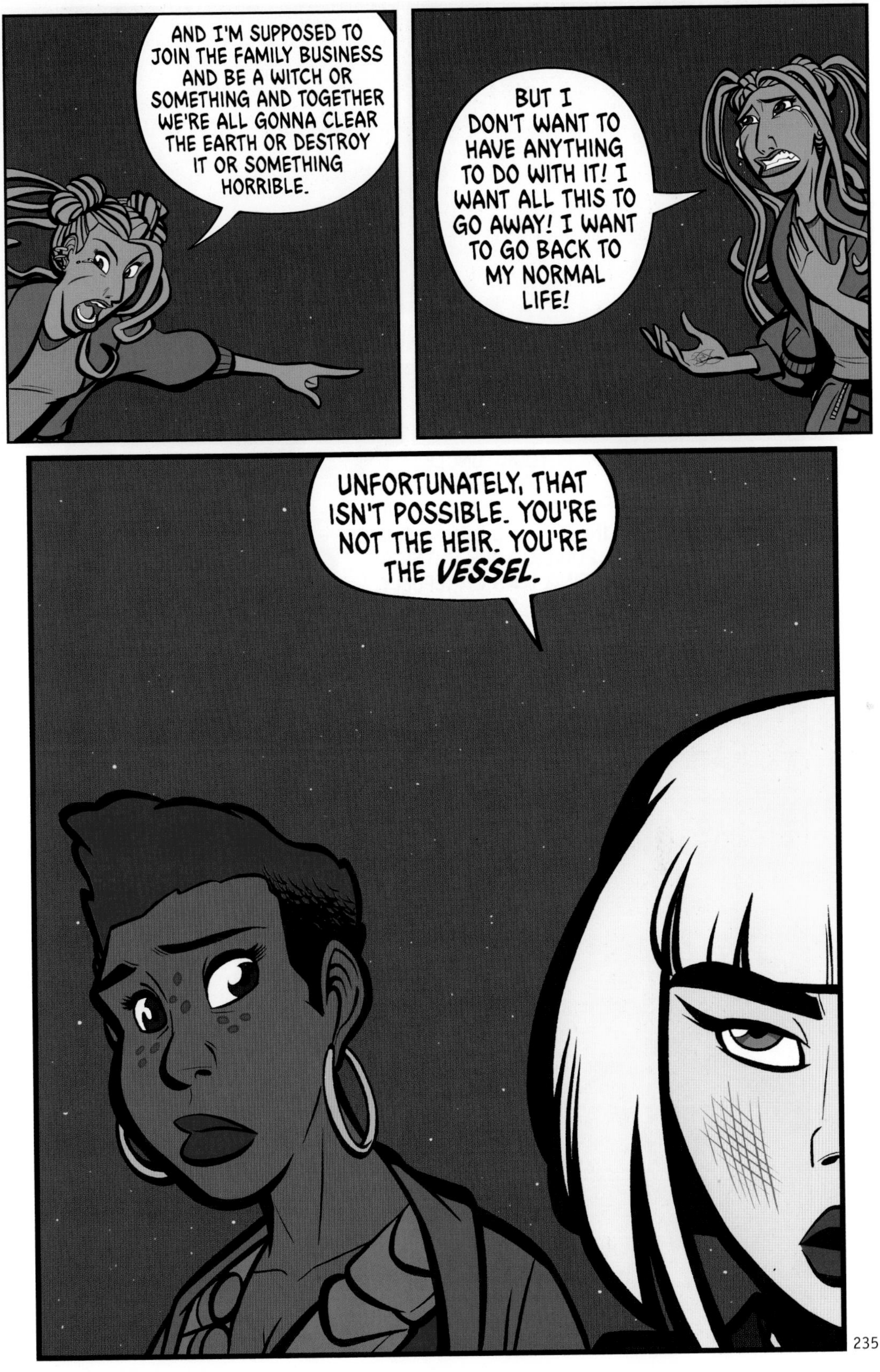
AND I'M SUPPOSED TO JOIN THE FAMILY BUSINESS AND BE A WITCH OR SOMETHING AND TOGETHER WE'RE ALL GONNA CLEAR THE EARTH OR DESTROY IT OR SOMETHING HORRIBLE.
BUT I DON'T WANT TO HAVE ANYTHING TO DO WITH IT! I WANT ALL THIS TO GO AWAY! I WANT TO GO BACK TO MY NORMAL LIFE!
UNFORTUNATELY, THAT ISN'T POSSIBLE. YOU'RE NOT THE HEIR. YOU'RE THE *VESSEL.*

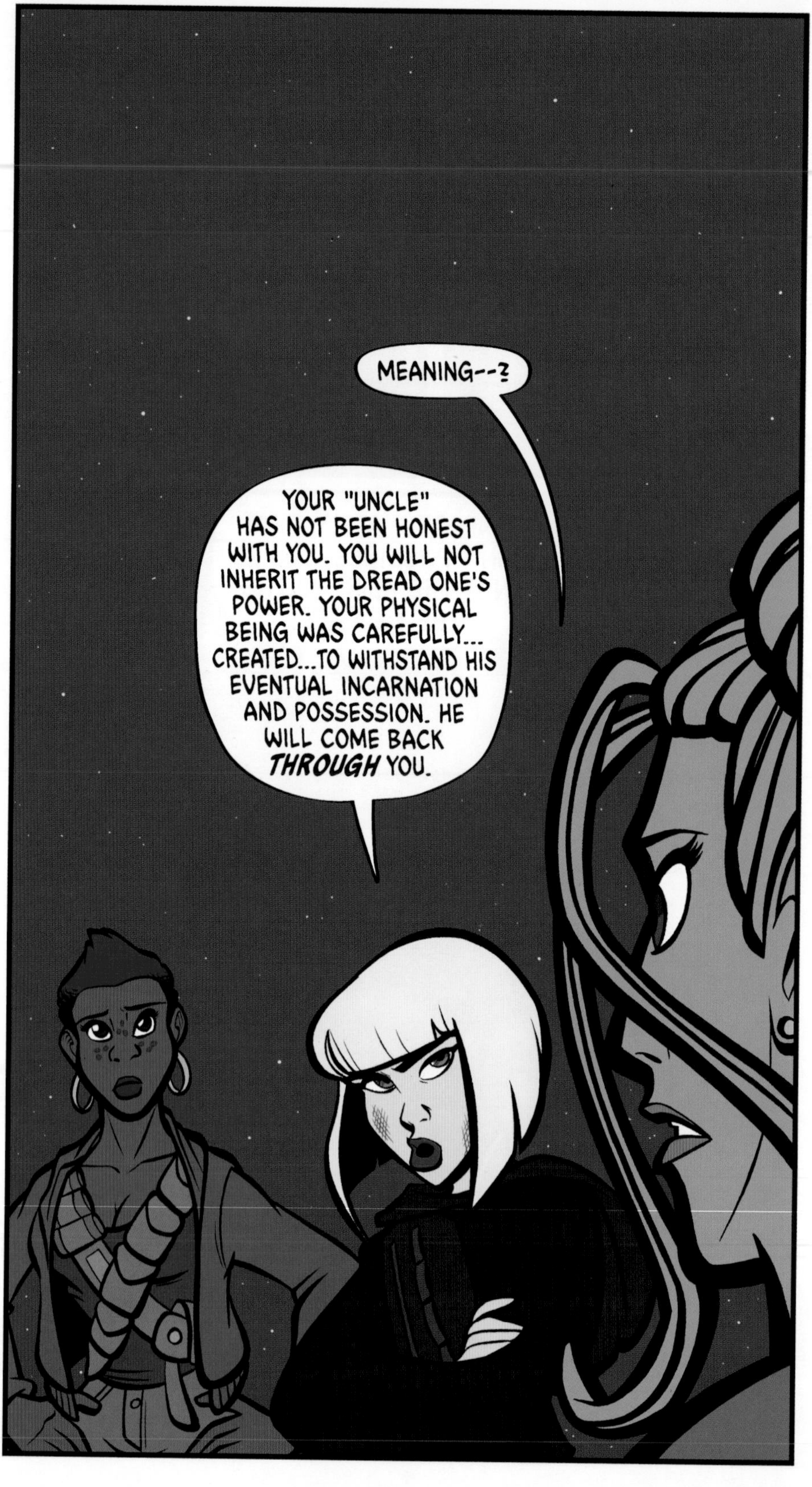
MEANING--?
YOUR "UNCLE" HAS NOT BEEN HONEST WITH YOU. YOU WILL NOT INHERIT THE DREAD ONE'S POWER. YOUR PHYSICAL BEING WAS CAREFULLY... CREATED...TO WITHSTAND HIS EVENTUAL INCARNATION AND POSSESSION. HE WILL COME BACK ***THROUGH*** YOU.

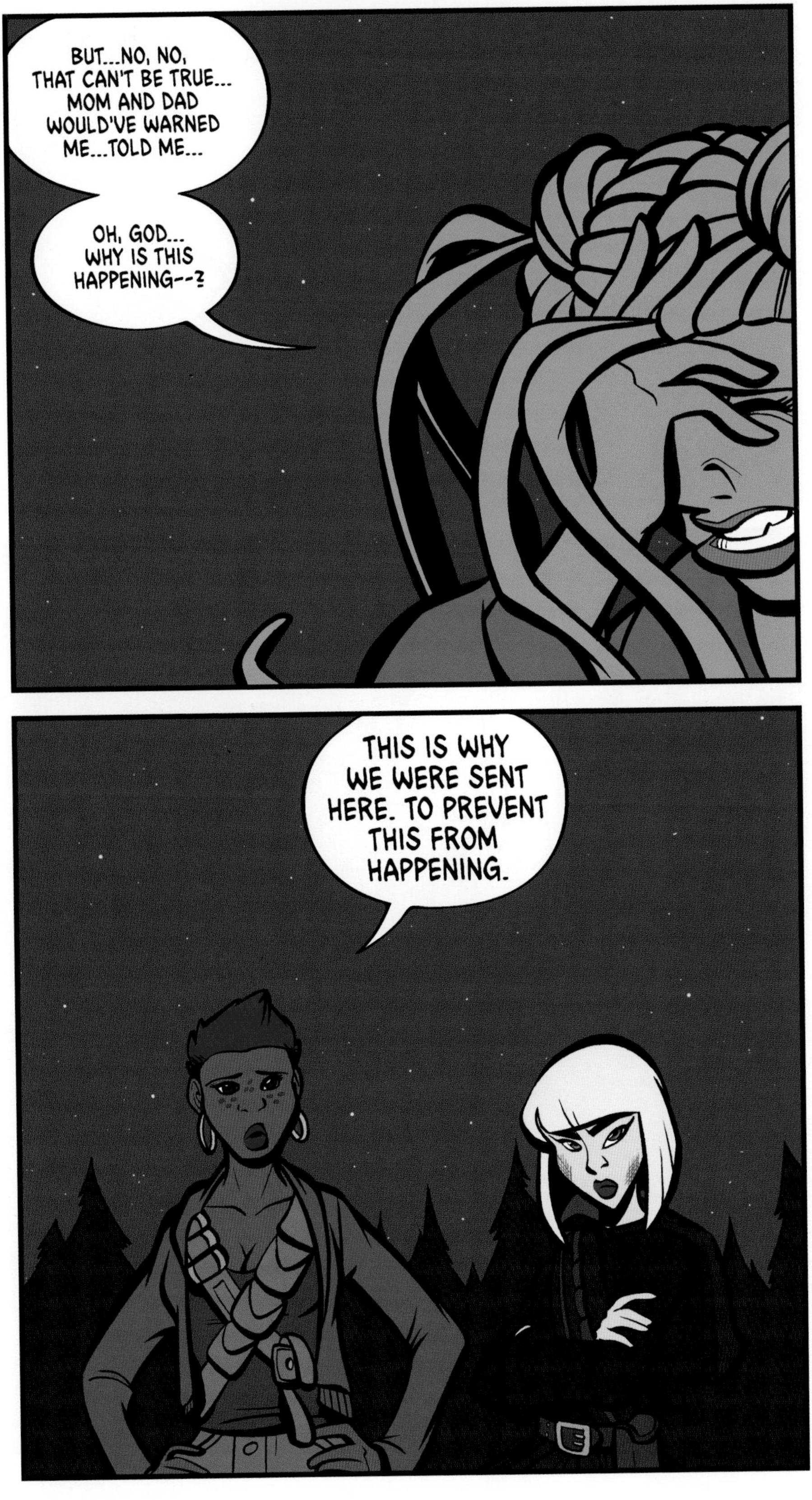
BUT...NO, NO, THAT CAN'T BE TRUE... MOM AND DAD WOULD'VE WARNED ME...TOLD ME...
OH, GOD... WHY IS THIS HAPPENING--?
THIS IS WHY WE WERE SENT HERE. TO PREVENT THIS FROM HAPPENING.

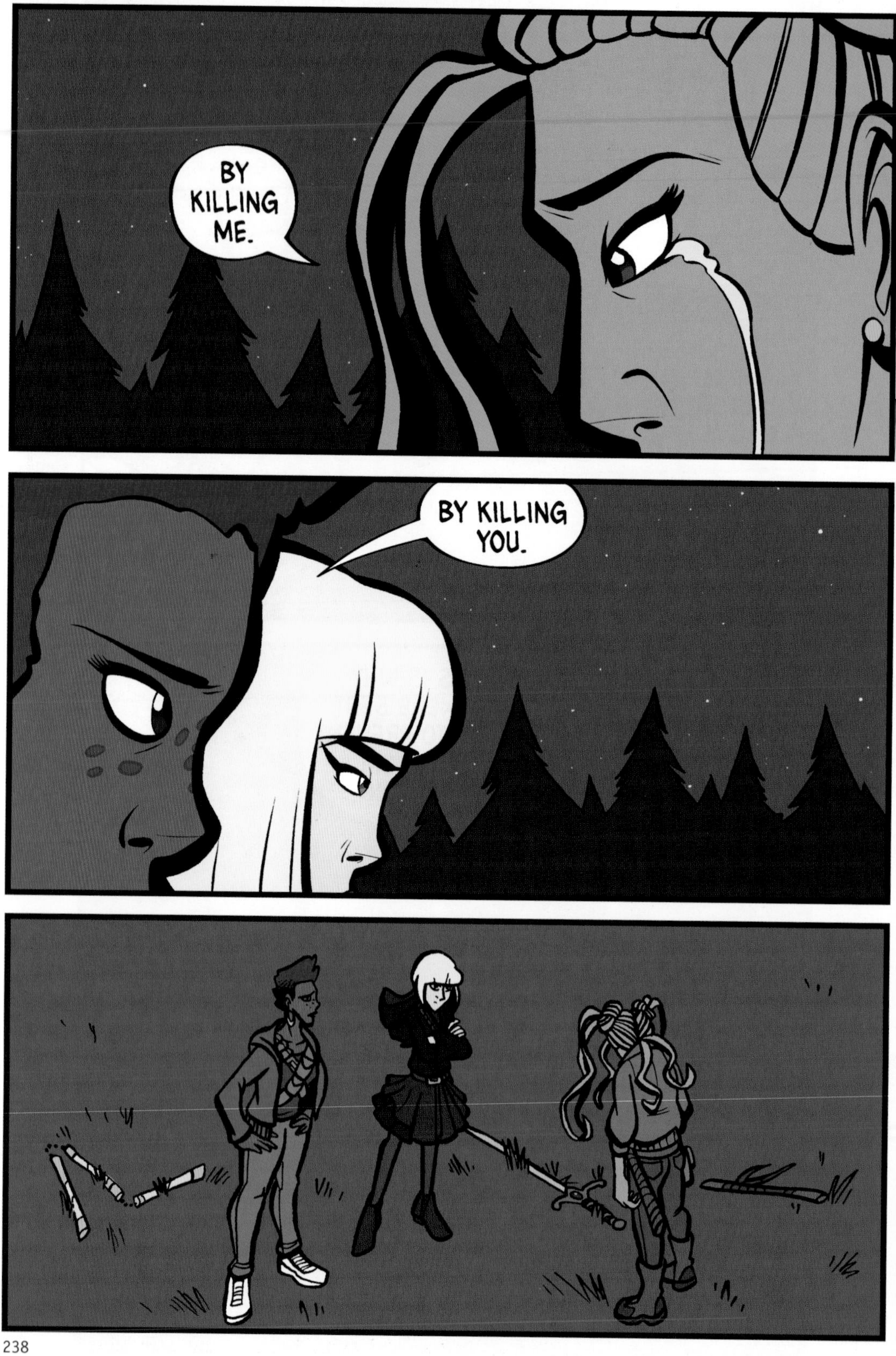
BY KILLING ME.
BY KILLING YOU.

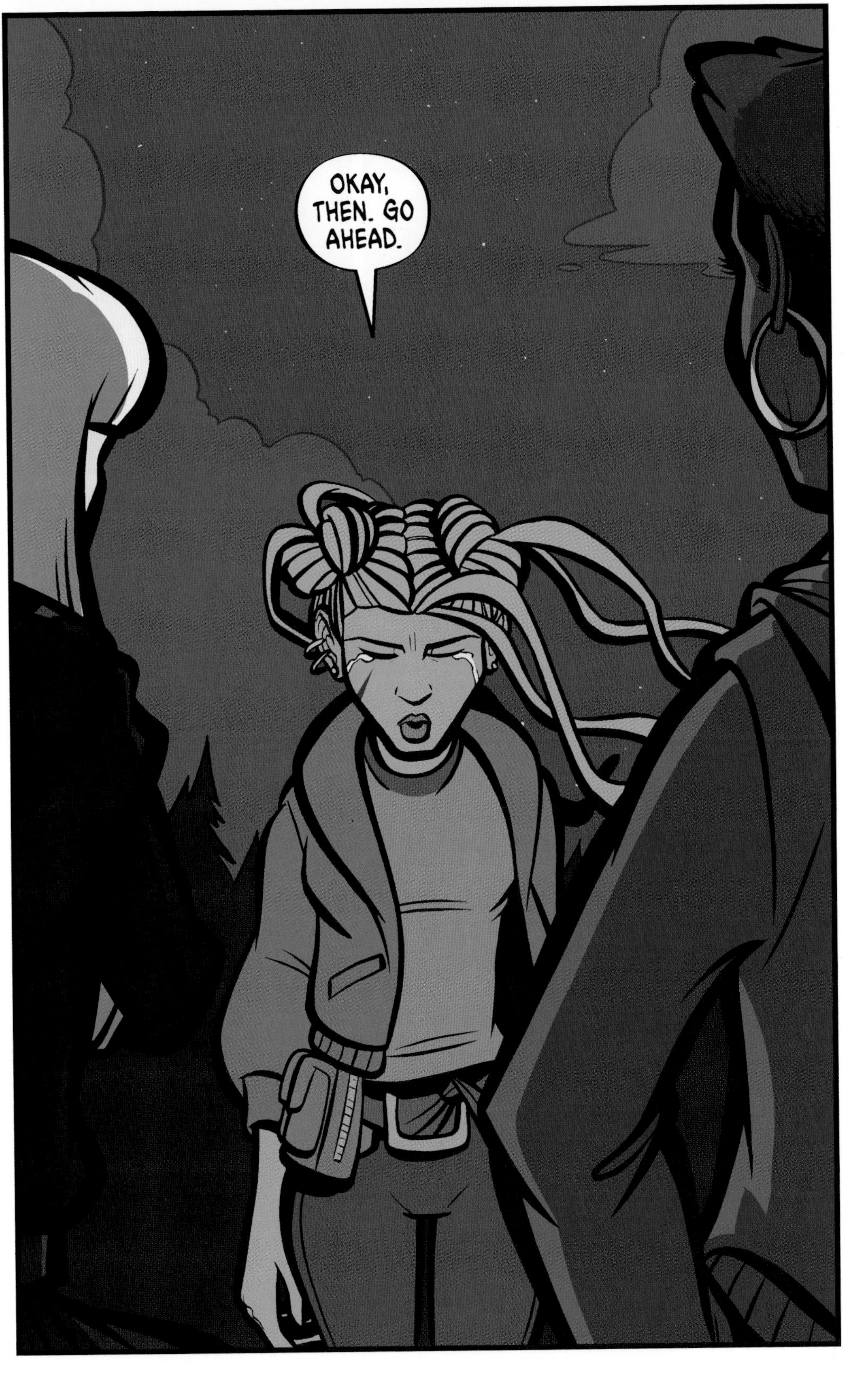
OKAY, THEN. GO AHEAD.

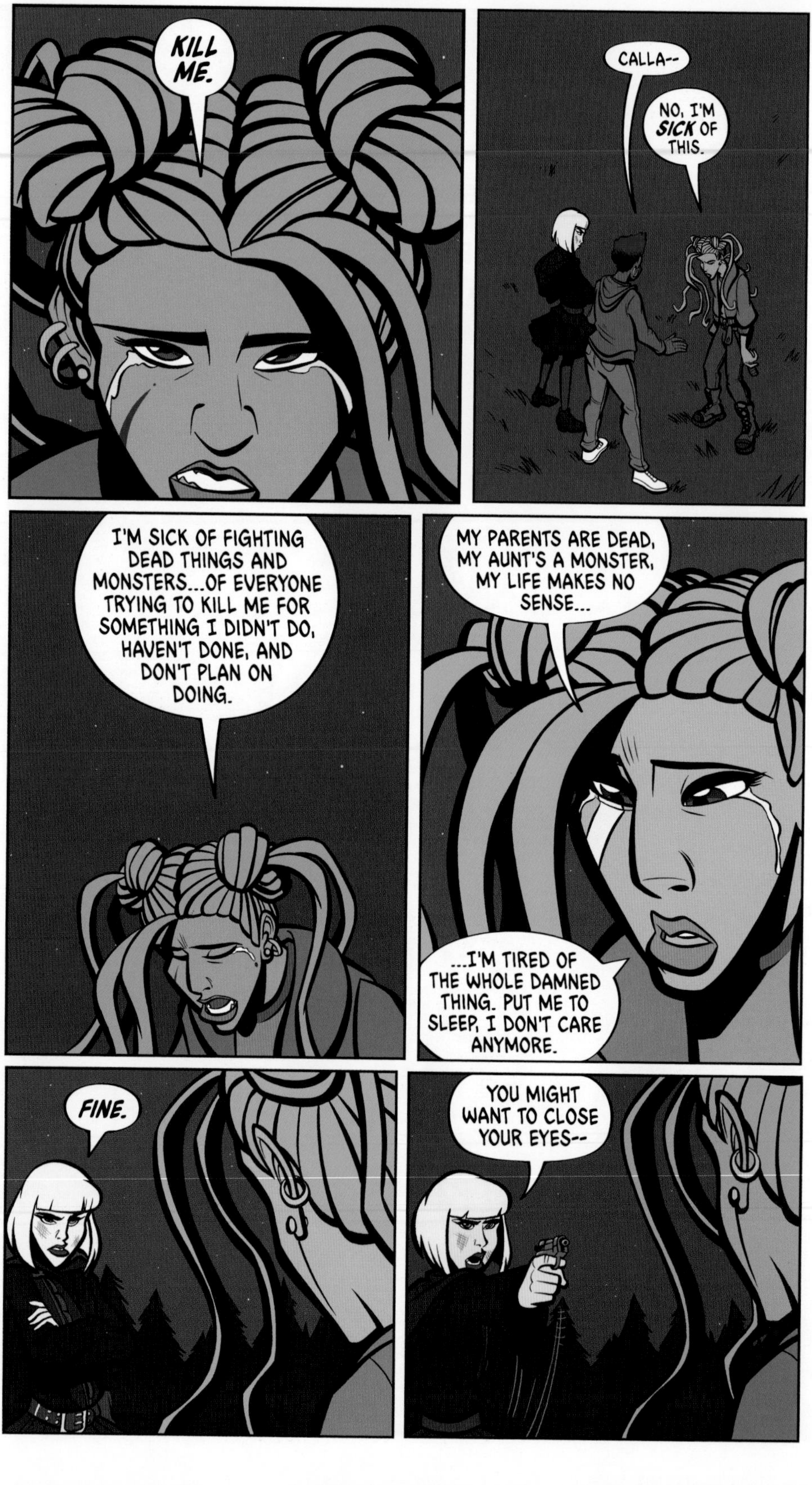
KILL ME.
CALLA--
NO, I'M SICK OF THIS.
I'M SICK OF FIGHTING DEAD THINGS AND MONSTERS...OF EVERYONE TRYING TO KILL ME FOR SOMETHING I DIDN'T DO, HAVEN'T DONE, AND DON'T PLAN ON DOING.
MY PARENTS ARE DEAD, MY AUNT'S A MONSTER, MY LIFE MAKES NO SENSE...
...I'M TIRED OF THE WHOLE DAMNED THING. PUT ME TO SLEEP, I DON'T CARE ANYMORE.
FINE.
YOU MIGHT WANT TO CLOSE YOUR EYES--

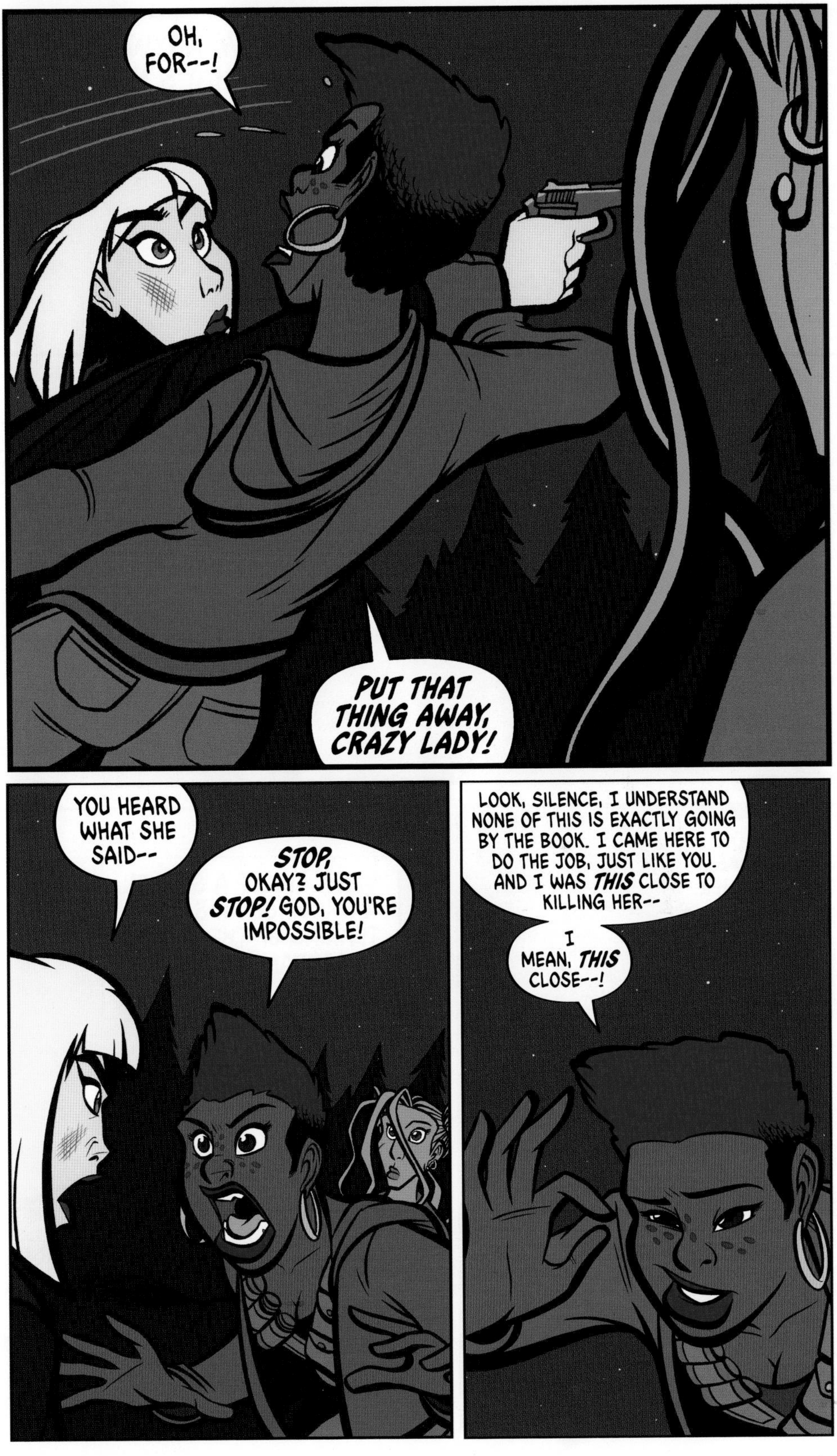
OH, FOR--!
PUT THAT THING AWAY, CRAZY LADY!
YOU HEARD WHAT SHE SAID--
STOP, OKAY? JUST STOP! GOD, YOU'RE IMPOSSIBLE!
LOOK, SILENCE, I UNDERSTAND NONE OF THIS IS EXACTLY GOING BY THE BOOK. I CAME HERE TO DO THE JOB, JUST LIKE YOU. AND I WAS THIS CLOSE TO KILLING HER--
I MEAN, THIS CLOSE--!

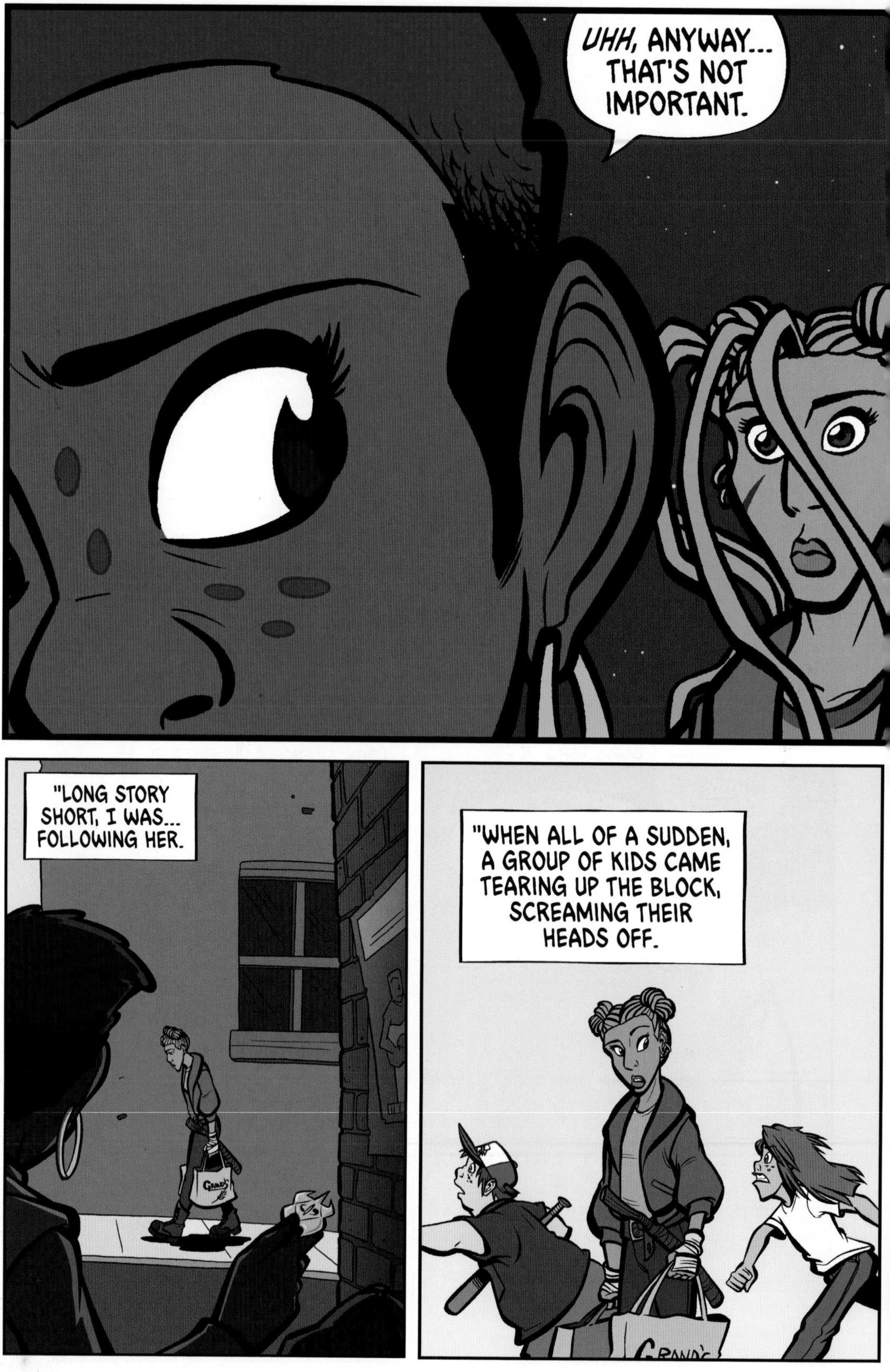
UHH, ANYWAY... THAT'S NOT IMPORTANT.
"LONG STORY SHORT, I WAS... FOLLOWING HER.
"WHEN ALL OF A SUDDEN, A GROUP OF KIDS CAME TEARING UP THE BLOCK, SCREAMING THEIR HEADS OFF.

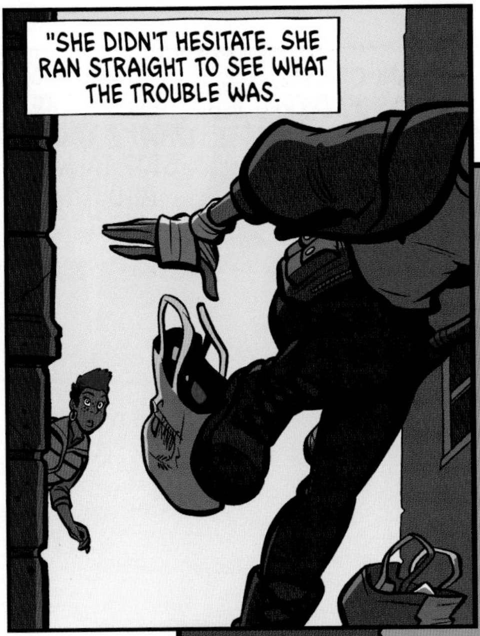
"SHE DIDN'T HESITATE. SHE RAN STRAIGHT TO SEE WHAT THE TROUBLE WAS.

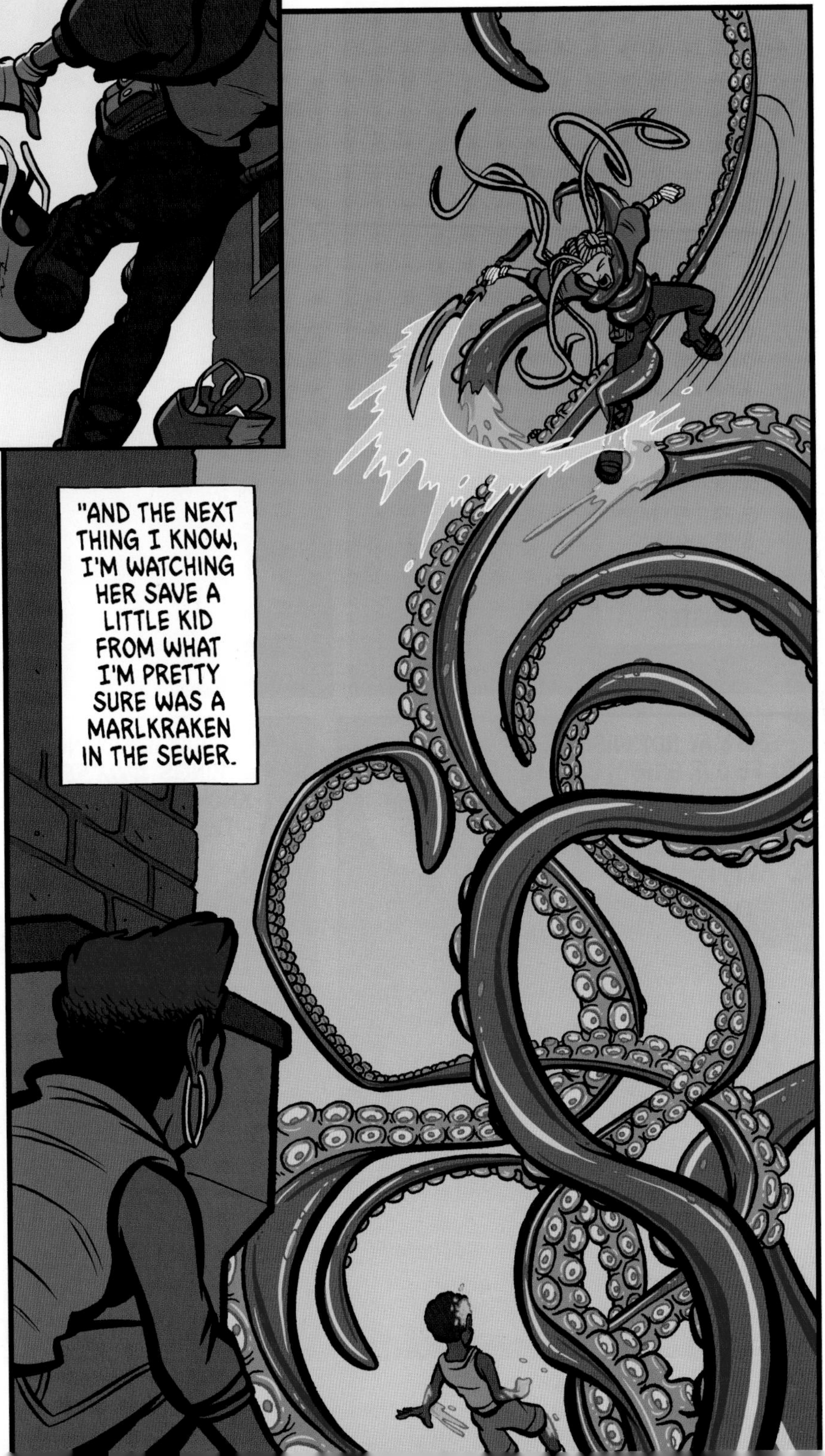
"AND THE NEXT THING I KNOW, I'M WATCHING HER SAVE A LITTLE KID FROM WHAT I'M PRETTY SURE WAS A MARLKRAKEN IN THE SEWER.

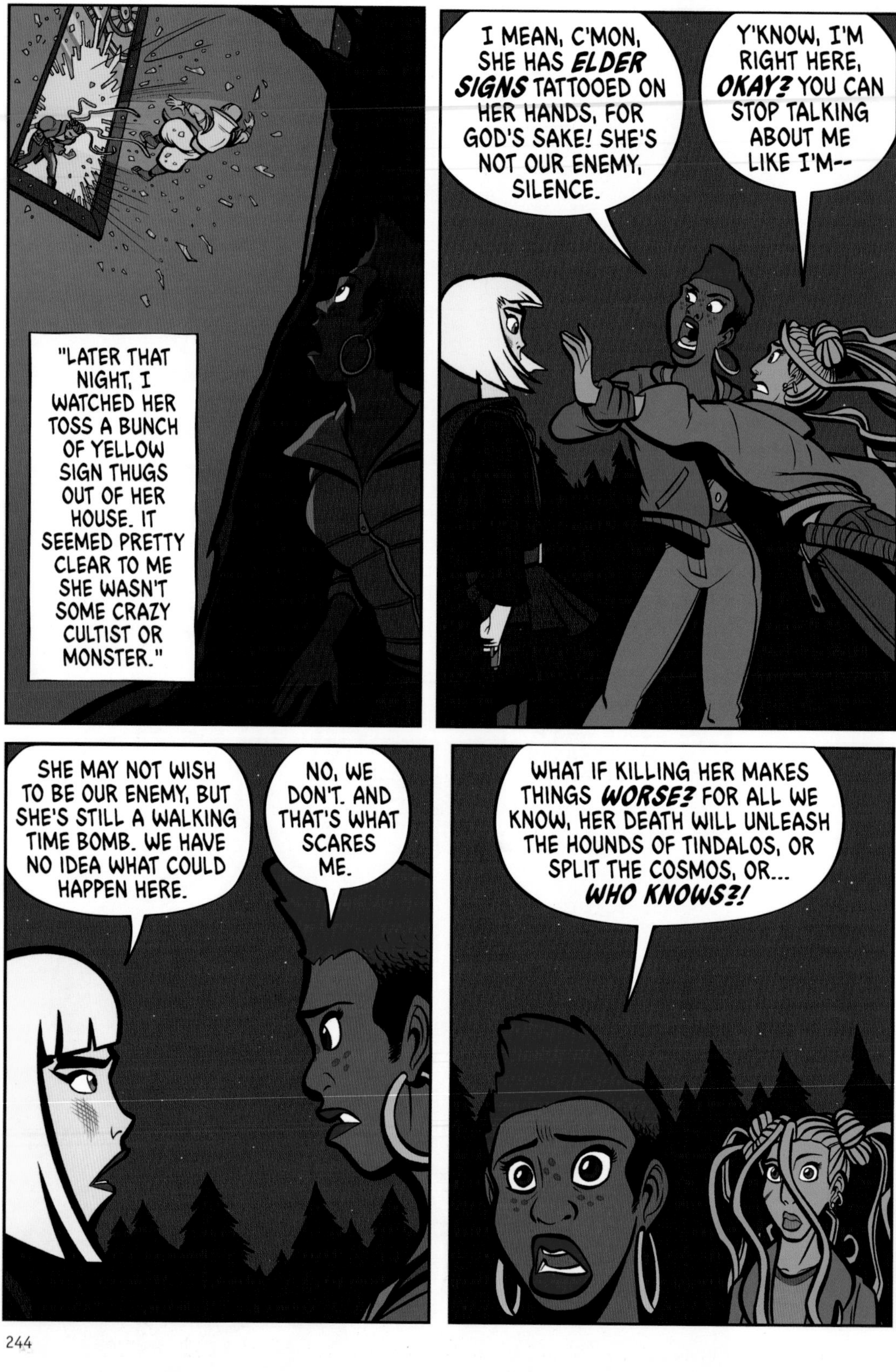
"LATER THAT NIGHT, I WATCHED HER TOSS A BUNCH OF YELLOW SIGN THUGS OUT OF HER HOUSE. IT SEEMED PRETTY CLEAR TO ME SHE WASN'T SOME CRAZY CULTIST OR MONSTER."
I MEAN, C'MON, SHE HAS ELDER SIGNS TATTOOED ON HER HANDS, FOR GOD'S SAKE! SHE'S NOT OUR ENEMY, SILENCE.
Y'KNOW, I'M RIGHT HERE, OKAY? YOU CAN STOP TALKING ABOUT ME LIKE I'M--
SHE MAY NOT WISH TO BE OUR ENEMY, BUT SHE'S STILL A WALKING TIME BOMB. WE HAVE NO IDEA WHAT COULD HAPPEN HERE.
NO, WE DON'T. AND THAT'S WHAT SCARES ME.
WHAT IF KILLING HER MAKES THINGS WORSE? FOR ALL WE KNOW, HER DEATH WILL UNLEASH THE HOUNDS OF TINDALOS, OR SPLIT THE COSMOS, OR... WHO KNOWS?!

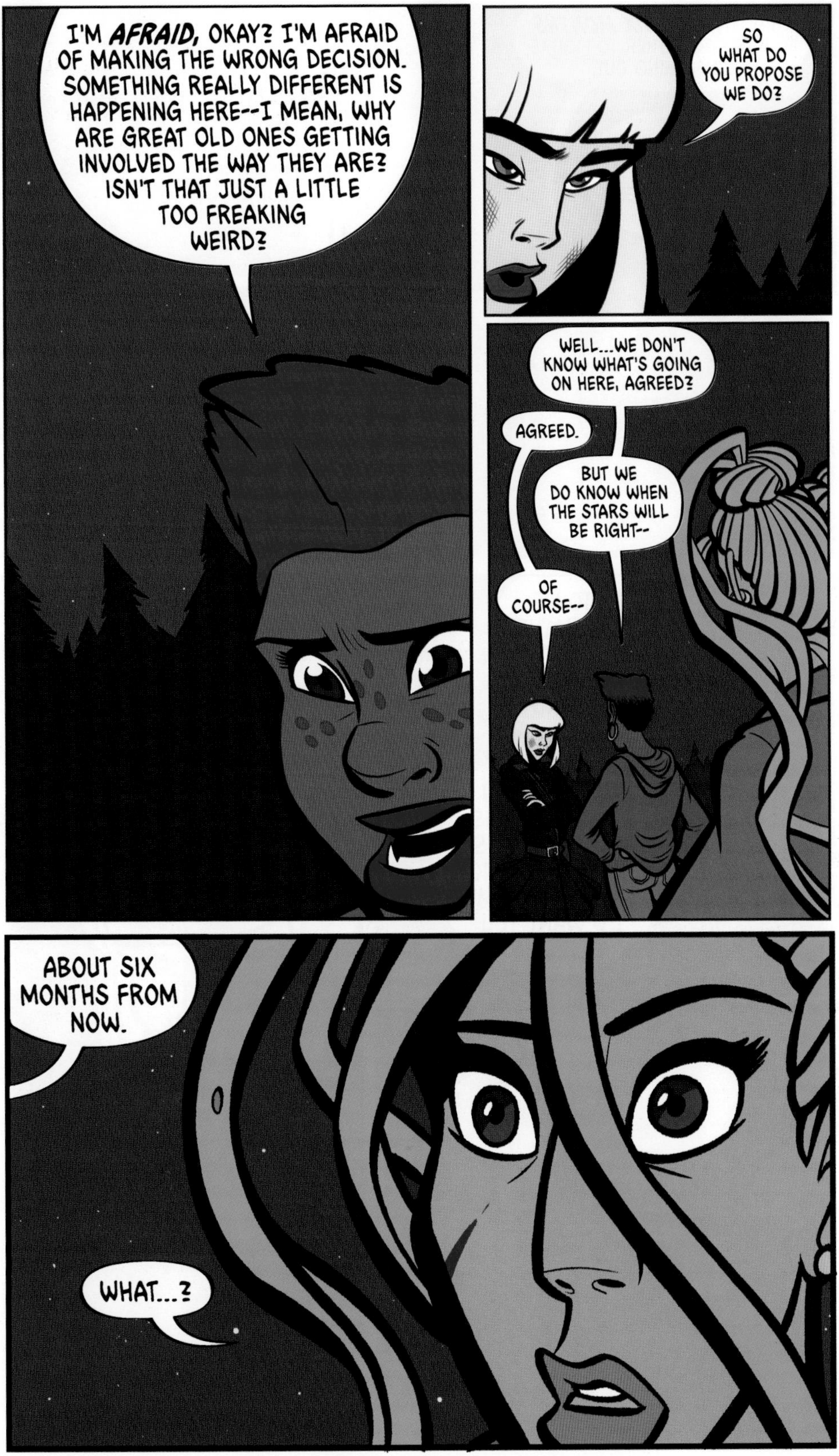
I'M *AFRAID,* OKAY? I'M AFRAID OF MAKING THE WRONG DECISION. SOMETHING REALLY DIFFERENT IS HAPPENING HERE--I MEAN, WHY ARE GREAT OLD ONES GETTING INVOLVED THE WAY THEY ARE? ISN'T THAT JUST A LITTLE TOO FREAKING WEIRD?
SO WHAT DO YOU PROPOSE WE DO?
WELL...WE DON'T KNOW WHAT'S GOING ON HERE, AGREED?
AGREED.
BUT WE DO KNOW WHEN THE STARS WILL BE RIGHT--
OF COURSE--
ABOUT SIX MONTHS FROM NOW.
WHAT...?

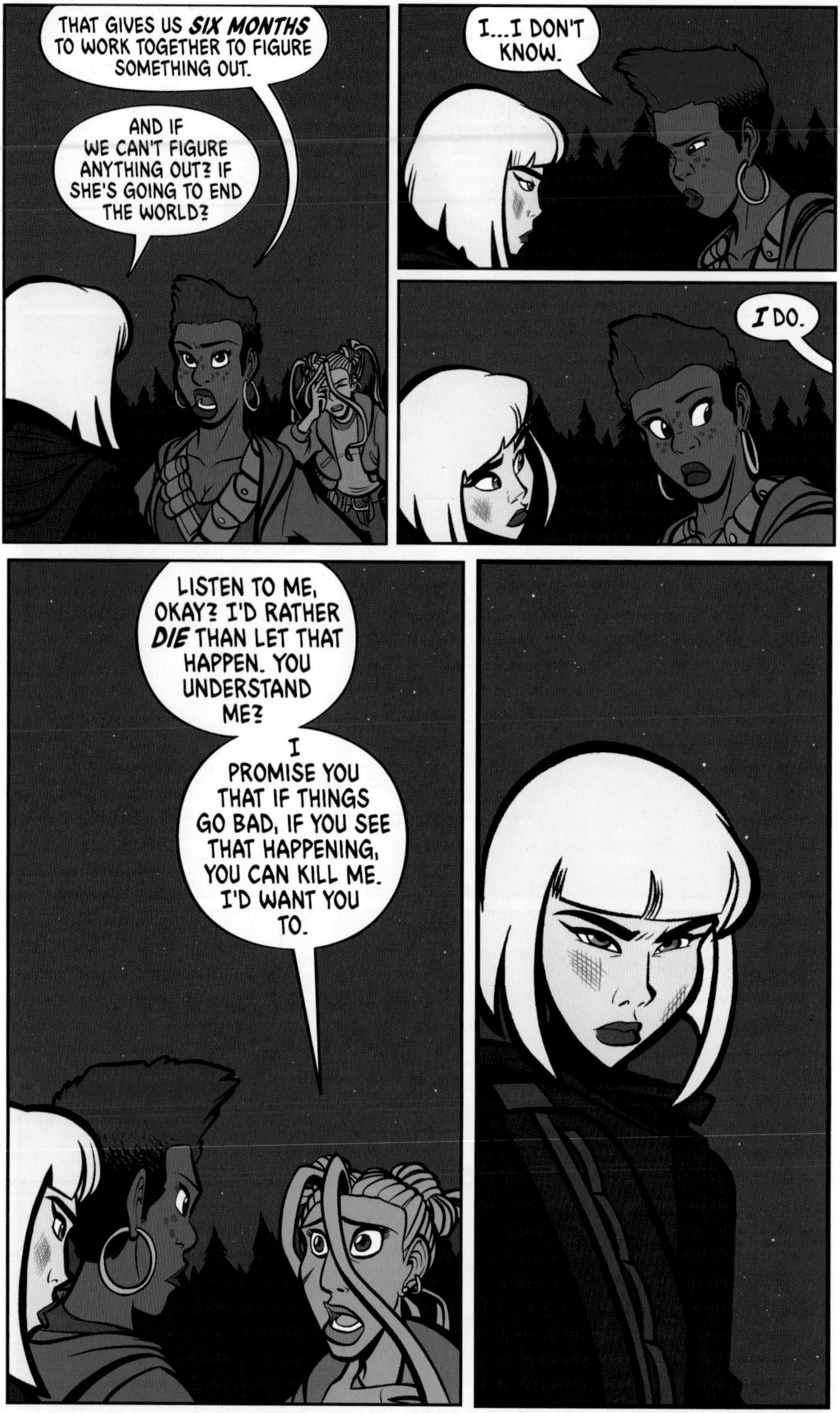
THAT GIVES US SIX MONTHS TO WORK TOGETHER TO FIGURE SOMETHING OUT.
AND IF WE CAN'T FIGURE ANYTHING OUT? IF SHE'S GOING TO END THE WORLD?
I...I DON'T KNOW.
I DO.
LISTEN TO ME, OKAY? I'D RATHER DIE THAN LET THAT HAPPEN. YOU UNDERSTAND ME?
I PROMISE YOU THAT IF THINGS GO BAD, IF YOU SEE THAT HAPPENING, YOU CAN KILL ME. I'D WANT YOU TO.

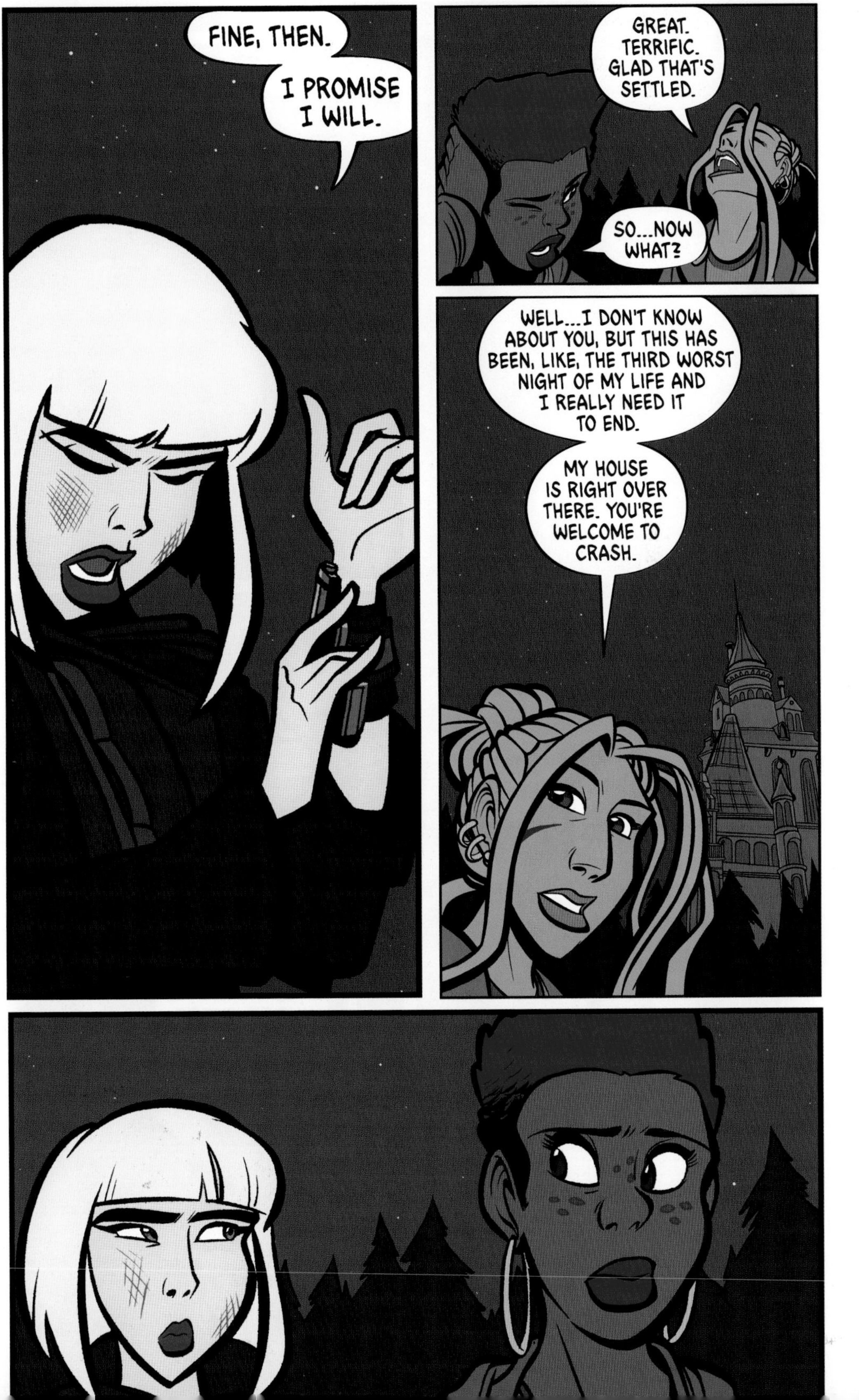
FINE, THEN.
I PROMISE I WILL.
GREAT. TERRIFIC. GLAD THAT'S SETTLED.
SO...NOW WHAT?
WELL...I DON'T KNOW ABOUT YOU, BUT THIS HAS BEEN, LIKE, THE THIRD WORST NIGHT OF MY LIFE AND I REALLY NEED IT TO END.
MY HOUSE IS RIGHT OVER THERE. YOU'RE WELCOME TO CRASH.

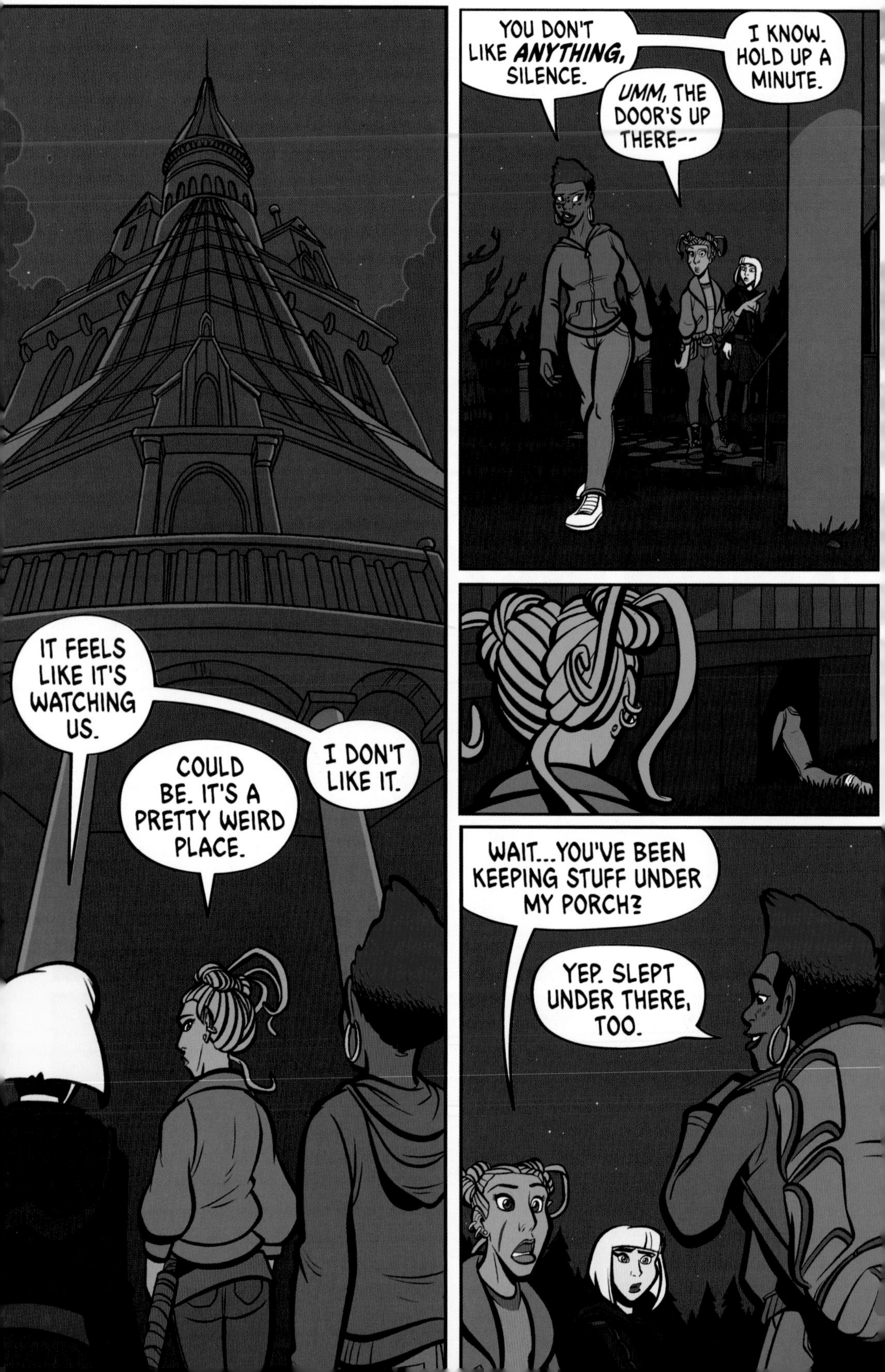

IT FEELS LIKE IT'S WATCHING US.
COULD BE. IT'S A PRETTY WEIRD PLACE.
I DON'T LIKE IT.
YOU DON'T LIKE ANYTHING, SILENCE.
UMM, THE DOOR'S UP THERE--
I KNOW. HOLD UP A MINUTE.
WAIT...YOU'VE BEEN KEEPING STUFF UNDER MY PORCH?
YEP. SLEPT UNDER THERE, TOO.

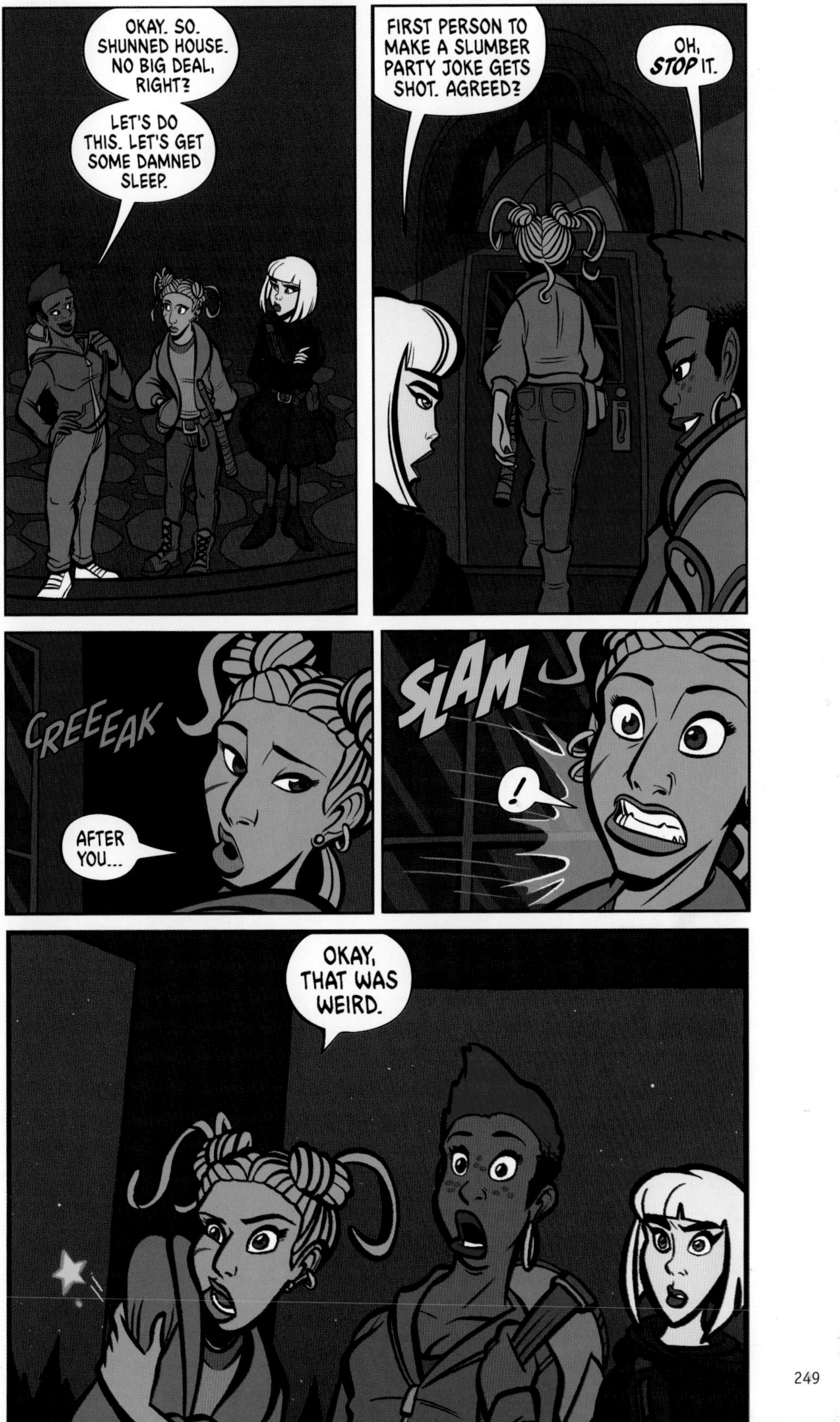
OKAY. SO. SHUNNED HOUSE. NO BIG DEAL, RIGHT?
LET'S DO THIS. LET'S GET SOME DAMNED SLEEP.
FIRST PERSON TO MAKE A SLUMBER PARTY JOKE GETS SHOT. AGREED?
OH, STOP IT.
CREEEAK
AFTER YOU...
SLAM
!
OKAY, THAT WAS WEIRD.

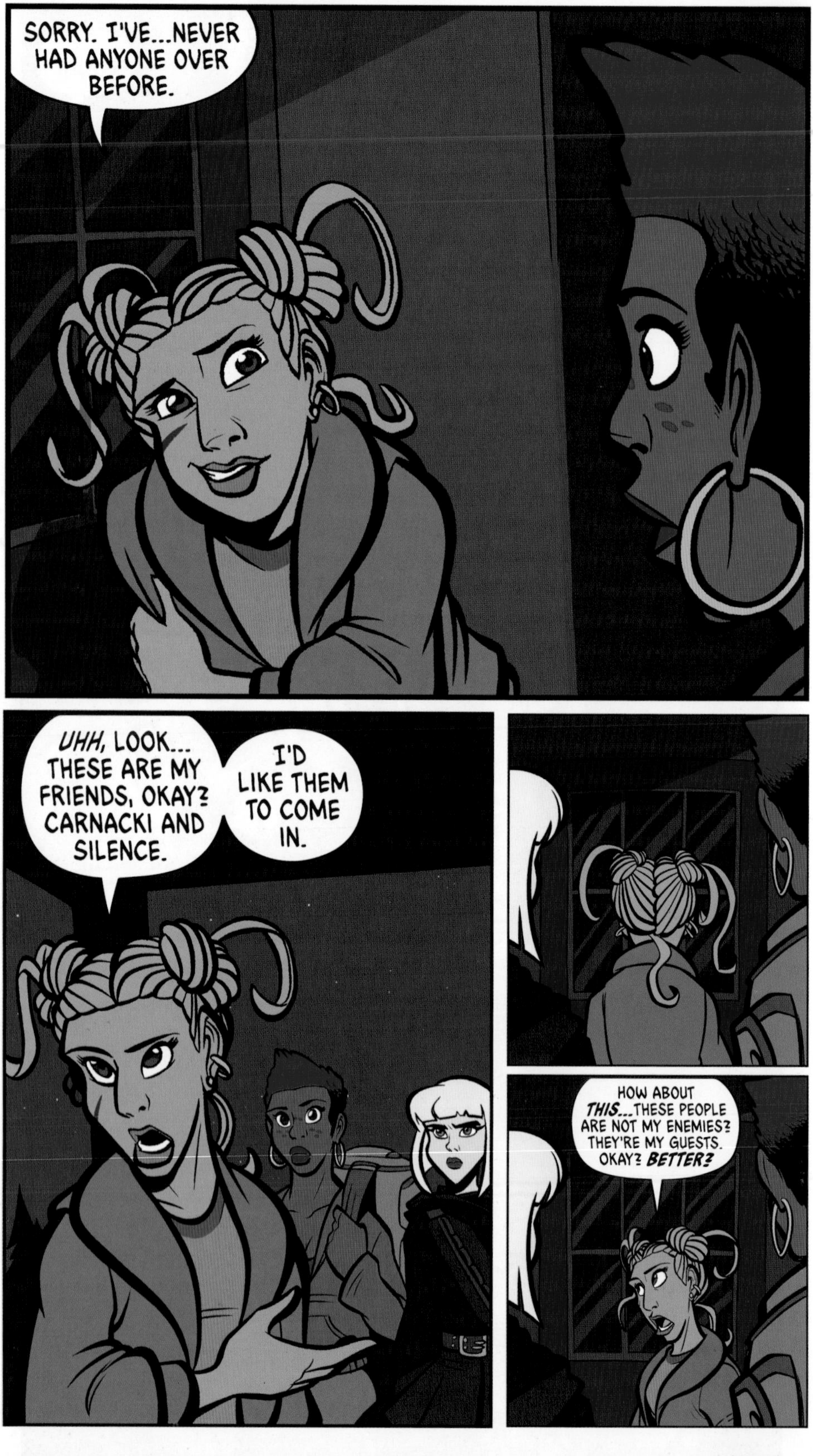
SORRY. I'VE...NEVER HAD ANYONE OVER BEFORE.
UHH, LOOK... THESE ARE MY FRIENDS, OKAY? CARNACKI AND SILENCE.
I'D LIKE THEM TO COME IN.
HOW ABOUT THIS...THESE PEOPLE ARE NOT MY ENEMIES? THEY'RE MY GUESTS. OKAY? BETTER?

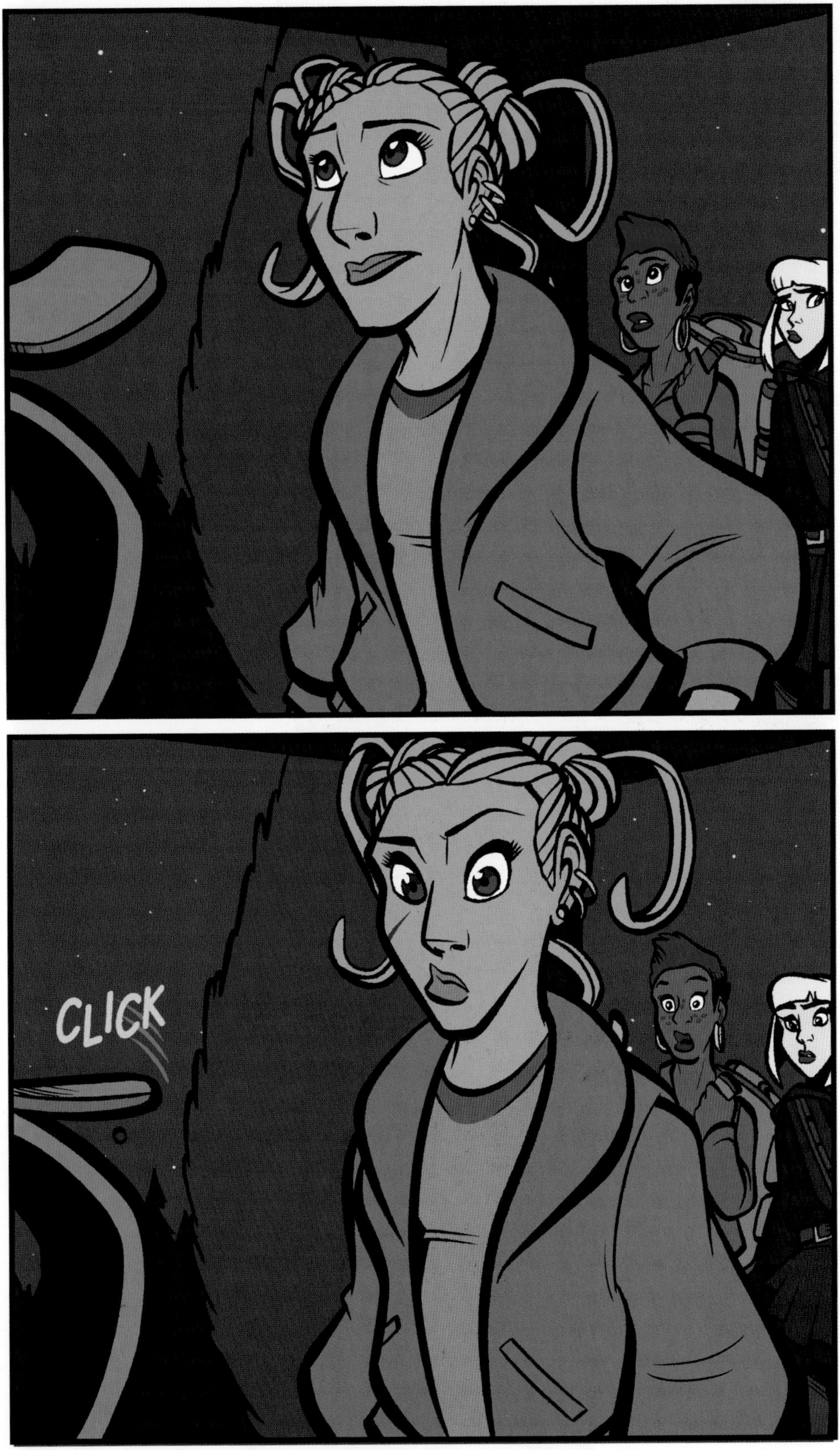
CLICK

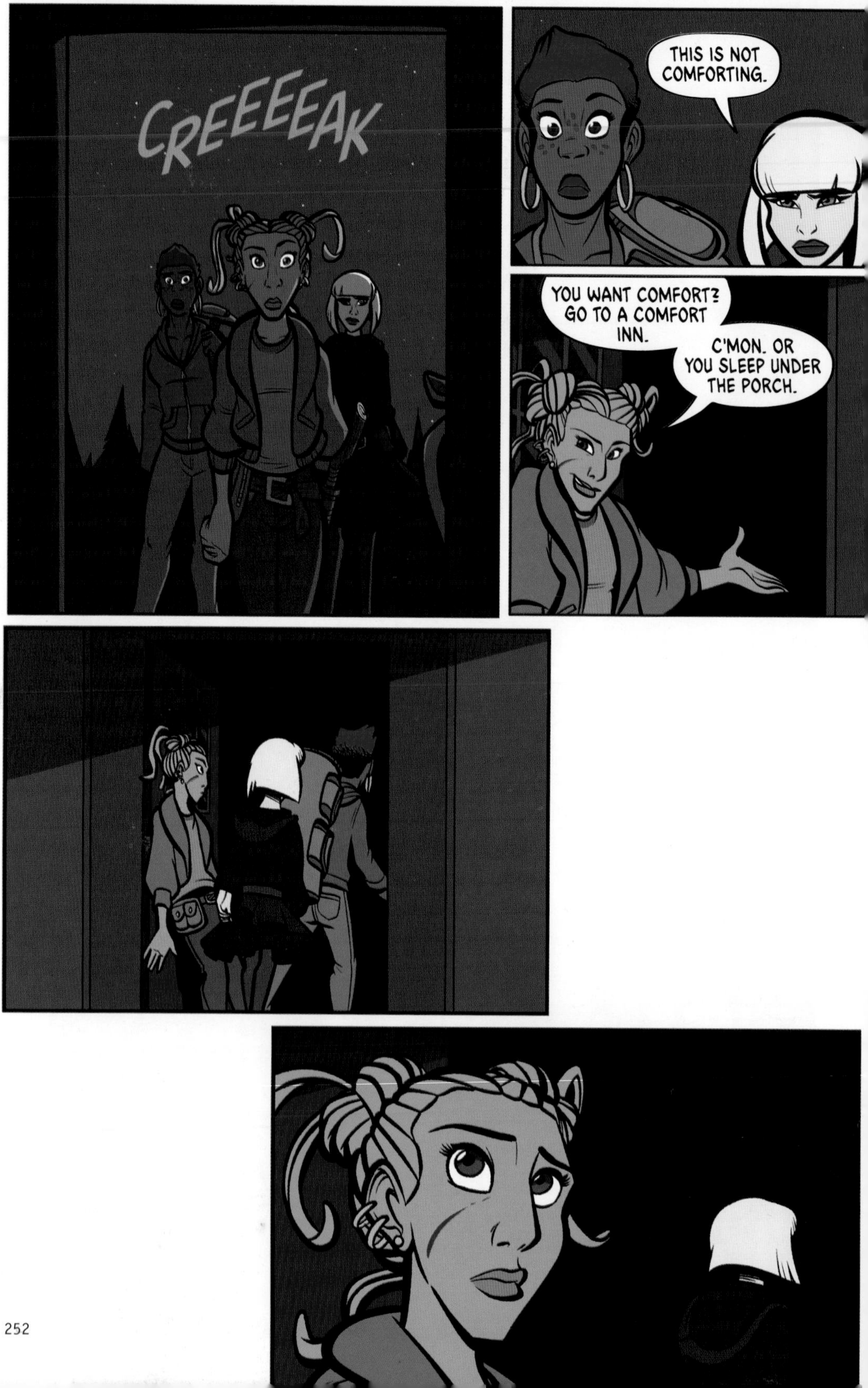

CREEEEEAK
THIS IS NOT COMFORTING.
YOU WANT COMFORT? GO TO A COMFORT INN.
C'MON. OR YOU SLEEP UNDER THE PORCH.

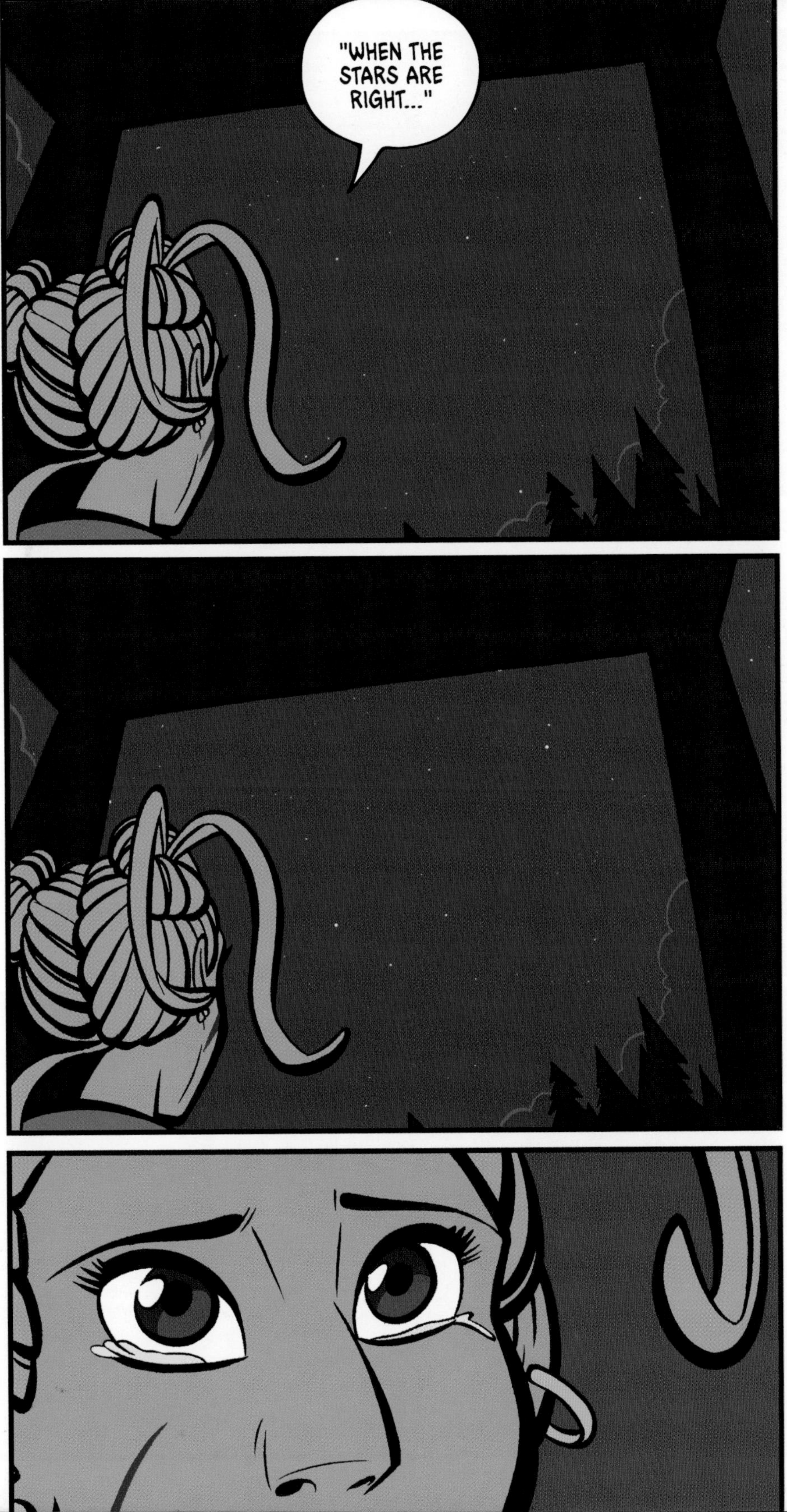
"WHEN THE STARS ARE RIGHT..."

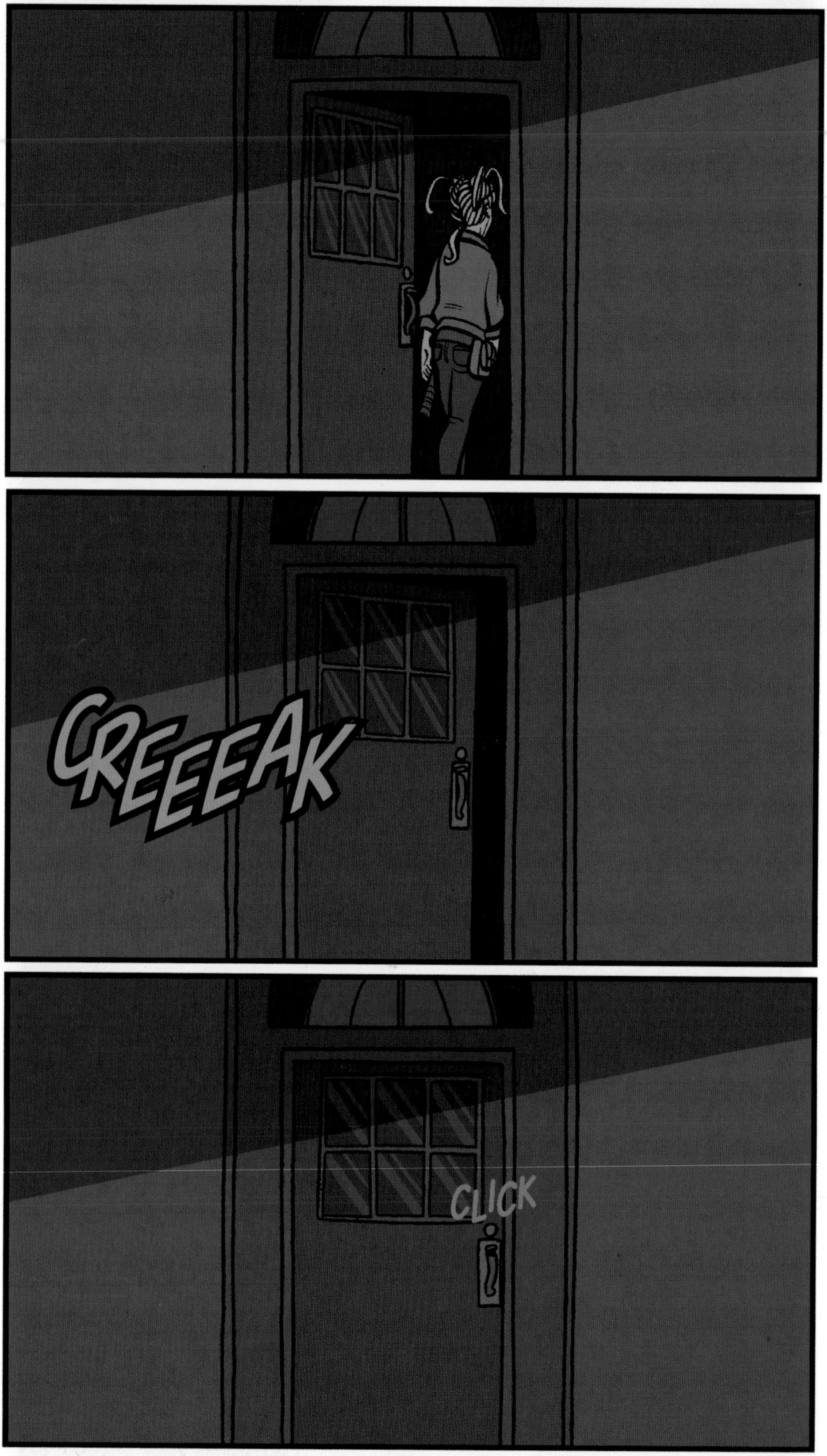
CREEEEAK
CLICK

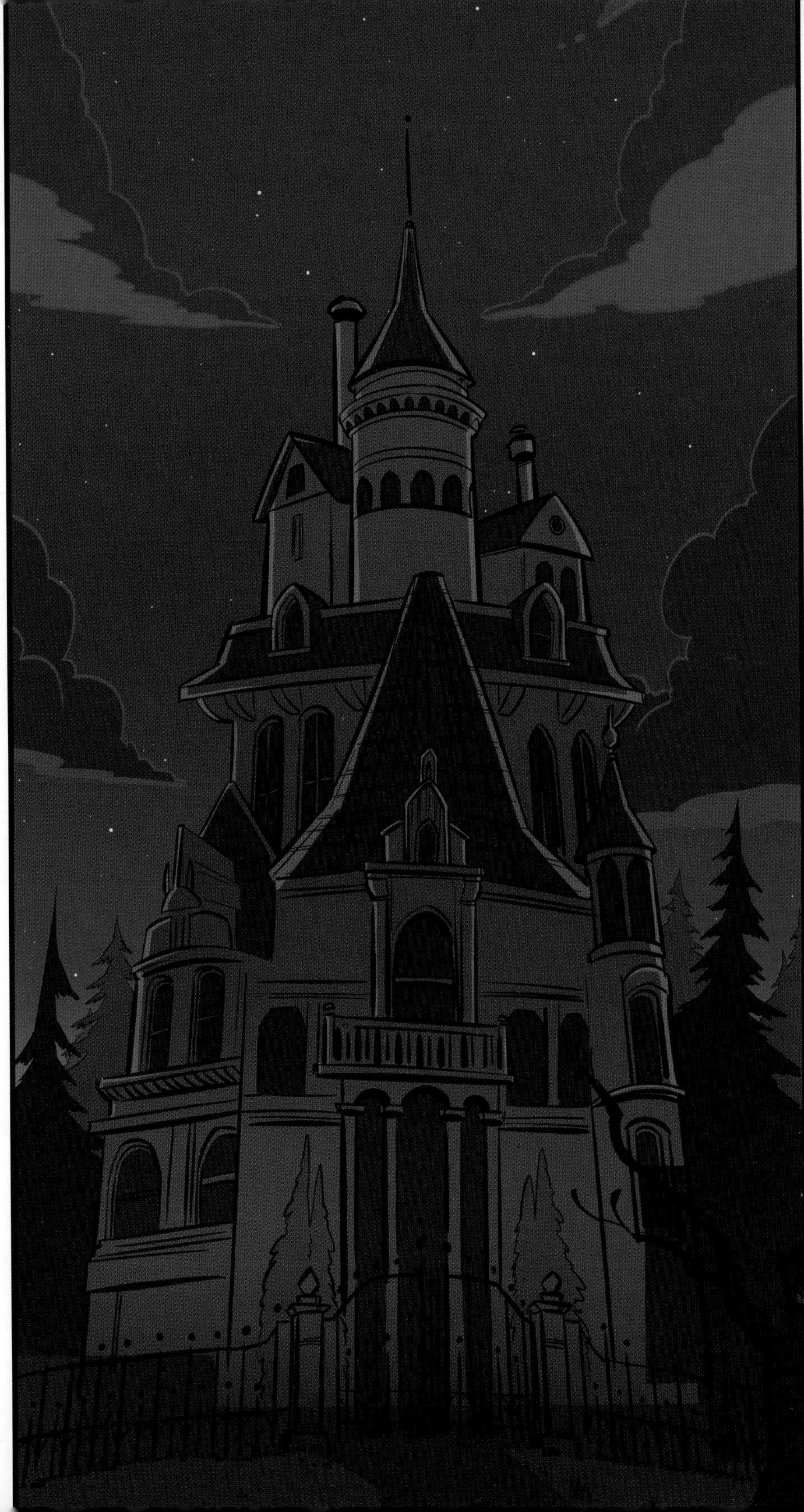